NOAH ... N,

in l... ...n't touch,
tryi... ...one mad,
and ... ...not dare
ima...

MICHAEL WHITACRE,

squandering his talents in a whirl of glitter and
glamor, watching love turn to adultery and divorce, searching for a way to salvage his self-
respect . . .

CHRISTIAN DIESTL,

a born hero, handsome, strong, fearless, for whom
women were easy prey and life was a perilous
challenge . . .

THE YOUNG LIONS

IRWIN SHAW

The Young Lions

A DELL BOOK

TO MY WIFE

Published by
Dell Publishing Co., Inc.
1 Dag Hammarskjold Plaza
New York, N.Y. 10017

Dell ® TM 681510, Dell Publishing Co., Inc.

ISBN: 0-440-19794-5

Reprinted by arrangement with Random House, Inc.

Manufactured in the United States of America

First Dell printing—August 1976
Second Dell printing—September 1976
Third Dell printing—October 1976
Fourth Dell printing—November 1976
Fifth Dell printing—November 1976
Sixth Dell printing—March 1977
Seventh Dell printing—December 1977
Eighth Dell printing—June 1978

Behold, I am against thee,
saith the Lord of hosts, and
I will burn her chariots
in the smoke, and the sword
shall devour thy young lions:
and I will cut off thy
prey from the earth,
and the voice of thy messengers
shall no more be heard.

NAHUM: 2, 13

CHAPTER ONE

THE TOWN SHONE IN the snowy twilight like a Christmas window, with the electric railway's lights tiny and festive at the foot of the white slope, among the muffled winter hills of the Tyrol. People smiled at each other broadly, skiers and natives alike, in their brilliant clothes, as they passed each other on the snow-draped streets, and there were wreaths on the windows and doors of the white and brown houses because this was the eve of the new and hopeful year of 1938.

Margaret Freemantle listened to her ski boots crunch in the packed snow as she walked up the hill. She smiled at the pure twilight and the sound of children singing somewhere in the village below. It had been raining in Vienna when she left that morning and people had been hurrying through the streets with that gloomy sense of being imposed upon that rain brings to a large city. The soaring hills and the clear sky and the good snow, the athletic, cozy gaiety of the village seemed like a personal gift to her because she was young and pretty and on vacation.

Her legs felt relaxed and pleasantly weary as she scuffed little spurts of snow in her path. The two cherry brandies she had drunk after the afternoon's skiing had warmed her throat and she could feel the warmth spreading out to her shoulders and arms in thin, rich tendrils under her sweaters.

"*Dort oben am Berge,*" the children sang, "*da wettert der Wind,*" their voices clear and plangent in the rare air.

"*Da sitzet Maria,*" Margaret sang softly to herself, "*und weiget ihr Kind.*" Her German was halting and as she sang she was pleased not only with the melody and delicacy of the song, but her audacity in singing in German at all.

She was a tall, thin girl, with a slender face. She had green eyes and a spattering of what Joseph called American freckles across the bridge of her nose. Joseph was coming up on the early train the next morning, and when she thought of him she grinned.

At the door of her hotel she stopped and took one last look at the rearing, noble mountains and the winking lights. She

7

breathed deeply of the twilight air. Then she opened the door and went in.

The main room of the small hotel was bright with holly and green leaves, and there was a sweet, rich smell of generous baking. It was a simple room, furnished in heavy oak and leather, with the spectacular, brilliant cleanliness found so often in the mountain villages, that became a definite property of the room, as real and substantial as the tables and chairs.

Mrs. Langerman was walking through the room, carefully carrying a huge cutglass punchbowl, her round, cherry face pursed with concentration. She stopped when she saw Margaret and, beaming, put the punchbowl down on a table.

"Good evening," she said in her soft German. "How was the skiing?"

"Wonderful," Margaret said.

"I hope you didn't get too tired." Mrs. Langerman's eyes crinkled slyly at the corners. "A little party here tonight. Dancing. A great many young men. It wouldn't do to be tired."

Margaret laughed. "I'll be able to dance. If they teach me how."

"Oh!" Mrs. Langerman put up her hands deprecatingly. "You'll have no trouble. They dance every style. They will be delighted with you." She peered critically at Margaret. "Of course, you are rather thin, but the taste seems to be in that direction. The American movies, you know. Finally, only women with tuberculosis will be popular." She grinned and picked up the punchbowl again, her flushed face pleasant and hospitable as an open fire, and started toward the kitchen. "Beware of my son, Frederick," she said. "Great God, he is fond of the girls!" She chuckled and went into the kitchen.

Margaret sniffed luxuriously of the sudden strong odor of spice and butter that came in from the kitchen. She went up the steps to her room, humming.

The party started out very sedately. The older people sat rather stiffly in the corners, the young men congregated uneasily in impermanent groups, drinking gravely and sparely of the strong spiced punch. The girls, most of them large, strong-armed creatures, looked a little uncomfortable and out of place in their frilly party finery. There was an accordionist, but after playing two numbers to which nobody danced he moodily stationed himself at the punchbowl and gave way to the phonograph with American records.

Most of the guests were townspeople, farmers, merchants, relatives of the Langermans, all of them tanned a deep red-brown by the mountain sun, looking solid and somehow immortal, even in their clumsy clothes, as though no seed of illness or decay could exist in that firm mountain flesh, no

8

premonition of death ever be admitted under that glowing skin. Most of the city people who were staying in the few rooms of the Langermans' inn had politely drunk one cup of punch and then had gone on to gayer parties in the larger hotels. Finally Margaret was the only non-villager left. She was not drinking much and she was resolved to go to bed early and get a good night's sleep, because Joseph's train was getting in at eight-thirty in the morning. She wanted to be fresh and rested when she met him. As the evening wore on, the party became gayer. Margaret danced with most of the young men, waltzes and American fox-trots. Along about eleven o'clock, when the room was hot and noisy and the third bowl of punch had been brought on, and the faces of the guests had lost the shy, out-door look of dumb, simple health and taken on an indoor glit-ter, she started to teach Frederick how to rhumba. The others stood around and watched and applauded when she had fin-ished, and old man Langerman insisted that she dance with him. He was a round, squat old man with a bald pink head, and he perspired enormously as she tried to explain in her mediocre German, between bursts of laughter, the mystery of the de-layed beat and the subtle Caribbean rhythm.

"Ah, God," the old man said when the song ended, "I have been wasting my life in these hills." Margaret laughed and leaned over and kissed him. The guests, assembled on the pol-ished floor in a close circle around them, applauded loudly, and Frederick grinned and stepped forward and put his arms up. "Teacher," he said, "me again."

They put the record on again and they made Margaret drink another cup of punch before they began. Frederick was clumsy and heavy-footed, but his arms around her felt pleasantly strong and secure in the spinning, warm dance.

The song ended and the accordionist, now freighted with a dozen glasses of punch, started up. He sang, too, as he played, and one by one the others joined him, standing around him in the firelight, their voices and the rich, swelling notes of the accordion rising in the high, beamed room. Margaret stood with Frederick's arm around her, singing softly, almost to her-self, her face flushed, thinking, how kind, how warm these peo-ple are, how friendly and childlike, how good to strangers, sing-ing the new year in, their rough outdoor voices tenderly curbed to the sweet necessities of the music.

"*Röslein, Röslein, Röslein rot, Röslein auf der Heide,*" they sang, old man Langerman's voice rising above the chorus, bull-like and ridiculously plaintive, and Margaret sang with them. She looked across the fireplace at the dozen singing faces. Only one person in the room remained still.

Christian Diestl was a tall, slender young man, with a solemn, abstracted face and close-cut hair, his skin burned dark

9

by the sun, his eyes light and almost golden with the yellow flecks you find in an animal's eyes. Margaret had seen him on the slopes, gravely teaching beginners how to ski, and had momentarily envied him the rippling, long way he had moved across the snow. Now he was standing a little behind and away from the singers, an open white shirt brilliant in contrast to his dark skin, soberly holding a glass and watching the singers with considering, remote eyes.

Margaret caught his glance. She smiled at him. "Sing," she said.

He smiled gravely back and lifted his glass. She saw him obediently begin to sing, although in the general confusion of voices she could not hear what addition he made to the music.

Now, with the hour and the strong punch and the imminence of a new year, the party had become less polite. In dark corners of the room couples kissed and pawed each other, and the voices grew louder and more confident and the songs became harder for Margaret to follow and understand, full of slang and double meanings that made the older women giggle, the men roar with laughter.

Then, just before midnight, old man Langerman stood up on a chair, called for silence, gave a signal to the accordionist, and said in an oratorical, slightly drunken tone, "As a veteran of the Western Front, wounded three times, 1915 to 18, I would like everyone to join me in a song." He waved to the accordionist, who went into the opening chords of *Deutschland, Deutschland über Alles*. This was the first time Margaret had ever heard the song sung in Austria, but she had learned it from a German maid when she was five. She still remembered the words and she sang with them, feeling drunk and intelligent and international. Frederick held her tighter and kissed her forehead, delighted that she knew the song, and old man Langerman, still on his chair, lifted his glass and offered a toast, "To America. To the young ladies of America!" Margaret drained her glass and bowed. "In the name of the young ladies of America," she said formally, "permit me to say that I am delighted."

Frederick kissed her neck, but before she could decide what to do about that, the accordionist struck up once more, ringing, primitive chords, and all the voices sang out, harshly and triumphantly, in the chorus. For a moment Margaret didn't know what the song was. It was one which she had heard only once or twice before, in surreptitious snatches in Vienna, and the male, roaring voices, obscured by drink, made the tangled German words hard to understand.

Frederick was standing stiffly next to her, clutching her, and she could feel his muscles straining with the passion of the

10

song. She concentrated on him and, finally, she recognized the song.

"Die Fahne hoch, die Reihen fest geschlossen," he sang, the cords standing out on his throat, *"S. A. marschiert in ruhig festen Schritt. Kameraden die Rotfront und Reaktion erschossen."*

Margaret listened, her face stiffening. She closed her eyes and felt weak and half strangled in the grinding music and tried to pull away from Frederick. But his arm was clamped around her and she stood there and listened. When she opened her eyes she looked across at the ski-teacher. He was not singing, but was watching her, his eyes somehow troubled and understanding.

The voices became louder and louder, full of threat and thunder, as they crashed to the end of the Horst Wessel song. Then men stood up straight, eyes flashing, proud and dangerous, and the women, joining in, sank like opera nuns before an operatic god. Only Margaret and the dark young man with the yellow-flecked eyes were silent when the last *"Marschieren mit uns in ihrem Geiste mit,"* rang through the room.

Margaret began to weep, silently, weakly, hating herself for the softness, clamped in Frederick's embrace, as the bells of the village churches rang out in thin, joyous pealing, echoing against the hills in the winter night air.

Old man Langerman, beet-red by now, the sweat running off his round bald dome, his eyes glistening as they might have glistened on the Western Front when first he arrived there in 1915, raised his glass. "To the Fuehrer," he said in a deep, religious voice.

"To the Fuehrer!" The glasses flashed in the firelight and the mouths were eager and holy as they drank.

"Happy New Year! Happy New Year! God bless you this year!" The high patriotic spell was broken, and the guests laughed and shook hands and clapped each other on the back, and kissed each other, cozy and intimate and unwarlike.

Frederick turned Margaret around and tried to kiss her, but she ducked her head. The tears turned into sobs and she broke away. She ran up the steps to her room on the floor above.

"American girls," she heard Frederick say, laughing. "They pretend they know how to drink."

The tears stopped slowly. Margaret felt weak and foolish and tried to ignore them, methodically washing her teeth and putting her hair up and patting cold water on the red stained eyes, so that in the morning, when Joseph came, she would be lively and as pretty as possible.

She undressed in the shining clean whitewashed room, with a thoughtful brown wood Christ hanging on a crucifix over the

11

bed. She put out the light, opened the window and scrambled into the big bed as the wind and the moonlight came soaring in off the powdery, bright mountains. She shivered once or twice in the cold sheets, but in a moment it was warm, under the piled feathers. The linen smelled like fresh laundry back home in her grandmother's house when she was a child, and the stiff white curtains whispered against the window frame. By now the accordionist was playing softly below, sad, autumn songs of love and departure, muffled and heartbreaking with so many doors between. In a little while she was asleep, her face serious and peaceful, childish and undefended in the cold air above the counterpane.

Dreams were often like that. A hand going softly over your skin. A dark, generalized body next to yours, a strange, anonymous breath against your cheek, a clasping, powerful arm, pressing you . . .

Then Margaret woke up.

"Be quiet," the man said, in German. "I won't harm you."

He has been drinking brandy, Margaret thought irrelevantly. I can smell it on his breath.

She lay still for a moment, staring into the man's eyes, little jets of light in the darkness of the eyesockets. The hand went over her belly softly and expertly, slid down her leg. She could feel his leg thrown over hers. He was dressed and the cloth was rough and heavy and scratched her. With a sudden jerk, she threw herself to the other side of the bed and sat up, but he was very swift and powerful and pulled her down again and covered her mouth with his hand. He chuckled.

"Little animal," he said, "little quick squirrel."

She recognized the voice now. "It's only me," Frederick said, "I am merely paying a little visit. Nothing to be frightened of." He took his hand tentatively from her mouth. "You won't scream," he whispered, still the small chuckle in his voice, as though he were being amused by a child. "There is no point in screaming. For one thing, everyone is drunk. For another, I will say that you invited me, and then maybe changed your mind. And they will believe me, because I have a reputation with the girls anyway, and you are a foreigner, besides . . ."

"Please go away," Margaret whispered. "Please. I won't tell anyone."

Frederick chuckled. He was a little drunk, but not as drunk as he pretended. "You are a graceful little darling girl. You are the prettiest girl who has come up here this season. . . ."

"Why do you want me?" Margaret desperately took the cue, trying to tense her body, make it stony, so that the inquisitive hand would meet only cold, antagonistic surfaces. "There are so many others who would be delighted."

12

"I want you." Frederick kissed her neck with what he obviously thought was irresistible tenderness. "I have a great deal of regard for you."

"I don't want you," Margaret said. Insanely, caught there next to that huge, tough body in the dark bed, deep in the night, she felt herself worrying that her German would fail her, that she would forget vocabulary, construction, idioms, and be taken because of that schoolgirl failure. "I don't want you."

"It is always more pleasant," Frederick said, "when the person pretends in the beginning she is unwilling. It is more ladylike, more refined." She felt him sure of himself, making fun of her. "There are many like that."

"I'll tell your mother," Margaret said, "I swear it."

Frederick laughed softly, the sound confident and easy in the quiet room. "Tell my mother," Frederick said. "Why do you think she always puts the pretty young girls in this room, with the shed under it, so it is simple to get in through the window?"

It isn't possible, Margaret thought, that little round, cherry-faced, beaming woman, who had hung crucifixes in all the rooms, that clean, industrious, church-going. . . . Suddenly, Margaret remembered how Mrs. Langerman had looked when the singing had gripped them all in the room below, the wild, obstinate stare, the sweating, sensual face swept by the coarse music. It *is* possible, Margaret thought, it is, this foolish eighteen-year-old boy couldn't have made it up. . . .

"How many times," she asked, talking swiftly, postponing the final moment as long as possible, "how many times have you climbed in here?"

He grinned and she could see the gleam of his teeth. For a moment his hand lay still as he answered, pleased with himself. "Often enough," he said. "Now I am getting very particular. It is a hard climb, and it's slippery with the snow on the shed. They have to be very pretty, like you, before I will do it."

The hand moved on, soft and knowing and insistent. Her own hands were pinned under her by his arm. At her core she felt flaming and weak, violated and dissolved all at once. She rolled her head and shoulders and tried to move her legs, but she couldn't. Frederick held her tight, smiling at her, pleased at this small, titillating resistance.

"You're so pretty," Frederick whispered, "you are so well joined together."

"I'm going to scream, I warn you."

"It will be terrible for you if you do," Frederick said. "Terrible. My mother will call you all sorts of names in front of the other guests, and will demand that you go out of her house at once, for luring her little eighteen-year-old son into your room and getting him into trouble. And your gentleman friend will

13

come here tomorrow and the whole town will be talking about it . . ." Frederick's voice was amused and confidential, "I really advise you not to scream."

Margaret closed her eyes and lay still. For a moment she had a vision of all the faces of the people at the party that evening, grinning, leering conspirators, disguised in their mountain health and cleanliness, plotting against her among themselves in their snowy fortress.

Suddenly Frederick rolled over and was on top of her. His clothes were open and she could feel the smooth, warm skin of his chest against her. He was huge. She felt smothered and lost beneath him. She felt the tears coming into her eyes and fought them back.

Slowly and methodically he was pulling her legs apart. Her hands were free now and she scratched at his eyes. She could feel the skin tearing and hear the rasping ugly sound. Again and again, swiftly, before he could grasp her hands, she ripped at his face.

"Bitch!" Frederick grabbed her hands, held them, hurting the wrists, in one great hand. He swung the other and hit her across the mouth. She felt the blood come. "Cheap little American bitch!" He was sitting astride her. She was lying rigid, staring up at him, triumphant, bloody and defiant, with the level moon lighting the scene in peaceful silver.

He hit her again, backhanded. With the taste of his knuckles, and the feel of bone against her mouth, she got a fleeting ugly whiff of the kitchen where he worked.

"If you don't go," she said clearly, although her head was dipping and whirling, "I'll kill you tomorrow. My friend and I will kill you. I promise you."

He sat above her, holding her hands in one of his. He was cut and bleeding, his long blond hair down over his eyes, his breath coming hard as he loomed over her, glaring at her. There was a moment of silence while he stared at her. Then his eyes swung indecisively. "Aaah," he said, "I am not interested in girls who don't want me. It's not worth the trouble."

He dropped her hands, pushed her face with the heel of his hand, cruelly and hard, and got off the bed, purposely hitting her with his knee as he crossed over. He stood at the window, arranging his clothing, sucking at his torn lip. In the calm light of the moon, he looked boyish and a little pathetic, disappointed and clumsy, buttoning his clothes.

He strode across the room heavily. "I am leaving by the door," he said. "After all, I have a right."

Margaret lay absolutely still, looking up at the ceiling.

Frederick stood at the door, loath to go without some shred of victory to take with him. Margaret could feel him groping heavily in his farmboy mind for some devastating thing to say

14

to her before leaving. "Aaah," he said, "go back to the Jews in Vienna."

He threw the door open and left without closing it. Margaret got up and quietly shut the door. She heard the heavy footsteps going down the stairs toward the kitchen, echoing and re-echoing through the old wooden walls of the sleeping, winter-claimed house.

The wind had died and the room was still and cold. Margaret shivered suddenly in her rumpled pajamas. She went over to the window and shut it. The moon had gone down and the night was paling, the sky, and mountains dead and mysterious in the graying air.

Margaret looked at the bed. One of the sheets was torn, and there were blood spots on the pillow, dark and enigmatic, and the bedclothes were rumpled and crushed. She dressed, shivering, her body feeling fragile and damaged, her wrist-bones aching in the cold. She got into her warmest ski-clothes, with two pairs of wool socks, and put her coat on over them. Still shivering and unwarmed, she sat in the small rocker at the window, staring out at the hills as they swam up out of the night, touched now on their pale summits by the first green light of dawn.

The green turned to rose. The light marched down until all the snow on the slopes glistened, bright with the arrival of morning. Margaret stood up and left the room, not looking at the bed. Softly she went down through the quiet house, with the last shades of night still lying in the corners and a weary smell of old celebration hanging over the lobby downstairs. She opened the heavy door and stepped out into the sleeping, white and indigo New Year.

The streets were empty. She walked aimlessly between the piled drifts on the side of the walks, feeling her lungs tender and sensitive under the impact of the thin dawn air. A door opened and a round little woman with a dustcap and apron stood there, red-cheeked and cheery. "Good morning, Fräulein," she said. "Isn't it a beautiful morning?"

Margaret glanced at her, then hurried on. The woman looked after her, her face first puzzled, then snubbed and angry, and she slammed the door loudly.

Margaret turned off the street and onto the road leading toward the hills. She walked methodically, looking at her feet, climbing slowly toward the ski-slopes, wide and empty now and glistening in the first light. She left the road and went across the packed surface toward the ski-hut, pretty, like a child's dream of Europe, with its heavy beams and low, peaked roof, crusted heavily with snow.

There was a bench in front of the hut and Margaret sank onto it suddenly feeling drained and incapable of further effort.

She stared up at the swelling, gentle slopes, curving creamily up to the high, forbidding rocks of the summit, now sharp and purple against the blue sky.

I will not think about it, she told herself. I will not. She stared stonily at the soaring mountain, consciously trying to make herself map out Christies and stem turns for an imaginary perfect descent. I will not think about it. Her tongue licked at the dried blood over her cut lip. Later on, perhaps, I will think about it, when I am calmer, not so shaken . . . The dangerous part was the deep snow along the edge of the ravine over to the right, because you'd be coming blind over that knoll and swinging wide to avoid that outcropping of rock and you might panic . . .

"Good morning, Miss Freemantle," a voice said beside her.

She jerked her head around. It was the ski-instructor, the slender, burned-dark young man whom she had smiled at and asked to sing when the accordionist played. Without thinking, she stood up and started away.

Diestl took a step after her. "Is anything wrong?" he asked. The voice, following her, was deep, polite and gentle. She stopped, remembering that of all the loud, shouting people the evening before, when Frederick had stood with his arm around her, braying at the top of his voice, only the ski-instructor had remained silent. She remembered the way he had looked at her when she wept, the sympathetic, shy, baffled attempt to show her that she was not alone at that moment.

She turned back to him. "I'm sorry." She even essayed a smile. "I was thinking and I suppose you frightened me."

"Are you sure nothing's the matter?" he asked. He was standing there, bareheaded, looking more boyish and more shy than he had at the party.

"Nothing." Margaret sat down. "I was just sitting here admiring the mountains."

"Perhaps you would prefer being left alone?" He even took a tentative step back.

"No," Margaret said. "Really not." She had suddenly realized that she had to talk about what had happened to someone, make some decision in her own mind about what it meant. It would be impossible to tell Joseph, and the ski-instructor invited confidence. He even looked a little like Joseph, dark and intellectual and grave. "Please stay," she said.

He stood before her, his legs slightly apart, his collar open and his hands bare, as though there were no wind and no cold. He was graceful and compact in his beautifully cut ski clothes. His skin seemed to be naturally olive-colored under the tan, and his blood pulsed a kind of coral-red under the clear tone of his cheeks.

The ski-instructor took out a pack of cigarettes and offered one to her. She took it and he lit it for her, deftly cupping the match against the wind, his hands firm and certain, masculine and olive-colored close to her face as he leaned over her.

"Thank you," she said. He nodded and lighted his own cigarette and sat down next to her. They sat there, leaning against the back of the bench, their heads tilted easily back, staring through half-closed eyes at the glory of the mountain before them. The smoke curled slantwise over them and the cigarette tasted rich and heavy against Margaret's morning palate.

"How wonderful!" she said.

"What?"

"The hills."

He shrugged. "The enemy," he said.

"What?" she asked.

"The enemy."

She looked at him. His eyes were slitted and his mouth was set in a harsh line. She looked back at the mountains.

"What's the matter with them?" she asked.

"Prison," he said. He moved his feet, in their handsome, strapped and buckled boots. "My prison."

"Why do you say that?" Margaret asked, surprised.

"Don't you think it's an idiotic way for a man to spend his life?" He smiled sourly. "The world is collapsing, the human race is struggling to remain alive, and I devote myself to teaching fat little girls how to slide down a hill without falling on their faces." What a country, Margaret couldn't help thinking, amused despite herself, even the athletes have *Weltschmerz*.

"If you feel so strongly," she said, "why don't you do something about it?"

He laughed, soundlessly, without pleasure.

"I tried," he said. "I tried in Vienna seven months. I couldn't bear it here any longer and I went to Vienna. I was going to get a sensible, useful job, if it killed me. Advice: don't try to get a useful job in Vienna these days. I finally got a job. Busboy in a restaurant. Carrying dishes for tourists. I came home. At least you can earn a respectable living here. That's Austria for you. For nonsense you can get paid well." He shook his head. "Forgive me," he said.

"For what?"

"For talking like this. Complaining to you. I'm ashamed of myself." He flipped his cigarette away and put his hands in his pockets, hunching his shoulders a little embarrassedly. "I don't know why I did. So early in the morning, perhaps, and we're the only ones awake on the mountain here. I don't know. Somehow . . . you seemed so sympathetic. The people up here . . ." He shrugged. "Oxen. Eat, drink, make money. I wanted to talk to you last night . . ."

"I'm sorry you didn't," said Margaret. Somehow, sitting

there next to him, with his soft, deep voice rolling over his precise German, considerately slow and clear for her uncertain ear, she felt less bruised now, restored and calm again.

"You left so suddenly," he said. "You were crying."

"That was silly," she said flatly. "It's merely a sign I'm not grown up yet."

"You can be very grown up and still cry. Cry hard and often." Margaret felt that he somehow wanted her to know that he, too, wept from time to time. "How old are you?" he asked, abruptly.

"Twenty-one," Margaret said.

He nodded, as though this were a significant fact and one to be reckoned with in all future dealings. "What are you doing in Austria?" he asked.

"I don't know . . ." Margaret hesitated. "My father died and left me some money. Not much, but some. I decided I wanted to see a little of the world before I settled down . . ."

"Why did you pick Austria?"

"I don't know. I was studying scene designing in New York and someone had been in Vienna and said there was a wonderful school there, and it was as good a place as any. Anyway, it was different from America. That was the important thing."

"Do you go to school in Vienna?"

"Yes."

"Is it good?"

"No." She laughed. "Schools are always the same. They seem to help other people, but never yourself."

"Still," he said, turning and looking gravely at her, "you like it?"

"I love it. I love Vienna. Austria."

"Last night," he said, "you were not very fond of Austria."

"No." Then she added, honestly, "Not Austria. Just those people. I wasn't very fond of them."

"The song," he said. "The Horst Wessel song."

She hesitated. "Yes," she said. "I wasn't prepared for it. I didn't think, up here, in a beautiful place like this, so far away from everything . . ."

"We're not so far away," he said. "Not so far away at all. Are you Jewish?"

"No." That question, Margaret thought, the sudden dividing question of Europe.

"Of course not," he said. "I knew you weren't." He pursed his lips thoughtfully and squinted out across the slope, in what was a characteristic grimace, puzzling and searching. "It's your friend," he said.

"What?"

"The gentleman who is coming up this morning."

"How did you know?"

"I asked," he said.

There was a little silence. What a curious mixture he is, Margaret thought, half bold, half shy, humorless and heavy, yet unexpectedly delicate and perceptive.

"He's Jewish, I suppose." There was no trace of judgment or animosity in the grave, polite voice as he spoke.

"Well . . ." Margaret said, trying to put it straight for him. "The way you people figure, I suppose he is. He's a Catholic, but his mother's Jewish, and I suppose . . ."

"What's he like?"

Margaret spoke slowly. "He's a doctor. Older than I, of course. He's very handsome. He looks like you. He's very funny, and he always keeps people laughing when they're with him. But he's serious, too, and he fought in the Karl Marx Apartments battle against the soldiers. He was one of the last to escape . . ." Suddenly she stopped herself. "I take it all back. It's ridiculous to go around telling stories like that. It can start a lot of trouble."

"Yes," the ski-instructor said. "Don't tell me any more. Still, he sounds very nice. Are you going to marry him?"

Margaret shrugged. "We've talked about it. But . . . No decision yet. We'll see."

"Are you going to tell him about last night?"

"Yes."

"And about how you got the cut lip?"

Margaret's hand went involuntarily to the bruise. She looked sidelong at the ski-instructor. He was squinting solemnly out at the hills. "Frederick paid you a visit last night, didn't he?" he said.

"Yes," Margaret said softly. "You know about Frederick?"

"Everyone knows about Frederick," the ski-instructor said harshly. "You're not the first girl to come down from that room with marks on her."

"Hasn't anything ever been done about it?"

The ski-instructor laughed harshly. "Charming, high-spirited youth. Most of the girls really love it, the story goes, even the ones who take some argument. A little, quaint individual touch to Mrs. Langerman's hotel. A village character. Everything for the skier. A funicular, five hand tows, eighteen feet of snow, and some mild local rape. I suppose he never goes too far. If, finally, the lady is really firmly opposed, he quits. He quit with you, didn't he?"

"Yes," Margaret said.

"You had a bad night altogether, didn't you? Bring the New Year in with joy and song in happy old Austria."

"I'm afraid," Margaret said, "it's all of a piece."

"What do you mean?"

19

"The Horst Wessel song, Nazis, forcing yourself into women's rooms, hitting them . . ."

"Nonsense!" Diestl's voice was loud and angry. "Don't talk like that."

"What did I say?" Margaret felt a little returning unreasonable twinge of uneasiness and fear.

"Frederick did not climb into your room because he was a Nazi." The ski-instructor was talking now in his usual, calm manner, patient and teacher-like, as he talked to children in his beginners' classes. "Frederick did that because he is a pig. He's a bad human being. For him it is only an accident that he is a Nazi. Finally, if it comes to it, he will be a bad Nazi, too."

"How about you?" Margaret sat absolutely still, looking down at her feet.

"Of course," the ski-instructor said. "Of course, I'm a Nazi. Don't look so shocked. You've been reading those idiotic American newspapers. We eat children, we burn down churches, we march nuns through the street naked and paint dirty pictures on their backs in lipstick and human blood, we have breeding farms for human beings, etcetera, etcetera . . . It would make you laugh, if it weren't so serious."

He was silent. Margaret wanted to leave, but she felt weak, and she was afraid she would stumble and fall if she got up now. Her eyes were hot and sandy and there was a tingling, uncertain feeling in her knees as though she hadn't slept in days. She blinked and looked out at the quiet white hills, receding and less dramatic now as the light grew stronger.

What a lie, she thought, the magnificent, peaceful hills in the climbing sun.

"I would like you to understand . . ." The man's voice was gentle, sorrowful and pleading. "It's too easy for you in America to condemn everything. You're so rich and you can afford so many luxuries. Tolerance, what you call democracy, moral positions. Here in Austria we cannot afford a moral position." He waited, as though for her to attack, but she remained silent, and he went on, his voice low and toneless and hard to understand, losing itself quickly in the immense shining emptiness. "Of course," he said, "you have a special conception. I don't blame you. Your young man is a Jew and you are afraid for him. So you lose sight of the larger issues. The larger issues . . ." he repeated, as though the sound of the words had a reassuring and pleasant effect on his inner ear. "The larger issue is Austria. The German people. It is ridiculous to pretend we are not Germans. It is easy for an American five thousand miles away to pretend we are not Germans. But not for us. This way we are a nation of beggars. Seven million people with no place to go, no future, at anyone's mercy, living like hotelkeepers off tourists and foreigners' tips. Americans just can't understand. People cannot live forever in humiliation. They will do whatever they have to do to regain their self-respect. Austria will only do that by going Nazi, by becoming a part of the Greater Germany." His voice had become more lively now, and the tone had come back into it.

"It's not the only way," Margaret said, arguing despite herself. But he seemed so sensible and pleasant, so accessible to reason . . . "There must be other ways than lying and murdering and cheating."

"My dear girl," the ski-instructor shook his head patiently and sorrowfully, "live in Europe ten years and then come and tell me that. If you still believe it. I'm going to tell you something. Until last year I was a Communist. Workers of the World, peace for all, to each according to his need, the victory of reason, brotherhood, brotherhood, etcetera, etcetera." He laughed. "Nonsense! I do not know about America, but I know about Europe. In Europe nothing will ever be accomplished by reason. Brotherhood . . . a cheap, street-corner joke, good for mediocre politicians between wars. And I have a feeling it is not so different in America, either. You call it lying, murdering, cheating. Maybe it is. But in Europe it is the necessary process. It is the only thing that works. Do you think I like to say that? But it is true, and only a fool will think otherwise. Then, finally, when things are in order, we can stop what you call the 'lying and murdering.' When people have enough to eat, when they have jobs, when they know that their money will be worth the same tomorrow as it is today and not one-tenth as much, when they know they have a government that is their own, that cannot be ordered around by anyone else, at anyone else's whim . . . when they can stop being defeated. Out of weakness, you get nothing. Shame, starvation. That's all. Out of strength, you get everything. And about the Jews . . ." He shrugged. "It is an unlucky accident. Somehow, someone discovered that that was the only way to come to power. I am not saying I like it. Myself, I know it is ridiculous to attack any race. Myself, I know there are Jews like Frederick, and Jews, say, like myself. But if the only way you can get a decent and ordered Europe is by wiping out the Jews, then we must do it. A little injustice for a large justice. It is the one thing the Comrades have taught Europe—the end justifies the means. It is a hard thing to learn, but, finally, I think, even Americans will learn it."

"That's horrible," Margaret said.

"My dear young lady," the ski-instructor swung around and took her hands, speaking eagerly and candidly, his face flushed and alive, "I am speaking abstractly and it sounds worse that way. You must forgive me. I promise you something. It will never come to that. You can tell your friend that, too. For a year or two, he will be a little annoyed. He may have to give up his business; he may have to move from his house. But once the thing is accomplished, once the trick has done what it is intended to do, he will be restored. The Jew is a means, not an end. When everything else is arranged, he will come back to his proper place. I absolutely guarantee. And don't believe the American newspapers. I was in Germany last year, and I tell you it is much worse in a journalist's mind than it is on the streets of Berlin."

"I hate it." Margaret said. "I hate them all."

The ski-instructor looked into her eyes, then shrugged, sorrowful and defeated, and swung slowly around. He stared thoughtfully at the mountains. "I'm sorry," he said. "You seem so reasonable and intelligent. I thought, maybe here is one American who would speak a good word when she got home, one American who would have some understanding . . ." He stood up. "Ah, I suppose it is too much to ask." He turned to her and smiled, pleasantly, his lean, agreeable face gentle and touching. "Permit me to make a suggestion. Go home to America. I'm afraid Europe will make you very unhappy." He scuffed at the snow. "It will be a little icy today," he said in a brisk businesslike voice. "If you and your friend are going to ski, I will take you down the west trail myself, if you like. It will be the best one today, but it is not advisable to go alone."

"Thank you." Margaret stood up, too. "But I think we won't stay."

"Is he coming on the morning train?"

"Yes."

The ski-instructor nodded. "He'll have to stay at least until three o'clock this afternoon. There are no other trains." He peered at her under his heavy eyebrows, bleached at the ends. "You don't wish to remain here for your holiday?"

"No," said Margaret.

"Because of last night?"

"Yes."

"I understand. Here." He took a piece of paper out of his pocket and a pencil, and wrote for a moment. "Here is an address you can use. It's only twenty miles from here. The three o'clock train stops there. It's a charming little inn, and a very good slope, quite advanced, and the people are very nice. Not political at all." He smiled. "Not horrible like us. There are no Fredericks there. You will be made very welcome. And your friend, too."

Margaret took the paper and put it in her pocket. "Thank you," she said. She couldn't help thinking, how decent and good this man is, despite everything. "I imagine we'll go there."

"Good. Have a pleasant holiday. And after that . . ." He

smiled at her and put out his hand. "After that, go home to America."

She shook his hand. Then she turned and started down the hill toward town. When she was at the bottom of the hill, she looked back. His first class had begun, and he was crouched over on his skis, laughing, patiently lifting a seven-year-old girl, in a red wool cap, from the snow where she had fallen.

Joseph got off the train, bubbling and joyful. He kissed her and gave her a box of pastries he had carried with insane care all the way from Vienna, and a new skiing cap in pale blue that he hadn't been able to resist. He kissed her again, and said, "Happy New Year, darling," and "God, look at your freckles," and "I love you, I love you," and "You are the most beautiful American in the world," and "I'm starving. Where is breakfast?" and breathed deeply and looked around him at the encircling mountains with pride and ownership and said, his arm around her, "Look! Look at that! Don't tell me there is anything like this in America!" and when she began to cry, helplessly, softly, he grew serious and held her, and kissed the tears, and said in his low, honest voice, "What? What is it, darling?"

Slowly, standing close to each other, in a corner of the little station, hidden from most of the people on the platform, she told him. She didn't tell him about Frederick, but about the singing the night before and the Nazi toasts, and that she couldn't stay there for another day, no matter what. Joseph kissed her forehead absently and stroked her cheek. His face lost the holiday bustle and gaiety that it had had when he got off the train. The fine bones of his cheeks and jaw suddenly showed sharp and hurtful under his skin, and his eyes looked sunken and deep as he spoke to her. "Ah," he said, "here, too. Indoors, outdoors, city, country . . ." He shook his head. "Margaret, Baby," he said gently, "I think you had better get away from Europe. Go home. Go back to America."

"No," she said, letting it come out, without thinking about it. "I want to stay here. I want to marry you and stay here."

Joseph shook his head, the soft, closely-cropped hair, graying a little, glistening where some drops of melting snow had fallen on it. "I must visit America," he said, softly. "I must visit the country that produces girls like you."

"I said I want to marry you." Margaret held his arms tight and hard.

"Some other time, Sweet," Joseph said tenderly. "We'll discuss it some other time."

But they never did.

They went back to Langermans', and had a huge breakfast, quietly sitting before a sparkling sunny window, with the Alps a majestic background for the bacon and eggs and potatoes

23

and pancakes and coffee Viennese style with globs of whipped cream. Frederick waited on them, discreetly and politely. He held Margaret's chair when she sat down and was quick to refill Joseph's cup when it was empty.

After breakfast Margaret packed, and told Mrs. Langerman that she and her friend had to leave. Mrs. Langerman clucked and said, "What a shame!" and presented the bill.

There was an item on the bill of nine schillings.

"I don't understand this," Margaret said. She was standing at the shiny oak desk in the lobby as she pointed out the neatly inked entry on the bill. Mrs. Langerman, bobbing, starched and brilliantly scrubbed, behind the desk, ducked her head and peered near-sightedly at the piece of paper.

"Oh." She looked up and stared without expression at Margaret. "Oh, that's for the torn sheets, *Liebchen*."

Margaret paid. Frederick was helping with her bags. She tipped him. He bowed as he helped her into the cab and said, "I hope you have enjoyed your visit."

Margaret and Joseph checked their bags at the station and walked around, looking at the shops until it was time to get their train.

As the train pulled out she thought she saw Diestl, graceful and dark, at the end of the platform, watching. She waved, but the figure didn't wave back. Somehow, though, she felt it would be like him to come down to the station and, without even greeting her, watch her go off with Joseph.

The inn Diestl had recommended was small and pretty, and the people charming. It snowed two of the three nights and there was fresh cover on the trails in the morning. Joseph had never been gayer or more delightful. Margaret slept secure and warm, with his arms around her all night, in the huge feather-bed that seemed to have been made for mountain honeymoons. They didn't talk about anything serious, and they didn't mention marriage again. The sun shone in the clear sky over the peaks all day long, every day, and the air was winey and intoxicating in the lungs. Joseph sang Schubert lieder for the other guests in front of the fire at night, his voice sweet and searching. There was a smell of cinnamon always in the house. Both of them were burned a deep brown, and even so, more freckles than ever before came out on her nose, and Margaret nearly wept when she went down to the station on the fourth day because they had to go to Vienna. The holiday was over.

CHAPTER TWO

IN NEW YORK CITY, too, the shining new year of 1938 was being welcomed. The taxicabs were bumper to bumper in the wet streets, their horns swelling and roaring, as though they were all some newly invented species of tin-and-glass animal, penned in the dark stone and concrete. In the middle of the city, trapped in the glare of the advertising signs, like prisoners caught by the warden's floodlights in the moment of attempted flight, a million people, clamped together, rolled slowly and aimlessly, in pale tides uptown and downtown. The electric sign that jittered nervously around the Times Building announced to the merrymakers below that a storm had destroyed seven lives in the Midwest, that Madrid had been shelled twelve times at the turn of the year, which conveniently for the readers of the *Times,* came several hours earlier to Madrid than it did to the city of New York.

The police, to whom the New Year could only mean more burglary, further rape, increasing death in traffic, added heat and snow, put on a show of bluff jollity at the street corners, but their eyes were cynical and weary as they herded the celebrating animals up one side of the Square and down the other.

The celebrants themselves, pushing lava-like and inexorable through the paper slush underfoot, threw confetti at each other, laden with the million germs of the city's streets, blew horns to tell the world that they were happy and unafraid, shouted hoarse greetings with thin good nature that would not last till morning. They had come from the fogs of England for this, the green mists of Ireland, the sand hills of Syria and Iraq, from the pogrom-haunted ghettoes of Poland and Russia, from the vineyards of Italy and the cod banks of Norway, and from every other island, city, and continent on the face of the earth. Later, they had come from Brooklyn and the Bronx, and East St. Louis and Texarkana, and from towns called Bimiji and Jaffrey and Spirit, and they all looked as though they had never had enough sun or enough sleep; they all looked as though their clothes had originally been bought for other people; they all looked as though they had been thrown into this cold, asphalt cage for someone else's holiday, not their own; they all looked as though deep in their bones they understood that winter would last forever, and that, despite the horns and the

25

laughter and the shuffling, religious promenade, they knew that 1938 would be worse than the year before it.

Pickpockets, whores, gamblers, pimps, confidence men, taxidrivers, bartenders and hotel owners did well, as did the producers of plays and champagne salesmen, beggars and nightclub doormen. Here and there could be heard the crashing of glass, as whiskey bottles were hurled out of hotel windows into the narrow areaways which provided light and air and a view of the world to the two-dollar rooms, five dollars for tonight, in which the old year was being discarded in transient merriment. A girl's throat was cut on 50th Street and an ambulance's siren made a brief peremptory contribution to the general celebration. From partly opened windows, yellow and bright, on the quieter streets, came the soprano, desert laughter of women, the Saturday-night and holiday-evening voice of the city, which, rasping and over-amused, somehow can only be heard in the dark, toward the cold hours of morning.

Later on, in the ageless January air underground, dank and flickering in the enclosed dark roar of the suburban subway trains, the crowd, by then compartmentalized, swaying and grimy-eyed, silent and bruised by sleep, smelling of streetcorner gardenias, garlic, onion, sweat, shoe polish, perfumes and labor, would flee to their lurking homes. But now they flowed up and down the bright streets, making noise with horns and rattles and tin whistles, irresistibly and steadfastly celebrating, because, for lack of a better reason, as the new year came in, they had proof that they had at least survived the old year and were alive for the next.

Michael Whitacre pushed his way through the crowds. He felt himself smiling mechanically and hypocritically at people as they jostled him. He was late, and he couldn't get a taxi, and he hadn't been able to avoid staying and having some drinks in one of the dressing rooms. The hurried gulping had left his head buzzing and his stomach burning.

The theatre had been wild. There had been a noisy, disinterested audience and an understudy had filled in the grandmother's part because Patricia Ferry had shown up too drunk to go on, and Michael had had a trying night keeping everything going. He was the stage manager for *Late Spring* and it had a cast of thirty-seven, with three children who always got colds, and five sets that had to be changed in twenty seconds. At the end of a night like this all he wanted to do was go home and sleep. But there was this damned party over on 67th Street, and Laura was there. Anyway, nobody ever just went to sleep on New Year's Eve.

He pushed through the worst of the crowd and walked briskly to Fifth Avenue and turned north. Fifth Avenue was less crowded and the air whipped down from the Park, lively and invigorating. The sky here was dark enough over the looming buildings so that he actually could see stars, pale and small, in the thin corridor of heaven visible over the street.

I must get a home in the country, he thought as he walked briskly, his shoes making a soft tapping on the cement, a little inexpensive place not far from the city, six, seven thousand, maybe, you could swing a loan, where I can get away for a few days at a time, where it's quiet and you can see all the stars at night and where you can go to sleep at eight o'clock when you feel like it. I must do it, he thought, I mustn't just think about it.

He got a glimpse of himself in a dimly lit shop window. He looked shadowy and unreal in the reflection, but, as usual, he was annoyed with what he saw. Self-consciously, he straightened his shoulders. I must remember not to slouch, he thought, and I must lose fifteen pounds. I look like a fat grocer.

He refused a taxi that stopped next to him, as he crossed at a corner. Exercise, he thought, and no drinking for at least a month. That's what does it. The drinking. Beer, martinis, have another. And the way your head felt in the morning. You weren't good for anything until noon and by that time you were out to lunch and there you were with a glass in your hand again. This was the beginning of a new year, a wonderful time to go on the wagon. It would be a good test of character. Tonight, at the party. Unobtrusively. Just not drinking. And in the house in the country no liquor closet at all. He felt much better now, resolved and powerful, although his dress trousers still felt uncomfortably tight as he strode past the rich windows toward 67th Street.

When he came into the crowded room, it was just past twelve. People were singing and embracing and that girl who passed out at all the parties was doing it again in the corner. Whitacre saw his wife in the crowd kissing a little man who looked like Hollywood. Somebody put a drink in his hand and a tall girl spilled some potato salad on his shoulder and said, "Excellent salad." She brushed vaguely at his lapel with a long, exquisite hand with crimson nails an inch and a half in length. Katherine came over with enough bosom showing to power a frigate in a mild breeze and said, "Mike, darling." She kissed him behind the ear, and said, "What are you doing tonight?" Michael said, "My wife arrived yesterday from the Coast." And Katherine said, "Ooops! Sorry. Happy New Year," and wandered off, her bosom dazzling three Harvard juniors with crew haircuts and white ties, who were related to the hostess and who were in town for the holiday.

Michael lifted his glass and drank half of its contents. It seemed to be Scotch into which someone had poured lemon

27

soda. Tomorrow, he thought, will be time enough for the wagon. After all, he had had three already, so this night was lost anyhow. Michael waited until he saw his wife finish kissing the bald little man, who wore a swooping Russian cavalryman's moustache.

Michael made his way across the room and came up behind his wife. She was holding the little man's hand, and saying, "Don't tell anyone, Harry, but the script stinks."

"You know me, Laura," the bald man said. "Do I ever tell anyone?"

"Happy New Year, darling," Michael kissed Laura's cheek.

Laura turned around, still holding the bald man's hand. She smiled. Even with the din of celebration all around her, and the drunks and commotion, there was that tenderness and melting, lovely welcome that always surprised and shook Michael, no matter how many times he saw it. She put up her free arm and drew Michael closer to her to kiss him. There was a single, hesitating moment when his cheek was next to hers, before she kissed him, when he could sense her sniffing inquisitively. He felt himself grow stolid and sullen, even as they kissed. She always does it, he thought. New Year, old year, makes no difference.

"I doused myself, before leaving the theatre," he said, pulling away and standing straight, "with two bottles of Chanel Number 5."

He saw Laura's eyelids quiver a little, hurt. "Don't be mean to me," she said, "in 1938. Why're you so late?"

"I stopped and had a couple."

"With whom?" The suspicious, pinched look that always came over Laura's face when she questioned him, corrupted its usual delicate, candid expression.

"Some of the boys," he said.

"That's all?" Her voice was light and playful, in the accepted tone in which you quizzed your husband in public in her circle.

"No," said Michael. "I forgot to tell you. There were six Polynesian dancing girls with walnuts in their navels, but we left them at the Stork."

"Isn't he funny?" Laura said to the bald man. "Isn't he terribly funny?"

"This is getting domestic," the bald man said. "This is when I leave. When it gets domestic." He waved his fingers at the Whitacres. "Love you, Laura, darling," he said, and burrowed into the crowd.

"I have a great idea," Laura said. "Let's not be mean to wives tonight."

Michael drained his drink, and put the glass down. "Who's the moustache?" he asked.

"Oh, Harry?"

28

"The one you were kissing."

"Harry. I've known him for years. He's always at parties." Laura touched her hair tenderly. "Here. On the Coast. I don't know what he does. Maybe he's an agent. He came over and said he thought I was enchanting in my last picture."

"Did he really say enchanting?"

"Uhuh."

"Is that how they talk in Hollywood these days?"

"I guess so." She was smiling at him, but her eyes flicked back and forth, looking over the room, as they always did everywhere but in their own home. "How did you think I was in my last picture?"

"Enchanting," Michael said. "Let's get a drink."

Laura stood up and took his arm and rubbed her cheek softly against his shoulder and said, "Glad I'm here?" and Michael grinned and said, "Enchanted." They both chuckled as they went toward the bar, side by side, through the mass of people in the center of the room.

The bar was in the next room, under an abstract painting of what was probably a woman with three magenta breasts, seated on a parallelogram.

Wallace Arney was there, graying and puffy, holding a teacup in his hand. He was flanked by a squat, powerful man in a blue-serge suit who looked as though he had been out in the weather for ten winters in a row. There were two girls, with flat, pretty faces and models' bony ungirdled hips, who were drinking whiskey straight.

"Did he make a pass at you?" Michael heard one of the girls saying as he came up.

"No," the other girl said, shaking her sleek, blonde hair.

"Why not?" the first girl asked.

"At the moment," the blonde girl said, "he's a Yogi."

Both girls stared reflectively at their glasses, then drained them and walked off together, stately and graceful as two panthers in the jungle.

"Did you hear that?" Michael asked Laura.

"Yes." Laura was laughing.

Michael asked the man behind the bar for two Scotches and smiled at Arney, who was the author of *Late Spring*. Arney merely continued to stare directly ahead of him, saying nothing, from time to time lifting the teacup to his lips, in an elegant, shaky gesture.

"Out," said the man in the blue-serge suit. "Out on his feet. The referee ought to stop the bout to spare him further punishment."

Arney looked around him, grinning and furtive, and pushed his teacup and saucer toward the man behind the bar. "Please," he said, "more tea."

The bartender filled his cup with rye and Arney peered around him once more before accepting it. "Hello, Whitacre," he said. "Mrs. Whitacre. You won't tell Felice, will you?"

"No, Wallace," Michael said. "I won't tell."

"Thank God," Arney said, "Felice has indigestion. She's been in the john for an hour. She won't let me have even a beer." His voice, hoarse and whiskey-riddled, wavered in self-pity. "Not even a beer. Can you imagine that? That's why I carry a teacup. From a distance of three feet, who can tell the difference? After all," he said defiantly, sipping from the cup, "I'm a grown man. She wants me to write another play." Now he was aggrieved. "Just because she's the wife of my producer she feels she has a right to throw a glass right out of my hand. Humiliating. A man my age should not be humiliated like that." He turned vaguely to the man in the blue-serge suit. "Mr. Parrish here drinks like a fish and nobody humiliates him. Everybody says, isn't it touching how Felice devotes herself to that drunken Wallace Arney? It doesn't touch me. Mr. Parrish and I know why she does it. Don't we, Mr. Parrish?"

"Sure, Pal," said the man in the blue suit.

"Economics. Like everything else." Arney waved his cup suddenly, splashing whiskey on Michael's sleeve. "Mr. Parrish is a Communist and he knows. The basis of all human action. Greed. Naked greed. If they didn't think they could get another play out of me, they wouldn't care if I lived in a distillery. I could bathe in tequila and absinthe and they'd say, 'Kiss my ass, Wallace Arney.' I beg your pardon, Mrs. Whitacre."

"That's all right," Laura said.

"Your wife is very pretty," Arney said. "Very pretty indeed. I've heard her spoken of here tonight in glowing terms." He leered at Michael knowingly. "Glowing terms. She has several old friends among the assembled guests here tonight. Haven't you, Mrs. Whitacre?"

"Yes," said Laura.

"Everybody has several old friends among the assembled guests," Arney said. "That's the way parties are these days. Modern society. A nest of snakes, hibernating for the winter, everybody wrapped around everybody else. Maybe that'll be the theme of my next play. Except I won't write it." He drank deeply. "Marvelous tea. Don't tell Felice." Michael took Laura's arm and started to leave. "Don't go, Whitacre," Arney said. "I know I'm boring you, but don't go. I want to talk to you. What do you want to talk about? Want to talk about Art?"

"Some other time," Michael said.

"I understand you're a very serious young man," Arney said doggedly. "Let's talk about Art. How did my play go tonight?"

"All right," said Michael.

"No," said Arney, "I won't talk about my play. I said Art

and I know what you think of my play. Everybody in New York knows what you think about my play. You shoot your mouth off too goddamn much and if it was up to me I'd fire you. I am being friendly at the moment, but I'd fire you."

"You're drunk, Wally," Michael said.

"I am not profound enough for you," Arney said, his pale-blue eyes watering, his lower lip, full and wet, quivering as he spoke. "Reach my age, Whitacre, and you try to be profound."

"I'm sure Michael likes your play very much," Laura said in a clear, soothing voice.

"You're a very pretty girl, Mrs. Whitacre," Arney said, "and you have many friends, but please keep your trap shut at the moment."

"Why don't you go lie down somewhere?" Michael said.

"Let's not get off the subject." Arney turned hazily and belligerently back to Michael. "I know what you go around saying at parties. 'Arney is a silly old has-been. Arney writes about people who vanished in 1929 in a style that vanished in 1829.' It isn't even very funny. I have plenty of critics. Why do I have to pay them out of my own money? I don't like young snots like you, Whitacre. You're not even young enough to be so snotty."

"Listen, Pal . . ." the man in the blue-serge suit began.

"You talk to him," Arney said to Parrish. "He's a Communist, too. That's why I'm not profound enough for him. All you have to do to be profound these days is pay fifteen cents a week for the *New Masses*." He put his arm around Parrish lovingly. "This is the kind of Communist I like, Whitacre," he said. "Mr. Parrish. Mr. Sunburned Parrish. He got sunburned in sunny Spain. He went to Spain and he got shot at in Madrid and he's going back to Spain and he's going to get killed there. Aren't you, Mr. Parrish?"

"Sure, Pal," Parrish said.

"That's the kind of Communist I like," Arney said loudly. "Mr. Parrish is here to get some money and some volunteers to go back and get shot with him in sunny Spain. Instead of being so goddamn profound at these fairy parties in New York, Whitacre, why don't you go be profound in Spain with Mr. Parrish?"

"If you don't keep quiet," Michael started to say, but a tall, white-haired woman with a regal, dark face swept between him and Arney and calmly and without a word knocked the teacup out of Arney's hand. It broke on the floor in a small, china tinkle. Arney looked at her angrily for a moment, then grinned sheepishly, ducking his head, looking shiftily at the floor. "Hello, Felice," he said.

"Get away from the bar," Felice said.

"Just drinking a little tea," Arney said. He turned and

31

shuffled off, fat and aging, his gray hair lank and sweating against his large head.

"Mr. Arney does not drink," Felice said to the bartender.

"Yes, Ma'am," said the bartender.

"Christ," said Felice to Michael, "I could kill him. He's driving me crazy. And fundamentally he's such a sweet man."

"A darling man," Michael said.

"Was he awful?" Felice asked anxiously.

"Darling," Michael said.

"Nobody'll invite him any place any more and everyone ducks him . . ." Felice said.

"I can't imagine why," said Michael.

"Even so," said Felice sadly, "it's awful for him. He sits in his room brooding, telling everyone who'll listen to him that he's a has-been. I thought this would be good for him and I could keep an eye on him." She shrugged, looking after Arney's rumpled, retreating figure. "Some men ought to have their hands cut off at the wrist when they reach for their first drink." She picked up her skirts in a courtly, old-fashioned gesture, and went off after the playwright in a rustle of taffeta.

"I think," Michael said, "I could stand a drink."

"Me, too," said Laura.

"Pal," said Mr. Parrish.

They stood silently at the bar, watching the bartender fill their glasses.

"The abuse of alcohol," Mr. Parrish said in a solemn, preacher-like voice, as he reached for his glass, "is the one thing that puts Man above the animal."

They all laughed and Michael raised his glass to Mr. Parrish before he drank.

"To Madrid," Parrish said, in an offhand, everyday way, and Laura said "To Madrid" in a hushed, breathy voice. Michael hesitated, feeling the old uneasiness, before he, too, said, "To Madrid."

They drank.

"When did you get back?" Michael asked. He felt uncomfortable, talking about it.

"Four days ago," Parrish said. He lifted the glass to his lips again. "You have very good liquor in this country," he said, grinning. He drank steadily, refilling his glass every five minutes, getting a little redder as time went by, but showing no other effects.

"When did you leave Spain?" Michael asked.

"Two weeks ago."

Two weeks ago, Michael thought, on the frozen roads, with the cold rifles and the makeshift uniforms and the planes overhead and the new graves. And now he's standing here in a blue suit like a truckdriver at his own wedding, rattling the ice cubes in his drink, with people talking about the last picture they made and what the critics said and what the doctor thought about the baby's habit of sleeping with his fist in his eyes, and a man with a guitar singing fake Southern ballads in the corner of the room in the heavy-carpeted, crowded, rich apartment eleven stories up in the unmarked, secure building, with a view of the Park through the tall windows, and the magenta girl with three breasts over the bar. And in a little while he would go down to the docks on the river that you could see from the windows and get on a boat and start back. And there were no marks on him of what he had been through, no hints in the good-natured, clumsy way in which he behaved, of what was ahead of him.

The human race, Michael thought, is insanely flexible. He was considerably older than Michael, and no doubt had led a much harder life, and yet he had been there, on the long marches and the bloody ground. He had killed and risked being killed, and was going back for more of the same . . . Michael jerked his head, despising himself for a moment as he realized that he was sorry Parrish was there, at this party, a red-faced, rough-handed, polite policeman to Michael's conscience.

". . . money is the important thing," Parrish was saying to Laura, "and political pressure. We can get plenty of guys who want to fight. But the British Government's impounded all the Loyalist gold in London, and Washington's really helping Franco. We have to sneak our fellows in, and it takes bribing and passage money and stuff like that. So one day, we were in the line outside University City, and it was cold, sweet God, it would freeze the nipples off a whale's belly, and they came to me and they said, 'Parrish, me lad, you're just wasting ammunition here anyway, and we haven't seen you hit a Fascist yet. So we decided, you're an eloquent lying son-of-a-bitch, go back to the States and tell some big, juicy, heartbreaking stories about the heroes of the Immortal International Brigade in the front line of the fight against the Fascists. And come back here with your pockets loaded.' So I get up at meetings and just let my imagination ramble, green and free. Before you know it, the people are dying with emotion and generosity, and what with the dough rolling in and all the girls, I think maybe I have found my true profession in the fight for liberty." He grinned, his brilliantly even false teeth shining happily in his face, and he pushed his empty glass toward the bartender. "Want to hear some bloody tales of the horrible war for freedom in tortured Spain?"

"No," said Michael, "not with that introduction."

"The truth," Parrish said, suddenly sober and unsmiling, "the truth is not for the likes of these." He swung around and surveyed the room. For the first time, Michael could sense, in

33

the cold, harsh, measuring eyes, something of what Parrish had been through. "The men running, the young boys that came five thousand miles suddenly surprised that they are actually dying, there, right there, themselves, with a bullet in their own sweet bellies. The French, stinking up the border and accepting bribes to let men walk on bleeding feet through the Pyrenees in the middle of the winter. The crooks and four-flushers and smart operators everywhere. On the docks. In the offices. Right up in battalion and company, right up next to you on the front line. The nice boys who see their pals get it and suddenly say, 'I must have made a mistake. This is different from the way it looked at Dartmouth.' "

A little plump forty-year-old woman in a school-girlish pink dress came up to the bar and took Laura's arm. "Laura, darling," she said, "I've been looking for you. It's your turn."

"Oh," Laura said, turning to the blonde woman, "I'm sorry if I kept you waiting, but Mr. Parrish was so interesting." Michael winced a little as Laura said "interesting." Mr. Parrish merely smiled at both women with an even, impartial lust.

"I'll be back in a few minutes," Laura told Michael. "Cynthia's been reading fortunes for the women and she's going to do mine now."

"See," Parrish said loudly, "if there's a forty-year-old Irishman with false teeth in your future."

"I'll ask," Laura said, laughing, and went off arm in arm with the fortune-teller. Michael watched her as she walked through the room, in her straight-backed, delicately sensual way, and caught two other men watching her, too. One was Donald Wade, a tall, pleasant-looking man, and the other was a man called Talbot, and they were both what Laura described as "ex-beaux" of hers. They seemed constantly to be invited to the same parties as the Whitacres. The term ex-beau was one which Michael sometimes puzzled over uneasily. What it really meant he was sure, was that Laura had had affairs with them, and wanted Michael to believe that she no longer had anything to do with them. He was suddenly annoyed at the whole situation, although at the moment, turning it over in his mind, there didn't seem to be very much to do about it.

"The girls of America," Parrish was saying, "are a song in a man's testicles."

Michael couldn't help laughing, as Parrish wagged his grizzled, solid head in solemn appreciation.

"Have a drink," Michael said.

"Pal," said Parrish.

They pushed their glasses at the bartender.

"When are you going back?" Michael asked.

Parrish looked around him, his blunt, open face taking on a ludicrous expression of guile. "Hard to say, Pal," he whispered.

34

"Not wise to say. The State Department, you know . . . Has its Fascist spies everywhere. As it is, I've forfeited my American citizenship, technically, by enlisting under the colors of a foreign power. Keep it to yourself, Pal, but I'd say a month, month and a half . . ."

"Are you going back alone?"

"Don't think so, Pal. Taking a nice little group of lads back with me." Parrish smiled benevolently. "The International Brigade is a wide-open growing concern." Parrish glanced at Michael reflectively, and Michael felt that the Irishman was measuring him, questioning in his own mind what Michael was doing there, in his fancy suit in this fancy apartment, why Michael wasn't at a machine gun this night instead of a bar.

"You looking at me?" Michael asked.

"No, Pal." Parrish wiped his cheek.

"Do you take my money?" Michael asked harshly.

"I'll take money," Parrish grinned, "from the holy hand of Pope Pius, himself."

Michael got out his wallet. He had just been paid, and he still had some money left over from his bonus. He put it all in Parrish's hand. It amounted to seventy-five dollars.

"Leave yourself carfare, Pal." Parrish carelessly stuffed it into a side pocket and patted Michael's shoulder. "We'll kill a couple of the bastards for you."

"Thanks." Michael put his wallet away. He didn't want to talk to Parrish any more. "You staying here at the bar?"

"Is there a good whorehouse in the building?" Parrish asked.

"No."

"Then I'll stay here," he said.

"See you later," Michael said. "I'm going to circulate."

"Sure, Pal," Parrish nodded coolly at him. "Thanks for the dough."

"Stuff it, Pal," Michael said.

"Sure, Pal." Parrish turned back to his drink, his wide, square shoulders a blue-serge bulwark in the froth of bare shoulders and satin lapels around him.

Michael walked slowly across the room toward a group in the corner. Long before he got there, he could see Louise looking at him, smiling tentatively at him. Louise was what Laura probably would call an "old girl" of his, except that, really, they had never stopped. Louise was married by now, too, but somehow, from time to time, for shorter or longer periods, she and Michael continued as lovers. There was a moral judgment to be made there some day, Michael felt. But Louise was one of the prettiest girls in New York, small, dark and clever-looking, and she was warm and undemanding. In a way she was dearer to him than his wife. Sometimes, lying next to each other, on winter afternoons in borrowed apartments, Louise would sigh, staring up at the ceiling, and say, "Isn't this wonderful? I suppose some day we ought to give it up." But neither she nor Michael took it seriously.

She was standing now next to Donald Wade. For a second, Michael got an unpleasant vision of the complexity of life, but it vanished as he kissed her and said, "Happy New Year."

He shook hands gravely with Wade, wondering, as always, why men thought they had to be so cordial to their wives' ex-lovers.

"Hello," Louise said. "Haven't seen you in a long time. You look very nice in your pretty suit. Where's Mrs. Whitacre?"

"Having her fortune told," Michael said. "The past isn't bad enough. She's got to have the future to worry about, too. Where's your husband?"

"I don't know." Louise waved vaguely and smiled at him in the serious private manner she reserved for him. "Around."

Wade bowed a little and moved off. Louise looked after him. "Didn't he use to go with Laura?" she asked.

"Don't be a cat," Michael said.

"Just wanted to know."

"The room," Michael said, "is loaded with guys who used to go with Laura." He surveyed the guests with sudden dissatisfaction. Wade, Talbot, and now another one had come in, a lanky actor by the name of Moran who had been in one of Laura's pictures. Their names had been linked in a gossip column in Hollywood and Laura had called New York early one morning to reassure Michael that it had been an official studio party, etcetera, etcetera...

"The room," Louise said, looking at him obliquely, "is full of girls who used to go around with you. Or maybe 'used to' isn't exactly what I mean."

"Parties these days," Michael said, "are getting too crowded. I'm not coming to them any more. Isn't there some place you and I can go and sit and hold hands quietly?"

"We can try," Louise said, and took his arm and led him down the hallway through the groups of guests, toward the rear of the apartment. Louise opened a door and looked in. The room was dark and she motioned Michael to follow. They tiptoed in, closed the door carefully behind them and sank onto a small couch. After the bright lights in the other rooms, Michael couldn't see anything here for a moment. He closed his eyes luxuriously, feeling Louise snuggle close to him, lean over and softly kiss his cheek.

"Now," she said, "isn't that better?"

There was a creaking of a bed across the room, and now, with his eyes growing more accustomed to the semi-light, Michael could see a figure heave itself clumsily up on one of the twin beds and reach out to the table between the beds.

There was the unmistakable rattle of a cup against a saucer and the figure lifted the cup and drank.

"Humiliation." The one word punctuated two long sips from the cup, and Michael recognized Arney, sitting up, his legs swung over the side of the bed. Arney leaned over, nearly toppling, and peered at the other bed. "Tommy," Arney said. "Tommy, are you up?"

"Yes, Mr. Arney," a ten-year-old voice came up sleepily from the pillow. It was the son of the Johnsons, whose home this was.

"Happy New Year, Tommy."

"Happy New Year, Mr. Arney."

"Don't let me disturb you, Tommy. I merely became sickened with adult society and I came here to wish the new generation a happy new year."

"Thank you very much, Mr. Arney."

"Tommy . . ."

"Yes, Mr. Arney." Tommy was waking up now and becoming more lively. Michael could feel Louise smothering giggles beside him, and he felt half amused, half annoyed at being caught dark and silent like this.

"Tommy," Arney was saying, "should I tell you a story?"

"I'd love a story," Tommy said.

"Let me see . . ." Arney sipped from the cup once more, with a loud rattling of crockery. "Let me see. I don't know any stories suitable for children."

"I like any kind of story," Tommy said. "I read *The Thin Man* last week."

"All right," Arney said grandly, "I will tell you a story unsuitable for children, Tommy. The story of my life."

"Were you ever knocked out by the butt end of a 45?" Tommy asked.

"Don't prompt me, Tommy," the playwright said, irritated. "If I was knocked out by the butt end of a 45 it will all come out in its proper time."

"I'm sorry, Mr. Arney." Tommy's voice was polite and hurt.

"Until I was twenty-eight years old," Arney began, "I was a young man of promise . . ."

Michael squirmed uneasily, feeling ashamed and idiotic listening to this, but Louise squeezed his hand warningly and he sat still.

"I had been educated in good schools, as they say in novels, Tommy. I worked hard and I could recognize quotations from all the English poets. Want a drink, Tommy?"

"No, thank you." Tommy was wide awake now, sitting up, fascinated.

"You are probably too young to remember the reviews of

my first play, Tommy. *The Long and the Short.* How old are you, Tommy?"

"Ten."

"Too young." There was the clatter of the teacup against the saucer. "I would quote some of them, but it might bore you. However, it would not be vanity to say that I was compared to Strindberg and O'Neill. You ever hear of Strindberg, Tommy?"

"No, sir."

"What the hell do they teach children in school these days?" Arney's voice was irritated and sharp. He sipped at his drink. "The story of my life, Tommy," he went on, somewhat mollified. "I was invited to all the best houses. I signed checks at four of the most expensive speakeasies in New York City. I had my picture in the papers on many separate occasions and I was asked to address committees and artistic organizations. I stopped speaking to all my old friends, and that was a relief, and I went to Hollywood and for a long time I made 3,500 dollars a week, and this was before the income tax, too. I discovered the bottle, Tommy, and I married a woman with a house in Antibes, France, and a brewery in Milwaukee. I betrayed her in 1931 with her best friend, and that was a mistake, because the lady was as bony as a mountain trout. . . ."

There was the noisy sucking on the cup. Michael knew he would just have to sit where he was in the dark and hope Arney wouldn't discover him.

"People say," Arney went on, musically now, his voice soft and nostalgic, "I left my talent in Hollywood, Tommy. And there's no doubt about it, that's the place to leave it if you have to leave it somewhere. But I don't believe them, Tommy. I don't believe them. I'm a has-been, and everybody avoids me. I don't go to a doctor because I'm sure he will tell me I am going to die in six months. My latest play would be kept from the stage in a well-regulated state, but it wasn't Hollywood that did it. I'm a weak, intelligent man, Tommy, and we don't live in the right age for weak, intelligent men. Take my advice, Tommy, grow up stupid. Strong and stupid."

Arney moved around heavily on the bed and stood up, his outline wavering against the dim light fading in through the window.

"Don't think for a minute, Tommy, that I'm complaining," Arney said in a loud, pugnacious voice. "I'm an old drunk, and everybody makes fun of me. I disappointed everybody I ever knew. But I'm not complaining. If I had it to do over again, Tommy, I'd do it just the way I did." He waved his arms and the cup and saucer fell to the carpet, breaking there. But Arney didn't seem to notice. "There's only one thing, Tommy," he said portentously, "one thing I'd do differently." He paused,

38

reflecting. Then he spoke, "I'd . . ." He stopped. "No, Tommy, you're too young."

He wheeled, majestically, his shoes cracking on the broken saucer, and started toward the door. Tommy lay quiet. Arney passed Louise and Michael and threw the door open. Light streamed in and Arney saw them sitting here. He smiled angelically. "Whitacre," he said, "Whitacre, old boy, how would you like to do an old man a favor? Go into the kitchen, Whitacre, old man, and get a cup and saucer and bring it here. Some son of a bitch broke mine."

"Sure," Michael said. He stood up and Louise stood with him. "Tommy," he said, as they went through the door, "go to sleep."

"Yes, sir," said Tommy, his voice sleepy but disturbed.

Michael sighed and closed the door and went looking for a cup and saucer.

The rest of the evening was confined to Michael's mind. Later on he didn't remember whether he had made a date with Louise for Tuesday afternoon or not, or whether Laura had told him that the fortune-teller had predicted they were going to be divorced or not. But he remembered seeing Arney appear at the other end of the room, smiling a little, whiskey dribbling down from his mouth on his chin. Arney, with his head slightly to one side, as though his neck was stiff, came walking, quite steadily, through the room, ignoring the other guests who were standing there, and came up next to Michael. He stood there, wavering for a moment, in front of the tall French window, then threw open the window and started to step out. His coat caught on a lamp. He stopped to disentangle it, and started out again. Michael watched him and knew that he should rush over and grab him. He felt himself starting to move sluggishly, his arms and legs dreamlike and light, although he knew that if he didn't move faster the playwright would be through the window and falling eleven stories before he could reach him.

Michael heard the quick scuff of shoes behind him. A man leaped past him and took the playwright in his arms. The two figures teetered dangerously on the edge, with the reflection of the night lights of New York a heavy red neon glow on the clouds outside. The window was slammed shut by someone else and they were safe. Then Michael saw that it was Parrish, who had been halfway across the room at the bar, who had come past him to save the playwright.

Laura was in Michael's arms, hiding her eyes, weeping. He was annoyed at her for being so useless and so demanding at a moment like that, and he was glad he could be annoyed at her because it kept him from thinking about how he had failed, although he knew he wouldn't be able to avoid thinking about it later.

They left soon after, with everyone very gay and offhand and pretending Arney had been playing a joke on his friends. Arney was lying on the floor, sleeping. He refused to go inside to a bed and he rolled off the couch every time he was raised to it. Parrish, smiling and happy, was at the bar once more, asking the bartender from the caterer's what union he belonged to.

Michael wanted to go home, but Laura said she was hungry, and somehow they were in a crowd of people and somebody had a car and everybody sat on everybody else's lap and he was relieved when they drew up to the big garish restaurant on Madison Avenue and he could get out of the crowded car.

They sat down in a shrill orange room with paintings of Indians for some reason all over the walls, and inexperienced waiters, hastily pressed into emergency service, stumbling erratically among the loud, still-celebrating diners. Michael felt drunk, his eyelids drooping with wooden insistence over his eyes. He didn't talk because he felt himself stuttering when he tried. He stared around him, his mouth curled in what he thought was lordly scorn for the world around him. Louise was at the table, he suddenly noticed, with her husband. And Katherine, with the three Harvard juniors. And Wade, he noticed, sitting next to Laura, holding her hand. Michael's head began to clear and ache at the same time. He ordered a hamburger and a bottle of beer.

This is disgraceful, he thought heavily, disgraceful. Ex-girls, ex-beaux, ex-nothing. Was it Tuesday afternoon he was to meet Louise, or Wednesday? And what afternoon was Wade to meet Laura? A nest of snakes hibernating for the winter, Arney had said. He was a silly, broken man, Arney, but he wasn't wrong there. There was no honor to this life, no form . . . Martinis, beer, brandy, Scotch, have another, and everything disappeared in a blur of alcohol—decency, fidelity, courage, decision. Parrish had to be one to jump across the room. Automatically. Danger, therefore jump. Michael had been right there, next to the window, and he had hardly moved, a small indecisive shuffling—no more. There he'd stood, too fat, too much liquor, too many attachments, a wife who was practically a stranger, darting in from Hollywood for a week at a time, full of that talk, doing God knows what with how many other men on those balmy orange-scented California evenings, while he frittered away the years of his youth, drifting with the easy tide of the theatre, making a little money, being content, never making the bold move . . . He was thirty years old and this was 1938. Unless he wanted to be driven to the same window as Arney, he had better take hold.

He got up and mumbled, "Excuse me," and started through

the crowded restaurant toward the men's room. Take hold, he said to himself, take hold. Divorce Laura, live a rigorous, ascetic life, live as he had when he was twenty, just ten years ago, when things were clear and honorable, and when you faced a new year, you weren't sick with yourself for the one just passed.

He went down the steps to the men's room. It would start right here. He'd soak his head with ice-cold water for ten minutes. The pale sweat would be washed off, the flush would die from his cheeks, his hair would be cool and in order on his head, he would look out across the new year with clearer eyes...

He opened the door to the men's room, and went to the washbowls and looked at himself with loathing in the mirror, at the slack face, the rumpled, conniving eyes, the weak, indecisive mouth. He remembered how he had looked at twenty. Tough, thin, alive, uncompromising . . . That face was still there, he felt, buried beneath the unpleasant face reflected in the mirror. He would quarry his old face out from the unsightly outcroppings of the years between.

He ducked his head and splashed the icy water on his eyelids and cheeks. He dried himself, his skin tingling pleasantly. Refreshed, he walked soberly up the steps to rejoin the others at the big table in the center of the noisy room.

CHAPTER THREE

ON THE WESTERN EDGE of America, in the sea-coast town of Santa Monica, among the flat sprawling streets and the shredding palms, the old year was coming to an end in soft, gray fog, rolling in off the oily water, rolling in over the scalloped surf breaking on the wet beaches, rolling in over the hot-dog stands, closed for the winter, and the homes of the movie stars, and the muffled coast road that led to Mexico and Oregon.

The streets of the town were deserted, left to the fog, as though the new year were a public disaster that all the inhabitants of the place were avoiding by wisely staying in their homes until the danger was past. Here and there a light shone wetly, and on some streets the fog was tinged the garish neon-red which has become the color of night-time city America. The flickering red tubes advertised restaurants, ice-cream parlors, moving-picture theatres, hotels, drive-ins, but their real effect in the soundless, sorrowful night was tragic and foreboding, as though the human race were being given a furtive glimpse, in the mist, of its last home, cavernous and blood-colored through gray, shuffling curtains.

The electric sign of the Sea View Hotel, from which at no time, even on the clearest days, could any body of water be observed, added its baleful, minor tone to the thin, sifting fog outside Noah's window. The light filtered into the darkened room and touched the damp plaster walls and the lithograph of Yosemite Falls above the bed. Splinters of red fell on Noah's father's sleeping face on the pillow, on the large, fierce nose, the curving, distended nostrils, the rigid, deep eyesockets, on the high, imposing brow, the bushy white hair, courtly moustache and Vandyke beard, like a Kentucky colonel's in the movies, ludicrous and out of place here, on a dying Jew in the narrow, hired room.

Noah would have liked to read as he sat there, but he didn't want to wake his father by putting on the light. He tried to sleep, sitting in the single, hard-upholstered chair, but his father's heavy breathing, roaring and uneven, kept him awake. The doctor had told Noah that Jacob was dying, as had the woman his father had sent away on Christmas Eve, that widow what was her name . . . Morton—but Noah didn't believe them. His father had had Mrs. Morton send him a telegram in Chicago, telling him to come at once. Noah had sold his overcoat and his typewriter and the old wardrobe trunk, to pay the bus fare. He had rushed out, sitting up all the way, and had arrived in Santa Monica light-headed and exhausted, just in time to be present for the big scene.

Jacob had brushed his hair and combed his beard, and had sat up in bed like Job arguing with God. He had kissed Mrs. Morton who was over fifty years old, and sent her from him, saying in his rolling, actorish voice, "I wish to die in the arms of my son. I wish to die among the Jews. Now we say good-bye."

That was the first time Noah had heard that Mrs. Morton wasn't Jewish. She wept, and the whole scene was like something from the second act of a Yiddish play on Second Avenue in New York. But Jacob had been adamant. Mrs. Morton had gone. Her married daughter had insisted on taking the weeping widow away to the family home in San Francisco. Noah was left alone with his father in the small room with the single bed on the side street a half mile from the winter ocean.

The doctor came for a few moments every morning. Aside from him, Noah didn't see anyone. He didn't know anyone else in the town. His father insisted that he stay at his side day and night, and Noah slept on the floor near the window, on a lumpy mattress that the hotel manager had grudgingly given him.

Noah listened to the heavy, tragic breathing, filling the medicine-smelling air. For a moment he was sure his father was awake and purposely breathing that way, labored and harsh, not because he had to, but because he felt that if a man lay dying, his every breath should announce that fact. Noah stared closely at his father's handsome patriarchal head on the dark pillow next to the dimly glinting array of medicine bottles. Once more Noah couldn't help feeling annoyed at the soaring, bushy, untrimmed eyebrows, the wavy, theatrical, coarse mane of hair, which Noah was sure his father secretly bleached white, the spectacular white beard on the lean, ascetic jaws. Why, Noah thought, irritably, why does he insist on looking like a Hebrew King, on an embassy to California? It would be different if he had lived that way . . . But with all the women he'd gone through in his long, riotous life, all the bankruptcies, all the money borrowed and never returned, all the creditors that stretched from Odessa to Honolulu, it was a sour joke on the world for his father to look like Moses coming down from Sinai with the stone tablets in his hands.

"Make haste," Jacob said, opening his eyes, "make haste, O God, to deliver me. Make haste to help me, O Lord."

That was another habit that had always infuriated Noah. Jacob knew the Bible by heart, both in Hebrew and English, although he was absolutely irreligious, and salted his speech with long, impressive quotations at all times.

"Deliver me, O my God, out of the hand of the wicked, out of the hand of the unrighteous and cruel man." Jacob rolled his head, facing the wall, and closed his eyes once more. Noah got up from his chair and went over to the bed and pulled the blankets up closer around his father's throat. But there was no sign from Jacob that he noticed any of this. Noah stared down at him for a moment, listening to the bitter breathing. Then he turned and went to the window. He opened the window and sniffed at the dank, rolling mist, freighted with the heavy smell of the sea. A car sped dangerously down the street between the straggling palms, and there was the sound of a horn blown in celebration, lost in the mist.

What a place, Noah thought irrelevantly, what a place to celebrate New Year's Eve! He shivered a little in the influx of cold air, but he kept the window open. He had been working in a mail-order house in Chicago as a filing clerk, and, being honest with himself, the excuse to come to California, even if it was to watch his father die, had been a welcome one. The sunny coast, the warm beaches, he had thought, the orchards tossing their leaves in the sun, the pretty girls . . . He grinned sourly as he looked around him. It had rained for a week.

And his father was prolonging his death-scene interminably. Noah was down to his last seven dollars and he had found out that creditors had a lien on his father's photographic studio. Even under the best of circumstances, even if everything were sold at high prices, they could only hope to recover thirty cents on the dollar. Noah had gone down to the shabby little studio near the ocean and had peered in through the locked plate-glass door. His father had specialized in very artistic, very terrible retouched portraits of young women. A hundred heavy-lidded local beauties draped in black velvet, with startling high lights and slumbrous eyes had peered back at him through the dusty neglected glass. It was the sort of business his father had had again and again, from one end of the country to another, the sort of business that had driven Noah's mother to an early death, the sort of business that appears and disappears in down-at-the-heel buildings for a season, makes a ragged little flourish for a few months then vanishes, leaving behind it only some inconclusive, tattered books, a smattering of debts, a stock of aging photographs and advertising signs that are finally burned in a back alley when the next tenant arrives.

In his day Jacob had also sold cemetery lots, contraceptive devices, real estate, sacramental wine, advertising space, second-hand furniture, bridal clothing, and had even once, improbably, set himself up in a ship chandler's store in Baltimore, Maryland. And at no one of these professions had he ever made a living. And in all of them, with his deft, rolling tongue, his archaic rhetoric, loaded with Biblical quotations, with his intense, handsome face and vital, broad-handed movements, he had always found women who made up for him the difference in what he secured by his own efforts from the economic battlefield around him and what it took to keep him alive. Noah was his only child, and Noah's life had been wandering and disordered. Often he had been deserted, often left for long periods with vague, distant relatives, or, lonely and persecuted, in shabby military schools.

"They are burning my brother Israel in the furnace of the heathen."

Noah sighed and closed the window. Jacob was lying rigid now, staring up at the ceiling, his eyes wide open. Noah put on the single light which he had shaded with pink paper that was a little singed now in spots and added its small smell to the general sick-room atmosphere when the light was on.

"Is there anything I can do for you, Father?" Noah asked.

"I can see the flames," Jacob said. "I can smell the burning flesh. I can see my brother's bones crumbling in the fire. I deserted him and he is dying tonight among the foreigners."

Noah couldn't help being annoyed with his father. Jacob hadn't seen his brother in thirty-five years, had, in fact, left him in Russia to support their mother and father when Jacob had made his way to America. From everything that Noah had heard, Jacob had despised his brother, and they had parted enemies. But two years before, somehow, a letter from his brother had reached him from Hamburg, where Jacob's brother had gone in 1919. The letter had been desperate and pleading. Noah had to admit that Jacob had done everything he could —had written countless letters to the Immigration Bureau, had gone to Washington and haunted the corridors of the State Department buildings, an improbable, bearded, anachronistic, holy vision, half rabbi, half river-gambler, among the soft-spoken, impervious young men from Princeton and Harvard who shuffled the papers vaguely and disdainfully on their polished desks. But nothing had come of it, and after the single, wild cry for help, there had been the dreadful silence of official Germany, and Jacob had returned to his sun and his photographic studio and his plump, widowed Mrs. Morton in Santa Monica and had said no more about it. But tonight, with the red-tinted fog sighing at the window, and the new year standing at the gate, and death, according to the doctor, a matter of hours, the deserted brother, caught in the welter of Europe, cried piercingly through the clouding brain.

"Flesh," Jacob said, his voice still rolling and deep, even on his last pillow, "flesh of my flesh, bone of my bone, you are being punished for the sins of my body and the sins of my soul."

O God, Noah thought, looking down at his father, why must he always speak like a blank-verse shepherd giving dictation to a secretary on a hill in Judea?

"Don't smile." Jacob peered sharply at him, his eyes surprisingly bright and knowing in the dark hollows of his face. "Don't smile, my son, my brother is burning for you."

"I'm not smiling, Father." Noah touched Jacob's forehead soothingly. The skin was hot and sandy and Noah could feel a small, twitching revulsion in his fingertips.

Jacob's face was contorted in oratorical scorn. "You stand there in your cheap American clothes and you think, 'What has he to do with me? He is a stranger to me. I have never seen him and if he dies, in the furnaces in Europe, what of it, people die every minute all over the world.' He is not a stranger to you. He is a Jew and the world is hunting him, and you are a Jew and the world is hunting you."

He closed his eyes in cold exhaustion and Noah thought, if he only talked in simple, honest language, you would be moved, affected. After all, a father dying, obsessed with the thought of a murdered brother five thousand miles away, a single man at his loneliest moment, feeling the ghost insecure and fleeting in his throat, mourning for the fate of his people all over the world, was a touching and tragic thing. And while it was true that to him, Noah, there was no sense of immediacy or personal tragedy in what was happening in Europe, intellectually and rationally he could feel the somber weight of it. But long years of his father's rhetoric, his father's stagy gesturing for effect, had robbed Noah of all ability to be moved by him. All he could think of as he stood there looking at the gray face, listening to the heaving breath, was, Good God, the old man is going to keep it up to the end.

"When I left him," his father said, without opening his eyes, "when I left Odessa in 1903, Israel gave me eighteen rubles and he said to me, 'You're no good. Congratulations. Take my advice. Stick to women. America can't be that different from the rest of the world. Women will be idiots there too. They will support you.' We didn't shake hands, and I left. He should have shaken my hand, no matter what, don't you think, Noah?" Suddenly his father's voice was changed. It was small and without timbre and it did not remind Noah of a stage performance.

"Noah . . ."

"Yes, Father?"

"Don't you think he should have shaken my hand?"

"Yes, Father."

"Noah . . ."

"Yes, Father. . . ."

"Shake my hand, Noah."

After a moment, Noah leaned over and picked up his father's dry, broad hand. The skin was flaked, and the nails, usually exquisitely cared for, pared and polished, were long and jagged and had crescents of dirt under them. They shook hands. Noah could feel the thin, restless, uneven pressure of the fingers.

"All right, all right . . ." Jacob said, suddenly peevish, and pulled his hand away, caught in some inexplicable vision of his own. "All right, enough." He sighed, stared up at the ceiling.

"Noah . . ."

"Yes?"

"Have you a pencil and paper?"

"Yes."

"Write this down . . ."

Noah went over to the table and sat down. He picked up a pencil and took out a sheet of flimsy white paper with an engraving of the Sea View Hotel on it, large, surrounded by sweeping lawns and tall trees, without basis of real life, but convincing and holiday-like on the stationery.

"To Israel Ackerman," Jacob said in a plain, business-like voice, "29 Kloster Strasse, Hamburg, Germany."

"But, Father," Noah began.

"Write it in Hebrew," Jacob said, "if you can't write German. He's not very well educated, but he'll manage to understand."

46

"Yes, Father." Noah couldn't write Hebrew or German, but he didn't see any sense in telling his father.

"My dear brother . . . Have you got that?"

"Yes, Father."

"I am ashamed of myself for not having written sooner," Jacob began, "but you can well imagine how busy I've been. Soon after coming to America . . . Have you got that, Noah?"

"Yes," Noah said, making aimless little scratches on the paper. "I have it."

"Soon after coming to America . . ." Jacob's voice rolled on, low and full of effort in the damp room, "I went into a large business. I worked hard, although I know you will not believe it, and I was promoted from one important position to another. In eighteen months I became the most valuable member of the firm. I was made a partner and I married the daughter of the owner of the business, a Mr. von Kramer, an old American family. I know you will be glad to know that we have a family of five sons and two daughters who are a joy and pride to their parents in our old age, and we have retired to an exclusive suburb of Los Angeles, a large city on the Pacific Ocean where it is sunny all the time. We have a fourteen-room house and I do not rise till nine-thirty every morning and I go to my club and play golf every afternoon. I know you will be interested in this information at this time . . ."

Noah felt a clot of emotion jammed in his throat. He had the wild notion that if he opened his mouth he would laugh, and that his father would die on peal after peal of his son's laughter.

"Noah," Jacob asked querulously, "are you writing this down?"

"Yes, Father." Somehow Noah managed to say it.

"It is true," Jacob went on in his calm, dictating voice, "that you are the oldest son and you were constantly giving advice. But now, oldest and youngest do not have the same meaning. I have traveled considerably, and I think maybe you can profit from some advice from me. It is important to remember how to behave as a Jew. There are many people in the world, and they are becoming more numerous, who are full of envy. They look at a Jew and say, 'Look at his table manners,' or 'The diamonds on his wife are really paste,' or 'See how much noise he makes in a theatre,' or 'His scales are crooked. You will not get your money's worth in his shop.' The times are getting more difficult and a Jew must behave as though the life of every other Jew in the world depended on every action of his. So he must eat quietly, using his knife and fork delicately. He must not put diamonds on his wife, especially paste ones. His scales must be the most honest in the city. He must walk in a digni-

47

fied and self-respecting manner. "No," Jacob cried, "cross all that out. It will only make him angry."

He took a deep breath and was silent for a long time. He didn't seem to move on his bed and Noah looked uneasily over at him to make sure he was still alive.

"Dear Brother," Jacob said, finally, his voice broken and hoarse, and unrecognizable, "everything I have told you is a lie. I have led a miserable life and I have cheated everyone and I drove my wife to her death and I have only one son and I have no hope for him and I am bankrupt and everything you have told me would happen to me has happened to me. . . ."

His voice stopped. He choked and tried to say something else, and then he died.

Noah touched his father's chest, searching for the beating of his heart. The skin was wrinkled and the bones of his chest were jagged and frail. The stillness under the parched, flaked skin and the naked bone was final.

Noah folded his father's hands on his chest, and closed the piercing, staring eyes, because he had seen people doing that in the movies. Jacob's mouth was open, with a realistic, alive expression, as though he were on the verge of speech, but Noah didn't know what to do about that, so he left it alone. As he looked down at his father's dead face, Noah could not help realizing that he felt relieved. It was over now. The demanding imperious voice was quiet. There would be no more gestures.

Noah walked around the room, flatly taking inventory of the things of value in it. There wasn't much. Two shabby, rather flashy double-breasted suits, a leather-bound edition of the King James Bible, a silver frame with a photograph of Noah, aged seven and on a Shetland pony, a small box with a pair of cufflinks and a tiepin, made of nickel and glass, a tattered red manila envelope with a string tied around it. Noah opened the envelope and took out the papers: twenty shares of stock in a radio-manufacturing corporation that had gone into bankruptcy in 1927.

There was a cardboard box on the bottom of the closet. Noah took it out and opened it. Inside, carefully wrapped in soft flannel, was a large, old-fashioned portrait camera, with a big lens. It was the one thing in the room which looked as though it had been treated with love and consideration, and Noah was grateful that his father had been crafty enough to hide it from his creditors. It might even pay for the funeral. Touching the worn leather and the polished glass of the camera, Noah thought, fleetingly, that it would be good to keep the camera, keep the one well-preserved remnant of his father's life, but he knew it was a luxury he could not afford. He put the camera back in the box, after wrapping it well, and hid the box under a pile of old clothes in the corner of the closet.

He went to the door and looked back. In the mean rays of the single lamp, his father looked forlorn and in pain on the bed. Noah turned the light off and went out.

He walked slowly down the street. The air and the slight exercise felt good after the week in the cramped room, and he breathed deeply, feeling his lungs fill, feeling young and healthy, listening to the soft muffled tap of his heels on the glistening sidewalks. The sea air smelt strange and clean in the deserted night, and he walked in the direction of the beach, the tang of salt getting stronger and stronger as he approached the cliff that loomed over the ocean.

Through the murk came the sound of music, echoing and fading, suddenly growing stronger, with tricks of the wind. Noah walked toward it and as he got to the corner, he saw that the music came from a bar across the street. People were going in and out under a sign that said, "No Extra Charge for the Holiday. Bring the New Year in at O'Day's."

The tune changed on the jukebox inside and a woman's low voice sang, "Night and day you are the one, Only you beneath the moon and under the sun," her voice dominating the empty, damp night with powerful, well-modulated passion.

Noah crossed the street, opened the door and went in. Two sailors and a blonde were at the other end of the bar, looking down at a drunk with his head on the mahogany. The bartender glanced up when Noah came in.

"Have you got a telephone?" Noah asked.

"Back there." The bartender motioned toward the rear of the room. Noah started toward the booth.

"Be polite, boys," the blonde was saying to the sailors as Noah passed. "Rub his neck with ice."

She smiled widely at Noah, her face green with the reflection from the jukebox. Noah nodded to her and stepped into the telephone booth. He took out a card that the doctor had given him. On it was the telephone number of a twenty-four-hour-a-day undertaker.

Noah dialed the number. He held the receiver to his ear, listening to the insistent buzzing in the earpiece, thinking of the phone on the dark, shiny desk, under a single shaded light in the mortuary office, ringing the New Year in. He was about to hang up when he heard a voice at the other end of the wire.

"Hello," the voice said, somehow vague and remote. "Grady Mortuary."

"I would like to inquire," Noah said, "about a funeral. My father just died."

"What is the name of the party?"

"What I wanted to know," said Noah, "is the range of prices. I haven't very much money and . . ."

"I will have to know the name of the party," the voice said, very official.

"Ackerman."

"Waterfield," said the thick voice on the other end. "First name, please . . ." and then, in a whisper, "Gladys, stop it! Gladys!" Then back into the phone, with the hint of a smothered laugh, "First name, please."

"Ackerman," said Noah. "Ackerman."

"Is that the first name?"

"No," said Noah. "That's the last name. The first name is Jacob."

"I wish," said the voice, with alcoholic dignity, "you would talk more clearly."

"What I want to know," said Noah loudly, "is what you charge for cremation."

"Cremation. Yes," the voice said, "we supply that service to those parties who wish it."

"What is the price?" Noah asked.

"How many coaches?"

"What?"

"How many coaches to the services?" the voice asked, saying "shervishes." "How many guests and relatives will there be?"

"One," said Noah. "There will be one guest and relative."

Night and Day came to an end with a crash and Noah couldn't hear what the man on the other end of the wire said.

"I want it to be as reasonable as possible," Noah said, desperately. "I don't have much money."

"I shee, I shee," the man at the Mortuary said. "One question, if I may. Does the deceased have any insurance?"

"No," said Noah.

"Then it will have to be cash, you understand. In advance, you understand."

"How much?" Noah shouted.

"Do you wish the remains in a plain cardboard box or in a silver plated urn?"

"A plain cardboard box."

"The cheapest price I can quote you, my dear friend . . ." The voice on the other end suddenly became large and coherent. ". . . is seventy six dollars and fifty cents."

"That will be an additional five cents for five minutes," the operator's voice broke in.

"All right." Noah put another nickel into the box and the operator said, "Thank you." Noah said, "All right. Seventy-six dollars and fifty cents." Somehow he would get it together. "The day after tomorrow. In the afternoon." That would give him time to go downtown on January second and sell the camera and the other things. "The address is Sea View Hotel. Do you know where that is?"

50

"Yes," the drunken voice said, "yes, indeedy. The Sea View Hotel. I will send a man around tomorrow and you can sign the contract . . ."

"Okay," Noah said, sweating, preparing to hang up.

"One more thing, my dear man," the voice went on. "One more thing. The last rites."

"What about the last rites?"

"What religion does the deceased profess?"

Jacob had professed no religion, but Noah didn't think he had to tell the man that. "He was a Jew."

"Oh." There was silence for a moment on the wire and then Noah heard the woman's voice say, gayly and drunkenly, "Come on, George, les have another little drink."

"I regret," the man said, "that we are not equipped to perform funeral services on Hebrews."

"What's the difference?" Noah shouted. "He wasn't religious. He doesn't need any ceremonies."

"Impossible," the voice said thickly, but with dignity. "We do not cater to Hebrews. I'm sure you can find many others . . . many others who are equipped to cremate Hebrews."

"But Dr. Fishbourne recommended you," Noah shouted, insanely. He felt as though he couldn't go through all this again with another undertaker, and he felt trapped and baffled. "You're in the undertaking business, aren't you?"

"My condolences to you, my dear man," the voice said, "in your hour of grief, but we cannot see our way clear . . ."

Noah heard a scuffle at the other end of the wire and the woman's voice say, "Let me talk to him, Georgie." Then the woman got on the phone. "Listen," she said loudly, her voice brassy and whiskey-rich, "why don't you quit? We're busy here. You heard what Georgie said. He don't burn Kikes. Happy New Year." And she hung up.

Noah's hands were trembling and he felt the sweat coming out on his skin. He put the receiver back on the hook with difficulty. He opened the door of the booth and walked slowly toward the door, past the jukebox, which was playing a jazz version of Loch Lomond, past the group of blonde and drunk and sailors at the bar. The blonde smiled at him and said, "What's the matter, Big Boy, wasn't she home?"

Noah hardly heard her. He walked slowly, feeling weak and tired, toward the unoccupied end of the bar near the door and sat on a stool.

"Whiskey," he said. When it came, he drank it straight and ordered another. The two drinks had an immediate, surging effect on him, blurring the outlines of the room, blurring the music and the other people in the bar into softer and more agreeable forms, and when the blonde, in her tight flowered yellow dress with red shoes and a little hat with a purple veil,

51

came down the bar toward him, swaying her full hips exaggeratedly, he grinned at her.

"There," the blonde said, touching his arm softly, "there, that's better."

"Happy New Year," Noah said.

"Honey . . ." The blonde sat down on the stool next him, jiggling her tightly girdled buttocks on the red leatherette seat, rubbing her knee against his. "Honey, I'm in trouble, and I looked around the bar and I decided you were the one man in the room I could depend on. Orange Blossom," she said to the bartender who had padded up to where she was sitting. "In time of trouble," she went on, holding Noah's arm at the elbow, looking earnestly at him through her veil, her small, blue, mascara'd eyes inviting and serious, "in time of trouble I like Italian men. They have more character. They're excitable, but they're sympathetic. And, to tell you the truth, Honey, I like an excitable man. Show me a man who doesn't get excited and I'll show you a man who couldn't make a woman happy for ten minutes a year. There are two things I look for in a man. A sympathetic character and full lips."

"What?" Noah asked, dazed.

"Full lips," the blonde said earnestly. "My name is Georgia, Honey, what's yours?"

"Ronald Beaverbrook," Noah said. "And I have to tell you . . . I'm not an Italian."

"Oh." The woman looked disappointed and she drank half her Orange Blossom in one smooth gulp. "I could have sworn. What are you, Ronald?"

"An Indian," Noah said. "A Sioux Indian."

"Even so," the woman said, "I bet you can make a woman very happy."

"Have a drink," Noah said.

"Honey," the woman called to the bartender. "Two Orange Blossoms. Double, Honey." She turned back to Noah. "I like Indians, too," she said. "The one thing I don't like is ordinary Americans. They don't know how to use a woman properly. On and off and bang, they're out of bed and they're putting on their pants and on their way home to their wives. Honey," she said, finishing her first drink, "Honey, why don't you go over to those two boys in blue and tell them you're taking me home? Take a beer bottle with you, in case they give you an argument."

"Did you come with them?" Noah asked. He was feeling very light-headed now, remote and amused, and he caressed the woman's hand lightly and smiled into her eyes as he talked. Her hands were calloused and worn and she was ashamed of them.

"It comes from working in the laundry," she said sadly. "Don't ever work in a laundry, Honey."

"Okay," said Noah.

"I came with that one." With a gesture of her head, the veil fluttering in the green and purple light of the jukebox, she indicated the drunk with his head on the bar. "Knocked out of the box in the first inning. I'll tell you something." She leaned close to Noah and whispered to him, and he got a strong impression of gin and onions and violet perfume, "The sailors are plotting against him. In the uniform of their country. They are going to roll him and they're planning to follow me and purse-snatch my purse in a dark alley. Take a beer bottle, Ronald, and go talk to them."

The bartender put down their drinks and the woman took out a ten-dollar bill and gave it to him. "This is on me," she said. "This is a poor lonely boy on New Year's Eve."

"You don't have to pay for me," Noah said.

"To us, Honey." She raised the glass three inches from his face, and looked over it, through her veil, melting and coquettish. "What's money for, Honey, if it isn't for the use of your friends?"

They drank and the woman put her hand on his leg and caressed his knee. "You're terribly stingy, Honey," she said. "We'll have to do something about that. Let's get out of here. I don't like this place any more. Let's go up to my little apartment. I got a bottle of Four Roses, just for you and me, and we can have our own private little celebration. Kiss me once, Honey." She leaned over again and closed her eyes determinedly. Noah kissed her. Her lips were soft and there was a taste of raspberry from her lipstick, along with the onion and gin. "I can't wait, Honey." She got down off the stool, quite steadily, and took his arm, and they walked, carrying their drinks to the rear of the bar.

The two sailors watched them coming. They were very young and there was a puzzled, disappointed look on their faces.

"Be careful of my friend," the woman warned them. "He's a Sioux Indian." She kissed Noah's neck behind the ear. "I'll be right out, Honey," she said. "I'm going to freshen up, so you'll love me." She giggled and squeezed his hand moistly, still holding her glass, walked, with her exaggerated, mincing gait, the flowers dancing over her girdled rear, into the ladies' room.

"What's she been giving you?" the younger of the two sailors asked. He didn't have his hat on and he had his hair cut so short that it looked like the first outcropping of fuzz on a baby's skull.

"She says," Noah said, feeling powerful and alert, "she says you want to rob her."

The sailor with the hat on snorted. "We rob her? That's hot. It's just the other way around, Brother."

"Twenty-five bucks," the young sailor said. "Twenty-five

apiece, she asked. She said she never did it before and she's married and she ought to get paid for the risks she's taking."

"Who does she think she is?" the one with the hat on demanded. "How much did she ask you?"

"Nothing," Noah said, and he felt an absurd sense of pride. "And she wants to throw in a bottle of Four Roses."

"How do you like that?" The older sailor turned bitterly to his partner.

"You going with her?" the younger one asked, avidly.

Noah shook his head. "No."

"Why not?" the young one asked.

Noah shrugged. "I don't know."

"Boy," the young one said, "you must be well serviced."

"Ah," said the sailor with the hat on, "let's get out of here. Santa Monica!" He stared accusingly at the other sailor. "We might just as well have stayed on the Base."

"Where's the Base?" Noah asked.

"San Diego. But *he* . . ." The older sailor gestured bitterly and derisively at the fuzz-topped one. . . . "he had us all fixed up in Santa Monica. Two widows with a private house. That's the last time I'll leave any arrangements to you."

"It's not my fault," the young one said doggedly. "How was I supposed to know they were kidding me? How was I supposed to know the address was a phony?"

"We walked around in this damn fog for three hours," the older sailor said, "looking for that fake address. New Year's Eve! I've had better New Years when I was seven years old on a farm in Oklahoma. Come on . . . I'm getting out of here."

"What about him?" Noah touched the drunk sleeping peacefully on the mahogany.

"That's the lady's problem."

The young sailor put on his little white hat with an air of severe purpose and the two boys went out. "Twenty-five bucks!" Noah heard the older one say as he slammed the door.

Noah waited a moment, then patted the sleeping drunk in a comradely fashion, and followed the sailors. He stood outside the door, breathing the soft wet air, feeling it chill his flushed face. Under a wavering, uncertain lamppost down the street he saw the two blue figures, forlornly disappearing into the fog. He turned and went in the other direction, the whiskey he had drunk hammering musically and pleasantly at his temples.

Noah opened the door with careful deliberation, silently, and stepped into the dark room. The smell was there. He had forgotten the smell. Alcohol, medicine, something sweet and heavy . . . He fumbled for the light. He felt the nerves in his hand twitching and he stumbled against a chair before he found the lamp.

His father lay rigid and frail on the bed, his mouth open as if to speak in the bare light. Noah swayed a little as he looked down at him. Foolish, tricky old man, with the fancy beard and the bleached hair and the leatherbound Bible.

Make haste, make haste, O God, to deliver me . . . What religion does the deceased profess? Noah felt a little dizzy. His mind didn't seem to be able to fix on any one thing, and one thought slid in on top of another, independent and absurd. Full lips. Twenty-five dollars for the sailors and nothing for him. He had never had particular luck with women, certainly nothing like that. Trouble probably made a man attractive, and the woman had sensed it. Of course she had been terribly drunk . . . Ronald Beaverbrook. The way the flowers had waved on her skirt as she rolled toward the ladies' room. If he had stayed he'd probably be snug in bed with her now, under the warm covers, the soft, fat, white flesh, onion, gin, raspberry. He had a piercing, sharp moment of regret that he was standing here in the naked room with the dead old man . . . If the positions had been reversed, he thought, if it was he lying there and the old man up and around, and the old man had got the offer, he was damned sure Jacob would be in that bed now, with the blonde and the Four Roses. What a thing to think of. Noah shook his head. His father, from whose seed he sprang. God, was he going to get to talk like him as he grew older?

Noah made himself look for a whole minute at his father's dead face. He tried to cry. Somehow, deserted this way, at the end of a year, on this winter night, a man, any man, had the right to expect a tear from his only son.

Noah had never really thought very much about his father, once he had got old enough to think about him at all. He had been bitter about him, but that was all. Looking at the pale, lined head, looming from the pillow like a stone statue, noble and proud as Jacob had always known he would look in death, Noah made a conscious effort to think of his father. How far Jacob had come searching for this narrow room on the shore of the Pacific. Out of the grimy streets of Odessa, across Russia and the Baltic Sea, across the ocean, into the sweat and clangor of New York. Noah closed his eyes and thought of Jacob, quick and lithe, as a young man, with that handsome brow and that fierce nose, taking to English with a quick, natural, overblown rhetorical instinct, striding down the crowded streets, his eyes lively and searching, with a ready bold smile for girls and partners and customers and travel . . . Jacob, unafraid, and dishonest, wandering through the South, through Atlanta and Tuscaloosa, quick-fingered, never really interested in money, but cheating for it, and finally letting it slip away, up the continent to Minnesota and Montana, laughing, smoking black cigars, known in saloons and gambling halls, making dirty jokes and quoting Isaiah in the same breath, marrying Noah's mother in Chicago, grave-eyed and responsible for a day, tender and delicate and perhaps even resolved to settle down and be an honorable citizen, with middle age looming over him, and his hair touched at the ends with gray. And Jacob singing to Noah in his rich, affected baritone, in the plush-furnished parlor after dinner, singing, "I was walking through the park one day, In the merry, merry month of May . . ."

Noah shook his head. Somewhere in the back of his mind, echoing and faraway, the voice, singing, young and strong, resounded, *"In the merry, merry month of May,"* and refused to be stilled.

And the inevitable collapse as the years claimed Jacob. The shabby businesses, getting shabbier, the charm fading, the enemies more numerous, the world tighter-lipped and more firmly organized against him, the failure in Chicago, the failure in Seattle, the failure in Baltimore, the final, down-at-the-heels, scrubby failure in Santa Monica . . . "I have led a miserable life and I have cheated everyone and I drove my wife to death and I have only one son and I have no hope for him and I am bankrupt . . ." And the deceived brother, crumbling in the furnace, haunting him across the years and the ocean, with the last, agonized breath. . . .

Noah stared, dry-eyed at his father. Jacob's mouth was open, intolerably alive. Noah jumped up, and crossed the room, wavering, and tried to push his father's mouth shut. The beard was stiff and harsh against Noah's hand, and the teeth made a loud, incongruous clicking sound as the mouth closed. But the lips fell open, ready for speech, when Noah took his hand away. Again and again, more and more vigorously, Noah pushed the mouth shut. The hinges of the jaw made a sharp little sound and the jaw felt loose and unmoored, but each time Noah took his hand away the mouth opened, the teeth gleaming in the yellow light. Noah braced himself against the bed with his knees to give himself more leverage. But his father, who had been contrary and stubborn and intractable with his parents, his teachers, his brother, his wife, his luck, his partners, his women, his son, all his life, could not be changed now.

Noah stepped back. The mouth hung open, pitiful and pale under the swirling white moustaches, under the noble arch of the deceptive dead head on the gray pillow.

Finally, and for the first time, Noah wept.

CHAPTER FOUR

CHRISTIAN FELT like an imposter, sitting in the little open scout car, with his helmet on his head. He held his light automatic machine pistol loosely over his knees as they sped cheerfully along the tree-bordered French road. He was eating cherries they had picked from an orchard back near Meaux. Paris lay just ahead over the ripples of frail green hills. To the French, who must be peering at him from behind the shutters of their stone houses along the road, he looked, he knew, like a conqueror and stern soldier and destroyer. He hadn't heard a shot fired yet, and here the war was already over.

He turned to talk to Brandt, sitting in the back seat. Brandt was a photographer in one of the propaganda companies and he had hitched on to Christian's reconnaissance squadron as far back as Metz. He was a frail, scholarly-looking man who had been a mediocre painter before the war. Christian had grown friendly with him when Brandt had come to Austria for the spring skiing. Brandt's face was burned a bright red and his eyes were sandy from the wind, and his helmet made him look like a small boy playing soldier in the family backyard. Christian grinned at him, jammed in there with an enormous Corporal from Silesia, who spread himself happily over Brandt's legs and photographic equipment in the cramped little seat.

"What're you laughing about, Sergeant?" Brandt asked.

"The color of your nose," Christian said.

Brandt touched the burned, flaked skin gingerly. "Down to the seventh layer," he said. "It is an indoor-model nose. Come on, Sergeant, hurry up and take me to Paris, I need a drink."

"Patience," Christian said. "Just a little patience. Don't you know there's a war on?"

The Silesian Corporal laughed uproariously. He was a high-spirited young man, simple and stupid, and aside from being anxious to please his superiors, he was having a wonderful time on his journey across France. The night before, very solemnly, he had told Christian, as they lay side by side on their blankets along the road, that he hoped the war didn't end too soon. He wanted to kill at least one Frenchman. His father had lost a leg at Verdun in 1916, and the Corporal, whose name was Kraus, remembered saying, at the age of seven, standing rigidly in front of his one-legged father after church on Christmas Eve, "I will die happy after I have killed a Frenchman." That had been fifteen years ago. But he still peered hopefully at each new town for signs of Frenchmen who might oblige him. He had been thoroughly disgusted back at Chanly, when a French Lieutenant had appeared in front of a café, carrying a white flag, and had surrendered sixteen likely candidates to them without firing a shot.

Christian glanced back, past Brandt's comic burning face, at the other two cars speeding smoothly along on the even, straight road at intervals of seventy-five meters behind them. Christian's Lieutenant had gone down another parallel road with the rest of the section, leaving these three cars under Christian's command. They were to keep moving toward Paris, which they had been assured would not be defended. Christian grinned as he felt himself swelling a little with pride at this first independent command, three cars and eleven men, with armament of ten rifles and tommyguns and one heavy machine gun.

He turned in his seat and watched the road ahead of him. What a pretty country, he thought. How industriously it has been taken care of, the neat fields bordered by poplars, the regular lines of the plowing now showing the budding green of June.

How surprising and perfect it all had been, he thought drowsily. After the long winter of waiting, the sudden superb bursting out across Europe, the marvelous irresistible tide of energy, organized and detailed down to the last salt tablet and tube of Salvarsan (each man had been issued three with his emergency field rations in Aachen, before they started out, and Christian had grinned at the Medical Department's estimate of the quality of French resistance). And how exactly everything had worked. The dumps and maps and water just where they had been told they would be, the strength of the enemy and the extent of his resistance exactly as predicted, the roads in precisely the condition they had been told they would be. Only Germans, he thought, remembering the complex flood of men and machines pouring across France, only Germans could have managed it.

There was the sound of an airplane over the hum of the scout car's engine. Christian looked up behind him and smiled. A Stuka, fifty feet in the air, was flying slowly along the road behind him. How graceful and sure it looked, with the two wheels like hawk's talons stretching eagerly forward under the belly. For a moment, looking up at the wings against the sky, Christian regretted that he hadn't gone into the Air Force. There was no doubt about it, they were the darlings of the Army and the people back home. And their living conditions were absurdly comfortable, like first-class accommodations at a fancy resort hotel. And the men themselves were wonderful types, the best in the country, young, careless, confident. Christian had seen them in the bars, and listened to them talk, in tight, exclusive groups, with their own peculiar, elliptical language, spending a lot of money, talking about what it was like over Madrid, and the day they hit Warsaw, and the girls in Barcelona, and what they thought of the new Messerschmitt, all of them seeming to be oblivious of the facts of death or defeat, as though those things could not exist in their close, aristocratic, dangerous, gay world.

The Stuka was above Christian now, and Christian could see the pilot's face, grinning over the cockpit, as he banked across the scout car. Christian grinned back, and waved, and the pilot waggled his wings before he flew on, unprotected and youthful and arrogant, down the tree-lined road stretching out ahead of them toward Paris.

Through Christian's head, as he sat easily in the front seat of the scout car, with the sound of the engine busy and reassuring in his ears, and the green-smelling wind in his hair, ran a theme of music he had heard at a concert when he was on leave in Berlin. It was from a clarinet quintet by Mozart, sorrowful and persuasive, like a young girl mourning decorously for a lost lover by a slowly moving river on a summer afternoon. As Christian listened to the interior music, his eyes half closed, the gold flecks in their depths only occasionally glinting for a moment, he remembered the clarinetist. He had been a small, sad-looking little man with a bald head and drooping sandy moustaches, like a henpecked husband in a cartoon.

Really, Christian thought playfully, at a time like this, I should be humming Wagner. It is probably a kind of treachery to the Greater Third Reich not to be singing Siegfried today. He didn't like Wagner very much, but he promised himself he would think of some Wagner after he got through with the clarinet quintet. Anyway, it would help keep him awake. His head fell onto his chest and he slept, breathing softly and smiling a little. The driver looked over at him, and grinned and jerked his thumb at Christian in friendly mockery for the benefit of the photographer and the Silesian corporal in the back. The Silesian corporal roared with laughter, as though Christian had done something irresistibly clever and amusing for his benefit.

The three cars sped along the road through the calm, shining countryside, deserted, except for occasional cattle and chickens and ducks, as though all the inhabitants had taken a holiday and gone to a Fair in the next town.

The first shot seemed to be part of the music.

The next five shots wakened him, though, and the sound of the brakes, and the tumbling sensation of the car skidding sideways to a halt in the ditch next to the road. Still almost asleep, Christian jumped out and lay behind the car. The others lay panting in the dust beside him. He waited for something to happen, somebody to tell him what to do. Then he realized that the others were looking anxiously at him. In command, he thought, the non-commissioned officer will take immediate stock of the situation and make his dispositions with simple, clear orders. He will betray no uncertainty and will at all times behave with confidence and aggressiveness.

"Anybody hurt?" he whispered.

"No," said Kraus. He had his finger on the trigger of his rifle and was peering excitedly around the front tire of the car.

"Christ," Brandt was saying nervously. "Jesus Christ." He was fumbling erratically with the safety on his pistol, as though he had never handled the weapon before.

"Leave it alone," Christian said sharply, "leave the safety on. You'll kill somebody this way."

"Let's get out of here," Brandt said. His helmet had tumbled off and his hair was dusty. "We'll all get killed."

"Shut up," Christian said.

There was a rattle of shots. Slugs tore through the scout car and a tire exploded.

"Christ," Brandt mumbled, "Christ."

Christian edged toward the rear of the car, climbing over the driver as he did so. This driver, Christian thought automatically, as he rolled over him, hasn't bathed since the invasion of Poland.

"For God's sake," he said irritably, "why don't you take a bath?"

"Excuse me, Sergeant," the driver said humbly.

Protected by the rear wheel of the car, Christian raised his head. A little clump of daisies waved gently, in front of him, magnified to a forest of prehistoric growths by their closeness. The road, shimmering a little in the heat, stretched away in front of him.

Twenty feet away a small bird landed and strutted, busy with its affairs, rustling its feathers, calling unmusically from time to time, like an impatient customer in a deserted store.

A hundred yards away was the road block.

Christian examined it carefully. It was squarely across the road in a place where the land on both sides rose quite steeply, and it was placed like a dam in a brook. There were no signs of life from behind it. It was in deep shadow, shaded by the rustling trees that grew on both sides of the road and made an arch over the barricade. Christian looked behind him. There was a bend in the road there, and the other two cars were nowhere to be seen. Christian was sure they had stopped when they heard the shots. He wondered what they were doing now and cursed himself for having fallen asleep and letting himself get into something like this.

The barricade was obviously hastily improvised, two trees with the foliage still on them, filled in with springs and mattresses and an overturned farm cart and some stones from the near-by fence. It was well placed in one way. The overhanging trees hid it from aerial observation; the only way you'd find out about it would be by coming on it as they had done.

It was a lucky thing the Frenchmen had fired so soon. Christian's mouth felt dusty. He was terribly thirsty. The cherries he had eaten suddenly made his tongue smart where it had been burned a little raw by cigarettes.

If they have any sense, he thought, they will be around on our flanks now and preparing to murder us. How could I do it? he thought, staring harshly at the two felled trees silent in the enigmatic shadow a hundred meters away, how could I have fallen asleep? If they had a mortar or a machine gun placed anywhere in the woods, it would be all over in five seconds. But there was no sound in front of them, just the bird hopping beyond the daisies on the asphalt, making its irritable sharp cry.

There was a noise behind him and he twisted around. But it was only Maeschen, one of the men from the other two cars, crawling up to them through the underbrush. Maeschen crawled correctly and methodically, as he had been taught in training camp, with his rifle cradled in his arms.

"How are things back there?" Christian asked. "Anybody hurt?"

"No," Maeschen panted. "The cars are up a dirt side road. Everybody's all right. Sergeant Himmler sent me up here to see if you were still alive."

"We're alive," Christian said grimly.

"Sergeant Himmler told me to tell you he will go back to battery headquarters and report that you have engaged the enemy and will ask for two tanks," Maeschen said, very correct, again as he had been taught in the long weary hours with the instructors.

Christian squinted at the barricade, low and mysterious in the green gloom between the aisle of trees. It had to happen to me, he thought bitterly. If they find out I was asleep, it will be court-martial. He had a sudden vision of disapproving officers behind a table, with the rustle of official papers before them and he standing there stiffly, waiting for the blow to fall.

It's damned helpful of Himmler, he thought ironically, to offer to go back for reinforcements, leaving me here getting my balls shot off. Himmler was a round, loud, jovial man who always laughed and looked mysterious when he was asked if he was any relation to Heinrich Himmler. Somehow it was part of the uneasy myth of the battery that they were related, probably uncle and nephew, and Sergeant Himmler was treated with touchy consideration by everyone. Probably at the end of the war, by which time Himmler would have risen to the rank of Colonel, mostly on the strength of the shadowy relationship, because he was a mediocre soldier, and would never get anywhere by himself, they'd find out there was nothing there at all, no connection whatever.

Christian shook his head. He had to concentrate on the job ahead of him. It was amazing how difficult it was. With your life hanging on every move you made, your brain kept sliding around: Himmler, the rank, heavy smell of the driver's body, like old laundry, the little bird hopping on the road, the pallor under the sunburn of Brandt's skin and the way he sprawled, biting into the ground, as though he could dig a trench for himself with his teeth.

There was no movement behind the barricade. It lay low on the road, its leaves flicking gently now and again in the wind.

"Keep covered," he whispered to the others.

"Should I stay?" Maeschen asked, anxiously.

"If you would be so kind," Christian said. "We serve tea at four."

Maeschen looked baffled and uneasy and blew some dust out of the breech of his rifle.

Christian pushed his machine pistol through the daisy clump and aimed at the barricade. He took a deep breath. The first time, he thought, the first shot of the war. He fired two short bursts. The noise was savage and mean against the trees and the daisies waved wildly before his eyes. Somewhere behind him he heard grunting, whimpering little noises. Brandt, he thought, the war photographer.

For a moment, nothing happened. The bird had disappeared and the daisies stopped waving and the echoes of the shots died down in the woods. No, Christian thought, of course they're not that stupid. They're not behind the block. Things couldn't be that easy.

Then, as he watched, he saw the rifles through chinks high in the barricade. The shots rang out and there was the vicious, searching whistle of the bullets around his head.

"No, oh no, oh, please no . . ." It was Brandt's voice. What the hell could you expect from a middle-aged landscape painter?

Christian made himself keep his eyes open. He counted the rifles as they fired. Six, possibly seven. That was all. As suddenly as they had begun they stopped.

It's too good to be true, Christian thought. They can't have any officers with them. Probably a half dozen boys, deserted by their lieutenant, scared but willing and easy to take.

"Maeschen!"

"Yes, Sergeant."

"Go back to Sergeant Himmler. Tell him to bring his car out onto the road. They can't be seen from here. They're perfectly safe."

"Yes, Sergeant."

"Brandt!" Christian didn't look back, but he made his voice as cutting and scornful as possible. "Stop that!"

"Of course," Brandt said. "Certainly. Don't pay any attention. I will do whatever you say I should do. Believe me. You can depend on me."

"Maeschen," Christian said.

"Yes, Sergeant."

"Tell Himmler I am going to move off to my right through these woods and try to come up on the block from behind. He is to cross the road where he is and do the same thing on his side with at least five men. I think there are only six or seven people behind that barricade and they are armed only with rifles. I don't think there's an officer with them. Can you remember all that?"

"Yes, Sergeant."

"I'll fire once at them, in fifteen minutes," Christian said, "and then demand that they surrender. If they find themselves being under fire from behind, I don't think they'll do much fighting. If they do, you're to be in position to block them on your side. I'm leaving one man here in case they come on up over the barricade. Have you got all that?"

"Yes, Sergeant."

"All right. Go ahead."

"Yes, Sergeant." Maeschen crawled away, his face ablaze with duty and determination.

"Diestl," Brandt said.

"Yes," Christian said coldly, without looking at him. "If you want, you can go back with Maeschen. You're not under my command."

"I want to go along with you." Brandt's voice was controlled. "I'm all right now. I just had a bad moment." He laughed a little. "I just had to get used to being shot at. You said you were going to ask them to give up. You'd better take me along. No Frenchman'll ever understand your French." Christian looked at him and they grinned at each other. He's all right, Christian thought, finally, he's all right.

"Come along," he said. "You're invited."

Then with Brandt dragging his Leica, with his pistol in his other hand, thoughtfully on safety, and Kraus eagerly bringing up the rear, they crawled off through a bed of fern into the woods toward their right. The fern was soft and dank-smelling. The ground was a little marshy and their uniforms were soon stained with green. There was a slight rise thirty meters away. After they had crawled over that, they could stand up and proceed, bent over, behind its cover.

There was a small continuous rustling in the wood. Two squirrels made a sudden, deadly racket leaping from one tree to another. The underbrush tore at their boots and trousers as they cautiously tried to walk a course parallel to the road.

It's not going to work, Christian thought, it's going to be a terrible failure. They can't be that stupid. It's a perfect trap and I've fallen perfectly into it. The Army will get to Paris all right, but I'll never see it. Probably you could lie dead here for ten years and no one would find you but the owls and the wood animals. He had been sweating out on the road, and when he was crawling, but now the chill gloom struck through his clothes and the sweat congealed on his skin. He clenched his teeth to keep them from chattering. The woods were probably full of Frenchmen, desperate, full of hate, slipping in and out behind the trees which they knew like the furniture in their own bedrooms, furiously happy to kill one more German before going down in the general collapse. Brandt, who had lived all his life on city pavements, sounded like a herd of cattle, blundering through the brush.

Why in God's name, Christian thought, did it have to happen this way? The first action. All the responsibility on his shoulders. Just this time the Lieutenant had to be off on his own. Every other moment of the war the Lieutenant had been there, looking down his long nose, sneering, saying, "Sergeant, is that how you have been taught to give a command?" and "Sergeant, is it your opinion that this is the correct manner in which to fill out a requisition form?" and "Sergeant, when I say I want ten men here at four o'clock, I mean four o'clock, not four-two, or four-ten, or four-fifteen. FOUR O'CLOCK, SERGEANT. Is that clear?" And now the Lieutenant was sailing happily along in the armored car, down a perfectly safe road, stuffed full of tactics and Clausewitz and disposition of troops and flanking movements and fields of fire and compass marches over unfamiliar terrain, when all he needed was a Michelin road map and a few extra gallons of gasoline. And here was Christian, a dressed-up civilian, really, stumbling through treacherous woods in an insane, improvised patrol against a strong position, with two men who had never fired a shot at anyone in their lives. . . . It was madness. It would never succeed. He remembered his optimism out on the road and marveled at it. "Suicide," he said, "absolute suicide."

"What's that?" Brandt whispered, and his voice carried through the rustling forest like a dinner gong. "What did you say?"

"Nothing," Christian said. "Keep quiet."

His eyes were aching now from the strain of watching each leaf, each blade of grass.

"Attention!" Kraus shouted crazily. "Attention!"

Christian dived behind a tree. Brandt crashed into him and the shot hit the wood over their heads. Christian swung around and Brandt blinked through his glasses and struggled with the safety catch on his pistol. Kraus was jumping wildly to one side, trying to disentangle the sling of his rifle from the branches of a bush. There was another shot, and Christian felt the sting on the side of his head. He fell down and got up again and fired at the kneeling figure he suddenly saw in the confusion of green and waving foliage behind a boulder. He saw his bullets chipping the stone. Then he had to change the clip in his gun and he sat on the ground, tearing at the breech, which was stiff and new. There was a shot to his left and he heard Kraus calling, wildly, "I got him, I got him," like a boy on his first hunt for pheasant, and he saw the Frenchman quite deliberately slide, face down, on the grass. Kraus started to run for the Frenchman, as though he were afraid another hunter would claim him. There were two more shots, and Kraus fell into a stiff bush and sprawled there, almost erect, with the bush quivering under him, giving his buttocks a look of electric life. Brandt had got the safety off his pistol and was firing erratically at a clump of bushes, his elbows looking rubbery and loose. He sat on the ground, with his glasses askew on his nose, biting his lips white, holding the elbow of his right arm with his left hand in an attempt to steady himself. By that time Christian had the clip in his pistol and started firing at the clump of bushes too. Suddenly a rifle came hurling out and a man sprang out with his hands in the air. Christian stopped firing. There was the quiet of the forest again and Christian suddenly smelled the sharp, dry, unpleasant fumes of the burnt powder.

"Venez," Christian called. "Venez ici." Somewhere inside of him, with the buzzing of his head and the ringing of his ears from the firing, there was a proud twinge at the sudden access of French.

The man, his hands still over his head, came toward them slowly. His uniform was soiled and open at the collar and his face was pasty and green with fright under the scrubbly beard. He kept his mouth open and the tongue licked at the corners of his mouth dryly.

"Cover him," Christian said to Brandt, who, amazingly, was snapping pictures of the advancing Frenchman.

Brandt stood up and poked his pistol out menacingly. The man stopped. He looked as though he were going to fall down in a moment and his eyes were imploring and hopeless as Christian passed him on the way over to the bush where Kraus hung. The bush had stopped vibrating and Kraus looked deader

65

now. Christian laid him out on the ground. Kraus had a surprised, eager look on his face.

Walking erratically, with his head aching from the slap of the bullet and the blood dripping over his ear, Christian went over to the Frenchman Kraus had shot. He was lying on his face with a bullet between his eyes. He was very young, Kraus's age, and his face had been badly mangled by the bullet. Christian dropped him back to the ground hurriedly. How much damage, he thought, these amateurs can do. No more than four shots fired between them in the whole war, and two dead to show for it.

Christian felt the scratch on his temple; it had already stopped bleeding. He went over to Brandt and told him to instruct the prisoner to go down to the block and tell them they were surrounded and demand the surrender of everyone there, upon pain of annihilation. My first real day in the war, he thought, while Brandt was translating, and I am delivering ultimatums like a Major General. He grinned. He felt lightheaded and uncertain of his movements, and from moment to moment he was not sure whether he was going to laugh or weep.

The Frenchman kept nodding again and again, very emphatically, and talking swiftly to Brandt, too swiftly for Christian's meager talent for the language.

"He says he'll do it," Brandt said.

"Tell him," Christian said, "we'll follow him and shoot him at the first sign of any nonsense."

The Frenchman nodded vigorously as Brandt told him this, as though it were the most reasonable statement in the world. They started out down through the forest toward the road block, past Kraus's body, looking healthy and relaxed on the grass, with the sun slicing through the branches, gilding his helmet with dull gold.

They kept the Frenchman ten paces ahead of them. He stopped at the edge of the forest, which was about three meters higher than the road and along which ran a low stone fence.

"Emile," the Frenchman called, "Emile . . . It's I. Morel." He clambered over the fence and disappeared from view. Carefully, Christian and Brandt approached the fence, and knelt behind it. Down on the road, behind the block, their prisoner was talking swiftly, standing up, to seven soldiers kneeling and lying on the road behind their barricade. Occasionally, one of them would stare nervously into the woods, and they kept their voices to a swift, trembling whisper. Even in their uniforms, with their guns in their hands, they looked like peasants congregated in a town hall to discuss some momentous local problem. Christian wondered what stubborn, despairing flare of patriotism or private determination had led them to make this

66

pathetic, inaccurate, useless stand, deserted, un-officered, clumsy, bloody. He hoped they would surrender. He did not want to kill any of these whispering, weary-looking men in their rumpled, shoddy uniforms.

Their prisoner turned and waved to Christian.

"C'est fait!" he shouted. *"Nous sommes finis."*

"He says, all right," Brandt said, "they're finished."

Christian stood up, to wave to them to put down their arms. But at that moment there were three ragged bursts from the other side of the road. The Frenchman who had done the negotiating fell down and the others started running back along the road, firing, and vanishing one by one into the woods.

Himmler, Christian thought bitterly. At exactly the wrong moment. If you needed him, he'd never . . .

Christian jumped over the wall and slid down the embankment toward the barricade. They were still shooting from the other side, but without effect. The Frenchmen had disappeared, and Himmler and his men didn't seem to have any mind for pursuit.

As Christian reached the road, the man who was lying there stirred. He sat up and stared at Christian. The Frenchman leaned stiffly over to the base of the barricade where there was a case of grenades. Awkwardly, he took one out of the box and pulled weakly at the pin. Christian turned around. The man's face was glaring up at him and he was pulling at the pin with his teeth. Christian shot him and he fell back. The grenade rolled away. Christian leaped at it and threw it into the woods. He waited for the explosion, crouched behind the barricade next to the dead Frenchman, but there was no sound. The pin had never come out.

Christian stood up. "All right," he called. "Himmler. Come on out here."

He looked down at the man he had just killed as Himmler and the others came crashing down out of the brush. Brandt took a picture of the corpse, because photographs of dead Frenchmen were still quite rare in Berlin.

I've killed a man, Christian thought. Finally. He didn't feel anything special.

"How do you like that?" Himmler was saying jubilantly. "That's the way to do it. This is an Iron Cross job, I'll bet."

"Oh, Christ," Christian said, "be quiet."

He picked up the dead man and dragged him over to the side of the road. Then he gave orders to the other men to tear down the barricade, while he went up with Brandt to where Kraus was lying in the forest.

By the time he and Brandt had carried Kraus back to the road, Himmler and the others had got most of the barricade down. Christian left the Frenchman who had been killed in the forest lying where he had died. He felt very impatient now, and anxious to move on. Somebody else would have to do the honors to the fallen enemy.

He laid Kraus down gently. Kraus looked very young and healthy, and there were red stains around his lips from the cherries, like a small boy who comes guiltily out of the pantry after pillaging the jam jars. Well, Christian thought, looking down at the large simple boy who had laughed so heartily at Christian's jokes, you killed your Frenchman. When he got to Paris, he would write Kraus's father to tell him how his son had died. Fearless, he would write, cheerful, aggressive, best type of German soldier. Proud in his hour of grief. Christian shook his head. No, he would have to do better than that. That was like the idiotic letters in the last war, and, there was no denying it, they had become rather comic by now. Something more original for Kraus, something more personal. We buried him with cherry stains on his lips and he always laughed at my jokes and he got himself killed because he was too enthusiastic . . . You couldn't say that either. Anyway, he would have to write something.

He turned away from the dead boy as the other two cars drove slowly and warily up the road. He watched them coming with impatient, superior amusement.

"Come on, ladies," he shouted, "there's nothing to be afraid of. The mice have left the room."

The cars spurted obediently and stopped at the road block, their motors idling. Christian's driver was in one of them. Their own car was a wreck, he said, the engine riddled, the tires torn. It could not be used. The driver was very red, although he had merely lain in the ditch while all the firing was going on. He spoke in gulps, as though it was hard to get his breath, two short, gasping words at a time. Christian realized that the man, who had been quite calm while the action was on, had grown terribly frightened now that it was over, and had lost control of his nerves.

Christian listened to his own voice as he gave orders. "Maeschen," he said, "you will stay here with Taub, until the next organization comes down this road." The voice is steady, Christian noted with elation, the words are crisp and efficient. I came through it all right. I can do it. "Maeschen, go up there into the woods about sixty meters and you will find a dead Frenchman. Bring him out and leave him with the other two . . ." He gestured to Kraus and the little man Christian had killed, lying side by side now along the road, "so that they can be correctly buried. All right." He turned to the others. "Get moving."

They climbed into the two cars. The drivers put them in gear, and they went slowly through the space that had been cleared in the block. There was some blood on the road and bits of mattress and trampled leaves, but it all looked green and peaceful. Even the two bodies lying in the heavy grass alongside the road looked like two gardeners who were catching a nap after lunch.

The cars gathered speed and pulled swiftly out of the shade of the trees. There was no more danger of sniping among the open, budding fields. The sun was shining warmly, making them sweat a little, quite pleasantly, after the chill of the woods. I did it, Christian thought. He was a little ashamed of the small smile of self-satisfaction that pulled at the corners of his mouth. I did it. I commanded an action. I am earning my keep, he thought.

Ahead of him, at the bottom of a slope some three kilometers away, was a little town. It was made of stone and was dominated by two church steeples, medieval and delicate, rising out of the cluster of weathered walls around them. The town looked comfortable and secure, as though people had been living there quietly for a long time. The driver of Christian's car slowed down as they approached the buildings. He looked nervously at Christian again and again.

"Come on," Christian said impatiently. "There's nobody there."

The driver obediently stepped on the accelerator.

The houses didn't look as pretty or comfortable from close up as they had from out in the fields. Paint was flaking off the walls, and they were dirty, and there was an undeniable strong smell. Foreigners, Christian thought, they are all dirty.

The street took a bend and they were out into the town square. There were some people standing on the church steps and some others in front of the café that surprisingly was open. "Chasseur et Pecheur" Christian read on the sign over the café. Hunter and Fisher. There were five or six people sitting at the tables and a waiter was serving two of them drinks on those little saucers. Christian grinned. What a war.

On the church steps, there were three young girls in bright skirts and low-cut waists.

"Ooo," the driver said, "ooo, la, la."

"Stop here," Christian said.

"*Avec plaisir, mon colonel,*" the driver said, and Christian looked at him, surprised and amused at his unsuspected culture.

The driver drew up in front of the church and stared unashamedly at the three girls. One of the girls, a dark, full-bodied creature, holding a bouquet of garden flowers in her hand, giggled. The other two girls giggled with her, and they stared with frank interest at the two carloads of soldiers.

Christian got out of the car. "Come on, Interpreter," he said to Brandt. Brandt followed him, carrying his camera.

Christian walked up to the girls on the church steps. *"Bon jour, Mesdemoiselles,"* he said, carefully taking off his helmet with a graceful, unofficial salute.

The girls giggled again and the big one said, in French that Christian could understand. "How well he speaks." Christian felt foolishly flattered, and went on, disdaining the use of Brandt's superior French.

"Tell me, Ladies," he said, only groping a little for the words, "are there any of your soldiers who have passed through here recently?"

"No, Monsieur," the big one answered, smiling, as though what she had just said were a coquettish invitation. "We have been deserted completely. Are you going to do us any harm?"

"We do not plan to harm anyone," Christian said, "especially three young ladies of such beauty."

"Now," Brandt said, in German, "now listen to that." Christian grinned. There was something very pleasant about standing there in this old town in front of the church in the morning sunlight, looking at the full bosom of the dark girl peeping from above her sheer blouse, and flirting with her in the unfamiliar language. It was one of the things you never thought about when you started off to war.

"My," the dark girl said, smiling at him, "is that what they teach you in military school in your country?"

"The war is over," Christian said solemnly, "and you will find that we are truly friends of France."

"Oh," said the dark girl, "what a marvelous propagandist." She looked at him invitingly, and for a moment Christian had a wild thought of perhaps staying in this town for an hour. "Will there be many like you following?"

"Ten million," said Christian.

The girl threw up her hands in mock despair. "Oh, my God," she said, "what will we do with them all? Here," she offered him the flowers, "because you are the first."

He looked at the flowers with surprise, then took them gently from her hand. What a young, human thing it was to do. How hopeful it was . . .

"Mademoiselle . . ." His French became halting. "I don't know how to say it . . . but . . . Brandt!"

"The Sergeant wishes to say," Brandt said smoothly and swiftly in his proper French, "that he is most grateful and takes this as a token of the great bond between our two great peoples."

"Yes," said Christian, jealous of Brandt's fluency. "Exactly."

"Ah," said the girl, "he is a Sergeant. The officer." She smiled even more widely at him, and Christian thought, amused, they are not so different from the ones at home.

There were steps behind him, clear and ringing on the cob-

70

blestones. Christian turned with the bouquet in his hand. He felt a glancing blow, light but sharp, on his fingers, and the flowers went spinning out of his grasp and scattered on the dirty stones at his feet.

An old Frenchman in a black suit and a greenish felt hat was standing there, a cane in his hand. The old man had a sharp, fierce face and a military ribbon in his lapel. He was glaring furiously at Christian.

"Did you do that?" Christian asked the old man.

"I do not talk to Germans," the old man said. The way he stood made Christian feel that he was an old, retired regular soldier, used to authority. His leathery face, wrinkled and weathered, added to the impression. The old man turned on the girls.

"Sluts!" he said. "Why don't you just lie down? Lift your skirts and be done with it!"

"Ah," the dark girl said sullenly, "be quiet, Captain, this is not your war."

Christian felt foolish standing there, but he didn't know what to do or say. This was not exactly a military situation, and he certainly couldn't use force on a seventy-year-old man.

"Frenchwomen!" The old man spat. "Flowers for Germans! They've been out killing your brothers and you present them with bouquets!"

"They're just soldiers," the girl said. "They're far away from home and they're so young and handsome in their uniforms." She was smiling impudently at Brandt and Christian by now, and Christian couldn't help laughing at her direct womanly reasoning.

"All right," he said, "old man. We no longer have the flowers. Go back to your drink." He put his arm in a friendly manner across the old man's shoulders. The old man shook the arm off violently.

"Keep your hands off me!" he shouted. *"Boche!"*

He strode across the square, his heels clicking fiercely on the cobbles. "Ooo, la, la," Christian's driver said, shaking his head reprovingly as the old man passed the car.

The old man paid no attention to him. "Frenchmen! French-women!" he shouted to the town at large as he stalked toward the café. "It's no wonder the *Boches* are here this time! No heart, no courage. One shot and they are running through the woods like rabbits. One smile and they are in bed for the whole German Army! They don't work, they don't pray, they don't fight, all they know how to do is surrender. Surrender in the line, surrender in the bedroom. For twenty years France has been practicing for this and now they have perfected it!"

"Ooo, la, la," said Christian's driver, who understood French. He bent over and picked up a stone and casually threw it across the square at the Frenchman. It missed him, but it went through the window of the café behind him. There was the sharp crash of the plateglass and then silence in the square. The old Frenchman didn't even look around at the damage. He sat down silently, leaning on the head of his cane. Ferociously and heart-brokenly he glared across at the Germans.

Christian walked over to the driver. "What did you do that for?" he asked quietly.

"He was making too much noise," the driver said. He was a big, ugly, insolent man, like a Berlin taxi-driver, and Christian disliked him intensely. "Teach them some respect for the German Army."

"Don't ever do anything like that again," Christian said harshly. "Understand?"

The driver stood a little straighter, but he didn't answer. He merely stared dully and ambiguously, with a lurking hint of insolence, into Christian's eyes.

Christian turned from him. "All right," he called. "On the road."

The girls were a little subdued now, and didn't wave as the cars lurched across the square and onto the road toward Paris.

Christian was a little disappointed when he drove up to the brown sculptured bulk of the Porte Saint Denis and saw the open square around it thronged with armored vehicles and gray uniforms, the men lounging on the concrete and eating from a field kitchen, for all the world like a Bavarian garrison town on a national holiday, preparing for a parade. Christian had never been in Paris, and he felt it would have been a marvelous climax to the war to be the first to drive through the historic streets, leading the Army into the ancient capital of the enemy.

He drove slowly through the lounging troops and the stacked rifles to the base of the monument. He signaled to Himmler in the car behind him to stop. This was the rendezvous point at which he had been ordered to wait for the rest of the company. Christian took his helmet off and stretched in his seat, taking a deep breath. The mission was finished.

Brandt leaped out of the car and busied himself taking pictures of troopers eating, leaning against the base of the monument. Even with his uniform and the black leather holster strapped around his waist, Brandt still looked like a bank-clerk on vacation, taking snapshots for the family album. Brandt had his own theories about pictures. He picked out the handsomest and youngest soldiers. He made a point of picking very blond boys most of the time, privates and lower-grade, non-commissioned officers. "My function," he had once told Christian, "is to make the war attractive to the people back home." He seemed to be having some success with his theories, because

72

he was up for a commission, and he was constantly receiving commendations from the propaganda headquarters in Berlin for his work.

There were two small children wandering shyly among the soldiers, the sole representatives of the French civilian population of Paris on the streets that afternoon. Brandt led them over to where Christian was cleaning his gun on the hood of the little scout car.

"Here," Brandt said, "do me a favor. Pose with these two."

"Get someone else," Christian protested. "I'm no actor."

"I want to make you famous," Brandt said. "Lean over and offer them some candy."

"I haven't any candy," Christian said. The two children, a boy and a girl who could not have been over five years old, stood at the wheel of the car, looking gravely up at Christian, with sad, deep black eyes.

"Here." Brandt took some chocolate out of his pocket and gave it to Christian. "The good soldier is prepared for everything."

Christian sighed and put down the dismantled barrel of the machine pistol. He leaned over the two shabby, pretty children.

"Excellent types," Brandt said, squatting, with the camera up to his eyes. "The youth of France, pretty, undernourished, sad, trusting. The good-natured, hearty, generous German sergeant, athletic, friendly, handsome, photogenic . . ."

"Get away from here," Christian said.

"Keep smiling, Beauty." Brandt was busily snapping a series of angles. "And don't give it to them until I tell you. Just hold it out and make them reach for it."

"I would like you to remember, Soldier," Christian said, grinning down at the somber, unsmiling faces below him, "that I am still your superior officer."

"Art," said Brandt, "above everything. I wish you were blond. You're a good model for a German soldier, except for the hair. You look as though you once had a thought in your head and that's hard to find."

"I think," said Christian, "I ought to turn you in for statements detrimental to the honor of the German Army."

"The artist," said Brandt, "is above these petty considerations."

He finished his pictures, working very fast, and said, "All right." Christian gave the candy to the children, who didn't say anything. They merely looked up at him solemnly and tucked the candy in their pockets and wandered off hand-in-hand among the steel treads and the boots and rifle butts.

An armored car, followed by three scout cars, came into the square and moved slowly alongside Christian's detachment. Christian felt a slight twinge of sorrow when he saw it was the Lieutenant. His independent command was over. He saluted and the Lieutenant saluted back. The Lieutenant had one of the smartest salutes in military history. You heard the rattle of swords and the jangle of spurs down the ages to the campaigns of Achilles and Ajax, when he brought his arm up. Even now, after the long ride from Germany, the Lieutenant looked shiny and impeccable, as though he had just come from the graduation exercises of Spandau, with his diploma in his white-gloved hand. Christian disliked the Lieutenant and felt uncomfortable before that rigid perfection. The Lieutenant was very young, twenty-three or -four, but when he looked around him with his cold, light-gray imperious stare, a whole world of bumbling, inaccurate civilians seemed to be revealed to his merciless observation. There were very few men who had ever made Christian feel inefficient, but the Lieutenant was one of them. As he stood at attention, watching the Lieutenant climb crisply down from the armored car, Christian hastily rehearsed his report, and felt all over again the inadequacy and sense of guilt and neglect of duty that he had felt walking through the forest into the trap.

"Yes, Sergeant?" The Lieutenant had a cutting, weary voice, a voice that might have belonged to Bismarck in military school. He didn't look around him; he had no interest in the old closed buildings of Paris around him; he might just as well have been on an enormous bare drillfield outside Königsberg as in the center of the capital of France on the first day of its investment by foreign troops since 1871. What an admirable, miserable character, Christian thought, what a useful man to have in your army.

"At ten hundred hours," Christian said, "we made contact with the enemy on the Meaux-Paris road. The enemy had a camouflaged road block and opened fire on our leading vehicle. We engaged him with nine men. We killed two of the enemy and drove the others in disorder from their position and demolished the block." Christian hesitated for the fraction of a second.

"Yes, Sergeant?" the Lieutenant said flatly.

"We had one casualty, Sir," Christian said, thinking, this is where I start my trouble, "Corporal Kraus was killed."

"Corporal Kraus," said the Lieutenant. "Did he perform his duty?"

"Yes, Sir." Christian thought of the lumbering boy, shouting enthusiastically, "I got him! I got him!" among the shaking trees. "He killed one of the enemy with his first shots."

"Excellent," said the Lieutenant. A frosty smile shone briefly on his face, twisting the long, angled nose for a moment. "Excellent."

He is delighted, Christian noted in surprise.

"I am sure," the Lieutenant was saying, "that there will be a decoration for Corporal Kraus."

"I was thinking, Sir," Christian said, "of writing a note to his father."

"No," said the Lieutenant. "That's not for you. This is the function of the Company Commander. Captain Mueller will do that. I will give him the facts. It is a delicate matter, this kind of letter, and it is important that the proper sentiments are expressed. Captain Mueller will say exactly the correct thing."

Probably, Christian thought, in the military college there is a course, "Personal Communications to Next of Kin. One hour a week."

"Sergeant," the Lieutenant said, "I am pleased with your behavior and the behavior of the rest of the men under your command."

"Thank you, Sir," said Christian. He felt foolishly pleased.

Brandt came over and saluted. The Lieutenant saluted back coldly. He didn't like Brandt, who never could look like a soldier. The Lieutenant made clear his feelings about men who fought the war with cameras instead of guns. But the directives from Headquarters down to the lower echelons about giving photographers all possible assistance were too definite to be denied.

"Sir," Brandt said, in his soft civilian voice, "I have been instructed to report with my film as soon as possible to the Place de l'Opera. The film is being collected there and is to be flown back to Berlin. I wonder if I might have a vehicle to take me there. I'll come back immediately."

"I'll let you know in a little while, Brandt," the Lieutenant said. He turned and strode across the square to where Captain Mueller, who had just arrived, was sitting in his amphibious car.

"Just crazy about me," Brandt said. "That lieutenant."

"You'll get the car," Christian said. "He's feeling pretty good."

"I'm crazy about him, too," Brandt said. "I'm crazy about all lieutenants." He looked around him at the soft stone colors of the tenements rising from the square, with the helmets and the gray uniforms and the large, lounging, armed men looking foreign and unnatural in front of the French signs and the shuttered cafés. "The last time I was in this place," Brandt said, reflectively, "was less than a year ago. I had on a blue jacket and flannel trousers. Everybody mistook me for an Englishman, so they were nice to me. There's a wonderful little restaurant just around that corner there and I drove up in a taxi and it was a mild summer night and I was with a beautiful girl with black hair and I'd slept with her for the first time that afternoon . . ." Brandt closed his eyes dreamily and leaned his head against the armored side of a tracked personnel carrier. "It was her notion

75

that the function of the female sex was to please men and she had a voice that made you want her if you heard it a block away, and she had the most remarkable breasts this side of the Danube. We had champagne before dinner and she was wearing a dark-blue dress. Very demure and young. When you looked at her it was impossible to believe you'd been in bed with her just an hour ago. We sat and held hands across the table and I think tears came into her eyes, and we had a marvelous omelet and a bottle of Chablis and I'd never heard of Lieutenant Hardenburg and I knew I was going to be back in bed with her in an hour and a half and I could have shot my brains out I felt so marvelous."

"Stop it," Christian said. "My morale is tottering."

"That was in the old days," Brandt said, his eyes still closed, "when I was a loathsome civilian. The old days, before I became a military figure."

"Open your eyes," Christian said, "and pull yourself out of that bed. Here comes the Lieutenant."

They both stood at attention as the Lieutenant strode up to them.

"It is agreed," the Lieutenant said to Brandt. "You can have the car."

"Thank you, Sir," Brandt said.

"I myself will go with you," said the Lieutenant. "And I will take Himmler and Diestl. There is talk of our unit being billeted in that neighborhood. The Captain suggested we look at the situation there." He smiled in what he obviously thought was a warm, intimate manner. "Also, we have earned a little sightseeing tour. Come."

He led the way over to one of the cars, Christian and Brandt following him. Himmler was already there, seated at the wheel, and Brandt and Christian climbed in back. The Lieutenant sat in front, stiff, erect, shining, representing the German Army and the German state on the boulevards of Paris.

Brandt made a little grimace and shrugged his shoulders as they started off toward the Place de l'Opera. Himmler drove with dash and certainty. He had spent several vacations in Paris, and he even spoke a kind of understandable French with a coarse, ungrammatical fluency. He pointed out places of interest, like a comic guide, cafés he had patronized, a vaudeville theatre in which he had seen an American Negress dancing naked, a street down which, he assured them, was the most fully equipped brothel in the world. Himmler was the combination comedian and politician of the company, a common type in all armies, and a favorite with all the officers, who permitted him liberties for which other men would be mercilessly punished. The Lieutenant sat stiffly beside Himmler, his eyes roam-

76

ing hungrily up and down the deserted streets. He even laughed twice at Himmler's jokes.

The Place de l'Opera was full of troops. There were so many soldiers, filling the impressive square before the soaring pillars and broad steps, that for a long time the absence of women or civilians in the heart of the city was hardly noticeable.

Brandt went into a building, very important and business-like with his camera and his film, and Christian and the Lieutenant got out of the car and stared up at the domed mass of the opera house.

"I should have come here before," the Lieutenant said softly. "It must have been wonderful in peace time."

Christian laughed. "Lieutenant," he said, "that's exactly what I was thinking."

The Lieutenant's chuckle was warm and friendly. Christian wondered how it was that he had always been so intimidated by this rather simple boy.

Brandt bustled out. "The business is finished," he said. "I don't have to report back till tomorrow afternoon. They're delighted in there. I told them what sort of stuff I took and they nearly made me a Colonel on the spot."

"I wonder," the Lieutenant said, his voice hesitant for the first time since 1935, "I wonder if it would be possible for you to take my picture standing in front of the Opera. To send home to my wife."

"It will be a pleasure," Brandt said gravely.

"Himmler," the Lieutenant said. "Diestl. All of us together."

"Lieutenant," Christian said, "why don't you do it alone? Your wife isn't interested in seeing us." It was the first time since they had met a year ago that he had dared contradict the Lieutenant in anything.

"Oh, no." The Lieutenant put his arm around Christian's shoulders and for a fleeting moment Christian wondered if he'd been drinking. "Oh, no. I've written her a great deal about you. She would be most interested."

Brandt made a fuss about getting the angle just right, with as much of the Opera as possible in the background. Himmler grinned clownishly at one side of the group, but Christian and the Lieutenant peered seriously into the lens, as though this were a moment of solemn historic interest.

After Brandt had finished they climbed back into their car and started toward the Porte Saint Denis. It was late afternoon and the streets looked warm and lonely in the level light, especially since there were long stretches in which there were no soldiers and no military traffic. For the first time since they had arrived in Paris, Christian began to feel a little uneasy.

"A great day," the Lieutenant said reflectively, up in the front seat, "a day of lasting importance. In years to come, we will look back on this day, and we will say to ourselves, 'We were there at the dawn of a new era!' "

Christian could sense Brandt, sitting beside him, making a small, amused grimace, but Brandt, perhaps because of the long years he had lived in France, had a standard attitude of cynicism and mockery toward all grandiose sentiment.

"My father," the Lieutenant said, "got as far as the Marne in 1914. The Marne . . . So close. And he never saw Paris. We crossed the Marne today in five minutes . . . A day of history . . ." The Lieutenant peered sharply up a side street. Involuntarily, Christian twisted nervously in the back seat to look.

"Himmler," the Lieutenant said, "isn't this the street?"

"What street, Lieutenant?"

"The house you talked about, the famous one?"

What a ferocious mind, Christian thought. Everything is engraved on it irrevocably. Gun positions, regulations for courts-martial, the proper procedure for decontamination of metal exposed to gas, the address of French brothels carelessly pointed out on a strange street two hours before. . . .

"It seems to me," the Lieutenant said carefully, as Himmler slowed the car down by imperceptible degrees, "it seems to me that on a day like this, a day of battle and celebration . . . In short, we deserve some relaxation. The soldier who does not take women does not fight . . . Brandt, you lived in Paris, have you heard of this place?"

"Yes, sir," said Brandt. "An exquisite reputation."

"Turn the car around, Sergeant," the Lieutenant said.

"Yes, Sir." Himmler grinned and swung the little car around in a dashing circle and made for the street he had pointed out.

"I know," said the Lieutenant gravely, "that I can depend upon you men to keep quiet about this."

"Yes, Sir," they all said.

"There is a time for discipline," the Lieutenant said, "and a time for comradeship. Is this the place, Himmler?"

"Yes, Sir," said Himmler. "But it looks closed."

"Come with me." The Lieutenant dismounted and marched across the sidewalk to the heavy oak door, his heels crashing on the pavement, making the narrow street echo and re-echo as though a whole company had marched past.

As he tapped on the door, Brandt and Christian looked at each other, grinning. "Next," Brandt whispered, "he'll be selling us dirty postcards."

"Sssh," said Christian.

After awhile the door opened and the Lieutenant and Himmler half pushed, half-argued their way in. It closed behind them and Christian and Brandt were left alone in the empty, shaded street, with night just beginning to touch the sky over their heads. There was no sound, and all the windows of the buildings were closed.

"I was of the impression," Brandt said, "that the Lieutenant invited us on this party."

"Patience," Christian said. "He is preparing the way."

"With women," said Brandt, "I prefer to prepare my own way."

"The good officer," Christian said gravely, "always sees that his troops are bedded down before he is himself."

"Go upstairs," Brandt said, "and read the Lieutenant that lecture."

The door of the building opened and Himmler waved to them. They got out of the car and went in. A Moorish-looking lamp cast a heavy purple light over the staircase and hanging tapestries along the walls inside.

"The Madam recognized me," Himmler said, clumping up the steps ahead of them. "A big kiss, and 'mon cher gar. . con' and all that. How do you like that?"

"Sergeant Himmler," Brandt said. "Well known in the brothels of five countries. Germany's gift to the cause of the Federation of Europe."

"Anyway," said Himmler, grinning, "I didn't waste my time in Paris. Here . . . into the bar. Girls aren't ready yet. We have to do a little drinking first. The horrors of war."

He pushed open a door and there was the Lieutenant, his gloves and helmet off sitting on a stool with his legs crossed, delicately picking at the goldfoil on a bottle of champagne. The bar was a very small room, done in a kind of lavender stucco, with crescent-shaped windows and tasseled hangings. There was a large woman who seemed to go with the room, all frizzed hair, fringed shawls and heavy painted eyelids. She was behind the bar, chattering away in French to the Lieutenant, who was nodding gravely, not understanding a word of what she was saying.

"*Amis,*" Himmler said, putting his arms around Brandt and Christian. "*Brave Soldaten.*"

The woman came out from behind the bar and shook hands and said they were very welcome and they must forgive her for the delay, but it had been an upsetting day, as they could understand, and the girls would make their appearance quite soon, quite, quite soon, and would they be so kind as to seat themselves and have a glass of wine, and wasn't it democratic, the men drinking and taking their pleasure with the officers, you would never find that in the French Army, and perhaps that was why they had won the war.

The girls hadn't arrived by the time the third bottle had disappeared, but by then it didn't make much difference.

"The French," the Lieutenant was saying, sitting stiff and

correct, his eyes now dark-green and opaque, like sea-worn bottle glass, "I disdain the French. They are not willing to die. That is why we are here drinking their wine and taking their women, because they prefer not to die. Comic . . ." He waved his glass in the air, in a gesture that was drunken but bitter. "This campaign. A comic, ridiculous campaign. Since I have been eighteen years old, I have been studying war. The art of war. At my fingertips. Supply. Liaison. Morale. Selection of disguised points for command posts. Theory of attack against automatic weapons. The value of shock. I could lead an army. Five years of my life. Then the moment comes." He laughed bitterly. "The great moment. The Army surges to the battle-line. What happens to me?" He stared at the Madam, who did not understand a word of German and was nodding happily, agreeing. "I do not hear a shot fired. I sit in an automobile and I ride four hundred miles and I go to a whorehouse. The miserable French Army has made a tourist out of me! A tourist! No more war. Five years wasted. No career. I'll be a Lieutenant till the age of fifty. I don't know anyone in Berlin. No influence, no friends, no promotion. Wasted. My father was better off. He only got to the Marne, but he had four years to fight in, and he was a Major when he was twenty-six, and he had his own battalion at the Somme, when every other officer was killed in the first two days. Himmler!"

"Yes, Sir," Himmler said. He was not drunk and he had a sly, amused look on his face as he listened to the Lieutenant.

"Himmler! Sergeant Himmler! Where is my girl! I want a French girl."

"Madam says you will have a girl in ten minutes."

"I disdain them," the Lieutenant said, sipping at his champagne uncertainly, spilling a little on his chin, "I completely disdain the French."

Two girls came into the room. One was a large, heavy blonde girl with an easy, full-mouthed smile. The other was small and slender and dark, with a brooding, almost Arab face, set off by the heavy makeup and bright red lipstick.

"Here they are," the Madame said caressingly. "Here are the little cabbages." She patted the blonde approvingly, like a horse dealer. "This is Jeanette. Just the type, eh? I predict she will have a great vogue while the Germans are in Paris."

"I'll take that one." The Lieutenant stood up, very straight, and pointed to the girl who looked like an Arab. She gave him a dark, professional smile and came over and took his arm.

Himmler had been looking at her with interest, too, but he resigned immediately to the privilege of rank, and put his arm around the big blonde. *"Chérie,"* he said, "how would you like a nice, healthy German soldier?"

"Where is there a convenient room?" the Lieutenant said in German. "Brandt, translate."

Brandt translated and the dark girl smiled at the others and led the Lieutenant, very formal and polite, through the door.

"Now," said Himmler, holding tightly onto the blonde, "now it's my turn. If you boys don't mind . . ."

"Not at all," said Christian. "No hurry at all."

Himmler grinned and went off with the blonde, saying, in his ferocious French, "Chérie, I love your gown . . ."

The Madam made her excuses and left, after putting out another bottle of champagne. Christian and Brandt sat alone in the orange-lit Moorish bar, staring silently at the frosted bottle in the ice bucket.

They drank without speaking. Christian opened the new bottle, wrestling with the cork, jumping a little, involuntarily, when it exploded out of the bottle with a loud noise. The champagne ran over on his hand, iced and foamy.

"Were you ever in a place like this before?" Brandt asked finally.

"No."

"War," said Brandt. "Makes great changes in a man's standard of living."

"Yes," said Christian.

"You want a girl?" Brandt asked.

"Not particularly."

"If you wanted a girl," Brandt said, "and Lieutenant Hardenburg wanted the same girl, what would you do?"

Christian gravely sipped at his drink. "I won't answer that question," he said.

"Neither will I," said Brandt. He played with the stem of his glass. "How do you feel?" he said after awhile.

"I don't know," said Christian. "Strange. A little strange."

"I feel sad," said Brandt. "Very sad. What was it the Lieutenant said?"

"Today is the dawn of a new era."

"I feel sad at the dawn of the new era." Brandt poured himself some wine. "Did you know that ten months ago I nearly became a French citizen?"

"No," said Christian.

"I lived in France ten years, off and on. Some other time I'll take you to the place on the Normandy coast I went in the summers. I painted all day long, thirty, sometimes forty canvases a summer. I was developing a little reputation in France, too. We must go to the gallery that showed my stuff. Maybe they still have some of the paintings, and you can take a look at them."

"I'll be very happy to," Christian said formally.

"I couldn't show my paintings in Germany. They were abstract. Non-objective art, they call it. Decadent, the Nazis call it." Brandt shrugged. "I suppose I am a little decadent. Not as decadent as the Lieutenant, but sufficient. How about you?"

"I am a decadent skier," Christian said.

"Every field," said Brandt, "to its own decadence."

The door opened and the small dark girl came in. She had on a pink wrap, fringed with feathers. She was grinning a little to herself. "Where is the Boss?" she asked.

"Back there some place." Brandt waved vaguely. "Can I help?"

"It is your Lieutenant," the girl said. "I need some translation. He wants something, and I am not quite sure what it is. I think he wants to be whipped, but I am afraid to start in unless I know for certain."

"Begin," said Brandt. "That is exactly what he wants. He is an old friend of mine."

"Are you sure?" The girl looked at both of them doubtfully.

"Absolutely," said Brandt.

"Good." The girl shrugged. "I will essay it." She turned at the door. "It is a little strange," she said, a hint of mockery in her voice, "the victorious soldier . . . The day of victory . . . A curious taste, wouldn't you say?"

"We are curious people," Brandt said. "You will discover that. Attend to your business."

The girl looked angrily at him for a moment, then smiled and went out.

"Did you understand?" Brandt asked Christian.

"Enough."

"Let's have a drink." Brandt poured for them both. "I answered the call of the Fatherland," he said.

"What?" Christian looked at him, puzzled.

"The war was about to begin, and there I was painting decadent, abstract landscapes on the French coast, waiting to become a French citizen." Brandt half closed his eyes, looking over his wine at the troubled, uncertain days of August, 1939. "The French are the most admirable people in the world. They eat well; they are independent; a man can paint any kind of picture he wants and they will not do anything to him; they have a glorious military history behind them and they know they are not going to do anything like that again. They are reasonable and miserly, a good atmosphere for art. Still, at the last minute, I became Corporal Brandt, whose pictures could not be shown in a German art gallery. Blood is thicker than . . . what? And here we are in Paris, welcomed by all the whores. I tell you something, Christian, finally we are going to lose. It is too immoral . . . the barbarians of the Elbe eating their sausage on the Champs Elysées."

"Brandt," said Christian, "Brandt . . ."

"The dawn of a new era," said Brandt. "Flagellation for the Wehrmacht. Tomorrow I take a sausage to the Etoile."

The door opened and Himmler came in. He had his jacket off and his collar was open and he was grinning and carrying the green gown that the blonde girl had been wearing.

"Next," he said. "The lady is waiting."

"Do you wish to follow in Sergeant Himmler's bedsteps?" Brandt asked.

"No," said Christian. "I do not."

"No offense meant, Sergeant," said Brandt, "but we will drink this one out."

Himmler looked sullenly at both of the men, the usual sly pattern of good humor vanishing from his face for a moment.

"I did it fast," he complained. "I didn't want to keep my pals waiting."

"Thoughtful," said Brandt. "Very thoughtful of you. At a time like that."

"She's pretty good," said Himmler. "A big soft one. Are you sure you don't want it?"

"Sure," said Christian.

"All right," said Himmler, "I'll go back for the second act."

"What did you do?" Brandt asked. "Tear the dress off her back?"

Himmler grinned. "I bought it from her," he said. "Nine hundred francs. She wanted fifteen hundred. I'm going to send it to my wife. She's just about the same size. Feel it . . ." He pushed it in front of Christian. "Real silk."

Christian fingered the material gravely. "Real silk," he said.

"Last chance." Himmler was at the door now, looking back.

"Thank you just the same," said Brandt.

"All right," said Himmler. "It's up to you."

"Himmler," said Christian, "we're leaving. You wait for the Lieutenant and drive him back. We'll walk."

"Don't you think you ought to wait for orders?" Himmler asked.

"I don't think this could be called a tactical situation," Christian said. "We'll walk back."

Himmler shrugged. "You're liable to get shot in the back, walking alone through the streets."

"Not tonight," said Brandt. "Later on, but not tonight." He stood up and Christian stood with him. They walked out.

It was dark outside. The blackout was thorough and no lights were showing. The moon hung over the rooftops, though, dividing each street into geometrical blocks of light and shadow. The atmosphere was mild and still and there was a hushed, empty air hanging over the city, broken occasionally by the sound of steel-treaded vehicles shifting in the distance, the noise

83

sudden and harsh, then dying down to nothingness among the dark buildings.

Brandt led the way. He was wobbling slightly, but he knew where he was and he walked with reassuring certainty in the direction of the Porte Saint Denis.

They did not speak. They walked side by side, their shoulders touching occasionally, their hobnailed shoes clattering on the pavements. Somewhere in the dark a window was slammed shut and Christian thought he heard a child crying, faintly and far away. They turned onto the wide, empty boulevard, walking close to the shuttered windows and the stacked tables and chairs of the closed sidewalk cafés. Far off down the boulevard they could see some lights, signs that the Army felt secure from all attack this evening in the heart of France. Through the sweet haze of the champagne the lights looked cozy and warm with comradeship to Christian, and he smiled dreamily to himself as he walked toward them at an even, regular pace, with Brandt beside him.

Paris, shining under the early moon, was frail and graceful through the mist of alcohol. He loved it. He loved the worn pavements. He loved the narrow streets winding off the boulevard like entrances into another century. He loved the churches crowded among the bars and brothels and grocery shops. He loved the spindly chairs thriftily upended on the tables in the shadows under the café awnings. He loved the people hiding now behind their drawn blinds. He loved the river he had not yet seen that poured through and dominated the city and he loved the restaurants he had not yet eaten in and the girls whom he had not yet met, but who would come out tomorrow, in the sunny morning, when the fear of the night had vanished, and would walk down these streets with their high heels and their impudent, clever clothes. He loved the legend of the city and the fact that it was one place on the face of the earth that lived up to the legend it had established in the hearts of men. He loved the fact that he had fought on the road to the city and had killed to get there and he loved the little shabby Frenchman he had killed and he loved Corporal Kraus, lying dead beside him, far from the farm in Silesia, with cherry stains on his lips. He loved the fact that he had been tested on the road and in the forest, that death had whistled past him, and he loved the war because in no other way could a man be truly tested, and he loved it that the war was going to end soon, because he did not want to die. He loved the days to come, because they were going to be peaceful and rich, and all the ideas for which he had been willing to risk his life would be put into law and made permanent and a new time of prosperity and order was beginning. He loved Brandt, walking almost correctly, next to his shoulder, because Brandt had whimpered with fear on the road and had conquered it and fought at his side, holding his shaking elbow with his hand, to steady it as he fired through the spring foliage at the man who would have killed Christian if he could. And he loved the hour, the calm, dark moonlit hour, when they walked side by side down the empty, pleasant street, the possessors of the town, and he knew finally that his life had not been wasted, that he had not been born merely to fritter away his days teaching a game to children and vacationists. He was of use and he had been used, and a man could ask no more of life.

"Look," Brandt said. He stopped and pointed.

Christian stopped too, and looked where Brandt was pointing. It was a stone church wall, angled against the moonlight, and written on it in large, chalk figures was the number 1918. Christian blinked and shook his head. He knew that there was a significance chalked there on the wall, but for a moment he could not make out what it was.

"1918," Brandt said. "They know. The French know."

Christian looked at the wall. He felt sad and suddenly tired, because he had been up since four o'clock in the morning and it had been an exhausting day. He walked heavily over to the wall and lifted his arm. With his sleeve, slowly and methodically he began to erase the large, chalked numbers.

CHAPTER FIVE

THE RADIO dominated everything. Even though it was sunny outside and the Pennsylvania hills were green and crisp in the fair June weather, and even though they kept saying the same thing over and over again in the little static-tortured machine, Michael found himself sitting indoors all day in the wall-papered living room with its spindly Colonial furniture. There were newspapers all around his chair. From time to time Laura came in and sighed in loud martyrdom as she bent and ostentatiously picked them up and arranged them in a neat pile. But Michael hardly paid any attention to her. He sat hunched over the machine, twisting the dial, hearing the variety of voices, mellow and ingratiating and theatrical, saying over and over again, "Buy Lifebuoy to avoid unpleasant body odors," and "Two teaspoonfuls in a glass before breakfast will keep you regular," and "It is rumored that Paris will not be defended. The German High Command is maintaining silence about the position of its spearheading columns against crumbling French resistance."

"We promised Tony," Laura was standing at the door, speaking in a patient voice, "that we'd have some badminton this afternoon."

Michael continued to sit silently hunched up, close to the radio.

"Michael!" Laura said loudly.

"Yes?" He didn't look around.

"Badminton," Laura said. "Tony."

"What about it?" Michael asked, his forehead wrinkled with the effort of trying to listen to her and the radio announcer at the same time.

"The net isn't up."

"I'll put it up later."

"How much later?"

"For God's sake, Laura!" Michael shouted, "I said I'd do it later."

"I'm getting tired," Laura said coldly, tears coming to her eyes, "of your doing everything later."

"Will you stop that?"

"Stop shouting at me." The tears started to roll down her cheeks and Michael felt sorry for her. They had planned this time in the country as a vacation during which, without telling each other, they had hoped to recapture some of the old friendship and affection they had lost in the disordered years since their marriage. Laura's contract had run out in Hollywood, and they hadn't taken up her option and, inexplicably, she couldn't get another job. She had been quite good about it, gay and uncomplaining, but Michael knew how defeated she felt, and he had resolved to be tender with her in the month in the country in the house that a friend had loaned them. They'd been there a week, but it had been a terrible week. Michael had sat listening to the radio all day and hadn't been able to sleep at night. He had paced the floor downstairs and sat up reading and had gloomily stalked around, red-eyed and weary, neglecting to shave, neglecting to help Laura with the work in keeping the pretty little house in order.

"Forgive me, darling," he said, and took her in his arms and kissed her. She smiled, although she was still crying.

"I hate to be a pest," Laura said, "but some things have to be done, you know."

"Of course," Michael said.

Laura laughed. "Now you're being noble. I love it when you're noble."

Michael laughed too, but he couldn't help feeling a little annoyed.

"Now you've got to pay up," Laura said, under his chin, "for being nice to me."

"What now?" Michael asked.

"Don't sound resigned," Laura said, "I hate it when you sound resigned."

Michael controlled himself purposefully and listened to his own voice being polite and pleasant as he spoke. "What do you want me to do?"

"First," Laura said, "turn off that damned radio."

Michael started to protest, but thought better of it. The announcer was saying, "The situation is still confused, but the British seem to have evacuated the greater portion of their Army safely, and it is expected that Weygand's counter-offensive will soon develop . . ."

"Michael, darling," Laura said warningly.

Michael turned the radio off.

"There," he said, "anything for you."

"Thanks," said Laura. Her eyes were dry and bright and smiling now. "Now, one more thing."

"What's that?"

"Shave."

Michael sighed and ran his hand over the little stubble on his jaw.

"Do I really need it?" he asked.

"You look as though you just came out of a Third Avenue flophouse."

"You've convinced me," Michael said.

"You'll feel better, too," Laura said, picking up the newspapers around Michael's chair.

"Sure," said Michael. Almost automatically, he sidled over toward the radio and put his hand down to the dials.

"Not for an hour," Laura pleaded, holding her hand over the dials. "One hour. It's driving me crazy. The same thing over and over."

"Laura, darling," Michael said, "it's the most important week of our lives."

"Still," she said, with crisp logic, "it doesn't help to drive ourselves out of our minds. That won't help the French, will it? And when you come down, darling, put up the badminton net."

Michael shrugged. "Okay," he said. Laura kissed his cheek lightly and ran her fingers through his hair. He started upstairs.

While he was shaving he heard some of the guests arrive. The voices floated up from the garden, lost from time to time in the sound of the water running in the basin. They were women's voices and they sounded musical and soft at this distance. Laura had invited two of the teachers from the nearby girls' school to which she had gone when she was fourteen. They both were Frenchwomen who had taught her and been good to her. As

Michael half-listened to the rising and falling voices, he couldn't help feeling how much more pleasant Frenchwomen sounded than most of the American women he knew. There was something modest and artful in the tone of their voices and the spacing of the words that fell much more agreeably on the ear than the self-assured clangor of American female speech. That, he thought, grinning, is an observation I will not dare make aloud.

He cut himself and felt annoyed and jangled again as he saw the small, persistent crimson seeping under his jaw.

From the large tree at the end of the garden came the cawing of crows. A colony of them had set up their nests there, and from time to time they clacked away, drowning out the other and more gentle noises of the countryside.

He went downstairs and stole quietly into the living room and turned the radio on, low. In a moment it warmed up, but for once there was only music. A woman's voice was singing "I got plenty of nuthin' and nuthin's plenty for me," on one station. A military band was playing the overture from *Tannhäuser* on the other station. It was a weak little radio and it was only possible to get two stations on it. Michael turned the radio off and went out into the garden to meet the guests.

Johnson was here, in a yellow tennis shirt with brown bars across it. He had brought along a tall, pretty girl, with a serious, intelligent face, and automatically, as Michael shook her hand, he wondered where Mrs. Johnson was this summer afternoon.

"Miss Margaret Freemantle . . ." Laura was conducting the introductions. Miss Freemantle smiled slowly, and Michael felt himself thinking bitterly: How the hell does Johnson get a girl as pretty as that?

Michael shook hands with the two Frenchwomen. They were sisters, both of them frail, and dressed in black, quite smartly, in a style that you felt must have been very fashionable some years before, although you could not remember exactly when. They were both in their fifties, with upswept lacquered hair and soft, pale complexions and amazing legs, slender and finely shaped. They had delicate, perfect manners, and long years of teaching young girls had given them an air of remote patience with the world. They always seemed to Michael like exquisitely mannered visitors from the nineteenth century, polite, detached, but secretly disapproving of the time and the country in which they found themselves. Today, despite the disciplined evidences of preparation for the afternoon, the clever rouging and eyeshadow, there was a wan, drawn look on their faces, and their attention seemed to wander, even in the middle of a conversation.

Michael looked at them obliquely, suddenly realizing what it must be like to be French today, with the Germans near Paris, and the city hushed listening for the approaching rumble of the guns, and the radio announcers breaking into the jazz programs and the domestic serials with bulletins from Europe, with the careful American pronunciation of names that were so familiar to them, Reims, Soissons, the Marne, Compiègne . . .

If only I was more delicate, Michael thought, if only I had more sense, if I wasn't such a heavy, stupid ox, I would take them aside and talk to them and somehow say the right words that would comfort them. But he knew that if he tried he would be clumsy and would say the wrong thing and embarrass them all and make everything worse than it had been. It was something nobody ever thought to teach you. They taught you everything else but tact, humanity, the healing touch.

". . . I don't like to say this," Johnson was saying in his fine, intelligent, reasonable voice, "but I think the whole thing is a gigantic fake."

"What?" Michael asked stupidly. Johnson was sitting gracefully on the grass, his knees drawn up boyishly, smiling at Miss Freemantle, making an impression on her. Michael could feel himself being annoyed because Johnson seemed to be succeeding in making an impression.

"Conspiracy," Johnson said. "You can't tell me the two greatest armies of the world just collapsed all of a sudden, just like that. It's been arranged."

"Do you mean," Michael asked, "they're handing over Paris to the Germans deliberately?"

"Of course," said Johnson.

"Have you heard anything recent?" the younger Frenchwoman, Miss Boullard, asked softly. "About Paris?"

"No," said Michael, as gently as he could manage. "No news yet."

The two ladies nodded and smiled at him as though he had just presented them with bouquets.

"It'll fall," Johnson said. "Take my word for it."

Why the hell, Michael thought irritably, do we have this man here?

"The deal is on," said Johnson. "This is camouflage for the sake of the people of England and France. The Germans'll move into London in two weeks and a month later they'll all attack the Soviet Union." He said this triumphantly and angrily.

"I think you're wrong," Michael said doggedly. "I don't think it's going to happen. Somehow it's going to work out differently."

"How?" Johnson asked.

"I don't know how." Michael felt he must seem silly in Miss Freemantle's eyes and the thought annoyed him, but he persisted. "Somehow."

"A mystic faith," Johnson said derisively, "that Father will take care of everything. The bogey man won't be allowed into the nursery."

"Please," said Laura, "do we have to talk about it? Don't we want to play badminton? Miss Freemantle, do you play badminton?"

"Yes," said Miss Freemantle. Her voice is low and husky, Michael thought, automatically.

"When are people going to wake up?" Johnson demanded. "When are they going to face the hard facts? There's a deal on to deliver the world. Ethiopia, China, Spain, Austria, Czechoslovakia, Poland . . ."

Those names, Michael thought, those gray names. They had been used so often that almost all emotional significance had been drained from them.

"The ruling class of the world," Johnson said, making Michael think of all the pamphlets he had ever seen, "is consolidating its power, and this is the way they decided to do it. A couple of guns fired off to fool the public, a few patriotic speeches by some old generals, and then the deal, signed, sealed and delivered."

He's probably right, Michael thought wearily, probably everything he says is more or less true, only a man couldn't afford to believe it until he was willing to throw himself into the river. There was a certain minimum gullibility it was necessary to preserve if you wanted to continue living. And, even so, having Johnson say those things in his passionate, educated, indoor voice, the kind of voice you always heard at the theatre on opening nights and in good restaurants and smart parties, was somehow objectionable. Michael wondered where that Irishman was, that drunk, Parrish, at the New Year's Eve party. He would probably say many of the same things that Johnson was saying. After all, it was more or less the Party line, but you could take it better from him. He was probably dead now, grinning in the ground some place near the Ebro River . . . Whatever happens, Michael thought maliciously, looking at Johnson in his chocolate-colored slacks and his bright yellow shirt, whatever happens *you* won't be buried any place, that's a cinch.

"Please," Laura said. "I'm dying to play badminton. Darling . . ." She touched Michael's arm. "The poles and the net and stuff are on the back porch."

Michael sighed and pushed himself heavily up from the ground. Still, Laura was probably right; it would be better than talking this afternoon.

"I'll help," Miss Freemantle said, standing up and starting after Michael.

"Johnson . . ." Michael couldn't resist a parting, defiant shot, "Johnson, has the possibility ever occurred to you that you might be wrong?"

90

"Of course," Johnson said with dignity. "But I'm not wrong now."

"Somewhere," Michael said, "there's got to be a little hope."

Johnson laughed. "Where do you shop for your hope these days?" he asked. "Have you got any to spare?"

"Yes," Michael said.

"What do you hope for?"

"I hope," Michael said, "that America gets into the war and . . ." He saw the two Frenchwomen staring at him seriously.

"The racquets," Laura said nervously, "are in that green wooden box, Michael . . ."

"You want Americans to get killed, too, in this swindle," Johnson said derisively. "Is that it?"

"If necessary," Michael said.

"That's something new for you," Johnson said. "Warmongering."

"It's the first time I thought of it," said Michael, coldly, standing over Johnson. "This minute."

"I get it," said Johnson. "A reader of the New York *Times*. Crazy to save civilization as we know it, and all that."

"Yop," said Michael. "I'm crazy to save civilization as we know it and all that."

"Come on, now," Laura pleaded. "Don't be ugly."

"If you're so eager," Johnson said, "why don't you just go over and join the British Army? Why wait?"

"Maybe I will," said Michael, "maybe I will."

"Oh, no." Michael turned, surprised. It was Miss Freemantle who had said it, and she was standing now, with her hand over her mouth, as though the words had been surprised out of her.

"Did you want to say something?" Michael asked.

"I . . . I shouldn't have," the girl said. "I didn't want to interfere, but . . ." She spoke very earnestly. "You mustn't keep saying we should fight." A female member of the Party, Michael thought heavily; that's where Johnson picked her up. You'd never guess it, though, she was so pretty.

"I suppose," Michael said, "if Russia got into it, you'd change your mind."

"Oh, no," said Miss Freemantle. "It doesn't make any difference." Wrong again, Michael thought, I'm going to stop making these brilliant one-second judgments.

"It doesn't do any good," the girl went on, hesitantly. "It never does. And all the young men go off and get killed. All my friends, my cousins . . . Maybe I'm selfish, but . . . I hate to hear people talking the way you do. I was in Europe, and that's the way they were talking there. Now, probably, a lot of the boys I knew then, that I used to go dancing with and on skiing trips . . . They're probably dead. What for? They just

91

talked and talked, until finally they'd got themselves to a point where the only thing they could do was kill each other. Forgive me," she said, very seriously. "I hadn't meant to shoot my mouth off. It's probably a silly female way of looking at the world. . . ."

"Miss Boullard . . ." Michael turned to the two Frenchwomen. "As women, what's your position?"

"Oh, Michael!" Laura sounded very irritated.

"Our position . . ." The younger one spoke, softly, her voice controlled and polite. "I'm afraid we do not have the luxury of choosing our position."

"Michael," Laura said, "for God's sake, go get that stuff."

"Sure." Michael shook his head.

"Roy," Laura said to Johnson, "you shut up, too."

"Yes, Ma'am," said Johnson, smiling. "Should I tell you the latest gossip?"

"Can't wait," said Laura, in a good approximation of a completely light, untroubled, garden party voice. Michael and Miss Freemantle started out toward the back of the house.

"Josephine's got a new one," Johnson said. "That tall blond boy with the expression. The movie actor, Moran." Michael stopped when he heard the name and Miss Freemantle nearly bumped into him. "Picked him up at an art gallery, according to her. Weren't you in a picture with him last year, Laura?"

"Yes," Laura said. Michael looked at her appraisingly, trying to see if the expression on her face changed as she talked about Moran. Laura's expression hadn't changed. "He's quite a promising actor," she said. "A little light, but quite intelligent."

You never knew with women, Michael thought, they would lie their way into heaven without the flicker of an eyelash.

"He's coming over here," Johnson said. "Moran. He's up here for the first production of the summer theatre and I invited him over. I hope you don't mind."

"No," said Laura, "of course not." But Michael was watching closely and he could see, for a fleeting instant, a swift tremor cross her face. Then she turned her head and Michael couldn't tell any more.

Marriage, he thought.

"Mr. John Moran," the younger Miss Boullard said. Her voice was lively and pleased. "Oh, I'm so excited! I think he's so wonderful. So masculine," she said, "such an important thing for an actor."

"I heard," Michael said sourly, "he's a fairy."

Good God, he thought, women. One moment on the verge of tears because her country was crumbling to the most shameful defeat in its history, the next moment dithering about a pretty, empty-headed movie actor. So masculine!

"He can't be a fairy," Johnson said. "Every time I see him he's with a different girl."

"Maybe he swings from both sides of the plate," Michael said. "Ask my wife." He peered at Laura, feeling ridiculous, but not being able to stop searching her face. "She worked with him."

"I don't know," Laura said, her voice clipped and social. "He's a Harvard graduate."

"I'll ask him," Michael said, "when he comes. Come on, Miss Freemantle, before my wife nags me again. We have work to do."

They walked side by side toward the back of the house. The girl was wearing a fresh perfume, and she walked in an easy, unaffected way that made Michael feel suddenly how young she was.

"When were you in Europe?" he asked. He didn't really care, but he wanted to hear her talk.

"A year ago," she said, "a little more than a year ago."

"How was it?"

"Beautiful," she said. "And terrible. We'll never be able to help them. No matter what we do."

"You agree with Johnson," Michael said. "Is that it?"

"No," she said. "Johnson just repeats what people tell him to say. He hasn't got a thought in his head."

Michael couldn't help smiling to himself, maliciously.

"He's very nice," her voice was rushed a little now and apologetic. Michael thought: Europe has done her a lot of good, she talks so much more softly and agreeably than most American women. "He's very decent and generous and deep down he means so well . . . But everything's so simple for him. If you've seen Europe at all, it doesn't seem that simple. It's like a person suffering from two diseases. The treatment for one is poison for the other." She spoke modestly and a little hesitantly. "Johnson thinks all you have to do is prescribe fresh air and public nurseries and strong labor unions and the patient will automatically recover," Miss Freemantle went on. "He says I'm confused."

"Everybody who doesn't agree with the Communists," Michael said, "is confused. That's their great strength. They're so sure of themselves. They always know what they want to do. They may be all wrong, but they act."

"I'm not so fond of action," Miss Freemantle said. "I saw a little of it in Austria."

"You're living in the wrong year, lady," Michael said, "you and me, both." They were at the back of the house and Miss Freemantle picked up the net and the racquets while Michael hoisted the two poles to his shoulders. They started back to the garden. They walked slowly. Michael felt a tingle

93

of intimacy alone there on the shady side of the house, screened by the rustling tall maples from the rest of the world.

"I have an idea," he said, "for a new political party, to cure all the ills of the world."

"I can't wait to hear," Miss Freemantle said gravely.

"The Party of the Absolute Truth," said Michael. "Every time a question comes up . . . any question . . . Munich, what to do with left-handed children, the freedom of Madagascar, the price of theatre tickets in New York . . . the leaders of the party say exactly what they think on that subject. Instead of the way it is now, when everybody knows that nobody ever says what he means on any subject."

"How big is the membership?"

"One," Michael said. "Me."

"Make it two."

"Joining up?"

"If I may." Margaret grinned at him.

"Delighted," Michael said. "Do you think the party'd work?"

"Not for a minute," she said.

"That's what I think, too," Michael said. "Maybe I'll wait a couple of years."

They were almost to the corner of the house now, and Michael suddenly hated the thought of going out among all those people, turning the girl over to the distant world of guests and hosts and polite conversation.

"Margaret," he said.

"Yes?" She stopped and looked at him.

She knows what I'm going to say, Michael thought. Good.

"Margaret," he said, "may I see you in New York?"

They looked at each other in silence for a moment. She has freckles on her nose, Michael thought.

"Yes," she said.

"I won't say anything else," Michael said softly, "now."

"The telephone book," the girl said. "My name's in the telephone book."

She turned and walked around the corner of the house, in that precise, straight, graceful walk, carrying the net and the racquets, her legs brown and slender under the swaying full skirt. Michael stood there for a moment, trying to make sure his face had fallen back into repose. Then he walked out into the garden after her.

The other guests had come, Tony and Moran and a girl who wore red slacks and a straw hat with a brim nearly two feet wide.

Moran was tall and willowy and had on a dark-blue shirt, open at the collar. He was a glowing brown from the sun and his hair fell boyishly over his eye when he smiled and shook hands with Michael. Why the hell can't I look like that?

Michael thought dully as he felt the firm, manly grip. Actors, he thought.

"Yes," he heard himself saying, "we've met before. I remember. New Year's Eve. The night Arney did his window act."

Tony looked strange. When Michael introduced him to Miss Freemantle he barely smiled, and he sat all hunched up, as though he were in pain, his face pale and troubled, his lank, dark hair tumbled uneasily on his high forehead. Tony taught French literature at Rutgers. He was an Italian, although his face was paler and more austere than one expects of Italian faces. Michael had gone to school with him and had grown increasingly fond of him through the years. He spoke in a shy, delicate voice, hushed and bookish, as though he were always whispering in a library. He was a good friend of the Boullard sisters, and had tea with them two or three times a week, formal and bi-lingual, but today they didn't even look at each other.

Michael started to put up one of the poles. He pushed it into the lawn as the girl in the red slacks was saying in her high, fashionable voice, "That hotel is just ghastly. One bathroom to the floor and beds you could use for ship-planking and a lot of idiotic cretonne with hordes, really hordes of bugs. And the prices!"

Michael looked at Margaret and shook his head in a loose, mocking movement, and Margaret smiled briefly at him, then dropped her eyes. Michael glanced at Laura. Laura was staring stonily at him. How the hell does she manage it? Michael thought. Never misses anything. If that talent were only put to some useful purpose.

"You're not doing it right," Laura said, "the tree'll interfere."

"Please," said Michael, "I'm doing this."

"All wrong," said Laura stubbornly.

Michael ignored her and continued working on the pole.

Suddenly the two Misses Boullard stood up, pulling at their gloves, with crisp, identical movements.

"We have had a lovely time," the younger one said. "Thank you very much. We regret, but we have to leave now."

Michael stopped work in surprise. "But you just came," he said.

"It is unfortunate," the younger Miss Boullard said crisply, "but my sister is suffering from a disastrous headache."

The two sisters went from person to person, shaking hands. They didn't shake hands with Tony. They didn't even look at him, but passed him as though he were not there. Tony looked at them with a strange, quivering expression, incongruous and somehow naked.

"Never mind," he said, picking up the old-fashioned straw

95

hat he had carried into the garden with him. "Never mind. You don't have to go, I'll leave."

There was a moment of nervous silence and nobody looked at Tony or the two sisters.

"We have enjoyed meeting you so much," the younger Miss Boullard said coolly to Moran. "We have admired your pictures again and again."

"Thank you," Moran said, boyish and charming. "It's kind of you . . ."

Actors, Michael thought.

"Stop it!" Tony shouted. His face was white. "For the love of God, Helene, don't behave this way!"

"There is no need," the younger Miss Boullard said, "to see us to the gate. We know the way."

"An explanation is necessary," Tony said, his voice trembling. "We can't treat our friends this way." He turned to Michael, standing embarrassedly next to the flimsy pole for the badminton net. "It's inconceivable," Tony said. "Two women I've known for ten years. Two supposedly sensible, intelligent women . . ." The two sisters finally turned and faced Tony, their eyes and mouths frozen in contempt and hatred. "It's the war, this damned war," Tony said. "Helene. Rochelle. Please. Be reasonable. Don't do this to me. I am not entering Paris. I am not killing Frenchmen. I am an American and I love France and I hate Mussolini and I'm your friend . . ."

"We do not wish to talk to you," the younger Miss Boullard said, "or to any Italians." She took her sister's hand. The two of them bowed slightly to the rest of them, and walked, rustling and elegant in their gloves and garden hats and stiff black dresses, toward the gate at the end of the garden.

The crows were making a lot of noise in the big tree fifty yards away and their cawing struck the ear, harsh and clamorous.

"Come on, Tony," Michael said, "I'm going to give you a drink."

Without a word, with his mouth set in a sunken line, Tony followed Michael into the house. He was still clutching the straw hat with the gaily striped band.

Michael got out two glasses and poured two big shots of whiskey. Silently he gave Tony one of the glasses. Outside, the conversation was starting again, and, over the noise of the crows, Michael heard Moran saying, earnestly, "Aren't they wonderful types? Right out of a 1925 French movie."

Tony sipped slowly at his drink, holding on to the stiff, old-fashioned straw hat, his eyes faraway and sorrowful. Michael wanted to go over to him and embrace him, the way he had seen Tony's brothers embrace each other in times of trouble, but he couldn't bring himself to do it. He turned the radio on and took a long sip of his whiskey as the machine warmed up, with a high, irritating crackle.

"You, too, can have lovely white hands," a soft, persuasive voice was saying. Then there was a click on the radio and a sudden dead silence and a new voice spoke, slightly hoarse, trembling a little. "We have just received a special bulletin," the voice said. "It has been announced that the Germans have entered Paris. There has been no resistance and the city has not been harmed. Keep tuned to this station for further news."

An organ, swelling and almost tuneless, took over, playing the sort of music that is described as "light-classical."

Tony sat down and placed his glass on a table. Michael stared at the radio. He had never been to Paris. He had never seemed to find the time or the money to go abroad, but as he squinted at the little veneer box shaking now with the music of the organ and the echo of the hoarse, troubled voice, he pictured what it must be like in the French city this afternoon. The broad sunny streets, so familiar to the whole world, the cafés, empty now, he supposed, the flashy, rhetorical monuments of old victories shining in the summer light, the Germans marching rigidly in formation, with the noise of their boots clanging against the closed shutters. The picture was probably wrong, he thought. It was silly, but you never thought of German soldiers in twos or threes, or in anything but stiff, marching phalanxes, like rectangular animals. Maybe they were stealing along the streets timidly, their guns ready, peering at the shut windows, dropping to the sidewalks at every noise.

Christ, he thought bitterly, why didn't I go over there when I had the chance . . . the summer of '36, or last spring? You kept postponing things and this is what happened. He thought of the books he had read about Paris. The bubbling 1920's, at the hilarious and desperate end of another war. The gay, doomed, witty expatriates at the famous bars, the pretty girls, the clever, cynical young men with a Pernod in one hand and an American Express check in the other. Now, it was all gone, under the tank-treads, and he had never seen it and probably would never see it.

He looked at Tony. Tony was sitting with his head up, crying. Tony had lived in Paris for two years and again and again he had outlined to Michael what they would do together on vacations there, the little restaurants, the beach on the Marne, the place where they had a superior light wine in carafes on scrubbed wooden tables . . .

Michael felt the wetness in his own eyes and fought it savagely. Sentimental, he thought, cheap, easy, and sentimental. I was never there. It's just another city.

"Michael . . ." It was Laura's voice. "Michael!" Her voice was insistent and irritating. "Michael!"

Michael finished his drink. He looked at Tony, nearly said something to him, then thought better of it, and left him sitting there. Michael walked slowly out into the garden. Johnson and Moran and Moran's girl and Miss Freemantle were sitting around stiffly, and you could tell the conversation was all uphill. Michael wished they would go home.

"Michael, darling," Laura came over to him and held his arms lightly, "are we going to play badminton this summer or wait till 1950?" Then, under her breath, privately and harshly for him, "Come on. Act civilized. You have guests. Don't leave the whole thing up to me."

Before Michael could say anything she had turned and was smiling at Johnson.

Michael walked slowly over to the second pole that was lying on the ground. "I don't know if any of you are interested," he said, "but Paris has fallen."

"No!" Moran said. "Incredible!"

Miss Freemantle didn't say anything. Michael saw her clasp her hands and look down on them.

"Inevitable," Johnson said gravely. "Anybody could see it coming."

Michael picked up the second pole and started pushing the sharp end into the ground.

"You're putting it in the wrong place!" Laura's voice was high and irritated. "How many times must I tell you it won't do any good there." She rushed over to where Michael was standing with the pole and grabbed it from his hands. She had a racquet in her hand and it slapped sharply against his arm. He looked at her stupidly, his hands still out, curved as they were when he was holding the pole. She's crying, he thought, surprised, what the hell is she crying about?

"Here! It belongs here!" She was shouting now, and banging the sharp end of the pole hysterically into the ground.

Michael strode over to where she was standing and grabbed the pole. He didn't know why he was doing it. He just knew he couldn't bear the sight of his wife crazily yelling and slamming the pole into the grass.

"I'm doing this," he said idiotically. "You keep quiet!"

Laura looked at him, her pretty, soft face churned with hatred. She picked up her arm and threw the badminton racquet at Michael's head. Michael stared heavily at it as it sailed through the air at him. It seemed to take a long time, arching and flashing against the background of trees and hedge at the end of the garden. He heard a dull, whipping crack, and he saw it drop to his feet before he realized it had hit him over his right eye. The eye began to ache and he could feel blood coming out on his forehead, sticking in his eyebrow. After a moment, some of it dripped down over the eye, warm and opaque. Laura was still standing in the same place, weeping, staring at him, her face still violent and full of hate.

Michael carefully laid the pole down on the grass and turned and walked away. Tony passed him, coming out of the house, but they didn't say anything to each other.

Michael walked into the living room. The radio was still sending forth the doughy music of the organ. Michael stood against the mantelpiece, staring at his face in the little convex mirror in a gold, heavily worked frame. It distorted his face, making his nose look very long and his forehead and chin receding and pointed. The red splash over his eye seemed small and far away in the mirror. He heard the door open and Laura's footsteps behind him as she came into the room. She went over to the radio and turned it off.

"You know I can't stand organ music!" she said. Her voice was trembling and bitter.

He turned to face her. She stood there in her gay cotton print, pale orange and white, with her midriff showing brown and smooth in the space between the skirt and the halter. She looked very pretty, slender and soft in her fashionable summer dress, like an advertisement for misses' frocks in *Vogue* magazine. The bitter, hard-set face, streaked with tears, was incongruous and shocking.

"That's all," Michael said. "We're finished. You know that."

"Good! Delightful! I couldn't be more pleased."

"While we're at it," Michael said, "let me tell you that I'm pretty sure about you and Moran, too. I was watching you."

"Good," said Laura. "I'm glad you know. Let me put your mind at rest. You're absolutely right. Anything else?"

"No," said Michael. "I'll get the five-o'clock train."

"And don't be so goddamn holy!" Laura said. "I know a couple of things about you, too! All those letters telling me how lonely you were in New York without me! You weren't so damned lonely. I was getting pretty tired of coming back and having all those women look at me, pityingly. And when did you arrange to meet Miss Freemantle? Lunch Tuesday? Shall I go out and tell her your plans are changed? You can meet her tomorrow . . ." Her face was sharp and rushed and the thin childish face was contorted with misery and anger.

"That's enough," Michael said, feeling guilty and hopeless. "I don't want to hear any more."

"Any more questions?" Laura shouted. "No other men you want to ask me about? No other suspects? Shall I write out a list for you?"

Suddenly she broke. She fell onto the couch. A little too gracefully, Michael noted coldly, like an ingenue. She dug her head into the pillow and wept. She looked spent and racked, sobbing on the couch, with her pretty hair spread in a soft fan around her head, like a frail child in a party dress. Michael had a powerful impulse to go over and take her in his arms and say, "Baby, Baby" softly, and comfort her.

He turned and went out to the garden. The guests had moved discreetly to the other end of the garden, away from the house. They were standing in a stiff, uncomfortable group, their bright clothes shining against the deep green background. Michael walked over to them, brushing the back of his hand against the cut over his eye.

"No badminton today," he said. "I think you'd better leave. The garden party has not been the success of the Pennsylvania summer season."

"We were just going," Johnson said, stiffly.

Michael didn't shake hands with any of them. He stood there, staring past the blurred succession of heads. Miss Freemantle looked at him once, then kept her eyes on the ground as she went past. Michael did not say anything to her. He heard the gate close behind them.

He stood there, on the fresh grass, feeling the sun make the cut over his eye sticky. Overhead the crows were making a metallic racket in the branches. He hated the crows. He walked over to the wall, bent down and carefully selected some smooth, heavy stones. Then he stood up and squinted at the tree, spotting the crows among the foliage. He drew back and threw a stone at three of the birds sitting in a black, loud row. His arm felt limber and powerful, and the stone sang through the branches. He threw another stone, and another, hard and swift, and the birds scrambled off the branches and flapped away, cawing in alarm. Michael threw a stone in a savage arc at the flying birds. They disappeared into the woods. For awhile there was silence in the garden, drowsy and sunny in the late summer afternoon.

CHAPTER SIX

NOAH WAS NERVOUS. This was the first party he had ever given, and he tried to remember what parties looked like in the movies and parties he had read about in books and magazines. Twice he went into the kitchenette to inspect the three dozen ice cubes he and Roger had bought at the drugstore. He looked at his watch again and again, hoping that Roger would get back from Brooklyn with his girl before the guests started to come, because Noah was sure that he would do some awful, gauche thing, just at the moment it was necessary to be relaxed and dignified.

He and Roger Cannon shared a room near Riverside Drive, not far from Columbia University in New York City. It was a large room, and it had a fireplace, although you couldn't light a fire there, and from the bathroom window, by leaning out only a little, you could see the Hudson River.

After his father's death, Noah had drifted back across the country. He had always wanted to see New York. There was nothing to moor him in any other place on the face of the earth, and he had been able to find a job in the city two days after he landed there. Then he had met Roger in the Public Library on Fifth Avenue.

It was hard to believe now that there had been a time when he didn't know Roger, a time when he had wandered the city streets for days without saying a word to anyone, a time when no man was his friend, no woman had looked at him, no street was home, no hour more attractive than any other hour.

He had been standing dreamily in front of the library shelves, staring at the dull-colored rows of books. He had reached up for a volume, he remembered it even now, a book by Yeats, and he had jostled the man next to him, and said "Excuse me." They had started to talk and had gone out into the rainy street together, and had continued talking. Roger had invited him into a bar on Sixth Avenue and they had had two beers and had agreed before they parted to have dinner together the next night.

Noah had never had any real friends. His shifting, erratic boyhood, spent a few months at a time among abrupt and disinterested strangers, had made it impossible to form any but the most superficial connections. And his stony shyness, reinforced by the conviction that he was a drab, unappealing child, had put him beyond all overtures. Roger was four or five years older than Noah, tall and thin, with a lean, dark, close-cropped head, and he moved with a certain casual air that Noah had always envied in the young men who had gone to the better colleges. Roger hadn't gone to college, but he was one of those people who seem to be born with confidence in themselves, secure and unshakable. He regarded the world with a kind of sour, dry amusement that Noah was trying now desperately to emulate.

Noah could not understand why, but Roger had seemed to like him. Perhaps, Noah thought, the truth was that Roger had pitied him, alone in the city, in his shabby suit, gawky, uncertain, fiercely shy. At any rate, after they had seen each other two or three times, for drinks in the horrible bars that Roger seemed to like, or for dinner in cheap Italian restaurants,

101

Roger, in his quiet, rather offhand way, had said, "Do you like the place you're living in?"

"Not much," Noah had said, honestly. It was a dreary cell in a rooming house on 28th Street, with damp walls and bugs and the toilet pipes roaring above his head.

"I've got a big room," Roger had said. "Two couches. If you don't mind my playing the piano every once in a while in the middle of the night."

Gratefully, still astonished that there was anyone in this crowded, busy city who could find profit, of any kind whatsoever, in his friendship, Noah had moved into the large, rundown room near the river. Roger was almost like the phantom friend lonely children invent for themselves in the long, unpeopled stretches of the night. He was easy, gentle, accomplished. He made no demands on anyone and he seemed to take pleasure, in his rambling, unostentatious way, in putting the younger man through a rough kind of education. He talked in a random, probing way, about books, music, painting, politics, women. He had been to France and Italy, and the great names of ancient cities and charming towns sounded intimate and accessible in his slow, rather harsh New England accent. He had dry, sardonic theories about the British Empire and the workings of democracy in the United States, and about modern poetry, and the ballet and the movies and the war. He didn't seem to have any ambition of his own. He worked, sporadically and not very hard, for a company that took polls for commercial products. He didn't pay much attention to money, and he wandered from girl to girl with slightly bored, good-humored lust. All in all, with his careless, somehow elegant clothes, and his crooked, reserved smile, he was that rare product of modern America, his own man.

He and Noah took rambling walks together along the river, and on the University campus. Roger had found Noah a good job through some friends as a playground director at a settlement house down on the East Side. Noah was making thirty-six dollars a week, more money than he ever had made before, and as they trudged along the quiet pavements late at night, side by side, with the cliffs of Jersey rearing up across the river, and the lights of the boats winking below them, Noah listened, thirsty and delighted, like an eavesdropper on an unsuspected, glowing world, as Roger said, "Then there was this defrocked priest near Antibes who drank a quart of Scotch every afternoon, sitting in the café on the hill, translating Baudelaire . . ." or "The trouble with American women is they all want to be captain of the team or they won't play. It comes from putting an inflated value on chastity. If an American woman pretends to be faithful to you, she thinks she has earned the right to chain you to the kitchen stove. It's better in Europe.

Everyone knows everyone else is unchaste, and there is a more normal system of values. Infidelity is a kind of gold standard between the sexes. There is a fixed rate of exchange and you know what things cost you when you go shopping. Personally, I like a submissive woman. All the girls I know say I have a feudal attitude toward women, and maybe they're right. But I'd rather they submitted to me than have me submit to them. One or the other is bound to happen, and I'm in no rush, I'll find a proper type eventually . . ."

Walking beside him, it seemed to Noah that life could not improve on his condition now . . . being young, at home on the streets of New York, with a pleasant job and thirty-six dollars a week, and a book-crowded room nearly overlooking the river, and a friend like Roger, urbane, thoughtful, full of strange information. The only thing lacking was a girl, and Roger had decided to fix even that. That was why they had planned the party.

Roger had had a good time all one evening casting about among his old address books for likely candidates for Noah. And now, tonight, they were coming, six of them, besides the girl that Roger was bringing himself. There were going to be some other men, of course, but Roger had slyly selected funny-looking ones or slow-witted ones among his friends, so that the competition would not be too severe. As Noah looked around the warm, lamp-lit room, with cut flowers in vases and a print by Braque on the wall, and the bottles and the glasses shining like a vision from a better world on the desk, he knew, with delicious, fearful certainty, that tonight he would finally find himself a girl.

Noah smiled as he heard the key in the door because now he would not have to face the ordeal of greeting the first guests by himself. The door opened and Roger came in. Roger had his girl with him, and Noah took her coat and hung it up without accident, not tripping over anything or wrenching the girl's arm. He smiled to himself inside the closet as he heard the girl saying to Roger, "What a nice room. It looks as though there hasn't been a woman in here since 1750."

Noah came back into the room. Roger was in the kitchenette getting some ice and the girl was standing in front of the picture on the wall, with her back to Noah. Roger was singing softly over the ice behind the screen, his nasal voice bumbling along on a song he sang over and over again, whose words went, "You make time and you make love dandy, You make swell molasses candy. But, honey, are you makin' any money, That's all I want to know."

The girl had on a plum-colored dress with a full skirt that caught the lamplight. She was standing, very serious and at home, with her back to the room, in front of the fireplace. She had pretty, rather heavy legs, and a narrow, graceful waist. Her hair was pulled to the back in a severe, feminine knot, like a pretty schoolteacher in the movies. The sight of her, the sound of ice, his friend's silly, good-humored song from behind the screen, made the room, the evening, the world, seem wonderfully domestic and dear and melancholy to Noah. Then the girl turned around. Noah had been too busy and excited really to look at her when she first came in and he didn't even remember what her name was. Seeing her now was like looking through a glass that is suddenly brought to focus.

She had a dark, pointed face and grave eyes. Somehow, as he looked at her, Noah felt that he had been hit, physically, by something solid and numbing. He had never felt anything like this before. He felt guilty and feverish and absurd.

Her name, Noah discovered later, was Hope Plowman, and she had come down from a small town in Vermont two years before. She lived in Brooklyn now with an aunt. She had a direct, serious way of talking, and she didn't wear any perfume and she worked as a secretary to a man who made printing machinery in a small factory near Canal Street. Noah felt a little irritated and foolish through the night, as he found out all these things, because it was somehow simple-minded and unworldly to be so riotously overcome by a rather ordinary smalltown Yankee girl who worked prosaically as a stenographer in a dull office, and who lived in Brooklyn. Like other shy, bookish young men, with their hearts formed in the library, and romance blooming only out of the volumes of poetry stuck in their overcoat pockets, it was impossible to conceive of Isolde taking the Brighton Express, Beatrice at the Automat. No, he thought, as he greeted the new guests and helped with the drinks, no, I am not going to let this happen. Most of all, she was Roger's girl, and even if any girl would desert that handsome, superior man, for an awkward craggy boy like himself, it was inconceivable that he, Noah, could repay the generous acts of friendships even by the hidden duplicity of unspoken desire.

But the other guests, men and women alike, were merely blurs, and he moved dreamlike and tortured among them, staring hungrily at the girl, the memory of her every calm, controlled movement burned on his brain, the crisp music of her every inflection singing with a terrible mixture of shame and jubilance in his ears. He felt like a soldier caught in his first battle, like an heir who has just been left a million dollars, like a believer who has just been excommunicated, like a tenor who has just sung Tristan for the first time at the Metropolitan Opera House. He felt like a man who has just been found in a hotel bedroom with the wife of his best friend, like a General leading his troops into a captured city, like Nobel prize winners, like condemned criminals being led to the gallows, like heavyweight champions who have just knocked out all contenders, like a swimmer drowning in the middle of the night, thirty miles from shore in a cold ocean, like a scientist who has just discovered the serum which will make the race immortal...

"Miss Plowman," he said, "would you like a drink?"

"No, thank you," she said. "I don't drink."

And he went off into a corner to ponder this and discover whether this was good or bad, hopeful or not.

"Miss Plowman," he said, later, "have you known Roger long?"

"Oh, yes. Nearly a year."

Nearly a year! No hope, no hope.

"He's told me a lot about you." The direct, dark gaze, the soft, definite voice.

"What did he say?" How lame, how hungry, how hopeless.

"He likes you very much..."

Treachery, treachery... Friend who snatched the lost waif among the library shelves, who fed and sheltered and loved ... Friend now, all thoughtless and laughing, at the center of the bright group, fingering the piano lightly, singing in the pleasant, intelligent voice, "Joshua fit the battle of Jericho, Jericho, Jericho..."

"He said," once more the troubling, dangerous voice ... "He said, when you finally woke up you would be a wonderful man..."

Ah, worse and worse, the thief armed with his friend's guarantee, the adulterer given the key to the wife's apartment by the trusting husband.

Noah stared blankly and wearily at the girl. Unreasonably, he hated her. At eight that evening he had been a happy man, secure and hopeful, with friend and home and job, with the past clean behind him, the future shining ahead. At nine he was a bleeding fugitive in an endless swamp, with the dogs baying at him, and a roster of crimes dark against his name on the books of the country. And she was the cause of it, sitting there, demure, falsely candid, pretending she had done nothing, knew nothing, sensed nothing. A little, unpretentious, rock-farm hill girl, who probably sat on her boss's knee in the office of the printing-machinery factory near Canal Street, to take dictation.

"... and the walls came tumbling down..." Roger's voice and the strong chords of the old piano against the wall filled the room.

Noah stared wildly away from the girl. There were six other girls in the room, young, with fair complexions and glowing hair, with soft bodies and sweet, attentive voices... They had

105

been brought here for him to choose from and they had smiled at him, full of kindness and invitation. And now, for all of him, they might as well have been six tailor's dummies in a closed store, six numbers on a page, six doorknobs. It could only happen to him, he thought. It was the pattern of his life, grotesque, savagely humorous, essentially tragic.

No, he thought, I will put this away from me. If it shatters me, if I collapse from it, if I never touch a woman as long as I live. But he could not bear to be in the same room with her. He went over to the closet in which his clothes hung side by side with Roger's, and got his hat. He would go out and walk around until the party had broken up, the merrymakers dispersed, the piano silent, the girl safe with her aunt beyond the bridge in Brooklyn. His hat was next to Roger's on the shelf and he looked with guilt and tenderness at the rakishly creased old brown felt. Luckily, most of the guests were grouped around the piano and he got to the door unobserved; he would make up some excuse for Roger later. But the girl saw him. She was sitting talking to one of the other girls, facing the door, and an expression of quiet inquiry came into her face as she looked at Noah, standing at the door, taking one last, despairing look at her. She stood up and walked over to him. The rustle of her dress was like artillery in his ears.

"Where are you going?" she asked.

"We . . . we . . ." he stuttered, hating himself for the ineptness of his tongue. "We need some more soda, and I'm going out to get it."

"I'll go with you," she said.

"No!" he wanted to shout. "Stay where you are! Don't move!" But he remained silent and watched her get her coat and a plain, rather unbecoming hat, that made tidal waves of pity and tenderness for her youth and her poverty sweep him convulsively. She went to Roger, sitting at the piano, and leaned over, holding his shoulder, to whisper into his ear. Now, Noah thought, blackly, now it will all be known, now it is over, and he nearly plunged out into the night. But Roger turned and smiled at him, waving with one hand, while still playing the bass with the other. The girl came across the room with her unpretentious walk.

"I told Roger," she said.

Told Roger! Told him what? Told him to beware strangers? Told him to pity no one, told him to be generous never, to cut down love in his heart like weed in a garden?

"You'd better take your coat," the girl said. "It was raining when we came."

Stiffly, silently, Noah went over and got his coat. The girl waited at the door and they closed it behind them in the dark hall. The singing and the laughter within sounded far away and forbidden to them as they walked slowly, close together, down the steps to the wet street outside.

"Which way is it?" she asked, as they stood irresolutely with the front door of the house closed behind them.

"Which way is what?" Noah asked, dazedly.

"The soda. The place where you can buy the soda?"

"Oh . . ." Noah looked distractedly up and down the gleaming pavements. "Oh. That. I don't know. Anyway," he said, "we don't need soda."

"I thought you said . . ."

"It was an excuse. I was getting tired of the party. Very tired. Parties bore me." Even as he spoke, he listened to his voice and was elated at the real timbre of sophistication and weariness with frivolous social affairs that he heard there. That was the way to handle this matter, he decided. With urbanity. Be cool, polite, slightly amused with this little girl . . .

"I thought that was a very nice party," the girl said, seriously.

"Was it?" Noah asked offhandedly. "I hadn't noticed." That was it, he told himself, gloomily pleased, that was the attack. Remote, slightly vague, like an English baron after an evening's drinking, frigidly polite. It would serve a double purpose. It would keep him from betraying his friend, even by so much as a word. And also, and he felt a delicious thrill of guilty promise at the thought, it would impress this simple little Brooklyn secretary with his rare and superior qualities.

"Sorry," he said, "if I got you down here in the rain under false pretenses."

The girl looked around her. "It's not raining," she said, practically.

"Ah." Noah regarded the weather for the first time. "Ah, so it is." There was something baffling about the grammar here, but the tone still was right, he felt.

"What are you going to do?" she asked.

He shrugged. It was the first time he had ever shrugged in his whole life. "Don't know," he said. "Take a stroll." Even his vocabulary suddenly took on a Galsworthian cast. "Often do. In the middle of the night. Very peaceful, walking along through the deserted streets."

"It's only eleven o'clock now," the girl said.

"So it is," he said. He would have to be careful not to say that again. "If you want to go back to the party . . ."

The girl hesitated. A horn blew out on the misty river and the sound, low and trembling, went to the core of Noah's bones.

"No," she said, "I'll take a walk with you."

They walked side by side, without touching, down to the tree-bordered avenue that ran high above the river. The Hudson, smelling of spring and its burden of salt that had swept

107

up from the ocean on the afternoon's tide, slipped darkly past the misty shores. Far north was the string of soaring lights that was the bridge to Jersey and across the river the Palisades loomed like a castle. There were no other strollers. Occasionally a car rushed by, its tires whining on the pavement, making the night and the river and themselves moving slowly along under the budding branches of the glistening trees, extraordinary and mysterious.

They walked in silence alongside the flowing river, their footsteps lonely and brave. Three minutes, Noah thought, looking at his shoes, four minutes, five minutes, without talking. He began to grow desperate. There was a sinful intimacy about their silence, an almost tangible longing and tenderness about the echoing sound of their footsteps and the quiet intake of their breath, and the elaborate precautions not to touch each other with shoulder or elbow or hand as they went downhill along the uneven pavement. Silence became the enemy, the betrayer. Another moment of it, he felt, and the quiet girl walking slyly and knowingly beside him, would understand everything, as though he had mounted the balustrade that divided street from river and there made an hour-long speech on the subject of love.

"New York City," he said hoarsely, "must be quite frightening to a girl from the country."

"No," she said, "it isn't."

"The truth is," he went on, desperately, "that it is highly overrated. It puts on a big act of being sophisticated and cosmopolitan, but at heart it's unalterably provincial." He smiled, delighted with the "unalterably."

"I don't think so," the girl said.

"What?"

"I don't think it's provincial. Anyway, not after Vermont."

"Oh . . ." He laughed patronizingly. "Vermont."

"Where have you been?" she asked.

"Chicago," he said, "Los Angeles, San Francisco . . . All over." He waved vaguely, with a debonair intimation that these were merely the first names that came to mind and that if he had gone through the whole list, Paris, Budapest and Vienna would certainly have been on it.

"I must say, though," he went on, "that New York has beautiful women. A little flashy, but very attractive." Here he thought with satisfaction, looking at her anxiously, here we have struck the right note. "American women, of course," he said, "are best when they're young. After that . . ." Once more he tried to shrug and once more he achieved it. "For myself," he said, "I prefer the slightly older Continental type. They are at their best when American women are bridge-playing harpies with spread behinds." He glanced at her a little nervously. But the girl's expression hadn't changed. She had broken off a twig from a bush and was absently running it along the stone fence, as though she were pondering what he had just said. "And by that time, too, a Continental woman has learned how to handle men . . ." He thought back hurriedly about the foreign women he had known. There was that drunk in the bar the night his father died. It was quite possible that she was Polish. Poland was not a terribly romantic place, but it was on the Continent all right.

"How does a Continental woman learn how to handle men?" the girl asked.

"She learns how to submit," he said. "The women I know say I have a feudal attitude . . ." Oh, friend, friend at the piano, forgive me for this theft tonight, I will make it up some other time . . .

After that it flowed freely. "Art," he said. "Art? I can't stand the modern notion that art is mysterious and the artist an irresponsible child."

"Marriage?" he said. "Marriage? Marriage is a desperate admission on the part of the human race that men and women do not know how to live in the same world with each other."

"The theatre," he said, "the American theatre? It has a certain lively, childish quality, but as for taking it seriously as an art form in the twentieth century . . ." He laughed loftily. "Give me Disney."

After awhile they looked around them and discovered that they had walked thirty-four blocks along the dark sliding river and that it had begun to rain again and that it was very late. Standing close to the girl, cupping a match to keep out the wind so that they could see what time it was on his wrist watch, with the small fragrance of the girl's hair mingling with the smell of the river in his nostrils, Noah suddenly decided to be silent. This was too painful, this wild flood of nonsensical talk, this performance of the jaundiced young blood dilettante and connoisseur.

"It's late," he said abruptly, "we'd better go back to the party."

But he couldn't resist the gesture of hailing a taxi that was cruising slowly past them. It was the first time he had taken a taxi in New York and he stumbled over the little let-down chairs, but he felt elegant and master of himself and social life as he sat far away from the girl on the back seat. She sat quietly in the corner. Noah sensed that he had made a strong impression on her and he gave the driver a quarter tip although the entire fare had only been sixty cents.

Once more they stood at the closed door of the house in which he lived. They looked up. The lights were out and no sound of conversation, music or laughter came from behind the closed windows.

"It's over," he said, his heart sinking with the realization that Roger would now be certain he had stolen his girl. "Nobody's there."

"It looks that way, doesn't it?" the girl said placidly.

"What'll we do?" Noah felt trapped.

"I guess you'll have to take me home," the girl said.

Brooklyn, Noah thought, heavily. Hours there and hours back, and Roger waiting accusingly in the dawn light in the rumpled room where late the party had been so merry, waiting with the curt, betrayed, final dismissal on his lips. The night had started out so wonderfully, so hopefully. He remembered the moment when he had been alone in the apartment waiting for the guests, before Roger had arrived. He remembered the warm expectancy with which he had inspected the shabby, shelf-lined room that had seemed at that moment so friendly and promising.

"Can't you go home alone?" he asked bleakly. He hated her standing there, pretty, a little drab, with the rain wilting on her hair and her clothes.

"Don't you dare talk like that," she said. Her voice was sharp and commanding. "I'm not going home alone. Come on."

Noah sighed. Now, aside from everything else, the girl was angry at him.

"Don't sigh like that," she said crisply. "Like a henpecked husband."

What's happened, Noah thought dazedly, how did I get here, how did this girl get the right to talk to me this way? . . .

"I'm going," she said, and turned with definiteness and started off toward the subway. He watched her for a moment, baffled, then hurried after her.

The trains were dank and smelly with the ghost of the rain that the riders brought in with them from the streets above. There was a taste of iron in the unchanging air and the bosomy girls who advertised toothpaste and laxatives and brassieres on the garish cards seemed foolish and improbable in the light of the dusty lamps. The other passengers in the cars, returning from unknown labors and unimaginable assignations, swayed on the stained yellow seats.

The girl sat tight-lipped and silent. When they had to change trains at a station she merely stood with unbending disapproval and walked out onto the platform, leaving Noah to shuffle lamely after her.

They had to change again and again, and wait interminably for new connections on the almost deserted platforms, with the water from the rain and leaking mains dripping down the graying tiles and rusted iron of the tunnels. This girl, Noah thought with dull hostility, this girl must live at the end of the city, five hundred yards past the ultimate foot of track, out among the dump heaps and cemeteries. Brooklyn, Brooklyn, how long was Brooklyn, stretched in the sleeping night from the East River to Gravesend Bay, from the oily waters of Greenpoint to the garbage scows of Canarsie. Brooklyn, like Venice, was clasped in the waters of the sea, but its Grand Canal was the Fourth Avenue Local.

How demanding and certain of herself this girl was, thought Noah, glaring at her, to drag a man she had just met so far and so long through the clanging, sorrowful labyrinth of the Borough's mournful underground. His luck, he thought, with a prescient, murky vision of himself, night after night on these grim platforms, night after night among the late-riding charladies and burglars and drunken merchant seamen who made up the subway dawn passenger lists, his luck, with one million women living within a radius of fifty blocks of him, to be committed to a sharp-tempered, unrelenting girl, who made her home at the dreary other end of the largest city known to man.

Leander, he thought, swam the Hellespont for another girl; but he did not have to take her home later in the evening, nor did he have to wait twenty-five minutes among the trash baskets and the signs that warned against spitting and smoking on DeKalb Avenue.

Finally, they got off at a station and the girl led him up the steps to the streets above.

"At last," he said, the first words he had spoken in an hour. "I thought we were down there for the summer season."

The girl stopped at the corner. "Now," she said coldly, "we take the street car."

"Oh, God!" Noah said. Then he began to laugh. His laughter sounded mad and empty across the trolley tracks, among the shabby store fronts and dingy brownstone walls.

"If you're going to be so unpleasant," the girl said, "you can leave me here."

"I have come this far," Noah said, with literary gravity. "I will go the whole way."

He stopped laughing and stood beside her, silent under the lamppost, with the raw wind smashing against them in rough wet gusts, the wind that had come across the Atlantic beaches and the polluted harbors, across the million acres of semi-detached houses, across the brick and wood wastes of Flatbush and Bensonhurst, across the sleeping, tortured souls of millions of their fellowmen, who in their uneasy voyage through life had found no gentler place to lay their heads.

A quarter of an hour later the trolley car rumbled toward them, a clanking eye of light in the distance. There were only three other passengers, dozing unhappily on the wood seats, and Noah sat formally beside the girl, feeling, in the lighted car, creaking along the dark streets, like a man on a raft, wrecked with strangers, relics of a poor ship that had foundered on a cold run among northern islands. The girl sat primly, staring straight ahead, her hands crossed in her lap, and Noah felt as though he did not know her at all, as though if he ventured to speak to her she would cry out for a policeman and demand to be protected against him.

"All right," she said, and stood up. Once more he followed her to the door. The car stopped and the door wheezed open. They stepped down to the wet pavement. The car pulled away, a mass of protesting bearings, clashing at the meager sleep of the natives, packed into their leaning houses. Noah and the girl walked away from the trolley tracks. Here and there along the mean streets there was a tree, fretted with green in surprising evidence that spring had come to this place this year.

The girl turned into a small concrete yard, under a high stone stoop. There was a barred iron door. She opened the lock with her key and the door swung open.

"There," she said, coldly. "We're home," and turned to face him.

Noah took off his hat. The girl's face bloomed palely out of the darkness. She had taken off her hat, too, and her hair made a wavering line around the ivory gleam of her cheeks and brow. Noah felt like weeping, as though he had lost everything that he had ever held dear, as he stood close to her in the poor shadow of the house in which she lived.

"I . . . I want to say . . ." he said, whispering, "that I do not object . . . I mean I am pleased . . . pleased, I mean, to have brought you home."

"Thank you," she said. She was whispering, too, but her voice was noncommittal.

"Complex," he said. He waved his hands vaguely. "If you only knew how complex. I mean, I'm very pleased, really . . ."

She was so close, so poor, so young, so frail, deserted, courageous, lonely . . . He put out his hands in a groping blind gesture and took her head delicately in his hands and kissed her.

Her lips were soft and firm and a little damp from the mist. Then she slapped him. The noise echoed meanly under the stone steps. His cheeks felt a little numb. How strong she is, he thought dazedly, for such a frail-looking girl.

"What made you think," she said coldly, "that you could kiss me?"

"I . . . I don't know," he said, putting his hand to his cheek to assuage the smarting, then pulling it away, ashamed of showing that much weakness at a moment like this. "I . . . I just did."

"You do that with your other girls," Hope said crisply. "Not with me."

"I don't do it with other girls," Noah said unhappily.

"Oh," Hope said. "Only with me. I'm sorry I look so easy."

"Oh, no," said Noah, mourning within him. "That isn't what I mean." Oh, God, he thought, if only there was some way to explain to her how I feel. Now she thinks I am a lecherous fool on the loose from the corner drugstore, quick to grab any girl who'll let me. He swallowed dryly, the English language clotted in his throat.

"Oh," he said, weakly. "I'm so sorry."

"I suppose you think," the girl began cuttingly, "you're so wonderfully attractive, so bright, so superior that any girl would just fall all over herself to let you paw her . . ."

"Oh, God." He backed away painfully, and nearly stumbled against the two steps that led down from the cement yard.

"I never in all my days," said the girl, "have come across such an arrogant, opinionated, self-satisfied young man."

"Stop . . ." Noah groaned. "I can't stand it."

"I'll say good night now," the girl said bitingly. "Mr. Ackerman."

"Oh, no," he whispered. "Not now. You can't."

She moved the iron gate with a tentative, forbidding gesture, and the hinges creaked in his ears.

"Please," he begged, "listen to me . . ."

"Good night." With a single, swift movement she was behind the gate. It slammed shut and locked. She did not look back, but opened the wooden door to the house and went through it. Noah stared stupidly at the two dark doors, the iron and the wood, then slowly turned, and brokenly started down the street.

He had gone thirty yards, holding his hat absently in his hand, not noticing that the rain had begun again and a fine drizzle was soaking his hair, when he stopped. He looked around him uneasily, then turned and went back toward the girl's house. There was a light on there now, behind the barred window on the street level, and even through the drawn blinds he could see a shadow moving about within.

He walked up to the window, took a deep breath, and tapped at it. After a moment, the blind was drawn aside and he could see Hope's face peering out. He put his face as close to the window as he could and made vague, senseless gestures to indicate that he wanted to talk to her. She shook her head irritably and waved to him to go away, but he said, quite loudly, with his lips close to the window. "Open the door. I've got to talk to you. I'm lost. Lost. LOST!"

He saw her peering at him doubtfully through the rain-streaked glass. Then she grinned and disappeared. A moment

113

later he heard the inside door being opened, and then she was at the gate. Involuntarily, he sighed.

"Ah," he said, "I'm so glad to see you."

"Don't you know your way?" she asked.

"I am lost," he said. "No one will ever find me again."

She chuckled.

"You're a terrible fool," she said, "aren't you?"

"Yes," he said humbly. "Terrible."

"Well," she said, very serious now, on the other side of the locked gate, "you walk two blocks to your left and you wait for the trolley, the one that comes from your left, and you take that to Eastern Parkway and then . . ."

Her voice swept on, making a small music out of the directions for escaping to the larger world, and Noah noticed as she stood there that she had taken off her shoes and was much smaller than he had realized, much more delicate, and more dear.

"Are you listening to me?" she asked.

"I want to tell you something," he said loudly, "I am not arrogant, I am not opinionated . . ."

"Sssh," she said, "my aunt's asleep."

"I am shy," he whispered, "and I don't have a single opinion in the whole world, and I don't know why I kissed you. I . . . I just couldn't help it."

"Not so loud," she said. "My aunt."

"I was trying to impress you," he whispered. "I don't know any Continental women. I wanted to pretend to you that I was very smart and very sophisticated. I was afraid that if I just was myself you wouldn't look at me. It's been a very confusing night," he whispered brokenly. "I don't remember ever going through anything so confusing. You were perfectly right to slap me. Perfectly. A lesson," he said, leaning against the gate, his face cold against the iron, close to her face. "A very good lesson. I . . . I can't say what I feel about you at the moment. Some other time, maybe, but . . ." He stopped. "Are you Roger's girl?" he asked.

"No," she said. "I'm not anybody's girl."

He laughed, an insane, creaking laugh.

"My aunt," she warned.

"Well," he whispered, "the trolley to Eastern Parkway. Good night. Thank you. Good night."

But he didn't move. They stared at each other in the shadowy, watery light from the lamppost.

"Oh, Lord," he said softly, full of anguish, "you don't know, you just don't know."

He heard the lock of the gate opening, and then the gate was open and he had taken the one step in. They kissed, but it wasn't like the first kiss. Somewhere within him something was

114

thundering, but he couldn't help feeling that perhaps, in the middle of it, she would step back and hit him again.

She moved slowly away from him, looking at him with a dark smile. "Don't get lost," she said, "on the way home."

"The trolley," he whispered, "the trolley to Eastern Parkway and then . . . I love you," he said. "I love you."

"Good night," she said. "Thanks for taking me home."

He stepped back and the gate closed between them. She turned and padded gently through the door in her stockinged feet. Then the door was shut and the street was empty. He started toward the trolley car. It didn't occur to him until he was at the door of his own room nearly two hours later, that he had never before in all his twenty-one years said "I love you" to anyone.

The room was dark and he could hear Roger's measured sleeping breath. Noah undressed swiftly and silently and slid into bed across the room from his friend. He lay there staring at the ceiling, caught in alternate waves of pleasure and agony as he thought first of the girl and the kiss at the gate, and of Roger and what he would say in the morning.

He was dozing off to sleep when he heard his name.

"Noah!"

He opened his eyes. "Hello, Roger," he said.

"You all right?"

"Yes."

Silence.

"Take her home?"

"Yes."

Silence in the dark room.

"We went out to get some sandwiches," Roger said. "You must have missed us."

"Yes."

Silence again.

"Roger . . ."

"Yes?"

"I feel I have to explain. I didn't mean to . . . Honest. I started out by myself and then . . . I don't quite remember . . . Roger, are you awake?"

"Yes."

"Roger, she told me something . . ."

"What?"

"She told me she wasn't your girl."

"Did she?"

"She said she wasn't anybody's girl. But if *she* is your girl. Or if you want her to *be* your girl . . . I . . . I'll never see her again. I swear, Roger. Are you awake?"

"Yes. She's not my girl. I won't deny, from time to time the

115

thought's crossed my mind, but who the hell could make that trip to Brooklyn three times a week?"

Noah wiped the sweat off his forehead in the dark. "Roger," he said.

"Yes."

"I love you."

"Go the hell to sleep." Then the chuckle across the shared dark room. Then silence again.

In the next two months Noah and Hope wrote each other forty-two letters. They worked near each other and met every day for lunch and almost every night for dinner, and they slipped away from their jobs on sunny afternoons to walk along the docks and watch the ships passing in and out of the harbor. Noah made the long, shuttling trip back and forth to Brooklyn thirty-seven times in the two months, but their real life was carried through the United States mails.

Sitting next to her, in no matter how dark and private a place, he could only manage to say, "You're so pretty," or "I love the way you smile," or "Will you go to the movies with me on Sunday night?" But with the heady freedom of blank paper, and through the impersonal agency of the letter-carrier, he could write, "Your beauty is with me day and night. When I look out in the morning at the sky, it is clearer because I know it is covering you, too; when I look up the river at the bridge, I believe it is a stronger bridge because you have once walked across it with me; when I look at my own face in the mirror, it seems to me it is a better face, because you have kissed it the night before."

And Hope, who had a dry, New England severity in her makeup that prevented her from offering any but the most guarded and reticent expressions of love in person, would write . . . "You have just left the house and I think of you walking down the empty street and waiting in the spring darkness for the trolley car, and riding in the train to your home. I will stay up with you tonight while you make your journey through the city. Darling, as you travel, I sit here in the sleeping house, with one lamp on, and think of all the things I believe about you. I believe that you are good and strong and just, and I believe that I love you. I believe that your eyes are beautiful and your mouth sad and your hands supple and lovely . . ."

And then, when they would meet, they would stare at each other, the glory of the written word trembling between them, and say, "I got two tickets for a show. If you're not doing anything tonight, want to go?"

Then, late at night, light-headed with the dazzle of the theatre, and love for each other, and lack of sleep, standing, embraced in the cold vestibule of Hope's house, not being able to go in, because her uncle had a dreadful habit of sitting up in

116

the living room till all hours of the morning reading the Bible, they would hold each other desperately, kissing until their lips were numb, the life of their letters and their real life together fusing for the moment in a sorrowing burst of passion.

They did not go to bed with each other. First of all, there seemed to be no place in the whole brawling city, with all its ten million rooms, that they could call their own and go to in dignity and honor. Then, Hope had a stubborn religious streak, and every time they veered dangerously close to consummation, she pulled back, alarmed. "Some time, some time," she would whisper. "Not now ..."

"You will just explode," Roger told him, grinning, "and blow away. It's unnatural. What's the matter with the girl? Doesn't she know she's the postwar generation?"

"Cut it out, Roger," Noah said sheepishly. He was sitting at the desk in their room, writing Hope a letter, and Roger was lying flat on his back on the floor, because the spring of the sofa had been broken five months ago and the sofa was very uncomfortable for a tall man.

"Brooklyn," Roger said. "That dark, mysterious land." Since he was on the floor anyway, he started doing some exercises for the abdomen, bringing his feet above his head and then letting them down slowly three times. "Enough," he said, "I feel healthier already. Sex," he said, "is like swimming. You either go in all the way or you stay out. If you just hang around the edge, letting the spray hit you, you get cold and nervous. One more month with that girl and you'll have to go to a psychoanalyst. Write her that and tell her I said so."

"Sure thing," said Noah. "I'm putting it down right now."

"If you're not careful," Roger said, "you're going to find yourself a married man."

Noah stopped typing. He had bought a typewriter on time payments when he found himself writing so many letters.

"No danger," he said. "I'm not going to get married." But the truth was he had thought about it again and again, and had even, in his letters, written tentatively about it to Hope.

"Maybe it wouldn't be so bad at that," Roger said. "She's a fine girl and it'd keep you out of the draft."

They had avoided thinking about the draft. Luckily, Noah's number was among the highest. The Army hung somewhere in the future, like a dark, distant cloud in the sky.

"No," said Roger, judiciously, from the floor, "I have only two things against the girl. One, she keeps you from getting any sleep. Two, you know what. Otherwise, she's done you a world of good."

Noah glanced at his friend gratefully.

"Still," Roger said, "she ought to go to bed with you."

117

"Shut up."

"Tell you what. I'll go away this week-end and you can have the place." Roger sat up. "Nothing could be fairer than that."

"Thanks," Noah said. "If the occasion arises, I'll take your offer."

"Maybe," Roger said, "I'd better talk to her. In the role of best friend, concerned for his comrade's safety. 'My dear young lady, you may not realize it, but our Noah is on the verge of leaping out the window.' Give me a dime, I'll call her this minute."

"I'll manage it myself," Noah said, without conviction.

"How about this Sunday?" Roger asked. "Lovely month of June, etcetera, the full moon of summer, etcetera . . ."

"This Sunday is out," said Noah. "We're going to a wedding."

"Whose?" Roger asked. "Yours?"

Noah laughed falsely. "Some friend of hers in Brooklyn."

"You ought to get a wholesale rate," Roger said, "from the Transit System." He lay back. "I have spoken. I now hold my peace."

He remained quiet for a moment while Noah typed.

"One month," he said. "Then the psychoanalyst's couch. Mark my words."

Noah laughed and stood up. "I give up," he said. "Let's go down and I'll buy you a beer."

Roger sprang to his feet. "My good friend," he said, "the virgin Noah."

They laughed and went out of the house, into the soft, calm summer evening, toward the frightful saloon on Columbus Avenue that they frequented.

The wedding on Sunday was held in a large house in Flatbush, a house with a garden and a small lawn, leading down to a tree shaded street. The bride was pretty and the minister was quick and there was champagne.

It was warm and sunny and everyone seemed to be smiling with the tender, unashamed sensuality of wedding guests. In corners of the large house, after the ceremony, the younger guests were pairing off in secret conversations. Hope had a new yellow dress. She had been out in the sun during the week and her skin was tanned. Noah kept watching her proudly and a little anxiously as she moved about, her hair dark and tumbled in a new coiffure, above the soft golden flash of her dress. Noah stood off to one side, sipping the champagne, a little shy, talking quietly again and again to the friendly guests, watching Hope, something inside his head saying, her hair, her lips, her legs, in a kind of loving shorthand.

He kissed the bride and there was a jumbled confusion of

118

white satin and lace and lipstick-taste and perfume and orange blossom. He looked past the bright, moist eyes and the parted lips of the bride to Hope, standing watching him across the room, and the shorthand within him noted her throat, her waist. Hope came over and he said, "There's something I've wanted to do," and he put out his hands to her waist, slender in the tight bodice of her new dress. He felt the narrow, girlish flesh and the intricate small motion of the hipbones. Hope seemed to understand. She leaned over gently and kissed him. He didn't mind, although several people were watching, because at a wedding everybody seemed licensed to kiss everyone else. Besides he had never before drunk champagne on a warm summer's afternoon.

They watched the bride and the groom go off in a car with streamers flying from it, the rice scattered around, the mother weeping softly at the doorstep, the groom grinning, red and self-conscious at the rear window. Noah looked at Hope and she looked at him and he knew they were thinking about the same thing.

"Why," he whispered, "don't we . . ."

"Sssh." She put her hand over his lips. "You've drunk too much champagne."

They made their good-byes and started off under the tall trees, between the lawns on which water sprinklers were whirling, the flashing fountains of water, brilliant and rainbow-like in the sun, making the green smell of the lawns rise into the waning afternoon. They walked slowly, hand in hand.

"Where are they going?" Noah asked.

"California," Hope said. "For a month. Monterey. He has a cousin there with a house."

They walked side by side among the fountains of Flatbush, thinking of the beaches of Monterey on the Pacific Ocean, thinking of the pale Mexican houses in the southern light, thinking of the two young people getting into their compartment on the train at Grand Central and locking the door behind them.

"Oh, God," Noah said. Then he grinned sourly. "I pity them," he said.

"What?"

"On a night like this. The first time. One of the hottest nights of the year."

Hope pulled her hand away. "You're impossible," she said sharply. "What a mean, vulgar thing to say . . ."

"Hope . . ." he protested. "It was just a little joke."

"I hate that attitude," Hope said loudly. "Everything's funny!" With surprise, he saw that she was crying.

"Please, darling." He put his arms around her, although two

119

small boys and a large collie dog were watching him interestedly from one of the lawns.

She shrugged away. "Keep your hands off me," she said. She started swiftly away.

"Please." He followed her anxiously. "Please, let me talk to you."

"Write me a letter," she said, through her tears. "You seem to save all your romance for the typewriter."

He caught up with her and walked in troubled silence at her side. He was baffled and lost, adrift on the irrational, endless female sea, and he did not try to save himself, but merely let himself drift with the wind and tide, hoping they would not wreck him.

But Hope would not relent, and all the long way home on the trolley car she sat stubborn and silent, her mouth set in bitter rejection. Oh, God, Noah thought, peering at her timidly as the car rattled on. Oh, God, she is going to quit me.

But she let him follow her into the house when she opened the two doors with her key.

The house was empty. Hope's aunt and uncle had taken their two small children on a three-day holiday to the country, and an almost exotic air of peace hung over the dark rooms.

"You hungry?" Hope asked dourly. She was standing in the middle of the living room and Noah had thought he would kiss her until he saw the expression on her face.

"I think I'd better go home," he said.

"You might as well eat," she said. "I left some stuff in the icebox for supper."

He followed her meekly into the kitchen and helped as unobtrusively as possible. She got out some cold chicken and made a salad and poured a pitcherful of milk. She put everything on a tray and said, curtly, "Outside," like a Sergeant commanding a platoon.

He took the tray out to the back garden, a twilit oblong now, that was bounded on two sides by a high board fence, and on the far end by the blank brick wall of a garage that had Virginia creeper growing all over it. There was a graceful acacia tree growing out of the garden, Hope's uncle had a small rock garden at one end and beds of common flowers, and there was a wood table with shielded candles and a long, sofa-like swing with a canopy. In the hazy blue light of evening, Brooklyn vanished like mist and rumor, and they were in a walled garden in England or France or the mountains of India.

Hope lit the candles and they sat gravely across from each other, eating hungrily. They hardly spoke while they ate, just polite requests for the salt and the milk pitcher. They folded their napkins and stood up on opposite sides of the table.

120

"We don't need the candles," Hope said. "Will you please blow out the one on your side?"

"Certainly," Noah said. He leaned over the small glass chimney that guarded the candle and Hope bent over the one on her side of the table. Their heads touched as they blew, together, and in the sudden darkness, Hope said, "Forgive me. I am the meanest female in the whole world."

Then it was all right. They sat side by side, in the swing, looking up at the darkening sky with the summer stars beginning to bloom above them one by one through the single tree. Far off the trolley, far off the trucks, far off the aunt, the uncle and the two children of the house, far off the newsboys crying beyond the garage, far off the world as they sat there in the walled garden in the evening.

Hope said, "No, we shouldn't" and "I'm afraid, afraid . . ." and "Darling, darling" and Noah was shy and triumphant and dazzled and humble and after it was over they lay there crushed and subdued by the wilderness of feeling through which they had blundered, and Noah was afraid that now that it was done she would hate him for it, and every moment of her silence seemed more and more foreboding and then she said, "See . . ." and she chuckled. "It wasn't too hot. Not too hot at all."

Much later, when it was time for him to go home, they went inside. They blinked in the light, and didn't quite look at each other. Noah bent over to turn the radio on because it gave him something to do.

They were playing Tchaikovsky on the radio, the piano concerto, and the music sounded rich and mournful, as though it had been especially composed and played for them, two people barely out of childhood, who had just loved each other for the first time. Hope came over and kissed the back of his neck as he stood above the radio. He turned to kiss her, when the music stopped, and a matter-of-fact voice said, "Special Bulletin from the Associated Press. The German advance is continuing along the Russian border at all points. Many new armored divisions have struck on a line extending from Finland to the Black Sea."

"What?" Hope said.

"The Germans," Noah said, thinking how often you say that word, how well known they've made themselves. "They've gone into Russia. That must have been what the newsboys were yelling . . ."

"Turn it off." Hope reached over and turned the radio off herself. "Tonight."

He held her, feeling her heart beating with sudden fierceness against him. All this afternoon, he thought, while we were

121

at the wedding and walking down that street, and all this evening, in the garden, it was happening, the guns going, the men dying. From Finland to the Black Sea. His mind made no comment on it. It merely recorded the thought, like a poster on the side of the road which you read automatically as you speed by in a car.

They sat down on the worn couch in the quiet room. Outside it was very dark and the newsboys crying on the distant streets were remote and inconsequential. "What's the day?" Hope asked.

"Sunday." He smiled. "The day of rest."

"I don't mean that," she said. "I know that. The date."

"June," he said, "the twenty-second of June."

"June twenty-second," the girl whispered. "I'm going to remember that date. The first time you made love to me."

Roger was still up when Noah got home. Standing outside the doorway, in the dark house, trying to compose his face so that it would show nothing of what had gone on that night, Noah heard the piano being softly played within. It was a sad jazz tune, hesitant and blue, and Roger was improvising on it so that it was difficult to recognize the melody. Noah listened for two or three minutes in the little hallway before he opened the door and went in. Roger waved to him with one hand, without looking around, and continued playing. There was only one lamp lit, in the corner, and the room looked large and mysterious as Noah sank slowly into the battered leather chair near the window. Outside, the city was sleeping along the dark streets. The curtains moved at the open window in the soft wind. Noah closed his eyes, listening to the running, somber chords. He had a strange impression that he could feel every bone and muscle and pore of his body, alive and weary, in trembling balance under his clothes, reacting to the music.

In the middle of a passage Roger stopped. He sat at the piano with his long hands resting on the keyboard, staring at the scratched and polished old wood. Then he swung around.

"The house is yours," he said.

"What?" Noah opened his eyes.

"I'm going in tomorrow," Roger said. He spoke as though he were continuing a conversation with himself he had been conducting for hours.

"What?" Noah looked closely at his friend to see if he had been drinking.

"The Army. The party's over. Now they begin to collect the civilians."

Noah felt dazed, as though he couldn't quite understand the words Roger was using. Another night, he felt, and I could understand. But too much has happened tonight.

"I suppose," Roger said, "the news has reached Brooklyn."

"You mean about the Russians?"

"I mean about the Russians."

"Yes."

"I am going to spring to the aid of the Russians," Roger said.

"What?" Noah asked, puzzledly. "Are you going to join the Russian Army?"

Roger laughed and walked over to the window. He stood there, holding onto the curtain, staring out. "Not exactly," he said. "The Army of the United States."

"I'll go in with you," Noah said suddenly.

"Thanks," said Roger. "Don't be silly. Wait until they call you."

"They haven't called you," said Noah.

"Not yet. But I'm in a hurry." Roger tied a knot reflectively in the curtain, then untied it. "I'm older than you. Wait until they come for you. It'll be soon enough."

"Don't sound," Noah said, "as though you're eighty years old."

Roger laughed and turned around. "Forgive me, Son," he said. Then he grew more serious. "I ignored it just about as long as it could be ignored," he said. "Today, when I heard it over the radio, I knew I couldn't ignore it any more. From now on, the only way I can make any sense to myself is with a rifle in my hand. From Finland to the Black Sea," he said, and Noah remembered the voice on the radio. "From Finland to the Black Sea to the Hudson River to Roger Cannon. We're going to be in soon, anyway. I want to rush to it. I've waited around for things all my life. This thing I want to take a running broad jump at. What the hell, I come from an Army family, anyway." He grinned. "My grandfather deserted at Antietam, and my old man left three illegitimate children at Soissons."

"Do you think it'll do any good?" Noah said.

Roger grinned. "Don't ask me that, Son," he said. "Never ask me that." Then he spoke more soberly. "It may be the making of me. Right now, as you may have noticed, I have no goal in life. That's a disease. In the beginning it's no worse than a pimple and you hardly notice it. Three years later the patient is paralyzed. Maybe the Army will give me a goal in life . . ." He grinned. "Like staying alive or making sergeant or winning some war. Do you mind if I play the piano some more?"

"Of course not," Noah said dully. He's going to die, a voice kept saying inside Noah's head, Roger is going to die, they're going to kill him.

Roger sat down at the piano once more and placed his hands reflectively on the keys. He played something Noah had never heard before.

"Anyway," said Roger above the music, "I'm glad to see you and the girl finally went and did it . . ."

"What?" Noah asked, hazily trying to remember if he had said anything. "What're you talking about?"

"It was sticking out all over your face," Roger said, grinning. "Like an electric sign." He played a long passage in the bass.

Roger disappeared into the Army the next day. He wouldn't let Noah go down to the recruiting station with him, and he left him all his belongings, all the furniture, all the books, and even all his clothes, although they were much too large for Noah. "I won't need any of this stuff," Roger said, looking around critically at the accumulation of the baggage of his twenty-six years. "It's just junk anyway." He stuffed a copy of the *New Republic* into his pocket to read on the subway ride down to Whitehall Street, smiling and saying, "Oh, what a frail weapon I have here," and waved at Noah and jammed his hat at his own private angle on the lean, close-cropped head, and once and for all left the room in which he had lived for five years. Noah watched him go, with a choked feeling in his throat, and a premonition that he would never have a friend again and that the best days of his life were past.

Occasionally Noah would get a dry, sardonic note from some camp in the South, and once a mimeographed company order announcing that Private Roger Cannon had been promoted to Private First Class, and then there was a long lapse until a two-page letter came from the Philippines, describing the red-light section of Manila and a half-Burmese, half-Dutch girl who had the *SS Texas* tattooed on her belly. There was a postscript, in Roger's sprawling handwriting. "P.S. Stay out of the Army. It is not for human beings."

There was, of course, one advantage, and Noah felt guiltily how much he was enjoying it. Now he and Hope had a place of their own. They were no longer night-prowlers, famished for each other, waiting sadly in cold vestibules for Bible-reading uncles to go to bed, lovers lacking a couch to bed their love in, sad-eyed children comically frustrated on the public concrete of the city.

In the months after Roger's departure, Noah felt that he had finally, after all these years, made the discovery of his body. It was stronger than he had known and capable of more feeling than he had ever expected. He even took to looking at it in the long mirror behind the door, and with the blessing of Hope's approval on it, it appeared infinitely more graceful and useful than it had seemed to him before. Oh, he thought gratefully, looking at his bare chest, oh, how lucky it is I have no hair on it.

Hope, with a private place that was so securely their own, was unexpectedly wanton. In the warm familiar darkness of the city summer the cold hills of her Vermont puritanism vanished in riotous smoke, and they matched hunger for hunger, claim for claim on the other's flesh. In the dizzying ebb and flow of love, in the shabby room which had become the dearest and most profound secret of their lives, the noise of the streets below, the shouting on the corners, the calls in the Senate, the gunfire on other continents, dwindled to a remote murmur of background music, drums and bugles in the camp of another army far away in another war.

CHAPTER SEVEN

CHRISTIAN FOUND it hard to keep his mind on the moving picture. It was a fairly good picture, too, about a detachment of troops in Berlin for one day in 1918 en route from the Russian Front to the Western Front. The Lieutenant in the picture was under strict orders to keep his men together at the station, but he understood how much they wanted to see their wives and sweethearts, after the ferocious battles in the East and the fatal battles-to-come in the West. At the risk of court-martial and death, he permitted them to go to their homes. If any one of them failed to get back to the station on time, the Lieutenant's life would be forfeit. The picture followed the various men. Some got drunk, some were tempted by Jews and defeatists to remain in Berlin, some were nearly persuaded by their wives, and for awhile it was touch-and-go whether the Lieutenant would survive the gamble. But finally, in the nick of time, the last soldier made the station just as the train was pulling out, and it was a solid band of comrades who started toward France, having vindicated their Lieutenant's faith in them. The picture was done very well. It cleverly demonstrated that the war had not been lost by the Army, but by the faint-hearts and the traitors at home, and it was full of touches of humor and pathos.

Even the soldiers who were sitting in the troop theatre all around Christian were moved by the actors playing soldiers in another war. The Lieutenant was a little too good to be true, of course, and Christian had never come across one quite like him. Lieutenant Hardenburg, Christian thought dryly, could profit by seeing this picture a few times. Since the one day of relaxation in the brothel in Paris, Hardenburg had grown more and more rigid with the lengthening of the war. Their regiment had had its armor taken from it and had been moved to Rennes. They had been stationed there, as policemen, more than anything else, while the war with Russia had started and all of Hardenburg's contemporaries were winning honors in the East.

One morning Hardenburg had read that a boy he had gone to officers' school with, whom they had called the Ox because he was so backward, had been made a Lieutenant Colonel in the Ukraine, and Hardenburg had nearly exploded with fury. He was still a Lieutenant, and even though he was living well, in a two-room apartment in one of the best hotels in town, and he had an arrangement with two women who lived on the same floor, and was making considerable money blackmailing illegal operators in meat and dairy products, Hardenburg was inconsolable. And an inconsolable Lieutenant, Christian thought grimly, made for an unhappy Sergeant.

It was a good thing Christian's leave was beginning tomorrow. Another unrelieved week of Hardenburg's snapping sarcasm might have driven Christian to some dangerous act of insubordination. Even now, Christian thought resentfully, when he knows I'm leaving on the seven-o'clock train for Germany in the morning he's put me on duty. There was a patrol scheduled for midnight to round up some French boys who were dodging labor service in Germany, and Hardenburg hadn't picked Himmler or Stein or any of the others for it. That nasty, thin grin, and, "I know you won't mind, Diestl. Keep you from being bored your last night in Rennes. You don't have to report till midnight."

The picture faded out on a closeup of the handsome young Lieutenant smiling tenderly and thoughtfully at his collected men as the train sped west, and there was real applause from the soldiers in the hall.

The newsreel came on. There were pictures of Hitler talking and the Luftwaffe dropping bombs on London and Goering pinning a medal on a pilot who had downed a hundred planes, and infantry advancing against a burning farm building on the road to Leningrad.

Automatically, Christian noticed the energy and precision with which the men carried out their assignments. They'd be in Moscow in another three months, he thought heavily, and he'd still be sitting in Rennes taking abuse from Hardenburg, arresting pregnant women who had insulted German officers in the cafés. Soon there would be snow all over Russia, and here he was, one of the best skiers in Europe, playing policeman in the mild climate of Western France. The Army was a marvelous instrument, but there was no doubt about it, it had some grave imperfections.

One of the men on the screen fell. It was hard to tell whether he was taking cover or had been hit, but he didn't get up, and the camera passed over him. Christian felt his eyes growing wet. He was a little ashamed of himself for it, but every time he saw these films of Germans fighting, while he sat safe and comfortable so far away, he had to curb a tendency to cry. And he always felt guilty and uneasy and was sharp-tempered with his men for days afterwards. It wasn't his fault that he was alive while others were dying. The Army performed its intricate functions in its own way, but he couldn't fight off the sense of guilt. And even the thought of going back home for two weeks was flavored by it. Young Frederick Langerman had lost a leg in Latvia and both sons of the Kochs had been killed and it would be impossible to avoid the measuring, contemptuous stares of his neighbors when he came back, well-fed and whole, with one half hour of semi-comic combat outside Paris behind him.

The war, he thought, had to end soon. Suddenly his civilian life, the easygoing, thoughtless days on the snowy slopes, the days without Lieutenant Hardenburg, seemed unbearably sweet and desirable. Well, the Russians were about to cash in, and then the British would finally see the light, and he would forget these boring, silly days in France. Two months after it was over people would stop talking about the war, and a clerk who had added figures in the quartermaster's office in Berlin for three years would get as much respect as a man who had stormed pillboxes in Poland, Belgium and Russia. Then, Hardenburg might show up some day, still a Lieutenant . . . or even better, discharged as unnecessary. And Christian would get him off alone in the hills and . . . He smiled sourly as he recognized the recurrent, childish dream. How long, he wondered, would they be likely to keep him in after the armistice was signed? Those would be the really difficult months, when the war was over and you just were waiting for the slow, enormous machinery of the Army's bureaucracy to release you.

The newsreel ended and a photograph of Hitler was thrown on the screen and everybody stood at attention and saluted and sang, "Deutschland, Deutschland, über Alles."

The lights went up and Christian moved slowly out among the crowd of soldiers. They all looked middle-aged, Christian thought bitterly, and like men who suffered from frailty and disease. Garrison troops, contemptuously left in a peaceful country while the better specimens of German manhood were out fighting the nation's battles thousands of miles away. And he was one of them. He shook his head irritably. He'd better stop this or he'd get as bad as Hardenburg.

There were still some Frenchmen and women on the dark streets and they hastily stepped down into the gutter as he approached. He was annoyed at them, too. Timidity was one of

127

the most irritating qualities in the human character. And it was a more or less needless and unfounded timidity, which was worse. He wasn't going to hurt them and the entire Army was under the strictest orders to behave correctly and with the utmost politeness to the French. Germans, he thought, as a man stumbled a little stepping down from the curb, Germans would never behave like that if there were a foreign army in Germany. Any foreign army.

He stopped. "Old man!" he said.

The Frenchman stopped. Even in the dark, the hunch of his shoulders and the hasty movements of his hands showed how frightened he was.

"Yes," the Frenchman said, his voice trembling a little, "yes, my colonel."

"I am not a Colonel," Christian said. What a childlike, infuriating form of flattery.

"Forgive me, Monsieur," the Frenchman said. "In the dark . . ."

"You don't have to step down in the street for me," Christian said.

"Yes, Sir," said the Frenchman. But he didn't move.

"Get up here," said Christian harshly. "Get up on the sidewalk."

"Yes, Sir," said the Frenchman. He stepped up tentatively. "I will show you my pass. My papers are in perfect order."

"I don't want to see your damned papers," Christian said.

"Whatever you say, Sir." The Frenchman spoke humbly.

"Ah," said Christian. "Go home."

"Yes, Sir." The Frenchman scurried off and Christian continued on his way. A new Europe, he thought ironically, a powerful federation of dynamic states. Not with material like this. God, if only the war would end. Or if he were sent some place where the guns could be heard. It was this garrison life. Half civilian, half military, with all the drawbacks of both. It rotted the soul, robbed a man of ambition, faith. Maybe his application for officers' school would come through and after he became a Lieutenant he would be sent to Russia or to Africa, and this period would fall into its proper perspective. He had put in his application three months ago and had heard nothing yet. Probably it was lying under a pile of papers on some fat corporal's desk on the Wilhelmstrasse.

God, it was so different from what he had expected the day he had left home, the day he had come into Paris . . . He remembered the stories from the last war. The iron-bound, tender friendships formed under fire, the grim sense of duty performed and the sporadic flares of exaltation. He remembered the end of *The Magic Mountain*. Hans Castorp, in 1914, running into the French fire across the flower-spotted field, singing

128

Beethoven. The book had ended too soon. There should have been a chapter showing Castorp three months later, checking off size 12 boots in a supply depot in Liége. Not singing anything.

The whole myth of comradeship in a war. He had had it for a moment with Brandt, on the road to Paris, and even, for a flicker in time, with Hardenburg going down the Boulevard des Italiens toward the Place de l'Opera. But now Brandt had been commissioned and was an important young officer with a flat in Paris, working on an Army magazine. And Hardenburg had lived up to all the worst expectations Christian had had of him in training. And the other men around him were swine. There was no getting away from it. They thanked God morning, noon and night they were in Rennes instead of outside Tripoli, or Kiev, and every one of them was busy making all sorts of black-market deals with the French and putting away piles of money for the depression after the war. How be comrades with men like that? Money-lenders. War-dodgers in uniform. Whenever any one of them was in danger of being sent to one of the fronts he pulled every wire imaginable, bribed regimental clerks, anything, to remain where he was. Christian was in an army of ten million men and he had never been so lonely in all his life. In Berlin on his leave he would go to the War Office. He knew a Colonel there, a man who had worked with him in Austria in the days before Anschluss, and he would ask him about a transfer to another and more active unit. Even if it meant giving up his rank . . .

He looked at his watch. He still had twenty minutes before having to report to the orderly room. There was a café open across the street and he suddenly needed a drink.

He opened the door. There were four soldiers drinking champagne at a table. They were red-faced and they had obviously been drinking a long time. They had their tunics unbuttoned and two of them needed shaves. Champagne, too. Certainly not on a private's pay. Probably were selling stolen German Army weapons to the French. The French weren't using them, of course, but there was no telling what might happen finally. Even the French might regain their courage. An army of black-market merchants, Christian thought bitterly, dealers in leather and ammunition and Normandy cheese and wine and veal. Leave them in France another two years and you wouldn't be able to distinguish them from the French except by their uniforms. The subtle, shabby victory of the Gallic spirit.

"A vermouth," Christian said to the proprietor, who was standing nervously behind the bar. "No, a brandy."

He leaned against the bar and stared at the four soldiers. The champagne was probably awful. Brandt had told him the French put any kind of label on any kind of miserable wine.

The Germans didn't know better, and it was the French way of fighting back, patriotism mixed, of course, with profit.

The four soldiers noticed Christian watching them. They became a little self-conscious and lowered their voices as they drank. Christian saw one of the men rub his hand guiltily across his unshaven cheek. The proprietor put the brandy down in front of Christian and he sipped at it, staring stonily at the four soldiers. One of the men took out his wallet to pay for a new bottle of champagne and Christian saw that it was bulging carelessly with francs. God, was it for these soft, conniving gangsters that Germans were hurling themselves against the Russian lines? Was it for these flabby shopkeepers that the Luftwaffe was burning over London?

"You!" Christian said, to the man with the wallet. "Come over here!"

The man with the wallet looked at his comrades thoughtfully. They were very quiet and they stared down into their glasses. The man with the wallet stood up slowly and stuffed his money away in a pocket.

"Move!" Christian said fiercely. "Get over here."

The soldier shuffled over to Christian, his face growing pale under his stubble.

"Stand up!" Christian said. "Stand at attention!"

The man stiffened, looking more frightened than ever.

"What's your name?" Christian snapped.

"Private Hans Reuter, Sergeant," the man said, in a low, nervous voice.

Christian took out a pencil and a slip of paper and wrote the name down. "Organization?" he asked.

The soldier swallowed unhappily. "147th Battalion of Pioneers," he said.

Christian wrote that down. "The next time you go out to drink, Private Reuter," he said, "you will shave and keep your tunic buttoned. You will also stand at attention when addressing your superiors. I'm submitting your name for disciplinary action."

"Yes, Sergeant."

"Dismissed."

Reuter sighed and turned back to his table.

"All of you," Christian called bitingly, "dress like soldiers!"

The men buttoned their tunics. They sat in silence.

Christian turned his back on them and stared at the proprietor.

"Another brandy, Sergeant?"

"No."

Christian put some money on the bar for the drink, finished the brandy. He stalked out without looking at the four soldiers sitting in the corner.

Lieutenant Hardenburg was sitting in the orderly room with his cap and gloves on. He sat erectly, as though he was on a horse, staring across the room at the Propaganda Ministry's map of Russia, with the battle lines, as of last Tuesday, drawn on it in victorious black and red strokes. The orderly room was in an old French police building, and there was a smell of ancient small crimes and unwashed French policemen that all the brisk cleanliness of the German Army had failed to eradicate. A single small bulb burned overhead and it was hot because the windows and blinds were closed for the blackout and the ghosts of all the petty criminals who had been beaten in the room seemed to be hovering in the stale air.

When Christian came into the room, a little, greasy man in the uniform of the French Milice was standing uneasily near the window, occasionally glancing at Hardenburg. Christian stood at attention and saluted, thinking: This cannot go on forever, this will end some day.

Hardenburg paid no attention to him and it was only because Christian knew him so well that he was sure Hardenburg was aware he was in the room, and waiting. Christian stood rigidly at the doorway, examining the Lieutenant's face.

As Christian watched Hardenburg, he knew that he hated that face worse than the faces of any of his enemies. Worse than Churchill, worse than Stalin, worse than any tank captain or mortar gunner in the British or Russian armies.

Hardenburg looked at his watch. "Ah," he said, without looking around, "the Sergeant's on time."

"Yes, Sir," said Christian.

Hardenburg strode over to the paper-littered desk and sat down behind it. He picked up one of the papers and said, "Here are the names and photographs of three men we have been looking for. They were called for Labor Service last month and have evaded us so far. This gentleman . . ." with a slight, cold gesture toward the Frenchman in the Milice uniform . . . "this gentleman pretends to know where all three can be found."

"Yes, Lieutenant," the Frenchman said eagerly. "Absolutely, Lieutenant."

"You will take a detail of five," Hardenburg said, going on as though the Frenchman were not in the room, "and pick up these three men. There is a truck and a driver in the courtyard and the detail is already in it."

"Yes, Sir," said Christian.

"You," said Hardenburg to the Frenchman. "Get out of here."

"Yes, Sir." The Frenchman gasped a little as he spoke, and went quickly out the door.

Hardenburg stared at the map on the wall. Christian felt himself begin to sweat in the warm room. All the lieutenants

131

in the German Army, he thought, and I had to get Hardenburg.

"At ease, Diestl." Hardenburg did not stop looking at the map.

Christian moved his feet slightly.

"Everything in order?" Hardenburg asked in a conversational tone. "You have all the proper papers for your leave?"

"Yes, Sir," said Christian. Now, he thought, this is going to happen. It's going to be canceled. Unbearable.

"You're going to Berlin first, before going home?"

"Yes, Sir."

Hardenburg nodded, without taking his eyes from the map. "Lucky man," he said. "Two weeks among Germans, instead of these swine." He made an abrupt gesture of his head, indicating the spot where the Frenchman had been standing. "I've been trying to get leave for four months. Can't be spared," he said bitterly. "Too important here." He almost laughed. "I wonder if you could do me a favor."

"Of course, Sir," said Christian, and then was angry with himself for the alacrity with which he spoke.

Hardenburg took out a set of keys from his pocket and unlocked one of the desk drawers. He lifted a small, carefully wrapped package out of the drawer and locked it methodically again. "My wife," he said, "lives in Berlin. I've written the address down here." He gave Christian a slip of paper. "I've uh . . . secured . . . a beautiful piece of lace here." He tapped the package gravely. "Very beautiful. Black. From Brussels. My wife is very fond of lace. I had hoped to be able to give it to her in person, but the prospect of leave . . ." He shrugged. "And the mail system." He shook his head. "They must have every thief in Germany in the post offices. After the war," he said angrily, "there should be a thorough investigation. However . . . I was thinking, if it wouldn't be too much trouble, my wife lives quite near the station . . ."

"I'd be delighted," Christian said stiffly.

"Thank you." Hardenburg handed Christian the package. "Give her my most tender regards," Hardenburg said. He smiled frostily. "You might even say I think of her constantly."

"Yes, Sir," said Christian.

"Very good. Now, about these three men." He tapped the sheet in front of him. "I know I can depend upon you."

"Yes, Sir."

"I have been instructed that it might be advisable to be a little rough in these matters from now on," Hardenburg said. "As an example to the others. Nothing serious, you understand, but a little shouting, a blow with the back of the hand, a show of guns . . ."

132

"Yes, Sir," said Christian, holding gently onto the package of lace, feeling it soft under the paper.

"That will be all, Sergeant." Hardenburg turned back to the map. "Enjoy yourself in Berlin."

"Thank you, Sir." Christian saluted. "Heil Hitler."

But Hardenburg was already lost among the armor on the rolling plains on the road to Smolensk, and he barely lifted his hand as Christian went out the door, stuffing the lace into his tunic and buttoning it to make sure the package would not fall out.

The first two men on the list were hiding out together in an unused garage. They grinned a little worriedly at the sight of the guns and soldiers, but they made no trouble.

The next address the Milice Frenchman directed them to was in a slum neighborhood. The house itself smelled of bad plumbing and garlic. The boy they dragged out of bed clung to his mother and they both screamed hysterically. The mother bit one of the soldiers and he hit her in the belly and knocked her down. There was an old man who sat at a table weeping, with his head in his hands. All in all, it was as unpleasant as could be. There was another man in the apartment, too, hiding in one of the closets. Christian suspected from the look of him that he was a Jew. His papers were out-of-date and he was so frightened he couldn't answer any questions at all. For a moment Christian was tempted to leave him alone. After all, he had only been sent out for the three boys, not to pick up random suspects, and if it turned out the man was a Jew it would mean concentration camp and eventual death. But the man from the Milice kept watching him and whispering, *"Juif, juif."* He'd be sure to tell Hardenburg and it would be just like Hardenburg to have Christian recalled from his leave to face charges of neglect of duty.

"You'd better come along," he said, as kindly as possible to the Jew. The man was fully dressed. He had been sleeping with all his clothes on, even his shoes, as though he had been ready to flee at a second's notice. He looked blankly around the room, at the middle-aged woman lying on the floor moaning and holding her belly, at the old man bowed over and weeping at the table, at the crucifix over the bureau, as though it was his last home and death was waiting for him the moment he stepped outside the door. He tried to say something, but his mouth merely hung open and went through the motions of speech without any sound coming from the pale lips.

Christian was glad to get back to the police barracks and deliver his prisoners over to the Duty Officer. He made out his report, sitting at Hardenburg's desk. It hadn't been so bad. Altogether, the whole business had only taken a little over three hours. He heard a scream from the back of the building as he was writing, and he frowned a little. Barbarians, he thought. As soon as you make a man a policeman you make him a sadist. He thought of going back there and stopping them, and even got up from the desk to do it, then thought better of it. There might be an officer back there and he'd get in trouble interfering.

He left a copy of the report on Hardenburg's desk, where he could see it in the morning, and left the building. It was a fine autumn night, and the stars were sharp in the sky above the buildings. The city looked better in the dark, too, and the square in front of the city hall was quite beautiful, spacious, well-proportioned, and empty under the moon. Things could be worse, Christian thought as he walked slowly across the pavement, I could be in worse places.

He turned off near the river and rang the bell of Corinne's house. The concierge came out grumbling, but kept respectfully silent, sleepy and bedraggled, when she saw who it was.

Christian went up the creaking old steps and knocked on Corinne's door. The door opened quickly, as though Corinne had been awake, waiting for him. She kissed him warmly. She was in a nightgown, almost transparent, and her heavy, firm breasts were warm from bed as Christian held her to him.

Corinne was the wife of a French Corporal who had been taken prisoner outside Metz in 1940 and was in a labor camp now near Königsberg. She was a large woman with thick ropes of dyed hair. When Christian had first met her in a café seven months ago he had thought she was striking and voluptuous-looking. But she was an affectionate, easygoing woman with a mild, placid style of making love, and from time to time as he lay beside her in the big double bed of the absent Corporal, Christian had the feeling that he had no need of traveling for wares like this. There must be five million peasant girls in Bavaria and the Tyrol, he felt, exactly as fat, exactly as firm, exactly as bovine. The fabled women of France, the quick-witted, mercurial, exciting girls who made a man's heart quicken when he thought of the flashing streets of Paris and the South, all seemed to have escaped Christian. Ah, he thought, as he sat on the heavy carved walnut chair in Corinne's bedroom, taking off his shoes, ah, I suppose you have to be an officer for that kind. He thought heavily of his application for officers' school, lost in the traps of Army communications, and he had to hide the expression of distaste on his face as he watched Corinne climb domestically into bed, her large buttocks shining in the lamplight. He put out the light and it was better. He opened the window, although Corinne had the usual French horror of the night air. As he got into bed next to her and she threw a large meaty leg across his, with a comfortable,

134

heavy sigh, like a fat woman taking off her corset, he heard, far off in the night sky, the distant throbbing of engines.

"*Chéri* . . ." Corinne began.

"Sssh," Christian said harshly. "Listen."

They listened to the sound of the men returning from the searchlight-crossed skies over London, returning from the frozen dark upper reaches of the British sky, returning from the balloons and night-fighters and the exploding shells. As Corinne put her hand with a milkmaid's heavy expertness on him, Christian felt once more near tears, as he had in the movie theatre when he watched the soldier drop on the Russian earth. He pulled Corinne on top of him, smothering the cold, bloody sound of the motors in the heavy, plain flesh.

Corinne got up and made him breakfast. There was real white bread he had brought from the shop that did the baking for the officer's mess. The coffee, of course, was ersatz, thin and black. He felt his mouth draw sourly as he drank it in the still-dark kitchen. Corinne looked sleepy and messy, with her heavy hair in disorder, but she moved around the kitchen deftly enough, putting the dishes in front of Christian.

Corinne sat down opposite him, her robe open loosely, showing a large expanse of the coarse, pale skin of her bosom.

"*Chéri*," she said, sipping her coffee noisily, "you will not forget me in Germany?"

"No," said Christian.

"You will be back in three weeks?"

"Yes."

"Definitely?"

"Definitely."

"You will bring me something from Berlin?" She coquetted heavily.

"Yes," said Christian, "I'll bring you something."

She smiled widely at him. The truth was, she was always asking for something, new dresses, black-market roasts, stockings, perfume, a little cash because the sofa needed recovering . . . When the corporal-husband comes back from Germany, Christian thought unpleasantly, he'll find his wife completely outfitted. There'll be a question or two he'll want to ask when he looks through the closets.

"*Chéri*," Corinne said, munching strongly and evenly on her bread, which she had soaked in the coffee, "I have arranged for my brother-in-law to meet you when you return."

"What's that?" Christian looked at her, puzzled.

"I told you about him," Corinne said. "My husband's brother. The one with the produce business. Milk and eggs and cheese. You know. He has a very nice offer from a broker in town here. He can make a fortune if the war lasts long enough."

135

"Good," said Christian. "I'm delighted to hear your family is doing well."

"*Chéri* . . ." Corinne looked at him reproachfully. "*Chéri,* don't be mean. It isn't as simple as that."

"What does he want from me?" Christian asked.

"The problem is, getting it into the city." Corinne spoke defensively. "You know the patrols on the roads, at the entrances. Checking up to see whether it is requisitioned material or not. You know."

"Yes?"

"My brother-in-law asked if I knew a German officer . . ."

"I'm not an officer."

"Sergeant, my brother-in-law said, was good enough. Somebody who could get some kind of pass from the authorities. Somebody who three times a week could meet his truck outside the city and drive in with it at night . . ." Corinne stood up and came around the table and played with his hair. Christian wriggled a little, certain she had neglected to wipe the butter off her fingers. "He is willing to share fifty-fifty in the profits," Corinne said, in a wheedling tone, "and later on, if you find it possible to secure some gasoline, and he can use two more trucks, you could make yourself a rich man. Everybody is doing it, you know, your own Lieutenant . . ."

"I know about my own Lieutenant," Christian said. God, he thought, her husband's brother, and the husband rotting in prison, and the brother anxious to go into business with the wife's German lover. The amenities of French family life.

"In matters of money, *Chéri,*" Corinne held him closely around the neck, "it is necessary to be practical."

"Tell your miserable brother-in-law," Christian said loudly, "that I am a soldier, not a black-market merchant."

Corinne took her arms away. "*Chéri,*" she said coldly, "there is no need to be insulting. All the others are soldiers too and they are making fortunes."

"I am not all the others," Christian shouted.

"I think," Corinne said, beginning to cry, "that you are tired of me."

"Oh, God," Christian said. He put on his tunic and picked up his cap. He wrenched the door open and went out.

Outside, in the dawn, smelling the cool, thin air, he felt less angry. After all, it had been a pleasant convenience, and a man could do much worse. Ah, he thought, it will wait till I get back from Germany.

He strode down the street, sleepy, but each moment more happily excited with the thought that at seven o'clock he would be on the train and leaving for home.

Berlin was glorious in the fall sunlight. Christian had never liked the city much, but today, as he walked out of the station, carrying his bag, there seemed to be an air of solidity and purpose, a dash and smartness to the uniforms and even the clothing of the civilians, a general sense of energy and well-being that was in refreshing contrast to the drabness and boredom of the French towns in which he had spent the last twelve months.

He got out the paper that had Mrs. Hardenburg's address on it. As he took it out of his pocket he remembered that he had neglected to turn in the pioneer private who had needed a shave. Well, he would have to remember that when he got back.

He debated with himself whether he should find a hotel first or deliver the package to Hardenburg's wife. He decided in favor of delivering the package. He would get that over with, and then, for two weeks, his time would be completely his own, with no hangovers or duties from the world he had left behind him at Rennes. As he walked through the sunny streets, he idly mapped out a program for himself for the next two weeks. Concerts and the theatre. There were agencies where soldiers could get tickets for nothing, and he would have to be careful of his money. It was too bad it was too early for skiing. That would have been the best thing. But he hadn't dared wait for his leave. In the Army, he had learned, he who waits is lost, and a leave delayed is more often than not a leave vanished.

The Hardenburg apartment was in a new, impressive-looking building. A uniformed attendant stood at the door and there were heavy carpets in the foyer. As he waited for the elevator, Christian wondered how the Lieutenant's wife managed to live so well.

He rang the bell on the fourth floor and waited. The door opened and a blonde woman with loose disheveled hair, which made her look as though she had just risen from bed, was standing there. "Yes?" she asked, her voice brusque and annoyed. "What do you want?"

"I'm Sergeant Diestl," Christian said, thinking: Not a bad life, just getting up at eleven in the morning. "I'm in Lieutenant Hardenburg's company."

"Yes?" The woman's voice was wary, and she did not open the door fully. She was dressed in a quilted silk robe of deep crimson and she kept pushing her hair back out of her eyes with a graceful, impatient gesture. Christian couldn't help thinking: Not bad for the Lieutenant, not bad at all.

"I've just arrived in Berlin on leave," Christian said, speaking slowly so that he could get a good look at her. She was a tall woman, with a long slender waist, and a full bosom that

137

the robe did not quite hide. "The Lieutenant has a gift for you. He asked me if I would deliver it."

The woman looked thoughtfully at Christian for a moment. She had large, cold gray eyes, well set in her head, but too deliberate, Christian thought, too full of calculation and judgment. Then she decided to smile.

"Ah," she said, and her voice was very warm. "I know who you are. The serious one on the steps of the Opera."

"What?" Christian asked, puzzled.

"The photograph," the woman said. "The day Paris fell."

"Oh, yes." Christian remembered. He smiled at her.

"Come in, come in . . ." She took his arm and pulled at it. "Bring your bag. It's so nice of you to come. Come in, come in . . ."

The living room was large. A huge plateglass window looked out over the surrounding roofs. The room was in a profound state of clutter at the moment, bottles, glasses, cigar and cigarette butts on the floor, a broken wineglass on a table, items of women's clothing strewn around on the chairs. Mrs. Hardenburg looked at it and shook her head.

"God," she said, "isn't it awful? You just can't keep a maid these days." She moved a bottle from one table to another and emptied an ashtray into the fireplace. Then she surveyed the room once more in despair. "I can't," she said, "I just can't." She sank into a deep chair, her long legs bare as they stuck out in front of her, her feet encased in high-heeled red fur mules.

"Sit down, Sergeant," she said, "and forgive the way this room looks. It's the war, I tell myself." She laughed. "After the war, I will remake my entire life. I will become a tremendous housekeeper. Every pin in place. But for the present . . ." She waved at the disorder. "We must try to survive. Tell me about the Lieutenant."

"Well," said Christian, trying to remember some noble or amusing fact about Hardenburg, and trying to remember not to tell his wife that he had two girls in Rennes or that he was one of the leading black-market profiteers in Brittany, "Well, he is very dissatisfied, as you know, with . . ."

"Oh." She sat up and leaned over toward him, her face excited and lively. "The gift. The gift. Where is it?"

Christian laughed self-consciously. He went over to his bag and got out the package. While he was bending over his bag he was aware of Mrs. Hardenburg's measuring stare. When he turned back to her she did not drop her eyes, but kept them fixed on him, directly and embarrassingly. He walked over to her and handed her the package. She didn't look at it but stared coolly into his eyes, a slight, equivocal smile on her lips. She looks like an Indian, Christian thought, a wild American Indian.

138

"Thanks," she said, finally. She turned then and ripped open the paper of the package. Her movements were nervous and sharp, her long, red-tipped fingers tearing in flickering movements over the wrinkled brown paper. "Ah," she said flatly. "Lace. What widow did he steal this from?"

"What?"

Mrs. Hardenburg laughed. She touched Christian's shoulder in a gesture of apology. "Nothing," she said. "I don't want to disillusion my husband's troops." She put the lace over her hair. It fell in soft black lines over the straight pale hair. "How does it look?" she asked. She tilted her head, close to Christian, and there was an expression on her face that Christian was too old not to recognize. He took a step toward her. She lifted her arms and he kissed her.

She pulled away. She turned without looking at him again and walked before him into the bedroom, the lace trailing down her back to her swinging waist. There's no doubt about it, Christian thought as he slowly followed her, this is better than Corinne.

The bed was rumpled. There were two glasses on the floor and a ridiculous picture of a naked shepherd making love to a muscular shepherdess on a hillside. But it was better than Corinne. It was better than any other woman Christian had ever had anything to do with, better than the American schoolgirls who used to come to Austria for the skiing, better than the English ladies who used to slip out of their hotels at night after their husbands were asleep, better than the buxom virgins of his youth, better than the night-prowling ladies of the Paris cafés, better than he had known women could be. I wish, he thought with grim humor, I wish the Lieutenant could see me now.

Finally, they lay side by side, spent, looking down at their bodies in the noon light.

"Ever since I saw that photograph," Mrs. Hardenburg said, "I have been waiting for you to appear." She twisted in the bed and leaned over the side. She pulled back with a half-full bottle. "There are clean glasses," she said, "in the bathroom."

Christian got up. There was a thick smell of scented soap in the bathroom and a pile of soiled pink underthings on the floor next to the basin. He got the glasses and went back to the bed.

"Go to the door," Mrs. Hardenburg said, "and walk back to me slowly."

Christian grinned a little self-consciously, then went back to the bathroom door. He turned and walked across the heavy carpet, carrying the glasses, suddenly feeling a little embarrassed in his nakedness under her critical scrutiny.

"There are so many fat old Colonels in Berlin," she said, "you forget a man can look like that."

She lifted the bottle. "Vodka," she said. "A friend of mine brought me three bottles from Poland."

He sat on the edge of the bed holding the glasses while she poured two large drinks. She placed the bottle down without putting the cork back. The drink tasted roaring and rich as it flowed down his throat. The woman downed hers with one swift gulp. "Ah," she said, "now we're alive." She leaned over and brought the bottle up again and silently poured for them both. "You took so long," she said, touching his glass with hers, "getting to Berlin."

"I was a fool," Christian said, grinning. "I didn't know."

They drank. The woman dropped her glass to the floor. She reached up and pulled him down on her. "I have an hour," she said, "before I have to go."

Later, still in bed, they finished the bottle and Christian got up and found another in a closet stocked with vodka from Poland and Russia, Scotch that had been captured at British Headquarters in 1940, champagnes and brandies and fine Burgundies in straw covers, slivovitz from Hungary, aquavit, chartreuse, sherry, Benedictine and white Bordeaux. He opened the bottle and put it down on the floor, convenient to the woman's hand. He stood over her, wavering a little, looking at the outstretched, savage body, slender but full-breasted. She stared gravely up at him, her eyes half-surrendering, half-hating. That was the most exciting thing about her, he decided suddenly, that look. As he dropped to the sheets beside her he thought: Finally, the war has brought me something good.

"How long," she said, in her deep voice, "how long are you going to stay?"

"In bed?" he asked.

She laughed. "In Berlin, Sergeant."

"I . . ." He began. He was going to tell her that his plan was to stay a week and then go home to Austria for the second week of his leave. "I," he said, "I'm staying two weeks."

"Good," she said dreamily. "But not good enough." She ran her hand lightly over his belly. "Perhaps I will talk to certain friends of mine in the War Office. Perhaps it would be a good idea to have you stationed in Berlin. What do you think of that?"

"I think," said Christian slowly, "it's a marvelous idea."

"And now," she said, "we have another drink. If it weren't for the war," her voice came softly over the sound of the liquor pouring into the glass, "if it weren't for the war, I'd never have discovered vodka." She laughed and poured a drink for him.

"Tonight," she said, "after twelve. All right?"

"Yes."

"You haven't got another girl in Berlin?"

"No, I haven't got another girl any place."

140

"Poor Sergeant. Poor lying Sergeant. I have a Lieutenant in Leipzig, a Colonel in Libya, a Captain in Abbeville, another Captain in Prague, a Major in Athens, a Brigadier General in the Ukraine. That is not taking into account my husband, the Lieutenant, in Rennes. He has some queer tastes, my husband."

"Yes."

"I, too, have some queer tastes. We'll go into that later. You . . . you're all right. You're energetic. You're simple, but you're energetic. You're responsive. Promising and responsive. After midnight."

"Yes."

"The war. A girl's gentlemen friends get scattered around in a war. You're the first Sergeant I've known since the war, though. Aren't you proud?"

"Ridiculous."

The woman giggled. "I'm going out with a full Colonel tonight and he is giving me a sable coat he brought back from Russia. Can you imagine what his face would be like if I told him I was coming home to a little Sergeant?"

"Don't tell him."

"I'll hint. That's all. Just a little hint. After the coat's on my back. Tiny little dirty hint. I think I'll have you made a Lieutenant. Man with your ability." She giggled again. "You laugh. I can do it. Simplest thing in the world. Let's drink to Lieutenant Diestl."

They drank to Lieutenant Diestl.

"What're you going to do this afternoon?" the woman asked.

"Nothing much," said Christian. "Walk around, wait for midnight."

"Waste of time. Buy me a little present." She got out of bed and went over to the table where she had dropped the lace. She draped the lace over her head. "A little pin," she said, holding the lace together under her throat, "a little brooch for here would be very nice, don't you think?"

"Yes."

"Marvelous shop," the woman said; "on Tauentzienstrasse corner Kurfürstendamm. They have a little garnet pin that might be very useful. You might go there."

"I'll go there."

"Good." The woman smiled at him and came slowly in her sliding naked walk over to the bed. She dropped down on one knee and kissed his throat. "It was very nice of the Lieutenant," she said whispering into the crease of Christian's throat, "very nice to send that lace. I must write him and tell him it was delivered safely."

Christian went to the shop on Tauentzienstrasse and bought a small garnet brooch. He held it in his hand, thinking of how it would look at Mrs. Hardenburg's throat. He grinned as he

141

realized he didn't know her first name. The brooch cost 240 marks, but he could cut down on his other expenses. He found a small rooming house near the station that was very cheap and he put his bag there. It was dirty and full of soldiers. But he wouldn't be spending much time there, anyway.

He sent a telegram to his mother, telling her that it was impossible to get home on his leave, and asking if she could lend him two hundred marks. It was the first time since he was sixteen that he had asked her for money, but he knew his family was doing very well this year, and they could spare it.

Christian went back to the boarding house and tried to sleep, but he kept thinking of the morning and sleep would not come. He shaved and changed his clothes and went out. It was five-thirty in the afternoon, still light, and Christian walked slowly down Friedrichstrasse, smiling as he listened to the bustling snatches of German spoken on all sides. He shook his head gently when he was approached by whores on the corners. The whores, he noticed, were spectacularly well-dressed, real fur-pieces and smartly designed coats. The conquest of France, he thought, has had a beneficial effect on one profession, at least.

As he walked pleasantly among the crowds, Christian had a stronger feeling than ever before that the war was going to be won. The city, which at other times had appeared so drab and weary, now seemed gay, energetic and invulnerable. The streets of London this afternoon, he thought, and the streets of Moscow, are probably very different from this. Every soldier, he thought, should be sent back on leave to Berlin. It would have a tonic effect on the entire Army. Of course, and he grinned inwardly as he thought it, it would be advisable for every soldier to be supplied with a Mrs. Hardenburg when he got off the train, and a half-bottle of vodka. A new problem for the quartermaster.

He bought a newspaper and went into a café and ordered a beer.

He read the newspaper. It was like listening to a brass band. There were triumphant stories about thousands of Russians being taken, stories of companies that had defeated battalions in the North, stories of armored elements that lived off the land and the foe, and made week-long sorties, without communications of any kind with the main body of the Army, slashing and disrupting the enemy's crumbling rear. There was a careful analysis by a retired Major General who cautioned against over-optimism. Russia would not capitulate, he said, in less than three months, and the wild talk of imminent collapse was harmful to morale at home and at the front. There was an editorial that warned Turkey and the United States in the same paragraph, and a confident assertion that, despite the frantic activities of the Jews, the people of America would refuse to be drawn into a war that they saw very clearly was none of their business. There was a story from Russia about how German soldiers had been tortured and burned by Soviet troops. Christian hurried through it, reading only the first line in each paragraph. He was on leave now, and he did not want to think about things like that for the next two weeks.

He sipped at his beer, a little disappointed because it seemed watery, but enjoying himself, with his body weary and satisfied, his eyes occasionally leaving the paper to look across the room at the chatting, bright couples. There was a Luftwaffe pilot in the café, with a pretty girl, and two good ribbons on his chest. Christian had a fleeting moment of regret, thinking, how much dearer this place and this holiday must seem to a man who had come down from the embattled skies than to himself, who had merely come from the police barracks, the double bed of Corinne's corporal, from the sharp tongue of Lieutenant Hardenburg. I must go and talk to Colonel Meister in the War Office, he thought, without conviction, about the possibilities of being transferred to a unit in Russia. Perhaps later in the week, when things are more settled . . .

Christian turned the page of the newspaper to the section devoted to music. There were four concerts scheduled for that night and he saw, with a nostalgic twinge of amusement, that the Mozart clarinet quintet was being played. I'll go, he thought, it's a perfect way to wait for midnight.

The attendant downstairs in the foyer of the Hardenburg building had a message for him. "The lady said to let you in. She hasn't returned yet."

They went up in the elevator together, both of them with grave, composed faces. The attendant said, "Good night, Sergeant," matter-of-factly, after he had opened the apartment door with a passkey.

Christian went in slowly. One light had been left burning and the blinds were drawn. The room had been arranged since he had left it, and looked quite handsome in an angular, modern way. Looking at Hardenburg, Christian thought, you'd never think he'd live in a place like this. Somehow you'd imagine high, dark old furniture, stiff chairs, plush and polished walnut.

Christian lay down on the sofa. He was tired. The music had bored him. The hall had been too warm, and crowded. After the first few moments of pleasure he had had to struggle to keep from dozing. Mozart had seemed tame and without flavor and as he half-closed his eyes in the warm hall, visions of Mrs. Hardenburg, long and naked, had kept swimming between him and the music. He stretched luxuriously on the couch, and fell asleep.

He was awakened by the sound of voices. He opened his

eyes and looked up, squinting in the light. Mrs. Hardenburg and another woman were standing over him, looking down at him, smiling.

"Lo, the weary Sergeant," Mrs. Hardenburg was saying. She bent down and kissed him. She had on a heavy fur coat, and her breath smelled strongly of liquor. The pupils of her eyes were dark and large in controlled drunkenness. She put her head next to his. "I've brought a friend, darling. Sergeant Diestl, Eloise."

Eloise smiled at him. Her eyes were shining, too, in a vague, swimming way. She sat down suddenly in a big chair, without taking her coat off.

"Eloise lives too far away to go home tonight," Mrs. Hardenburg said. "She's going to stay with us. You'll love Eloise and she'll love you. She knows all about you." She stood up and held her arms out, the soft wide sleeves of her coat falling back from her wrists. "How do you like it, Sergeant?" she asked. "Isn't it beautiful?"

Christian sat up. "Beautiful," he said. He felt confused. He couldn't help staring at Eloise stretched out in the chair. Eloise was blonde, too, but soft and fat blonde.

"Hello, Sergeant," Eloise said. "Pretty Sergeant."

Christian rubbed his hand over his eyes. I'd better get out of here, he thought, this is no place for me.

"You don't know the trouble I had," Mrs. Hardenburg giggled, "keeping that Colonel out of here."

"Next trip back from Russia," Eloise said, "I get a fur coat, too."

"What time is it?" Christian asked.

"Two, three," Mrs. Hardenburg said.

"Four," said Eloise, looking at her watch. "Time to go to bed."

"I think," said Christian warily, "I'd better leave . . ."

"Sergeant . . ." Mrs. Hardenburg looked at him reproachfully and threw her arms around him, the fur silky against his neck. "You can't do this to us. And after what we went through with the Colonel. He's going to make you a Lieutenant."

"Major," said Eloise. "I thought he was going to make him a Major."

"Lieutenant," Mrs. Hardenburg said with dignity. "And have you attached to the General Staff here. All arranged."

"He's crazy about Gretchen," Eloise said. "Do anything for her."

Gretchen, Christian thought, that's her name.

"What we need," Gretchen said, "is one drink. Darling, we're on brandy. You know where the closet is." Suddenly she seemed completely sober. Her speech was cool and careful. She brushed the hair back from her eyes and stood very tall in the magnificent coat and a long white evening dress in the center of the room. Christian couldn't help staring at her hungrily.

"There . . ." Gretchen smiled briefly and touched his lips casually with her fingertips, "that's the way to look at a woman. The closet, darling."

Well, one drink, Christian thought. He walked into the other room to the closet with the brandy in it.

A blaze of light on his closed eyelids woke him. He opened his eyes. The sun was streaming in through the large window. He turned his head slowly. He was alone in the disheveled bed. The smell of perfume made him swallow dryly. He was thirsty and his head began to ache. The night came back to him in sodden globs of memory. The coat, the two girls, the Colonel who was going to make him a Lieutenant, the jumble of twisting, perfumed bodies . . . He closed his eyes painfully. He had heard stories of women like that, and he remembered the rumors about depraved Berlin after the last war, but it was different when it happened to yourself . . .

The door from the bathroom opened and Gretchen came in. She was fully dressed, in a black suit, and her hair was bound by a black ribbon, girlishly. Her eyes were clear and shining. She looked fresh and brand-new in the bright morning sunlight. She smiled at Christian and came over to him and sat on the bed.

"Good morning," she said. Her voice was pleasant and reserved.

"Hello." Christian managed to smile. Gretchen's shining neatness made him feel shabby and ill. "Where's the other lady?"

"Eloise?" Gretchen absently stroked his hand. "Oh, she had to go to work. She likes you."

She likes me, Christian thought grimly, and she likes you and she likes any other man or woman or beast of the field she can lay her hands on. "What're you doing all dressed?" Christian asked.

"I've got to go to work, too," Gretchen said. "You didn't think I was an idle woman, did you?" she asked, grinning. "In the middle of a war?"

"What do you work at?"

"In the Ministry of Propaganda." Gretchen's face became very serious, with a devoted, earnest expression Christian hadn't seen there before. "The Women's Division."

Christian blinked. "What do you do for them?"

"Oh," said Gretchen. "I write speeches, talk on the radio. Right now, we're conducting a campaign. A lot of girls, you'd be surprised how many, sleep with the foreigners."

"What foreigners?" Christian asked puzzledly.

"The ones we import to work. In the factories. On the farms. I'm not supposed to talk about it, especially to soldiers . . ."

"That's all right," Christian said, grinning. "I have no illusions."

"But rumors get around, and it's very bad for the morale of the men at the front." She spoke like a bright little schoolgirl reciting her lessons for the day. "We get long secret reports from Rosenberg on it. It's very important."

"What do you tell them?" By now Christian was really interested in this new facet of Gretchen's character.

"Oh, the ordinary thing." Gretchen shrugged. "There's nothing much new you can say any more. The purity of the German bloodstock. The theory of racial characteristics. The position of the Poles and Hungarians and Russians in European history. The worst thing is trying to handle the French. The girls have a weakness for the French."

"What do you do about them?"

"Venereal disease. We quote statistics showing the incidence of syphilis in Paris, and stuff like that."

"Does it work?"

"Not much." Gretchen smiled.

"What are you going to do today?"

"I have a radio interview today," she said, "with a woman who just had her tenth baby. We've got a Major General to give her the bonus over the air." Gretchen looked at her watch. "I've got to go now." She stood up.

"Will I see you tonight?" Christian asked.

"Sorry, darling." She was in front of a mirror giving final, subtle touches to her hair. "I'm busy tonight."

"Break it." Christian hated it, but there was a bare note of pleading in his voice.

"Sorry, darling. It's an old friend. A Colonel just back from Africa. It would break his heart."

"Later. After you're through with him . . ."

"Sorry," Gretchen said briskly. "It's going to be terribly late. It's a big party."

"Tomorrow, then?"

Gretchen looked consideringly over at him, then smiled. "You're awfully anxious, aren't you?"

"Yes," Christian said.

"Have a good time last night?" She went back to pushing at her hair as she stared in the mirror.

"Yes."

"You're a nice man. That's a nice little pin you got me." She came over and leaned down and kissed him lightly. "Not a bad little pin at all. There's a pretty little pair of earrings that go with it in the same shop . . ."

146

"I'll have them for you," Christian said coldly, despising himself for the bribe. "Tomorrow night."

Gretchen touched his lips with her fingertips in her characteristic gesture. "Very nice man indeed." Christian wanted to put up his arms and pull her down to him, but he knew better than to try. "Should I bring Eloise?" Gretchen asked, smiling.

Christian closed his eyes for a moment, remembering the violent and drunken happenings of the night before. It was sickly and perverse and in ordinary times he would be ashamed of himself for it, but, now . . . "Yes," he said slowly. "Why not?"

Gretchen giggled. "Now I have to run." She started for the door. She stopped there. "You need a shave," she said. "There's a razor in the medicine cabinet and some American shaving soap." She smiled. "The Lieutenant's. I know you won't mind using it." She waved at him and went through the door, on her way to the Major General and the woman who had successfully delivered herself of her tenth child.

The next week passed in a riotous haze for Christian. The city around him, the millions going to and fro, the clang of trolley car and bus, the placards outside the newspaper offices, the Generals and politicians in their gleaming uniforms who sped by him in the long armored cars in the street, the shifting hordes of soldiers on leave and on duty, the bulletins on the radio of miles gained and men killed in Russia—all seemed to him shadowy and remote. Only the apartment on Tiergarten Strasse, only the wild pale body of Lieutenant Hardenburg's wife seemed substantial and real. He bought her the earrings, sent home for more money and bought her a gold chain bracelet, and a sweater from a soldier who had carried it back from Amsterdam.

She had gotten into the habit of calling him demandingly at any hour of the day or night at the boarding house where he was living, and he forsook the avenues and the theatres and merely lay on his bed, waiting for the phone to ring downstairs in the grimy hall, waiting to rush through the streets to her.

Her home became for him the one fixed place in a shadowy, reeling world. At times when she left him alone, waiting for her in her apartment, he roamed restlessly through the rooms, opening closets and desk-drawers, peering at mail, looking at photographs hidden between books. He had always been a private man and one who had a deep sense of others' privacy, but it was different with her. He wanted to devour her and all her thoughts, possessions, vices, desires.

The apartment was crammed with loot. A student of economics could have pieced together the story of German conquest in Europe and Africa merely from the stores tucked away carelessly in Gretchen's apartment, brought there by the

147

procession of rigid, shining-booted, be-ribboned officers whom Christian occasionally saw delivering Gretchen in heavy official cars as he peered jealously out the window to the main door below. Aside from the rich profusion of bottles that he had seen the first day, there were cheeses from Holland, sixty-five pairs of French silk stockings, quarts of perfume, jeweled clasps and ceremonial daggers from all parts of the Balkans, brocaded slippers from Morocco, baskets of grapes and nectarines flown from Algiers, three fur coats from Russia, a small Titian sketch from Rome, two sides of smoked Danish bacon hanging in the pantry behind the kitchen, a whole shelf of Paris hats, although he had never seen Gretchen wear a hat, an exquisite worked-silver coffee urn from Belgrade, a heavy leather desk that an enterprising Lieutenant had somehow shipped from a captured villa in Norway.

The letters, negligently dropped on the floor or slipped under magazines on the tables, were from the farthest reaches of the new German Empire, and although written in the widest variety of literary styles, from delicate and lyric poems from young scholars on duty in Helsinki to stiff, pornographic memorials from aging professional military men serving under Rommel in the Western desert, they all bore the same burden of longing and gratitude. Each letter, too, bore promises . . . a bolt of green silk bought in Orleans, a ring found in a shop in Budapest, a locket with a sapphire stone picked up in Tripoli. . . .

Eloise was mentioned in some of the letters, and other girls, sometimes half-humorously, sometimes with a wondering echo of past sensuality. Christian had come to recognize Eloise and the other girls as almost normal . . . or at least normal for Gretchen. She was beyond the bounds of ordinary behavior, put there by her extraordinary beauty, her appetite, her superhuman energy. It was true that in the morning she often took Benzedrine and other drugs to restore the violent flame of her energy which she squandered so light-heartedly. Also, sometimes in the morning she gave herself huge injections with a hypodermic needle of Vitamin B, which, she said, cured her immediately of hangovers.

The amazing thing about her was that only three years before she had been a demure young schoolteacher in Baden, instructing ten-year-old children in geography and arithmetic. She had been shy, she told Christian. Hardenburg had been the first man she had ever slept with, and she had refused him until he married her. But when he brought her to Berlin, just before the beginning of the war, a woman photographer had seen her in a night club and had asked to take her picture for some posters she was doing for the Propaganda Ministry. The photographer had seduced her, in addition to making her face and figure quite famous as a model for a typical German girl, who,

148

in the series of photographs, worked extra hours in munitions factories, attended party meetings regularly, gave to the Winter Fund, cleverly prepared attractive menus in the kitchen with ersatz foods. Since that time she had risen dizzily in the wartime Berlin social world. Hardenburg had been sent off to a regiment early in his wife's career. Now that he had seen the situation at home, Christian understood better why Hardenburg was considered so valuable in Rennes and found it so difficult to get leave to return home. Gretchen was invited to all the important parties and had met Hitler twice and was on terms of intimacy with Rosenberg, although she assured Christian it did not include the final, or what was for Gretchen the semi-final one.

Christian refused to make a judgment on Gretchen's morality. From time to time, as he lay in his darkened room in the boarding house, waiting for the ring of the telephone below, he had reflected upon what his mother would call Gretchen's mortal sin. Although he had left the church early, remnants of his mother's bitter religious morality would occasionally rear up through the flood of the years in Christian's mind, and at times like that he would find himself reflecting harshly on Gretchen's activities. But he put those random, half-begun judgments from him. Gretchen was above ordinary morality, beyond it. A person of such vitality, such appetite, such raging energy, could not be fettered by the niggling considerations of what was, after all, a dying and outworn code. To judge Gretchen by the word of Jesus was to judge a bird by a snail, a tank captain by a village traffic regulation, a general by the civil laws against manslaughter.

Hardenburg's letters from Rennes were stiff, almost military documents, empty, windy, cold. Christian couldn't help smiling as he read them, knowing that Hardenburg, if he survived the war, would be a forgotten and carelessly discarded article in Gretchen's swirling past. For the future, Christian had plans that he only half-admitted to himself. Gretchen had told him one night, casually, between one drink and the next, that the war would be over in sixty days and that someone high in the Government, she wouldn't tell Christian his name, had offered her a three-thousand-acre tract in Poland. There was a seventeenth-century stone mansion, untouched by war, on it, and seven hundred acres were under cultivation, even now.

"How would you be," she had asked, half-joking, lying back on the sofa, "at running an estate for a lady?"

"Wonderful," he had said.

"You wouldn't wear yourself out," she had said, smiling, "with your agricultural duties?"

"Guaranteed." He had sat down beside her and put his hand

under her head and caressed the firm, fair skin at the base of her neck.

"We'll see. We'll see . . ." Gretchen had said. "We might do worse . . ."

That would be it, Christian thought. A great wild estate, with the money rolling in, and Gretchen mistress of the old house . . . They wouldn't marry, of course. Marrying Gretchen was an act of supererogation. A kind of private Prince Consort, with hand-made riding boots and twenty horses in the stables and the great and wealthy of the new Empire coming down from the capitals for the shooting . . .

The luckiest moment of my life, Christian thought, when Hardenburg unlocked that desk and took the package of black lace out of it in the police barracks in Rennes. Christian hardly thought of Rennes any more. Gretchen had told him she had talked to a Major General about his transfer and commission and it was in the works. Hardenburg was a miserable phantom of the past now, who might reappear for one delicious moment in the future to be dismissed with a curt murderous phrase. The luckiest day of my life, Christian thought, turning with a smile to the door, which had just been opened. Gretchen stood there in a golden dress, with a wrap of mink thrown easily over her shoulders. She was smiling and holding out her arms, saying, "Now, isn't this a nice thing to find waiting for a girl when she gets home from her day's work?"

Christian went over and kicked the door shut and took her into his arms.

Then, three days before his leave was due to expire, although he wasn't worried, Gretchen had said it was all being fixed, the phone rang in the boarding house and he rushed down the stairs to answer it. It was her voice. He smiled as he said, "Hello, darling."

"Stop that." Her voice was harsh, although she seemed to be talking in a whisper, "And don't say my name over the phone."

"What?" he asked, dazedly.

"I'm speaking from a phone in a café," she said. "Don't try to call me at home. And don't come there."

"But you said, eight o'clock tonight."

"I know what I said. Not eight o'clock tonight. Or any night. That's all. Stay away. Good-bye."

He heard the click as she hung up. He stared at the instrument on the wall, then put up the receiver slowly. He went to his room and lay down on the bed. Then he got up and put on his tunic and went out. Any place, he thought, but this room.

He walked hazily through the streets, hopelessly going over in his mind Gretchen's whispered, final conversation, and all the acts and words that might have led up to it. The night be-

150

fore had been, for them, an ordinary night. She had appeared at the apartment at one o'clock, quite drunk, in her controlled, nervous way, and they had drunk some more until about two, and then they had gone to bed together. It had been as good as it had ever been, and she had dropped off to sleep, lying beside him, and had kissed him brightly and affectionately at eleven in the morning, when she left for work, and said, "Tonight, let's start earlier. Eight o'clock. Be here."

There was no hint in this. He stared at the blank faces of the buildings and the hurried, swarming faces of the people around him. The only thing to do was to wait for her outside her apartment house and ask her, point-blank.

At seven o'clock that night he took up his station behind a tree across the street from the entrance to her apartment house. It was a damp night, with a drizzle. In half an hour he was soaked, but he paid little attention to it. A policeman came by for the third time at ten-thirty and looked inquisitively at him.

"Waiting for a girl." Christian managed a sheepish grin. "She's trying to shake a parachute major."

The policeman grinned at him. "The war," he said. "It makes everything difficult." He shook his head commiseratingly and moved on.

At two o'clock in the morning, one of the familiar official cars drove up and Gretchen and an officer got out. They talked for a moment on the sidewalk. Then they went in together and the car drove away.

Christian looked up through the drizzle at the black-dark side of the building and tried to figure out which window was the one that belonged to Gretchen's apartment, but it was impossible to tell in the blackness.

At eight o'clock in the morning, the long car drove up again and the officer came out and got into it. Lieutenant Colonel, Christian noted automatically. It was still raining.

He nearly crossed the street to the apartment house. No, he thought, that would ruin it. She'd be angry and throw me out and that would be the end of it.

He stayed behind the tree, his eyes clammy with sleep, his uniform soaked, staring up at the window which was revealed now in the gray light.

At eleven o'clock she came out. She had on short rubber boots and a belted light raincoat, with a cape attached, like a soldier's camouflage equipment. She looked fresh, as always in the morning, and young and schoolgirlish in her rain outfit. She started to walk briskly down the street.

He caught up with her after she turned the corner.

"Gretchen," he said, touching her elbow.

She wheeled nervously. "Get away from me!" she said. She looked apprehensively around her and spoke in a whisper.

151

"What's the matter?" he said, pleadingly. "What have I done?"

She began walking again, swiftly. He walked after her, keeping a little behind her.

"Gretchen, darling . . . ."

"Listen," she said. "Get away. Keep away. Isn't that clear?"

"I've got to know," he said. "What is it?"

"I can't be seen talking to you." She stared straight ahead of her as she strode down the street. "That's all. Now get out. You've had a nice leave, and it'll be up in two days anyway; go back to France and forget this."

"I can't," he said. "I can't. I've got to talk to you. Any place you say. Any time."

Two men came out of a store on the other side of the street and walked swiftly, parallel to them, in the same direction they were going.

"All right," Gretchen said. "My place. Tonight at eleven. Don't use the front door. You can walk up the back stairs through the basement. The entrance is on the other street. The kitchen door will be unlocked. I'll be there."

"Yes," said Christian. "Thank you. That's wonderful."

"Now leave me alone," she said. He stopped and watched her walk away, without looking back, in her bright, nervous walk, accentuated by the boots and the belted rubber coat. He turned and went slowly back to his boarding house. He lay down on the bed without taking off his clothes and tried to sleep.

At eleven o'clock that night, he climbed the dark back stairs. Gretchen was sitting at a table writing something. Her back was very straight in a green wool dress, and she didn't even look around when Christian came into the room. Oh, God, he thought, it is the Lieutenant all over again. He walked lightly over behind her chair and kissed the top of her head, smelling the scented hair.

Gretchen stopped writing and turned around in the chair. Her face was cool and serious.

"You should have told me," she said.

"What?" he asked.

"You may have gotten me into a lot of trouble," she said. Christian sat down heavily. "What did I do?"

Gretchen stood up and began to walk up and down the room, the wool skirt swinging at her knees.

"It wasn't fair," she said, "letting me go through all that."

"Go through what?" Christian asked loudly. "What are you talking about?"

"Don't shout!" Gretchen snapped at him. "God knows who's listening."

"I wish," said Christian, keeping his voice low, "that you'd let me know what's happening."

"Yesterday afternoon," Gretchen said, standing in front of him, "the Gestapo sent a man to my office."

"Yes?"

"They had been to see General Ulrich first," Gretchen said significantly.

Christian shook his head wearily. "Who in God's name is General Ulrich?"

"My friend," said Gretchen, "my very good friend, who is probably in very hot water right now because of you."

"I never saw General Ulrich in all my life," Christian said.

"Keep your voice low." Gretchen paced over to the sideboard and poured herself four fingers of brandy. She did not offer Christian a drink. "I'm a fool to have let you come here at all."

"What has General Ulrich got to do with me?" Christian demanded.

"General Ulrich," Gretchen said deliberately, after taking a large swallow of the brandy, "is the man who tried to put through your application for a direct commission and a transfer to the General Staff."

"Well?"

"The Gestapo told him yesterday that you were a suspected Communist," Gretchen said, "and they wanted to know what his connection with you was and why he was so interested in you."

"What do you want me to say?" Christian demanded. "I'm not a Communist. I was a member of the Nazi Party in Austria in 1937."

"They knew all that," said Gretchen. "They also knew that you had been a member of the Austrian Communist Party from 1932 to 1936. They also knew that you made trouble for a Regional Commissioner named Schwartz right after the Anschluss. They also knew that you had an affair with an American girl who had been living with a Jewish socialist in Vienna in 1937."

Christian sank wearily back into the chair. The Gestapo, he thought, how meticulous and inaccurate they could be.

"You're under observation in your Company," Gretchen said. "They get a report on you every month." She grinned sourly. "It may please you to know that my husband reports that you are a completely able and loyal soldier and strongly recommends you for officers' school."

"I must remember to thank him," Christian said flatly, "when I see him."

"Of course," said Gretchen, "you can never become an officer. They won't even send you to fight against the Russians. If your unit is shifted to that front, you will be transferred."

153

What a winding, hopeless trap, Christian thought, what an impossible, boring catastrophe.

"That's it," Gretchen said. "Naturally, when they found out that a woman who worked for the Propaganda Ministry, who was friendly, officially and otherwise, with many high-ranking military and official personnel..."

"Oh, for God's sake," Christian said irritably, standing up, "stop sounding like a police magistrate!"

"You understand my position..." It was the first time Christian had heard a defensive tone in Gretchen's voice. "People've been shipped off to concentration camps for less. You must understand my position, darling."

"I understand your position," Christian said loudly, "and I understand the Gestapo's position, and I understand General Ulrich's position, and they all bore me to death!" He strode over to her and towered over her, raging, "Do you think I'm a Communist?"

"That's beside the point, darling," Gretchen said carefully. "The Gestapo thinks you may be. That's the important thing. Or at least, that you may not be quite ... quite reliable. Don't blame me, please ..." She came over to him and her voice was soft and pleading. "It would be different if I was an ordinary girl, in an ordinary unimportant job ... I could see you whenever I pleased, I could go any place with you ... But this way, it's really dangerous. You don't know. You haven't been back in Germany for so long, you have no idea of the way people suddenly disappear. For nothing. For less than this. Honestly. Please... don't look so angry..."

Christian sighed and sat down. It would take a little time to get accustomed to this. Suddenly he felt he was not at home any longer; he was a foreigner treading clumsily in a strange, dangerous country, where every word had a double meaning, every act a dubious consequence. He thought of the three thousand acres in Poland, the stables, the hunting week-ends. He smiled sourly. He'd be lucky if they let him go back to teach skiing.

"Don't look like that," Gretchen said. "So ... so despairing."

"Forgive me," he said. "I'll sing a song."

"Don't be harsh with me," she said humbly. "What can I do about it?"

"Can't you go to them? Can't you tell them? You know me, you could prove..."

She shook her head. "I can't prove anything."

"I'll go to them. I'll go to General Ulrich."

"None of that!" Her voice was sharp. "You'll ruin me. They told me not to tell you anything about it. Just to stop seeing you. They'll make it worse for you, and God knows what

154

they'll do to me! Promise me you won't say anything about it to anyone."

She looked so frightened, and, after all, it wasn't her doing. "I promise," he said slowly. He stood up and looked around the room that had become the real core of his life. "Well," and he tried to grin, "I won't say that it hasn't been a nice leave."

"I'm so terribly sorry," she whispered. She put her arms around him gently. "You don't have to go . . . just yet . . ."

They smiled at each other.

But an hour later she thought she heard a noise outside the door. She made him get up and dress and go out the back door, the way he'd come, and she was very vague about when he could see her again.

Christian sat in the corner of the crowded compartment, his face set and abstracted, his eyes closed, as the train drew closer to Rennes. There was a heavy, rank smell in the train, because it was night and all the windows were closed and the blinds drawn, a thick, sour smell of soldiers who never had enough changes of linen or frequent enough opportunities to bathe, who ate and slept and lived in the same clothes for months on end. Suddenly he hated the smell with a nerve-tearing, intolerable intensity. A civilized man, he thought, should not have to live in such constant foulness. The least a man should expect to get from the twentieth century was that the air he breathed not be a continual offense in his nostrils. He opened his eyes and looked gloomily at the sprawling men around him. Slack, slightly drunken, sleeping faces. Sleep redeemed some faces, made them gentle, child-like, but not these faces. There was an air of slyness, of cheating and timid cunning that sleep seemed to intensify on these flabby, ugly features. God, Christian thought, feeling the muscles of his jaw jumping in distaste, I must get out of this . . .

He closed his eyes again. Another few hours, he thought, and Rennes again, Lieutenant Hardenburg again, the thick, unexciting face of Corinne again, the patrols again, the weeping Frenchmen, the lounging soldiers in the cafés, the soggy routine again . . . He felt like standing up on his seat and screaming at the top of his voice. And nothing he could do about it. He couldn't even help win or lose the war, shorten or lengthen it by a minute. And every time he got into bed, and closed his eyes and tried to sleep, the image of Gretchen began to roar in his waking blood, tantalizing, hopeless . . . She had refused to see him again after that night. She had been polite on the phone, although frightened, and had said she'd really love to see him, but there was an old friend who had just come back from Norway . . . (That old friend, who kept returning from Tunis or Reims or Smolensk, always with a rich, expensive gift that Christian couldn't match . . .) That might be the way to do it. The next time he got to Berlin to have a lot of money, be able to get her a fur coat, a leather suit, the new phonograph she had mentioned. That might be it, Christian thought, eyes closed among the stinking soldiers, with the rattle of the wheels below in the French night . . . enough money might do the trick. I'll tell Corinne, he thought, to bring her brother-in-law around. It was time to stop being a fool about this. Next time I get to Berlin, he thought, I am going to have my pockets stuffed. A little gasoline, Corinne had said, and her brother-in-law could run three trucks. Brother-in-law will get that gasoline, Christian thought grimly, without delay. He smiled a little and even managed to drop off to sleep in the next ten minutes as the train rolled slowly on toward Brittany.

Lieutenant Hardenburg was in the orderly room when Christian reported in the next morning. He looked thinner and more alert, as though he had been exercising. He was striding back and forth with a springy, energetic step, and he smiled with what was for him great amiability, as he returned Christian's salute.

"Did you have a good time?" he asked, his voice friendly and pleasant.

"Very good, Sir," Christian said.

"Mrs. Hardenburg wrote me," the Lieutenant said, "that you delivered the lace."

"Yes, sir."

"Very good of you."

"It's nothing, Sir."

The Lieutenant peered at Christian, a little shyly, Christian thought. "Did she uh . . . look well?" he asked.

"She looked very fit, Sir," Christian said gravely.

"Ah, good. Good." The Lieutenant wheeled nervously in what was almost a pirouette, in front of the map of Africa that had supplanted the map of Russia on the wall. "Delighted. She has a tendency to work too hard, overdo things. Delighted," he said vaguely and spiritedly. "Lucky thing," he said, "lucky thing you took your leave when you did."

Christian didn't say anything. He was in no mood to engage in a long, social conversation with Lieutenant Hardenburg. He hadn't seen Corinne yet and he was impatient to get her and tell her to get in touch with her brother-in-law.

"Yes," Lieutenant Hardenburg said, "very lucky." He grinned inexplicably. "Come over here, Sergeant," he said mysteriously. He went to the barred grimy window and stared out. Christian followed him and stood next to him.

"I want you to understand," Hardenburg whispered, "that all

156

this is extremely confidential. Secret. I really shouldn't be telling you this, but we've been together a long time and I feel I can trust you . . ."

"Yes, Sir," Christian said cautiously.

Hardenburg looked around him carefully, then leaned a little closer to Christian. "Finally," he said, the jubilance plain in his voice, "finally, it's happened. We're moving." He turned his head sharply and looked over his shoulder. The clerk, who was the only other person in the room, was thirty feet away. "Africa," Hardenburg whispered, so low that Christian barely heard him. "The Africa Corps." He grinned widely. "In two weeks. Isn't it marvelous?"

"Yes, Sir," Christian said, flatly, after awhile.

"I know you'd be pleased," said Hardenburg.

"Yes, Sir."

"There'll be a lot to do in the next two weeks. You're going to be a busy man. The Captain wanted to cancel your leave, but I felt it would do you good, and you could make up for the time you'd lost . . ."

"Thank you very much, Sir," said Christian.

"Finally," said Hardenburg triumphantly, rubbing his hands. "Finally." He stared unseeingly through the window, his eyes on the dust clouds rising from the armored tread on the roads of Libya, his ears hearing the noise of cannon on the Mediterranean coast. "I was beginning to be afraid," Hardenburg said softly, "that I would never get to see a battle." He shook his head, raising himself from his delicious reverie. "All right, Sergeant," he said, in his usual, clipped voice. "I'll want you back here in an hour."

"Yes, Sir," said Christian. He started to go, then turned. "Lieutenant," he said.

"Yes?"

"I wish to submit the name of a man in the 147th Pioneers for disciplinary action."

"Give it to the clerk," said the Lieutenant. "I'll send it through the proper channels."

"Yes, Sir," said Christian and went over to the clerk and watched him write down the name of Private Hans Reuter, unsoldierly appearance and conduct, complaint brought by Sergeant Christian Diestl.

"He's in trouble," the clerk said professionally. "He'll get restricted for a month."

"Probably," said Christian and went outside. He stood in front of the barracks door for a moment, then started for Corinne's house. Halfway there, he halted. Ridiculous, he thought. What's the sense in seeing her now?

He walked slowly back along the street. He stopped in front of a jeweler's shop, with a high small window. In the window

157

there were some small diamond rings and a gold pendant with a large topaz on the end of it. Christian looked at the topaz, thinking: Gretchen would like that. I wonder how much it costs.

CHAPTER EIGHT

THERE WERE BOYS and young men all over the halls, lounging, smoking, spitting, talking loudly in the concrete accents of the New York streets, saying, in the grimy cold corridor that smelled of sweat and public use, "Uncle Sam, here's Vincent Kelly," and "There I was lissenin' to the foolball game and this bastidd breaks in and he says, the Japs went and hit Hickam Field. And I got so excited I didn't lissen no more and then I said to my wife, I said, 'Where the hell is Hickam Field?' and that's the first words I said in the war."

And other voice said, "Nuts, they'll grab you later on, anyway. My motto is get in on the ground floor. My old man was in on the Marines the last time and he said, 'The ratings'll all go to the first guys that show up.' That's the way it was in the last one, he said, you didn't have to be smart, you just had to be early."

And they said, "I wouldn't mind seeing those Islands. One thing I can't stand is Noo Yawk in the winter. Summertime they'd have to come and get me, but I got a outside job, anyway, with the Gas Company, and no army could be worse than that."

And they said, "Have a drink. This war is great. The dame I was with said, 'My aching back, they're killing American boys' an' I said, 'I'm joinin' up in the mawning to fight for democracy, Clara,' and she cried and I laid her, right there in her own bedroom, with her husband's picture watchin' in a sailor suit. I been tryin' to lay that broad for three weeks and I was thrown out at first base every time I got up to the plate. But last night she was like a cage full of overflowin' tigers, and she nearly bust the springs loose from the bed with patriotism."

And they said, "The hell with the Navy. I want to be some place where I can dig a hole."

Noah stood among the patriots, waiting his turn to be interviewed by the recruiting officer. He had taken Hope home late and it had been a bad time when he told her what he was going to do, and he had slept poorly, with one of his old dreams about being put up against a wall and machine-gunned, and he had risen in the dark to go down to Whitehall Street to enlist, hoping to be early enough to avoid getting caught in the crowd he was sure would be besieging the place. As he looked around at the others he wondered how the draft had missed them all, but that was almost the limit of speculation his weary mind could manage at the moment. In the days before the attack he had tried not to think it out, but, remorselessly, his conscience had made the decision for him. If the war began, he could not hesitate. As an honorable citizen, as a believer in the war, as an enemy of Fascism, as a Jew . . . He shook his head. There it was again. That should have nothing to do with it. Most of these men were not Jews, and yet here they were at six-thirty of a winter's morning, the second day of the war, ready to die. And they were better, he knew, than they sounded. The rough jokes, the cynical estimates, were all on the surface, embarrassed attempts to hide the true depths of the feeling that had brought them to this place. As an American, then. He refused to put himself at this moment into any special category. Perhaps, he thought, I will ask to be sent to the Pacific. Not against Germany. That would prove to them that it wasn't because he was a Jew . . . Nonsense, nonsense, he thought, I'll go where they send me.

A door opened and a fat sergeant with a beery face came out and shouted irritably, "All right, all right, you guys. Stop spittin' on the floor, this is government property. And stop shovin'. Nobody's goin' to be left behind. The Army's got plenty of room for everybody. Come in, one by one, through this door, when I give you the word. And leave your bottles outside. This is a United States Army installation."

It took all day. He was shipped to Governor's Island in an Army ferry that had a General's name on it. He stood on the crowded deck, his nose running with the cold, watching the harbor traffic on the slate waters. He wondered what obscure act of heroism or flattery the General had done in his day to deserve this minute honor. The Island was busy and thronged with soldiers who were grimly carrying guns, as though they expected to have to repel a landing party of Japanese marines at any moment.

Noah had told Hope he would try to call her at her office some time during the day, but he didn't want to lose his place in the slow line that went past the bored, short-tempered doctors.

"Christ," the man next to Noah said, looking down the long line of naked, scrawny, flabby aspirants for glory, "is this what's going to defend the country? Christ, we've lost the war."

Noah grinned a little self-consciously, and threw his shoul-

159

ders back, measuring himself secretly in his nakedness against the others. There were three or four powerful young men, who looked as though they had played football, and one enormous man with a clipper in full sail tattooed on his chest, but Noah was pleased to see that he compared favorably with most of the rest. He had become acutely conscious of his body in the last few months. The Army, he thought as he waited to get his chest x-rayed, will probably build me up considerably. Hope will be pleased. Then he grinned. It was an elaborate, round-about way to put yourself in condition, to have your country go to war against the Empire of Japan.

The doctors paid little attention to him. His vision was normal, he did not have piles, flat feet, hernia, or gonorrhea. He did not have syphilis or epilepsy, and in a minute and a half interview a psychiatrist decided he was sane enough for the purposes of modern warfare. His joints articulated well enough to please the Surgeon General and his teeth met in an efficient enough manner to insure his being able to chew Army food and there were no scars or lesions evident anywhere on his skin.

He dressed, glad to get his clothes on once again, thinking, tomorrow it will be a uniform, and went up, in the slow-moving line, to the sallow, harassed-looking medical officer who sat at a yellow desk, stamping 1A, Limited Service, or Rejected, on the medical records.

I wonder, Noah was thinking, as the doctor bent over his record, I wonder if I'll be sent to some camp near New York so I can see Hope on passes . . .

The doctor picked up one of the stamps and tapped it several times on a pad. Then he hit Noah's record and pushed it toward him. Noah looked down at it. REJECTED was smeared across it in blurred purple letters. Noah shook his head and blinked. It still said REJECTED.

"What . . . ?" he began.

The doctor looked up at him, not unkindly. "Your lungs, son," he said. "The x-ray show scar tissue on both of them. When did you have t.b.?"

"I never had t.b."

The doctor shrugged. "Sorry, son," he said. "Next."

Noah walked slowly out of the building. It was evening now, and the wind was cruel and full of December as it swept off the harbor across the old fort and the barracks and parade ground that stood over the sea approaches to the city. The city itself was a clot of a million lights across the dark stretch of water. New levees of draftees and volunteers came pouring off the ferries, shuffling off to the waiting doctors and the final purple stamps.

Noah shivered and put his collar up, clutching the sheet of

paper with his record on it, pulling at his hand in the wind. He felt numb and purposeless, like a schoolboy deserted among the dormitories on Christmas Eve, with all his friends off to celebrations in their homes. He put his hand inside his coat and inside his shirt. He touched the skin of his chest and felt the firm skeleton of his ribs. It felt solid and reliable, even with tips of cold wind whipping at it through his opened clothing. Tentatively, he coughed. He felt strong and whole.

He moved slowly to the ferry slip and stepped aboard past the MP with the winter hat with the earmuffs and the rifle. The ferry was almost empty. Everybody, he thought dully, as the ferry with the dead General's name painted on it slid across the narrow black stretch of water toward the looming city, everybody is going the other way.

Hope wasn't home when he got there. The uncle who read the Bible was sitting up in his underwear in the kitchen, reading, and he peered ill-naturedly at Noah, whom he did not like, and said, "You here? I thought you'd be a Colonel by now."

"Is it all right," Noah asked wearily, "if I stay here and wait for her?"

"Suit yourself," the uncle said, scratching himself under the arm, above the Book, open to the gospel according to Luke on the table before him. "I don't guarantee when she'll be home. She's a girl who's developed some mighty fast habits, as I write her parents in Vermont, and the hours of the night don't seem to make much impression on her." He grinned nastily at Noah. "And now her fellah's goin' in the Army, or leastwise, she thinks he is, she's probably out scoutin' out some new ground, wouldn't you say?"

There was some coffee heating on the stove, and a half-filled cup before him, and the smell was tantalizing to Noah, who hadn't eaten since noon. But the uncle made no offer and Noah wouldn't ask for it.

Noah went into the living room and sat down in the velour easy chair with the cheap lace antimacassars on it. It had been a long day and his face smarted from the cold and wind, and he slept, sitting up, not hearing the uncle shuffling loudly about the kitchen, banging cups and occasionally reading aloud in his nasal, scratching voice.

The noise of the outside gate being opened, one of the deep familiar noises of his world, woke him from his sleep. He blinked his eyes and stood up just as Hope came into the room. She was walking slowly and heavily. She stopped short when she saw him standing there in the middle of the living room.

Then she ran to him and he held her close to him.

"You're here," she said.

Her uncle loudly slammed the door between the kitchen and the living room. Neither of them paid any attention to the noise.

Noah rubbed his cheek in her hair.

"I was in your room," Hope said. "All this time. Looking at all your things. You didn't call. All day. What's happened?"

"They won't take me," Noah said. "I have scars on my lungs. Tuberculosis."

"Oh, my God," Hope said.

CHAPTER NINE

THE CLASHING SOUND of a lawnmower awoke Michael. He lay for a moment in the strange bed, remembering where he was, remembering what had happened yesterday, smelling the clipped fragrance of the California grass. "Probably," the movie writer on the edge of the swimming pool at Palm Springs had said yesterday afternoon, "probably ten guys are home writing it now. The butler comes into the garden with the tea and he says, 'Lemon or cream?' and the little nine-year-old girl comes in, carrying her doll, and says, 'Daddy, please fix the radio. I can't get the funnies. The man keeps talking about Pearl Harbor. Daddy, is Pearl Harbor near where Grandma lives?' And she bends the doll over and it says, 'Mamma'."

It was silly, Michael thought, but more true than not. Large events seemed to announce themselves in clichés. The arrival of universal disaster in the ordinary traffic of life always seemed to come in a rather banal, overworked way. And on Sunday, too, as people were resting after the large Sabbath dinner, after coming out of the churches where they had mumbled dutifully to God for peace. The enemy seemed to take a sardonic delight in picking Sunday for his most savage forays, as though he wanted to show what an ironic joke could be played over and over again on the Christian world. After the Saturday night drunkenness and fornication and the holy morning prayer and bicarbonate of soda.

Michael, himself, had been playing tennis in the blazing desert sun with two soldiers who were stationed at March Field. When the woman had come out of the clubhouse, saying, "You'd better come in and listen to the radio. There's an awful lot of static, but I think I heard that the Japanese have attacked us," the two soldiers had looked at each other and had put their racquets away and had gone in and packed their bags and had started right back for March Field. The ball before the battle of Waterloo. The gallant young officers waltzing, kissing the bare-shouldered ladies good-bye, then off to the guns on the foaming horses, with a rattle of hoofs and scabbards and a swirling of capes in the Flanders night more than a century ago. An old chestnut, then, probably, but Byron had done it big just the same. How would Byron have handled the morning in Honolulu and this next morning at Beverly Hills?

Michael had meant to stay in Palm Springs another three days, but after the tennis game he had paid his bill and rushed back to town. No capes, no horses, just a rented Ford with a convertible top that went down when you pushed a button. And no battle waiting, just the hired-by-the-week ground-floor apartment overlooking the swimming pool.

The noise of the mower came right up to the French windows that opened on the small lawn. Michael turned and looked at the machine and the gardener. The gardener was a small fifty-year-old Japanese, bent and thin with his years of tending other people's grass and flower beds. He plodded after the machine mechanically, his thin, wiry arms straining against the handle.

Michael couldn't help grinning. A hell of a thing to wake up to the day after the Japanese Navy dropped the bombs on the American fleet . . . a fifty-year-old Jap advancing on you with a lawnmower. Michael looked more closely and stopped smiling. The gardener had a set, gloomy expression on his face, as though he were bearing a chronic illness. Michael remembered him from the week before, when he had gone about his chores with a cheery, agreeable smile, and had even hummed from time to time, tunelessly, as he had pruned the oleander bush outside the window.

Michael got out of bed and went to the window, buttoning his pajama top. It was a clear, golden morning, with the tiny crispness that is Southern California's luxurious substitute for winter. The green of the lawn looked very green and the small red and yellow dahlias along the border shone like gleaming bright buttons against it. The gardener kept everything in sharp definite lines out of some precise sense of Oriental design, and made the garden look like colored cups laid out on a billiard table.

"Good morning," Michael said. He didn't know the man's name. He didn't know any Japanese names. Yes—one. Sessue Hayakawa, the old movie star. What was good old Sessue Hayakawa doing this morning?

The gardener stopped the lawnmower and came slowly up from his somber dream to stare at Michael.

"Yes, Sir," he said. His voice was flat and high, and there

163

was no welcome in it. His little dark eyes, set among the brown wrinkles, looked, Michael thought, lost and pleading. Michael wanted to say something comforting and civilized to this aging, laboring exile who had overnight found himself in a land of enemies, charged with the guilt of a vile attack three thousand miles away.

"It's too bad," Michael said, "isn't it?"

The gardener looked blankly at him, as though he had not understood at all.

"I mean," said Michael, "about the war."

The man shrugged. "Not too bad," he said. "Everybody say, 'naughty Japan, goddamn Japan.' But not too bad. Before, England wants, she take. America wants, she take. Now Japan wants." He stared coldly at Michael, direct and challenging. "She take."

He turned and turned the mower with him and started across the lawn slowly, with the cut grass flying in a fragrant green spray around his ankles. Michael watched him for a moment, the bent humble back, the surprisingly powerful legs, bare up to the knee in torn denim pants, the creased, sun-worn neck rising out of the colorless sweaty shirt.

Michael shrugged. Perhaps a good citizen, in time of war, should report utterances like this to the proper authorities. Perhaps this aged gardener in his ragged clothes was really a full commander in the Japanese Navy, cleverly awaiting the arrival of the Imperial Fleet outside San Pedro Harbor before showing his hand. Michael grinned. The movies, he thought, there is no escape for the modern mind from their onslaught.

He closed the French windows and went in and shaved. While he was shaving, he tried to plan what he would do from now on. He had come to California with Thomas Cahoon, who was trying to cast a play. They were conferring about revisions with the author, too, Milton Sleeper, who could only work at night on the play, because he worked during the day for Warner Brothers as a scenario writer. "Art," Cahoon had said, acidly, "is in great shape in the twentieth century. Goethe worked all day on a play, and Chekhov and Ibsen, but Milton Sleeper can only give it his evenings."

Somehow, Michael thought, as he scraped at his face, when your country goes to war, you should be galvanized into some vast and furious action. You should pick up a gun, board a naval vessel, climb into a bomber for a five-thousand-mile flight, parachute into the enemy's capital . . .

But Cahoon needed him to put the play on. And, there was no escaping this fact, Michael needed the money. If he went into the Army now, his mother and father would probably starve, and there was Laura's alimony . . . Cahoon was giving him a percentage of the play this time, too. It was a small percentage, but if it was a hit it would mean that money would be coming in for a year or two. Perhaps the war would be short and the money would last it out. And if it was a tremendous smash, say, like *Abie's Irish Rose* or *Tobacco Road,* the war could stretch on indefinitely. It was a dreadful thing to think of, though—a war that ran as long as *Tobacco Road.*

Too bad he didn't have the money now, though. It would have been so satisfactory to go to the nearest Army post after hearing the news on the radio and enlist. It would have been a solid, unequivocal gesture which you could look back at with pride all your life. But there were only six hundred dollars in the bank, and the income-tax people were bothering him about his return for 1939, and Laura had been unpredictably greedy about the divorce settlement. He had to give her eighty dollars a week for her whole life, unless she got married, and she had taken all the cash he had in his account in New York. He wondered what happened to alimony when you joined the Army. Probably an MP taps you on the shoulder as you lie crouched in a trench on the mainland of Asia, and says, "Come on, Soldier, we've been looking for you." He remembered the story a British friend of his told him about the last war. The friend had been at the Somme, and on the third day of the battle, with nearly no one left in his company, and no sign anywhere of any respite of relief, he had received a letter from home. With trembling hands, near tears, he had opened it. It was from the British equivalent of the Internal Revenue Department, saying, "We have written you again and again with regard to your non-payment of thirteen pounds seven in tax for the year 1914. We regret to tell you that this is absolutely the last warning. If we do not hear from you we shall have to institute legal steps." The friend, muddy, hollow-eyed, ragged, survivor of the death of all the men around him, deafened with the continuing roar of the guns, had gravely written on the face of the letter, "Come and get it. The War Office will be pleased to give you my address." He had given it to the Company Clerk to mail and had turned to the Germans in front of him.

As Michael dressed he tried to think about other things. There was something inglorious about sitting, a little hung-over from last night's nervous drinking, in this over-fancy, pink-chiffon, rented bedroom, done in Hollywood whorehouse style, uneasily going over your finances on this morning of decision, like a bookkeeper who has lifted fifty dollars from the till and is worrying about how to get it back before the auditors arrive. The men at the guns in Honolulu were probably in even more severe financial shape, but he was sure they weren't worrying about it this morning. Still, it was impractical to go down and enlist immediately. It was ridiculous, but patriotism, like almost every other generous activity, was easier for the rich, too.

While he was dressing he heard the colored man who did the cleaning come in and rattle the bottles in the small cabinet in the dining alcove. War hasn't changed him, Michael thought, he's stealing the gin just the same.

Michael put on his tie and went out into the living room. The colored man was running a carpet sweeper. He was standing in the middle of the floor, staring up at the ceiling, and pushing the carpet sweeper about in long, vague gestures, in all directions. There was a powerful smell of gin in the air and the colored man wavered in a benign, pendulum-like movement as he worked.

"Good morning, Bruce," Michael said pleasantly. "How do you feel?"

"Morning, Mr. Whitacre," Bruce said dreamily. "Feel the same. Feel exactly the same."

"They going to get you in the Army?" Michael asked.

"Me, Mr. Whitacre?" Bruce stopped sweeping and shook his head. "Not old Bruce. The man says, 'Join up, Brother,' but old Bruce don't join. Too old, too full of clap and rheumatism. And even if I was as young as the leaping colt and strong as the roaring lion, you wouldn't catch me enlisting for this war. Mebbe the next, but not this one. No, Sir."

Michael pulled back a little because in his vehemence Bruce had swayed, close and gin-smelling, toward him. Michael looked at him puzzledly. He always felt a little embarrassed with Negroes, and guilty. He never seemed to strike a candid, everyday, honest conversational tone with them.

"No, Sir," Bruce went on, swaying, "not this one at all. Not if they gave me a solid silver gun and spurs of shining gold. This is the war of the Unrighteous, as it is predicted in the Books of Prophecy, and I would not lift my hand in it to wound my fellowman."

"But," Michael said, trying to put it in simple terms to get through the gin cloud, somehow feeling that on a day like this a man should debate this question with his neighbor, "they're killing Americans, Bruce."

"Maybe they are. Haven't seen for myself yet. Don't know for certain. Only what I read in the white papers. Maybe they *are* killing Americans. Likely, they was provoked. Maybe they tried to get into a hotel and the white men said, no yellow men here, and the yellow men finally got mad and they schemed awhile and they said, 'White men don't let us in the hotel, let's take the hotel.' No, man . . ." He ran the carpet sweeper briskly twice over the carpet, then stopped and leaned on it again. "This ain't the war for me. The next one is the one I'm waiting for."

"When will that be?" Michael asked.

"1956," Bruce said promptly. "Armageddon. The war of the

166

races. The colored against the white." He looked drunkenly and religiously up at the ceiling. "First day of *that* war, I present myself at the recruiting office and I say to the colored general, 'General, make use of my strong right arm.' "

California, Michael thought crazily. You only meet people like this in California.

He left Bruce, who had fallen into a somber, reflective silence, leaning on the handle of the carpet sweeper in the middle of the room.

Outside, across the street, on a vacant lot that rose quite steeply above the rest of the ground around it, there were two Army trucks and an anti-aircraft gun and soldiers in helmets were digging in. The gun, poking its long, covered muzzle up at the sky, and the busy soldiers scraping out an emplacement as though they were already under fire, struck Michael as incongruous and comic. This, too, must be a local phenomenon. It was impossible to believe that any place else in the country, the Army was going to these melodramatic lengths. And, somehow, soldiers and guns had always seemed to Michael, as they did to most Americans, like instruments for a kind of boring, grown-up game, not like anything real. And this particular gun was stuck between a woman's Monday washline, brassieres and silk stockings and pantie girdles, and the back door of a Spanish bungalow, with the morning's milk still on the steps.

Michael walked toward Wilshire Boulevard, toward the drugstore where he usually had his breakfast. There was a bank building on the corner, with a line of people outside the door, waiting for the bank to open. A young policeman was keeping them in order, saying over and over again, "Ladies and Gentlemen. Ladies and Gentlemen. Keep your places. Don't worry. You'll all get your money."

Michael went up to the policeman, curiously. "What's going on here?" he asked.

The policeman looked sourly at him. "The end of the line, Mister," he said pointing.

"I don't want to get inside," said Michael. "I haven't any money in this bank. Or," and he grinned, "in any other bank."

The policeman smiled back at him, as though this expression of poverty had made sudden friends of them. "They're gettin' it out," he gestured with his head to the line of people, "before the bombs fall on the vaults."

Michael stared at the people in the line. They stared back with hostility, as though they suspected anyone who talked to the policeman of being in conspiracy to defraud them of their money. They were well dressed, and there were many women among them.

"Back east," the policeman said in a loud, contemptuous

stage whisper. "They're all heading back east as soon as they get it out. I understand," he said very loudly, so that everyone in the line could hear him, "that ten Japanese divisions have landed at Santa Barbara. The Bank of America is going to be used as headquarters for the Japanese General Staff, starting tomorrow."

"I'm going to report you," a severe middle-aged woman in a pink dress and a wide blue straw hat said to the policeman. "See if I don't."

"The name, Lady, is McCarty," said the policeman.

Michael smiled as he moved on toward his breakfast, but he walked reflectively past the plateglass windows of the shops, some of which already had strips of plaster across them to protect from concussion the silver tea sets and evening gowns displayed in them. The rich, he thought, are more sensitive to disaster than others. They have more to lose and they are quicker to run. It would never occur to a poor man to leave the West Coast because there was a war on somewhere in the Pacific. Not out of patriotism, perhaps, or fortitude, but merely because he couldn't afford it. Also, the rich were accustomed to pay other people to do their manual work for them, and their dirty jobs, and a war was the hardest labor and the dirtiest job of all. He thought of the gardener, who had lived in this country for forty years, and Bruce, drunk on gin and prophecy, whose grandfather had been freed in South Carolina in 1863, and he remembered the grasping, tight, hostile expressions on the women in the line before the bank and he thought of himself sitting on the edge of the pink bed worrying about tax and alimony. Are these the people, created in greatness by the work of Jefferson and Franklin, he thought, are these the bitter farmers and hunters and craftsmen who came out of the wilderness, furious for liberty and justice, is this the new world of giants sung by Whitman?

He went into the drugstore and ordered orange juice, toast and coffee.

He met Cahoon at one o'clock at the famous restaurant in Beverly Hills. It was a large dark room, done in the curving, startling style affected by movie-set designers. It looks, Michael thought, standing at the bar, surveying the crowded civilian room, in which one uniform, on a tall infantry sergeant, stood out strangely, it looks like a bathroom decorated by a Woolworth salesgirl for a Balkan queen. The image pleased him and he gazed with more favor on the tanned fat men in the tweed jackets and the smooth, powdered, beautiful women with startling hats who sat about the room, their eyes pecking at each new arrival. There was an air of celebration and generosity hanging over the room, and people clapped each other on the back and talked jovially and louder than usual and bought each other drinks. It reminded Michael, more than anything else, of the cocktail hour in fashionable bars in New York on the afternoon before New Year's Eve, when everyone was stoking up for the night of hope and merrymaking ahead.

There were rumors and anecdotes about the war already. A famous director walked through the room with a set face, whispering here and there that of course he didn't want it spread around, but we hadn't a ship in the Pacific, and a fleet had been spotted 300 miles off the Oregon coast. And a writer had heard a producer in the MGM barbershop sputter, through the lather on his face, "I'm so mad at those little yellow bastards, I feel like throwing up my job here and going—going—" The producer had hesitated, groping for the most violent symbol of his feeling of outrage and duty. Finally, he had found it, "—going right to Washington." The writer was having a great success with the story. He was going to table after table with it, cleverly leaving on the burst of laughter it provoked, to move on to new listeners.

Cahoon was quiet and abstracted and Michael could tell that he was in pain from his ulcer, although he insisted upon drinking an old-fashioned at the bar before going to their table. Michael had never seen Cahoon take a drink before.

They sat down at one of the booths to wait for Milton Sleeper, the author of the play Cahoon was working on, and for Kirby Hoyt, a movie actor whom Cahoon hoped to induce to play in it. "One of the most irritating things about this town," Cahoon growled. "Everybody insists on doing business over lunch. You can't sign a barber without stuffing his face first."

Pharney came ambling down the room, smiling, and shaking hands in a royal passage across the booths. He was an agent for a hundred and fifty of the highest-priced actors and writers and directors in Hollywood, and this restaurant was his regal domain and lunchtime his solemn hour of audience. He knew Michael well, and again and again had tried to persuade him to come out and learn the business, promising him fame and fortune as a director.

"Hello," Pharney said, shaking hands, smiling in the insolent, good-natured way that he had found impressed people into giving more money than they had intended for his clients. "How do you like it?" he asked, as though the war were a production he had himself supervised and of which he was very proud.

"Best little old war," Michael said, "I ever was in."

"How old're you?" Pharney peered shrewdly at Michael.

"Thirty-three."

"I can get you two stripes," Pharney said, "in the Navy. Public Relations. Radio stuff. Want it?"

"Christ," said Cahoon, "does the Navy use agents, too?"

"Friend of mine," Pharney said, unoffended. "Full Captain. Well?" He turned back to Michael.

"Not at the moment," said Michael. "I'm not ready to go in for two or three months."

"In three months," Pharney said, grinning across them at two glittering beauties in the next booth, "In three months you'll be tending gardens in Yokahama."

"The truth is," Michael said hesitantly, trying to make it sound unheroic, "I think I want to go in as a private in the Army."

"My perishing ass," Pharney said, "what for?"

"It's a long story," said Michael, feeling immodest and embarrassed. "I'll tell you another time."

"Hamburger," Pharney said cheerfully. "That's all a private in the Army is. Grind him down fine and don't mind if there's a little fat in it. Have a good war." He waved and was off, down the saluting line of booths.

Cahoon stared gloomily at two comedians who were making their way along the bar, laughing loudly and shaking hands with all the drinkers. "This town," he said, "I'd give the Japanese High Command five hundred dollars and two seats to the opening nights of all my plays if they'd bomb it tomorrow. Mike," he said, without looking at Michael, "I'm going to say something very selfish."

"Go ahead," Michael said.

"Don't go in till we get this play on. I'm too tired to get a show on by myself. And you've been in on it since the beginning. Sleeper's a horrible jerk, but he's got a good play there, and it ought to be done . . ."

"Don't worry," Michael said softly, half afraid already that he was leaping at this honorable excuse in friendship's name to remain aloof from the war for another season. "I'll hang around."

"They'll get along without you," Cahoon said, "for a couple of months. We'll win the war anyway."

He stopped talking. Sleeper was threading his way through the crowd toward their booth. Sleeper dressed like a forceful young writer, dark-blue work shirt and a tie that was off to one side. He was a handsome, heavy-set, arrogant man, who had written two inflammatory plays about the working class several years before. He sat down without shaking hands.

"Christ," he growled, "why do we have to meet in this Chanel douche bag?"

"Your secretary," Cahoon said, mildly, "made the date."

"My secretary," Sleeper said, "has two ambitions. She wants to lay a Hungarian producer at Universal and she wants to make a gentleman out of me. She's the kind of girl who's

170

always saying she doesn't like your shirts. Know that kind?"

"I don't like your shirts, either," said Cahoon. "You make two thousand dollars a week, you don't have to wear things like that."

"Double Scotch," Sleeper said to the waiter. "Well," he said loudly, "Uncle Sam has finally backed his tail into the service of humanity."

"Did you rewrite Scene Two yet?" Cahoon asked.

"For Christ's sake, Cahoon!" Sleeper said. "Do you think a man can work at a time like this?"

"Just thought I'd ask," said Cahoon.

"Blood," said Sleeper, sounding, Michael thought, like a character in one of his plays. "Blood on the palm trees, blood on the radio, blood on the decks, and he asks about the second scene! Wake up, Cahoon. A cosmic moment. Thunder in the bowels of the earth. The human race is twisting, tortured and bleeding in its uneasy sleep."

"Save it," said Cahoon, "for the trial scene."

"Cut it." Sleeper glowered heavily under his heavy, handsome eyebrows. "Cut those brittle, Broadway jokes. That time's passed, Cahoon, passed forever. The first bomb yesterday dropped right in the middle of the last wisecrack. Where's the Ham?" He looked around him restlessly, tapping the table in front of him.

"Hoyt said he'd be a little late," Michael said. "He'll be here."

"I've got to get back to the studio," said Sleeper. "Freddie asked me to come in this afternoon. The studio's thinking of making a picture about Honolulu to awaken the American people."

"What're you going to do?" Cahoon asked. "Are you going to have time to finish the play?"

"Of course I am," said Sleeper. "I told you I would, didn't I?"

"Yes," said Cahoon. "That was before the war started. I thought you might go in. . . ."

Sleeper snorted. "To do what? Guard a viaduct in Kansas City?" He took a long sip of the Scotch the waiter placed before him. "The artist doesn't belong in uniform. The function of the artist is to keep alive the flame of culture, to explain what the war is about, to lift the spirits of the men who are grappling with death. Anything else," he said, "is sentimentality. In Russia they don't take the artist. Write, they say, play, paint, compose. A country in its right mind doesn't put its national treasures in the front line. What would you think if the French had put the Mona Lisa and Cezanne's self-portrait in the Maginot Line? You'd think they were crazy, wouldn't you?"

"Yes," Michael said, because Sleeper was glaring at him.

"Well," Sleeper shouted, "why the hell should they put a new Cezanne, a living Da Vinci there? Christ, even the Germans keep their artists at home! God, I get so weary of this argument!" He finished his Scotch and looked furiously around him. "I can't stand a tardy Ham," Sleeper said. "I'm going to order my lunch."

"Pharney," said Cahoon, smiling slightly, "can get you two stripes in the Navy."

"Screw Pharney," said Sleeper. "Flesh-peddling provocateur. Ham and eggs," he said to the waiter, "and asparagus with Hollandaise sauce. And a double Scotch."

Hoyt came in while Sleeper was ordering and made his way quickly to their table, shaking hands with only five people in his passage.

"Sorry, old man," Hoyt said as he slipped onto the green leather bench behind the table. "Sorry I'm late."

"Why the hell," Sleeper asked pugnaciously, "can't you get any place on time? Wouldn't your public like it?"

"Confusing day at the studio, old man," Hoyt said. "Couldn't break away." He had a clipped British accent which had never varied in the seven years he had been in the United States. He had taken out American citizenship papers when the war began in 1939, but otherwise he seemed exactly the same handsome, talented young toff, via Pall Mall out of the Bristol slums, who had got off the boat in 1934. He looked distracted and nervous and ordered a very light lunch. He did not order a drink because he had a tiring afternoon ahead of him. He was playing an RAF Squadron Leader and there was a complicated scene in a burning plane over the Channel, with process shots and difficult closeups.

Lunch was a tense affair. Hoyt had promised to re-read the play over the week-end and give Cahoon his final decision about whether he would appear in it. He was a good actor and just right for the part, and if he didn't play it, it would be a difficult job to find another man. Sleeper kept drinking double Scotches gloomily and Cahoon poked drably at his food.

Michael saw Laura at a table across the room with two other women, and nodded coolly at her. It was the first time he'd seen her since the divorce. That eighty bucks a week, he thought, won't go far if she pays for her own lunch in this place. He was angry at her for being improvident and then was annoyed at himself for worrying about it. She looked very pretty and it was hard to remember that he was angry at her and also hard to remember that he had ever loved her. Another face, he thought, that will pull vaguely and sadly at the heart when glimpsed by accident at one end of the country or another.

"I've re-read the play, Cahoon," Hoyt said, a little hurriedly, "and I must say I think it's just beautiful."

"Good." Cahoon started to smile broadly.

". . . But," Hoyt broke in a little breathlessly, "I'm afraid I can't do it."

Cahoon stopped smiling and Sleeper said, "Oh, Christ."

"What's the matter?" Cahoon asked.

"At the moment . . ." Hoyt smiled apologetically. "With the war and all. Change of plans, old man. Truth is, if I went into a play, I'm afraid the bloody draft board'd clap its paws on me. Out here . . ." He took a mouthful of salad. "Out here, it's a somewhat different case. Studio says they'll get me deferred. The word is from Washington that movies'll be considered in the national interest. Necessary personnel, y' know . . . Don't know about the stage. Wouldn't like to take a chance. You understand my position . . ."

"Sure," said Cahoon flatly. "Sure."

"Christ," said Sleeper. He stood up. "Got to go back to Burbank," he said. "In the national interest."

He walked out heavily and bit unsteadily.

Hoyt looked after him nervously. "Never liked that chap," he said. "Not a gentleman." He chewed tensely on his salad.

Rollie Vaughn appeared at the table, red-faced and beaming, with a glass of brandy in his hand. He was English, too, older than Hoyt, and was playing a Wing Commander in Hoyt's picture. But he was not on call for the afternoon and could safely drink.

"Greatest day in England's history," he said happily, beaming at Hoyt. "The days of defeat are over. Days of victory ahead. To Franklin Delano Roosevelt." He lifted his glass and the others politely lifted theirs, and Michael was afraid that Rollie was going to heave the glass into the fireplace, now that he was in the RAF at Paramount. "To America!" Rollie said, lifting his glass again. What he's really drinking to, Michael thought unpleasantly, is the Japanese Navy, for getting us in. Still, you couldn't blame an Englishman . . .

"We will fight them on the beaches," said Rollie loudly, "we will fight them on the hills." He sat down. "We will fight them in the streets . . . No more Cretes, no more Norways . . . No more getting pushed out of any place."

"I wouldn't talk like that, old man," Hoyt said. "I had a private conversation not long ago. Chap in the Admiralty. You'd be surprised at the name if I could tell it to you. He explained to me about Crete."

"What did he say about Crete?" Rollie stared at Hoyt, a slight belligerence showing in his eyes.

"All according to the over-all plan, old man," said Hoyt. "Inflict losses and pull out. Cleverest thing in the world. Let them have Crete. Who needs Crete?"

Rollie stood up majestically. "I'm not going to sit here," he said harshly, a wild light in his eye, "and hear the British Armed Forces insulted by a runaway Englishman."

"Now, now," Cahoon said soothingly. "Sit down."

"What did I say, old boy?" Hoyt asked nervously.

"British blood spilled to the last ounce," Rollie banged the table. "Desperate, bloody stand to save the land of an ally. Englishmen dying by the thousand . . . and he says it was planned that way! 'Let them have Crete!' I've been watching you for some time, Hoyt, and I've tried to be fair in my mind, but I'm afraid I've finally got to believe what people're saying about you."

"Now, old man," Hoyt was very red in the face and his voice was high and rattled. "I think you're the victim of a terrible misunderstanding."

"If you were in England," Rollie said, bitingly, "you'd sing a different tune. They'd have you up before the law before you'd have a chance to get out more than ten words. Spreading despondency and alarm. Criminal offense, you know, in time of war."

"Really," Hoyt said weakly, "Rollie, old man . . ."

"I'd like to know who's paying you for this," Rollie stuck his chin out challengingly close to Hoyt's face. "I really would like to know. Don't think this is going to die in this restaurant. Every Englishman in this town is going to hear about it, never fear! Let them have Crete, eh?" He slammed his glass down on the table and stalked back to the bar.

Hoyt wiped his sweating face with his handkerchief and looked painfully around him to see how many people had heard the tirade. "Lord," he said, "you don't know how difficult it is to be an Englishman these days. Insane, neurotic cliques, you don't dare open your mouth . . ." He got up. "I hope you'll excuse me," he said, "but I really must get back to the studio."

"Of course," Cahoon said.

"Terribly sorry about the play," said Hoyt. "But you see how it is."

"Yes," said Cahoon.

"Cherrio," said Hoyt.

"Cherrio," said Cahoon, with a straight face.

He and Michael watched the elegant, 7500-dollar-a-week back retreating past the bar, retreating past the defender of Crete, retreating to the Paramount Studios, to the prop plane afire that afternoon against the processed clouds ten miles off the Hollywood-Dover coast.

Cahoon sighed. "If I didn't have ulcers when I came in here," he said, "I'd have them now." He called for the check.

Then Michael saw Laura walking toward their table. Michael looked down at his plate with great interest, but Laura stopped in front of him.

"Invite me to sit down," she said.

Michael looked coldly up at her, but Cahoon smiled and said, "Hello, Laura, won't you join us?" and she sat down facing Michael.

"I'm going anyway," Cahoon said before Michael could protest. He stood up, after signing the check. "See you tonight, Mike," he said, and wandered slowly off toward the door. Michael watched him go.

"You might be more pleasant," Laura said. "Even if we're divorced we can be friendly."

Michael stared at the Sergeant who was drinking at the bar. The Sergeant had watched Laura walk across the room and was looking at her now, frankly and hungrily.

"I don't approve of friendly divorces," Michael said. "If you have to get a divorce it should be a mean, unfriendly divorce."

Laura's eyelids quivered. Oh, God, Michael thought, she still cries.

"I just came over to warn you," Laura said, her voice trembling.

"Warn me about what?" Michael asked, puzzled.

"Not to do anything rash. About the war, I mean."

"I won't do anything rash."

"I think," said Laura softly, "you might offer me a drink."

"Waiter," said Michael, "two Scotch and soda."

"I heard you were in town," Laura said.

"Did you?" Michael stared at the Sergeant, who had not taken his eyes off Laura since she sat down.

"I was hoping you'd call me," she said.

Women, Michael thought, their emotions were like trapeze artists falling into nets. Miss the rung, fall through the air, then bounce up as high and spry as ever.

"I was busy," Michael said. "How are things with you?"

"Not bad," Laura said. "They're testing me for a part at Fox."

"Good luck."

"Thanks," Laura said.

The Sergeant swung around fully at the bar so that he wouldn't have to crane his neck to see Laura. She did look very pretty, with a severe black dress and a tiny hat on the back of her head, and Michael didn't blame the Sergeant for looking. The uniform accentuated the expression of loss and loneliness and dumb desire on his face. Here he is, Michael thought, adrift in the war, maybe on the verge of being sent to die on some jungle island that nobody ever heard of, or to rot there month after month and year after year in the dry, womanless clutch of the Army, and he probably doesn't know a girl between here and Dubuque, not much older than he, sitting in this fancy place with a beautiful girl . . . Probably behind that lost, staring expression there are visions of me unconcernedly drinking with one pretty girl after another in the rich bars of his native land, in bed with them, between the crisp civilized sheets, while he sweats and weeps and dies so far away . . .

Michael had an insane notion that he wanted to go up to the Sergeant and say to him, "Look here, I know what you're thinking. You're absolutely wrong. I'm not going to be with that girl tonight or any other night. If it was up to me, I'd send her out with you tonight, I swear I would." But he couldn't do that. He could just sit there and feel guilty, as though he had been given a prize that someone else had earned. Sitting beside his lovely ex-wife, he knew that this was still another thing to sour his days; that every time he entered a restaurant with a girl and there was a soldier unescorted, he would feel guilty; and that every time he touched a woman with tenderness and longing, he would feel that she had been bought with someone else's blood.

"Michael," Laura said softly, looking with a little smile over her drink, "what are you doing tonight? Late?"

Michael took his eyes away from the Sergeant. "Working," he said. "Are you through with your drink? I have to go."

CHAPTER TEN

IT MIGHT HAVE BEEN bearable without the wind. Christian moved heavily under his blanket, tasting the sand on his cracked lips. The wind picked the sand off the flinty, rolling ridges and hurled it in malicious bursts at you, into your eyes, your throat, your lungs.

Christian sat up slowly, keeping his blanket around him. It was just getting light and the pitiless cold of night still gripped the desert face. His jaws were quivering with the cold and he moved about, stiffly, still sitting, to get warm.

Some of the men were actually sleeping. Christian stared at them with wonder and loathing. Just under the ridge Hardenburg and five of the men were lying. Hardenburg was peering over the ridge at the convoy through his glasses, only the very top of his head above the jagged rocky line. Every line of Hardenburg's body, even through the swathing of the big, thick overcoat, was alert, resilient. God, Christian thought, doesn't he ever have to sleep? What a wonderful thing it would be if Hardenburg got killed in the next ten minutes. Christian played deliciously with the idea for a moment, then sighed. Not a chance. All the rest of them might get killed that morning, but not Hardenburg. You could take one look at Hardenburg and know that he was going to be alive when the war ended.

Himmler crawled cautiously down from his position under the ridge next to Hardenburg, careful not to raise any dust. He shook the sleeping men to awaken them and whispered to them. Slowly they began to move around, with elaborate, measured motions, as though they were in a dark room crowded with many delicate glass ornaments.

Himmler reached Christian on his hands and knees. He moved his knees around in front of him and sat down next to Christian very deliberately.

"He wants you," Himmler whispered, although the British were three hundred meters away.

"All right," Christian said, without moving.

"He's going to get us all killed," Himmler said. He had lost a great deal of weight and his face was raw under the stubble of his beard and his eyes seemed caged and desperate. He hadn't made a joke or clowned for the officers since the first shell was fired over their heads outside Bardia three months before. It was as though another man, a thinner, despairing cousin, had taken possession of Sergeant Himmler's body upon his arrival in Africa, leaving the rotund, jovial ghost of the old Himmler comfortably moored in some shadowy haven back in Europe, waiting to claim possession of the Sergeant's body if and when he ever returned. "He just lies up there," Himmler whispered, "watching the Tommies, singing to himself."

"Singing?" Christian shook his head to clear it.

"Humming. Smiling. He hasn't closed his ears all night. Ever since that convoy stopped out there last night, he's just lain there and kept his glasses on them, smiling." Himmler looked bleakly over at the Lieutenant. "Wouldn't go for them last night. Oh, no. Too easy. Afraid we might miss one of them. Has to lay up here for ten hours, to wait till it gets light, so we can get every one of them. It'll look better in the report." Himmler spat unhappily into the restlessly swirling sand. "He'll get us all killed, you wait and see."

"How many Tommies are there?" Christian asked. He finally dropped his blanket and shivered as he picked up his carefully wrapped machine pistol.

"Eighty," Himmler whispered. He looked around him bitterly. "And thirteen of us. Thirteen. Only that son of a bitch would take thirteen men out on a patrol. Not twelve, not fourteen, not . . ."

"Are they up yet?" Christian broke in.

"They're up," Himmler said. "Sentries all over the place. It's just a miracle they haven't spotted us so far."

"What is he waiting for?" Christian looked at the Lieutenant, lying tensely, like a crouching animal, just under the ridge.

"You ask him," Himmler said. "Maybe for Rommel to come down and watch this personally and give him a medal after breakfast."

The Lieutenant slid down from the top of the ridge and waved impatiently for Christian. Christian crept slowly up toward him, with Himmler following.

"Had to set the mortar himself," Himmler grumbled. "Couldn't trust me. I'm not scientific enough for him. He's been crawling over and playing with the elevation all night. I swear to God, if they examined him for lunacy, they'd have him in a strait-jacket in two minutes."

"Come on, come on," Hardenburg whispered harshly. As Christian came up to him, he could see that Hardenburg's eyes were glowing with what could only be happiness. He needed a shave and his cap was sandy, but he looked as though he had slept at least ten refreshing hours.

"I want everyone in position," Hardenburg said, "in one minute. No one will make a move until I tell them. The first shots will be from the mortar and I will give a hand signal from up here."

Christian, on his hands and knees, nodded.

"On the signal, the two machine guns will be raised to the top of the ridge and will begin firing, and continuous fire will be kept up by the riflemen until I give the command to stop. Is that clear?"

"Yes, Sir," Christian whispered.

"When I want corrections on the mortar I will call them myself. The crew will keep their eyes open and watch me at all times. Understand?"

"Yes, Sir," said Christian. "When will we go into action, Sir?"

"When I am good and ready," Hardenburg said. "Make your rounds, see that everything is in order and come back to me."

"Yes, Sir." Christian and Himmler turned and crawled over to where the mortar was set up, with the shells piled behind it and the men crouched beside it.

"If only," Himmler whispered, "that bastard gets a slug up his ass I will die happy today."

"Keep quiet," Christian said. Himmler's nervousness was unsettling. "You do your job, and let the Lieutenant take care of himself."

"Nobody has to worry about me," Himmler said. "Nobody can say I don't do my job."

"Nobody said it."

"You were about to say it," Himmler said pugnaciously, glad to have this intimate enemy to argue with for the mo-

178

ment—to take his mind off the eighty Englishmen three hundred meters away.

"Keep your mouth shut," Christian said. He looked at the mortar crew. They were cold and shivering. The new one, Schoener, kept opening and closing his mouth in an ugly, trembling yawn, but they seemed ready. Christian repeated the Lieutenant's instructions and crawled on. Making certain to raise no dust, he approached the machine-gun crew of three on the right end of the ridge.

The men were ready. The waiting, through the night, with the eighty Englishmen, just over the scanty ridge, had told on everyone. The vehicles, the two scout cars and the tracked carrier, were just barely hidden by the small rise. If an RAF plane on an early patrol appeared in the sky, and came down to investigate, they would all be lost. The men kept peering nervously, as they had done all the previous day, too, into the clear, limitless sky, lit now by the growing light of dawn. Luckily, the sun was behind them, low and blinding. For another hour the British on the ground would have a difficult time locating them against its glare.

This was the third patrol through the British lines that Hardenburg had taken them on in five weeks, and Christian was sure that the Lieutenant was volunteering again and again at Battalion Headquarters for the job. The line here, far over on the right of the shifting front, among the waterless, roadless sand and scrub, was lightly manned. It was a succession of small posts and wandering, mingled patrols, more than anything else, not like the densely packed ground near the coast, with its precious road and water points, where there were full-dress artillery and aerial sweeps all day and night.

Here, there was a sensation of uneasy stillness, a premonition of disaster hanging over the landscape.

In a way, Christian thought, it was better in the last war. The slaughter was horrible in the trenches, but everything was organized. You got your food regularly, you had a feeling that matters were arranged in some comprehensible order, the dangers came through regular and recognizable channels. In a trench, Christian thought, as he slowly approached Hardenburg, lying once more just under the crest of the ridge, peering over it through his glasses, you were not so much at the mercy of a wild glory-seeker like this one. Finally, Christian thought, in 1960 this maniac will be in command of the German General Staff. God help the German soldier then.

Christian dropped carefully to the sand beside the Lieutenant, keeping his head down under the sky-line. There was a slight, sour smell from the leaves of the desiccated brush that clung to the sharp soil of the ridge.

"Everything is ready, Lieutenant," Christian said.

"Good," said Hardenburg, without moving.

Christian took off his cap. Slowly, very slowly, he raised his head until his eyes were over the line of the ridge.

The British were brewing tea. They had a dozen fires going in small tins that had been half-filled with sand, and then soaked with gasoline. The fires flared palely. The men grouped around them and waited with their enamel dixies. The white of the enamel picked up little glitters of sunshine and gave a curious impression of restless movement to the groups. They looked very small, three hundred meters away. Their trucks and cars in their desert paint looked like battered toys.

There was a man on duty at the machine gun mounted on a circular bar above the cab of each truck. But aside from that, the entire scene had a kind of picnic quality, city people who had left their women at home on a Sunday to rough it for a morning. The blankets on which the men had slept still lay about the vehicles and here and there Christian could see men shaving out of half cups of water. They must have a lot of water, Christian thought automatically, to waste it like that.

There were six trucks, five open and laden with boxes of rations, and one covered. Ammunition in that one, probably. The sentries had drifted in toward the fires, still holding their rifles. How safe they must feel, Christian thought, thirty miles behind their own lines, on a routine run to the posts to the south. They had dug no holes for themselves and there was no cover anywhere, except behind the trucks. It was incredible that eighty men could move about so long and so unconcernedly under the guns of an enemy who was only waiting the move of a hand to kill them. And it was grotesque that they were shaving and making tea. Well, if it was going to be done, now was the time to do it.

Christian looked at the Lieutenant. There was a slight, fixed smile on his face, and he was humming, as Himmler had said. The smile was almost a fond one, like the smile of a grown-up watching the touching, clumsy movements of an infant in a play-pen. But Hardenburg made no sign. Christian settled himself in the sand, squinting to keep the men below in focus, and waited.

The water boiled below and little gusts of steam spurted up into the wind. Christian saw the Tommies domestically measuring out the tea into the water, and sugar from sacks, and tinned milk. They would make a richer tea, he thought, if they knew they wouldn't need the rest for lunch, or dinner.

He saw a man from each of the groups around the fires carry back the cans and sacks and carefully stow them away in the trucks. One by one, the Tommies dipped into the steaming brew and came up with their cups full. Occasionally, a twist of the wind would bring the faint sound of talk or laughter, as the men sat on the ground taking their breakfast. Christian ran his tongue over his lips, watching them, envying them. He hadn't had anything to eat for twelve hours and he hadn't had a hot drink since he left their own command post. He could almost smell the rich, heavy savor of the steam, almost taste the thick, cloudy drink.

Hardenburg didn't stir. Still the smile, still the tuneless humming. What in the name of God was he waiting for? To be discovered? To have to fight, instead of merely killing at leisure? To be caught by a plane? Christian looked around him. The other men were crouched in stiff, unnatural positions, staring with worried eyes at the Lieutenant. The man on Christian's right swallowed dryly. The sound was foolishly loud and metallic.

He's enjoying it, Christian thought, looking back once more to Hardenburg. The Army has no right to put a man like that in command of its soldiers. It's bad enough without that.

Here and there among the British around the trucks men began to fill pipes and light cigarettes. It gave an added air of contentment and security to the small tableau, and at the same time made Christian's palate ache for a cigarette. Of course, it was difficult at this distance to observe the men very closely, but they seemed like the ordinary, run-of-the-mill type of English soldier, rather scrawny and small in their overcoats, moving about in their phlegmatic, deliberate way.

Some of them finished their breakfasts and industriously scrubbed their kits with sand before moving over to the trucks and starting to roll their blankets. The men at the machine guns on the trucks swung down to get their breakfast. There were two or three minutes when the guns on all the vehicles were left unattended. Now, Christian thought, this is what he was waiting for. Quickly he glanced around to see that everything was in readiness. The men had not moved. They were still crouched painfully in the same positions they had taken before.

Christian looked at Hardenburg. If he had noticed that the British guns were not manned he did nothing to show it. Still the same small smile, still the humming.

His teeth, Christian noted, are the ugliest thing about him. Big, wide, crooked, with spaces between them, you could be sure that when he drank anything he made a lot of noise about it. And he was so pleased with himself. It stuck out all over him, as he lay there smiling behind the binoculars, knowing that every man's eyes were straining on him, waiting for the signal that would release them from the torture of delay, knowing they hated him, were afraid of him, could not understand him.

Christian blinked and looked once more, hazily now, at the British, trying to erase the image of Hardenburg's thin, ironic face from his eyeballs. By now new sentries had slowly swung up to their positions behind the guns. One of them was bare-headed. He had blond hair and he was smoking a cigarette. He had opened his collar, warming himself in the heightening sun. He looked very comfortable, lounging with the small of his back against the iron bar, his cigarette dangling from his lips, his hands lightly resting on the gun, which was pointing directly toward Christian.

Well, now, Christian thought heavily, he's missed that chance. Now what is he waiting for? I should have inquired about him. Christian thought, when I had the chance. From Gretchen. What's driving him? What is he after? What turned him so sour? What is the best way to deal with him? Come on, come on, Christian pleaded within him, as two British soldiers, both of them officers, started out from the convoy with shovels and toilet paper in their hands. Come on, give the signal . . .

But Hardenburg didn't move.

Christian felt himself swallowing dryly. He was cold, colder than when he had awakened and he felt his shoulders shaking in little spasms and there was nothing to do about it. His tongue filled his mouth in a puffy lump, and he could taste the sand inside his lip. He looked down at his hand, lying on the breech of his machine pistol, and he tried to move his fingers. They moved slowly and weirdly, as though they were under someone else's control. I won't be able to do it, he thought crazily. He'll give the signal and I'll try to lift the gun and I won't be able to. His eyes burned and he blinked again and again until tears came, and the eighty men below, and the trucks and the fires, all blurred into a wavering mass.

This was too much. Too much. Lying here so long, watching men you were going to kill wake up, cook their breakfast, light cigarettes, go to relieve their bowels. There were fifteen or twenty men now, spread out, away from the trucks, with their trousers down . . . The soldier's regime, in any army . . . If you didn't do it in ten minutes after breakfast you probably wouldn't find time during the rest of the day . . . When you marched off to war, to the drums and the bugles and the flut-tering of banners, down the clean, scrubbed streets, you never realized that what it would mean was lying in wait for ten hours in the cold, cutting sand of a desert that not even the Arabs had ever crossed before, watching twenty Englishmen with their trousers down, squatting over sanitary little holes in the Cyrenaican desert. Let Brandt take *this picture for the Frankfurter Zeitung*.

He heard a curious, lilting sound next to him. He turned slowly. It was Hardenburg chuckling.

Christian turned back, but he closed his eyes. It has to end, he thought, it has to end. The chuckling had to end, the British at their morning labors had to end, Lieutenant Hardenburg had to end, Africa, the sun, the wind, the war . . .

Then there was the noise behind him. He opened his eyes and a moment later he saw the explosion of the mortar shell. He knew that Hardenburg had given the signal. The shell hit right on the blond boy who had been smoking and he disappeared.

The truck started to burn. Shell after shell exploded among the other trucks. The machine guns were pushed over the ridge and opened up, raking the convoy. The little figures seemed to stagger stupidly in all directions. The men who had been squatting at their toilets were pulling at their trousers and running clumsily, tripping and falling, with their buttocks gleaming whitely against the sandy glitter of the desert. One man ran straight at the ridge, as though he didn't know where the firing was coming from. Suddenly he saw the machine guns, when he was no more than a hundred meters away. After a moment of complete, stunned immobility, he turned, holding his trousers up with one hand and tried to get away. Someone casually, as a kind of afterthought, cut him down.

Hardenburg chuckled again and again, between calling out corrections for the mortar. Two shells hit the ammunition truck and it blew up in a wide ball of smoke. Pieces of steel whistled over their heads for a whole minute. Men were lying strewn all over the ground in front of the trucks. A Sergeant seemed to have got about a dozen men together and they started to lumber through the sand toward the ridge, firing wildly from the hip. Someone shot the Sergeant. He fell down and kept shooting from a sitting position until someone else shot him again. He rolled over, his head in the sand.

The squad the Sergeant had led broke and started to run back, but they were all cut down before they got anywhere near the trucks. Two minutes later there was not a single shot coming from the Tommies. The smoke from the burning trucks poured back, away from the ridge, in the stiff wind. Here and there a man moved brokenly, like a squashed bug.

Hardenburg stood up and held up his hand. The firing stopped. "Diestl," he ordered, staring out at the burning trucks and the dead Englishmen, "the machine guns will continue firing."

Christian stood beside him. "What was that, Sir?" he asked dully.

"The machine guns will continue firing."

Christian looked down at the wrecked convoy. By now, except for the flames coming from the trucks, there was no movement visible. "Yes, Sir," Christian said.

"Rake the entire area," Hardenburg said. "We're going down

there in two minutes. I don't want anything left alive there. Understood?"

"Yes, Sir," Christian said. He went over first to the machine gun on the right, and then to the other one and said, "Keep firing, until you are ordered to stop."

The men at the guns gave him a strange, sidelong glance, then shrugged and went to work. In the silence, with not a word being spoken and no shouts or other gunfire to blend with it, the noise of the guns, nervous and irritable, seemed disturbing and out of place. One by one the men who were not handling the guns stood up on the crest of the ridge, watching the bullets skip along the ground, tear at the already dead and the wounded near the trucks, making them jump with eccentric spasms on the windswept sand.

A British soldier lying near one of the breakfast fires was hit. He sat up and threw his head back and screamed. The sound floated up to the ridge, surprising and personal in the methodical rhythm of the guns. The men at the guns stopped firing as the Tommy screamed, his head back, his hands waving blindly in front of him.

"Continue firing!" Hardenburg said sharply.

The guns took up again and the Tommy was hit by both of them. He fell back, his last scream sliced in half by a spurt of bullets in his throat.

The men watched silently, the same look of fascination and horror on all the faces.

Only Hardenburg didn't look like that. His lips were curled, his teeth showing, his breath came in rather hurried, uneven gasps, his eyes were half-closed. Christian tried to remember where he had seen that look before . . . abandoned, lost in pleasure. Then he remembered. Gretchen. When he had made love to her . . . They must be cousins, Christian thought, they really look tremendously alike . . .

The guns went on and on, the even, chattering noise by now almost like the everyday sound of a factory in the next block. Two of the men on the ridge took out cigarettes and lit them, very matter-of-factly, already a little bored with the monotony of the scene.

The life of the soldier, Christian thought, looking at the twitching bodies below. If they had stayed home in England it wouldn't have happened to them. Tomorrow it might be himself lying on the sand and some Cockney from the East Side of London putting a pound of lead into him. He felt a sudden wave of superiority. You felt superior to the Poles and the Czechs and the Russians and the Italians, but most of all you felt superior to the dead. He remembered the handsome, languid young Englishmen who used to come to Austria for the skiing, talking in the cafés in that flat, loud tone that drowned out all other speech in self-assured clamor. He hoped that those young lords were represented today among the officers lying face down in the bloody sand with belly torn and buttocks showing.

Hardenburg waved his hand. "Cease firing," he said.

The guns stopped. The gunner nearest Christian was sweating. He sighed loudly and wiped his face and leaned wearily on the barrel in the quiet.

"Diestl," said Hardenburg.

"Yes, Sir."

"I want five men. And you." Hardenburg started down, sliding a little in the heavy sand, toward the still field below.

Christian motioned to the five men nearest him and they followed the Lieutenant.

Hardenburg walked deliberately, as though he were going to address a parade, toward the trucks. His pistol was in its holster and his hands swung in stiff little arcs at his side. Christian and the others followed just behind him. They came to the Englishman who had foolishly run toward them, holding onto his belt. The Englishman had been hit several times in the chest. His ribs were shattered and sticking in white and red splinters among the blood-soaked rags of his jacket, but he was still alive. He looked up quietly from the sand. Hardenburg took out his pistol, pulled the bolt to load it, and casually shot twice, without taking careful aim, at the Englishman's head. The Englishman's face disappeared. He grunted once. Hardenburg put the pistol back in his holster and strolled on.

Next there was a group of six men. They all seemed to be dead, but Hardenburg said, "Make sure," and Christian fired some shots into them mechanically. He felt nothing.

They reached the line of breakfast fires. Christian observed the careful way in which the tins had been punched with holes to get the best possible results out of the makeshift stoves. God knows how many gallons of tea had been brewed there. There was a heavy smell of tea, and the smell of burned wool and burning rubber, and the smell of roasted flesh from the trucks, where several men had been caught in the fire. One man had jumped out of a truck, all ablaze. He was lying on one elbow, with his blackened and burnt head up in an alert, searching pose. The mortars had hit around here, too, and there were a pair of naked legs torn off at the hips and exploded out of their trousers, mixed with tea and canned corned beef and spilt sugar.

One man had had his head almost severed from his body and he was sitting against a wheel. Christian stared at the lolling head. The face was one of a working man, with strong muscular jaws and that expression of sly stubbornness and surface servility that was so common on British faces. The man had had an upper plate and it was half-hanging out of his mouth, giving a mocking twist to his lips. He was clean-shaven, the jaws red and scraped under the graying hair of his temples. One of the shavers, Christian thought. The neat soldier. One like that in all squads. He needn't have bothered this morning.

Here and there an arm moved, or a groan could be heard. The detail spread out, and the shots came from all over the area. Hardenburg went to the lead car, which had obviously been used by the officer in command of the convoy, and rummaged around inside for papers. He took some maps and some typewritten orders and a photograph of a blonde woman with two children that was tucked in the mapcase. Then he set fire to the car.

He and Christian stood watching the car burn.

"We were lucky," Hardenburg said. "They stopped in just the right place." He grinned, Christian grinned too. This wasn't like the half-farcical approach to Paris. This wasn't the black-marketing and police-work of Rennes. This was what they were here for, this is what the war was like, these dead around him were measurable, substantial, valuable. The Americans were not going to help these Englishmen very much.

"All right," Hardenburg called to the others. "Any you've missed can walk home. Back up the hill."

He and Christian started back. The men on the ridge were outlined against the sky, standing there, watching them. How vulnerable they looked, Christian thought anxiously, how lonely, how much he needed them . . .

They passed the officer lying with his naked buttocks sticking up into the air. The flesh was slender and pale and had a look of surprised aristocracy.

Hardenburg grinned. "Do you remember," Hardenburg asked, "what he looked like, squatting there, worrying about being constipated, when he heard the first shot? And how he looked when he tried to run? Trying to wave and hold up his pants at the same time . . . A Captain in His Majesty's Forces . . . I'll bet they never taught him how to handle a situation like that at Sandhurst!"

Hardenburg laughed. As he laughed, the humor of the recollection struck him more and more forcibly. Finally he had to stop walking and stood still, bent over, his hands on his knees, gasping weakly, his laughter rolling wildly out into the wind.

Christian started to laugh, too, although at first he didn't want to. But then the laughter caught him in its tide, and he rocked helplessly as it swept him. The others, seeing their Lieutenant and Sergeant overcome by laughter, began to laugh, too. First they giggled, then the infection became too strong, and finally all of them, the five men with Christian and Hardenburg, and the men standing next to the guns on the ridge, were roaring together, the sound sweeping over the torn ground, the quiet bodies, the subsiding breakfast fires, the scattered guns, the comic shovels, the burning trucks, the dead man sitting propped up against the wheel, with his head almost off at the ear and the false upper plate dangling from his twisted lips.

CHAPTER ELEVEN

THE TRAIN RATTLED slowly along between the drifts and the white hills of Vermont. Noah sat at the frosted window, with his overcoat on, shivering because the heating system of the car had broken down. He stared out at the slowly changing, forbidding scenery, gray in the cloudy wastes of Christmas dawn. He had not been able to get a berth because the train was crowded, and he felt grimy and stiff. The water had frozen in the men's room and he hadn't been able to shave. He rubbed the stubble on his cheek and knew that it was black and ugly and that his eyes were rimmed with bloodshot red and that there were smoke smudges on his collar. This is a hell of a way, he thought, to present myself to her family.

With each mile he felt more and more uncertain. At one station, where they had stopped for fifteen minutes, there had been another train en route back to New York, and he had had a wild impulse to jump out and climb aboard and rush back to the city. With the discomfort of the journey, the cold and the snoring passengers and the sight of the grim hills breaking out of the cloudy night, more and more of his confidence had left him. Never, he was saying to himself, this will never work.

Hope had gone on ahead to prepare the way. She had been up here for two days now, and by this time she must have told her father that she was going to get married, and that she was going to marry a Jew. It must have gone off all right, Noah thought, forcing himself to be optimistic in the dusty car, otherwise she would have sent me a telegram. She's let me come up here, so it must be all right, it must be . . .

After the Army had rejected him, Noah had, as reasonably as he could, decided to rearrange his life in as rational and useful a way as possible. He had begun to spend three or four evenings a week in the library, reading blueprints for marine-construction work. Ships, they cried in the newspapers and on the radio, ships and more ships. Well, if he couldn't fight, he could at least build. He had never studied a blueprint in his life, and he had only the vaguest notion of what the processes of welding and riveting were; and, according to all authorities, it took months of intensive training for a man to become proficient at any of those things, but he studied with cold fury, memorizing, reciting to himself, making himself draw plans from memory again and again. He was at home with books and he learned quickly. In another month, he felt, he could go into a shipyard and bluff his way onto the scaffolding and earn his keep.

And in the meantime, there was Hope. He felt a little guilty about planning his private happiness at a time when all his friends were going down into the horrors of war, but his abstinence would not bring Hitler to defeat any sooner, nor would the Emperor of Japan surrender any earlier if he, Noah, remained single—and Hope had been insistent.

But she was very fond of her father. He was a devout churchgoer, a hardbitten Presbyterian elder, rooted stubbornly all his life in this harsh section of the world, and she would not marry without his consent. Oh, God, Noah thought, staring across the aisle at a Marine Corporal who was sleeping, sprawled there, with his mouth open and his feet up in the air, Oh, God, why is the world so complicated?

There was a brickyard along the tracks, and a glimpse of one of those tightly-put-together, unpromising white streets with steeples rising at both ends. Then there was Hope, standing on the platform, searching the sliding, frosted windows for his face.

He jumped down from the train before it stopped. He skidded a little on a patch of frozen snow, and nearly dropped the battered imitation-leather bag he was carrying as he fought to hold his balance. An old man who was pushing a trunk said to him testily, "That's ice, young man. Ice. You can't toe-dance on it."

Then Hope hurried up to him. Her face was wan and disturbed. She didn't kiss him. She stopped three feet away from him. "Oh, my, Noah," she said, "you need a shave."

"The water," he said, feeling irritated, "was frozen."

They stood there uncertainly facing each other. Noah looked hastily around to see if she was alone. Two or three other people had got off at the station, but it was early and no one had come to greet them and they were already hurrying off. Aside from the old man with the trunk, Noah and Hope had the station to themselves as the train started to pull out.

It's no good, Noah thought, they've sent her down by herself to break the news.

"Did you have a good trip?" Hope said artificially.

"Very nice," Noah answered. She seemed strange and cold, bundled up in an old mackinaw and a scarf drawn tight over her hair. The northern wind cut across from the frozen hills, slicing through his overcoat as though it were the thinnest cotton.

"Well," Noah said, "do we spend Christmas here?"

"Noah . . ." Hope said softly, her voice trembling with the effort to keep it steady. "Noah, I didn't tell them."

"What?" Noah asked stupidly.

"I didn't tell them. Not anything. Not that you were coming. Not that I wanted to marry you. Not that you're Jewish. Not that you're alive."

Noah swallowed. What a silly, aimless way to spend Christmas, he thought foolishly, looking at the uncelebrating hills.

"That's all right," he said. He didn't know what that meant, but Hope looked so forlorn standing there in her tightly drawn scarf, with her face pinched by the morning cold, that he felt he had to comfort her some way. "That's perfectly all right," he said, in the tone of a host telling a clumsy guest who has dropped a water glass that no great harm has been done. "Don't worry about it."

"I meant to," Hope said. She spoke so low that he had difficulty understanding her, with the wind snatching at her words. "I tried to. Last night, I was on the point . . ." She shook her head. "We came home from church and I thought I would be able to sit down in the kitchen with my father. But my brother came in, he's over from Rutland with his wife and their children, for the holidays. They started to talk about the war, and my brother, he's an idiot anyway, my brother began to say that there were no Jews fighting in the war and they were making all the money, and my father just sat there nodding. I don't know whether he was agreeing or just getting sleepy the way he does at nine o'clock every night, and I just couldn't bring myself . . ."

"That's all right," Noah kept saying stupidly, "that's perfectly all right." He moved his hands vaguely in their gloves because they were getting numb. I must get breakfast soon, he thought, I need some coffee.

"I can't stay here with you," Hope said. "I've got to get back. Everybody was asleep when I left the house, but they'll probably be up by now, and they'll wonder where I am. I've got to go to church with them, and I'll try to get my father alone after church."

"Of course," Noah said, with lunatic briskness. "Exactly the thing to do."

"There's a hotel across the street." Hope pointed to a three-story frame building fifty yards away. "You can go in there and get something to eat and freshen up. I'll come and get you around eleven o'clock. Is that all right?" she asked anxiously.

"Couldn't be better," Noah said. "I'll shave." He smiled brightly, as though he had just thought of some brilliantly clever notion.

"Oh, Noah, darling . . ." She came closer to him, and put her hands in clumsy anguish to his face. "I'm so sorry. I've failed you, I've failed you."

"Nonsense," he said softly, "nonsense." But in his heart he knew she was right. She *had* failed him. He was surprised more than anything else. She had always been so dependable, she had so much courage, she had always been so frank and candid in everything she did with him. But mixed with the disappointment and the hurt at being damaged this way on this cold Christmas morning, he was a little glad that for once she had failed. He was certain that he had failed her again and again and would, from time to time, fail her in the future. There was a juster balance between them now, and there would be something for which he could always forgive her.

"Don't worry, darling." He smiled at her, grimed and weary. "I'm sure it will all be fine. I'll wait for you over there." He gestured toward the hotel. "Go to church. And . . ." he grinned sadly, "pray a couple of prayers for me."

She smiled, near tears, then wheeled and strode away, in her crisp walk that even the heavy overshoes and the uncertain footing underneath could not mar. He watched her disappear around a corner on her way back to the waking house in which her doubtful father and her talkative brother were even now waiting for her. He picked up his bag and made his way across the icy street to the hotel. As he opened the door of the hotel he stopped. Oh, God, he thought, I forgot to wish her Merry Christmas.

It was twelve-thirty before there was a knock on the door of the gray little room with the flaking, painted iron bed and the cracked washstand that Noah had rented for two and a half dollars. That left him three dollars and seventy-five cents to celebrate the holiday with. He had his ticket back to the city though. He had not counted on having to pay for a room. Still, it was not so bad. Meals, he had discovered, were cheap in Vermont. Breakfast had been only thirty-five cents, with two eggs. He had groaned as he had gone wearily over his finances. Aside from war and love and the savage division between Jew and Gentile which had existed for almost 2000 years now until this stony Christmas morning, and the ordinary reluctance of a father to deliver his daughter over to a stranger, there was the weary arithmetic of living through the holiday with less than five dollars in your pocket.

Noah opened the door, composing his face into what he thought was a quiet smile, with which to greet Hope. But it wasn't Hope. It was a wrinkled, red-faced old man who worked for the hotel.

"Lady and gentleman," the man said briefly, "down in the lobby." He turned and sauntered off.

Noah looked anxiously at his face in the mirror, combed his short hair back in three jerky movements, straightened his tie, and left the room. Why, he asked himself as he went uneasily down the creaking stairs that smelled of wax and bacon fat, why would a man in his right mind say yes to me? Three dollars to my name, with an alien religion, and a body that had been discarded as worthless by the government of the republic, and no profession, no real ambition except to live with and love his daughter. No family, no accomplishments, no friends, with a face that must seem harsh and foreign to this man, and a voice that nearly stuttered and was stained with the common accents of bad schools and low company from one end of America to the other. Noah had been in towns like this before and he knew what sort of men grew from them. Proud, private to themselves and their own kind, hard, with family histories that went back as far as the stones and planks of the towns themselves, looking with fear and scorn at the rootless foreign hordes which filled the cities. Noah had never felt more of a stranger anywhere on the long face of the continent than he did at the moment when he stepped down into the hotel lobby from the stairway and saw the man and the girl sitting on the wooden rockers, looking out through the small plateglass window at the frozen street.

The two people stood up when they heard Noah come into the lobby. She's pale, Noah's mind registered, with a sense of catastrophe, very pale. He walked slowly toward the father and daughter. Mr. Plowman was a tall, stooped man, who looked as though he had worked with stone and iron all his life and had risen no later than five in the morning for the last sixty years. He had an angular, reserved face, and weary eyes behind silver-rimmed glasses, and he gave no sign either of welcome or hostility, as Hope said, "Father, this is Noah."

He put his hand out, though. Noah shook it. The hand was tough and horny. I'm not going to beg. Noah thought, no matter what. I'm not going to lie. I'm not going to pretend I'm anything much. If he says yes, fine. If he says no . . . Noah refused to think about that.

"Very glad," her father said, "to make your acquaintance."

They stood in an uneasy group, with the old man who served as clerk watching them with undisguised interest.

"Seems to me," Mr. Plowman said, "might not be a bad idea for myself and Mr. Ackerman to have a little talk."

"Yes," Hope whispered, and the tense, uncertain timbre of her voice made Noah feel that all was lost.

Mr. Plowman looked around the lobby consideringly. "This might not be the best place for it," he said, staring at the clerk, who stared back curiously. "Might take a little walk around town. Mr. Ackerman might like to see the town, anyway."

"Yes, Sir," Noah said.

"I'll wait here," said Hope. She sat down suddenly in the rocker. It creaked alarmingly in the still lobby. The clerk made a severe, disapproving grimace at the sound and Noah was sure that he was going to hear the complaining wooden noise in his bad moments for many years.

"We'll be back in a half hour or so, Daughter," Mr. Plowman said.

Noah winced a little at the "Daughter." It was like a bad play about life on the farm in 1900, and he had an unreal sense of melodrama and heavy contrivance as he held the door open and he and Mr. Plowman went out into the snowy street. He caught a glimpse of Hope sitting behind the window, staring anxiously at them, and then they were walking slowly and deliberately past the closed shop-fronts on the cleared sidewalks, in the harsh, windy cold.

They walked without speaking for almost two minutes, their shoes making a dry crunching on the scraps of snow that the shovels had left on the pavements. Then Mr. Plowman spoke. "How much," he asked, "do they charge you in the hotel?"

"Two-fifty," Noah said.

"For one day?" Mr. Plowman asked.

"Yes."

"Highway robbers," Mr. Plowman said. "All hotelkeepers."

Then he fell back into silence and they walked quietly once more. They walked past Marshall's Feed and Grain store, past the drugstore of F. Kinne, past J. Gifford's Men's Clothing shop, past the law offices of Virgil Swift, past John Harding's butcher shop and Mrs. Walton's Bakery, past the furniture and undertaking establishment of Oliver Robinson, and N. West's grocery store.

Mr. Plowman's face was set and rigid, and as Noah looked from his sharp, quiet features, noncommittally arranged under the oldfashioned Sunday hat, to the storefronts, the names went into his brain like so many spikes driven into a plank by a methodical, impartial carpenter. Each name was an attack. Each name was a wall, an announcement, an arrow, a reproof. Subtly, Noah felt, in an ingenious quiet way, the old man was showing Noah the close-knit, homogeneous world of plain English names from which his daughter sprang. Deviously, Noah felt, the old man was demanding, how will an Ackerman fit here, a name imported from the broil of Europe, a name lonely, careless, un-owned and dispossessed, a name without a father or a home, a name rootless and accidental.

It would have been better to have the brother here, Noah thought, talking, fulminating, with all the old, familiar, ugly, spoken arguments, rather than this shrewd, silent Yankee attack.

They passed the business section, still in silence. A weathered red brick school building reared up across a lawn, covered with dead ivy.

"Went to school there," Mr. Plowman said, with a stiff gesture of his head. "Hope."

A new enemy, Noah thought, looking at the plain old building, crouched behind its oak trees, another antagonist lying in wait for twenty-five years. There was some motto carved into the weathered stone above the portal and Noah squinted to read it. "Ye shall know the truth," the faded letters proclaimed to the generations of Plowmans who had walked under it to learn how to read and write and how their forefathers had set foot on the rock of Plymouth in the blustery weather of the seventeenth century. "Ye shall know the truth, and the truth shall make you free." Noah could almost hear his own father reading the words, the dead voice ringing out of the tomb with rhetorical, flaring relish.

"Cost twenty-three thousand dollars," Mr. Plowman said, "back in 1904. WPA wanted to tear it down and put up a new one in 1935. We stopped that. Waste of the taxpayers' money. Perfectly good school."

They continued walking. There was a church a hundred yards down the road, its steeple rising slender and austere into the morning sky. That's where it's going to happen, Noah thought despairingly. This is the shrewdest weapon coming up. There are probably six dozen Plowmans buried in that yard, and I'm going to be told in their presence.

The church was made of white wood and lay delicately and solidly on its sloping snowy lawns. It was balanced and reserved and did not cry out wildly to God, like the soaring cathedrals of the French and the Italians, but rather addressed Him in measured, plain terms, brief, dryly musical, and to the point.

"Well," said Mr. Plowman while the church was still fifty yards away, "we've probably gone far enough." He turned. "Like to go back?"

"Yes," Noah said. He was dazed and puzzled, and walked automatically, almost unseeingly, as they started back toward the hotel. The blow had not fallen yet, and there was no indication when it would fall. He glanced at the old man's face. There was a look of concentration and puzzlement there, among the granite lines, and Noah felt that he was searching painfully in his mind for the proper, cold, thoughtful words with which to dismiss his daughter's lover, words that would be fair but decisive, reasonable but final.

"You're doing an awful thing, young fellow," Mr. Plowman said, and Noah felt his jaw grow rigid as he prepared to fight. "You're putting an old man to the test of his principles. I won't deny it. I wish to God you would turn around and get on the

193

train and go back to New York and never see Hope again. You won't do that, will you?" He peered shrewdly at Noah.

"No," said Noah. "I won't."

"Didn't think you would. Wouldn't've been up here in the first place if you would." The old man took a deep breath, stared at the cleared pavements before his feet, as he walked slowly at Noah's side. "Excuse me if I've given you a pretty glum walk through town," he said. "A man goes a good deal of his life living more or less automatically. But every once in a while, he has to make a real decision. He has to say to himself, now, what do I really believe, and is it good or is it bad? The last forty-five minutes you've had me doing that, and I'm not fond of you for it. Don't know any Jews, never had any dealings with them. I had to look at you and try to decide whether I thought Jews were wild, howling heathen, or congenital felons, or whatever . . . Hope thinks you're not too bad, but young girls've made plenty of mistakes before. All my life I thought I believed one man was born as good as another, but thank God I never had to act on it till this day. Anybody else show up in town asking to marry Hope, I'd say, 'Come out to the house. Virginia's got turkey for dinner . . .' "

They were in front of the hotel now. Noah hadn't noticed it, listening to the old man's earnest voice, but the door of the hotel opened and Hope came quickly out. The old man stopped and wiped his mouth reflectively as his daughter stood there staring at him, her face worried and set-looking.

Noah felt as though he had been confined to a sickbed for weeks, and the list of names on the storefronts, the Kinnes and Wests and Swifts marshalled behind him, and the name on the tombstones in the churchyard, and the cold unrelenting church itself, and the deliberate voice of the old man, suddenly, all together, with the pale, harrowed sight of Hope herself, became intolerable. He had a vision of his warm, tumbled room near the river, with the books and the old piano, and he longed for it with an aching intensity.

"Well?" Hope said.

"Well," her father said slowly. "I just been telling Mr. Ackerman, there's turkey for dinner."

Slowly, Hope's face broke into a smile. She leaned over and kissed her father. "What in Heaven took so long?" she asked, and, dazedly, Noah knew it was going to be all right, although at the moment he was too spent and weary to feel anything about it.

"Might as well take your things, young man," Mr. Plowman said. "No sense giving those robbers all your money."

"Yes," Noah said. "Yes, of course." He moved slowly and dreamily up the steps into the hotel. He opened the door and looked back. Hope was holding her father's arm. The old man was grinning. It was a little forced and a little painful, but it was a grin.

"Oh," said Noah, "I forgot. Merry Christmas."

Then he went in to get his bag.

CHAPTER TWELVE

THE DRAFT BOARD was in a large bare loft over a Greek restaurant. The smell of frying oil and misused fish swept up in waves. The floor was dirty. There were only two bare lights glaring down on the rickety wooden camp chairs and the cluttered desks with the two plain secretaries boredly typing forms. A composition wall divided the waiting room from the section where the board was meeting, and a hum of voices filtered through. There were about a dozen people sitting on the camp chairs, grave, almost middle-aged men in good business suits, an Italian boy in a leather jacket with his mother, several young couples, holding hands defensively. They all look, Michael thought, as though they are at bay, resentful, bitter, staring at the frayed paper American flag and the mimeographed and printed announcements on the walls.

They all sit, Michael thought, like people with dependents or deferable physical ailments. And their women, the wives and mothers, glared accusingly at all the other men, as though they were on the verge of saying, "I can see through you. You're in perfect health and you have plenty of money hidden away in the vault, and you want my son or my husband to go instead of you. Well, you're not going to get away with it."

The door from the board room opened, and a small dark-eyed boy came out with his mother. The mother was crying and the boy was red-faced, half-angry, half-frightened. Everyone in the room looked at him, coldly and measuringly, already seeing the still form on the battlefield, the white wood cross, the Western Union messenger ringing the doorbell with the telegram in his hand. There was no pity in their glances, only a harsh satisfaction that seemed to say, "Well, there's one son of a bitch that didn't fool them."

There was a buzz from the machine on the desk of one of the secretaries. She stood up and looked bleakly out across the room. "Michael Whitacre," she called. Her voice was rasping and bored. She was an ugly girl with a large nose and a great

195

deal of lipstick. Michael noticed, as he stood up, that her legs were bowed and her stockings were crooked and wrinkled.

"Whitacre," she called again, her voice bristling and impatient. He waved to her and smiled. "Control yourself, darling," he said. "I'm on my way."

She stared at him with cold superiority. Michael couldn't blame her. Added to the automatic insolence of a government employee was the heady sense of power that she was sending men out to die for her, who obviously had never had a man look kindly at her in her life. Each oppressed minority, Negroes, Mormons, Nudists, loveless women, Michael thought as he approached the door, to its own peculiar compensations. It would take a saint to behave well on a draft board.

As he opened the door, Michael noticed with surprise that he was trembling a little. Ridiculous, he thought, annoyed with himself, as he faced the seven men sitting at the long table. They swung around and looked at him. Their faces were the other side of the draftee's coin. To match the fear and resentment and argument waiting in the outside room, here were unrelenting suspicion, shrewd, constantly reinforced hardness. There isn't one of them, Michael thought, staring unsmilingly at their unwelcoming faces, that I would ever talk to under any other circumstances. My neighbors. Who picked them? Where did they come from? What made them so eager to send their fellow-citizens off to war?

"Sit down, please, Mr. Whitacre," said the chairman. He motioned glumly to the vacant chair at the head of the table. He was an old man, fat, with a face that had heavy, cold dewlaps, and angry, peering eyes. Even when he said "Please," there was a peremptory challenge in his voice. What war, Michael thought, as he walked to his chair, did you fight in?

The other faces swung around at him, like the guns of a cruiser preparing for a bombardment. Amazing, Michael thought, as he sat down, I've lived in this neighborhood for ten years and I've never seen a single one of these faces before. They must have been lying in wait, lurking secretly in the cellars, for this moment.

There was an American flag on the long wall behind the board, real cloth this time, a garish spot of color in the drab room, behind the gray and blue business suits of the board and their yellow complexions. Michael had a sudden vision of thousands of such rooms all over the country, thousands of such graying, cold-faced, suspicious men with the flag behind their balding heads, facing thousands of resentful, captured boys. It was probably the key scene of the moment, 1942's most common symbol, the lines of terror and violence and guile brought to this single point, shabby, loveless, with only the promise of

196

wounds and death to add any stature or nobility to the proceedings.

"Now, Mr. Whitacre," the chairman said, fumbling nearsightedly with a dossier, "you claim a 3A exemption here because of dependency." He peered at Michael angrily, as though he had just said "Where is the gun with which you shot the deceased?"

"Yes," Michael said.

"We have found out," the chairman said loudly, "that you are not living with your wife." He looked triumphantly around him, and several of the other members of the board nodded eagerly.

"We are divorced," Michael said.

"Divorced!" the chairman said. "Why did you hide that fact?"

"Look," Michael said, "I'm going to save you a lot of time. I'm going to enlist."

"When?"

"As soon as the play I'm working on is put on."

"When will that be?" a little fat man at the other end of the table asked in a sour voice.

"Two months," said Michael. "I don't know what you down on that paper, but I have to provide for my mother and father, and I have to pay alimony . . ."

"Your wife," the chairman said bitterly, looking down at the papers before him, "makes five hundred and fifty dollars a week . . ."

"When she works," Michael said.

"She worked thirty weeks last year," the chairman said.

"That's right," Michael said wearily. "And not a week this year."

"Well," said the chairman, with a wave, "we have to consider the probable earnings. She's worked for the last five years and there's no reason to suppose she won't continue. Also," he glared down once more at the papers in front of him, "you claim your mother and father as dependents."

"Yes," said Michael, sighing.

"Your father, we have discovered, has a pension of sixty-eight dollars a month."

"That's right," said Michael. "Have you ever tried to support two people on sixty-eight dollars a month?"

"Everybody," said the chairman with dignity, "has to expect to make some sacrifices at a time like this."

"I'm not going to argue with you," said Michael. "I told you I'm going to enlist in two months."

"Why?" said a man down at the other end. He peered glitteringly through pince-nez glasses at Michael, as though ready to ferret out this last subterfuge.

Michael looked around him at the seven glowering faces. He grinned. "I don't know why," he said. "Do you?"

"That will be all, Mr. Whitacre," the chairman said.

Michael got up and walked out of the room. He felt the eyes of all seven men on him, angry, resentful. They feel cheated, he realized suddenly, they would have much preferred to trap me into it. They were all prepared.

The people waiting in the outside room looked up at him, surprised, because he had come out so quickly. He grinned at them. He wanted to make a joke, but it would be too cruel to the taut, harried boys waiting so painfully.

"Good night, darling," he said to the ugly girl behind the desk. He couldn't resist that. She looked at him with the unbreakable superiority of the person who will not be called upon to die over the man who may.

Michael was still smiling as he started down the steps through the thick fumes of the Greek cuisine, but he felt depressed. The first day, he thought, I should have gone in the first day. I shouldn't've exposed myself to a scene like that. He felt soiled and suspect as he walked slowly through the mild late winter night, among the strolling couples oblivious to the tattered, shabby war being fought between one soul and another, in their name, in the dirty loft over the Greek restaurant half a block away.

Two mornings later, when he went down for his mail, there was a card from his draft board. "As per your request," it read, "you will be reclassified as 1A on May 15." He laughed as he read it. They have salvaged victory out of the ruins of their campaign, he thought. But he felt relieved as he went upstairs again in the elevator. There were no more decisions to be made.

CHAPTER THIRTEEN

NOAH OPENED HIS EYES in the soft dawn light and looked at his wife. She sleeps, he thought, as though she were keeping a secret. Hope, he thought, Hope, Hope. She must have been one of those grave little girls, walking through that white clapboard town, always looking as though she was hurrying to some private destination. She probably had little caches of things stuffed away in the odd corners of her room, too. Feathers, dried flowers, old fashion plates from *Harper's Bazaar,* drawings of women with bustles, that sort of thing. You didn't know anything about little girls. Would be different if you had sisters. Your wife came to you out of a locked vault of experience. Might just as well have come from the mountains of Tibet or a French nunnery. While he was smoking cigarettes under the roof at Colonel Drury's Military Academy for Boys, We Take the Boy and Return the Man, what was she doing, walking gravely past the churchyard with all the Plowmans tucked in under the old grass? If there was a plan to anything, she was preparing for him then, preparing for this moment of sleeping beside him in the dawn light. And he had been preparing for her. If there was a plan. Impossible to believe. If Roger hadn't somehow met her (how *did* he meet her? Must ask). If Roger hadn't half-ironically decided to have a party to get him a girl. If Roger had brought one of the dozen other girls he knew, they wouldn't be lying here together this morning. Accident, the only law of life. Roger. "You make time and you make love dandy. You make swell molasses candy. But honey, are you makin' any money. That's all I want to know." Caught in the Philippines, Bataan, if he had lived that long. And here they were in Roger's room, in Roger's bed, because it was more comfortable. Noah's old bed slanted to the right. It all started when he reached up to the copy of Yeats' *The Herne's Egg and Other Plays* on the library shelf. If he had reached for another book, he wouldn't've bumped into Roger and he wouldn't have lived here and he wouldn't've met Hope and she probably would be lying in another bed now, with another man watching her, thinking, I love her, I love her. If you thought about it you stared into the shouting pit of madness. No plan to anything. No plan to loving or dying or fighting or anything. The equation: Man plus his intentions equals Accident. Impossible to believe. The plan must be there, but cleverly camouflaged, the way a good playwright disguises his plot. At the moment you die perhaps everything is clear to you, you say, oh, now I see, that's why that character was introduced in the first act.

Bataan. Hard to think of Roger saying "Yes, Sir" to anybody. Hard to think of Roger in a helmet. Always thought of him with that tipped, broken, brown felt hat across his head. Hard to think of Roger in a muddy hole. Hard to think of a man who could play Beethoven on the piano being shelled in the jungle. Hard to think of Roger losing, even in a war. Roger was a born victor, because victory in anything never seemed very important to him, it amused him. Hard to think of Roger being torn apart by a mortar shell, screaming, or falling with machine-gun bullets in his chest. Hard to think of Roger surrendering. "Oh, my God," you could imagine him saying, grinning crookedly at the Jap who made the request, "are you kidding?" Hard to think of Roger's grave under the palm trees,

Roger's skull laid bare by time in the jungle mold. Had Roger ever kissed Hope? Probably. How many other men? The secret face on the pillow. The locked vault. How many men had she wanted, and what visions had she manufactured as she lay waiting in her single bed in Vermont and Brooklyn? And how many of the other men lay dead in the Pacific? And how many of the others, boys and men had she touched, longed for, had unspeakable dreams about, were walking alive now and would be dead this year or next somewhere in the world?

What time was it? Six-fifteen. Another five minutes in bed. This was going to be a kind of holiday today. No nervous thunder of the riveters, no wind on the scaffolds, none of the hiss and flare of the welders in the shipyard in Passaic. He had to go to his draft board today, and once more to Governor's Island to be examined. The system kept repeating itself, like a bankteller with a bad memory, adding the same line of figures over and over again. Once more the Wassermann, once more the careless finger pressing the testicles, "Cough," no hernia, once more the bored psychiatrist. "Have you ever had relations with men?" What a degrading way to phrase that question. The Army's belief that relations with your fellowman could only be unnatural. What about his relations with Roger, and Vincent Moriarity, the foreman on his shift at the shipyard, who bought him beers and boasted that he pulled down the British flag over the post office in Dublin, Easter week, 1916? What about his relations with his wife's father, who had sent him his own edition of the collected works of Emerson as a wedding gift? What of his relations with his own father, who had wandered half across the world from Odessa, full of lust and lies and prophecy, and who now was a small box of ashes neglected on a mausoleum shelf in California? What of his relations with Hitler and Roosevelt, with Thomas Jefferson and Shakespeare, with Colonel Drury in the crumbling gray buildings outside Detroit, who drank a quart of bourbon every afternoon, who had once told the graduating class, "There is only one virtue. Courage. I am not interested in a man who is not quick to take offense." What of his relations to his own son, not yet conceived, but latent and attendant here in this dawn bed between Hope and himself? Would his son be quick to take offense? Offense at what? Who would give him offense and what the cause and how decided? Was there a grave waiting for him somewhere, too, on some far island? Was there a bullet, not yet made, that would bring down his son, not yet born? Was there an unconceived soul somewhere on another continent, who later in the century would peer out across rifle sights at the heart of his son? And what God would the minister address at the funeral service? Christ, Jehovah, Who? Maybe an uneasy double address, like a careful gambler's hedged bet. "To

200

Whatever God It May Concern—kindly accept this dead boy into Whatever Hereafter You happen to run." Ridiculous to lie here next to a girl you have just scarcely married, worrying about how your child, who has not yet announced his coming, is going to be buried. Other problems, though, before that. Would he be christened? Would he be circumcised? "You circumcised dog!" in *Ivanhoe*, in the first term in high school. In Budapest, in the pogroms, when the Revolutionary Government was overthrown in 1920, the crowds tore down the trousers of suspected Jews and murdered every male who had been circumcised. The poor Christians who had had it done for sanitary reasons. Probably hated the Jews as heartily as any of their executioners, and yet there they were, dying in that approximate hatred. Must stop thinking about the Jews. If you let yourself fall into a reverie, on no matter what subject, it finally came around to that. Wonder if there was ever a time when a Jew could avoid that? What century? The fifth century before Christ, perhaps.

Six-twenty. Time to get up. The doctors were waiting on the green island, the ferry with the General's name, the x-ray technicians, the rubber stamp with Rejected on it. What did they do in older wars? Before x-ray. How many men fought at Shiloh with scars on their lungs, all unknowing? How many men came to Borodino with stomach ulcers? How many at Thermopylae who would be turned back by their draft boards today for curvature of the spine? How many 4F's perished outside Troy? Time to get up.

Hope stirred beside him. She turned to him and put her arm across his chest. She came slowly out from the backstage of sleep and ran her hand lightly, in half-slumbering possession, down her ribs and his stomach.

"Bed," she murmured, still in the grip of the last dream, and he grinned at her and gathered her close to him.

"What time is it?" she whispered, her lips close to his ear. "Is it morning? Do you have to go?"

"It's morning," he said. "And I have to go. But," and he smiled as he said it, and pressed the familiar, slender body, "but I think the government can wait another fifteen minutes."

Hope was washing her hair when she heard the key in the lock. She had come home from work and seen that Noah hadn't returned yet from Government's Island, and she had puttered around the house, without switching on a lamp, in the summer twilight, waiting for him to get back.

With her head bent over the basin, and the soapy water dripping onto her closed eyelids, she heard Noah come into the big room.

"Noah," she called, "I'm in here," and she wrapped a towel

around her head and turned to him, naked except for that. His face was sober and controlled. He held her loosely, gently touching the base of her neck, still wet from the rinsing.

"It happened," she said.

"Yes," he said.

"The x-ray?"

"Didn't show anything, I guess." His voice was remote and calm.

"Did you tell them?" she asked. "About the last time?"

"No."

She wanted to ask why not, but she stopped herself, because in a confused, intuitive way, she knew.

"You didn't tell them that you had a defense job, either, did you?"

"No."

"I'll tell them," she said loudly. "I'll go down myself. A man with scars on his lungs can't be . . ."

"Sssh," he said. "Sssh."

"It's silly," she said, trying to talk reasonably, like a debater. "What good will a sick man do in the Army? You'll only crack up. It'll just be another burden for them. They can't make you a soldier . . ."

"They can try." Noah smiled slowly. "They sure can try. The least I can do is give them a chance. Anyway," and he kissed her behind the ear, "anyway, they've already done it. I was sworn in at eight o'clock tonight."

She pulled back. "What're you doing here then?"

"Two weeks," he said. "They give you two weeks to settle your affairs."

"Will it do any good," Hope asked, "for me to argue with you?"

"No," he said very softly.

"Goddamn them!" Hope said. "Why don't they get things straight the first time? Why," she cried, addressing the draft boards and the Army doctors and the regiments in the field and the politicians in all the capitals of the world, addressing the war and the time and all the agony ahead of her, "why can't they behave like sensible human beings?"

"Sssh," Noah said. "We only have two weeks. Let's not waste them. Have you eaten yet?"

"No," she said. "I'm washing my hair."

He sat down on the edge of the tub, smiling wearily at her. "Finish your hair," he said, "and we'll go out to dinner. There's a place I heard about on Second Avenue where they have the best steaks in the world. Three dollars apiece, but they're . . ."

She threw herself down at his knees and held him tightly. "Oh, darling," she said, "oh, darling . . ."

He stroked her bare shoulder as though he were trying to

memorize it. "For the next two weeks," he said, his voice almost not trembling, "we will go on a holiday. That's how we'll settle my affairs." He grinned at her. "We'll go up to Cape Cod and swim and we'll hire bicycles and we'll eat only three-dollar steaks at every meal. Please, please, darling, stop crying."

Hope stood up. She blinked twice. "All right," she said. "It's stopped. I won't cry again. It'll take me fifteen minutes to get ready. Can you wait?"

"Yes," he said. "But hurry. I'm starved."

She took the towel off her head and finished washing her hair. Noah sat on the edge of the tub and watched her. From time to time Hope got glimpses of his drawn, thin face in the mirror. She knew that she was going to remember the way his face looked then, lost and loving as he sat perched on the porcelain rim, in the cluttered, garishly lit room, remember for a long, long time.

They had their two weeks on Cape Cod. They stayed at an aggressively clean tourist house with an American flag on a pole on the lawn in front of it. They ate clam chowder and broiled lobster for dinner. They lay on the pale sand and swam in the dancing, cold water and went to the movies religiously at night, without commenting on the newsreels to each other, without saying anything about the charging, tremulous voices describing death and defeat and victory on the flickering screen. They rented bicycles and rode slowly along the seaside roads and laughed when a truckload of soldiers passed and whistled at Hope's pretty legs, and called to Noah, "Pretty soft, Bud. What's your draft number, Bud? We'll see you soon!"

Their noses peeled and their hair got sticky with salt, and their skin, when they went to bed at night, smelled ocean-fragrant and sunny in the immaculate sheets of the shingled cottage in which they lived. They hardly spoke to anyone else, and the two weeks seemed to stretch through the summer, through the year, through every summer they had ever known, and all time seemed to go in a gentle spiral on sandy roads, between scrub firs, in a gleam of summer light on brisk waves and under the stars of cool summer evenings stirred by a holiday wind that came off the Vineyard and off Nantucket and off a sunny ocean disturbed only by gulls and the sails of small boats and the splash of flying fish playing in the water.

Then the two weeks were up and they went back to the city. The people there seemed pallid and wilted, defeated by the summer, and they felt healthy and powerful in comparison.

The final morning, Hope made coffee for them at six o'clock. They sat across from each other, sipping the hot, bitter liquid out of the huge cups that were their first joint domestic investment. Hope walked with Noah down the quiet, shining streets, still cool with the memory of night, to the drab unpainted store that had been taken over by the draft board.

They kissed, thoughtfully, already remote from each other, and Noah went in to join the quiet group of boys and men who were gathered around the desk of the middle-aged man who was serving his country in its hour of need by waking early twice a month to give the last civilian instructions and the tickets for the free subway ride to the groups of men departing from the draft board for the war.

Noah went out in the shuffling, self-conscious line, with the fifty others, and walked with them the three blocks to the subway station. The people on the street, going about their morning business, on their way to their shops and offices, on their way to the day's marketing and the day's cooking and money-making, looked at them with curiosity and a little awe, as the natives of a town might look at a group of pilgrims from another country who happen to pass through their streets, on their journey to an obscure and fascinating religious festival.

Noah saw Hope across the street from the entrance to the subway station. She was standing in front of a florist's shop. The florist was an old man slowly putting out pots of geraniums and large blue vases of gladioli in the windows behind her. She had on a blue dress dotted with white flowers. The morning wind brushed it softly against her body in front of the blossoms shining through the glass behind her. Because of the sun reflecting from the glass, Noah could not tell what her face was like. He started to cross the street to her, but the leader that the man at the draft board had assigned to the group called anxiously, "Please, boys, stick together, please," and Noah thought, what could I tell her, what could she tell me? He waved to her. She waved back, a single, lifting gesture of the bare brown arm. In the shadow she created with the movement, Noah could see she wasn't crying.

What do you know, he said to himself, she isn't crying. And he went down into the subway, between a boy named Tempesta and a thirty-five-year-old Spaniard whose name was Nuncio Aguilar.

CHAPTER FOURTEEN

THE RED-HEADED WOMAN he hadn't kissed four years ago leaned over, smiling, in Michael's last dream and kissed him. He awoke, warmly remembering the dream and the red-headed woman.

The morning sun angled past the sides of the closed Venetian blinds, framing the windows in a golden dust. Michael stretched.

Outside the room he heard the murmur of the seven million people walking through the streets and corridors of the city. Michael got up. He padded over on the carpeted floor to the window and pulled up the blinds.

The sun filled the back gardens with an early summer wealth, soft and buttery on the faded brick of the old buildings, on the dusty ivy, on the bleached striped awnings of the small terraces filled with rattan furniture and potted plants. A little round woman, in a wide orange hat and old fat slacks that clung cheerfully to her round behind, was standing over a potted geranium on the terrace directly across from Michael. She reached thoughtfully down and snipped off a blossom. Her hat shook sorrowfully as she looked at the mortal flower in her hand. Then she turned and walked through curtained French windows into her house, her cheerful behind shaking, middle-aged and healthy, in her city garden.

Michael grinned, pleased that it was sunny, and that the red-headed woman had finally kissed him, and that there was a fat little woman with an absurd sweet behind mourning over faded geraniums on the other side of the sunny back gardens.

He washed, dousing himself with cold water, then walked barefoot, in his pajamas, across the carpeted floor through the living room, to the front door. He opened it and picked up the *Times*.

In the polite print of the *Times*, which always reminded Michael of the speeches of elderly and successful corporation lawyers, the Russians were dying but holding on the front page, there were new fires along the French coast from English bombs, Egypt was reeling, somebody had discovered a new way to make rubber in seven minutes, three ships had sunk quietly into the Atlantic Ocean, the Mayor had come out against meat, married men could be expected to be called up into the Army, the Japanese were in a slight lull.

Michael closed the door. He sank onto the couch and turned away from the blood on the Volga, the drowned men of the Atlantic, the sand-blinded troops of Egypt, from the rumors of rubber and the flames in France and the restrictions on roast beef, to the sporting page. The Dodgers, steadfast—though weary and full of error—had passed through another day of war and thousand-edged death, and despite some nervousness down the middle of the diamond and an attack of wildness in the eighth, had won in Pittsburgh.

The phone rang and he went into the bedroom and picked it up.

"There's a glass of orange juice in the icebox," Peggy's voice came over the wire. "I thought you'd like to know."

"Thanks," Michael said. "I noticed some dust on the books on the right-hand shelves, though, Miss Freemantle . . ."

"Nuts," Peggy said.

"There's a lot in what you say," Michael said, delighted with Peggy's voice, familiar and full of pleasure over the phone. "Are they working you hard?"

"The flesh off the bones. You were taking it mighty easy when I left. Flat on your back, with all the covers off. I kissed you good-bye."

"What a nice girl you are. What did I do?"

There was a little pause and then, for a moment, Peggy's voice was sober and a little troubled. "You put your hands over your face and you mumbled, 'I won't, I won't . . .'"

The little half-smile that had been playing about Michael's face died. He rubbed his ear thoughtfully. "The sleeping man betrays us unashamed morning after morning."

"You sounded frightened," Peggy said. "It frightened me."

"'I won't, I won't,'" Michael said reflectively. "I don't know what it was I wouldn't . . . Anyway, I'm not frightened now. The morning's bright, the Dodgers won, my girl made me orange juice . . ."

"What're you going to do today?" Peggy asked.

"Nothing much. Wander around. Look at the sky. Look at the girls. Drink a little. Make my will . . ."

"Oh, shut up!" Peggy's voice was serious.

"Sorry," Michael said.

"Are you glad I called you?" Peggy's voice was consciously a little coquettish now.

"Well I suppose there was no way of avoiding it," Michael said languidly.

"You know what you can do."

"Peggy!"

She laughed. "Do I get dinner tonight?"

"What do you think?"

"I think I get dinner. Wear your gray suit."

"It's practically worn through at the elbows."

"Wear your gray suit. I like it."

"O.K."

"What'll I wear?" For the first moment in the conversation Peggy's voice became uncertain, little girlish, worried.

Michael laughed softly.

"What're you laughing at?" Peggy asked harshly.

"Say it again. Say 'What'll I wear?' again for me."

"Why?"

"Because it makes me laugh and remember you and makes

206

me sorry and tender for you and all women living to hear you say, 'What'll I wear?' "

"My," said Peggy, very pleased, "you got out of the right side of the bed this morning, didn't you?"

"I certainly did."

"What'll I wear? The blue print or the beige suit with the cream blouse or the . . ."

"The blue print."

"It's *so* old."

"The blue print."

"All right. Hair up or down?"

"Down."

"But . . ."

"Down!"

"God," Peggy said, "I'll look like something you dragged out of the Harlem River. Aren't you afraid some of your friends'll see us?"

"I'll take my chances," Michael said.

"And don't drink too much . . ."

"Now, Peggy . . ."

"You'll be going around saying good-bye to all your good friends . . ."

"Peggy, on my life . . ."

"They'll pour you into the Army from a bucket. Be careful."

"I'll be careful."

"Glad I called?" Peggy sounded again like a flirtatious girl languishing behind a fan at the high-school prom.

"I'm glad you called," Michael said.

"That's all I wanted to know. Drink your orange juice." And she hung up.

Michael put the receiver down slowly, smiling, remembering Peggy. He sat for a moment, thinking of her.

Then he got up and went out through the living room to the kitchen. He put some water on to boil and measured out three heaping spoonsful of coffee, his nose grateful for the ever-beautiful smell of the coffee imprisoned in the can. He drank his orange juice in long cold gulps, between getting out bacon and the eggs and cutting the bread for toast. He hummed wordlessly as he prepared his breakfast. He liked making his own breakfasts, private in his single house, with his pajamas flapping about him and the floor cool under his bare feet. He put five strips of bacon in a large pan and set a small flame going under it.

The telephone rang in the bedroom.

"Oh, Hell," Michael said. He moved the bacon pan off the flame and walked through the living room, noticing almost unconsciously, as he did again and again, what a pleasant room it was, with its high ceilings and broad windows facing each other, and the books piled into the bookcases all over the room, with the faded spectrum of the publishers' linen covers making a subtle and lovely pattern, wavering along the walls.

Michael picked up the phone and said, "Hello."

"Hollywood, California, calling Mr. Whitacre."

"This is Mr. Whitacre."

Then Laura's voice, across the continent, still deep and artful. "Michael? Michael, darling . . ."

Michael sighed a little. "Hello, Laura."

"It's seven o'clock in the morning in California," Laura said, a little accusingly. "I got up at seven in the morning to speak to you."

"Thanks," Michael said.

"I heard about it," Laura said vehemently. "I think it's awful. Making you a private."

Michael grinned. "It's not so awful. There're a lot of people in the same boat."

"Almost everybody out here," Laura said, "is at least a Major."

"I know," Michael said. "Maybe that's a good reason for being a private."

"Stop being so damned special!" Laura snapped. "You'll never be able to make it. I know what your stomach's like."

"My stomach," Michael said gravely, "will just have to join the Army with the rest of me."

"You'll be sorry the day after tomorrow."

"Probably." Michael nodded.

"You'll be in the guardhouse in two days," Laura said loudly. "A Sergeant'll say something you don't like and you'll hit him. I know you."

"Listen," Michael said patiently. "Nobody hits Sergeants. Not me or anybody else."

"You haven't taken an order from anybody in your whole life, Michael. I know you. That was one of the reasons it was impossible to live with you. After all, I lived with you for three years and I know you better than any . . ."

"Yes, Laura, darling," Michael said patiently.

"We may be divorced and all that," Laura went on rapidly, "but there's no one in the whole world I'm fonder of. You know that."

"I know that," Michael said, believing her.

"And I don't want to see you killed." She began to cry.

"I won't be killed," Michael said gently.

"And I hate to think of you being ordered around. It's wrong . . ."

Michael shook his head, wondering once again at the gap between the real world and a woman's version of the world. "Don't you worry about me, Laura, darling," he said. "And it was very sweet of you to call me."

208

"I've decided something," Laura said firmly. "I'm not going to take any more of your money."

Michael sighed. "Have you got a job?"

"No. But I'm seeing MacDonald at MGM this afternoon, and ..."

"O.K. When you work, you don't take any money. That's fine." Michael rushed past the point, not letting Laura speak. "I read in the paper you're going to get married. That true?"

"No. Maybe after the war. He's going into the Navy. He's going to work in Washington."

"Good luck," Michael murmured.

"There was an assistant director from Republic they took right into the Air Corps. First Lieutenant. He won't leave Santa Anita for the duration. Public relations. And you're going to be a private ..."

"Please, Laura darling," Michael said. "This call will cost you five hundred dollars."

"You're a queer, stupid man and you always were."

"Yes, darling."

"Will you write me where they station you?"

"Yes."

"I'll come and visit you."

"That will be wonderful." Michael had a vision of his beautiful ex-wife in her mink coat and her almost famous face and figure, waiting outside Fort Sill, Oklahoma, with the soldiers whistling at her as they went past, while he rushed from a formation to meet her.

"I feel all mixed up about you." Laura was crying softly and honestly. "I always did and I always will."

"I know what you mean." Michael remembered the way Laura looked fixing her hair in front of a mirror and how she looked dancing and the holidays they'd had. For a moment he was moved by the distant tears, and regretted the lost years behind him, the years without war, the years without separations ...

"What the hell," he said softly. "They'll probably put me in an office some place."

"You won't let them," she sobbed. "I know you. You won't let them."

"You don't let the Army do anything. It does what it wants and you do what it wants. The Army isn't Warner Brothers, darling."

"Promise me ... promise me ..." The voice rose and fell and then there was a click and the connection was cut off. Michael looked at the phone and put it down.

Finally he got up and went into the kitchen and finished making his breakfast. He carried the bacon and eggs and toast and coffee, black and thick, into the living room and put it down on the wide table set in front of the great sunny window.

He turned the radio on. Brahms was being played, a piano concerto. The music poured out of the machine, round, disputatious and melancholy.

He ate slowly, smearing marmalade thickly on the toast, enjoying the buttery taste of the eggs and the strong taste of the coffee, proud of his cooking, listening with pleasure to the mournful sweet thunder of the radio.

He opened the *Times* to the theatrical pages. It was full of rumors of endless plays and endless actors. Each morning he read the theatrical page of the *Times* with growing depression. Each morning the recital of baffled hope and money lost and sorrowful critical reproach of his profession made him feel a little silly and restless.

He pushed the paper aside and lit the day's first cigarette and took the last sip of coffee. He turned the radio off. It was playing Respighi by now, anyway, and Respighi quit the morning air with a dying fall and left the sunlit house in fragrant silence as Michael sat at the breakfast table, smoking, staring dreamily out at the gardens and the diagonal glimpse of street and working people below.

After awhile, he got up and shaved and showered.

Then he put on a pair of old flannels and a soft old blue shirt, gently and beautifully faded from many launderings. Most of his clothes were already packed away, but there were still two jackets hanging in the closet. He stood there thoughtfully, trying to make up his mind for a moment, then picked the gray jacket, and put it on. It was a worn old jacket, soft and light on his shoulders.

Downstairs his car was waiting at the curb, its paint and chromium glistening from the garage's industry. He started the motor and pushed the button for the top. The top came down slowly and majestically. Michael felt the usual touch of amusement at the grave collapsing movement.

He drove up Fifth Avenue slowly. Every time he rode up through the city on a working day, he felt once again some of the same slightly malicious pleasure he had experienced the first day he had driven in his first, brand-new car, top down, up the Avenue, at noon, looking at the working men and women thronging to their lunches, and feeling wealthy and noble and free.

Michael drove up the broad street, between the rich windows, frivolous and wealthy and elegantly suggestive in the sun.

Michael left his car at the door of Cahoon's apartment house, giving the keys to the doorman. Cahoon was going to use the car and take care of it until Michael returned. It would have been more sensible to sell the car, but Michael had a superstitious feeling that the bright little machine was a token of his gayest civilian days, long rides in the country in the springtime, and careless holidays, and that he must somehow preserve it as a charm against his return.

On foot, feeling a little bereft, he walked slowly across town. The day stretched ahead of him with sudden emptiness. He went into a drugstore and called Peggy.

"After all," he said, when he heard her voice, "there's no law that says I can't see you twice in the same day."

Peggy chuckled. "I get hungry about one," she said.

"I'll buy you lunch, if that's what you want."

"That's what I want." Then, more slowly, "I'm glad you called. I have something very serious to say to you."

"All right," Michael said. "I feel pretty serious today. One o'clock."

He hung up, smiling. He walked out into the sunlight and headed downtown, toward his lawyer's office, thinking about Peggy. He knew what the serious talk she wanted to have at lunch would be about. They had known each other for about two years, rich, warm years, a little desperate because day by day the war came closer and closer. Marriage in this bloody year was a cloudy and heartbreaking business. Marry and die, graves and widows; the husband-soldier carrying his wife's photograph in his pack like an extra hundred pounds of lead; the single man mourning furiously in the screaming jungle night for the forsworn moment, the honorable ceremony, the blinded veteran listening for his wife's chained footstep . . .

"Hey, Michael!" A hand slapped him on the shoulder. He turned. It was Johnson, in a rough felt hat with a colored band, and a full knitted tie and a beautiful cream-colored shirt under the soft blue jacket. "I've been wanting to see you forever . . . Aren't you ever home?"

"Not recently. I took a vacation." From time to time, Michael liked to see Johnson and have dinner with him and listen to him argue in his deep, actorish voice. But ever since the bitterness of the arguments about the Nazi-Soviet pact, Michael had found it almost impossible to talk civilly for a whole evening with Johnson or any of his friends.

". . . and I sent you this petition," Johnson was saying, gripping Michael's arm as they walked downtown swiftly, because Johnson never did anything slowly. "And it's so important and your name should be on it."

"What's the petition?"

"To the President. For the second front. Everybody's signing it." Real anger showed in Johnson's face. "It's a crime, the way we're letting the Russians bear the whole brunt . . ."

Michael didn't say anything.

"Don't you believe in the second front?" Johnson asked.

"Sure," Michael nodded. "If they can swing it."

"They can swing it all right."

"Maybe. Maybe they're afraid they'll lose too many men. Maybe," Michael said, suddenly realizing that tomorrow he would be in khaki and eligible for the landing on the beach of Europe, "maybe it'll cost a million, a million and a half lives . . ."

"So it'll cost a million, a million and a half lives," Johnson said loudly, walking even more quickly down the street. "It's worth it . . . A major diversion. Even two million lives . . ."

Michael looked at his friend strangely, his friend with the deep, indoor voice, and his 4F neatly on his draft registration card, calling so debonairly for the blood of other men on this handsome city boulevard, feeling religious and just because far away on another continent the Russians were fighting like lions. What would a Russian soldier, crouched behind a broken wall in Stalingrad, facing the oncoming tank, grenade in hand, think of this soft-voiced patriot in his fuzzy hat who called him brother, on the unruined street in the unruined city in America?

"Sorry," Michael said. "I'd like to do all I can to help the Russians, but I think I'd better leave it up to the professionals."

Johnson finally stopped walking. He dropped his hand from Michael's arm and stood there, his face tightened with anger and disdain. "I'm going to tell you something frankly, Michael," he said. "I'm ashamed of you."

Michael nodded soberly, embarrassed because he couldn't say what was in his heart without hurting Johnson forever.

"For a long time," Johnson said, "I've seen this coming. I've seen you growing soft . . ."

"Sorry," Michael said. "I've been sworn in as a soldier of the Republic, and soldiers of the Republic do not send petitions to their Commander in Chief, instructing him on questions of high strategy."

"That's an evasion."

"Maybe it is. So long . . ." Michael turned and walked away. After ten steps Johnson called, coolly, "Good luck, Michael." Michael waved without looking back.

He thought of Johnson and his other friends with displeasure. Either they were insensitively militant like Johnson, in their untouchable civilian occupations, or, under a thin veneer of patriotism, they were cynical and resigned. And this was no time for resignation, Michael felt. This was no time for saying no or perhaps. This was a time for a great yea-saying. That was a good thing about getting into the Army. He would get away from the over-sensitive resigners, the poetic despairers, the polite suicides. He had come of age at a time of critics, in a country of critics. Everyone criticized books and poetry and plays and government and the policies of England, France, and Russia. America for the last twenty years had been a perpetual drama-critics circle, saying over and over again, "Yes, I know 3000 died at Barcelona, but how clumsy the second act . . ." Age of critics, country of critics. He had begun to feel it was a sour age and a barren country because of it. This was a time for roaring rhetoric, savage vengeance, melodramatic shouting of boasts and assurance down the corridors of night. This was a time for roistering and wild-eyed soldiers, crazy with faith, oblivious of death. Michael could see no faith-madness around him. Civilians saw too much of the cheapness of war for faith . . . the chicanery and treachery of the lovers of six percent, of the farm bloc and business bloc and labor bloc. He had gone into the good restaurants and seen the great boom of heavy eaters, the electric excitement and pleasure of the men and women who were making good money and spending it before the Government claimed it. Stay out of the Army and you had to turn critic. He wanted to be a critic only of the enemy.

He felt silly sitting in the paneled room across the desk from his lawyer, reading through his will. Outside the window, high up in the tall building, the city shone in the everyday sunlight, the brick towers rearing into the soft blue haze, the streams of smoke from the boats on the river, the same city, looking exactly as it had always looked, and here he was, with his glasses on, reading ". . . one-third of the aforementioned estate to my former wife, Miss Laura Roberts. In the event of her marriage, this bequest is voided and the amount reserved in her interest will be joined to the residual amount left in the name of the executor and divided in this manner . . ."

He felt so healthy and whole and the language was so portentous and ugly. He looked across at Piper, his lawyer. Piper was growing bald and had a pudgy, pale complexion like the inside of a classroom in torts and grievances. Piper was signing a batch of papers, his pudgy mouth pursed, happily making money, happily confident that with his three children and his recurrent arthritis he was never going to war. Michael regretted that he had not written out the will himself, in his own hand, in his own language. It was somehow shameful to be represented to the future in the dry and money-sly words of a bald lawyer who would never hear a gun fired any place. A will should be a short, eloquent, personal document that reflected the life of the man who signed it and whose last possessions and last wishes were being memorialized in it. "To my mother, for the love I bear her, and for the agony she has endured and will later endure in my name and the name of my brothers . . .

"To my ex-wife, whom I humbly forgive and who will, I hope, forgive me in the same spirit of remembrance of our good days together . . .

"To my father, who has lived a hard and tragic life, and who has behaved so bravely in his daily war, and whom, I hope, I shall see once more before he dies . . ."

But Piper had covered eleven typewritten pages, full of whereases, and in the events of, and now if Michael died, he would be known to the future as a long list of many-syllabled modifying clauses, and cautious businessman's devices.

Perhaps later, Michael thought, if I *really* think I am going to be killed, I shall write another one, better than this. He signed the four copies.

Piper pressed the buzzer on his desk and two secretaries came in. One was a notary and carried her seal with her. She stamped the papers methodically, and they both signed as witnesses. Again Michael had the feeling it was all wrong, that this should be done by good friends who had known him a long time and who would feel bereaved if he died.

Michael looked at the date on the calendar. The thirteenth. He grinned a little sourly. He was not a superstitious man, but perhaps this was carrying it too far.

The secretaries went out, and Piper stood up. They shook hands and Piper said, "I will keep an eye on things and I will mail you a monthly report on what you have earned, and what I have spent."

Sleeper's play, in which Cahoon had given him a five percent interest, was doing very well, and it would undoubtedly sell to the movies, and there would be money coming in from it for two years. "I will be the richest private," Michael said, "in the American Army."

"I still think," Piper said, "that you ought to let me invest it for you."

"No, thank you," said Michael. He had gone over that again and again with Piper, and Piper still couldn't understand. Piper had some very good steel stocks himself and wanted Michael to buy some, too. But Michael had a stubborn, although vague and slightly shamefaced opposition to making money out of money, of profiting by the labor of other men. He had tried once to explain it to Piper, but the lawyer was too sensible for talk like that, and now Michael merely smiled and shook his head. Piper shrugged and put out his hand. "Good luck," he said. "I'm sure the war will be over very soon."

"Of course," said Michael. "Thanks."

He left quickly, glad to get out of the lawyer's office. He always felt trapped and restless when talking to lawyers or doing any business with them, and the feeling was even worse today.

He rang for the elevator. It was full of secretaries on the way to lunch, and there was a smell of powder, and the eager, released bubble of voices. As the elevator swooped down the forty stories, he wondered, again, how these young, bright, lively people could endure being locked in among the type-writers, the books, the Pipers, the notaries' seals and the legal language all their lives.

As he walked north along Fifth Avenue, toward the restrau-rant where he was to meet Peggy, he felt relieved. Now he was through with all his official business. For this afternoon, and all the night, until six-thirty the next morning when he had to report to his draft board, life was quit of all claims on him. The civil authorities had relinquished him and the military authorities had not yet taken him up. It was one o'clock now. Seventeen and a half hours, unanchored, between one life and the next.

He felt lightfooted and free and he looked fondly about him at the sunny wide street and the hurrying people, like a plan-tation owner with a good breakfast under his belt strolling over the wide lawns of his estate and looking out over the stretch-ing rich acres of his property. Fifth Avenue was his lawn, the city his estate, the shopwindows were his granaries, the Park his greenhouse, the theatres his workshop, all well taken care of, busy, in their proper order . . .

He thought of a bomb falling in the bright space between the Cathedral and Rockefeller Center and peered a little thoughtfully at the people beside him on the crowded avenue to see if there was any hint or premonition in their faces of that possible disaster. But the faces were as they always had been, preoccupied, all confident that bombs might fall on Saville Street, on the Place Vendôme, on Unter den Linden, on Plaza Victor Emmanuel, on Red Square, but the world would never depart so far from its reasonable and appointed routine as to break one window in Saks'.

Michael walked along the gray cathedral sides to Madison Avenue. Nobody on Madison Avenue looked as though the possibility that a bomb might fall there had ever entered their heads. Two Air Force Lieutenants in summer uniforms were walking with new-found military stiffness in front of the Co-lumbia Broadcasting Building, and Michael imagined that in their faces he saw the realization that no place was invulner-able, not even the stone and flower courtyard of the Rocke-feller's, or the tall castle of the broadcasters. But the Lieu-tenants passed him quickly, and perhaps all that he saw in their faces was anxiety that the girls they were going to meet might order the most expensive dishes on the menu for lunch.

Michael stopped in front of a hat store. It was a good store and the hats cost fifteen and twenty-five dollars, soft rich browns and gray felts with quiet bands. No helmets there, no ugly little limp overseas caps, at whatever price, no headgear, garrison, no braid for the Air Force or the Infantry or the Medical Corps. That was going to be a problem in the Army. You had to wear a hat in the Army, and Michael had never worn a hat, even in the rain and the snow. Hats gave him a headache. If the war lasted five years could he expect to have a headache that lasted five years?

He moved on more briskly toward the restaurant in which Margaret was probably already waiting. The various unexpected problems of a war. Like the business of the hats. And then the other things. He was a light and uneasy sleeper. The slightest noise kept him awake, and it was very difficult to sleep in the same room with anyone else. In the Army there were always at least fifty men sleeping in the same room with you . . . Could he expect to postpone his sleep until the war was over? And the silly problem of the bathroom. Like most well-brought-up persons of twentieth-century America, the ritual of the private bathroom with the locked door was one of the pillars of existence. Were all those important bodily functions supposed to cease until Hitler surrendered, while he, Michael, stared in loathing and revulsion at the long row of soldiers squatting over the open toilets in serried, grotesque ranks? He sighed, saddened a little on the sunny Avenue. It would be easier, he thought, to stand and die in a blood-sodden trench, knowing no help would ever come, than to walk into an enlisted man's latrine and . . . The modern world, he thought resentfully, prepares you very poorly for the tests it puts you to.

And then, the question of sex. Perhaps it was a matter of habit, as so many authorities insisted, but it was a deep habit and firmly ingrained. Married or single, in the pleasant freedom of the 1930's and '40's, ever since he was seventeen years old, he had constant and agreeable relations with women. The two or three periods of a week or more when he had for one reason or another to do without women had been restless and unhappy times, with the riotous juices of his youth clouding in insistent thunder in his loins, making him irritable and nervous, preventing him from working, preventing him finally from thinking about anything else. In the manhordes of the Army, in the strict barracks, on the long marches and drill fields, in the foreign bivouacs ahead, there were hardly likely to be women convenient to the whims of a private soldier under the anonymous helmet and the anonymous title. Gene Tunney, the ex-heavyweight champion, had come out for celibacy for the soldiers of the Republic, solemnly announcing that medical authorities now agreed that it did no damage to the health. What would Freud have said to the conqueror of Dempsey? Michael grinned. He could grin now, but he knew that later in the year, as he lay awake and furious on his narrow bed, in the masculine, snoring night of the barracks, the humor of the situation would not appeal to him so strongly.

Sweet and fitting, Democracy, in thy name, it may be to die but the other sacrifices, he thought, may be more difficult to manage.

He turned down the two steps to the entrance of the little French restaurant. Through the window, he could see Peggy already sitting at the bar.

The restaurant was crowded and they sat at the bar next to a slightly drunken sailor with bright red hair. Always, when he met Peggy like this, Michael spent the first two or three minutes silently looking at her, enjoying the quiet eagerness of her face, with its broad brow and arched eyes, admiring the simple, straight way she did her hair and the pleasant way she wore her clothes. All the best things about the city somehow seemed to have an echo and reflection in the tall, straight, dependable girl . . . And, now, when Michael thought about the city, it was inextricably mixed in his mind with the streets he had walked down with her, the houses they had entered, the plays they had seen together, the galleries they had gone to, the bars they had sat at late in the winter afternoons, when the cold had made the windows tinkle and the first drink had sunk in cool glory down their throats. Looking at her, her cheeks flushed with her walk, her eyes bright with pleasure at seeing him, her long competent hands reaching out to touch his sleeve, it was impossible to believe that that eagerness or pleasure would ever wane, that there ever would be a time when he would return here and not find her, unchanged, unchanging . . .

He looked at her and all the sad, grotesque thoughts that had dogged him uptown from the notarized will in his lawyer's office left him. He smiled gravely at her and touched her hand and slid onto the stool beside her.

"What are you doing this afternoon?" he said.

"Waiting."

"Waiting for what?"

"Waiting to be asked."

"All right," Michael said. "You're asked. An old-fashioned," he said to the bartender. He turned back to Peggy. "Man I know," he said, "hasn't a thing to do until six-thirty tomorrow morning."

"What will I tell the people at my office?"

"Tell them," he said gravely, "you are involved in a troop movement."

"I don't know," Peggy said. "My boss is against the war."

"Tell him the troops are against the war, too."

"Maybe I won't tell him anything," said Peggy.

"I will call him," Michael said, "and tell him that when you

217

were last seen you were floating toward Washington Square in a bourbon old-fashioned."

"He doesn't drink."

"Your boss," said Michael, "is a dangerous alien."

They clicked glasses gently. Then Michael noticed that the red-headed sailor was leaning against him, peering at Peggy.

"Exactly," said the sailor.

"If you please," Michael said, feeling free to speak harshly to men in uniform now, "this lady and I are having a private party."

"Exactly," said the sailor. He patted Michael's shoulder and Michael remembered the hungry Sergeant staring at Laura at lunchtime in Hollywood the day after the beginning of the war. "Exactly," the sailor repeated. "I admire you. You have the right idea. Don't kiss the girls in the town square and go off to fight the war. Stay home and lay them. Exactly."

"Now, see here," said Michael.

"Excuse me," said the sailor. He put some money down on the bar and put on his cap, very straight and white on top of his red hair. "It just slipped out. Exactly. I am on my way to Erie, Pennsylvania." He walked out of the bar, very erect.

Michael watched him walk out. He couldn't help smiling, and when he turned back to Peggy he was still smiling. "The Armed Services," he began, "makes confidants of every . . ." Then he saw she was crying. She sat straight on the high stool in her pretty brown dress and the tears were welling slowly and gravely down her cheeks. She didn't put up her hands to touch them or wipe them off.

"Peggy," Michael said quietly, gratefully noticing that the bartender was ostentatiously working with his head ducked at the other end of the bar. Probably, Michael thought, as he put out his hand to touch Peggy, bartenders get used to seeing a great many tears these days and develop a technique to handle them.

"I'm sorry," Peggy said. "I started to laugh but this is the way it came out."

Then the headwaiter came over in a little Italian flurry, and said, "Your table now, Mr. Whitacre."

Michael carried the drinks and followed Peggy and the waiter to a table against the wall. By the time they sat down Peggy had stopped crying, but all the eagerness was gone out of her face and Michael had never seen her face looking like that.

They ate the first part of their meal in silence. Michael waited for Peggy to recover. This was not like her at all. He had never seen her cry before. He had always thought of her as a girl who faced whatever happened to her with quiet stoicism. She had never complained about anything or fallen into the irrational emotional fevers he had more or less come to expect from the female sex, and he had developed no technique with her for soothing her or rescuing her from depression. He looked at her from time to time as they ate, but her face was bent stubbornly over her food.

"I'm sorry," she said finally, as they were drinking their coffee, and her voice was surprisingly harsh, "I'm sorry for the way I behaved. I know I should be gay and offhand and kiss the brave young soldier off. 'Go get your goddamn head shot off, darling, I'll be waiting with a martini in my hand.'"

"Peggy," Michael said, "shut up."

"Wear my glove on your arm," Peggy said, "as you do KP."

"What's the matter, Peggy?" Michael asked foolishly, because he knew what the matter was.

"It's just that I'm so fond of wars," said Peggy flatly. "Crazy about wars." She laughed. "It would be awful if people were having a war and someone I knew wasn't being shot in it."

Michael sighed. He felt weary now, and helpless, but he couldn't help realizing that he wouldn't have liked it if Peggy was one of those patriotic women who jumped happily into the idea of the war, as into the arrangements for a wedding.

"What do you want, Peggy?" he said, thinking of the Army waiting implacably for him at six-thirty the next morning, thinking of the other armies on both sides of the world waiting to kill him. "What do you want from me?"

"Nothing," said Peggy. "You've given me two precious years of your time. What more could a girl want? Now go off and let them blow you up. I'll hang a gold star outside the ladies' room of the Stork Club."

The waiter was standing over them. "Anything else?" he asked, smiling with an Italian fondness for prosperous lovers who ate expensive lunches.

"Brandy for me," said Michael. "Peggy?"

"Nothing, thanks," Peggy said. "I'm perfectly happy."

The waiter backed off. If he hadn't caught the boat at Naples, in 1920, Michael thought, he'd probably be in Libya today, rather than on 56th Street.

"Do you want to know what I want to do this afternoon?" Peggy asked harshly.

"Yes."

"I want to go some place and get married." She stared across the small, wine-stained table at him, angry and challenging. The girl at the next table, a full blonde in a red dress, was saying to the beaming white-haired man she was lunching with, "You must introduce me to your wife some day, Mr. Cawpowder. I'm sure she's absolutely charming."

"Did you hear me?" Peggy demanded.

"I heard you."

The waiter came over to the table and put the small glass

down. "Only three more bottles left," he said. "It is impossible to get any brandy these days."

Michael glanced up at the waiter. Unreasonably, he disliked the dark, friendly, stupid face. "I'll bet," he said, "they have no trouble getting it in Rome."

The waiter's face quivered, and Michael could almost hear him saying unhappily to himself, "Ah, here is another one who is blaming me for Mussolini. This war, oh, this sickness of a war."

"Yes, Sir," the waiter said, smiling, "it is possible that you are right." He backed away, trying to disclaim, by the tortured small movements of his hands and the sorrowful upper lip, that he had any responsibility for the Italian Army, the Italian Fleet, the Italian Air Force.

"Well?" Peggy said loudly.

Michael sipped his brandy slowly, in silence.

"O.K.," said Peggy. "I catch on."

"I just don't see the sense," Michael said, "of getting married now."

"You're absolutely right," Peggy said. "It's just that I'm tired of seeing single men get killed."

"Peggy." Michael covered her hand softly with his. "This isn't at all like you."

"Maybe it is," said Peggy. "Maybe all the other times weren't like me. Don't think," she said coldly, "you're going to come back in five years with all your goddamn medals and find me waiting for you, with a welcoming smile on my face."

"O.K.," Michael said wearily. "Let's not talk about it."

"I'm going to talk about it," Peggy said.

"O.K.," said Michael. "Talk about it."

He could see her fighting back tears as her entire face dissolved and softened. "I was going to be very gay," she said, her voice trembling. "Going to war? Let's have a drink . . . I would've managed too, but that damned sailor . . . The trouble is, I'm going to forget you. There was another man, in Austria, and I thought I'd remember him till the day I died. He was probably a better man than you, too, braver and more gentle, and a cousin of his wrote me last year from Switzerland that they'd killed him in Vienna. I was going out to the theatre with you the night I got the letter, and first I thought, 'I can't go out tonight,' but then you were at the door and I looked at you and I didn't really remember the other man at all. He was dead, but I didn't remember very much about him, although at one time I asked him to marry me, too. I seem to have terrible luck in that department, don't I?"

"Stop it," Michael whispered, "please, Peggy, stop it."

But Peggy went on, the mist of tears barely held back in the deep, remembering eyes. "I'm silly," she said. "I'd probably have forgotten him even if we had been married, and I'd probably forget you, if you stayed away long enough. Probably just a superstition on my part. I guess I feel if you're married and it's there, all settled and official, to come home to, you'll come home. Ridiculous . . . His name was Joseph. He had no home, nothing. So, naturally, they killed him." She stood up abruptly. "Wait for me outside," she said. "I'll be right down."

She fled out of the small, dark room with the little bar near the window and the old-fashioned maps of the wine sections of France hung around the smoky walls. Michael left some money on the table for the bill, and a big tip to try to make up to the Italian waiter for being ugly to him, and walked slowly out into the street.

He stood in front of the restaurant, thoughtfully smoking a cigarette. No, he thought finally, no. She's wrong. I'm not going to carry that burden, too, or let her carry it, either. If she was going to forget him, that was merely another price you paid for the war, another form of casualty. It was not entered on the profit-and-loss balances of men killed and wounded and treasure destroyed, but it was just as surely a casualty. It was hopeless and crippling to try to fight it.

Peggy came out. Her hair shone in the sun as though she had combed it violently upstairs, and her face was composed and smiling.

"Forgive me," she said, touching his arm. "I'm just as surprised by it as you are."

"That's all right," Michael said. "I'm no prize today myself."

"I didn't mean a word of what I said. You believe that, don't you?"

"Of course," said Michael.

"Some other time," Peggy said, "I'll tell you about the man in Vienna. It's an interesting story. Especially for a soldier."

"Sure," said Michael politely. "I'd love to hear it."

"And now," Peggy looked up the street and waved to a taxicab that was slowly coming down from Lexington Avenue, "I think I'd better go back to work for the rest of the afternoon. Don't you?"

"There's no need . . ."

Peggy smiled at him. "I think it's a good idea," she said. "Then tonight, we'll meet as though we never had lunch today at all. I'd prefer it that way. You can find plenty of things to do this afternoon, can't you?"

"Of course," Michael said.

"Have a good time, darling." She kissed him lightly. "And wear your gray suit tonight." She got into the cab without looking back and the car drove loudly off toward Third Avenue. Michael watched it turn the corner under the splintered bright

221

shadows of the L. Then he walked slowly west on the shady side of the street.

He had put off thinking about Peggy, half consciously, half unconsciously. There were so many other things to think about. The war made a miser out of a man, he saved all his emotions for it. But that was no excuse, either. He still wanted to postpone thinking about her. He knew himself too well to imagine that for two, three, four years he could remain faithful to a photograph, a letter a month, a memory . . . And he didn't want to make any claims on her. They were two sensible, forthright, candid people, and here was a problem that millions of people all around them were facing one way or another, and they couldn't handle it any better than the youngest, the most naïve, the most illiterate backwoodsman come down from his hills to pick up a rifle, leaving his Cora Sue behind him . . . He knew that they wouldn't talk about it any more, either that night or any night before the end of the war, but he knew that in the nights of memory and recapitulation ahead of him on continents he had never traveled before, he would suffer as he thought of this early summer afternoon and a bitter voice would cry within him, "Why didn't you do it? Why not? Why not?"

He shook his head to clear it, and walked with defiant briskness between the brown buildings, gracious and friendly in the spacious light. He passed an old man, walking painfully with a cane. The old man had a wool muffler on and a long, dark coat, although it was a warm day. There were livermarks on the old man's skin, and his hands were yellow on his cane, and his eyes, as he looked at Michael, were watery and bitter, as though any young man briskly walking the streets was an affront to him, muffled and limping on the edge of the grave.

The look was surprising, and Michael almost stopped to peer again, to see if perhaps the old man was known to him and was nursing a more personal injury. But the old man was a stranger, and Michael walked on, more slowly. Fool, Michael thought. You've had the whole banquet, all the courses, the soup, the fish, the white wine, the red, the Burgundy and the Bordeaux, the game, the roast, the salad, the cheese, and now you've come to the dessert and brandy, and because you've found the sweet bitter and the drink harsh, you hate the men who have come more lately than you to the table. I'd change with you, Old Man, Michael thought. The days you've lived through. The best days of America. The optimistic days, the short wars, the little killing, the bracing, invigorating, early-century weather . . . You married and sat down to dinner with many children in the same house for twenty uninterrupted years, and only foreigners fought in the wars then. Don't envy me, Old Man, don't envy me. What good fortune, what a gift to be seventy and nearly dead in 1942! I pity you now because of your heavy coat on the old bones, the warm wool around the frozen throat, the shaking hand on the necessary cane . . . but perhaps I should pity myself more. Warm as I am, with my steady hands, and my certain step . . . I will never freeze on a summer's day, and my hand will never shake from age. I come to Intermission and I do not return to the Theatre for the Second Act.

There was the crisp sound of high heels beside him and Michael looked at the woman who was passing him. She had on a wide straw hat with a deep green band and the light, thrown on her face through the brim, was softened and rosy. Her dress was of a light, cool green and clung in nude, delightful wrinkles to her hips. She was barelegged and brown. She made a point of not paying any attention to Michael's polite but admiring glance. She passed him quickly and walked in front of him. Michael's eyes lingered pleasantly on the trim, pretty figure and he smiled as her hand went inevitably up to her hair and patted it and arranged it in helpless, agreeable response to the fact that a young man was looking at her and finding her beautiful.

Then Michael grinned. No, he thought, Old Man. I've been making it all up. Go die, Old Man, with my blessing. I'll sit the meal out with pleasure.

He was whistling later in the afternoon as he approached the bar where he was to meet Cahoon and say good-bye to him before he left for the wars.

CHAPTER FIFTEEN

THIS IS WHAT they said along the bar where they sold three-point-two beer in the PX at Fort Dix in the State of New Jersey on a night in the fateful, warm summer of 1942.

"I got one eye. Actually one eye. I told the bastidds and they said One A and here I am."

And they said, "I am the father of a ten-year-old girl. You're separated from your wife, they said, One A. The State is jumping with young single men without children and they persecuted me."

And they said, "In the old country, they wanted to draft you, you went to an expert and he ruptured you. One little pull of the finger and you had a hernia would keep you out of fifty wars. But in America they take one look and they say, 'Son, we'll fix your balls just as good as new in two days. One A.' "

And they said, "You call this beer? As soon as the government steps in, everything stinks, even the beer."

And they said, "It's a question of pull. You could beat Joe Louis in two rounds, and they'd defer you for delicate health, you know somebody on the draft board."

And they said, "I got ulcers so bad, every time I hear the telephone ring, my gut bleeds. It don't show on the x-rays, they said, One A. They won't be satisfied till they have my life. I wonder will they bury me at Arlington Cemetery. They'll send me a purple heart for hyperacidity and give me a military funeral and they can stuff it up their ass. I ain't et any of their food yet, but I can't hold out forever. One of those meals, bologna and cheese and peanut butter they pass out, and they got a dead soldier on their hands. I warned them, but they said, One A."

And they said, "I don't mind servin' my country, but what I don't like is they deduct twenty-two dollars a month and send it to my wife. I been separated from my wife eleven years, and she slept with every man and boy between here and Salt Lake, and they deduct twenty-two dollars."

And they said, "When I get out I'm goin' to kill the chairman of my draft board. I told him I want to join the Coast Guards, my application is in, I like the sea, but he said, 'One A, you better learn to like the land.' "

And they said, "Listen to me, Bud, when you stand formation, stand in the middle. Not in the front, not in the back, not on the sides. In the middle, see. Then they don't pick you for details, see. And stay away from your tent except at night, because they go around snoopin', and anybody they see on his back, they grab him and put him to work, unloadin' trucks in the warehouses."

And they said, "I could have had a commission, only it would of taken a little time, and the draft board was hungry for me, red, raving hungry."

And they said, "Did you see those two guys marchin' back and forth with full packs in front of the orderly room? They been there for five days like that, back and forth, back and forth, they must of walked two hundred miles by now. They went into Trenton for a couple of beers, and the Sergeant caught them, and they have to walk until they're shipped. For a couple of glasses of beer. And they call this a free country."

And they said, "When they take you in front of the interviewer, you tell him you can type. Makes no difference can you type, can't you type. You tell him you can type. This Army is crazy for typists. One thing you can be sure, they don't put typewriters any place where they can be shot at. You tell them you can't type, they put you in the Infantry and you can write home and tell your Ma to start shoppin' for a nice gold star for the window."

And they said, "This Army pays more attention to a man's instrument than a Spanish bride on a hot night on the Equator. I been in the Army twelve hours now and they've looked at it three times already. Who do they expect us to fight—the Japs or the field hockey team at Vassar?"

And they said, "They got all the ratings in the Air Force."

And they said, "You don't get killed in the Artillery."

And they said, "This is the worst company at Fort Dix. They found the cook buggering a KP and they court-martialed him and reduced him to the rank of Staff Sergeant."

And they said, "This is the first night I'll be sleeping away from my wife since 1931. I don't think I can manage it."

And they said, "Hey, look, they give you condoms for nothing in this joint."

And they said, "What do you know, you can buy the Bible for a quarter. Paper covered."

And they said, "Oh, Christ, they're closin' up."

Michael walked down the spit-covered steps of the PX onto the worn soil of New Jersey, under the calm, starlit summer-sky. Heavy with beer, in the stiff green fatigue suit that smelled like the back room of a haberdashery store, with his feet feeling clumsy and anchored in the new square shoes that already were blistering his heel, he moved down the company street between the tents, past the two sullen figures marching slowly back and forth under heavy packs in payment for the Trenton beers, past the crap game that had started yesterday and would go on until the men died or the Japanese surrendered, past the lonely, rumpled figures that stood next to the guy ropes looking soberly up at the dark sky, past the men packing their civilian clothes into bundles to give to the Red Cross, past the privates, first class, who did the actual work of running the company and who seemed like rare and lofty persons, endowed with incredible privileges, who were now calling hoarsely, "Lights out in ten minutes, Soldiers! Lights out in ten minutes!"

He went into his tent, bare and lonely under the single forty-watt bulb, and slowly undressed and got under the rough blanket in his underwear because he had been ashamed to go to war carrying pajamas.

The man from Elmira, who slept next to the tent opening, put out the light. He had been there three weeks already because he was a veterinarian and the Army was trying to place him at a post where he could be useful with mules, and it was hard to find that many mules in this up-to-date war. The man from Elmira put out the light because he was the veteran of the establishment and naturally took command of matters like that.

The man to the right of Michael was already snoring. He was a Sicilian who pretended he could read and write and he was going to wait here for ninety days to be made a citizen before the Army decided what it was going to do with him.

The men in the other beds had communicated nothing to Michael. They lay in the darkness, listening to the Sicilian snore, listening to Taps weep out over the public-address system, enormous and sorrowful over the herded shabby acres of men who were no longer civilians and not yet soldiers, and who now, finally, in a generally loose and approximate way, were to be prepared to die.

I'm here, Michael thought, smelling the Army blanket under his chin, it's happened. I should have rushed into it and I didn't and I could have dodged it and I didn't. Here I am, in this tent, under the stiff blanket, as I always knew I would be. This tent, this blanket, these snoring men have been waiting for me for thirty-three years, and now they have caught up with me and I have caught up with them. The expiration has begun. I have begun to pay up. Pay for my opinions, pay for my easy life, for the good meals and the soft beds, pay for the easy girls and all the easy money. Pay for the thirty-three year holiday that ended this morning when the Sergeant said, "You. Pick up that butt."

He found it easy to drift off to sleep, although there were shouts and whistles and drunken weeping all about him. And he slept without dreams all that night.

CHAPTER SIXTEEN

THE GENERAL had come down to inspect the line, exuding confidence, so they all knew something was up. Even the Italian General in the party of ten bulky, binoculared, goggled, scarved, glittering officers had exuded confidence, so they knew it was something big. The General had been particularly hearty, laughing uproariously when he talked to the soldiers, patting them heavily on the shoulder, even pinching the cheek of an eighteen-year-old boy who had just come up as a replacement in Himmler's squad. This was a certain sign that a great many men were going to be killed, one way or another, very soon.

There were other signs, too. Himmler, who had been at Divisional Headquarters two days ago, had heard on the radio that the British had been burning papers again at their headquarters in Cairo. The British seemed to have an unlimited number of papers to burn. They had burned them in July, and then again in August, and here it was October, and they were still burning them.

Himmler had also heard the man on the radio say that the overall strategy was for them to break through to Alexandria and Jerusalem and finally to join up with the Japanese in India. It was true that this seemed a little grandiose and ambitious to men who had been sitting in the same place in the bitter sun for months, but there was a reassuring sound to the plan. At least it gave evidence that the General *had* a plan.

The night was very quiet. Occasionally there was a random small rattle of fire, or a flare, but that was all. There was a moon and the pale sky, crusted with the mild glitter of the stars, blended gently with the shadowy expanse of the desert.

Christian stood alone, loosely holding the machine pistol in the crook of his arm, looking out toward the anonymous shadows behind which lay the enemy. There was no sound from them in the sleeping night, and no sound from the thousands of men all about him.

Night had its advantages. You could move around quite freely without worrying that some Englishman had you in his glasses and was debating with himself whether or not you were worth a shell or two. Also, the smell died down. The smell was the salient fact about war in the desert. There was not enough water for anything but drinking, and not enough for that, and nobody bathed. You sweated all day, in the same clothes, week in and week out, and your clothes rotted with it, and became stiff on your back, and you had a steady rash of prickly heat that itched and burned, but your nose suffered worst of all. The human race was only bearable when the obscene juices of living were being constantly washed away. You became dulled to your own smell, of course, otherwise you would kill yourself, but when you joined any group, the smell hit you, in a solid, jolting attack.

So the night was solace. There had been little enough solace since he had arrived in Africa. They had been winning, it was true, and he had marched from Bardia to this spot, some seventy miles from Alexandria. But somehow, while agreeable, victory did not have a personal quality to a soldier in the line. No doubt victory meant a great deal to the well-uniformed officers at the various headquarters and they probably celebrated over large dinners with wines and beer when towns were taken, but victories for you still meant that there was a good chance that you would die in the morning, and that you would still live in a shallow, gritty hole, and that the other men who lived by your side would stink just as unbearably in the hot wind of triumph as in defeat.

The only good time had been the two weeks in Cyrene, when he had been sent back with malaria. It had been cooler there, and green, and there was swimming in the Mediterranean.

When Himmler had reported that he had heard the expert on the radio announce that the plan of the German General Staff was to go through Alexandria and Cairo to join up in India with the Japanese, Knuhlen, who had come out with a recent draft of replacements, and who had taken over some of Himmler's old position of comedian to the company, had said, "Anybody who wants can go join up with the Japs. Myself, if nobody minds, I'll stop in Alexandria and join up with some of that Italian ass I hear they have running all over the streets there."

Christian grinned in the darkness as he remembered Knuhlen's rough witticism. There are probably few jokes, he thought, being told tonight on the other side of the minefield.

Then there was a flash for a hundred miles, and a second later, the sound. He fell to the sand, just as the shells exploded all around him.

He opened his eyes. It was dark, but he knew he was moving and he knew that he was not alone, because there was the smell. The smell was like untended pissoirs in Paris and clotted wounds and the winter clothes of the children of the poor. He remembered the sound of the shells over his head, and he closed his eyes again.

It was a truck. There was no doubt about that. And somewhere the war was still on, because there was the sound of artillery, going and coming, not very far off. And something bad had happened, because a voice in the darkness near him was weeping and saying between sobs, "My name is Richard Knuhlen, my name is Richard Knuhlen," over and over again, as though the man were trying to prove to himself that he was a normal fellow who knew exactly who he was and what he was doing.

Christian stared up in the opaque darkness at the heavy-smelling canvas that swayed and jolted above him. The bones of his arms and legs felt as though they had been broken. His ears felt smashed against his head, and for awhile he lay on the board floor in the complete blackness contemplating the fact that he was going to die.

"My name is Richard Knuhlen," the voice said, "and I live

at Number 3, Carl Ludwig Strasse. My name is Richard Knuhlen and I live at . . ."

"Shut up," Christian said, and immediately felt much better. He even tried to sit up, but that was too ambitious, and he lay back again, to watch the sky-rocketing waves of color under his eyelids.

The weeping stopped, and somebody said, "We are going to join up with the Japanese. And I know where." And laughed wildly again and again. "In Rome!" the voice said, laughing. "On Benito's balcony in Rome. I have to tell that expert that," and then Christian realized that it was Himmler talking, and he remembered a great deal of what had happened in the last ten days.

The barrage had been bad the first night, but everyone was fairly well dug in, and only Meyer and Heiss had been hit. There had been flares and searchlights and the light of a tank burning between them, and small gasoline fires before them where the Tommies were trying to mark a path through the minefield for the tanks and infantry behind the barrage, small dark figures appearing in sudden flashes, busily jumping around so far away. Their own guns had started in behind them. Only one tank had got close. Every gun within a thousand meters of them had opened up on it. When the hatch was opened a minute later they saw with surprise that the man who tried to climb out was burning brightly.

The whole attack on their sector, after the barrage died down, had only lasted two hours, three waves with nothing more to show for it than seven immobile tanks, charred, with broken treads, at aggressive angles in the sand, and many bodies strewn peacefully around them. Everybody had been pleased. They had only lost five men in the company, and Hardenburg had grinned widely when he went back to battalion to report in the quiet of the morning.

But at noon, the guns had started on them again, and what looked like a whole company of tanks had appeared in the minefield, jiggling uncertainly in the swirling dust and sand. This time the line had been overrun, but the British infantry had been stopped before it reached them, and what was left to the tanks had pulled back, turning maliciously from time to time to rake them before rumbling out of range. And before they could take a deep breath, the British artillery had opened on them again. It had caught the medical parties out in the open, tending the wounded. They were all screaming and dying and no one could leave his hole to help them. That was probably when Knuhlen had begun to cry and Christian remembered thinking, dazedly and somehow surprised: They are very serious about this.

Then he had begun to shake. He had braced himself crazily

with his hands rigid against the sides of the hole he was in. When he looked over the rim of the hole there seemed to be thousands of Tommies running at him and blowing up on mines, and those little bug-like gun carriers scurrying around among them in eccentric lines, their machine guns going, and he had felt like standing up and saying, "You are making a serious mistake. I am suffering from malaria and I am sure you would not like to be guilty of killing an invalid."

It went on for many days and nights, with the fever coming and going, and the chills in the middle of the desert noon, and from time to time you thought with dull hostility: They never told you it could last so long and they never told you you would have malaria while it was happening.

Then, somehow, everything died down, and he thought: We are still here. Weren't they foolish to try it? He fell asleep, kneeling in the hole. One second later Hardenburg was shaking him and peering down into his face, saying, "Goddamn you, are you still alive?" He tried to answer, but his teeth were shaking crazily in his jaws and his eyes wouldn't really open. So he smiled tenderly at Hardenburg who grabbed him by the collar and dragged him like a sack of potatoes along the ground as he nodded gravely at the bodies lying on both sides. He was surprised to see that it was quite dark and a truck was standing there, with its motor going, and he said, quite loudly, "Keep it quiet there." The man beside him was sobbing and saying, "My name is Richard Knuhlen," and much later, on the dark board floor under the smelly canvas, in all the heavy, bone-shaking jolting, he was still crying and still saying it over and over again, "My name is Richard Knuhlen and I live at Number 3 Carl Ludwig Strasse." When he finally really woke up and saw that perhaps he was not going to die at the moment and realized that he was in full retreat and still had malaria, he thought, abstractedly: I would like to see the General now. I wonder if he is still confident.

Then the truck stopped and Hardenburg appeared at the back and said, "Everybody out. Everybody!"

Slowly the men moved toward the rear of the truck, heavily, as though they were walking in thick mud. Two or three of them fell when they jumped down over the tailboard and just lay there uncomplainingly as other men jumped and fell on them. Christian was the last one out of the truck. I am standing, he thought with deliberate triumph. I am standing.

Hardenburg looked at him queerly in the moonlight. Off to both sides there was a flash of guns and there was a general rumble in the air, but the small victory of having landed correctly made everything seem quite normal for the moment.

Christian looked keenly at the men struggling to their feet and standing in sleepwalking poses around him. He recognized

230

very few of them, but perhaps their faces would come back to him in daylight. "Where's the company?" he asked.

"This is the company," Hardenburg said. His voice was unrecognizable. Christian had a sudden suspicion that someone was impersonating the Lieutenant. It looked like Hardenburg, but Christian resolved to go into the matter more deeply when things became more settled.

Hardenburg put out his hand and pushed roughly at Christian's face with the heel of his palm. His hand smelled of grease and gunoil and the sweat of his cuff. Christian pulled back a little, blinking.

"Are you all right?" Hardenburg said.

"Yes, Sir," he said. "Perfectly, Sir." He would have to think about where the rest of the company was, but that would wait until later, too.

The truck started to slither into movement on the sandy track, and two of the men trotted heavily after it.

"Stand where you are!" Hardenburg said. The men stopped and stood there, staring at the truck, which gathered speed and wound loudly over the shining sand toward the west. They were at the bottom of a small rise. They stood in silence and watched the truck climb, with a clashing of bearings past Hardenburg's motorcycle, up the rise. It shone along the top of it for a moment, huge, rolling, home-like, then disappeared on the other side.

"We dig in here," Hardenburg said, with a stiff wave of his hand to the white glitter of the rise. The men stared stupidly at it.

"Right now," Hardenburg said. "Diestl," he said, "stay with me."

"Yes, Sir," said Christian, very smart. He went over to Hardenburg, elated with the fact that he could move.

Hardenburg started up the rise with what seemed to Christian superhuman briskness. Amazing, he thought dully, as he followed the Lieutenant, a thin, slight man like that, after the last ten days ...

The men followed slowly. With rigid gestures of his arm, Hardenburg indicated to each of them where they should dig in. There were thirty-seven of them and Christian remembered again that he must inquire later what had happened to the rest of the company. Hardenburg stretched them out very thin, in a long, irregular line, one-third of the way up the rise. When he had finished he and Christian turned and looked back at the bent slow figures digging in. Christian suddenly realized that if they were attacked they would have to stand where they were, because there was no possibility of retreating up the exposed slope from the line where Hardenburg had set them. Then he began to realize what was happening.

231

"All right, Diestl," Hardenburg said. "You come with me."

Christian followed the Lieutenant back to the track. Without a word, he helped Hardenburg push the motorcycle up the track to the top of the rise. Occasionally a man would stop digging and turn and peer thoughtfully at the two men working the motorcycle slowly up to the crest of the slope behind them. Christian was panting heavily when they finally stopped pushing the machine. He turned, with Hardenburg, and looked at the sliver of a line of toiling men below him. The scene looked peaceful and unreal, with the moon and the empty desert and the doped movements of the shovelers, like a dream out of the Bible.

"They'll never be able to fall back," he said, almost unconsciously, "once they're engaged."

"That's right," Hardenburg said flatly.

"They're going to die there," said Christian.

"That's right," said Hardenburg. Then Christian remembered something Hardenburg had said to him as far back as El Agheila. "In a bad situation that must be held as long as possible, the intelligent officer will place his men so that they have no possibility of retreat. If they are placed so that they must either fight or die, the officer has done his job."

"What happened?" Christian asked.

Hardenburg shrugged. "They broke through on both sides of us."

"Where are they now?"

Hardenburg looked wearily at the flash of gunfire to the south and the flicker farther off to the north. "You tell me," he said. He bent and peered at the gas gauge on the motorcycle. "Enough for a hundred kilometers," he said. "Are you well enough to hold on in back?"

Christian wrinkled his forehead, trying to puzzle this out, then slowly managed to do it. "Yes, Sir," he said. He turned and looked at the stumbling, sinking line of figures down the hill, the men whom he was going to leave to die there. For a moment, he thought of saying to Hardenburg, "No, Sir, I will stay here." But really, nothing would be gained by that.

A war had its own system of balances, and he knew that it was not cowardice on Hardenburg's part, or self-seeking on his own, to pull back and save themselves for another day. These men would fight a small, pitiful action, perhaps delay a British company for an hour or so on the bare slope, and then vanish. If he and Hardenburg stayed, they would not be able, no matter what their efforts, to buy even ten minutes more than that hour. That was the way it was. Perhaps the next time it would be himself left on a hill without hope and another on the road back to problematical safety.

"Stay here," Hardenburg said. "Sit down and rest. I'll go and tell them we're going back to find a mortar platoon to support us."

"Yes, Sir," said Christian and sat down suddenly. He watched Hardenburg slide briskly down toward where Himmler was slowly digging. Then he fell sideways and was asleep before his shoulder touched the ground.

Hardenburg was shaking him roughly. He opened his eyes and looked up. He knew that it would be impossible to sit up, then stand up, then take one step after another. He wanted to say, "Please leave me alone," drop off again to sleep. But Hardenburg grabbed him by his coat, at his neck, and pulled hard. Somehow Christian found himself standing. He walked automatically, his boots making a noise like his mother's iron over stiff and frozen laundry at home, and helped Hardenburg move the motorcycle. Hardenburg swung his leg over the saddle with great agility and began kicking the starting pedal. The machine sputtered again and again, but it did not start.

Christian watched him working furiously with the machine in the waning, dry moonlight. It wasn't until the figure was close to him that Christian looked up and realized that they were being watched. It was Knuhlen, the man who had been weeping in the truck, who had stopped shoveling and had followed the Lieutenant up the slope. Knuhlen didn't say anything. He just stood there, watching blankly as Hardenburg kicked again and again at the pedal.

Hardenburg saw him. He took a slow deep breath, swung his leg back and stood next to the machine.

"Knuhlen," he said, "get back to your post."

"Yes, Sir," said Knuhlen, but he didn't move.

Hardenburg walked over to Knuhlen and hit him hard on the nose with the side of his fist. Knuhlen's nose began to bleed. He made a wet, snuffling sound, but he did not move. His hands hung at his sides as though he had no further use for them. He had left his rifle and his entrenching tool at the hole he had been digging down the slope. Hardenburg stepped back and looked curiously and without malice at Knuhlen, as though he represented a small problem in engineering that would have to be solved in due time. Then Hardenburg stepped over to him again and hit him very hard twice. Knuhlen fell slowly to his knees. He kneeled there looking blankly up at Hardenburg.

"Stand up!" Hardenburg said.

Slowly Knuhlen stood up. He still did not say anything and his hands still hung limply at his hips.

Christian looked at him vaguely. Why don't you stay down? he thought, hating the baggy, ugly soldier standing there in silent, longing reproach on the crest of the moonlit rise. Why don't you die?

"Now," Hardenburg said, "get back down that hill."

But Knuhlen just stood there, as though words no longer entered the channels of his brain. Occasionally he sucked in some of the blood dripping into his mouth. The noise was surprising coming from that bent, silent figure. This was like some of the modern paintings Christian had seen in Paris. Three haggard, silent, dark figures on an empty hill under a dying moon, with sky and land cold and dark and almost of the same mysterious glistening, unearthly substance all around.

"All right," Hardenburg said, "come with me."

He took the motorcycle handlebars and trundled it down the other side of the rise away from the shovelers below. Christian took a last look at the thirty-six men scraping at the desert's face in their doped, rhythmic movements. Then he followed Hardenburg and Knuhlen along the down-sloping path.

Knuhlen walked in a dumb, scuffling manner, behind the rolling motorcycle. They walked about fifty meters in silence. Then Hardenburg stopped. "Hold this," he said to Christian.

Christian took the handlebars and balanced the machine against his legs. Knuhlen had stopped and was standing in the sand, staring patiently once more at the Lieutenant. Hardenburg cleared his throat as though he were going to make a speech, then walked up to Knuhlen, looked at him deliberately, and clubbed him twice, savagely and quickly, across the eyes. Knuhlen sat down backwards this time, without a sound, and remained that way, staring up dully and tenaciously at the Lieutenant. Hardenburg looked down at him thoughtfully, then took out his pistol and cocked it. Knuhlen made no move and there was no change on the dark, bloody face in the dim light.

Hardenburg shot him once. Knuhlen started to get up to his feet slowly, using his hands to help him. "My dear Lieutenant," he said in a quiet, conversational tone. Then he slid face down into the sand.

Hardenburg put his pistol away. "All right," he said.

Then he came back to the motorcycle, and swung himself into the saddle. He kicked the pedal. This time it started.

"Get on," he said to Christian.

Carefully, Christian swung his leg over and settled himself on the pillion seat of the motorcycle. The machine throbbed jumpily under him.

"Hold on tight," Hardenburg said. "Around my middle."

Christian put his arms around Hardenburg. Very strange, he thought, hugging an officer at a time like this, like a girl going for an outing into the woods with a motorcycle club on a Sunday afternoon. So close, Hardenburg smelled frightfully, and Christian was afraid he was going to vomit.

Hardenburg put the machine into gear and it sputtered and

roared and Christian wanted to say, "Please keep quiet," because something like this should be done quietly, and it was discourteous to the thirty-seven men who had to stay behind to advertise so blatantly that they were being left alone to die and that other men would still be alive when they were bleached bones on the hill from which no escape was possible.

Thirty-six now, Christian thought, remembering the laborious small pits facing the British, facing the tanks and the armored cars. Three dozen. Three dozen soldiers, he thought, holding tight to the Lieutenant on the jolting machine, trying to remember not to have an attack of fever or chills, three dozen soldiers, at how much a dozen.

Hardenburg reached a level place, and he accelerated the motor. They sped across the empty plain glowing in the last level rays of the sinking moon, surrounded by the flicker of guns on all horizons. Their speed created a great deal of wind, and Christian's cap blew off, but he did not mind, because the wind also made it impossible to smell the Lieutenant any more.

They rode north and west for a half hour. The flickering on the horizon grew stronger and brighter as the motorcycle slithered along the winding track among the dunes and the occasional patches of scrub grass. There were some burnt-out tanks along the track, and here and there a cannibalized truck, its naked driveshaft poking up into the dim air like an anti-aircraft gun. There were some new graves, obviously hastily dug, with a rifle, bayonet-down in the ground, and a cap or helmet hanging from the butt, and there were the usual crashed planes, blackened and wind-ripped, with the bent propellers and the broken wings vaguely reflecting glints of the moon from their ragged metal surfaces. But it wasn't until they reached a road considerably to the north, running almost due west, that they met up with any other troops. Then they suddenly were in a long regimental convoy of trucks, armored cars, scout cars, carriers and other motorcycles, moving slowly along the narrow track, in overpowering clouds of dust and exhaust fumes.

Hardenburg pulled off to one side, but not too far, because there was no telling, with all the fighting that had gone back and forth over this ground, where you might run over a mine. He stopped the motorcycle and Christian nearly dropped off with the tension of speed no longer holding him to the seat. Hardenburg swung around and held Christian, steadying him.

"Thank you," Christian said formally and light-headedly. He was having a chill now, and his jaws were clamped in a cold spasm around his swollen tongue.

"You can get into one of those trucks," Hardenburg shouted, waving with a ridiculous expenditure of energy, to the procession slowly droning past. "But I don't think you should."

"Whatever you say, Lieutenant." Christian smiled with frozen amiability, like a drunk at a polite and rather boring garden party.

"I don't know what their orders are," Hardenburg shouted, "and they may have to turn off and fight at any moment . . ."

"Of course," said Christian.

"It's a good idea to hold onto our own transportation," Hardenburg said. Christian was vaguely grateful that the Lieutenant was being so kind about explaining everything to him.

"Yes," said Christian, "yes, indeed."

"What did you say?" Hardenburg shouted as an armored car roared past.

"I said . . ." Christian hesitated. He did not remember what he had said. "I am agreeable," he said, nodding ambiguously. "Absolutely agreeable."

"Good," said Hardenburg. He unknotted the handkerchief that Christian had around his throat. "Better put this around your face. For the dust." He started to tie it behind Christian's head.

Christian put his hands up slowly and pushed the Lieutenant's hands away. "Pardon me," he said, "for a moment." Then he leaned over and vomited.

The men in the trucks going by did not look at him or the Lieutenant. They merely stared straight ahead as though they were riding in a wintry parade in a dying man's dream, without interest, curiosity, destination, hope.

Christian straightened up. He felt much better, although the taste in his mouth was considerably worse than it had been before. He put the handkerchief up around over the bridge of his nose so that it covered the entire lower part of his face. His fingers worked heavily on the knot in back, but finally he made it.

"I am ready," he announced.

Hardenburg had his handkerchief around his face by this time. Christian put his arms around the Lieutenant's waist, and the motorcycle kicked and spun in the sand and jolted into the procession behind an ambulance with three pairs of legs showing through the torn door.

Christian felt very fond of the Lieutenant, sitting iron-like on the seat in front of him, looking, with his handkerchief mask, like a bandit in an American Western movie. I ought to do something, Christian thought, to show him my appreciation. For five minutes, in the shaking dust, he tried to think of how he could demonstrate his gratitude to the Lieutenant. Slowly, the idea came to him. I will tell him, Christian thought, about his wife and myself. That is all I have to offer.

236

Christian shook his head. Silly, he thought, silly, silly. But now he had thought of the idea, he could not escape it. He closed his eyes; he tried to think of the thirty-six men digging slowly in the sand to the south; he tried to think of all the beer and cold wine and ice water he had drunk in the last five years, but again and again he felt himself on the verge of shouting over the clanking of the traffic around him, "Lieutenant, I had your wife when I went on leave from Rennes."

The procession stopped, and Hardenburg, who had decided to remain, for safety, in the middle of the convoy, put his foot down and balanced the machine in neutral. Now, thought Christian crazily, now I am going to tell him. But at that moment, two men got out of the ambulance in front of them and dragged a body out by the feet and put it down by the side of the road. They moved heavily and wearily and dragged it by the ankles out of the way of the vehicles. Christian stared at them over the edge of his handkerchief. The two men looked up guiltily. "He is not alive," one of the men said earnestly, coming over to Christian. "What's the sense of carrying him if he is not alive?"

Then the convoy started and the ambulance ground into first speed. The two men had to run, their water bottles flapping against their hips, and they were dragged for quite a distance before they managed to scramble into the body of the ambulance over the other legs jutting out through the torn door. Then it was too noisy to tell Hardenburg about his wife.

It was hard to remember when the firing started. There was a ragged crackling near the head of the column and the vehicles stopped. Then Christian realized that he had been hearing the noise for what seemed like a long time without understanding what it was.

Men jumped heavily from the thin-skinned vehicles and scattered into the desert on both sides of the road. A wounded man fell out of the ambulance and crawled, digging his fingers into the ground, dragging one useless leg, to a little clump of grass ten meters to the right. He lay there, busily hollowing out a little space in front of him with his hands. Machine guns started all around them and the armored vehicles swung without any recognizable plan to both sides and opened fire wildly, in all directions. A man without a cap walked swiftly up and down near them alongside the deserted trucks, with their motors still going, bellowing, "Answer it! Answer it, you bastard." He was bald and capless and his dome shone whitely in the moonlight. He was waving a swagger stick insanely in the air. He must be at least a colonel, Christian thought.

Motor shells were dropping sixty meters away. A fire started in one of the carriers there. In the light Christian could see men being dragged roughly away from the road. Hardenburg drove the motorcycle alongside the ambulance and stopped it. He peered sharply across the desert, the little v of the handkerchief whipping around his chin like a misplaced beard.

The British were using tracers in their machine guns and and light artillery now. The lazy, curving streaks were sweeping in, seeming to gather speed as they neared the convoy. It was impossible for Christian to figure out where they were firing from. It is very disorderly, he thought reproachfully, it is impossible to fight under ridiculous conditions like this. He started to get off the motorcycle. He would merely walk away from this and lie down and wait for something to happen to him.

"Stay here!" Hardenburg shouted, although he was only twelve inches from him. More disorder, Christian thought, resentfully sitting back on the pillion. He felt for his gun but he did not remember what he had done with it. There was an acrid, biting smell of disinfectant coming from the ambulance, mixed with the smell of the dead. Christian began to cough. A shell whistled in and hit nearby and Christian ducked against the metal side of the ambulance. A moment later he felt a tap on his back. He put his hand up, knocking a hot spent fragment of shrapnel from his shoulder. In reaching back, he found his gun slung over his shoulder. He was heavily trying to disentangle it when Hardenburg kicked the machine into movement. Christian nearly fell off. The barrel of the gun hit him under the chin and he bit his tongue and tasted the blood, salty and hot, from the cut his teeth had made. He clung to Hardenburg. The motorcycle careened off among the crouching figures and the noise and the intermittent explosions. A stream of tracers from a great distance arched toward them. Hardenburg held the bucking machine on a straight course under the tracers and they pulled out of the glare of the flaming trucks.

"Very disorderly," Christian murmured. Then he got angry with Hardenburg. If he wanted to go riding into the British Army, let him do it. Why did he have to drag Christian with him? Craftily, Christian decided to fall off the machine. He tried to pick up his foot, but his trouser leg seemed to be caught on a protruding strip of metal and he couldn't lift his knee. Vaguely, ahead of them, and to one side, he saw the dark outlines of tanks. Then the tanks swung their guns around. A machine gun from one of the turrets opened on them, and there was the sickening whistle as the bullets screamed behind their heads.

Christian bent down and pressed his head crookedly against the Lieutenant's shoulder. The Lieutenant was wearing a leather harness and the buckles scraped against Christian's cheekbone. The machine gun swung around again. This time the bullets were hitting in front of them, knocking up puffs of moonlit dust, and bouncing up with thick savage thuds.

Then Christian began to cry, clinging to the Lieutenant, and he knew he was afraid, and that he could do nothing to save himself and they would be hit and he and the Lieutenant and the motorcycle would crash in a single, smoking mass, burnt cloth and blood and gasoline in a dark pool on the sand, and then there was someone shouting in English, and waving wildly nearby. Hardenburg was grunting and bending over more than ever. Then the whistles came from behind them, and suddenly they were alone on a pale streak of road, with the noise dying down far to the rear.

Finally, Christian stopped crying. He sat up straight when Hardenburg sat up, and he even managed to look with some interest at the open road peeling out in front of the bouncing motorcycle. His mouth tasted very queer, with the vomit and the blood, and his cheek was stinging him as sand flew up under his handkerchief and ground into the bruises there. But he took a deep breath, feeling much better. For a moment, he did not even feel tired.

Behind him the glare and the firing died down quickly. In five minutes they seemed to have the desert to themselves, all the long, quiet, moonlit waste from the Sudan to the Mediterranean, from Alamein to Tripoli.

He held Hardenburg affectionately. He remembered that he had wanted to tell the Lieutenant something before all this had started, but, at the moment, what he had intended to say escaped him. He took the handkerchief off his face and looked around him and felt the wind whipping the spit out of the corners of his mouth, and he felt quite happy and at peace with the world. Hardenburg was a strange man, but Christian knew he could depend upon him to get him some place safely. Just where he would get him and at what time, Christian did not know, but there was no need to worry. How lucky it was that Captain Mueller, in command of their company, had been killed. If he had been alive it would have been Mueller and Hardenburg on the motorcycle now, and Christian would still be back on that hill with the three dozen other dead men . . .

He breathed deeply of the dry, rushing air. He was sure now that he was going to live, perhaps even for quite a long time.

Hardenburg handled the motorcycle very well, and they covered a good deal of ground, skidding, bouncing into the air, but steadily going north and west with the sky behind them lightening in the pink streaks of dawn. The road and the desert were empty except for the usual wreckage, all picked neat and clean by the salvage battalions. There was still the noise of firing behind them, but faraway, moaning and re-echoing in eccentric rhythms, dying down for minutes at a time.

The sun came up. Hardenburg, now that he could see, increased the speed of the machine, and Christian had to concentrate to hold on.

"Are you sleepy?" Hardenburg asked, talking loudly, turning his head so that Christian could hear him over the cough of the engine.

"A little," Christian admitted. "Not too bad."

"You'd better talk to me," Hardenburg said. "I nearly fell asleep just now."

"Yes, Sir," said Christian. He opened his mouth as if to say something, but closed it again. He tried to prepare some conversation in his head, but it was absolutely blank.

"Go ahead," shouted Hardenburg irritably. "Talk!"

"Yes, Sir," said Christian. Then, helplessly. "About what?"

"Anything. The weather." Christian looked around at the weather. It was the same weather they had had for six months. "It's going to be a hot day," he said.

"Louder," shouted Hardenburg, looking straight ahead. "I can't hear you."

"I said it's going to be a hot day," Christian screamed into the Lieutenant's ear.

"That's better," Hardenburg said. "Yes. Very hot."

Christian tried to think of another subject.

"Come on," Hardenburg said impatiently.

"What else would you like to talk about?" Christian asked. His mind felt drugged and incapable of this exhausting intellectual effort.

"Good God! Anything! Did you go to the Greek whorehouse they set up in Cyrene?"

"Yes, Sir," said Christian.

"How was it?"

"I don't know," said Christian. "I waited in line and they closed up three men in front of me."

"Did anybody you know go?"

Christian thought hard. "Yes," he said, "a Corporal with a head wound."

"How did he like it?"

Christian tried to remember. "I think he said the Greek girls were not much. They had no spirit. Also," Christian remembered now, "he said it was too official. He had difficulty managing it under the time limit. And the girl didn't do anything. Just lay there. He thought the Army ought to get volunteers, not just anybody they can put their hands on."

"Your friend is an idiot," Hardenburg said viciously.

"Yes, Sir," said Christian. He fell silent.

"Come on." Hardenburg waved his head sharply, as though

240

to clear his eyes. "Keep talking. What did you do on your leave in Berlin?"

"I went to the opera," Christian said promptly, "and I went to the concerts."

"You're an idiot, too."

"Yes, Sir," said Christian, thinking, warily, he is getting terribly light-headed.

"Any girls in Berlin?"

"Yes, Sir." Christian thought carefully. "I met a girl who worked in an airplane factory."

"Did you have an affair with her?"

"Yes."

"How was it?"

"Excellent," Christian said loudly, peering anxiously out across the Lieutenant's bent head at the desert stretching in a growing glitter ahead of them.

"Good," said the Lieutenant. "What was her name?"

"Marguerite," said Christian, after a slight hesitation.

"Was she married?"

"I don't think so," Christian said. "She didn't say."

"Sluts," Hardenburg said addressing the girls of Berlin. "Have you ever been to Alexandria?"

"No, Sir," Christian said.

"I was looking forward to going there," said Hardenburg.

"I don't think we'll ever get there now," Christian said.

"Keep quiet!" shouted Hardenburg. The motorcycle took an alarming twist before he righted it. "We'll get there! Do you hear me! I said we'll get there! And get there soon! Do you hear me?"

"Yes, Sir," shouted Christian into the wind streaming back across the Lieutenant's head.

The Lieutenant twisted in his seat. His face was contorted and his eyes gleamed between the crusted lids. His mouth was open and his teeth were a garish white against the black lips. "I order you to keep quiet!" he shouted insanely, as though he were on a windy drill field, discipling a full company of raw troops. "Keep your goddamn mouth shut or I'll . . ."

Then the handlebars jerked to one side. The front wheel skidded around and the Lieutenant's hands bounced away from the grips. Christian felt himself falling and lunged forward, grasping the Lieutenant. The impact knocked the Lieutenant over the bucking front wheel and the machine skidded crazily off the track, the engine roaring loudly. Suddenly it dipped to one side and crashed. Christian felt himself flying through the air, screaming, but somewhere inside of him a voice was saying quietly, This is too much, too much. Then he hit and he felt a numbness in his shoulder, but he got up to one knee.

The Lieutenant was lying under the motorcycle, whose front

wheel was still spinning. The back wheel was a mass of twisted junk. The Lieutenant was lying quietly, blood spurting from a gash in his forehead, with his legs at a very queer angle under the machine. Christian walked slowly over to him, and started pulling at him. But that didn't work. So he laboriously lifted the motorcycle and toppled it over to the other side, away from Hardenburg. Then he sat down and rested. After a minute or so, he took out his first-aid kit and put a bandage clumsily over the blood on the Lieutenant's forehead. It looked very neat and professional for a moment. But then the blood came through and it looked like all the other bandages he had ever seen.

Suddenly the Lieutenant sat up. He looked once at the machine, and said crisply, "Now we walk." But when he tried to get up he couldn't. He looked at his legs reflectively. "Nothing serious," he said, as though to convince himself. "I assure you, it is nothing serious. Are you all right?"

"Yes, Sir," said Christian.

"I think," said the Lieutenant, "I had better rest for ten minutes. Then we shall see." He lay back with his hands clutching the sodden bandage over his forehead.

Christian sat next to him. He watched the front wheel of the motorcycle slowly stop spinning. It had been making a small, whining noise, that grew lower and lower in tone. When the wheel stopped, there was no more sound. No sound from the motorcycle, no sound from the armies intertwined with each other somewhere else on the continent.

The face of the desert looked fresh and cool in the new sun. Even the wrecks looked simple and harmless in the fresh light. Christian slowly uncorked his canteen. He drank one mouthful of water carefully, rolling it around on his tongue and teeth before swallowing it. The sound of his swallowing was loud and wooden. Hardenburg opened one eye to see what he was doing.

"Save your water," he said automatically.

"Yes, Sir," said Christian, thinking with admiration: That man would give an order to the devil who was shoveling him through the door of the furnace in hell. Hardenburg, he thought, what a triumph of German military education. Orders spurted from him like blood from an artery. At his last gasp he would be laying his plans for the next three actions.

Finally Hardenburg sighed and sat up. He patted the wet bandage on his head. "Did you put this on?" he asked.

"Yes, Sir."

"It will fall off the first time I move," Hardenburg said coldly, objectively criticizing, without anger. "Where did you learn to put on bandages?"

"Sorry, Sir," said Christian. "I must have been a bit shaken myself."

242

"I suppose so," Hardenburg said. "Still, it's silly to waste a bandage." He opened his tunic and took out an oilskin case. From the case he took a sharply folded terrain map. He spread the map on the desert floor. "Now," he said, "we see where we are."

Wonderful, Christian thought, fully equipped for all eventualities.

Hardenburg blinked from time to time as he studied the map. He grimaced with pain as he held the bandage on. But he figured rapidly, mumbling to himself. He folded the map and put it back briskly into the case and carefully tucked it away inside his tunic. "Very well," he said. "This track joins with another one, leading west, perhaps eight kilometers away. Do you think you can make it?"

"Yes, Sir," said Christian. "How about you?"

Hardenburg looked at him disdainfully. "Don't worry about me. On your feet," he barked, again to the phantom company he was continually addressing.

Christian rose slowly. His shoulder and arm pained considerably, and he could move the arm only with difficulty. But he knew he could walk several of the eight kilometers, if not all of them. He watched Hardenburg push himself up from the sand with a furious effort. The sweat broke out on his face and the blood began to come through the bandage on his forehead again. But when Christian leaned over to try to help him, Hardenburg glared at him, and said, "Get away from me, Sergeant!"

Christian stepped back and watched Hardenburg struggle to raise himself. He dug his heels into the grainy sand as though getting ready to take the shock of being hit by an onrushing giant. Then, with his right elbow held rigid, he pushed ferociously, with cold purpose, at the ground. Slowly, inch by inch, with the pain shouting mutely from his livid face, he raised himself till he was half-bent over, but off the ground. With a wrench, he pulled himself upright and stood there, wavering, but erect, the sweat and blood mixed with the grime on his face in a thick, alarming compost. He was weeping, Christian noticed with surprise, the tears making harsh lines down the nameless paste on his cheeks. His breath came hard, in dry, tortured sobs, but he set his teeth. In a grotesque, clumsy movement, he faced north.

"All right," he said. "Forward march."

He started out along the thick sand of the track, ahead of Christian. He limped, and his head bobbed crazily to one side as he walked, but he continued steadily, without looking back.

Christian followed him. He was feverishly thirsty. The gun slung over his shoulder seemed maliciously heavy, but he resolved not to drink or ask for a rest until Hardenburg did so first.

They shuffled slowly, in a broken, deliberate tandem, across the sand, among the occasional rusting wrecks, toward the road to the north where other Germans might be beating their way back from the battle. Or where the British might be waiting for them.

Christian thought impersonally and calmly about the British. They did not seem real or menacing. Only two or three things were real at the moment: the coppery taste in his throat, like sour brewery mash, the crippled, animal-like gait of Hardenburg before him, the sun rising higher and higher and with increasing, malevolent heat, behind their backs. If the British were waiting on the track that was a problem that would have to be solved in its own time. He was too occupied to grapple with it now.

They were sitting down for the second rest, stunned, sun-lacerated, their eyes dull with agony and fatigue, when they saw the car on the horizon. It was coming fast, with a swirl of dust like a plume behind it. In two minutes they saw that it was a smart open staff car, and a moment later they realized it was Italian.

Hardenburg pushed himself up with a bone-cracking effort. He limped slowly out into the middle of the track and stood there, breathing heavily, but staring calmly at the onrushing machine. He looked wild and threatening with the bloody bandage angled across his forehead, and his purple, sunken eyes. His bloodstained hands hooked ready at his sides.

Christian stood up, but did not go into the center of the track beside Hardenburg.

The car raced toward them, its horn blowing loudly, losing itself somehow in the emptiness and sounding like the echo of a warning. Hardenburg didn't move. There were five figures in the open car. Hardenburg stood cold and motionless, watching them. Christian was sure the car was going to run the Lieutenant down and he opened his mouth to call, when there was a squeal of brakes and the long, smart-looking machine skidded to a stop an arm's length in front of Hardenburg.

There were two Italian soldiers in front, one driving and the other crouched beside him. In the rear there were three officers. They all stood up and shouted angrily at Hardenburg in Italian.

Hardenburg did not move. "I wish to speak to the ranking officer here," he called coldly in German.

There was more Italian. Finally a dark, stout Major said, in bad German. "That is me. If you have anything you wish to say to me, come over here and say it."

"You will kindly dismount," Hardenburg said, standing absolutely still, in front of the car.

The Italians chattered among themselves. Then the Major opened the rear door and jumped down, fat and wrinkled in what had once been a pretty uniform. He advanced belligerently on Hardenburg. Hardenburg saluted grandly. The salute looked theatrical coming from this scarecrow in the glaring emptiness of the desert. The Major clicked his heels in the sand and saluted in return.

"Lieutenant," the Major said nervously, looking at Hardenburg's tabs, "we are in a great hurry. What is it you wish?"

"I am under orders," Hardenburg said coldly, "to requisition transportation for General Aigner."

The Major opened his mouth sadly, then clicked it shut. He looked hurriedly about him, as though he expected to see General Aigner spring suddenly from the blank desert.

"Nonsense," the Major said finally. "There is a New Zealand patrol coming up this road and we cannot delay . . ."

"I am under specific orders, Major," said Hardenburg in a sing-song voice. "I do not know anything about a New Zealand patrol."

"Where is General Aigner?" the Major looked around uncertainly again.

"Five kilometers from here," Hardenburg said. "His armored car threw a tread and I am under specific orders . . ."

"I have heard it!" the Major screamed. "I have already heard about the specific orders."

"If you will be so kind," Hardenburg said, "you will order the other gentlemen to dismount. The driver may remain."

"Get out of the way," said the Major. He started back toward the car. "I have heard enough of this nonsense."

"Major," said Hardenburg coldly and gently. The Major stopped and faced him, sweating. The other Italians stared at him worriedly, but not understanding the German.

"It is out of the question," said the Major, his voice trembling. "Absolutely out of the question. This is an Italian Army vehicle and we are on a mission to . . ."

"I am very sorry, Sir," said Hardenburg. "General Aigner outranks you and this is German Army territory. You will kindly deliver your vehicle."

"Ridiculous!" the Major said, but faintly.

"At any rate," Hardenburg said, "there is a road block ahead, and the men there have orders to confiscate all Italian transport. By force if necessary. You will then have to explain what three field grade officers are doing at a moment like this so far from their organizations. You will also have to explain why you took it upon yourself to disregard a specific order from General Aigner who is in command of all troops in this sector."

He stared coldly at the Major. The Major raised his hand in a strangled gesture. Hardenburg's expression had not changed at all. It still was weary, disdainful, rather bored. He turned his back on the Major and walked toward the car. Miraculously he even managed for these five steps not to limp.

"Furi!" he said, opening the door to the front of the car. "Out! The driver will remain," he said in Italian. The man beside the driver looked around beseechingly at the officers in the rear of the car. They avoided the man's glance and stared nervously at the Major, who had followed Hardenburg.

Hardenburg tapped the soldier in the front seat on the arm. *"Furi,"* he repeated calmly.

The soldier wiped his face. Then, looking down at his boots, he got out of the car and stood unhappily next to the Major. They looked amazingly alike, two soft, dark, disturbed Italian faces, handsome and unmilitary and worried.

"Now," Hardenburg gestured to the other two officers, "you gentlemen . . ." The wave of his arm was unmistakable.

The two officers looked at the Major. One of them spoke rapidly in Italian. The Major sighed and answered in three words. The two officers got out of the car and stood beside the Major.

"Sergeant," Hardenburg called without looking over his shoulder.

Christian came up and stood at attention.

"Clean the back of the car out, Sergeant," Hardenburg ordered, "and give these gentlemen everything that belongs to them, personally."

Christian looked into the back of the car. There were water cans, three bottles of Chianti, two boxes of rations. Methodically, one by one, he lifted the rations and the bottles and put them at the Major's feet on the side of the road. The three officers stared glumly down at their possessions being unloaded onto the desert sand.

Christian fingered the water cans thoughtfully. "The water, too, Lieutenant?" he asked.

"The water, too," Hardenburg said without hesitation.

Christian put the water cans beside the ration boxes.

Hardenburg went to the rear of the car, where there were rolls of bedding strapped against the metal. He took out his knife. With three swift slashes he cut the leather thongs holding them onto the car. The canvas rolls dropped open into the dust. One of the officers started to speak angrily in Italian, but the Major silenced him with an abrupt wave of his hand. The Major stood very erect in front of Hardenburg. "I insist," he said in German, "upon a receipt for the vehicle."

"Naturally," Hardenburg said gravely. He took out his map. He tore off a small rectangular corner and wrote slowly on the back of it. "Will this do?" he asked. He read aloud in a clear, unhurried voice. "Received from Major So and So . . . I am leaving the place blank, Major, and you can fill it in at your leisure . . . one Fiat staff car, with driver. Requisitioned by order of General Aigner. Signed, Lieutenant Siegfried Hardenburg."

The Major snatched the paper and read it over carefully. He waved it. "I will present this at the proper place," he said loudly, "in the proper time."

"Of course," Hardenburg said. He stepped into the rear of the car. "Sergeant," he said, sitting down, "sit back here."

Christian got into the car and sat down beside the Lieutenant. The seat was made of beautifully sewn tan leather and there was a smell of wine and toilet water. Christian stared impassively ahead of him at the burned brown neck of the driver in the front seat. Hardenburg leaned across Christian and slammed the door. "*Avanti*," he said calmly to the driver.

The driver's back tensed for a moment and Christian saw a flush spreading up the bare neck from below the collar. Then the driver delicately put the car in gear. Hardenburg saluted. One by one, the three officers returned the salute. The private who had been sitting beside the driver seemed too stunned to lift his hand.

The car moved smoothly ahead, the dust from its spinning wheels tossing lightly over the small group on the side of the road. Christian felt an almost involuntary muscular pull to turn around, but Hardenburg's hand clamped on his arm. "Don't look!" Hardenburg snapped.

Christian tried to relax into the seat. He waited for the sound of shots, but they didn't come. He looked at Hardenburg. The Lieutenant was smiling, a small, frosty smile. He was enjoying it, Christian realized with slow surprise. With all his wounds and with his company lost behind him and God knows what ahead of him, Hardenburg was enjoying the moment, savoring it, delighting in it. Christian couldn't smile, but he sank back into the soft leather, feeling his racked bones settling luxuriously in his resting flesh.

"What would have happened," he asked after awhile, "if they had decided to hold onto the car?"

Hardenburg smiled, his eyelids half-lowered in sensuous enjoyment as he spoke. "They would have killed me," he said. "That is all."

Christian nodded gravely. "And the water," he said. "Why did you let them have the water?"

"Ah," Hardenburg said, "that would have been just a little

247

too much." He chuckled as he settled back in the rich leather.

"What do you think will happen to them?" Christian asked.

Hardenburg shrugged carelessly. "They will surrender and go to British prison. Italians love to go to prison. Now," he said, "keep quiet. I wish to sleep."

A moment later, his breath coming evenly, his bloody, filthy face composed and childlike, he was sleeping. Christian remained awake. Someone, he thought, ought to watch the desert and the driver who sat rigidly before them, holding the speeding, powerful car on the road.

Merse Matruh was like a candy-box in which a death had taken place. They tried to find someone to report to, but the town was a chaos of trucks and staggering men and broken armor among the ruins. While they were there a squadron of planes came over and dropped bombs on them for twenty minutes. There were more ruins and an ambulance train was spilled open, with men shouting like animals from the twisted wreckage, and everybody seemed intent only upon pressing west, so Hardenburg ordered the driver into the long, slowly moving stream of vehicles and they made their way toward the outskirts of the town. There was a control post there, with a gaunt-eyed Captain with a long sheet of paper mounted on a board. The Captain was taking down names and organization designations from the caked and exhausted men streaming past him. He looked like a lunatic accountant trying to balance impossible accounts in a bank that was tottering in an earthquake. He did not know where their Division Headquarters were, or whether they still existed. He kept saying in a loud, dead voice, through the cake of dust around his lips, "Keep moving. Keep moving. Ridiculous. Keep moving."

When he saw the Italian driver he said, "Leave that one here with me. We can use him to defend the town. I'll give you a German driver."

Hardenburg spoke gently to the Italian. The Italian began to cry, but he got out of the car, and stood next to the Captain with the long sheet of paper. He took his rifle with him, but held it sadly near the muzzle, dragging it in the dust. It looked harmless and inoffensive in his hands as he stared hopelessly at the guns and the trucks and the tottering soldiers rolling past him.

"We will not hold Matruh forever," Hardenburg said grimly, "with troops like that."

"Of course," the Captain said crazily. "Naturally not. Ridiculous." And he peered into the dust and put down the organization numbers of two anti-tank guns and an armored car that rumbled past him, smothering him in a fog of dust.

But he gave them a tank driver who had lost his tank and a

248

Messerschmitt pilot who had been shot down over the town to ride with them, and told them to get back to Solum as fast as possible, there was a likelihood things were in better shape that far back.

The tank driver was a large blond peasant who grasped the wheel solidly as he drove. He reminded Christian of Corporal Kraus, dead outside Paris long ago with cherry stains on his lips. The pilot was young, but bald, with a gray, shrunken face, and a bad twitch that pulled his mouth to the right twenty times a minute. "This morning," he kept saying, "this morning I did not have this. It is getting worse and worse. Does it look very bad?"

"No," said Christian, "you hardly notice it."

"I was shot down by an American," the pilot said, wonderingly. "Imagine that. The first American I ever saw." He shook his head as though this was the final and most devastating point scored against German arms in all the campaigns in Africa. "I didn't even know they were here. Imagine that!"

The blond peasant was a good driver. They darted in and out of the heavier traffic, making good time on the bombed and pitted road alongside the shining blue waters of the Mediterranean, stretching, peaceful and cool, to Greece, to Italy, to Europe . . .

It happened the next day.

They still had their car and they had siphoned gasoline out of a wrecked truck along the road, and they were in a long, slow line that was moving in fits and starts up the winding, ruined road that climbs from the small, wiped out village of Solum to the Cyrenaican escarpment. Down below, the fragments of walls gleamed white and pretty about the keyhole-shaped harbor, where the water shone bright green and pure blue as it sliced into the burned land. Wrecks of ships rested in the water, looking like the deposit of ancient wars, their lines wavering gently and peacefully in the slight ripples.

The pilot was twitching worse than ever now and insisted upon looking at himself in the rearview mirror all the time, in an effort to catch the twitch at the moment of inception and somehow freeze it there to study it. So far he had not been successful, and he had screamed in agony every time he fell off to sleep the night before. Hardenburg was getting very impatient with him.

But there were signs that order was being restored down below. There were anti-aircraft guns set up about the town, and two battalions of infantry could be seen digging in on the eastern edge, and a General had been seen striding back and forth near the harbor, waving his arms about and delivering himself of orders.

Certain armored elements had been held out of the column that stretched back as far as the eye could reach. They were being assembled in a reserve area behind the infantry and small figures could be seen from the height pouring fuel and handing up ammunition to the men working in the turrets.

Hardenburg was standing up in the rear of the car, surveying everything keenly. He had even managed to shave in the morning, although he was running a high fever. His lips were cracked and covered with sores, he had a new bandage on his forehead, but he looked once more like a soldier. "This is where we stop them," he announced. "This is as far as they go."

Then the planes had come in low from the sea, the drumming of their engines drowning out the slow roar of the armor on the climbing road. They came in regular, arrow-like formation, like stunt-fliers at a carnival. They looked slow and vulnerable. But somehow, no one was firing at them. Christian could see the bombs dropping in twisting, curling arcs. Then the mountainside was exploding. A truck deliberately toppled over above them, and went crashing ponderously into the ravine a hundred meters below. One boot flew in a long, tumbling curve out from it, as though it had been thrown out from the truck by a man who was resolved to save the first thing that came to his hand from the wreck.

Then the bomb hit close by. Christian felt himself being lifted, and he thought: It is not fair, after having come so far and so hard, it is not at all fair. Then he knew he was hurt, except that there was no pain, and he knew that he was going to go out, and it was quite peaceful and delicious to relax into the spinning, many-colored, but painless chaos. Then he was out.

Later, he opened his eyes. Something was weighing him down and he pushed against it, but there was no use. There was the yellow smell of cordite and the brassy smell of burned rock and the old smell of dying vehicles, burning rubber and leather and singed paint. Then he saw a uniform and a bandage and he realized that it must be Lieutenant Hardenburg, and Lieutenant Hardenburg was saying calmly, "Get me to a doctor." But only the voice and the tabs and the bandage was Lieutenant Hardenburg because there was no face there at all. There was just a red and white pulpy mass, with the calm voice coming somehow through the red bubbles and the white strips of whatever it had been that held the side of Lieutenant Hardenburg's face together. Dreamily, Christian tried to remember where he had seen something like that before. It was hard to remember because he had a tendency to go out again, but finally it came back to him. It was like a pomegranate, roughly and inaccurately broken open, veined and red and with the juice running from the glistening, ripe globules past the knife down onto the shining ivory plate. Then he began to hurt and he didn't think about anything else for a long time.

CHAPTER SEVENTEEN

"THEY ASSURE ME," the voice behind the bandages was saying, "that in two years they can give me a face. I am not under any illusions. I will not look like a motion-picture actor, but I am confident it will be a serviceable face."

Christian had seen some of the serviceable faces that the surgeons patched onto the wrecked skulls delivered to their tables, and he was not as confident as Hardenburg, but he merely said, "Of course, Lieutenant."

"It is already almost definite," the voice went on, "that I will see out of my right eye within a month. By itself that is a victory, even if it was as far as they could go."

"Certainly, Lieutenant," Christian said in the darkened room of the villa on the pretty island of Capri, standing in the winter sunlight of the Bay of Naples. He was sitting between the beds, with his right leg, bandaged and stiff in front of him, just touching the marble floor and his crutches leaning against the wall.

The case in the other bed was a Burn, an armored-division burn, very bad, and the Burn merely lay still under his ten meters of bandage, filling the high-ceilinged cool room with the usual smell, which was worse than the aroma of the dead, but which Hardenburg could not smell, because he had nothing left to smell with. An economically-minded nurse had realized this fortunate fact and had placed them side by side, since the hospital, once a vacation spot of a prosperous Lyons silk manufacturer, was being crowded more and more every day with the surgically interesting products of the fighting in Africa.

Christian was in a larger hospital down the hill, devoted to the common soldiers, but they had given him his crutches a week ago, and he now felt like a free man.

"It is very good of you, Diestl," said Hardenburg, "to come and visit me. As soon as you get hurt people have a tendency to treat you as though you were eight years old, and your brain goes to rot along with everything else."

"I was very anxious to see you," Christian said, "and tell you in person how grateful I am for what you did for me. So when I heard you were on the Island, too, I . . ."

"Nonsense!" It was amazing how much the same, clipped, precise, snarling, Hardenburg's voice was, although the whole façade that had shielded the voice was now gone. "Gratitude is out of order. I did not save you out of affection, I assure you."

"Yes, Sir," said Christian.

"There were two places on that motorcycle. Two lives could be saved that might be useful somewhere later on. If there was someone else there who I thought would be more valuable later, I guarantee I would have left you."

"Yes, Sir," said Christian, staring at the smooth, white, unfeatured bandages wrapped so neatly about the head that he had last seen red and dripping on the hill outside Solum, with the noise of the British planes dying away in the distance.

The nurse came in. She was a motherly-looking woman of about forty, with a kindly, fat face. "Enough," she said. Her voice was not motherly, but bored and business-like. "The visit is over for the day."

She stood at the door, waiting to make sure that Christian left. Christian stood slowly, taking hold of his crutches. They made a sodden, wooden noise on the marble floor.

"At least," said Hardenburg, "I will be able to walk on my own two feet."

"Yes, Sir," Christian said. "I'll visit you again, if you are agreeable, Lieutenant."

"If you wish," said the voice behind the bandages.

"This way, Sergeant," said the nurse.

Christian tapped his way out clumsily, because he had only recently learned how to handle the crutches. It was very good to be out in the corridor, where you could not smell the Burn.

"She will not be too disturbed," Hardenburg was saying through the white muffling wall of bandage, "by the change in my appearance." He was talking about his wife. "I have written her and told her I was hit in the face and she said she was proud of me and that it would alter nothing."

No face, Christian thought, that is quite a change in appearance. But he said nothing. He sat between the two beds, with his leg out, and his crutches in their accustomed place against the wall.

Now he came to visit the Lieutenant almost every day. The Lieutenant talked, hour after hour, through the white darkness of the bandages, and Christian said, "Yes, Sir," and "No, Sir," and listened. The Burn still smelled just as badly, but after the first few gagging moments each time, Christian found himself able to bear it and even, after awhile, to forget it. Locked in his blindness, Hardenburg talked calmly and reflectively for hours on end, slowly unwinding the tissue of his life for his own and Christian's benefit, as though now, in this enforced and brutal holiday, he was taking inventory of himself, weighing himself, judging his past triumphs and errors and mapping out the possibilities of his future. It grew more and more fascinating for Christian, and he found himself spending half-days in the evil-smelling room, following the spiraling, oblique uncovering of a life that he felt to be more and more significantly locked with his own. The sickroom became a combination of lecture room and confessional, a place in which Christian could find his own mistakes clarified, his own vague hopes and aspirations crystallized, understood, categorized. The war was a dream on other continents, an unreal grappling of shadows, muffled trumpets in a distant storm, and only the room with the two swathed and stinking figures overlooking the sunny, blue harbor, was real, true, important.

"Gretchen will be very valuable to me," Hardenburg was saying, "after the war. Gretchen, that's the name of my wife."

"Yes, Sir," said Christian, "I know."

"How do you know? Oh, yes, I sent you to deliver a package."

"Yes, Sir," said Christian.

"She is quite handsome, Gretchen, isn't she?"

"Yes, Sir. Quite handsome."

"Very important," said Hardenburg. "You would be amazed at the number of careers that have been ruined in the Army by dowdy wives. She is also very capable. She has a knack for handling people . . ."

"Yes, Sir," said Christian.

"Did you have an opportunity to talk to her?"

"For about ten minutes. She questioned me about you."

"She is very devoted," said Hardenburg.

"Yes, Sir."

"I plan to see her in eighteen months. My face will be well enough along by then. I do not wish to shock her unnecessarily. Very valuable. She has a knack of being at home wherever she finds herself, of being at ease, saying the correct thing . . ."

"Yes, Sir."

"To tell you the truth, I was not in love with her when I married her. I was very much attached to an older woman. Divorced. With two children. Very attached. I nearly married her. It would have ruined me. Her father was a laborer in a metal factory and she herself had a tendency to fat. In ten years she will be monstrous. I had to keep reminding myself that in ten years I expected to have Ministers and Generals as guests in my home and that my wife would have to serve as hostess. She had a vulgar streak, too, and the children were impossible.

Still, even now, thinking of her, I feel a sinking, weak sensation. Have you ever been like that about a woman?"

"Yes, Sir," said Christian.

"It would have been ruinous," said the voice behind the bandages. "A woman is the most common trap. A man must be sensible in that department as in anything else. I despise a man who will sacrifice himself for a woman. It is the most sickly form of self-indulgence. If it were up to me, I would have all the novels burned, too, all of them, along with *Das Kapital* and the poems of Heine."

And another time, on a wet day, with the Bay outside the window gray and hidden in the sweep of winter rain . . . "After this one is over, we must leap into another war. Against the Japanese. It is always necessary to subdue your allies. It is something that is left out of *Mein Kampf*, perhaps, out of shrewdness on the author's part. And after that, it will be necessary to permit some nation, somewhere, to grow strong, so that we can always have an enemy who will be quite difficult to beat. To be great, a nation must always be stretched to the limits of its endurance. A great nation is always on the verge of collapse and always eager to attack. When it loses that eagerness, history begins to tap out the name on the tombstone. The Roman Empire stands as a perfect example for any intelligent people forever. The moment a people changes from, 'Whom shall I hit next?' to 'Who will be the next to hit me?' it is on the road to the dust-heap. Defense is only a coward's anagram for defeat. There is no successful defense to anything. Our civilization, so called, which is merely a combination of laziness and an unwillingness to die, is the great evil. England is the dessert on the Roman dinner. It is never possible to enjoy the fruits of war in peace. The fruits of war can only be enjoyed in further war, or you lose everything. When the British gazed around and said, 'Look what we have won. Now let us hold onto it,' an empire slipped through their fingers. It is always necessary to remain barbarians, because it is the barbarians who always win.

"We Germans have the best chance of all. We have an elite of daring and intelligent men, and we have a large, energetic population. It is true that other nations, say the Americans, have as many daring and intelligent men, and a population that is at least as energetic. But we are more fortunate, for one reason, and we shall conquer because of it. We are docile and they are not and probably never will be. We do what we are told and so we become an instrument in the hands of our leaders that can be used for decisive acts. The Americans can be made an instrument for a year, five years, but then they break up. The Russians are dangerous, merely because of their size.

254

Their leaders are stupid, as they always have been, and the energy of the people is canceled out by ignorance. It is only the size that is dangerous, and I do not believe it to be crucial."

The voice spun on, like the voice of a thoughtful scholar in a university library, reading from a well-loved book that had almost been memorized by the reader. The rain hit the window in soft, wet spurts, obscuring the harbor. The Burn in the next bed lay without moving, deep in its frightful smell, deep past hearing or caring or remembering anything.

"In several ways," Hardenburg was saying, "this wound of mine was a fortunate occurrence." It was another afternoon, still and dreamlike, with the sun late in the sky, and the entire landscape deep blue, water, air and mountains transparent and luminous outside the window. "Somehow, I was not very lucky in the Army—and this wound will mean I will not be tied to the Army any more. Somehow, I was never in the right spot in the Army. As you know, I was only promoted once, while men who had gone to school with me were promoted five times. There is no use complaining. It has nothing to do with favoritism or merit. It is merely a question of where you happen to be at certain moments. At a particular headquarters when the General there is given a lucky command. At a particular place in the line when the enemy attacks. How the despatches are worded on some mornings and who chances to read them that morning and how he is feeling at the moment . . . Well, it was becoming clear I was not lucky in that direction. Now they will not send me back into the Army. It is bad for the morale to have men commanded by an officer with a maimed face. Perfectly sensible. You do not march a company through a military cemetery before an attack if you can help it. Simple discretion. But a wounded face will be of value later, just the same. I intend going into politics. I had intended doing it later, through the Army, but I will save twenty years this way. Positions of leadership when the war is over will only be open to men who can prove they have served the Fatherland well on the battlefield. I will not have to wear my medals on my lapel. My face will be my medal. Pity, respect, gratitude, fear—my face will produce them all. There will be a world to be governed when this is over, and the Party will find my face as good a symbol as any to represent them in other countries.

"The idea of my face does not disturb me. When they take the bandages off I am going to get up and look at it in the mirror. I am quite certain that it is going to be horrible. Horror should not annoy a soldier any more than the sight of a hammer annoys a carpenter. It is sentimental to pretend that horror is not the tool of the soldier, just as the hammer is the tool of the carpenter. We live off death and the threat of death and we must take it calmly and use it well. For the purpose of our country we need an empty Europe. It is a mathematical problem and the equalizing sign is slaughter. If we believe in the truth of the answer we must not draw back from the arithmetic which solves the equation.

"Wherever we go everyone must realize that we are quick to kill. It is the most satisfactory key to dominion. Eventually I came to enjoy killing, as a pianist enjoys the Czerny which keeps his fingers limber for the Beethoven. It is the most valuable equipment in any military man, and when an officer loses it he should ask to be cashiered and returned to civilian life to take up bookkeeping.

"I have read some of your letters to your friends back home and I have been revolted by them. You are much older than I am, of course, and have been exposed to a great deal of Europe's nonsense, and I see your letters are full of talk about the great days of peace and prosperity for all the world that will come when the war is over. That is all very well for women and politicians, but a soldier should know better. He should not want peace, because peace is a buyer's market for a soldier, and he should know that prosperity can only be unilateral. We can be prosperous only if all Europe is a pauper, and a soldier should be delighted with that concept. Do I want the illiterate Pole, drunk on potato alcohol in the winter mud of his village, to be prosperous? Do I want the stinking goatherd in the Dolomites to be rich? Do I want a fat Greek homosexual to teach Law at Heidelberg? Why? I want servants, not competitors. And failing that, I want corpses. It is only because we are still part politicians, we Germans, selling ourselves to the world for an outdated and unnecessary vote of confidence, that we talk like that. In ten years we can display ourselves as what we are —soldiers, and nothing more, and then we can dispense with this nonsense. The soldier's world is the only real world. Any other world is something off the shelf of a library—rhetoric and old bindings. Flabby wishes and banquet speeches at a table at which all the guests have fallen asleep. Ten thousand shelves of books cannot stop one light tank. The Bible has been printed a billion times, perhaps, and a single patrol of five men in an armored car can break the ten commandments fifty times in a half hour in a Ukrainian village and celebrate that night over two cases of captured wine.

"War is the most fascinating of all pursuits, because it most completely fits the final nature of man, which is predatory and egotistic. I can say it because I have given my face for it, and no one can accuse me of loving it safely from a distance and for its rewards alone.

"I do not think we are going to lose this war, because we cannot afford to. But if we do lose it we will lose it because we

256

were not harsh enough. If we announced to the world that for every day of war, we would kill one hundred thousand Europeans, and kept our promise, how long do you think the war would last? And not Jews, because everyone is used to seeing Jews killed and everyone is more or less secretly delighted with us for our efficiency in that field. And the supply of Jews is not inexhaustible, no matter how generously we compute grandmothers. No. Europeans, Frenchmen, Poles, Russians, Dutchmen, English prisoners of war. We should print the lists of names with photographs, on good paper, and drop them over London instead of bombs. We are suffering because our conduct is not yet as mature as our philosophy. We kill Moses, but pretend to tolerate Christ, and we risk everything for that brainless pretense.

"When we overcome remorse we shall be the greatest people in Western history. We may do it without that, but in the meanwhile we are dragging a hidden anchor.

"I tell you these things because you're going back to the Army and I am not. I have had a chance these last months to think all these things out and I can use disciples. After the last war it took a wounded Corporal to save Germany from its defeat. After this war it may take a wounded Lieutenant to save Germany from its victory. You can write me from the front and I can lie back here while my face mends and feel that I have not been useless. I am younger than you, but I am far more mature because I have not done a thing since I was fifteen years old without relating it to my purpose. You have drifted and modified and sentimentalized and it has kept you in inconclusive adolescence. The reasonable modern man is the man who has learned to press things immediately, in a single step of logic, to their reasonable conclusions. I have done that and you have not, and until you learn to do so, you will be a child in a room full of grownups.

"Killing is an objective act and death is a state beyond right and wrong. I can kill a nineteen-year-old Lieutenant two months out of Oxford and leave three dozen Germans to die on a hill with exactly the same calculations, because I know these things. Each contributes as he can, all thirty-seven of them by dying in a particular way and at a particular time that I find convenient or necessary. I will weep over none of them, unless I am watched by a company who will be encouraged to die the same evening by my tears.

"If you think that I admire the German soldier you are wrong. He is better than other soldiers because he can be hammered harder without wearing through and because he will permit himself to be trained more thoroughly because he lacks imagination. But his courage is a trick that is played upon him, like any other soldier's courage, and his victory will mean no

257

more beer for him than before, and no less labor, and he does not know these things. An army finally is no more than the function of its numbers multiplied by the quality of its leaders. Clausewitz said that, and for once he was right. The German soldier is not responsible either for the fact that there are ten million more like him, or for the fact that he has the most gifted men in Europe guiding him. The birth rate of Central Europe takes care of the first and accident and the ambition of a thousand men takes care of the second.

"The German soldier has the good luck that at this balancing moment in history he is being led by men who are a little mad. Hitler falls into fits before the maps at Berchtesgaden. Goering was dragged from the sanitarium for dope addicts in Sweden. Roehm, Rosenberg, all the rest, would make old Dr. Freud rub his hands in Vienna if he peeked out and saw them waiting in his anteroom. Only the irrational vision of a madman could understand that an empire could be won in ten years merely by promising to institutionalize the pogrom. After all, Jews have been murdered for twenty centuries without any important result. We are being led against the sane and reasonable armies of men who could not deviate from the rules if they burst a kidney in the effort, and we are being led by men exalted by opium fumes and by gibbering Corporals who picked up their lessons in military affairs from serving tea in a trench to a broken Captain twenty-five years ago at Passchendaele. How can we expect to lose?

"If I had epilepsy or if I had been treated once for amnesia or paranoia I would have higher hopes for my success in Europe in the next thirty years, and I would serve my country better . . ."

The doctor was a gray-haired man. He looked seventy years old. He had pouches under his eyes of wrinkled purple skin, like the flesh of swamp flowers, and his hands shook as he poked harshly at Christian's knee. He was a Colonel and he looked too old even for a Colonel. There was brandy on his breath and the small, watery spurts of his eyes suspiciously searched Christian's scarred leg and Christian's face for the malingering and deception the doctor had found so often in thirty years of examining ailing soldiers of the Army of the Kaiser, the Army of the Social Democrats, and the Army of the Third Reich. Only the doctor's breath, Christian thought, has remained the same over the thirty years. The Generals have changed, the Sergeants have died, the philosophies have veered from north to south, but the Colonel's breath bears the same rich freight by a dark bottle out of Bordeaux that it did when Emperor Franz Josef stood beside his brother monarch in Vienna to review the first Saxony Guards on their way into Serbia.

"You'll do," said the Colonel, and the medical orderly busily marked down two ciphers on Christian's card. "Excellent. It doesn't look so good to the eye, but you can march fifty kilometers a day and never feel it. Eh?"

"I did not say anything, Colonel," said Christian.

"Full field duty," the Colonel said, peering harshly at Christian, as though Christian had contradicted him. "Eh?"

"Yes, Sir," said Christian.

The Colonel tapped the leg impatiently. "Roll down your trousers, Sergeant," he said. He watched Christian stand up and push his trouser leg down into place. "What was your profession, Sergeant, before the war?"

"I was a skiing instructor, Sir."

"Eh?" The Colonel glared at Christian as though he had just insulted him. "What was that?"

"Skiing, Sir."

"Eh," said the Colonel flatly. "You will not ski with that knee any more. It is for children anyway." He turned away from Christian and washed his hands, with meticulous thoroughness, as though Christian's bare pale flesh had been unutterably filthy. "Also, from time to time, you will find yourself limping. Eh, why not? Why shouldn't a man limp?" He laughed, showing yellow false teeth. "How will people know you have been in the war otherwise?"

He scrubbed busily at his hands in the large enamel sink that smelled so strongly of disinfectant as Christian went out of the room.

"You will kindly get me a bayonet," Hardenburg said. Christian was sitting at his side, looking at his leg, stretched, still stiff and dubious, out in front of him. In the next bed the Burn lay, lost as always in his silent Antarctic of bandage and his tropical and horrible smell. Christian had just told Hardenburg that he was leaving the next day for the Front. Hardenburg had said nothing, but had merely lain still and rigid, his smooth, swathed head like a frightening and morbid egg on the pillow. Christian had waited for a moment and then had decided that Hardenburg had not heard him. "I said, Lieutenant," he repeated, "that I was leaving tomorrow."

"I heard you," Hardenburg said. "You will kindly get me a bayonet."

"What was that, Sir?" Christian asked thinking: It only sounds like bayonet because of the bandages.

"I said I want a bayonet. Bring it to me tomorrow."

"I am leaving at two o'clock in the afternoon," Christian said.

"Bring it in the morning."

Christian looked at the overlapping, thin lines where the bandage crossed over itself on the round, smooth surface, but there was no expression there, of course, to give him a clue to what Hardenburg was thinking, and as usual, nothing was to be learned from the everlasting, even tone of the hidden voice. "I don't have a bayonet, Sir," he said.

"Steal one tonight. There is no complication there. You can steal one, can't you?"

"Yes, Sir."

"I don't want the scabbard. Just bring me the knife."

"Lieutenant," said Christian, "I am very grateful to you and I would like to be of service to you in every way I can, but if you are going to . . ." He hesitated. "If you are going to kill yourself, I cannot bring myself to . . ."

"I am not going to kill myself," the even, muffled voice said. "What a fool you are. You've listened to me for nearly two months now. Do I sound like a man who is going to kill himself?"

"No, Sir, but . . ."

"It's for him," Hardenburg said.

Christian straightened in the small armless wooden chair. "What's that, Sir?"

"For him, for him," Hardenburg said impatiently. "The man in the other bed."

Christian turned slowly and looked at the Burn. The Burn lay quiet, motionless, communicating nothing, as he had lain for two months. Christian turned back to the equal clot of bandage behind which lay the Lieutenant. "I don't understand, Sir," he said.

"He asked me to kill him," Hardenburg said. "It's very simple. He hasn't any hands left. Or anything left. And he wishes to die. He asked the doctor three weeks ago and the idiot told him to stop talking like that."

"I didn't know he could speak," Christian said dazedly. He looked at the Burn again, as though this newly discovered accomplishment must now somehow be apparent in the frightful bed.

"He can speak," Hardenburg said. "We have long conversations at night. He talks at night."

What discussions, Christian thought, must have chilled the Italian night air in this room, between the man who had no hands and no anything else left and the man without a face. He shivered. The Burn lay still, the covers shrouded over the fail frame. He hears now, Christian thought, staring at him, he understands every word we are saying.

"He was a watchmaker, in Nuremberg," Hardenburg said. "He specialized in sporting watches. He has three children and he has decided he wants to die. Will you kindly bring the bayonet?"

"Even if I bring it," Christian said, fighting to preserve himself from the bitter complicity of this eyeless, voiceless, finger-less, faceless suicide, "what good will it do? He couldn't use it anyway."

"I will use it," said Hardenburg. "Is that simple enough for you?"

"How will you use it?"

"I will get out of bed and go over to him and use it. Now will you bring it?"

"I didn't know you could walk . . ." Christian said dazedly. In three months, the nurse had told him, Hardenburg might expect to take his first steps.

With a slow, deliberate motion, Hardenburg threw back the covers from his chest. As Christian watched him rigidly, as he might watch a corpse that had just risen in its grave and stepped out, Hardenburg pushed his legs in a wooden, mechanical gesture, over the side of the bed. Then he stood. He was dressed in baggy, stained flannel pajamas. His bare feet were pallid and splotched on the marble floor of the Lyons silk manufacturer.

"Where is the other bed?" Hardenburg asked. "Show me the other bed."

Christian took his arm delicately and led him across the narrow space until Hardenburg's knees touched the other mattress. "There," Hardenburg said flatly.

"Why?" Christian asked, feeling as though he were putting questions to ghosts fleeing past a window in a dream. "Why didn't you tell anybody you could walk?"

Standing there, wavering a little in the yellowing flannel, Hardenburg chuckled behind his casque of bandage. "It is always necessary," he said, "to keep a certain amount of crucial information about yourself from the authorities who control you." He leaned over and felt lightly around on the blanket covering the chest of the Burn. Then his hand stopped. "There," a voice said from behind the icedrift of bandage above the counterpane. The voice was hoarse and lacking in human timbre. It was as though a dying bird, a panther drowning slowly in its own blood, an ape crucified on a sharp branch in a storm in the jungle, had at last accomplished speech with one final word. "There."

Hardenburg's hand stopped, pale yellow and bony, like a weathered and ancient x-ray of a hand on the white counter-pane.

"Where is it?" he asked harshly. "Where is my hand, Diestl?"

"On his chest," Christian whispered, staring fixedly at the ivory, spread fingers.

"On his heart," Hardenburg said. "J—ust above his heart. We have practiced this every night for two weeks." He turned, with blind certainty, and crossed to his bed and climbed into it. He pulled the covers up to where the helmet of bandage, like ar-

261

chaic armor, rose from his shoulders. "Now bring the bayonet. Don't worry about yourself. I will hide it for two days after you have gone, so that nobody can accuse you of the killing. And I will do it at night, when no one comes into the room for eight hours. And he will keep quiet." Hardenburg chuckled. "The watchmaker is very good at keeping quiet."

"Yes, Sir," said Christian quietly, getting up to leave, "I will bring the bayonet."

He brought the crude knife the next morning. He stole it at a canteen in the evening while its owner was singing "Lili Marlene" loudly over beer with two soldiers from the Quartermaster Corps. He carried it under his tunic to the marble villa of the silk manufacturer, and slid it under the mattress as Hardenburg directed. He only looked back once from the door, after he had said good-bye to the Lieutenant, looked back once at the two white blind figures lying still in the parallel beds in the tall-ceilinged rather gay room with the Bay shining and sunny outside through the high, elegant windows.

As he limped down the corridor, away from the room, his boots making a heavy, plebeian sound on the marble, he felt like a scholar who has finally been graduated from a university whose every book he has memorized and sucked dry.

CHAPTER EIGHTEEN

"ATTENTION!" A VOICE called from the door, dramatic and alarming, and Noah stiffened rigidly in front of his bunk.

Captain Colclough came in, followed by the Top Sergeant and Sergeant Rickett, and began his Saturday inspection. He walked slowly down the scrubbed middle of the barracks, between the stiff rows of barbered and laundered soldiers. He peered heavily at their hairlines and the shine on their shoes, with a hostile impersonality, as though these were not men he was inspecting, but enemy positions. The blazing Florida sunshine struck in through the bare windows.

The Captain stopped in front of the new man, Whitacre.

"Eighth General Order," Colclough said, staring coldly at Whitacre's necktie.

"To give the alarm," Whitacre said, "in case of fire or disorder."

"Rip that man's bed," Colclough said. Sergeant Rickett

stepped between the bunks and tore down Whitacre's bed. The sheets made a dry, harsh sound in the still barracks.

"This is not Broadway, Whitacre," Colclough said. "You are not living at the Astor Hotel. The maid does not come in here in the morning. You have to learn to make a satisfactory bed, here."

"Yes, Sir," Whitacre said.

"Keep your goddamn mouth shut!" Colclough said. "When I want you to talk I will give you a direct question and you will answer. Yessir, or Nosir."

Colclough moved down the aisle, his heels strident on the bare floor. The Sergeants moved softly behind him as though noise, too, was a privilege of rank.

Colclough stopped in front of Noah. He stared ponderously at him. Colclough had a very bad breath. It smelled as though something were rotting slowly and continuously in Colclough's stomach. Colclough was a National Guard officer from Missouri who had been an undertaker's assistant in Joplin before the war. His other customers, Noah thought crazily, probably did not mind the breath. He swallowed, hoping to drown the wild laughter that surged in his throat as the Captain glared at his chin for lurking signs of beard.

Colclough looked down at Noah's footlocker, at the sharply folded socks and the geometrically arranged toilet articles.

"Sergeant," he said, "remove the tray."

Ricket bent over and picked up the tray. Underneath were the rigidly folded towels, the stiffly arranged shirts, the woolen underwear, and under the other things, the books.

"How many books have you got there, Soldier?" Colclough asked.

"Three."

"Three, what?"

"Three, Sir."

"Are they government issue?"

Under the woolen underwear there were *Ulysses* and the *Collected Poems of T. S. Eliot* and the dramatic opinions of George Bernard Shaw. "No. Sir," said Noah, "they are not government issue."

"Only items of government issue, Soldier," said Colclough, his breath charging at Noah's face, "are to be exposed in footlockers. Did you know that, Soldier?"

"Yes, Sir," Noah said.

Colclough bent down and knocked the woolen underwear roughly to one side. He picked up the worn gray copy of *Ulysses*. Involuntarily, Noah bent his head to watch the Captain.

"Eyes front!" Colclough shouted.

Noah stared at a knothole across the barracks.

Colclough opened the book and leafed through some of the pages. "I know this book," he said. "It is a filthy, dirty book." He threw it on the floor. "Get rid of it. Get rid of all of them. This is not a library, Soldier. You're not here to read." The book lay open, face down, its pages crumpled on the floor, isolated in the middle of the barracks. Colclough brushed past Noah, between the double bunks, over to the window. Noah could sense him moving heavily around behind his back. He had a queer, exposed twitching sensation at the base of his spine.

"This window," Colclough said loudly, "has not been washed. This goddamn barracks is a goddamn pigpen." He strode out to the aisle again. Without stopping to inspect the rest of the men waiting silently before their cots, he walked to the end of the barracks, followed lightly by the Sergeants. At the door he turned around.

"I'm going to teach you men to keep a clean house," he said. "If you have one dirty soldier you're going to learn it's up to all of you to teach him to be clean. This barracks is confined to quarters until reveille tomorrow morning. There will be no passes given to anyone for the week-end and there will be an inspection tomorrow morning at nine o'clock. I advise you to make sure the barracks is in proper order by that time."

He turned and went out.

"Rest!" Sergeant Rickett shouted and followed the Top Sergeant and the Captain out of the building.

Slowly, conscious of the hundred accusing, deprived eyes upon him, Noah moved out to the middle of the aisle, where the book was lying. He bent over and picked it up and absently smoothed the pages. Then he walked over to the window that had been the cause of all the trouble.

"Saturday night," he heard in tones of bitter anguish from the other side of the room. "Confined on Saturday night! I got a date with a waitress that is on the verge and her husband arrives tomorrow morning! I feel like killing somebody!"

Noah looked at the window. It sparkled colorlessly, with the flat, dusty, sunbitten land behind it. On the lower pane in the corner a moth had somehow managed to fling itself against the glass and had died there in a small spatter of yellow goo. Reflectively, Noah lifted the moth off.

He heard steps behind him above the rising murmur of voices, but he continued standing there, holding the suicidal moth, feeling the dusty, unpleasant texture of the shattered wings, looking out over the glaring dust and the distant, weary green of the pinewoods on the other side of the camp.

"All right, Jew-boy." It was Rickett's voice behind him. "You've finally done it."

Noah still did not turn around. Outside the windows he saw

a group of three soldiers running, running toward the gate, running with the precious passes in their pockets, running to the waiting buses, the bars in town, the complaisant girls, the thirty-hour relief from the Army until Monday morning.

"About face, Soldier," Rickett said. The other men fell silent, and Noah knew that everyone in the room was looking at him. Slowly Noah turned away from the window and faced Rickett. Rickett was a tall, thickly built man with light-green eyes and a narrow colorless mouth. The teeth in the center of his mouth were missing, evidence of some forgotten brawl long ago, and it gave a severe twist to the Sergeant's almost lifeless mouth and played a curious, irregular lisping trick to his flat Texas drawl.

"Now, Tholdier," Rickett said, standing with his arms stretching from one bunk to another in a lounging, threatening position, "now Ah'm gawnta take you unduh mah puhsunal wing. Boyth." He raised his voice for the benefit of the listening men, although he continued to stare, with a sunken, harsh grin, at Noah. "Boyth, Ah promise you, this ith the last tahm little Ikie heah is goin' tuh interfeah with this ba'acks' Saturday nights. That's a solemn promith, Ah thweath t' Gahd. Thith ithn't a shitty thynagogue on the East Side, Ikie, thith ith a ba'ack in the Ahmy of the United Thtates of Americuh, and it hath t' be kep' shahnin' clean, white-man clean, Ikie, white-man clean."

Noah stared fixedly and incredulously at the tall, almost lipless man, slouching in front of him, between the two bunks. The Sergeant had just been assigned to their company the week before, and had seemed to pay no attention to him until now. And in all Noah's months in the Army, his Jewishness had never before been mentioned by anyone. Noah looked dazedly at the men about him, but they remained silent, staring at him accusingly.

"Lethun one," Rickett said, in the lisp that at other times you could joke about, "begins raht now, promptly and immediutly. Ikie, get into yo' fatigues and fetch yo'self a bucket. You are gahnta wash evry window in this gahdam ba'ack, and you're gahnta wash them lihk a white, churchgoin' Christian, t' mah thatishfaction. Get into yo' fatigues promptly and immediutly, Ikie, and start workin'. And ef these here windows ain't shahnin' like a whore's belly on Christmath Eve when Ah come around to inthpect them, bah Gahd, Ah promith you you'll regret it."

Rickett turned languidly and walked slowly out of the barracks. Noah went over to his bunk and started taking off his tie. He had the feeling that every man in the barracks was watching him, harshly and unforgivingly, as he changed into his fatigues.

Only the new man, Whitacre, was not watching him, and he was painfully making up his bunk, which Rickett had torn down at the Captain's orders.

Just before dusk, Rickett came around and inspected the windows.

"All raht, Ikie," he said finally. "Ah'm gahn t' be lenie it with yuh, this one tahm. Ah accept the windows. But, remembuh, Ah got mah eye on yuh. Ah'll tell yuh, heah an' now, Ah ain't got no use for Niggerth, Jewth, Mexicans or Chinamen, an' from now on you're goin' to have a powerful tough row to hoe in this here company. Now get your ass inside and keep it there. An' while you're at it, you better burn those bookth, like the Captain sayth. Ah don't mind tellin' you at thith moment that you ain't too terrible popular with the Captain, either, and if he seeth those bookth again, Ah wouldn't answer fo' yo' lahf. Move, Ikie. Ah'm tahd of lookin' at your ugly face."

Noah walked slowly up the barracks steps and went through the door, leaving the twilight behind him. Inside, men were sleeping, and there was a poker game in progress on two pulled-together footlockers in the center of the room. There was a smell of alcohol near the door, and Riker, the man who slept nearest the door, had a wide, slightly drunken grin on his face.

Donnelly, who was lying in his underwear on his bunk, opened one eye. "Ackerman," he said loudly, "I don't mind your killing Christ, but I'll never forgive you for not washing that stinking window." Then he closed his eye.

Noah smiled a little. It's a joke, he thought, a rough joke, but still a joke. And if they take it as something funny, it won't be too bad. But the man in the next bed, a long thin farmer from South Carolina, who was sitting up with his head in his hands, said quickly, with an air of being very reasonable, "You people got us into the war. Now why can't you behave yourselves like human beings?" and Noah realized that it wasn't a joke at all.

He walked deliberately toward his bunk, keeping his eyes down, avoiding looking at the other men, but sensing that they were all looking at him. Even the poker players stopped their game when he passed them and sat down on his bunk. Even Whitacre, the new man, who looked like quite a decent fellow, and who had, after all, suffered that day at the hands of Authority, too, sat on his re-made bed and stared with a hint of anger at him.

Fantastic, Noah thought. This will pass, this will pass . . .

He took out the olive-colored cardboard box in which he kept his writing paper. He sat on his bunk and began to write a letter to Hope.

"Dearest," he wrote, "I have just finished doing my house-

266

work. I have polished nine hundred and sixty windows as lovingly as a jeweler shining a fifty-carat diamond for a bootlegger's girl. I don't know how I would measure in a battle against a German infantryman or a Japanese Marine, but I will match my windows against their picked troops any day . . ."

"It's not the Jew's fault," said a clear voice from the poker game, "they're just smarter than everyone else. That's why so few of them are in the Army. And that's why they're making all the money. I don't blame them. If I was that smart I wouldn't be here neither. I'd be sitting in a hotel suite in Washington watching the money roll in."

There was silence then, and Noah could tell that all the players were looking at him, but he did not look up from his letter.

"We also march," Noah wrote slowly. "We march uphill and downhill, and we march during the day and during the night. I think the Army is divided into two parts. The fighting Army and the marching and window-washing Army, and we happen to be assigned to the second part. I have developed the springiest arches ever to appear in the Ackerman family."

"The Jews have large investments in France and Germany," another voice said from the poker game. "They run all the banks and whorehouses in Berlin and Paris, and Roosevelt decided we had to go protect their money. So he declared war." The voice was loud and artificial, and aimed like a weapon at Noah's head, but he refused to look up.

"I read in the papers," Noah wrote, "that this is a war of machines, but the only machine I have come across so far is a mop-wringer . . ."

"They have an international committee," the voice went on. "It meets in Poland, in a town called Warsaw, and they send out orders all over the world from there: Buy this, sell this, fight this country, fight that country. Twenty old rabbis with beards . . ."

"Ackerman," another voice said, "did you hear that?"

Noah finally looked across the bunks at the poker players. They were twisted around, facing him, their faces pulled by grins, their eyes marble-like and derisive.

"No," said Noah, "I didn't hear anything."

"Why don't you join us?" Silichner said with elaborate politeness. "It's a friendly little game and we're involved in an interesting discussion."

"No, thank you," Noah said. "I'm busy."

"What we'd like to know," said Silichner, who was from Milwaukee and had a trace of a German accent in his speech, as though he had spoken it as a child and never fully recovered from it, "is how you happened to be drafted. What happened—weren't there any fellow-members of the lodge on the board?"

Noah looked down at the paper in his hand. It isn't shaking, he thought, looking at it in surprise, it's as steady as can be.

"I actually heard," another voice said, "of a Jew who volunteered."

"No," said Silichner, wonderingly.

"I swear to God. They stuffed him and put him in the Museum."

The other poker players laughed loudly, in artificial rehearsed amusement.

"I feel sorry for Ackerman," Silichner said. "I actually do. Think of all the money he could be making selling black-market tires and gasoline if he wasn't in the infantry."

"I don't think," Noah wrote with a steady hand to his wife far away in the North, "that I have told you about the new Sergeant we got last week. He has no teeth and he lisps and he sounds like a debutante at a Junior League meeting when he . . ."

"Ackerman!"

Noah looked up. A Corporal from another barracks was standing beside his bunk. "You're wanted in the orderly room. Right away."

Very deliberately, Noah put the letter he was writing back in the olive-colored box and tucked the box away in his footlocker. He was conscious of the other men watching him closely, measuring his every move. As he walked past them, keeping himself from hurrying, Silichner said, "They're going to give him a medal. The Delancey Street Cross. For eating a herring a day for six months."

Again there were the rehearsed, artificial volleys of laughter.

I will have to try to handle this, Noah thought as he went out the door into the blue twilight that had settled over the camp. Somehow, somehow . . .

The air was good after the cramped, heavy smell of the barracks, and the wide silence of the deserted streets between the low buildings was sweet to the ear after the grating voices inside. Probably, Noah thought, as he walked slowly alongside the buildings, probably they are going to give me some new hell in the orderly room. But even so he was pleased at the momentary peace and the momentary truce with the Army and the world around him.

Then he heard a quick scurry of footsteps from behind a corner of the building he was passing, and before he could turn around he felt his arms pinned powerfully from behind.

"All right, Jew-boy," whispered a voice he almost recognized, "this is dose number one."

Noah jerked his head to one side and the blow glanced off his ear. But his ear felt numb and he couldn't feel the side of his face. They're using a club, he thought wonderingly as he

268

tried to twist away, why do they have to use a club? Then there was another blow and he began to fall.

When he opened his eyes, it was dark and he was lying on the sandy grass between two barracks. His face was collapsed and wet. It took him five minutes to drag himself over to the wall of the building and pull himself up along its side to a sitting position.

Michael was thinking of beer. He walked deliberately behind Ackerman, in the dusty heat, thinking of beer in glasses, beer in schooners, beer in bottles, kegs, pewter mugs, tin cans, crystal goblets. He thought of ale, porter, stout, then returned to thinking of beer. He thought of the places he had drunk beer in his time. The round bar on Sixth Avenue where the Regular Army Colonels in mufti used to stop off on the way uptown from Governor's Island, where they served beer in glasses that tapered down to narrow points at the bottom and where the bartender always iced the glass before drawing the foaming stuff out of the polished spigots. The fancy restaurant in Hollywood with prints of the French Impressionists behind the bar, where they served it in frosted mugs and charged seventy-five cents a bottle. His own living room, late at night, reading the next morning's paper in the quiet pool of light from the lamp, as he stretched, in slippers, in the soft corduroy chair before going to bed. At baseball games at the Polo Grounds in the warm, hazy summer afternoons, where they poured the beer into paper cups so that you couldn't throw the bottles at the umpires.

Michael marched steadily. He was tired and ferociously thirsty. His hands were numb and swollen, as they always were by the fifth mile of any hike, but he did not feel too bad. He heard Ackerman's harsh, grunting breath, and saw the way the boy rolled brokenly from side to side as he climbed the gentle slope of the road.

He felt sorry for Ackerman. Ackerman had obviously always been a frail boy, and the marches and problems and fatigues had worn the flesh off his bones, so that he now looked like a stripped-down version of a soldier, reedy and breakable. Michael felt a little guilty as he stared fixedly at the heaving, bent back. The long months of training had thinned Michael down, too, but with an athlete's leanness, leaving his legs steel-like and powerful, his body hard and resilient. It seemed unjust that in the same column, just in front of him, there was a man whose every step was suffering, while he felt so comparatively fit. Also, there had been the sickening hazing that Ackerman had been submitted to in the last two weeks. The constant ill-tempered jokes, the mock political discussions within Ackerman's hearing, in which men had said loudly. "Hitler is probably wrong most of the time, but you've got to hand it to him, he knows what to do about the Jews . . ."

Michael had tried once or twice to interrupt with a word of defense, but because he was new in the company, and came from New York and most of the men were Southerners, they ignored him and continued with their cruel game.

There was another Jew in the company, a huge man by the name of Fein, who wasn't bothered at all. He wasn't popular, but he wasn't annoyed. Perhaps his size had something to do with it. And he was good-natured and dangerous-looking. He had large, knotty hands and seemed to take everything easily and without thought. It would be hard to get Fein to take offense at anything, or even realize that he was being offended, so there would be little pleasure in baiting him. And if he did take offense he probably would do a tremendous amount of damage. So he was quietly left in peace by the men who bedeviled Ackerman. The Army, Michael thought.

Perhaps he'd been wrong to tell the man who had interviewed him at Fort Dix that he wanted to go into the infantry. Romantic. There was nothing romantic about it once you got into it. Sore feet, ignorant men, drunkenness, "Ah'm goin' to teach you how to pick up yo' rahfle and faght fo' yo' lahf . . ."

"I think I can put you into Special Service," the interviewer had said, "with your qualifications . . ." That would probably have meant a job in New York in an office all during the war. And Michael's self-consciously noble reply. "Not for me. I'm not in this Army to sit at a desk." What was he in the Army for? To cross the state of Florida on foot? To re-make beds that an ex-undertaker's assistant found not made to his liking? To listen to a Jew being tortured? He probably would have been much more useful hiring chorus girls for the USO, would have served his country better in Shubert Alley than here on this hot, senseless road. But he had to make the gesture. A gesture wore out so quickly in any army.

The Army. If you had to put what you thought of it in a phrase, a sentence, a paragraph . . . what would you say? It would be impossible. The Army was composed of ten million splinters. Splinters in motion, splinters that never coalesced, that never went in the same direction. The Army was the Chaplain who gave you the talk after they showed you the sex hygiene picture. First the horrible closeups of the riddled penis, then the man of God in his Captain's uniform, in front of the blank screen where lately the shabby whores and the vile flesh had been shown. "Men, the Army has to be practical . . ." The chanting Baptist voice, in the sweltering plank auditorium. "The Army says, 'Men will expose themselves. Therefore we show you this picture and show you how a prophylaxis station works.

270

But I am here to say that God is better than a prophylaxis, religion is healthier than lust . . ."

One splinter. Another splinter. The ex-high-school teacher from Hartford with the sallow face and the wild eyes, as though he feared assassination each night. He had whispered to Michael, "I'm going to tell you the truth about myself. I'm a Conscientious Objector. I don't believe in war. I refuse to kill my fellowman. So they put me on KP. I've been on KP for thirty-six days in a row. I've lost twenty-eight pounds and I'm still losing, but they are not going to force me to kill my fellowman."

The Army. The Regular at Fort Dix who had been in the Army thirteen years, playing on Army baseball and football teams in time of peace. Jock-strap soldiers, they called them. A big, tough-looking man with a round belly from beer drunk at Cavite and Panama City and Fort Riley, Kansas. Suddenly, he had fallen into disfavor in the orderly room and had been transferred out of the Permanent Party and had been put on orders to a regiment. The truck had driven up and he had put his two barracks bags on it, and then he had started to scream. He had fallen to the ground and wept and screamed and frothed at the mouth, because it was not a football game he was going to today, but a war. The Top Sergeant, a two-hundred-and-fifty-pound Irishman who had been in the Army since the last war, had come out of the orderly room and looked at him with shame and disgust. He kicked him in the head to quiet him, and had two men lift him and throw him, still twitching and weeping, into the back of the truck. The Sergeant then turned to the recruits who were silently watching and had said, "That man is a disgrace to the Regular Army. He is not typical. Not at all typical. Apologize for him. Get the hell out of here!"

The orientation lectures. Military courtesy. The causes of the war which You Are Fighting. The expert on the Japanese question, a narrow, gray-faced professor from Lehigh, who had told them that it was all a question of economics. Japan needed to expand and take over the Asiatic and Pacific markets and we had to stop her and hold onto them ourselves. It was all according to the beliefs that Michael had had about the causes of war for the last fifteen years. And yet, listening to the dry, professional voice, looking at the large map with spheres of influence and oil deposits and rubber plantations clearly marked out, he hated the professor, hated what he was saying. He wanted to hear that he was fighting for liberty or morality or the freedom of subject peoples, and he wanted to be told in such ringing and violent terms that he could go back to his barracks, go to the rifle range in the morning believing it. Michael looked at the men sitting wearily beside him at the lecture. There was no sign on those bored, fatigue-doped faces that they cared one way or another, that they understood, that they felt they needed the oil or the markets. There was no sign that they wanted anything but to be permitted to go back to their bunks and go to sleep . . .

In the middle of the speech Michael had resolved to get up and speak in the question period scheduled after the speaker had finished. But by the time the professor had said, "In conclusion, we are in a period of centralization of resources, in which . . . uh . . . large groups of capital and national interests in one part of the globe are . . . uh . . . in inevitable conflict with other large groups in other parts of the globe, and in defense of the American standard of living, it is absolutely imperative that we have . . . uh . . . free and unhampered access to the wealth and buying power of China and Indonesia . . ." Michael had changed his mind. He had wanted to say, as he thought, "This is horrible. This is no faith to die by," but he was tired, and like all the other men around him, he wanted to go back to his barracks and go to sleep.

The Army was several beautiful things too.

The flag dipping at Retreat, with the anthem over the public-address system making you dimly think of other bugles that other Americans had listened to for a hundred years at equal moments.

The soft Southern voices on the barracks stoop, after Taps, the ends of the cigarettes glowing in the dark, the voices counting over the treasures of former lives, the names of children, the color of a wife's hair, the shape of a home . . . And your feeling at that obscure, lonely hour no longer separate or apart, no longer judge or critic, no longer weighing words and motives, but blindly and faithfully living, weary and at peace in the heart of a troubled time . . .

In front of Michael, as he marched, Ackerman stumbled. Michael quickened his pace and held Ackerman by the arm. Ackerman looked at him coldly. "Let go," he said, "I don't need any help from anybody."

Michael took his hand away and dropped back. One of those Jews, he thought angrily, one of the proud ones. He watched Ackerman's rolling, staggering walk without sympathy as they crossed the brow of the hill.

"Sergeant," Noah said, standing before the desk in the orderly room behind which the First Sergeant was reading *Superman*, "I would like permission to speak to the Company Commander."

The First Sergeant did not look up. Noah stood stiff in his fatigues, grimy and damp with sweat after the day's march. He looked over at the Company Commander, sitting three feet

272

away, reading the sports page of a Jacksonville newspaper. The Company Commander didn't look up.

Finally the First Sergeant glanced at Noah. "What do you want, Soldier?" he asked.

"I would like permission," Noah said, trying to speak clearly through the downpulling weariness of the day's march, "to speak to the Company Commander."

The First Sergeant looked blankly at him. "Get out of here," he said.

Noah swallowed dryly. "I would like permission," he began stubbornly, "to speak to . . ."

"Get out of here," the Sergeant said evenly, "and when you come back, remember to wear your class A uniform. Now get out."

"Yes, Sergeant," Noah said. The Company Commander did not raise his eyes from the sports page. Noah went out of the small, hot room into the growing twilight. It was hard to know about the uniform. Sometimes the Company Commander saw men in fatigues and sometimes not. The rule seemed to change every half hour. He walked slowly back to his barracks past the lounging men and the loud sound of many small radios blaring tinnily forth with jazz music and detective serials.

When he got back to the orderly room, in his class A uniform, the Captain wasn't there. So Noah sat on the grass across the street from the orderly-room entrance and waited. In the barracks behind him a man was singing, softly, "I didn't raise my boy to be a soldier, the dying mother said . . ." and two other men were having a loud argument about when the war would end.

"1950," one of the men kept saying. "The fall of 1950. Wars always end right as winter sets in."

And the other man was saying, "Maybe the German war, but after that the Japs. We'll have to make a deal with the Japs."

"I'll make a deal with anyone," a third voice said. "I'll make a deal with the Bulgarians or the Egyptians or the Mexicans or anybody."

"1950," the first man said loudly. "Take my word for it. And we'll all get a bullet up our ass first."

Noah stopped listening to them. He sat on the scrub grass in the darkness, with his back against the wooden steps, half asleep, waiting for the Captain to return, thinking about Hope. Her birthday was next week. Tuesday, and he had ten dollars saved up and hidden away at the bottom of his barracks bag, for a gift. What could you get for ten dollars in town that you wouldn't be ashamed to give your wife? A scarf, a blouse . . . He thought of how she would look in a scarf. Then he thought of how she would look in a blouse, preferably a white one, with her slender throat rising from the white stuff and the dark hair

273

capping her head. Maybe that would be it. You ought to be able to get a decent blouse, even in Florida, for ten dollars.

Colclough came back. He moved heavily up the orderly-room steps. You could tell he was an officer at a distance of fifty yards, just by the way he moved his behind.

Noah stood up and followed Colclough into the orderly-room. The Captain was sitting at his desk with his cap on, frowning impressively at some papers in his hand.

"Sergeant," Noah said quietly. "I would like permission to speak to the Captain."

The Sergeant looked bleakly at Noah. Then he stood up and went the three steps over to the Captain's desk. "Sir," he said, "Private Ackerman wants to talk to you."

Colclough didn't look up. "Tell him to wait," he said.

The Sergeant turned to Noah. "The Captain says for you to wait."

Noah sat down and watched the Captain. After a half hour, the Captain nodded to the Sergeant.

"All right," the Sergeant said. "Make it short."

Noah stood up, saluted the Captain. "Private Ackerman," he said, "has permission from the First Sergeant to speak to the Captain."

"Yes?" Colclough did not look up.

"Sir," said Noah, nervously, "my wife is arriving in town Friday night, and she has asked me to meet her in the lobby of the hotel, and I would like to have permission to leave camp on Friday night."

Colclough didn't say anything for a long time. "Private Ackerman," he said finally, "you are aware of the Company rule. The entire Company is restricted on Friday nights to prepare for inspection . . ."

"I know, Sir," said Noah, "but this was the only train she could get a reservation on, and she expects me to meet her, and I thought, just this once . . ."

"Ackerman," Colclough finally looked at him, the pale spot on the end of his nose white and twitching, "in the Army, duty comes first. I don't know whether I can ever teach that to one of you people, but I'm goddamn going to try. The Army don't care whether you ever see your wife or not. When you're not on duty you can do whatever you please. When you are on duty, that's all there is to that. Now get out of here."

"Yes, Sir," said Noah.

"Yes, Sir, what?" Colclough asked.

"Yes, Sir. Thank you, Sir," Noah said, remembering the lecture on military courtesy. He saluted and went out.

He sent a telegram, although it cost eighty-five cents. But there was no answer in the next two days from Hope, and there was no way of knowing whether she had received it or not.

He couldn't sleep all Friday night, in the scrubbed barracks, lying there knowing that Hope was only ten miles from him after all these months, waiting for him in the hotel, not knowing, perhaps, what had happened to him, not knowing about people like Colclough or the blind authority and indifference of the Army, on which love had no claims, tenderness made no impression. Anyway, he thought dreamily, as he finally dozed off right before reveille, I'll see her this afternoon. And maybe it was all for the best. The last traces of my black eye may disappear by then, and I won't have to explain to her about how I got it . . .

The Captain was due in five minutes. Nervously, Noah checked the corners of his bunk, the arrangement of the towels in his footlocker, the shine on the windows behind the bunk. He saw the man next to him, Silichner, buttoning the top button of the raincoat which hung in its ordered line among his clothes. Noah had made certain before breakfast that all his clothes were buttoned correctly for the inspection, but he looked once more at his own clothes. He swung his overcoat back and then blinked. His blouse, which he had checked just an hour ago, was open from the top button down. Frantically, he worked on the buttons. If Colclough had seen the blouse open he would have been certain to restrict Noah for the weekend. He had done worse to others for less, and he had made very clear the fact that he was not fond of Noah. The raincoat, too, had two buttons undone. Oh, God, Noah thought, don't let him come in yet, not until I'm finished.

Suddenly Noah wheeled around. Riker and Donnelly were watching him, grinning a little. They ducked their heads and flicked at spots of dust on their shoes. That's it, thought Noah bitterly, they did it to me. With everyone in the barracks in on it, probably. Knowing what Colclough would do to me when he found it . . . Probably they slipped back early after breakfast and slipped the buttons out of their holes.

He checked each bit of clothing carefully, and leaped to the foot of his bunk just as the Sergeant shouted "Attention!" from the door.

Colclough looked him over coldly and carefully and stared for a long time at the rigid perfection of his footlocker. He went over behind him and fingered every piece of the clothing hanging from the rack. Noah heard the cloth swishing as Colclough let the coats fall back into place. Then Colclough stamped past him, and Noah knew it was going to be all right.

Five minutes later the inspection was over and the men started to pour out of the barracks toward the bus station. Noah took down his barracks bag and reached in to the small oilskin sack at the bottom in which he saved his money. He drew the sack out and opened it. There was no money in it. The ten-dollar bill was gone. In its place there was a single piece of torn paper. On it there was one word, printed in oily pencil. "Tough."

Noah stuffed the paper into his pocket. Methodically he hung the barracks bag up. I'll kill him, he thought, I'll kill the man who did that. No scarf, no blouse, no anything. I'll kill him.

Dazedly he walked toward the bus station. He wanted to let the men from his barracks leave on another bus. He did not want to see them this morning. He knew he would get into trouble if he stood beside Donnelly or Silichner or Rickett or any of the others, and this morning was no time for trouble.

He waited for twenty minutes in the long line of impatient soldiers and got into the gasoline-smelling bus. There was no one from his company there, and suddenly the faces, shaved and scrubbed and happy with release, seemed like the faces of friends. The man standing next to him, a huge soldier with a broad, smiling face, even offered him a drink out of a pint bottle of rye he carried in his pocket.

Noah smiled at him. "No, thank you," he said. "My wife just arrived in town and I haven't seen her yet. I don't want to meet her with alcohol on my breath."

The man grinned broadly, as though Noah had just said something most flattering and agreeable. "Your wife," he said. "How do you like that? When was the last time you saw her?"

"Seven months ago," Noah said.

"Seven months ago!" The man's face grew sober. He was very young and his skin was fair, like a girl's, on his tough, agreeable face. "Seven months and this is the first time." He bent over to the man who was sitting in the seat against which Noah was standing. "Soldier," he said, "get up and let this married man sit down. He hasn't seen his wife for seven months and she's waiting for him now and he needs all his strength."

The other man grinned and stood up. "You should have told me in the beginning," he said.

"No," said Noah, embarrassed but laughing. "I'll do all right. I don't have to sit down . . ."

The man with the bottle pushed him down with an imperious, gentle hand. "Soldier," he said solemnly, "this is a direct order. Sit down and preserve yourself."

Noah sat down and all the men around him grinned at him.

"You wouldn't happen to have a photograph of the lady?" the big man said.

"Well," said Noah, "the fact is . . ." He got out his wallet and showed the big man the photograph of Hope. The soldier looked at it soberly.

"A garden on a morning in May," he pronounced. "By God,

I'm going to get me married, myself, before I let them shoot me."

Noah put the wallet back, smiling at him, feeling, somehow, that this was an omen, that from now on things would be different, that he had reached the bottom and begun to climb up to the other side.

When the bus stopped in town in front of the post office, the large man, with elaborate care, helped him down the bus steps to the shabby street, and patted him gently and encouragingly on the shoulder. "Go along, now, Sonny," the man said, "and have a very nice week-end. And you forget that there is such a thing as the United States Army until reveille Monday morning."

Smiling, Noah waved at him, and hurried toward the hotel where Hope was waiting for him.

She was in the crowded lobby, among the surging khaki and the other wives.

Noah saw her before she saw him. She was peering, a little short-sightedly, through the milling soldiers and women and dusty potted palms. She looked pale and anxious. The smile that broke over her face when he came up behind her and lightly touched her elbow and said, "Mrs. Ackerman, I presume," was on the brink of tears.

They kissed as though they were all alone.

"Now," Noah said softly, "now, now . . ."

"Don't worry," she said, "I'm not going to cry."

She stood back, holding him at arm's length, and peered at him. "It's the first time," she said, "the first time I've seen you in uniform."

"How do I look?"

Her mouth trembled a little. "Horrible," she said.

Then they both laughed.

"Let's go upstairs," he said.

"We can't."

"Why not?" Noah asked, feeling a clutching sense of disaster.

"I couldn't get a room here. Full up. That's all right." She touched his face and chuckled at the despair she saw there. "We have a place. A rooming house down the street. Don't look like that."

They joined hands and went out of the hotel. They walked down the street silently, looking at each other from time to time. Noah was conscious of the polite, approving stares of the soldiers they passed who had no wives, no girls, and were only going to get drunk that afternoon.

The rooming house needed painting. The porch was overgrown with grape vines and the bottom step was broken. "Be

277

careful," Hope said. "Don't fall through. This would be an awful time to break your leg."

The door was opened for them by the landlady. She was a thin old woman in a dirty gray apron. She stared coldly at Noah, exuding a smell of sweat, age and dishwater. "This your husband?" she asked, her bony hand on the doorknob.

"Yes," said Hope. "This is my husband."

"Ummm," said the landlady, and did not smile when Noah grinned politely at her. The landlady watched them as they mounted the stairs.

"This is worse than inspection," Noah whispered as he followed Hope toward the door of their room.

"What's inspection?" Hope asked.

"I'll tell you," Noah said, "some other time."

Then the door closed behind them. The room was small, with one window with a cracked pane. The wallpaper was so old and faded that the pattern looked as though it somehow was growing out of the wall. The bed was chipped white iron and there were obvious lumps under the grayish spread. But Hope had put a small bunch of jonquils in a glass on the dresser and her hairbrush was there, sign of marriage and civilization, and she had put a small photograph of Noah, laughing, in a sweater, taken on a summer holiday, under the flowers.

They avoided looking at each other, embarrassed.

"I had to show her our marriage license," Hope said. "The landlady."

"What?" Noah asked.

"Our marriage license. She said you had to fight tooth and nail to maintain a respectable establishment with a hundred thousand drunken soldiers loose on the town."

Noah grinned and shook his head wonderingly. "Who told you to bring the license down?"

Hope touched the flowers. "I carry it around with me," she said, "all the time, these days. In my handbag. To remind me . . ."

Noah walked slowly over to the door. There was an iron key in the lock. He turned it. The clumsy noise of the primitive tumblers screeched through the room. "There," he said, "I've been thinking about doing this for seven months. Locking a door."

Suddenly Hope ducked her head. But she brought it up again quickly, and Noah saw she was holding a small box in her hands. "Here," she said, "I brought you something."

Noah took the box in his hands. He thought of the ten dollars for the gift, and the note at the bottom of his barracks bag, the ragged slip of paper with the sardonic "Tough" on it. As he opened the box, he made himself forget the ten dollars. That could wait until Monday.

278

There were chocolate cookies in the box.

"Taste them," Hope said. "I'm happy to say I didn't make them myself. I got my mother to bake them and send them on to me."

Noah bit into one of the cookies and they tasted like home. He ate another one. "It was a wonderful idea," he said.

"Take them off," Hope said fiercely. "Take off those damned clothes."

The next morning they went out for breakfast late. After breakfast they strolled through the few streets of the small town. People were coming home from church and children in their best clothes were walking in restless, bored dignity among the faded lawns. You never saw children in camp, and it gave a homely and pleasant air to the morning.

A drunken soldier walked with severe attention to his feet, along the sidewalk, glowering at the churchgoers fiercely, as though daring them to criticize his piety or his right to be drunk before noon on a Sunday morning. When he reached Hope and Noah, he saluted grandly, and said, "Sssh. Don't tell the MP's," and marched sternly ahead.

"Man yesterday," Noah said, "on the bus, saw your picture."

"What was the report?" Hope picked softly at his arm with her fingertips. "Negative or positive?"

"'A garden,' he said, 'a garden on a morning in May.'"

Hope chuckled. "This Army," she said, "will never win the war with men like that."

"He also said, 'By God, I'm going to get married myself, before they shoot me.'"

Hope chuckled again and then grew sober thinking about the last two words. But she didn't say anything. She could only stay one week and there was not time to be wasted talking about matters like that.

"Will you be able to come in every night?" she asked.

Noah nodded. "If I have to bribe every MP in the area," he said. "Friday night I may not be able to manage it, but every other night . . ." He looked around regretfully at the shabby, mean town, dusty in the sun, with the ten saloons lining the streets in neon gaudiness. "It's too bad you don't have a better place to spend the week. . . ."

"Nonsense," Hope said. "I'm crazy about this town. It reminds me of the Riviera."

"You ever been on the Riviera?"

"No."

Noah squinted across the railroad tracks where the Negro section sweltered, privies and unpainted board among the rutted roads. "You're right," he said. "It reminds me of the Riviera, too."

"You ever been to the Riviera?"

"No."

They grinned. Then they walked in silence. For a moment Hope leaned her head on his shoulder. "How long?" she asked. "How long do you think?"

He knew what she was talking about, but he asked, "How long what?"

"How long is it going to last? The war . . ."

A small Negro child was sitting in the dust, gravely caressing a rooster. Noah squinted at him. The rooster seemed to doze, half hypnotized by the movement of the gentle black hands.

"Not long," Noah said. "Not long at all. That's what everybody says."

"You wouldn't lie to your wife, would you?"

"Not a chance," Noah said. "I know a Sergeant at Regimental Headquarters and he says they don't think we'll ever get a chance to fight at all, our division. He says the Colonel's sore as can be, because the Colonel is bucking for BG."

"What's BG?"

"Brigadier General."

"Am I very stupid, not knowing?"

Noah chuckled. "Yep," he said. "I'm crazy about stupid women."

"I'm so glad," Hope said. "I'm delighted." They turned around without signaling each other, as though they had simultaneous lines to the same reservoir of impulses, and started walking back toward the rooming house. "I hope the son of a bitch never makes it," Hope said dreamily, after awhile.

"Makes what?" Noah asked, puzzled.

"BG."

They walked in silence for a minute.

"I have a great idea," Hope said.

"What?"

"Let's go back to our room and lock the door." She grinned at him and they walked a little faster toward their rooming house.

There was a knock on the door and the landlady's voice clanged through the peeling wood. "Mrs. Ackerman. Mrs. Ackerman, I would like to see you for a moment, please."

Hope frowned at the door, then shrugged her shoulders. "I'll be right down," she called.

She turned to Noah. "You stay right where you are," she said. "I'll be back in a minute."

She kissed his ear, then unlocked the door and went out. Noah lay back on the bed, staring through mild, half-closed eyes up at the stained ceiling. He dozed, with the Sunday afternoon coming to a warm, drowsy close outside the window, with

280

a locomotive whistle sounding somewhere far off and lonely soldiers' voices singing, "You make time and you make love dandy, You make swell molasses candy, But, honey, are you makin' any money, That's all I want to know," on the street below. Drowsily, he knew he'd heard that song before. Then he remembered Roger and that Roger was dead. But before he could think much about it, he fell asleep.

He was wakened by the slow closing of the door. He opened his eyes a slit, smiling gently as he saw Hope standing above him.

"Noah," she said, "you have to get up."

"Later," he said. "Much later. Come on down here."

"No," she said, and her voice was flat. "You've got to get up now."

He sat up. "What's the matter?"

"The landlady," Hope said. "The landlady says we have to get out right away."

Noah shook his head to clear it because he knew he was not getting this straight. "Now," he said, "let's hear it again."

"The landlady says we have to get out."

"Darling," Noah said patiently, "you must have gotten it a little mixed up."

"It's not mixed up." Hope's face was strained and tense. "It's absolutely straight. We have to get out."

"Why? Didn't you take this room for a week?"

"Yes," said Hope, "I took it for a week. But the landlady says I got it under false pretenses. She said she didn't realize we were Jews."

Noah stood up and slowly went over to the bureau. He looked at his smiling picture under the jonquils. The jonquils were getting dry and crackly around the edges.

"She said," Hope went on, "that she suspected from the name, but that I didn't look Jewish. Then when she saw you she began to wonder. Then she asked me and I said, of course we were Jewish."

"Poor Hope," Noah said softly. "I apologize."

"None of that," Hope said. "I never want to hear anything like that from you again. Don't you ever apologize to me for anything."

"All right," Noah said. He touched the flowers vaguely, with a drifting small movement of his fingers. The jonquils felt tender and dead. "I suppose we ought to pack," he said.

"Yes," said Hope. She got out her bag and put it on the bed and opened it. "It's nothing personal," Hope said. "It's a rule of the house, the landlady said."

"I'm glad to know it's nothing personal," Noah said.

"It's not so bad." Hope began to put the pink soft clothes into her bag, in the crisp folded way she had of packing anything. "We'll just go down the street and find another place."

Noah touched the hairbrush on the dresser. It had a worn silver back, with a heavy old-fashioned design of Victorian leaves on it. It shown dully in the dusty, shaded light of the room. "No," he said, "we won't find another place."

"But we can't stay here . . ."

"We won't stay here and we won't find another place," Noah said, keeping his voice even and emotionless.

"I don't know what you mean." Hope stopped her packing and looked at him.

"I mean that we'll walk down to the terminal and we'll find out when a bus is leaving for New York and you'll get on it."

There was silence in the room. Hope just stood there, looking solemn and reflective, staring at the rosy underclothes tucked away in the bag on the bed. "You know," she whispered, "this is the only week I can get in God knows how long. And we don't know what will happen to you. You may be shipped to Africa, to Guadalcanal, any place, next week, and . . ."

"I think there's a bus leaving at five o'clock," Noah said.

"Darling . . ." Hope did not move from her sober, thoughtful position in front of the bed. "I'm sure we could find another place in this town . . ."

"I'm sure we could," Noah said. "But we're not going to. I don't want you in this town. I want to be left alone here, that's all. I can't love you in this town. I want you to get out of it and stay out of it! The sooner the better! I could burn this town or drop bombs on it, but I refuse to love you in it!"

Hope came over to him swiftly and held him. "Dearest," she shook him fiercely, "what's happened to you? What have they been doing to you?"

"Nothing," Noah shouted. "Nothing! I'll tell you after the war! Now pack your things and let's get out of here!"

Hope dropped her hands. "Of course," she said, in a low voice. She went back to folding her clothes and placing them precisely in her bag.

Ten minutes later they were ready. Noah went out carrying her valise and the small canvas bag in which he kept his extra shirt and shaving kit. He didn't look back as he went out onto the landing, but Hope turned at the door. The lowering sun was slanting through the breaks in the unhinged shutter in thin, dusty gold. The jonquils remained in their glass on the dresser, bending over a little now, as though the weight of approaching death had made their blossoms heavy. But otherwise the room was as it had been when first she entered it. She closed the door softly and followed Noah down the stairs.

The landlady was on the porch, still in the gray apron. She said nothing when Noah paid her, merely standing there in her smell of sweat, age and dishwater, looking with silent, harsh righteousness at the soldier and the young girl who walked slowly up the quiet street toward the bus station.

There were some men sleeping in the barracks when Noah got there. Donnelly was snoring drunkenly near the door, but no one paid any attention to him. Noah took down his barracks bag and with maniacal care he went through every article there, the extra shoes, the wool shirts, the clean fatigues, the green wool gloves, the can of shoe-dubbing. But the money wasn't there. Then he got down the other barracks bag, and went through that. The money wasn't there. From time to time he glanced up sharply, to see if any of the men were watching him. But they slept, in the snoring, hateful, unprivate, everlasting way. Good, he thought, if I caught any of them looking at me, I would kill them.

He put the scattered things back into the bags, then took out his box of stationery and wrote a short note. He put the box on his bunk and strode down to the orderly room. On the bulletin board outside the orderly room, along with the notices about brothels in town that were out of bounds and regulations for wearing the proper uniforms at the proper times, and the list of promotions that had come through that week, there was a space reserved for lost-and-found notices. Noah tacked his sheet of paper up on top of a plea by PFC O'Reilly for the return of a six-bladed penknife that had been taken from his footlocker. There was a light hanging outside the orderly room, and in its frail glare, Noah re-read what he had written.

> To the Personnel of Company C . . . Ten dollars has been stolen from the barracks bag of Private Noah Ackerman, 2nd Platoon. I am not interested in the return of the money and will press no charges. I wish to take my satisfaction, in person, with my own hands. Will the soldier or soldiers involved please communicate with me immediately.
> Signed,
> Private Noah Ackerman

Noah read what he had written with pleasure. He had a feeling as he turned away, that he had taken the one step that would keep him from going mad.

The next evening, as he was going to the mess hall for supper, Noah stopped at the bulletin board. His notice was still there. And under it neatly typed, was a small sheet of paper. On the sheet of paper, there were two short sentences.

> We took it, Jew-Boy. We're waiting for you.
> Signed,

P. Donnelly   B. Cowley
J. Wright   W. Demuth
L. Jackson   E. Riker
M. Silichner   R. Henkel
P. Sanders   T. Brailsford

Michael was cleaning his rifle when Noah came up to him.

"May I talk to you for a moment?" Noah said.

Michael looked up at him with annoyance. He was tired and, as usual, he felt incompetent and uncertain with the intricate clever mechanism of the old Springfield.

"What do you want?" Michael asked.

Ackerman hadn't said a word to him since the moment on the hike.

"I can't talk in here," Noah said, glancing around him. It was after supper, and there were thirty or forty men in the barracks, reading, writing letters, fiddling with their equipment, listening to the radio.

"Can't it wait?" Michael asked coldly. "I'm pretty busy just now . . ."

"Please," Noah said. Michael glanced up at him. Ackerman's face was set in withered, trembling lines, and his eyes seemed to be larger and darker than usual. "Please . . ." he repeated. "I've got to talk to you. I'll wait for you outside."

Michael sighed. "O.K.," he said. He put the rifle together, wrestling with the bolt, ashamed of himself, as always, because it was so difficult for him. God, he thought, feeling his greasy hands slip along the oily stubborn surfaces, I can put on a play, discuss the significance of Thomas Mann, and any farm boy can do this with his eyes closed better than I can . . .

He hung the rifle up and went outside, wiping the oil off his hands. Ackerman was standing across the Company street in the darkness, a small, slender form outlined by a distant light. Ackerman waved to him in a conspiratorial gesture, and Michael slowly approached him, thinking, I get all the nuts . . .

"Read this," Noah said as soon as Michael got close to him. He thrust two sheets of paper into Michael's hand.

Michael turned so he could get some light on the papers. He squinted and read first the notice that Noah had put up on the bulletin board, which he had not read before, and the answer, signed by the ten names. Michael shook his head and read both notes over carefully.

"What the hell is this?" he asked irritably.

"I want you to act as my second," Noah said. His voice was dull and heavy, and even so, Michael had to hold himself back from laughing at the melodramatic request.

"Second?" he asked incredulously.

"Yes," said Noah. "I'm going to fight those men. And I don't

284

trust myself to arrange it myself. I'll lose my temper and get into trouble. I want it to be absolutely correct."

Michael blinked. Of all the things you thought might happen to you before you went into the Army, you never imagined anything like this. "You're crazy," he said. "This is just a joke."

"Maybe," said Noah flatly. "Maybe I'm getting tired of jokes."

"What made you pick on me?" Michael asked.

Noah took a deep breath and Michael could hear the air whistling into the boy's nostrils. He looked taut and very handsome in a rough-cut, archaic, tragic way in the blocked light and shadows from the hanging lamp across the street. "You're the only one," Noah said, "I felt I could trust in the whole Company." Suddenly he grabbed the two sheets of paper. "O.K.," he said, "if you don't want to help, the hell with you . . ."

"Wait a minute," Michael said, feeling dully that somehow he must prevent this savage and ludicrous joke from being played out to its limit. "I haven't said I won't help."

"O.K., then," Noah said harshly. "Go in and arrange the schedule."

"What schedule?"

"There are ten of them. What do you want me to do—fight them in one night? I have to space them. Find out who wants to fight me first, who wants to fight me second, and so on. I don't care how they come."

Michael took the sheets of paper silently from Noah's hand and looked at the names on the list. Slowly he began to place the names. "You know," he said, "that these are the ten biggest men in the company."

"I know."

"Not one of them weighs under a hundred and eighty pounds."

"I know."

"How much do you weigh?"

"A hundred and thirty-five."

"They'll kill you."

"I didn't ask you for advice," Noah said evenly. "I asked you to make the arrangements. That's all. Leave the rest to me."

"I don't think the Captain will allow it," Michael said.

"He'll allow it," said Noah. "That son of a bitch will allow it. Don't worry about that."

Michael shrugged. "What do you want me to arrange?" he asked. "I can get gloves and two-minute rounds and a referee and . . ."

"I don't want any round or any referees," Noah said. "When one of the men can't get up any more, the fight will be over."

Michael shrugged again. "What about gloves?"

285

"No gloves. Bare fists. Anything else?"

"No," said Michael. "That's all."

"Thanks," Noah said. "Let me hear how you make out."

Without saying good-bye, he walked stiffly down the Company street. Michael watched the shadowy, erect back vanishing in the darkness. Then he shook his head once and walked slowly toward the barracks door, looking for the first man, Peter Donnelly, six feet one, weight one hundred and ninety-five, who had fought heavyweight in the Golden Gloves in Miami in 1941 and had not been put out until the semi-final round.

Donnelly knocked Noah down. Noah sprang up and jumped in the air to reach Donnelly's face. Donnelly began to bleed from the nose and he sucked in the blood at the corner of his mouth, with a look of surprise and anger that supplanted the professional expression he had been fighting with until now. He held Noah's back with one hand, ignoring the fierce tattoo of Noah's fist on his face, and pulled him toward him. He swung, a short, chopping vicious blow, and the men watching silently went "Ah." Donnelly swung again as Noah fell and Noah lay at his feet on the grass.

"I think," Michael said, stepping forward, "that that's enough for this . . ."

"Get the hell out of here," Noah said thickly, pushing himself up from the ground with his two hands.

He stood before Donnelly, wavering, blood filling the socket of his right eye. Donnelly moved in and swung, like a man throwing a baseball. There was the noise again, as it hit Noah's mouth, and the men watching went "Ah," again. Noah staggered back and fell against them, where they stood in a tight, hard-eyed circle, watching. Then he slid down and lay still. Michael went over to him and kneeled down. Noah's eyes were closed and he was breathing evenly.

"All right." Michael looked up at Donnelly. "Hurray for you. You won." He turned Noah over on his back and Noah opened his eyes, but there was no light of reason in them as they stared thoughtlessly up at the evening sky.

Quietly the circle of watching men broke up and started to drift away.

"What do you know," Michael heard Donnelly say as Michael put his hand under Noah's armpit and lifted him slowly to his feet. "What do you know, the little bastard gave me a bloody nose."

Michael stood at the latrine window, smoking a cigarette, watching Noah, bent over one of the sinks, washing his face with cold water. Noah was bare to the waist, and there were

286

huge red blotches on his skin. Noah lifted his head. His right eye was closed by now, and the blood had not stopped coming from his mouth. He spat, and two teeth came out, in a gob of red.

Noah didn't look at the teeth, lying in the basin. He dried his face thoughtfully with his towel, the towel staining quickly.

"All right," Michael said, "I think that did it. I think you'd better cancel the rest . . ."

"Who's the next man on the list?"

"Listen to me," Michael said. "They'll kill you finally."

"The next man is Wright," Noah said flatly. "Tell him I'll be ready for him three nights from now." Without waiting for Michael to say anything, Noah wrapped the towel around his bare shoulders and went out the latrine door.

Michael looked after him, shrugged, took another drag on his cigarette, threw the cigarette away and went into the soft evening. He did not go into the barracks because he didn't want to see Ackerman again that evening.

Wright was the biggest man in the company. Noah did not try to avoid him. He stood up, in a severe, orthodox boxing pose, and flashed swiftly in and out among the flailing slow hands, cutting Wright's face, making him grunt when he hit him in the stomach.

Amazing, Michael thought, watching Noah with grudging admiration, he really knows how to box, where did he pick it up?

"In the belly," Rickett called from his post in the inner circle of the ring, "in the belly, you dumb bastard!" A moment later it was all over, because Wright swung sideways, all his weight behind a round, crushing swing. The knotted, hammer-like fist crashed into Noah's side. Noah tumbled across the cleared space to fall on his hands and knees, face down, tongue hanging thickly out of his open mouth, gasping helplessly for air.

The men who were watching looked on silently.

"Well?" said Wright, belligerently, standing over Noah. "Well?"

"Go home," Michael said. "You were wonderful."

Noah began to breathe again, the air struggling through his throat in hoarse, agonized whistles. Wright touched Noah contemptuously with his toe and turned away, saying, "Who's going to buy me a beer?"

The doctor looked at the x-rays and said that two ribs were broken. He taped Noah's chest with bandage and adhesive, and made Noah lie still in the infirmary bed.

"Now," Michael said, standing over Noah in the ward, "now, will you quit?"

"The doctor says it will take three weeks," Noah said, the speech coming painfully through his pale lips. "Arrange the next one for then."

"You're crazy," said Michael. "I won't do it."

"Deliver your goddamn lectures some place else," Noah whispered. "If you won't do it, you can leave now. I'll do it myself."

"What do you think you're doing?" Michael asked. "What do you think you're proving?"

Noah said nothing. He stared blankly and wildly across the ward at the man with a broken leg who had fallen off a truck two days before.

"What are you proving?" Michael shouted.

"Nothing," Noah said. "I enjoy fighting. Anything else?"

"No," said Michael. "Not a thing."

He went out.

"Captain," Michael was saying, "it's about Private Ackerman."

Colclough was sitting very erect, the little roll of fat under his chin lapping over his tight collar, making him look like a man who was slowly being choked.

"Yes," Colclough said, "What about Private Ackerman?"

"Perhaps you have heard about the . . . uh . . . dispute . . . that Private Ackerman is engaged in with ten members of the Company."

Colclough's mouth lifted a little in an amused grin. "I've heard something about it," he said.

"I think Private Ackerman is not responsible for his actions at this time," Michael said. "He is liable to be very seriously injured. Permanently injured. And I think, if you agreed with me, it might be a good idea to try to stop him from fighting any more . . ."

Colclough put his finger in his nose. He picked slowly at some obstacle there, then pulled his finger out and examined the treasure he had withdrawn. "In an army, Whitacre," he said in the even, sober tone which he must have heard from officiating ministers at so many funerals in Joplin, "a certain amount of friction between the men is unavoidable. I believe that the healthiest way of settling that friction is by fair and open fighting. These men, Whitacre, are going to be exposed to much worse than fists later on, much worse. Shot and shell, Whitacre," he said with grave relish. "Shot and shell. It would be unmilitary to forbid them to settle their differences now in this way, unmilitary. It is my policy, also, Whitacre, to allow as much freedom in handling their affairs as possible to the

288

men in my Company, and I would not think of interfering."

"Yes, Sir," said Michael. "Thank you, Sir."

He saluted and went out.

Walking slowly down the Company street, Michael made a sudden decision. He could not remain here like this. He would apply for Officer Candidates' School. When he had first come into the Army, he had resolved to remain an enlisted man. First, he felt that he was a little too old to compete with the twenty-year-old athletes who made up the bulk of the candidate classes. And his brain was too set in its ways to take easily to any further schooling. And, more deeply, he had held back from being put into a position where the lives of other men, so many other men, would depend upon his judgment. He had never felt in himself any talent for military command. War, in all its thousand, tiny, mortal particulars, seemed to him, even after all the months of training, like an impossible, deadly puzzle. It was all right to work at the puzzle as an obscure, single figure, at someone else's command. But to grapple with it on your own initiative . . . to send forty men at it, where every mistake might be compounded into forty graves . . . But now there was nothing else to do. If the Army felt that men like Colclough could be entrusted with two hundred and fifty lives, then no over-nicety of self-assessment, no modesty or fear of responsibility should hold one back. Tomorrow, Michael thought, I'll fill in the form and hand it in to the orderly room. And, he thought grimly, in my Company, there will be no Ackermans sent to the infirmary with broken ribs . . .

Five weeks later, Noah was back in the infirmary again. Two more teeth had been knocked out in his mouth, and his nose had been smashed. The dentist was making him a bridge so that he could eat, and the surgeon kept taking crushed pieces of bone out of his nose on every visit.

By this time Michael could hardly speak to Noah. He came to the infirmary and sat on the end of Noah's bed, and they both avoided each other's eyes, and were glad when the orderly came through, crying, "All visitors out."

Noah had worked his way through five of the list by now, and his face was crooked and lumpy, and one ear was permanently disfigured in a flat, creased cauliflower. His right eyebrow was split and a white scar ran diagonally across it, giving the broken eyebrows a wild, interrogating twist. The total effect of his face, the steady, wild eyes, staring out of the dark, broken face, was infinitely disturbing.

After the eighth fight, Noah was in the infirmary again. He had been hit in the throat. The muscles there had been temporarily paralyzed and his larynx had been injured. For two days the doctor was of the opinion that he would never be able to speak again.

"Soldier," the doctor had said, standing over him, a puzzled look on his simple college-boy face, "I don't know what you're up to, but whatever it is I don't think it's worth it. I've got to warn you that it is impossible to lick the United States Army singlehanded . . ." He leaned down and peered troubledly at Noah. "Can you say anything?"

Noah's mouth worked for a long time, without sound. Then a hoarse, croaking small noise came from between the swollen lips. The doctor bent over closer. "What was that?" he asked.

"Go peddle your pills, Doc," Noah said, "and leave me alone."

The doctor flushed. He was a nice boy but he was not accustomed to being talked to that way any more, now that he was a Captain.

He straightened up. "I'm glad to see," he said stiffly, "that you've regained the gift of speech."

He wheeled and stalked out of the ward.

Fein, the other Jew in the Company, came into the ward, too. He stood uneasily next to Noah's bed, twisting his cap in his large hands.

"Listen, Pal," he said, "I didn't want to interfere here, but enough's enough. You're going at this all wrong. You can't start swinging every time you hear somebody say Jew bastard . . ."

"Why not?" Noah grimaced painfully at him.

"Because it ain't practical," Fein said. "That's why. First of all, you ain't big enough. Second of all, even if you was as big as a house and you had a right hand like Joe Louis, it wouldn't do no good. There's a certain number of people in this world that say Jew bastard automatically, and nothing you do or I do or any Jew does will ever change 'em. And this way, you make the rest of the guys in the outfit think all Jews're crazy. Listen, they're not so bad, most of 'em. They sound a lot worse than they are, because they don't know no better. They started out feeling sorry for you, but now, after all these goddamned fights, they're beginning to think Jews are some kind of wild animal. They're beginning to look at *me* queer now . . ."

"Good," Noah said hoarsely. "Delighted."

"Listen," Fein said patiently, "I'm older than you and I'm a peaceful man. I'll kill Germans if they ask me to, but I want to live in peace with the guys around me in the Army. The best equipment a Jew can have is one deaf ear. When some of these bastards start to shoot their mouths off about the Jews that's the ear you turn that way, the deaf one . . . You let them live and maybe they'll let you live. Listen, the war ain't going to last forever, and then you can pick your company. Right now,

290

the government says you got to live with these miserable Ku Kluxers, O.K., what're you going to do about it? Listen, Son, if all the Jews'd been like you we'd've all been wiped out 2000 years ago . . ."

"Good," Noah said.

"Ah," Fein said disgustedly, "maybe they're right, maybe you are cracked. Listen, I weigh two hundred pounds, I could beat anyone in this Company with one hand tied behind me. But you ain't noticed me fightin', do you? I ain't had a fight since I put on the uniform. I'm a practical man!"

Noah sighed. "The patient is tired, Fein," he said. "He's in no condition to listen to the advice of practical men."

Fein stared at him heavily, groping despairingly with the problem. "The question I ask myself," he said, "is what do you want, what in hell do you want?"

Noah grinned painfully. "I want every Jew," he said, "to be treated as though he weighed two hundred pounds."

"It ain't practical," Fein said. "Ah, the hell with it, you want to fight, go ahead and fight. I'll tell you the truth, I feel I understand these Georgia crackers who didn't wear shoes till the Supply Sergeant put them on their feet better than I understand you." He put on his cap with ponderous decision. "Little guys," he said, "that's a race all by itself. I can't make head or tail of them."

And he went out, showing, in every line of his enormous shoulders and thick neck and bullet head, his complete disapproval of the battered boy in the bed, who by some trick and joke of Fate and registration was somehow linked with him.

It was the last fight and if he stayed down it would be all over. He peered bloodily up from the ground at Brailsford, standing above him in pants and undershirt. Brailsford seemed to flicker against the white ring of faces and the vague wash of the sky. This was the second time Brailsford had knocked him down. But he had closed Brailsford's eye and made him cry out with pain when he hit him in the belly. If he stayed down, if he merely stayed where he was on one knee, shaking his head to clear it, for another five seconds, the whole thing would be over. The ten men would be behind him, the broken bones, the long days in the hospital, the nervous vomiting on the days when the fights were scheduled, the dazed, sick roaring of the blood in his ears when he had to stand up once more and face the onrushing, confident, hating faces and the clubbing fists.

Five seconds more, and it would be proved. He would have done it. Whatever he had set out to demonstrate, and it was dim and anguished now, would have been demonstrated. They would have to realize that he had won the victory over them. Nine defeats and one default would not have been enough. The spirit only won when it made the complete tour of sacrifice and pain. Even these ignorant, brutal men would realize now, as he marched with them, marched first down the Florida roads, and later down the roads swept by gunfire, that he had made a demonstration of will and courage that only the best of them could have been capable of . . .

All he had to do was to remain on one knee.

He stood up.

He put up his hands and waited for Brailsford to come at him. Slowly, Brailsford's face swam into focus. It was white and splotched now with red, and it was very nervous. Noah walked across the patch of grass and hit the white face, hard, and Brailsford went down. Noah stared dully at the sprawled figure at his feet. Brailsford was panting hard, and his hands were pulling at the grass.

"Get up, you yellow bastard," a voice called out from the watching men. Noah blinked. It was the first time anyone but himself had been cursed on this spot.

Brailsford got up. He was fat and out of condition, because he was the Company Clerk and always managed to find excuses to duck out of heavy work. His breath was sobbing in his throat. As Noah moved in on him, there was a look of terror on his face. His hands waved vaguely in front of him.

"No, no . . ." he said pleadingly.

Noah stopped and stared at him. He shook his head and plodded in. Both men swung at the same time, and Noah went down again. Brailsford was a large man and the blow had hit high on Noah's temple. Methodically, sitting with his legs crumpled under him, Noah took a deep breath. He looked up at Brailsford.

The big man was standing above him, his hands held tightly before him. He was breathing heavily, and he was whispering, "Please, please . . ." Sitting there, with his head hammering, Noah grinned, because he knew what Brailsford meant. He was pleading with Noah to stay down.

"Why, you miserable hillbilly son of a bitch," Noah said clearly. "I'm going to knock you out." He stood up and grinned as he saw the flare of anguish in Brailsford's eyes when he swung at him.

Brailsford hung heavily on him, clinching, swinging with a great show of willingness. But the blows were soft and nervous and Noah didn't feel them. Clutched in the big man's fat embrace, smelling the sweat rolling off his skin, Noah knew that he had beaten Brailsford merely by standing up. After this it was merely a matter of time. Brailsford's nerve had run out.

Noah ducked away and lashed out at Brailsford's middle. The blow landed and Noah could feel the softness of the clerk's belly as his fist dug in.

Brailsford dropped his hands to his sides and stood there, weaving a little, a stunned plea for pity in his eyes. Noah chuckled. "Here it comes, Corporal," he said, and drove at the white, bleeding face. Brailsford just stood there. He wouldn't fall and he wouldn't fight and Noah merely stood flat on the balls of his feet, hooking at the collapsing face. "Now," he said, swinging with all his shoulder, all his body behind the driving, cutting blow. "Now. Now." He gained in power. He could feel the electric life pouring down his arms into his fists. All his enemies, all the men who had stolen his money, cursed him on the march, driven his wife away, were standing there, broken in nerve, bleeding before him. Blood sprayed from his knuckles every time he hit Brailsford's staring, agonized face.

"Don't fall, Corporal," Noah said, "don't fall yet, please don't fall," and swung again and again, faster and faster, his fists making a sound like mallets wrapped in wet cloth. And when he saw Brailsford finally begin to sway, he tried to hold him with one hand long enough to hit him twice more, three times, a dozen, and he sobbed when he no longer could hold the rubbery bloody mess up. Brailsford slipped to the ground.

Noah turned to the watching men. He dropped his hands. No one would meet his eyes. "All right," he said loudly. "It's over."

But they didn't say anything. As though at a signal, they turned their backs and started to walk away. Noah stared at the retreating forms, dissolving in the dusk among the barracks walls. Brailsford still lay where he fell. No one had stayed with him to help him.

Michael touched Noah. "Now," Michael said, "let's wait for the German Army."

Noah shook off the friendly hand. "They all walked away," he said. "The bastards just walked away." He looked down at Brailsford. The clerk had come to, although he still lay face down on the grass. He was crying. Slowly and vaguely he moved a hand up to his eyes. Noah went over to him and kneeled beside him.

"Leave your eye alone," he ordered. "You'll rub dirt in it this way." He started to pull Brailsford to his feet and Michael helped him. They had to support the clerk all the way to the barracks and they had to wash his face for him and clean the cuts because Brailsford just stood in front of the mirror with his hands at his side, weeping helplessly.

The next day Noah deserted.

Michael was called down to the orderly room.

"Where is he?" Colclough shouted.

"Where is who, Sir?" Michael asked, standing stiffly at attention.

293

"You know goddamn well who I mean," Colclough said. "Your friend. Where is he?"

"I don't know, Sir," said Michael.

"Don't hand me that!" Colclough shouted. All the Sergeants were in the room behind Michael, staring gravely at their Captain. "You were his friend, weren't you?"

Michael hesitated. It was hard to describe their relationship as friendship.

"Come on, Soldier! You were his friend."

"I suppose so, Sir."

"I want you to say yessir or nosir, that's all, Whitacre! Were you his friend or weren't you?"

"Yes, Sir, I was."

"Where did he go?"

"I don't know, Sir."

"You're lying to me!" Colclough's face had grown very pale and his nose was twitching. "You helped him get out. Let me tell you something, Whitacre, in case you've forgotten your Articles of War. The penalty for assisting at or failing to report desertion is exactly the same as for desertion. Do you know what the penalty for that is in time of war?"

"Yes, Sir."

"What is it?" Suddenly Colclough's voice had become quiet and almost soft. He slid down in his chair and looked up gently at Michael.

"It can be death, Sir."

"Death," said Colclough, softly. "Death. Listen, Whitacre, your friend is as good as caught already. When we catch him, we'll ask him if you helped him desert. Or even if he told you he was *going* to desert. That's all that's necessary. If he told you and you didn't report it, that is just the same as assisting at desertion. Did you know that, Whitacre?"

"Yes, Sir," Michael said, thinking, this is impossible, this could not be happening to me, this is an amusing anecdote I heard at a cocktail party about the quaint characters in the United States Army.

"I grant you, Whitacre," Colclough said reasonably, "I don't think a court-martial would condemn you to death just for not reporting it. But they might very well put you in jail for twenty years. Or thirty years. Or life. Federal prison, Whitacre, is not Hollywood. It is not Broadway. You will not get your name in the columns very often in Leavenworth. If your friend just happens to say that he happened to tell you he planned to go away, that's all there is to it. And he'll get plenty of opportunities to say it, Whitacre, plenty . . . Now . . ." Colclough spread his hands reasonably on the desk. "I don't want to make a big thing out of this. I'm interested in preparing a company to fight and I don't want to break it up with things like this. All you have to do is tell me where Ackerman is, and we'll forget all about it. That's all. Just tell me where you think he *might* be . . . That's not much, is it?"

"No, Sir," Michael said.

"All right," Colclough said briskly. "Where did he go?"

"I don't know, Sir."

Colclough's nose started to twitch again. He yawned nervously. "Listen, Whitacre," he said, "don't have any false feelings of loyalty to a man like Ackerman. He was not the type we wanted in the Company, anyway. He was useless as a soldier and he was not trusted by any of the other men in the Company and he was a constant source of trouble from beginning to end. You'd have to be crazy to risk spending your life in jail to protect a man like that. I don't like to see you do it, Whitacre. You're an intelligent man and you were a success in civilian life and you can be a good soldier, Whitacre, in time, and I want to help you . . . Now . . ." And he smiled winningly at Michael. "Where is Private Ackerman?"

"I'm sorry, Sir." Michael said. "I don't know."

Colclough stood up. "All right," he said quietly. "Get out of here, Jew-lover."

"Yes, Sir," Michael said. "Thank you, Sir."

He saluted and went out.

Brailsford was waiting for Michael outside the mess hall. He leaned against the building, picking his teeth and spitting. He had grown fatter than ever, but a look of uncertain grievance had set up residence in his features, and his voice had taken on a whining, complaining note since Noah had beaten him. Michael saw him waving to him as Michael came out the door, heavy with the porkchops and potatoes and spaghetti and peach pie of the noonday meal. He tried to pretend he had not seen the Company Clerk. But Brailsford hurried after him, calling, "Whitacre, wait a minute, will you?" Michael turned and faced Brailsford.

"Hello, Whitacre," Brailsford said. "I've been looking for you."

"What's the matter?" Michael asked.

Brailsford looked around him nervously. Other men were coming out of the mess hall and passing them in a food-anchored slow flood. "We better not talk here," he said. "Let's take a little walk."

"I have a couple of things to do," Michael said, "before formation . . ."

"It'll only take a minute." Brailsford winked solemnly. "I think you'll be interested."

Michael shrugged. "O.K.," he said, and walked side by side with the Company Clerk toward the parade ground.

"This Company," Brailsford said. "I'm getting good and pissed-off with it. I'm working on a transfer. There's a Sergeant at Regiment who's up for a medical discharge, arthritis, and I've been talking to a couple of people over there. This Company gives me the willies . . ." Michael sighed. He had planned to go back to his bunk and lie down in the precious twenty minutes after dinner.

"Listen," he said, "what's on your mind?"

"Ever since that fight," Brailsford said, "these bastards have been pissing on me. Listen, I didn't want to sign my name on that list. It was a joke, see, that's what they told me, the ten biggest guys in the Company, and I was one of them. I got nothing against the Jew. They told me he'd never fight. I didn't want to fight. I'm no fighter. Every kid in town used to lick me, even though I was big. What the hell, that ain't no crime, not being a pugilist, is it?"

"No," said Michael.

"Also," Brailsford said, "I have no resistance. I had pneumonia when I was fourteen, and ever since then I have no resistance. I'm even excused from hikes by the doctor. Try and tell that bastard Rickett that," he said bitterly. "Or any of the others. They treat me like I sold military secrets to the German Army, ever since Ackerman knocked me out. I stood there and took it as long as I could, didn't I? I stood there and he hit me and hit me and I didn't go down for a long time, isn't that true?"

"Yes," said Michael.

"That Ackerman is ferocious," Brailsford said. "He may be small, but he's wild. I don't like to have no dealings with people like that. After all, he gave Donnelly a bloody nose, didn't he, and Donnelly was in the Golden Gloves. What the hell do they expect from me?"

"All right," Michael said. "I know all about that. What's on your mind now?"

"I ain't got no future in this Company, no future at all." Brailsford threw away his toothpick and stared sorrowfully across the dusty parade ground. "And what I want to tell you is neither have you . . ."

Michael stopped. "What's that?" he said sharply.

"The only people that've treated me like a human being," Brailsford said, "are you and the Jew that night, and I want to help you. I'd like to help him, too, if I could, I swear I would . . ."

"Have you heard anything?" Michael asked.

"Yeah," said Brailsford. "They got him at Governor's Island, in New York, last night. Remember, nobody is supposed to know this, it's secret, but I know because I'm in the orderly room all the time . . ."

"I won't tell anybody." Michael shook his head, thinking of

Noah in the hands of the Military Police, wearing the blue fatigues with the big white P for prisoner stenciled on the back, and the guards with the shotguns walking behind him. "Is he all right?"

"I don't know. They didn't say. Colclough gave us all a drink of Three Feathers to celebrate. That's all I know. But that ain't what I wanted to talk to you about. I wanted to tell you something about yourself." Brailsford paused, obviously sourly pleased with the effect he was going to make in a moment. "Your application for OCS," he said, "the one you put in a long time ago . . ."

"Yes?" Michael asked. "What about it?"

"It came back," Brailsford said. "Yesterday. Rejected."

"Rejected?" Michael said dully. "But I passed the Board and I . . ."

"It came back from Washington, rejected. The other two guys from the Company was passed, but yours is finished. The FBI said no."

"The FBI?" Michael stared sharply at Brailsford to see if this was some elaborate joke that was being played on him. "What's the FBI got to do with it?"

"They check up, on everybody. And they checked up on you. You're not officer material, they said. You're not loyal."

"Are you kidding me?" Michael said.

"Why the hell would I want to kid you?" Brailsford asked aggrievedly. "I don't go in for jokes no more. You're not loyal, they said, and that's all there is to it."

"Not loyal." Michael shook his head puzzledly. "What's the matter with me?"

"You're a Red," said Brailsford. "They got it in the record. Dossier, the FBI calls it. You can't be trusted with information that might be of value to the enemy."

Michael stared out across the parade ground. There were men lying on the dusty patches of grass, and two soldiers were lazily throwing a baseball to each other. Across the parched brown and dead green the flag whipped in a light wind at the top of its pole. Somewhere in Washington at this moment there was a man sitting at a desk, probably looking at the same flag on the wall of his office, and that man had calmly and without remorse written on his record . . . "Disloyal. Communist affiliation. Not recommended."

"Spain," Brailsford said, "it's got something to do with Spain. I sneaked a look at the report. Is Spain Communist?"

"Not exactly," Michael said.

"You ever been in Spain?"

"No. I helped organize a committee that sent ambulances and blood banks over there."

"They got you," Brailsford said. "They got you cold. They

won't tell you, either, they'll just say you don't have the proper qualities of leadership or something like that. But I'm telling you."

"Thanks," Michael said. "Thanks a lot."

"What the hell," Brailsford said, "at least you treat me like a human being. Take a tip. Try and wrangle yourself a transfer. I ain't got no future in this here Company, but you got a lot less. Colclough is crazy on the subject of Reds. You'll do KP from now on till we go overseas, and you'll be first scout on every advance in combat, and I wouldn't give a used condom for your chances of coming out alive."

"Thanks, Brailsford," Michael said. "I think I'll take your advice."

"Sure," Brailsford said. "A man's got to protect his ass in this Army. It's a cinch the Army ain't interested in protecting it." He took out another toothpick and poked between his teeth. He spat, reflectively. "Remember," he said, "I ain't said a word."

Michael nodded and watched Brailsford lounge slowly along the edge of the parade ground, back to the orderly room in which he had no future.

Far away, thin and metallic over the whispering thousand miles of wire, Michael heard Cahoon's voice, saying, "Yes, this is Thomas Cahoon. Yes, I'll accept a collect call from Private Whitacre . . ."

Michael closed the door of the telephone booth of the Rawlings·Hotel. He had made the long trip into town because he did not want to make the call from camp, where somebody might overhear him. "Please limit your call to five minutes," the operator said. "There are others waiting."

"Hello, Tom," he said. "It's not poverty. It's just that I don't have the necessary quarters and dimes."

"Hello, Michael," Cahoon said, sounding very pleased. "It's all right. I'll take it off my income tax."

"Tom," Michael said, "listen very carefully. Do you know anybody in the Special Services Division in New York, the people who put on shows and camp entertainments and things like that?"

"Yes." Cahoon said. "Quite a few people. I work with them all the time."

"I'm tired of the infantry," Michael said. "Will you try to arrange a transfer for me? I want to get out of this country. There are Special Services units going overseas every day. Can you get me into one of them?"

There was a slight pause at the other end of the wire. "Oh," Cahoon said, and there was a tinge of disappointment and reproof in his voice. "Of course. If you want it."

"I'll send you a special-delivery letter tonight," Michael said. "Serial number, rank, and organization designation. You'll need that."

"Yes," said Cahoon. "I'll get right on it." Still the slight coolness in his voice.

"I'm sorry, Tom." Michael said. "I can't explain why I'm doing this over the phone. It will have to wait until I get there."

"You don't have to explain anything to me," Cahoon said. "You know that. I'm sure you have your reasons."

"Yes," said Michael. "I have my reasons. Thanks again. Now I have to get off. There's an expectant Sergeant here who wants to call the maternity ward of the Dallas City Hospital."

"Good luck, Michael," Cahoon said, and Michael could sense the effort at warmth that Cahoon put into the words, almost convincingly.

"Good-bye. I hope I see you soon."

"Of course," Cahoon said. "Of course you will."

Michael hung up and opened the door of the booth. He stepped out and a large, sad-looking Technical Sergeant, with a handful of quarters, flung himself onto the small bench under the phone.

Michael went out into the street and walked down the saloon-lined pavement, in the misty neon glow, to the USO establishment at the end of the block. He sat at one of the spindly desks among the sprawling soldiers, some of them sleeping in wrenched positions in the battered chairs, others writing with painful intensity at the desks.

I'm doing it, Michael thought, as he pulled a piece of paper toward him and opened his fountain pen, I'm doing what I said I'd never do, what none of these weary, innocent boys could never do. I'm using my friends and their influence and my civilian privileges. Cahoon is right perhaps to be disappointed. It was easy to imagine what Cahoon must be thinking now, sitting near the phone, in his own apartment, over which he had just spoken to Michael. Intellectuals, Cahoon probably was thinking, they're all alike, no matter what they say. When it finally gets down to it, they pull back. When the sound of the guns finally draws close, they suddenly find they have more important business elsewhere ...

He would have to tell Cahoon about Colclough, about the man in the office at the FBI, who approved of Franco, but not of Roosevelt, who had your ultimate fate at the tip of his pencil, and against whom no redress, no appeal was possible. He would have to tell him about Ackerman and the ten bloody fights before the pitiless eyes of the Company. He would have to tell him what it was like to be under the command of a man who wanted to see you killed. Civilians couldn't really understand things like that, but he would have to try to tell. It was the big difference between civilian life and life in a military establishment. An American civilian always could feel that he could present his case to some authorities who were committed to the idea of justice. But a soldier . . . You lost any hope of appeal to anyone when you put on your first pair of Army shoes. "Tell it to the Chaplain, Bud, and get a TS slip." TS. Tough shit.

He would try to explain it to Cahoon, and he knew Cahoon would try to understand. But even so, at the end, he knew that that little echo of disappointment would never finally leave Cahoon's voice. And, being honest with himself, Michael knew that he would not blame Cahoon, because the echo of disappointment in himself would never fully leave his own consciousness, either.

He started to write the letter to Cahoon, carefully printing out his serial number and organization, feeling, as he wrote the familiar ciphers that would seem so unfamiliar to Cahoon, that he was writing a letter to a stranger.

CHAPTER NINETEEN

"I'm AFRAID this may sound crazy," Captain Lewis read, "and I'm not crazy, and I don't want anyone to think that I am. This is being written in the main reading room of the New York Public Library on Fifth Avenue and 42nd Street at five o'clock in the afternoon. I have a copy of the Articles of War in front of me on the table and a volume of Winston Churchill's biography of the Duke of Marlborough and the man next to me is taking notes from Spinoza's *Ethics*. I tell you these things to show you that I know what I am doing and that my powers of reason and observation are in no way impaired . . ."

"In all my time in the Army," Captain Lewis said to the WAC secretary who sat at the next desk, "I never read anything like this. Where did we get this from?"

"The Provost Marshal's office sent it over," the WAC said. "They want you to go and look at the prisoner and tell them whether you think he's faking lunacy or not."

"I am going to finish writing this letter," Captain Lewis read, "and then I am going to get on the subway to the Battery and take the ferry to Governor's Island, and give myself up."

Captain Lewis sighed, and for a moment he was sorry that

he had studied psychiatry. Almost any other job in the Army, he felt, would be simpler and more rewarding.

"First of all," the letter went on, in the nervous, irregular handwriting on the flimsy paper, "I want to make it clear that no one helped me leave the camp, and no one knew that I was going to do it. My wife is not to be bothered, either, because I have refrained from going to see her or getting in touch with her in any way since I arrived in New York. I had to figure this question out and I did not wish to be swayed one way or another by any claims of sentiment. No one in New York has sheltered me or even spoken to me since I arrived two weeks ago, and I have not even by accident met anyone I ever knew. I have walked around most of the day and slept at night in various hotels. I still have seven dollars, which would have kept me going for three or four more days, but slowly my mind has been made up on the proper course that I must follow, and I do not wish to delay any longer."

Captain Lewis looked at his watch. He had a date for lunch in the city and he didn't want to be late. He got up and put on his coat and tucked the letter into his pocket, to be read on the ferry.

"If anybody wants to know where I am," Captain Lewis said to the WAC, "I am visiting the hospital."

"Yes, Sir," the girl said gravely.

Captain Lewis put on his cap and went out. It was a sunny, windy day, and across the harbor New York City, rooted in the green water, stood secure against the gale. Captain Lewis experienced the usual little twinge when he saw the city standing there, peaceful, tall and shining, and hardly the place for a soldier to spend the war. But he saluted with snap and precision in answer to the salutes of the enlisted men who passed him on the way down to the ferry, and he felt more soldierly by the time he went forward to the section of the upper deck reserved for officers and their families. Captain Lewis was not a bad man, and he suffered often from pangs of guilt and conscience, which he dutifully recognized. He would undoubtedly have been brave and useful if the Army had put him into a place of danger and responsibility. But he was having a good time in New York. He lived at a good hotel at a cut military rate; his wife remained home in Kansas City with the children, and he was sleeping with two girls who worked as models and did Red Cross things on the side, both of them prettier and more expert than any girl he had ever known before. Every once in a while he woke up gloomily in the morning and resolved that his time-wasting must come to a halt, that he must ask for a more active assignment in a combat zone, or at least take some steps to inject some real vitality into his own work on the Island. But after a morning or two of grumbling and cleaning out his desk and complaining to Colonel Bruce, he relaxed again and drifted back into the easygoing routine as before.

"I have searched myself," Captain Lewis read in the officers' section of the ferry, as it throbbed at its moorings, "for the reasons that I have acted as I have done, and I believe I can state them honestly and understandably. The immediate cause of my action is the fact that I am a Jew. The men of my Company were mostly from the South, for the most part quite uneducated. Their attitude of mild hostility, which I believe had begun to wear away in respect to me, was suddenly fanned by a new Sergeant who was put in command of my platoon. Still, as I have said, I believe I would have taken this action even if I were not a Jew, although that brought it to a crisis and made it impossible for me to continue living among them."

Captain Lewis sighed and looked up. The ferry was moving toward the lower point of Manhattan. The city looked clean and everyday and dependable, and it was hard to think of a boy roaming its streets, loaded with all this misery, preparing to go to the reading room of the Library and there spill it out onto paper for the Provost Marshal to read. God only knew what the MP's had made out of the document.

"I believe," the letter went on, "that I must fight for my country. I did not think so when I left camp, but I realize now that I was wrong then, that I did not see the issues clearly because of my preoccupation with my own troubles and a sense of bitterness which was suddenly made unbearably strong by something that happened on my last night in the camp. The hostility of the Company had crystallized into a series of fist-fights with me. I had been called upon to fight by ten of the largest men in the Company. I felt that I had to accept that challenge.

"I had gone through nine of the fights, however, fighting honorably, and asking for no quarter. In the last fight, I managed to beat the man who was opposing me. He knocked me down several times, but in the end, I knocked him out, as a culmination of many weeks of fighting. The Company, which had watched all the fights, had before this left me on the ground, full of congratulations for the winner. In this instance, when I faced them, looking, perhaps foolishly, for some spark of admiration or grudging respect for what I had done, they merely turned, as one man, and walked away. It seemed to me as I stood there that I could not bear the fact that all I had done, all I had gone through to gain a place in the Company, had been absolutely wasted.

"At that moment, looking at the backs of the men at whose side I was expected to fight and perhaps die, I decided to desert.

"I realize now that I was wrong. I realize now that I believe in this country and in this war, and an individual act like this is not possible. I must fight. But I think I have the right to ask for a transfer to another division, where I can be among men who are more anxious to kill the enemy than they are to kill me.

Respectfully,
Noah Ackerman, Private, US Army."

The ferry docked and Captain Lewis slowly rose to his feet. Thoughtfully he folded the letter and put it into his pocket, as he crossed the gangplank to the wharf. Poor boy, he thought, and he had an impulse to call off the lunch and go right back to the Island and seek Noah out. Ah, well, he thought, as long as I'm here now, I might as well have lunch and see him later. But I'll make it quick, he thought, and get back early.

But the girl he was lunching with had the afternoon off, and he had three old-fashioneds while waiting for a table, and after that the girl wanted to go home with him. She had been a little cool to him the last three times he had been out with her and he felt he couldn't risk leaving her now. Besides his head was a little fuzzy by now and he told himself he would have to be absolutely clear and sober when he went to see Noah, he owed it to the boy, it was the least he could do. So he went home with the girl and called his office and told Lieutenant Klauser to sign out for him after Retreat that afternoon.

He had a very good time with the girl and by five o'clock he decided that he had been foolish to think that she had grown cool toward him, very foolish indeed.

The visitor was very pretty, although a great deal of worry seemed to be under severe control in her steady dark eyes. Also, Lewis saw, she was pregnant. And from the look of her clothes, she was poor. Lewis sighed. This was going to be even worse than he expected.

"It was very good of you," Hope said, "to get in touch with me. They haven't let me see Noah all this time, and they don't let him write me, and they won't deliver my letters to him." Her voice was cool and steady, and there was no tone of complaint in it.

"The Army," Lewis said, feeling ashamed of all the men around him, all the uniforms, guns, buildings. "It does things its own peculiar way, Mrs. Ackerman. You understand."

"I suppose so," Hope said. "Is Noah well?"

"Well enough," Lewis said diplomatically.

"Are they going to let me see him?"

"I think so," Lewis said. "That's what I wanted to talk to you about." He frowned at the WAC secretary, who was watching them from her desk with frank interest. "If you please, Corporal," Lewis said.

"Yes, Sir." The WAC rose reluctantly and went slowly out of the room. She had fat legs and the seams of her stockings were crooked, as always. Why is it, Lewis thought automatically, why is it the dogs are the ones who join up? Then he realized what he was thinking and frowned nervously, as though somehow the grave, steady-eyed girl seated erectly in the stiff chair by the side of his desk could somehow read his thoughts and, in the middle of her terrible dilemma, be shocked and disgusted by him.

"I suppose," Lewis said, "that you know something of what has gone on, even though you haven't seen or heard from your husband."

"Yes," said Hope. "A friend of his, a Private Whitacre, who was down in Florida with him, passed through New York and he came to see me."

"Unfortunate," Lewis said. "Most unfortunate." Then he flushed, because the barest hint of an ironic smile played across the corners of the girl's mouth at his sympathy. "Now," he said briskly, "this is the situation. Your husband has asked to be transferred to another organization . . . Technically, he can be tried by a court-martial on the charge of desertion."

"But he didn't desert," Hope said. "He gave himself up."

"Technically," Lewis said, "he deserted, because at the time he left his post, he did not intend to return."

"Oh," said Hope. "There's a rule for everything, isn't there?"

"I'm afraid there is," Lewis said uncomfortably. The girl made him uneasy sitting there, staring steadily at him. It would have been easier if she cried. "However," he went on stiffly, "the Army realizes that there are extenuating circumstances . . ."

"Oh, God," Hope said, laughing dryly. "Extenuating circumstances."

". . . and in recognition of that," Lewis insisted, "the Army is willing not to press the court-martial and return your husband to duty."

Hope smiled, a grave, warm smile. What a pretty girl, Lewis thought, much prettier than either of the two models . . .

"Well, then," Hope said, "there's no problem, is there? Noah wants to be returned to duty and the Army is willing . . ."

"It isn't as simple as that. The General in command of the base from which your husband deserted insists that he be returned to the Company in which he was serving, and the authorities here will not interfere."

"Oh," Hope said flatly.

"And your husband refuses to go back. He says he would stand trial before going back."

"They'll kill him," Hope said dully, "if he goes back. Is that what they want?"

"Now, now," Lewis said, feeling that since he was wearing the uniform and the two bright Captain's bars, he had to defend the Army to a certain extent, anyway. "It's not as bad as that."

"No?" Hope asked bitterly. "Just how bad would you say it was, Captain?"

"I'm sorry, Mrs. Ackerman," Lewis said humbly. "I know how you feel. And remember, I'm trying to help . . ."

"Of course," Hope said, touching his arm impulsively with her hand. "Forgive me."

"If he stands trial, he is quite certain to be sent to jail." Lewis paused. "For a long time. For a very long time." He did not say that he had written a biting letter to the Inspector General's office about this matter, and had put it in his desk to be reworked the next morning to get it perfect and that he had begun to think, as he re-read the letter, that he was sticking his neck out awfully far, and that the Army had a quiet way of sending obstreperous officers, officers who found it necessary to make complaints about their superiors, to unpleasant places like Assam or Iceland or New Guinea. And he neglected to tell Hope that he had put the letter in his pocket and had re-read it four times during the day and then had torn it up at five o'clock in the afternoon and had gone out and gotten drunk that night. "Twenty years, Mrs. Ackerman," he said as gently as possible, "twenty-five years. Courts-martial have a tendency to harshness . . ."

"I know why you called me here," Hope said in a dead voice. "You want me to convince Noah to go back to his Company."

Lewis swallowed. "That, more or less, is it, Mrs. Ackerman."

Hope stared out the window. Three prisoners in blue fatigues were heaving garbage into a truck. Two guards stood behind them, with shotguns under their arms.

"Are you a psychiatrist in civilian life, too, Captain?" she asked suddenly.

"Why . . . uh . . . yes," Lewis said, flustered by the unexpected question.

Hope laughed sharply. "Aren't you ashamed of yourself today?" she asked.

"Please," Lewis said, stiffly. "Please. I have a job to do and I do it the best way I know how."

Hope stood up. She stood up heavily, carrying the child within her a little awkwardly. Her dress was too small for her and hung grotesquely in front. Lewis had a sudden vision of Hope desperately trying to alter her clothes because she could not afford to buy maternity dresses.

"All right," she said, "I'll do it."

"Good." Lewis beamed at her. After all, he told himself, this was the best possible way for everybody, and the boy would not suffer too badly. He almost believed it, too, as he picked up the phone to call Captain Mason in the Provost Marshal's office and tell him to get Ackerman ready for a visitor.

He asked for Mason's extension and listened to the ringing in the receiver. "By the way," he said to Hope, "does your husband know about . . . the child?" Delicately he avoided looking at the girl.

"No," Hope said. "He hasn't any idea."

"You might . . . uh . . . use that as an argument," Lewis said, holding the buzzing phone to his ear. "In case he won't change his mind. For the child's sake . . . a father in prison, disgraced . . ."

"It must be wonderful," Hope said, "to be a psychiatrist. It makes you so practical."

Lewis could feel his jaw growing rigid with embarrassment. "I didn't mean to suggest anything that . . ." he began.

"Please, Captain," Hope said, "keep your silly mouth closed."

Oh, God, Lewis mourned within him, the Army, it makes idiots of every man in it. I would never have behaved so badly in a gray suit. "Captain Mason," a voice said in the receiver.

"Hello, Mason," Lewis said gratefully. "I have Mrs. Ackerman here. Will you get Private Ackerman down to the visitors' room right away?"

"You have five minutes," the MP said. He stood at the door of the bare room, which had bars on the windows and two small wooden chairs in the middle of the floor.

The main problem was not to cry. He looked so small. The other things, the queer, smashed shape of his nose, the grotesque broken ear, the split, torn eyebrow were bad, but what was hard to conquer was that he looked so small. The stiff blue fatigues were much too large for him and he seemed lost and tiny in them. And they made him seem heartbreakingly humble. Everything about him was humble. Everything but his eyes. The soft way he came into the room. The mild, hesitant little smile as he saw her. The embarrassed, hasty kiss, with the MP watching. His low, mild voice, when he said, "Hello." It was dreadful to think of the long, cruel process which had produced such humility in her husband. But his eyes flared wildly and steadily.

They sat almost knee to knee on the two stiff chairs like two old ladies having tea in the afternoon.

"Well, now," Noah said softly. "Well, now." He grinned at her gently. There were the sorrowful gaps, between the healed gums, where the teeth had been knocked out, and they gave a horrible air of stupidity and rudimentary cunning to the

306

wrecked face. But Whitacre had prepared her for the missing teeth, and her expression didn't change at all. "Do you know what I think about all the time in here?"

"What?" Hope asked. "What do you think about?"

"Something you once said."

"What was that?"

" 'You see, it wasn't too hot, not too hot at all.' " He grinned at her, and not crying became a big problem again. "I remember just how you said it."

"What a thing," Hope said, trying to smile, too. "What a thing to remember."

They stared at each other in silence, as though they had exhausted all conversation.

"Your aunt and uncle," Noah said. "They still live in Brooklyn? The same garden . . ."

"Yes," Hope said. The MP moved a little at the door, scratching his back against the wood. The rough cloth made a sliding sound on the wood. "Listen," Hope said, "I've been talking to Captain Lewis. You know what he wants me to do . . ."

"Yes," Noah said. "I know."

"I'm not going to try to tell you, one way or another," Hope said. "You do what you have to do."

Then she saw Noah staring at her, his eyes slowly dropping to her stomach, tight against the belt of the old dress. "I wouldn't promise him anything," she went on, "not a thing . . ."

"Hope," Noah said, staring fixedly at the swelling belt. "Tell me the truth."

Hope sighed. "All right," she said. "Five more months. I don't know why I didn't write you when I could. I have to stay in bed most of the time. I had to give up my job. The doctor says I'll probably have a miscarriage if I keep on working. That's probably why I didn't let you know. I wanted to be sure it was going to be all right."

Noah looked at her gravely. "Are you glad?" he asked.

"I don't know," Hope said, wishing the MP would fall to the floor in a dead faint. "I don't know anything. Don't let this influence you one way or another."

Noah sighed. Then he leaned over and kissed her forehead. "It's wonderful," he said. "Absolutely wonderful."

Hope glared at the MP, the bare room, the barred window. "What a place," she said, "what a place to learn something like this."

The MP stolidly scratched his back along the frame of the door. "One more minute," he said.

"Don't worry about me," Hope said, swiftly, her words tumbling over each other. "I'll be all right. I'm going to my parents. They'll take care of me. Don't you worry at all."

Noah stood up. "I'm not worried," he said. "A child . . ." He waved vaguely, in a stiff, boyish gesture, and even now, in this grim room, Hope had to chuckle at the dear, familiar movement. "Well, now . . ." Noah said. "Well, what do you know?" He walked over to the window, and looked out through the bars at the enclosed clapboard courtyard. When he turned back to her his eyes seemed blank and lusterless. "Please," he said, "please go to Captain Lewis and tell him I'll go any place they send me."

"Noah . . ." Hope stood up, half in protest, half in relief.

"All right," the MP said. "Time's up." He opened the door.

Noah came over to her and they kissed. She took his hand and held it for a moment against her cheek. But the MP said, "All right, Lady," and she went through the door. She turned before the MP could close it again and saw Noah standing there, thoughtfully watching her. He tried to smile, but it didn't come out a smile. Then the MP closed the door, and she didn't see him again.

CHAPTER TWENTY

"I'M GOING to tell you the truth," Colclough was saying. "I'm sorry to see you back. You're a disgrace to this Company and I don't think we can make a soldier out of you in a hundred years. But by God, I'm going to try, if I have to break you in half doing it."

Noah stared at the twitching pale spot gleaming at the end of the Captain's nose. It was all the same, the same glaring light in the orderly room, the same stale joke pinned on the wall over the Top Sergeant's desk, "The Chaplain's number is 145. Get your TS cards punched there." Colclough had the same voice and he seemed to be saying the same thing, and even the smell of badly seasoned wood, dusty papers, sweaty uniforms, gun oil and beer, hung in the orderly room. It was hard to realize that he had ever been away or that anything had happened or anything changed.

"Naturally, you have no privileges." Colclough was speaking slowly, with solemn enjoyment. "You will get no passes and no furloughs. You will be on KP every day for the next two weeks, and after that you will have Saturday and Sunday KP from then on. Is that clear?"

"Yes, Sir," Noah said.

"You have the same bunk you had before. I warn you, Ackerman, you will have to be five times more soldier than anybody else in this outfit, just to keep alive. Is that clear?"

"Yes, Sir," Noah said.

"Now get out of here. I don't want to see you in this orderly room again. That's all."

"Yes, Sir. Thank you, Sir." Noah saluted and went out. He walked slowly down the familiar Company street toward his old barracks. He felt a constriction in his throat as he saw its lights shining through the bare windows fifty yards away and the familiar figures moving around within.

Suddenly he wheeled. The three men who were following him stopped in the darkness. But he recognized them. Donnelly, Wright, Henkel. He could see them grinning at him. They moved softly and almost imperceptibly toward him, in a spaced, dangerous line.

"We are the welcoming committee," Donnelly said. "The Company decided you should have a nice old-fashioned welcome when you got back, and now we are going to give it to you."

Noah reached into his pocket. He ripped out the spring knife that he had bought in town on the way to camp. He pressed the button and the six-inch blade whickered out of its sheath. It caught the light, gleaming new and bright and deadly in his hand. The three men stopped when they saw the knife.

"The next man that touches me," Noah said quietly, "gets this. If anybody in this Company ever touches me again I'm going to kill him. Pass the good word along."

He stood erect, the knife held at hip level in front of him.

Donnelly looked at the knife, then he looked at the other two men. "Ah," he said, "let's leave him alone. For the time being. He's nuts." Slowly they moved away. Noah remained standing with the knife in front of him.

"For the time being," Donnelly said loudly. "Don't forget I said for the time being."

Noah grinned, watching them until they turned a corner and disappeared. He looked down at the long, wicked blade. Confidently he snapped it closed and put it in his pocket. As he walked toward the barracks, he realized suddenly that he had discovered the technique of survival.

But he hesitated for a long moment at the barracks door. From inside he could hear a man singing, "And then I hold your hand, And then you understand . . ."

Noah threw the door open and stepped in. Riker, near the door, saw him. "My God," he said, "look who's here."

Noah put his hand into his pocket and felt the cold bone handle of the knife.

"Hey, it's Ackerman," Collins, across the room, said. "What do you know?"

Suddenly they were crowding around him. Noah backed un-ostentatiously against the wall, so that no one could get behind him. He fingered the little button that sprang the knife open.

"How was it, Ackerman?" Maynard said. "Did you have a good time? Go to all the night clubs?"

The others laughed, and Noah flushed angrily, until he listened carefully to the laughter, and slowly realized that it did not sound threatening.

"Oh, Christ, Ackerman," Collins said, "you should have seen Colclough's face the day you went over the hill! It was worth joining the Army for. And did he eat Rickett's ass out!" All the men roared in fond memory of the day of glory.

"How long were you gone, Ackerman?" Maynard asked. "Two months?"

"Four weeks," Noah said.

"Four weeks!" Collins marveled. "Four weeks vacation! I wish I had the guts to do it myself, I swear to God . . ."

"You look great, kid," Riker clapped his shoulder. "It's done you a world of good."

Noah stared at him, disbelievingly. This was another trick, and he kept his hand firmly on the knife.

"After you left," Maynard said, "three other guys took the hint and went AWOL. You set a style there, a real style. The Colonel came down and ate Colclough's ass out, right in front of everybody, wanted to know what the hell sort of company he was running, with everybody jumping the fence, the worst record of any company in camp, and all that crap. I thought Colclough was going to slit his throat."

"Here," Burnecker said, "we found these under the barracks and I saved 'em for you." He held out a small, burlap-wrapped package. Slowly Noah opened the package, staring at Burnecker's widely grinning baby face. The three books were still there, slightly moldy, but readable.

Noah shook his head slowly. "Thanks," he said, "thanks, boys," and put the books down. He did not dare to turn and show the watching men what was going on in his face. Dimly, he realized that his personal armistice with the Army had been made. It had been made on lunatic terms, on the threat of the knife and the absurd prestige of his opposition to authority, but it was real, and standing there, looking cloudily down on the tattered books on his bunk, with the voices of the other men a loud blur behind him, he knew that it probably would last, and might even grow into an alliance.

CHAPTER TWENTY-ONE

THE PLATOON LIEUTENANT had been killed in the morning and Christian was in command when the order came to fall back. The Americans had not been pushing much and the battalion had been beautifully situated on a hill overlooking a battered village of two dozen houses in which three Italian families grimly continued to live.

"I have begun to understand how the Army operates," Christian heard a voice complain in the dark, as the platoon clanked along, scuffling in the dust. "A Colonel comes down and makes an examination. Then he goes back to Headquarters and reports. 'General,' he says, 'I am happy to report that the men have warm, dry quarters, in safe positions which can only be destroyed by direct hits. They have finally begun to get their food regularly, and the mail is delivered three times a week. The Americans understand that their position is impregnable and do not attempt any activity at all.' 'Ah, good,' says the General. 'We shall retreat.'"

Christian recognized the voice. Private Dehn, he noted down silently for future reference.

He marched dully, the Schmeisser on its sling already becoming a nagging burden on his shoulder. He was always tired these days, and the malaria headaches and chills kept coming back, too mildly to warrant hospitalization, but wearying and unsettling. Going back, his boots seemed to sound as he limped in the dust, going back, going back . . .

At least, he thought heavily, we don't have to worry about the planes in the dark. That pleasure would be reserved for later, when the sun came up. Probably back near Foggia, in a warm room, a young American Lieutenant was sitting down now to a breakfast of grapefruit juice, oatmeal, ham and eggs, and real coffee with cream, preparing to climb into his plane a little later and come skimming over the hills, his guns spitting at the black, scattered blur of men, crouched insecurely in shallow holes along the road, that would be Christian and the platoon.

As he plodded on, Christian hated the Americans. He hated them more for the ham and eggs and the real coffee than for the bullets and the planes. Cigarettes, too, he thought. Along

311

with everything else, they have all the cigarettes they want, too. How could you beat a country that had all those cigarettes?

His tongue ached ferociously for the healing smoke of a cigarette. But he only had two cigarettes in his pack, and he had rationed himself to one a day.

Christian thought of the faces of the American pilots he had seen, men who had been shot down behind the German lines and had waited to be taken, insolently smoking cigarettes, with arrogant smiles on their empty, untouched faces. Next time, he thought, next time I see one of them, I'm going to shoot him, no matter what the orders are.

Then he stumbled in a rut. He cried out as the pain knotted in his knee and hip.

"Are you all right, Sergeant?" asked the man behind him.

"Don't worry about me," Christian said. "Stay on the side of the road."

He limped on, not thinking about anything any more, except the road in front of him.

The runner from battalion was waiting at the bridge, as Christian had been told he would.

The platoon had been walking for two hours, and it was broad daylight by now. They had heard planes, on the other side of the small range of hills the platoon had been skirting, but they had not been attacked.

The runner was a Corporal, who had hidden himself nervously in the ditch alongside the road. The ditch had six inches of water in it, but the Corporal had preferred safety to comfort, and he rose from the ditch muddy and wet. There was a squad of Pioneers on the other side of the bridge, waiting to mine it after Christian's platoon had gone through. It was not much of a bridge, and the ravine which it crossed was dry and smooth. Blowing the bridge wouldn't delay anyone more than a minute or two, but the Pioneers doggedly blew everything blowable, as though they were carrying out some ancient religious ritual.

"You're late," said the Corporal nervously. "I was afraid something had happened to you."

"Nothing has happened to us," said Christian shortly.

"Very well," said the Corporal. "It's only another three kilometers. The Captain is going to meet us, and he will show you where you are to dig in." He looked around nervously. The Corporal always looked like a man who expects to be shot by a sniper, caught in an open field by a strafing plane, exposed on a hill to a direct hit by an artillery shell. Looking at him, Christian was certain that the Corporal was going to be killed very shortly.

Christian gestured to the men and they started over the bridge behind the Corporal. Good, Christian thought dully, another three kilometers and then the Captain can start making decisions. The squad of Pioneers regarded them thoughtfully from their ditch, without love or malice.

Christian crossed the bridge and stopped. The men behind him halted automatically. Almost mechanically, without any conscious will on his part, his eye began to calculate certain distances, probable approaches, fields of fire.

"The Captain is waiting for us," said the Corporal, peering shiftily past the platoon, down the road on which later in the day the Americans would appear. "What are you stopping for?"

"Keep quiet," Christian said. He walked back across the bridge. He stood in the middle of the road, looking back. For a hundred meters the road went straight, then curved back around a hill, out of sight. Christian turned again and stared through the morning haze at the road and the hills before them. The road wound in mounting curves through the stony sparsely bushed hills in that direction. Far off, eight hundred, a thousand meters away, on an almost cliff-like drop, there was an outcropping of boulders. Among those boulders, his mind registered automatically, it would be possible to set up a machine gun and it would also be possible to sweep the bridge and its approach from there.

The Corporal was at his elbow. "I do not wish to annoy you, Sergeant," the Corporal said, his voice quivering, "but the Captain was specific. No delays, at all, he said, I will not take any excuses."

"Keep quiet," said Christian.

The Corporal started to say something. Then he thought better of it. He swallowed and rubbed his mouth with his hand. He stood at the first stone of the bridge and stared unhappily toward the south.

Christian walked slowly down the side of the ravine to the dry stream bed below. About ten meters back from the bridge, he noticed, his mind still working automatically, the slope leading down from the road was quite gentle, with no deep holes or boulders. Under the bridge the stream bed was sandy and soft, with scattered worn stones and straggling underbrush.

It could be done, Christian thought, it would be simple. He climbed slowly up to the road again. The platoon had cautiously got off the bridge by now and were standing at the edge of the road on the other side, ready to jump into the Pioneers' ditches at the sound of an airplane.

Like rabbits, Christian thought resentfully, we don't live like human beings at all.

The Corporal was jiggling nervously up and down at the entrance to the bridge. "All right, now, Sergeant?" he asked. "Can we start now?"

Christian ignored him. Once more he stared down the straight

313

hundred meters toward the turn in the road. He half closed his eyes and he could almost imagine how the first American, flat on his belly, would peer around the bend to make sure nothing was waiting for him. Then the head would disappear. Then another head, probably a Lieutenant's (the American Army seemed to have an infinite number of Lieutenants they were willing to throw away), would appear. Then, slowly, sticking to the side of the hill, peering nervously down at their feet for mines, the squad, or platoon, or maybe even the company would come around the bend, and approach the bridge.

Christian turned and looked again at the clump of boulders high up on the cliff-like side of the hill a thousand meters on the other side of the bridge. He was almost certain that from there, aside from being able to command the approach to the bridge and the bridge itself, he could observe the road to the south where it wound through the smaller hills they had just come through. He would be able to see the Americans for a considerable distance before they moved behind the hill from which they would have to emerge on the curve of the road that led up to the bridge.

He nodded his head slowly, as the plan, full-grown and thoroughly worked out, as though it had been fashioned by someone else and presented to him, arranged itself in his mind. He walked swiftly across the bridge. He went over to the Sergeant who was in command of the Pioneers.

The Pioneer Sergeant was looking at him inquisitively. "Do you intend to spend the winter on this bridge, Sergeant?" the Pioneer said.

"Have you put the charges under the bridge yet?" Christian asked.

"Everything's ready," said the Pioneer. "One minute after you're past we light the fuse. I don't know what you think you're doing, but I don't mind telling you you're making me nervous, parading up and down this way. The Americans may be along at any minute and then . . ."

"Have you a long fuse?" Christian asked. "One that would take, say, fifteen minutes to burn?"

"I have," said the Pioneer, "but that isn't what we're going to use. We have a one-minute fuse on the charges. Just long enough so that the man who sets them can get out of the way."

"Take it off," said Christian, "and put the long fuse on."

"Listen," said the Pioneer, "your job is to take these scarecrows back over my bridge. My job is to blow it up. I won't tell you what to do with your platoon, you don't tell me what to do with my bridge."

Christian stared silently at the Sergeant. He was a short man who miraculously had remained fat. He looked like the sort of fat man who also had a bad stomach, and his air was testy and

314

superior. "I will also require ten of those mines," Christian said, with a gesture toward the mines piled haphazardly near the edge of the road.

"I am putting those mines in the road on the other side of the bridge," said the Pioneer.

"The Americans will come up with their detectors and pick them up one by one," said Christian.

"That's not my business," said the Pioneer sullenly. "I was told to put them in here and I am going to put them in here."

"I will stay here with my platoon," said Christian, "and make sure you don't put them in the road."

"Listen, Sergeant," said the Pioneer, his voice shivering in excitement, "this is no time for an argument. The Americans . . ."

"Pick those mines up," Christian said to the squad of Pioneers, "and follow me."

"See here," said the Pioneer in a high, pained voice, "I give orders to this squad, not you."

"Then tell them to pick up those mines and come with me," said Christian coldly, trying to sound as much like Lieutenant Hardenburg as possible. "I'm waiting," he said sharply.

The Pioneer was panting in anger and fear now, and he had caught the Corporal's habit of peering every few seconds toward the bend, to see if the Americans had appeared yet. "All right, all right," he said. "It doesn't mean anything to me. How many mines did you say you want?"

"Ten," said Christian.

"The trouble with this Army," grumbled the Pioneer, "is that there are too many people in it who think they know how to win the war all by themselves." But he snapped at his men to pick up the mines, and Christian led them down into the ravine and showed them where he wanted them placed. He made the men cover the holes carefully with brush and carry away the sand they had dug up in their helmets.

Even while he supervised the men down below, he noticed, with a grim smile, that the Pioneer Sergeant himself was attaching the long fuses to the small, innocent-looking charges of dynamite under the span of the bridge.

"All right," said the Pioneer gloomily, when Christian came up on the road again, the mines having been placed to his satisfaction, "the fuse is on. I do not know what you are trying to do, but I put it on to please you. Now, should I light it now?"

"Now," said Christian, "please get out of here."

"It is my duty," said the Pioneer pompously, "to blow up this bridge and I shall personally see that it is blown up."

"I do not want the fuse lighted," Christian said, quite pleasantly now, "until the Americans are almost here. If you wish

315

personally to stay under the bridge until that time, I personally welcome you."

"This is not a time for jokes," said the Pioneer with dignity.

"Get out, get out," Christian shouted at the top of his voice, fiercely, menacingly, remembering with what good effect Hardenburg had used that trick. "I don't want to see you here one minute from now. Get back or you're going to get hurt!" He stood close to the Pioneer, towering ferociously above him, his hands twitching, as though he could barely restrain himself from knocking the Pioneer senseless where he stood.

The Pioneer backed away, his pudgy face paling under his helmet. "Strain," he said hoarsely. "No doubt you have been under an enormous strain in the line. No doubt you are not quite yourself."

"Fast!" said Christian.

The Pioneer turned hurriedly and strode back to where his squad was again assembled on the other side of the bridge. He spoke briefly, in a low voice, and the squad clambered up from the ditch. Without a backward glance they started down the road. Christian watched them for a moment, but did not smile, as he felt like doing, because that might ruin the healthful effect of the episode on his own men.

"Sergeant." It was the Corporal, the runner from battalion, again, his voice drier and higher than ever. "The Captain is waiting..."

Christian wheeled on the Corporal. He grabbed the man's collar and held him close to him. The man's eyes were yellow and glazed with fright.

"One more word from you," Christian shook him roughly, and the man's helmet clicked painfully down over his eyes, onto the bridge of his nose. "One more word and I will shoot you." He pushed him away.

"Dehn!" Christian called. A single figure slowly broke away from the platoon on the other side of the bridge and came toward Christian. "Come with me," said Christian, when Dehn had reached him. Christian half-slid, half-walked down the side of the ravine, carefully avoiding the small minefield he and the Pioneers had laid. He pointed to the long fuse that ran from the dynamite charge down the northern side of the arch.

"You will wait here," he said to the silent soldier standing beside him, "and when I give the signal, you will light that fuse."

Christian heard the deep intake of breath as Dehn looked at the fuse. "Where will you be, Sergeant?" he asked.

Christian pointed up the mountain to the outcropping of boulders about eight hundred meters away. "Up there. Those boulders below the point where the road turns. Can you see it?"

There was a long pause. "I can see it," Dehn whispered finally.

The boulders glittered, their color washed out by distance and sunlight, against the dry green of the cliff. "I will wave my coat," said Christian. "You will have to watch carefully. You will then set the fuse and make sure it is going. You will have plenty of time. Then get out on the road and run until the next turn. Then wait until you hear the explosion here. Then follow along the road until you reach us."

Dehn nodded dully. "I am to be all alone down here?" he asked.

"No," said Christian, "we will supply you with two ballet dancers and a guitar player."

Dehn did not smile.

"Is it clear now?" Christian asked.

"Yes, Sergeant," said Dehn.

"Good," Christian said. "If you set off the fuse before you see my coat, don't bother coming back."

Dehn did not answer. He was a large, slow-moving young man who had been a stevedore before the war, and Christian suspected that he had once belonged to the Communist party.

Christian took a last look at his arrangements under the bridge, and at Dehn standing stolidly, leaning against the curved damp stone of the arch. Then he climbed up to the road again. Next time, Christian thought grimly, that soldier will be less free with criticism.

It took fifteen minutes, walking swiftly, to reach the clump of boulders overlooking the road. Christian was panting hoarsely by the time he got there. The men behind him marched doggedly, as though resigned to the fact that they were doomed to march, bent under their weight of iron, for the rest of their lives. There was no trouble about straggling, because it was plain to even the stupidest man in the platoon that if the Americans got to the bridge before the platoon turned away out of sight behind the boulders, the platoon would present a fair target, even at a great distance, to the pursuers.

Christian stopped, listening to his own harsh breathing, and peered down into the valley. The bridge was small, peaceful, insignificant in the winding dust of the road. There was no movement to be seen any place, and the long miles of broken valley seemed deserted, forgotten, lost to human use.

Christian smiled as he saw that his guess had been right about the vantage point of the boulders. Through a cut in the hills it was possible to see a section of the road some distance from the bridge. The Americans would have to cross that before they disappeared momentarily from sight behind a spur of rock,

317

around which they would then have to turn and appear again on the way to the bridge. Even if they were going slowly and cautiously, it would not take them more than ten or twelve minutes to cover the distance, from the spot at which they would first come into sight, to the bridge itself.

"Heims," Christian said, "Richter. You stay with me. The rest of you go back with the Corporal." He turned to the Corporal. The Corporal now looked like a man who expects to be killed, but feels that there is a ten percent chance he may postpone the moment of execution till tomorrow. "Tell the Captain," Christian said, "we will get back as soon as we can."

"Yes, Sergeant," the Corporal said, nervous and happy. He started walking, almost trotting, to the blessed safety of the turn in the road. Christian watched the platoon file by him, following the Corporal. The road was high on the side of the hill now. When they walked, the men were outlined heroically and sadly against the shreds of cloud and wintry blue sky, and when they made their turns, one by one, in toward the hill, they seemed to step off into windy blue space.

Heims and Richter were a machine-gun team. They were standing heavily, leaning against the roadside boulders, Heims holding the barrel and a box of ammunition, and Richter sweating under the base and more ammunition. They were dependable men, but, looking at them, standing there, sweating in the cold, their faces cautious but noncommittal, Christian felt suddenly that he would have preferred, at this moment, to have with him now the men of his old platoon, dead these long months in the African desert. He hadn't thought about his old platoon for a long time, but somehow, looking at the two machine gunners, left behind on another hill this way, brought to mind the night more than a year before when the thirty-six men had thoughtfully and obediently dug the lonely holes which would a little later be their graves.

Somehow, looking at Heims and Richter, he felt that these men could not be depended upon to do their jobs as well. They belonged, by some slight, subtle deterioration in quality, to another army, an army whose youth had left it, an army that seemed, with all its experience, to have become more civilian, less willing to die. If he left the two men now, Christian thought, they would not stay at their posts for long. Christian shook his head. Ah, he thought, I am getting silly. They're probably fine. God knows what they think of me, besides.

The two men leaned, thickly relaxed against the stones, their eyes warily on Christian, as though they were measuring him and trying to discover whether he was going to ask them to die this morning.

"Set it up here," Christian said, pointing to a level spot between two of the boulders which made a rough v at their joining. Slowly but expertly the men set up the machine gun.

When the gun was set up, Christian crouched down behind it and traversed it. He shifted it a little to the right and peered down the barrel. He adjusted the sight for the distance, allowing for the fact that they would be shooting downhill. Far below, caught on the fine iron line of the sight, the bridge lay in sunlight that changed momentarily to shadows as rags of clouds ghosted across the sky.

"Give them plenty of chance to bunch up near the bridge," Christian said. "They won't cross it fast, because they'll think it's mined. When I give you the signal to fire, aim at the men in the rear, not at the ones near the bridge. Do you understand?"

"The ones in the rear," Heims repeated. "Not the ones near the bridge." He moved the machine gun slowly up and down on its rocker. He sucked reflectively at his teeth. "You want them to run forward, not back in the direction they are coming from . . ."

Christian nodded.

"They won't run across the bridge, because they are in the open there," said Heims thoughtfully. "They will run for the ravine, under the bridge, because they are out of the field of fire there."

Christian smiled. Perhaps he had been wrong about Heims, he thought, he certainly knew what he was doing here.

"Then they will run into the mines down there," said Heims flatly. "I see."

He and Richter nodded at each other. There was neither approval or disapproval in their gesture.

Christian took off his coat, so that he would be able to wave it in signal to Dehn, under the bridge, as soon as he saw the Americans. Then he sat on a stone behind Heims who was sprawled out behind the gun. Richter knelt on one knee, waiting with a second belt of cartridges. Christian lifted the binoculars he had taken from the dead Lieutenant the evening before. He fixed them on the break between the hills. He focused them carefully, noticing that they were good glasses.

There were two poplar trees, dark green and funereal, at the break in the road. They swayed glossily with the wind.

It was cold on the exposed side of the hill, and Christian was sorry he had told Dehn he would wave his coat at him. He could have used his coat now. A handkerchief would probably have been good enough. He could feel his skin contracting in the cold and he hunched inside his stiff clothes uncomfortably.

"Can we smoke, Sergeant?" Richter asked.

"No," said Christian, without lowering the glasses.

Neither of the men said anything. Cigarettes, thought Christian, remembering, I'll bet he has a whole pack, two packs. If he gets killed or badly wounded in this, Christian thought, I must remember to look through his pockets.

They waited. The wind, sweeping up from the valley, circled weightily within Christian's ears and up his nostrils and inside his sinuses. His head began to ache, especially around the eyes. He was very sleepy. He felt that he had been sleepy for three years.

Heims stirred as he lay outstretched, belly down, on the rockbed in front of Christian. Christian put down the glasses for a moment. The seat of Heim's trousers, blackened by mud, crudely patched, wide and shapeless, stared up at him. It is a sight, Christian thought foolishly, repressing a tendency to giggle, a sight completely lacking in beauty. The human form divine.

His forehead burned. The malaria. Not enough the English, not enough the French, the Poles, the Russians, the Americans, but the mosquitoes, too. Perhaps, he thought feverishly and cunningly, perhaps when this is over, I will have a real attack, one that cannot be denied, and they will have to send me back. He raised the glasses once more to his eyes, waiting for the chills to come, inviting the toxin in his blood to gain control.

Then he saw the small mud-colored figures slowly plodding in front of the poplars. "Quiet," he said warningly, as though the Americans could hear Heims and the other man if they happened to speak.

The mud-colored figures, looking like a platoon in any army, the fatigue of their movement visible even at this distance, passed in two lines, on each side of the road across the binoculars' field of vision. Thirty-seven, thirty-eight, forty-two, forty-three, Christian counted. Then they were gone. The poplars waved as they had waved before, the road in front of them looked exactly the same as it had before. Christian put down the glasses. He felt wide awake now, unexcited.

He stood up and waved his coat in large, deliberate circles. He could imagine the Americans moving in their cautious, slow way along the edge of the ridge, their eyes always nervously down on the ground, looking for mines.

A moment later he saw Dehn scramble swiftly out from beneath the bridge and run heavily up to the road. Dehn ran along the road, slowing down perceptibly as he tired, his boots kicking up minute puffs of dust. Then he reached a turn and he was out of sight.

Now the fuse was set. It only remained for the Americans to behave in a normal, soldierly manner.

Christian put on his coat, grateful for the warmth. He plunged his hands in his pockets, feeling cozy and calm.

The two men at the machine gun lay absolutely still.

Far off there was the drone of plane engines. High, to the

southwest, Christian saw a formation of bombers moving slowly, small specks in the sky, moving north on a bombing mission. A pair of sparrows swept, chirping, across the face of the cliff, darting in a flicker of swift brown feathers across the sights of the gun.

Heims belched twice. "Excuse me," he said politely.

They waited. Too long, Christian thought anxiously, they're taking too long. What are they doing back there? The bridge will go up before they get to the bend. Then the whole thing will be useless.

Heims belched again. "My stomach," he said aggrievedly to Richter. Richter nodded, staring down at the magazine on the gun, as though he had heard about Heims's stomach for years.

Hardenburg, Christian thought, would have done this better. He wouldn't have gambled like this. He would have made more certain, one way or another. If the dynamite didn't go off, and the bridge wasn't blown, and they heard about it back at Division, and they questioned that miserable Sergeant in the Pioneers and he told them about Christian . . . Please, Christian prayed under his breath to the Americans, come on, come on, come on . . .

Christian kept the glasses trained on the approach to the bridge. The glasses shook, and he knew that the chills were coming, although he did not feel them at that moment. There was a rushing, tiny noise, near him, and, involuntarily, he put the glasses down. A squirrel scurried up to the top of a rock ten feet away, then sat up and stared with beady, forest eyes at the three men. Another time, another place, Christian remembered, the bird strutting on the road through the woods outside Paris, before the French road block, the overturned farm cart and the mattresses. The animal kingdom, curious for a moment about the war, then returning to its more important business.

Christian blinked and put the glasses to his eyes again. The Americans were out on the road now, walking slowly, crouched over, their rifles ready, every tense line shouting that their flesh inside their vulnerable clothing understood that they were targets.

The Americans were unbearably slow. They were taking infinitely small steps, stopping every five paces. The dashing, reckless young men of the New World. Christian had seen captured newsreels of them in training, leaping boldly through rolling surf from landing barges, flooding onto a beach like so many sprinters. They were not sprinting now. "Faster, faster," he found himself whispering, "faster . . ." What lies the American people must believe about their soldiers!

Heims belched. It was a rasping, ugly, old man's noise. Each man reacted to a war in his own way, and Heims's reaction was from the stomach. What lies the people at home believed about

321

Heims and his comrades, *What were you doing when you won the Iron Cross? Mother, I was belching.* Only Heims and he and Richter knew what the truth was, only they and the forty-three men tenderly approaching the old stone of the bridge that had been put up by slow Italian laborers in the sunlight of 1840. They knew the truth, the machine gunners and himself, and the forty-three men shuffling through the dust across the gunsights eight hundred meters away, and they were more connected by that truth than to anyone else who wasn't there that morning. They knew of each other that their stomachs were contracting in sour spasms, and that all bridges are approached with timidity and a sense of doom . . .

Christian licked his lips. The last man was out from behind the bend now, and the officer in command, the inevitable childish Lieutenant, was waving to a man with the mine detector, who was moving regretfully up toward the head of the column. Slowly, foolishly, they were bunching, feeling a little safer closer together now, feeling that if they hadn't been shot yet they were going to get through this all right.

The man with the mine detector began to sweep the road twenty meters in front of the bridge. He worked slowly and very carefully, and as he worked, Christian could see the Lieutenant, standing in the middle of the road, put his binoculars to his eyes and begin to sweep the country all around him. Zeiss binoculars, no doubt, Christian's mind registered automatically, made in Germany. He could see the binoculars come up and almost fix on their boulders, as though some nervous, latent military sense in the young Lieutenant recognized instinctively that if there were any danger ahead of him, this would be the focus of it. Christian crouched a little lower, although he was certain that they were securely hidden. The binoculars passed over them, then wavered back.

"Fire," Christian whispered. "Behind them. Behind them."

The machine gun opened up. It made an insane shocking noise as it broke the mountain stillness, and Christian couldn't help blinking again and again. Down on the road two of the men had fallen. The others were still standing there stupidly, looking down in surprise at the men on the ground. Three more men fell on the road. Then the Americans began to run down the slope toward the ravine and the protection of the bridge. They are sprinting now, Christian thought, where is the cameraman? Some of the Americans were carrying and dragging the men who had been hit. They stumbled and rolled down the slope, their rifles thrown away, their arms and legs waving grotesquely. It was remote and disconnected, and Christian watched almost disinterestedly, as though he were watching the struggle of a beetle dragged down into a hole by ants.

Then the first mine went off. A helmet hurtled end over end, twenty meters straight up in the air, glinting dully in the sunlight, its straps whipping in its flight.

Heims stopped firing. Then the explosions came one on top of another, echoing and re-echoing along the walls of the hills. A large dirty cloud of dust and smoke bloomed from the bridge.

The noise of the explosions died slowly, as though the sound was moving heavily through the draws and along the ridges to collect in other places. The silence, when it came, seemed unnatural, dangerous. The two sparrows wheeled erratically, disturbed and scolding, across the gun. Down below, from beneath the arch of the bridge, a single figure came walking out, very slowly and gravely, like a doctor from a deathbed. The figure walked five or six meters, then just as slowly sat down on a rock. Christian looked at the American through his glasses. The man's shirt had been blown off him, and his skin was pale and milky. He still had his rifle. While Christian watched, the American lifted his rifle, still with that lunatic deliberation and gravity. Why, thought Christian with surprise, he's aiming at us!

The sound of the rifle was empty and flat and the whistle of the bullets was surprisingly close over their heads. Christian grinned. "Finish him," he said.

Heims pressed the trigger of the machine gun. Through his glasses, Christian could see the darting spurts of dust, flickering along a savage, swift line in an arc around the American. The American did not move. Slowly, with the unhurried care of a carpenter at his workbench, he was putting a new clip in his rifle. Heims swung the machine gun, and the arc of dust splashes moved closer to the American, who still refused to notice them. The American got the clip in his rifle and lifted it once more to his naked shoulder. There was something insane, disturbing, about the shirtless, white-skinned man, an ivory blob against the green and brown of the ravine, sitting comfortably on the stone with all his comrades dead around him, firing in the leisurely and deliberate way at the machine gun he could not quite make out with his naked eye, paying no attention to the continuous, snapping bursts of bullets that would, in a moment or two, finally kill him.

"Hit him," Christian murmured irritably. "Come on, hit him."

Heims stopped firing for a moment. He squinted carefully and jiggled the gun. It made a sharp, piercing squeak. The sound of the rifle came from the valley below, meaningless and undangerous, although again and again there was the whine of a bullet over Christian's head, or the plunk as it hit the hard-packed dirt below him.

Then Heims got the range and fired one short burst. The American put down his gun drunkenly. He stood up slowly and took two or three sober steps in the direction of the bridge. Then he lay down as though he were tired.

At that moment, the bridge went up. Chunks of stone spattered against the trees along the road, slicing white gashes in them and knocking branches off. It took a long time for the dust to settle, and when it did, Christian saw the lumpy, broken mud-colored uniforms sticking out here and there, at odd angles, from the debris. The half-naked American had disappeared under a small avalanche of earth and stones.

Christian sighed and put down his glasses. Amateurs, he thought, what are they doing in a war?

Heims sat up and twisted around. "Can we smoke now?" he asked.

"Yes," said Christian, "you can smoke."

He watched Heims take out a pack of cigarettes. Heims offered one to Richter, who took it silently. The machine gunner did not offer a cigarette to Christian. The miserly bastard, thought Christian bitterly, and reached in and took out one of his two remaining cigarettes.

He held the cigarette in his mouth, tasting it, feeling its roundness, for a long time before he lit it. Then, with a sigh, feeling, well, I've earned it, he lit the cigarette. He took a deep puff and held the smoke in his lungs as long as he could. It made him feel a little dizzy, but relaxed. I must write about this to Hardenburg, Christian thought, taking another pull at the cigarette, he'll be pleased, he wouldn't have been able to do better himself. He leaned back comfortably, taking a deep breath, smiling at the bright blue sky and the pretty little clouds racing overhead in the mountain wind, knowing that he would have at least ten minutes to rest before Dehn got there. What a pretty morning, he thought.

Then he felt the long quivering shiver sliding down his body. Ah, he thought deliciously, the malaria, and this is going to be a real attack, they're bound to send me back. A perfect morning. He shivered again, then took another pull at his cigarette. Then he leaned back happily against the boulder at his back, waiting for Dehn to arrive, hoping Dehn would take his time climbing the slope.

CHAPTER TWENTY-TWO

"ON YOUR FEET, Private Whitacre," the Sergeant said, and Michael rose and followed him. They went in to a large room,

324

with high, dark-paneled doors. The room was lit by tall candles that reflected back a thousand times in yellow buds from the pale green mirrors with which the room was lined.

There was the long, polished table, with the one chair drawn up in the middle, just as Michael had always known it would be. He sat down on the chair, with the Sergeant standing behind him. There was an inkwell before him and a plain wooden pen.

Another door opened and the two Germans came in. They were full Generals and they had on magnificent uniforms. Their decorations, their boots, their spurs, their monocles gleamed softly in the candlelight. They marched up to the table, in perfect formation, stopped, with a memorable clicking of heels, and saluted.

Michael saluted gravely, from his chair. One of the Generals unbuttoned his tunic and slowly drew out a stiff piece of rolled parchment. He gave it to the Sergeant. The Sergeant unrolled it. It made a dry noise in the still room. The Sergeant laid it on the table in front of Michael.

"The surrender papers," the Sergeant said. "You have been chosen to accept the surrender for the Allies."

Michael nodded gravely. Offhandedly he glanced over the documents. They seemed to be in order. He picked up the pen and dipped it in the inkwell. "Michael Whitacre, 32403008, Private First Class, U.S.A." he wrote in a bold, sprawling signature, at the bottom of the page, under the two German signatures. The pen scratched unmusically in the silence. Michael put the pen down. He stood up.

"That will be all, gentlemen," he said flatly.

The two Generals saluted. They quivered when they saluted. Michael did not return the salute. He stared a little over their heads at the sea-green mirrors behind them.

The Generals about-faced precisely. They marched out. There was a defeated Prussian rhythm of boots on the bare, shining floor, and an ironic tinkle of spurs. The heavy door opened and they went out. The door closed. The Sergeant vanished. Michael was left alone in the candlelit room, with the single chair, the long, gleaming table, the inkwell, the stiff, yellowish square of parchment with his signature on it.

"Drop your ——'s and grab your socks," the heavy voice shouted. "Rise and shine! Rise and shine!"

There was the shrill, cutting sound of whistles, all through the old house and from the other houses along the street, and the groaning, despairing moans of soldiers awaking in the darkness.

Michael opened his eyes. He was in a lower bunk and he stared up at the slats and straw mattress of the bunk above him. The man in the upper bunk was a nervous sleeper and a slow cascade of dust and straw splinters came down on Michael every night.

Michael swung his feet out of the bunk. He sat heavily on the edge, feeling his tongue sour behind his teeth, smelling the dreadful, unwashed, cold sweat and wool smell of the twenty men in the room. It was five-thirty in the morning and the blackout blinds were still drawn tightly across the never-opened windows.

Shivering, Michael dressed, his mind numb to the groans and swearing and obscene noises of the Army all around him preparing itself to face the day.

Blinking, he put on his overcoat and stumbled down the rickety stairs of the old house that had been taken over for enlisted men's billets. He stepped out into the bone-seeking chill of the London morning. All along the street other men were soddenly grouping for the reveille roll call. Not far from where Michael stood there was a house with a bronze plaque on it that announced that William Blake had lived and worked there in the nineteenth century. What would William Blake's reactions have been to reveille? What would William Blake have thought if he had looked out his window at the huddled, swearing, beersick men from the other side of the ocean, who were standing there, shivering, under the barrage balloons, still invisible in the high, thin, dark fog? What would William Blake have said to the Sergeant who called, greeting the fresh morning of a new day in the long progress of humanity toward grace, "Drop your ———'s and grab your socks?"

"Galiani."

"Here."

"Abernathy."

"Here."

"Tatnall."

"Here."

"Kammergaard."

"Here."

"Whitacre."

"Here."

William Blake, I am here, John Keats, I am here. Samuel Taylor Coleridge, I am here. King George, I am here. General Wellington, I am here. Lady Hamilton, I am here. Oh, to be in England now that Whitacre's there. Lawrence Sterne, I am here. Prince Hal, I am here. Oscar Wilde, I am here. Here with helmet, gasmask, and PX ration card, here, injected for tetanus, typhus, typhoid, and smallpox, here, instructed how to behave in an English home (food is low and second helpings must be refused), here, warned against the syphilis of the Saxon nymphs of Piccadilly, here, with brass buttons burned of varnish and polished bright to compete with the British Army.

Here, Paddy Finucane, dead in the Channel in the crashed Spitfire, here Montgomery, here Eisenhower, here Rommel, ready at my typewriter, armed with carbon copies, here, here, here, England, here by way of Washington and Local Board 17, here by way of Miami and Puerto Rico and Trinidad and the Guianas and Brazil and Ascension Island, here by way of the ocean in which the submarines surface at night to fire, like sharks in a dream, at the planes flying without lights in the streaming darkness ten thousand feet above, here history, here my past, here among the ruins and the Midwestern voices shouting "Taxi, *taxi*" in the blacked-out midnights. Here, Neighbor William Blake, here is an American, God help us all.

"Dismiss!"

Michael went into the house and made up his bunk. He shaved and mopped the latrine and picked up his messkit and went slowly, in an aluminum jangling, through the awakening, gray streets in the first sober light of the London morning, to breakfast in a large red house that in other times had been inhabited by the family of an earl. Overhead there was the steady drone of a thousand engines, as the Lancasters crossed the Thames on the way home from Berlin. There was grapefruit juice for breakfast, oatmeal, powdered eggs and bacon, thick, underdone, swimming in its own grease. Why, thought Michael, as he ate, why can't they teach an Army cook how to make coffee? How can we live on coffee like this?

"The ——th Fighter Group wants a comedian and some dancers," Michael said to Captain Mincey, his superior officer, sitting at the desk in the room that was lined with pictures of all the famous people who had passed through London for the USO. "And they don't want any more drunks. Johnny Sutter was potted up there last month, and he insulted a pilot in the ready room and was knocked out twice."

"Send them Flanner," Mincey said, weakly. Mincey had asthma and he drank too much, and the combination of Scotch and the climate of London always left him a little forlorn in the morning.

"Flanner has dysentery and he refuses to leave the Dorchester."

Mincey sighed. "Send them that lady accordionist," Mincey said, "what's her name, with the blue hair."

"They want a comedian."

"Tell them we only have accordionists." Mincey sniffed, pushing a tube full of medicine up his nose.

"Yes, Sir," said Michael. "Miss Roberta Finch cannot continue up into Scotland. She had a nervous breakdown in Salisbury. She keeps taking her clothes off in the enlisted men's mess and tries to commit suicide."

"Send that crooner to Scotland," Mincey sighed, "and make out a full report on Finch and send it back to Headquarters in New York, so we'll be covered."

"The MacLean troupe is in Liverpool Harbor," Michael said, "but their ship is quarantined. A seaman came down with meningitis and they can't come ashore for ten days."

"I can't bear it," said Captain Mincey.

"There is a confidential report," Michael said, "from the ——nd Heavy Bombardment Group. Larry Crosett's band played there last Saturday and got into a poker game Sunday night. They took eleven thousand dollars from the Group and Colonel Coker says he has evidence they used marked cards. He wants the money back or he is going to prefer charges."

Mincey sighed weakly, poking the glass tube into his other nostril. He had run a night club in Cincinnati before the war and he often wished he was back in Ohio among the comedians and specialty dancers. "Tell Colonel Coker I am investigating the entire matter," he said.

"A Chaplain at the Troop Carrier Command," Michael said, "objects to the profanity used in our production of *Folly of Youth*. He says the leading man says damn seven times and the ingenue calls one of the characters a son of a bitch in the second act."

Mincey shook his head. "I told that ham to cut out all profanity in this theatre of operations," Mincey said. "And he swore he would. Actors!" He moaned. "Tell the Chaplain I absolutely agree and the offending individuals will be disciplined."

"That's all for now, Captain," Michael said.

Mincey sighed and put his medicine in his pocket. Michael started out of the room.

"Wait a minute, Whitacre." Mincey said.

Michael turned around. Mincey regarded him sourly, his asthma-oppressed eyes and nose red and watery. "For Christ's sake, Whitacre," Mincey said, "you look awful."

Michael looked down without surprise at his rumpled, over-large blouse and his baggy trousers. "Yes, Captain," Michael said.

"I don't give a damn for myself," Mincey said. "For all of me you could come in here in blackface and a grass skirt. But when officers come in from other outfits, they get a bad impression."

"Yes, Sir," said Michael.

"An outfit like this," Mincey said, "has to look more military than the paratroopers. We have to shine. We have to glisten. You look like a KP in the Bulgarian Army."

"Yes, Sir," said Michael.

"Can't you get yourself another blouse?"

"I've asked for one for two months, now," Michael said. "The Supply Sergeant won't talk to me any more."

"At least," Mincey said, "polish your buttons. That's not much to ask, is it?"

"No, Sir," said Michael.

"How do we know," Mincey said, "General Lee won't show up here some day?"

"Yes, Sir," said Michael.

"Also," Mincey said, "you always have too many papers on your desk. It gives a bad impression. Put them in the drawers. Only have one paper on your desk at any one time."

"Yes, Sir."

"One more thing," Mincey said damply. "I wonder if you have some cash on you. I got caught with the check at Les Ambassadeurs last night, and I don't collect my per diem till Monday."

"Will a pound do?"

"That all you got?"

"Yes, Sir," said Michael.

"O.K." Mincey took the pound. "Thanks. I'm glad you're with us, Whitacre. This office was a mess before you came. If you'd only look more like a soldier."

"Yes, Sir," said Michael.

"Send in Sergeant Moscowitz," Mincey said. "That son of a bitch is loaded with dough."

"Yes, Sir," said Michael. He went into the other office and sent Sergeant Moscowitz in to see the Captain.

That was how the days passed in London, in the winter of 1944.

"Oh, my offense is rank," the King said, when Polonius had gone, *"it smells to heaven;*
It hath the primal eldest curse upon't,—
A brother's murder!"
In the little shadow boxes on each side of the stage, put there for that purpose, the sign "Air Raid Alert" was flashed, and a moment later came the sound of sirens, and immediately after, in the distance, toward the coast, the rumble of gunfire.

"Pray can I not," the King went on.
Though inclination be as sharp as will
My stronger guilt defeats my strong intent . . ."
The sound of gunfire came rapidly nearer as the planes swept across the suburbs. Michael looked around him. It was an opening night, and a fashionable one, with a new Hamlet, and the audience was decked out in its wartime best. There were many elderly ladies who looked as though they had seen every opening of Hamlet since Sir Henry Irving. In the rich glow from the stage there was an answering glow from the audience

of white piled hair and black net. The old ladies, and everyone else, sat quiet and motionless as the King strode, torn and troubled, back and forth across the dark room at Elsinore.

"Forgive me my foul murder?" the King was saying loudly. *"That cannot be; since I am still possess'd*
Of those effects for which I did the murder,—
My crown, mine own ambition, and my queen."

It was the King's big scene and he obviously had worked very hard on it. He had the stage all to himself and a long, eloquent soliloquy to get his teeth into. He was doing very well, too, disturbed, intelligent, cursed, with Hamlet in the wings making up his mind whether to stab him or not.

The sound of guns marched across London toward the theatre, and there was the uneven roar of the German engines approaching over the gilt dome. Louder and louder spoke the King, speaking across the three hundred years of English rhetoric, challenging the bombs, the engines, the guns. No one in the audience moved. They listened, as intent and curious as though they had been sitting at the Globe on the afternoon of the first performance of Mr. Shakespeare's new tragedy.

"In the corrupted currents of this world," the King shouted, *"offense's gilded hand may shove by justice;*
And oft 'tis seen the wicked prize itself
Buys out the law; But 'tis not so above;
There is no shuffling,—"

A battery of guns opened up just behind the back wall of the theatre, and there was a double explosion of bombs not far off. The theatre shivered gently. *". . . there the action lies in his true nature,"* said the King loudly, not forgetting any of his business, moving his hands with tragic grace just as the director had instructed him, speaking slowly, trying to space his words between the staccato explosions of the guns.

" . . . and we ourselves," the King said, in a momentary lull while the men outside were reloading, *"Even to the teeth and forehead . . ."* Then rocket guns opened up outside in their horrible, whistling speech that always sounded like approaching bombs, and the King paced silently back and forth, waiting till the next lull. The howling and thunder diminished for a moment to a savage grumbling. *"What then?"* the King said hastily, *"what rests?*
Try what repentance can: what can it not?"

Then he was overwhelmed once more and the theatre shook and trembled in the whirling chorus of the guns.

Poor man, Michael thought, remembering all the opening nights he had ever been through, poor man, his big moment, after all these years. How he must hate the Germans!

". . . O wretched state!" swam dimly out of the trembling and crashing. *"O bosom black as death."*

The planes stuttered on overhead. The battery behind the theatre sent a last revengeful salvo curling into the noisy sky. The rumble of guns was taken up, farther away, by the batteries near Hampstead. Against their diminishing background, like military drums being played at a general's funeral on another street, the King went on, slow, composed, royal as only an actor can be royal, *"O limed soul, that struggling to be free*

"Art more engaged! Help, angels!" he said in the blessed quiet, *"make assay*

Bow, stubborn knees, and, heart with strings of steel,
Be soft as sinews of the new-born babe!
All may be well."

He knelt at the altar and Hamlet appeared, graceful and dark in his long black tights. Michael looked around him. Every face was calmly and interestedly watching the stage; the old ladies and the uniforms did not stir.

I love you, Michael wanted to say, I love you all. You are the best and strongest and most foolish people on earth and I will gladly lay down my life for you.

He felt the tears, complex and dubious, sliding down his cheeks as he turned to watch Hamlet, torn by doubt, put up his sword rather than take his uncle at his prayers.

Far off a single gun spoke into the subsiding sky. Probably, thought Michael, it is one of the women's batteries, coming, like women, a little late for the raid, but showing their intentions are of the best.

London was burning in a bright circlet of fires when Michael left the theatre and started walking toward the Park. The sky flickered and here and there an orange glow was reflected off the clouds. Hamlet was dead by now. *"Now cracks a noble heart,"* Horatio had said. *"Good night, sweet prince. And flights of angels sing thee to thy rest."* Horatio had also said his final words on carnal, bloody, and unnatural acts: of accidental judgments, casual slaughters, while the last Germans were crashing over Dover, and the last Englishmen were burning in their homes as the curtain slowly dropped and the ushers ran up the aisles with flowers for Ophelia and the rest of the cast.

In Piccadilly, the whores strolled by in battalions, flashing electric torches on passing faces, giggling harshly, calling, "Hey, Yank, two pounds, Yank."

Michael walked slowly through the shuffling crowds of whores and MP's and soldiers, thinking of Hamlet saying of Fortinbras and his men, *"Witness this army, of such mass and charge,*

Led by a delicate and tender prince,
Whose spirit with divine ambition puff'd

> *Makes mouths at the invisible event;*
> *Exposing what is mortal and unsure*
> *To all that fortune, death and danger there,*
> *Even for an egg-shell."*

What mouths we make at the invisible event, Michael thought, grinning to himself, staring through the darkness at the soldiers bargaining with the whores, what regretful, doubtful mouths! We expose all that is mortal and unsure, and for more than an eggshell, but how differently from Fortinbras and his twenty thousand offstage men at arms! Ah, probably Shakespeare was laying it on. Probably no army, not even that of good old Fortinbras, returned from the Polack wars, ever was quite as dashing and wholehearted as the dramatist made out. It supplied a good speech and conveniently fitted Hamlet's delicate situation, and Shakespeare had put it in, although he must have known he was lying. We never hear what a Private First Class in Fortinbras' infantry thought about his tender and delicate prince, and the divine ambition that puff'd him. That would make an interesting scene, too. . . . Twenty thousand men, that for a fantasy and trick of fame, Go to their graves like beds, was it? There were graves waiting not so far off for more than twenty thousand of the men around him, Michael thought, and maybe for himself, too, but perhaps in the three hundred years the fantasy and the trick had lost some of their power. And yet we go, we go. Not in the blank verse, noble certainty so admired by the man in the black tights, but we go. In a kind of limping, painful prose, in legal language too dense for ordinary use or understanding, a judgment against us, more likely than not, by a civil court that is not quite our enemy and not quite our friend, a writ handed down by a nearly honest judge, backed by the decision of a jury of not-quite-our peers, sitting on a case that is not exactly within their jurisdiction. "Go," they say, "go die a little. We have our reasons." And not quite trusting them and not quite doubting them, we go. "Go," they say, "go die a little. Things will not be better when you finish, but perhaps they will not be much worse." Where is the Fortinbras, to toss a plume and strike a noble pose, and put the cause into good round language for us? *N'existe pas,* as the French put it. Out of stock. Out of stock in America, out of stock in England, quiet in France, too cunning in Russia. Fortinbras had vanished from the earth. Churchill made a good try of it, but when you finally sounded him there was a hollow and old-fashioned ring to him like a bugle blowing for a war three years ago. The mouth we make at the invisible event today is twisted into a skeptical grin. This is the war of the sour mouth, Michael thought, and yet there will be enough of us dead in it to please any bloodthirsty paying customer at the Globe in the early 1600's.

Michael walked slowly alongside the Park, thinking of the swans, settling down now on the Serpentine, and the orators who would be out again on Sunday, and the gun crews brewing tea and relaxing now that the planes had fled England. He remembered what an Irish Captain on leave in London, from a Dover battery which had knocked down forty planes, had said of the London anti-aircraft outfits. "They never hit anybody," he said in a contemptuous soft burr. "It's a wonder London isn't completely destroyed. They're so busy planting rhododendrons around the emplacements and shining the barrels so they'll look pretty when Miss Churchill happens to pass by, that it's bugger-all gunnery."

The moon was coming up now, over the old trees and the scarred buildings, and there was a tinkle of glass where some soldiers and their girls were walking over a window that had been blown out in the raid.

"Bugger-all gunnery," Michael said softly to himself, turning into the Dorchester, past the huge doorman with the decorations from the last war on his uniform. "Bugger-all gunnery," Michael repeated, delighted with the phrase.

There was dance music swinging into the lobby, and the old ladies and their nephews solemnly drinking tea, and pretty girls floating through on the way to the American bar on the arms of American Air Forces officers, and Michael had the feeling, looking at the scene, that he had read all about this before, about the last war, that the characters, the setting, the action, were exactly the same, the costumes so little different that the eye hardly noticed it. By a trick of time, he thought, we become the heroes in our youthful romances, but always too late to appear romantic in them.

He walked upstairs to the large room where the party was still in progress and where Louise had said she'd be waiting for him.

"Look," said a tall, dark-haired girl near the door, "a Private." She turned to a Colonel next to her. "I told you there was one in London." She turned back to Michael. "Will you come to dinner next Tuesday night?" she asked. "We'll lionize you. Backbone of the Army."

Michael grinned at her. The Colonel next to her did not seem pleased with Michael. "Come, my dear." He took the girl firmly by the arm. "I'll give you a lemon if you come," the girl said over her shoulder, receding in silk undulations with the Colonel. "A real whole lemon."

Michael looked around the room. Six Generals, he noticed, and felt very uncomfortable. He had never met a General before. He looked uneasily down at his ill-fitting blouse and the not-quite polished buttons. He would not have been surprised if one of the Generals had come over to him and taken his name, rank, and serial number for not having his buttons polished properly.

He did not see Louise for the moment, and he felt shy at going up to the bar, among the important-looking strangers at the other end of the room, and asking for a drink. When he had passed his sixteenth birthday he had felt that he was over being shy for the rest of his life. After that he had felt at home everywhere, had spoken his mind freely, felt that he was acceptable enough, if no more, to get by in any company. But ever since he had joined the Army, a later-day shyness, more powerful and paralyzing than anything he had known as a boy, had developed within him, shyness with officers, with men who had been in combat, among women with whom otherwise he would have felt perfectly at ease.

He stood hesitantly a little to one side of the door, staring at the Generals. He did not like their faces. They looked too much like the faces of businessmen, smalltown merchants, factory owners, growing a little fat and overcomfortable, with an eye out for a new sales campaign. The German Generals have better faces, he thought. Not better, abstractly, he thought, but better for Generals. Harder, crueler, more determined. A General should have one of two faces, he thought. Either he should look like a heavyweight prizefighter, staring out coldly with dumb animal courage at the world, through battered, quick slits of eyes, or he should look like a haunted man out of a novel by Dostoievski, malevolent, almost mad, with a face marked by evil raptures and visions of death. Our Generals, he thought, look as though they might sell you a building lot or a vacuum cleaner, they never look as though they could lead you up to the walls of a fortress. Fortinbras, Fortinbras, did you never migrate from Europe?

"What're you thinking about?" Louise asked.

He turned. She was standing at his side. "The faces of our Generals," he said. "I don't like them."

"The trouble with you is," Louise said, "you have the enlisted man's psychology."

"How right you are." He stared at Louise. She was wearing a gray plaid suit with a black blouse. Her red hair, bright and severe over the small, elegant body, shone among the uniforms. He never could decide whether he loved Louise or was annoyed with her. She had a husband some place in the Pacific of whom she rarely spoke, and she did some sort of semi-secret job for the OWI, and she seemed to know every bigwig in the British Isles. She had a deft, tricky way with men, and was always being invited to weekends at famous country houses where garrulous military men of high rank seemed to spill a great many dangerous secrets to her. Michael was sure, for example, that she knew when D Day was going to come, and which targets in

Germany were to be bombed for the next month, and when Roosevelt would meet Stalin and Churchill again. She was well over thirty, although she looked younger, and before the war had lived modestly in St. Louis, where her husband had taught at a college. After the war, Michael was certain, she would run for the Senate or be appointed Ambassadress to somewhere, and when he thought of it, he pitied the husband, mired on Bougainville or New Caledonia, dreaming of going back to his modest home and quiet wife in St. Louis.

"Why," Michael asked, smiling soberly at her, conscious that two or three high-ranking officers were watching him stonily as he talked to Louise, "why do you bother with me?"

"I want to keep in touch with the spirit of the troops," Louise said. "The Common Soldier and How He Grew. I may write an article for the *Ladies' Home Journal* on the subject."

"Who's paying for this party?" Michael asked.

"The OWI," Louise said, holding his arm possessively. "Better relations with the Armed Forces and our noble Allies, the British."

"That's where my taxes go," Michael said. "Scotch for the Generals."

"The poor dears," Louise said. "Don't begrudge it to them. Their soft days are almost over."

"Let's get out of here," Michael said. "I can't breath."

"Don't you want a drink?"

"No. What would the OWI say?"

"One thing I can't stand about enlisted men," Louise said, "is their air of injured moral superiority."

"Let's get out of here." Michael saw a British Colonel with gray hair bearing down on them, and tried to get Louise started toward the door, but it was too late.

"Louise," said the Colonel, "we're going to the Club for dinner, and I thought if you weren't busy . . ."

"Sorry," Louise said, holding lightly onto Michael's arm. "My date arrived. Colonel Treanor, PFC Whitacre."

"How do you do, Sir," said Michael, standing almost unconsciously at attention, as he shook hands.

The Colonel, he noticed, was a handsome, slender man with cold, pale eyes, with the red tabs of the General Staff on his lapel. The Colonel did not smile at Michael.

"Are you sure," he said rudely, "that you're going to be busy, Louise?"

He was staring at her, standing close to her, his face curiously pale, as he rocked a little on his heels. Then Michael remembered the name. He had heard a long time ago that there was something on between Louise and him, and Mincey, in the office, had once warned Michael to be more discreet when Mincey had seen Louise and Michael together at a bar. The

Colonel was not in command of troops now, but was on one of the Supreme Headquarters Planning Boards, and, according to Mincey, was a powerful man in Allied politics.

"I told you, Charles," Louise said, "that I'm busy."

"Of course," the Colonel said, in a clipped, somewhat drunken way. He wheeled, and went off toward the bar.

"There goes Private Whitacre," Michael said softly, "on landing barge Number One."

"Don't be silly," Louise snapped.

"Joke."

"It's a silly joke."

"Righto. Silly joke. Give me my purple heart now." He grinned at Louise to show her he wasn't taking it too seriously. "Now," he said, "now that you have blasted my career in the Army of the United States, may we go?"

"Don't you want to meet some Generals?"

"Some other time," said Michael. "Maybe around 1960. Go get your coat."

"O.K.," said Louise. "Don't go away. I couldn't bear it if you went away." Michael looked speculatively at her. She was standing close to him, oblivious of all the other men in the room, her head tilted a little to one side, looking up at him very seriously. She means it, Michael thought, she actually means it. He felt disturbed, tender and wary at the same time. What does she want? The question skimmed the edges of his mind, as he looked down at the bright, cleverly arranged hair, at the steady, revealing eyes. What does she want? Whatever it is, he thought rebelliously, I don't want it.

"Why don't you marry me?" she said.

Michael blinked and looked around him at the glitter of stars and the dull glint of braid. What a place, he thought, what a place for a question like that!

"Why don't you marry me?" she asked again, quietly.

"Please," he said, "go get your coat." Suddenly he disliked her very much. Suddenly he felt sorry for the schoolteacher husband in the Marine uniform faraway in the jungle. He must be a nice, simple, sorrowful man, Michael thought, who probably would die in this war out of simple bad luck.

"Don't think," Louise said, "that I'm drunk. I knew I was going to ask you that from the minute you walked in here tonight. I watched you for five minutes before you saw me. I knew that's what I wanted."

"I'll put a request through channels," Michael said as lightly as possible, "for permission from my Commanding Officer . . ."

"Don't joke, damn you," Louise said. She turned sharply and went to get her coat.

He watched her as she walked across the room. Colonel Treanor stopped her and Michael saw him arguing swiftly and secretly with Louise and hold her arm. She pulled away and went on to the dressing rooms. She walked lightly, Michael noticed, with a prim, stiff grace, her pretty legs and small feet very definite and womanly in their movements. Michael felt baffled and wished he had the courage to go to the bar for a drink. It had all been so light and comradely, offhand and without responsibility, just the thing for a time like this, this time of waiting, this time before the real war, this time of being ludicrous and ashamed in Mincey's ridiculous office. It had been off-hand and flattering, in exactly the proper proportions, and Louise had cleverly erected a thin shield of something that was less than and better than love to protect him from the comic, unending abuse of the Army. And, now, it was probably over. Women, Michael thought resentfully, can never learn the art of being transients. They are all permanent settlers at heart, making homes with dull, instinctive persistence in floods and wars, on the edges of invasions, at the moment of the crumbling of states. No, he thought, I will not have it. For my own protection I am going to get through this time alone . . .

The hell with it, he thought, Generals or no Generals. He strode, upright and swift, through the room to the bar.

"Whiskey and soda, please," he said to the bartender, and drank the first gulp down in a long, grateful draught.

A Colonel in the Supply Service of the British Army was talking to an RAF Wing Commander at Michael's elbow. They paid no attention to him. The Colonel was a little drunk. "Herbert, old man," the Colonel was saying, "I was in Africa and I can speak with authority. The Americans are fine at one thing. Superb. I will not deny it. They are superb at supply. Lorries, oil dumps, traffic control, superb. But, let us face it, Herbert, they cannot fight. If Montgomery were realistic he would say to them, 'Chaps, we will hand over all our lorries to you, and you hand over all your tanks and guns to us. You will haul and carry, chaps, because you're absolutely first-rate at it, and we will jolly well do the fighting, and we'll all be home by Christmas.'"

The Wing Commander nodded solemnly and both the officers of the King ordered two more whiskeys. The OWI, Michael thought grimly, staring at the Colonel's pink scalp shining through the thin white hair on the back of his head, the OWI is certainly throwing away the taxpayer's money on these particular allies.

Then he saw Louise coming out into the room in a loose gray coat. He put down his drink and hurried over to her. Her face wasn't serious any more, but curled into its usual slightly questioning smile, as though she didn't believe one half of what the world told her. At some moment in the dressing room, Michael thought, as he took her arm, she had looked into the mirror and told herself, I am not going to show anything more tonight, and switched on her old face, as smoothly and perfectly as she was now pulling on her gloves.

"Oh, my," Michael said, grinning, piloting her to the door. "Oh, my, what danger I am in."

Louise glanced at him, then half-understood. She smiled reflectively. "Don't think you're not," she said.

"Lord, no," said Michael. They laughed together and walked out through the lobby of the Dorchester, through the old ladies drinking tea with their nephews, through the young Air Forces Captains with the pretty girls, through the terrible, anchored English jazz, that suffered so sadly because there were no Negroes in England to breathe life into it, and tell the saxophonists and drummers, "Oh, Mistuh, are you off! Mistuh, lissen here, *this* is the way it goes, just turn it loose, Mistuh, turn that poor jailbird horn loose out of yo' hands . . ." Michael and Louise walked jauntily, arm in arm, back once more, and perhaps only for a moment, on the brittle happy perimeter of love. Outside, across the Park, in the fresh cold evening air, the dying fires the Germans had left behind them sent a holiday glow into the sky.

They paced slowly toward Piccadilly.

"I decided something tonight," Louise said.

"What?" Michael asked.

"I have to get you commissioned. At least a Lieutenant. It's silly for you to remain an enlisted man all your life. I'm going to talk to some of my friends."

Michael laughed. "Save your breath," he said.

"Wouldn't you like to be an officer?"

Michael shrugged. "Maybe. I haven't thought about it. Even so—save your breath."

"Why?"

"They can't do it."

"They can do anything," Louise said. "And if I ask them . . ."

"Nothing doing. It will go back to Washington, and it will be turned down."

"Why?"

"Because there's a man in Washington who says I'm a Communist."

"Nonsense."

"It's nonsense," Michael said, "but there it is."

"*Are* you a Communist?"

"About like Roosevelt," said Michael. "They'd kept him from being commissioned, too."

"Did you try?"

"Yes."

338

"Oh, God," Louise said, "what a silly world."

"It's not very important," said Michael. "We'll win the war anyway."

"Weren't you furious," Louise asked, "when you found out?"

"A little, maybe," said Michael. "More sad than furious."

"Didn't you feel like chucking the whole thing?"

"For an hour or two, maybe," said Michael. "Then I thought, What a childish attitude."

"You're too damned reasonable."

"Maybe. Not really, though, not so terribly reasonable," said Michael. "I'm not really much of a soldier, anyway. The Army isn't missing much. When I went into the Army, I made up my mind that I was putting myself at the Army's disposal. I believe in the war. That doesn't mean I believe in the Army. I don't believe in any army. You don't expect justice out of an army, if you're a sensible, grown-up human being, you only expect victory. And if it comes to that, our Army is probably the most just one that ever existed. I believe the Army will take care of me to the best of its abilities, that it will keep me from being killed, if it can possibly manage it, and that it will finally win as cheaply as human foresight and skill can arrange. Sufficient unto the day is the victory thereof."

"That's a cynical attitude," Louise said. "The OWI wouldn't like that."

"Maybe," said Michael. "I expected the Army to be corrupt, inefficient, cruel, wasteful, and it turned out to be all those things, just like all armies, only much less so than I thought before I got into it. It is much less corrupt, for example, than the German Army. Good for us. The victory we win will not be as good as it might be, if it were a different kind of army, but it will be the best kind of victory we can expect in this day and age, and I'm thankful for it."

"What're you going to do?" Louise demanded. "Stay in that silly office, stroking chorus girls on the behind for the whole war?"

Michael grinned. "People have spent wars in worse ways," he said. "But I don't think I'll only do that. Somehow," he said thoughtfully, "somehow the Army will move me some place, finally, where I will have to earn my keep, where I will have to kill, where I may be killed."

"How do you feel about it?" Louise demanded.

"Frightened."

"Why're you so sure it will happen?"

Michael shrugged. "I don't know," he said. "A premonition. A mystic sense that justice must be done by me and to me. Ever since 1936, ever since Spain, I have felt that one day I would be asked to pay. I ducked it year after year, and every

339

day that sense grew stronger; the payment would be demanded of me, without fail."

"Do you think you've paid yet?"

"A little," Michael grinned. "The interest on the debt. The capital remains untouched. Some day they're going to collect the capital from me, and not in the USO office, either." They turned down into St. James's Street, with the Palace looming dark and medieval at the other end, and the clock glistening palely, a soft gray blur, among the battlements.

"Maybe," Louise said, smiling, in the darkness, "maybe you're not the officer type, after all."

"Maybe I'm not," Michael agreed gravely.

"Still," said Louise, "you could at least be a Sergeant."

Michael laughed. "How the times have slid downhill," he said. "Madam Pompadour in Paris gets a Marshal's baton for her favorite. Louise M'Kimber slips into the King's bed for three stripes for her PFC."

"Don't be ugly," Louise said with dignity. "You're not in Hollywood now."

"Roll me over," sang three young British sailors who swung abreast diagonally across the wide street, *"in the clover, Lay me down, and do it again."*

"I was thinking about Dostoievski before I met you tonight," Michael began.

"I hate cultured men," said Louise firmly.

"In Dostoievski, who was it, Prince Mishkin, tried to marry a whore out of a sense of his own sin and his own guilt."

"I only read the *Daily Express,"* said Louise.

"The times have grown less drastic," Michael said. "I don't marry anyone. I merely remain a private for my guilt. It's not so hard. After all, there are eight million like me . . ."

"Oh, this is number four," sang the sailors, swinging down toward the palace, *"and she asked him for more, Oh, Roll me over and do it again."*

Michael and Louise turned down a side street, on which only one house had been bombed. The young voices, sweet and hoarse, despite their song, grew muffled and lonesome as the sailors wandered away.

The Canteen of the Allies, for all its imposing name, was merely three small basement rooms decked with dusty bunting, with a long plank nailed onto a couple of barrels that did service for a bar. In it, from time to time, you could get venison chops and Scotch salmon and cold beer from a tin washtub that the proprietress kept full of ice in deference to American tastes. The Frenchmen who came there could usually find a bottle of Algerian wine at legal prices. Almost everyone could get credit if he needed it, and a girl whether he needed it or not.

Four or five hungry-eyed ladies, nearing middle age, whose husbands all seemed to be serving in Italy in the Eighth Army, ran the place on a haphazard voluntary basis, and it conveniently and illegally served liquor after the closing hour.

When Michael and Louise entered, someone was playing the piano in the back room. Two English Sergeant pilots were singing softly at the bar. An American WAC Corporal was being helped, drunk, to the bathroom. An American Lieutenant Colonel by the name of Pavone, who looked like a middle-aged burlesque comedian and who had been born in Brooklyn and had somehow run a circus in France in the 1930's, and had served in the French cavalry in the beginning of the war, and who continually smoked large expensive cigars, was making what sounded like a speech to four war correspondents at a large table. In a corner, almost unnoticed, a huge dark Frenchman, who, it was reputed, dropped by parachute into France two or three times a month for British Intelligence, was eating martini glasses, something he did when he got drunk and felt moody late at night. In the small kitchen off the back room, a tall, fat American Top Sergeant in the MP's, who had taken the fancy of one of the ladies who ran the place, was frying himself a panful of fish. A two-handed poker game was being played at a small table near the kitchen between a correspondent and a twenty-three-year-old Air Forces Major who had just come back from bombing Kiel that afternoon, and Michael heard the Major say, "I raise you a hundred and fifty pounds." Michael watched the Major gravely write out an IOU for a hundred and fifty pounds and put it in the middle of the table. "I see you and raise you a hundred and fifty," said his opponent, who wore an American correspondent's uniform, but who sounded like a Hungarian. Then he wrote out an IOU and dropped it on the small flimsy pile in the middle of the table.

"Two whiskeys, please," said Michael to the British Lance Corporal who served behind the bar when he was in London on leave.

"No more whiskey, Colonel," said the Lance Corporal, who had no teeth at all, and whose gums, Michael thought, must be in sad shape from British Army rations. "Sorry."

"Two gins."

The Lance Corporal, who wore a wide, spotted grayish apron over his heavy battledress, deftly and lovingly poured the two drinks.

From the piano in the other room, quivering male voices sang,

> "My father's a black market grocer,
> My mother makes illegal gin,
> My sister sells sin on the corner,
> Kee-rist, how the money rolls in!"

341

Michael raised his glass to Louise. "Cheers," he said. They drank.

"Six bob, Colonel," said the Lance Corporal.

"Put it on the book," said Michael. "I'm busted tonight. I expect a large draft from Australia. I have a kid brother who's a Major there in the Air Forces, on flying pay and per diem."

The Lance Corporal laboriously scratched Michael's name down in a gravy-spotted ledger and opened two bottles of warm beer for the Sergeant pilots, who, attracted by the melody from the next room, drifted back that way, holding their glasses.

"I wish to address you in the name of General Charles de Gaulle," said the Frenchman, who for the moment had given up chewing on martini glasses. "You will all kindly stand up for General Charles de Gaulle, leader of France and the French Army."

Everyone stood up absently for the General of the French Army.

"My good friends," said the Frenchman loudly and with a thick Russian accent, "I do not believe what the newspapers say. I hate newspapers and I hate all newspapermen." He glared fiercely at the four correspondents around Colonel Pavone. "General Charles de Gaulle is a democrat and a man of honor." He sat down and looked muddily at a half-chewed martini glass.

Everyone sat down again. From the back room, the voices of the RAF clattered into the bar. *"There's a Lancaster leaving the Ruhr,"* they sang, *"bound for old Blighty's shore, heavily laden with terrified men, Shit-scared and prone on the floor . . ."*

"Gentlemen," said the proprietress. She had been asleep, on a chair along the wall, with her glasses hanging from one ear. She opened her eyes, grinned at the company, and said, pointing to the WAC, who was returning from the bathroom, "That woman has stolen my scarf." Then she fell asleep again. In a moment, she was snoring loudly.

"What I like about this place," Michael said, "is the atmosphere of sleepy old England that is so strong here. Cricket," said Michael, "tea being served in the vicar's garden, the music of Delius."

". . . *oh, they've shot off my ballocks,"* sang the RAF in the other room, *"and screwed my hydraulics, Oh, Bless them, lads, bless them all . . ."*

A stout Major General in Services of Supply, who had just arrived in England that afternoon from Washington, entered the bar. A large young woman with long teeth and a flowing black veil was on his arm. A drunken Captain with a large moustache followed him carefully.

"Ah," the Major General said, heading straight for Louise, with a wide, warm smile on his face, "my dear Mrs. M'Kimber." He kissed Louise. The woman with the long teeth smiled seductively at everyone. She had something wrong with her eyes, and she blinked them, quickly, again and again, all the time. Later on, Michael found out that her name was Kearney and that her husband had been a pilot in the RAF and had been shot down over London in 1941.

"General Rockland," Louise said, "I want you to meet PFC Whitacre. He loves Generals."

The General shook Michael's hand heartily, nearly crushing it, and Michael was sure the General must have played football at West Point at one time. "Glad to meet you, Boy," said the General. "I saw you at the party, sneaking out with this handsome young woman."

"He insists on being a Private," said Louise, smiling. "What can we do about it?"

"I hate professional Privates," said the General and the Captain behind him nodded gravely.

"So do I," said Michael. "I'd be delighted to be a Lieutenant."

"I hate professional Lieutenants, too," said the General.

"Very well, Sir," said Michael. "If you wish, you can make me a Lieutenant Colonel."

"Maybe I will," said the General, "maybe I will. Jimmy, take that man's name."

The Captain who had come in with the General, fumbled through his pockets and took out a card advertising a private black-market taxi service. "Name, rank, and serial number," he said automatically.

Michael gave him his name, rank and serial number and the Captain put the card back carefully in an inside pocket. He was wearing bright red suspenders, Michael saw, as the blouse flipped back.

The General had Louise over in a corner by now, pinned against the wall, his face close to hers. Michael started toward them, but the long-toothed girl stepped into his path, smiling softly and blinking. "My card," she said. She handed Michael a small, stiff white card. Michael stared down at it. Mrs. Ottilie Munsell Kearney, he read, Regent 4027.

"I'm in every morning until eleven," Mrs. Kearney said, smiling without ambiguity at him. Then she wheeled away, her veil blowing, and went from table to table, distributing cards.

Michael got another gin and went over to the table where Colonel Pavone was sitting with the correspondents, two of whom Michael knew.

". . . after the war," Pavone was saying, "France is going to go left, and there is nothing we can do about it and nothing

England can do about it and nothing Russia can do about it. Sit down Whitacre, we have whiskey."

Michael drained his glass, then sat down and watched one of the correspondents pour him four fingers of Scotch.

"I'm in Civil Affairs," Pavone said, "and I don't know where they're going to send me. But I'll tell you here and now, if they send me to France, it will be a big joke. The French have been governing themselves for a hundred and fifty years, and they'll just laugh at any American who tells them even where to put the plumbing in the city hall."

"I raise you five hundred pounds," said the Hungarian correspondent at the other table.

"I'll see you," said the Air Forces Major. They both wrote out IOU's.

"What happened, Whitacre?" Pavone asked. "The General get your girl?"

"Only on a short lease," said Michael, glancing toward the bar, where the General was leaning heavily against Louise and laughing hoarsely.

"The Privilege of Rank," said Pavone.

"The General loves girls," said one of the four correspondents. "He was in Cairo two weeks and he had four Red Cross girls. They gave him the Legion of Merit when he returned to Washington."

"Did you get one of these?" Pavone waved one of Mrs. Kearney's cards.

"One of my most treasured souvenirs," said Michael gravely, producing his card.

"That woman," said Pavone, "must have an enormous printing bill."

"Her father," said one of the correspondents, "is in beer. They have plenty of dough."

"I don't want to join the Air Force," sang the RAF in the back room, *"I don't want to go to war. I'd rather hang around the Piccadilly Underground, Living off the earnings of a high born—ladeeee . . ."*

The air-raid sirens blew outside.

"Jerry is getting very extravagant," said one of the correspondents. "Just yesterday I wrote an article proving conclusively that the Luftwaffe was through. I added up all the percentages of aircraft production reported destroyed by the Eighth Air Force, the Ninth Air Force, the RAF, and all the fighter planes knocked down in raids, and I found out that the Luftwaffe is operating on minus one hundred and sixty-eight percent of its strength. Three thousand words."

"Are you frightened by air raids?" a short, fat correspondent by the name of Ahearn asked Michael. He had a very serious round face, mottled heavily with much drinking. "This is not a random question," said Ahearn. "I am collecting data. I am going to write a long piece for *Collier's* on fear. Fear is the great common denominator of every man in this war, on all sides, and it should be interesting to examine it in its pure state."

"Well," Michael began, "let me see how I . . ."

"Myself," Ahearn leaned seriously toward Michael, his breath as solid as a brewery wall, "I find that I sweat and see everything much more clearly and in more detail than when I am not afraid. I was on board a naval vessel, even now I cannot reveal its name, off Guadalcanal, and a Japanese plane came in at ten feet off the water, right at the gun station where I was standing. I turned my head away, and I saw the right shoulder of the man next to me, whom I'd known for three weeks and seen before in all stages of undress. I noticed at that moment, something I had never noticed before. On his right shoulder he had a padlock tattooed in purple ink, with green vine leaves entwined in the bolt, and over that on a magenta scroll, Amor Omnia Vincit, in Roman script. I remember it with absolute clarity, and if anyone wished I could reproduce it line for line and color for color on this tablecloth. Now, about you, are things more clear or less clear when you are in danger of your life?"

"Well," said Michael, "the truth is I haven't . . ."

"I also find difficulty breathing," said Ahearn, staring sternly at Michael. "It is as though I am very high in an airplane, speeding through very thin air, without an oxygen mask." He turned suddenly away from Michael. "Pass the whiskey, please," he said.

"I am not very interested in the war," Pavone was saying. The guns in the distance coughed the overture to the raid. "I am a civilian, no matter what the uniform says. I am more interested in the peace later."

The planes were overhead by now, and the guns were loud outside the house. The planes seemed to be coming over in ones and twos, and diving low over the streets. Mrs. Kearney was handing a card to the MP Top Sergeant who was coming from the kitchen now with his fish.

"The war," said Colonel Pavone, "is a foregone conclusion. Therefore I am not interested in it. From the moment I heard the Japanese had hit us at Pearl Harbor, I knew we were going to win . . ."

"Oh, what a beautiful mornin'," sang an American voice near the piano, *"Oh, what a beautiful day. I got a beautiful feelin', Everything's goin' my way . . ."*

"America cannot lose a war," said Pavone. "You know it, I know it, by now even the Japs and the Germans know it. I repeat," he said, making his clown's grimace, pulling heavily on

345

his cigar, "I am not interested in the war. I am interested in the peace, because that issue is still in doubt."

Two Polish Captains came in, in their harsh, pointed caps, that always reminded Michael of barbed wire and spurs, and went, with set, disapproving faces, over to the bar.

"The world," said Pavone, "will swing to the left. The whole world, except America. The world will swing, not because people read Karl Marx, or because agitators will come out of Russia, but because, after the war is over, that will be the only way they can turn. Everything else will have been tried, everything else will have failed. And I am afraid that America will be isolated, hated, backward, we will all be living there like old maids in a lonely house in the woods, locking the doors, looking under the beds, with a fortune in the mattress, not being able to sleep, because every time the wind blows and a floor creaks, we will think the murderers are breaking in to kill us and take our treasure . . ."

The Hungarian correspondent came over to the table to fill his water tumbler with whiskey. "I have my own private theory," he said. "Later on, I am going to have it published in *Life* Magazine. How to Save the Capitalist System in America, by Laszlo Czigly." A battery in Green Park nearby made a great clatter for a moment and the Hungarian drank and looked reproachfully at the ceiling. "I call it The Guided Tour System of Democracy," he said, when the noise had died a little. "Look around us now . . ." He threw his arm wide in a spacious gesture. "What do we see? Unparalleled prosperity. Every man who wants to work, with a good job. Every woman, who in normal times could not be trusted to rinse rubber nipples, now doing precision tooling at eighty-seven dollars a week. Mississippi traffic policemen who in peacetime made eleven hundred dollars a year, now full Colonels, with pay starting at six hundred and twenty a month. College boys who were a drain on the family fortune, now Majors in the Air Forces, making five hundred and seventy dollars a month. Factories working night and day, no unemployment, everybody eating more meat, going to more movies, getting laid more often than ever before. Everybody alert, happy, in good physical condition. What is the source of all these benefits? The war. But, you say, the war cannot last forever. Alas, that is true. The Germans will finally betray us and collapse and we will go back to closed factories, unemployment, low pay, disaster. There are two ways of handling the situation. Either keep the Germans fighting forever, and you cannot trust them to do that . . . or . . ." And he took a long drink of his whiskey, and smiled widely. "Or, pretend the the war is always on. Keep the factories working. Keep producing fifty thousand airplanes a year, at two-fifty an hour for everyone who picks up a wrench, keep producing tanks at a hundred thousand dollars a tank, keep producing aircraft carriers at seven million dollars apiece. Ah, you say, then you have the problem of overproduction. The Czigly System takes care of everything. As of the moment, the Japanese and the Germans absorb our production, prevent us from glutting our markets. They shoot down our planes. They sink our aircraft carriers, they tear holes in our clothing. It is a simple problem. We must be our own Germans, our own Japs. Each month, we collect the necessary amount of B-17's, the allotted number of aircraft carriers, the specified number of tanks . . . and what do we do with them?" He looked proudly and drunkenly around his audience. "We sink them in the ocean, and we order new ones immediately. Now," he said, very seriously, "the most delicate problem—the human element. Overproduction of goods, you say, that is not an insoluble problem. But overproduction of human beings—there we tread on dangerous ground. One hundred thousand men a month, two hundred thousand men a month, I do not know how many, are now being disposed of. In peacetime, there will be a certain objection to killing them off, even if it keeps the economy in A Number One working order. Certain organizations would protest, the Church would take a stand, even I can comprehend the difficulties. No, I say, let us be humane, let us remember we are civilized human beings. Do not kill them. Merely keep them in the Army. Pay them their salaries, promote them, decorate the Generals, give allotments to their wives, and merely keep them out of America. Send them, under proper guidance, in large numbers to one country after another. They promote good will, they spread prosperity, they spend American money abroad in large sums, they make pregnant a great many lonely foreign women with good democratic New World seed, they set an example for the local manhood of vigor and directness that is most useful. Most of all, they do not compete with American labor on the home scene. From time to time, permit large groups of them to be demobilized and be sent home. There they will take up their old lives with their wives and mothers-in-law and their civilian employers. They will see quickly how foolish they were. They will clamor to be taken back into the Army. But we take back only the best; we have finally only ten or twelve million of our finest examples, touring the world; we have left in America only the slightly slow, the slightly stupid, who do not compete too fiercely with each other, and so that nervous tension which has been complained about so often in American life, slowly relaxes, slowly disappears . . ."

There was a high whistle outside and above, a roaring, crowding, thundering, clattering scream, that grew out of the blackness like a train wreck in a storm, and hurtled toward them. Everyone hit the floor.

The explosion crashed through every eardrum. The floor heaved. There was the sound of a thousand windowpanes blowing out. The lights flickered, and in the crazy moment before they went out, Michael saw the sleeping proprietress slide sideways out of her chair, her glasses still hanging from one ear. The explosion rumbled on in waves, each one less strong, as buildings collapsed, walls broke, brick tumbled into living rooms and areaways. The piano in the back room hummed as though ten men had struck chords on it all at once.

"I raise you five hundred," the Hungarian's voice came from the floor, and Michael laughed, because he realized that he was alive, and that they had not been hit.

The lights flickered on. Everyone got to his feet. Somebody lifted the proprietress from the floor and put her back on the chair, still sleeping. She opened her eyes and stared coldly out in front of her. "I think it's despicable," she said, "stealing an old woman's scarf while she sleeps." She closed her eyes again.

"Pest," said the Hungarian, "I have lost my drink." He poured himself another tumblerful of whiskey.

"You see," said Ahearn, standing up next to Michael, "I am sweating profusely."

The two Polish Captains put on their pointed caps. They looked around them disdainfully, then started out. At the door they stopped. On the wall was a poster of Roosevelt, Churchill, Chiang Kai-shek, and Stalin. One of the Poles reached up and tore off the picture of Stalin. Then he ripped the picture in quarters, swiftly, and threw it back into the room, in angular confetti. "Bolshevik pigs!" he shouted.

The Frenchman who ate martini glasses got up from the floor and threw a chair at the Poles. It clattered on the wall next to the pointed caps. The Poles turned and fled.

"Salauds!" shouted the Frenchman, wavering at his table. "Come back here and I will cut your testicles off!"

"Those gentlemen," said the proprietress, keeping her eyes closed, "are to be denied admission to these premises from now on."

Michael looked over to the end of the bar. The Major General had his arms comfortingly around Louise and was tenderly patting her buttocks. "There, there, little woman," he was saying.

"All right, General." Louise was smiling icily. "The battle is over. Disengage."

"The Poles," said the Hungarian. "Children of nature. However, there is no denying it, they are as brave as lions." The Hungarian bowed and returned, quite steady, to the table where the Air Forces Major was sitting. The Hungarian sat down and wrote out an IOU for a thousand pounds and shuffled the cards three times.

The siren went off, indicating, in its long, pulsating wailing, that the raid was over.

Then Michael began to shake. He gripped the bottom of his chair with his hands and he set his teeth, but they clattered in his jaws. He smiled woodenly at Pavone, who was relighting his cigar.

"Whitacre," said Pavone, "what the hell do you do in the Army? Whenever I see you, you're holding up a bar some place."

"I don't do anything much, Colonel," Michael said, then kept quiet, because one more word would have been too much, and his jaw would have worked loose.

"Can you speak French?"

"A little.".

"Can you drive a car?"

"Yes, Sir."

"Would you like to work for me?" Pavone asked.

"Yes, Sir," said Michael, because Pavone outranked him.

"We'll see, we'll see," said Pavone. "The man I had working for me is up for court-martial on charges of perversion, and I think he's going to be found guilty."

"Yes, Sir."

"Call me up in a couple of weeks," said Pavone. "It may turn out to be interesting."

"Thank you, Sir," said Michael.

"Do you smoke cigars?"

"Yes, Sir."

"Here." Pavone held out three cigars and Michael took them. "I don't know why I think so, but I think you have an intelligent look in your eye."

"Thanks."

Pavone looked over at General Rockland. "You'd better get back there," Pavone said, "before the General rapes your girl."

Michael stuffed the cigars into his pocket. He had considerable trouble with the pocket button because his fingers were shaking as though he were plugged into an electric circuit.

"I am still sweating," Ahearn was saying as Michael left the table, "but everything is extraordinarily clear."

Michael stood respectfully but firmly next to General Rockland. He coughed discreetly. "I'm afraid, Sir," he said, "I have to take the lady home. I promised her mother I'd bring her back by midnight."

"Your mother in London?" The General demanded of Louise.

"No," said Louise. "But PFC Whitacre knew her back in St. Louis."

The General laughed hoarsely and good-naturedly. "I know when I'm being given the business," he said. "Her mother.

That's a new one." He clapped Michael heavily on the back. "Good luck, Son," he said, "glad to have met you." He peered around the room. "Where's Ottilie?" he demanded. "Is she giving out those damned cards here, too?" He strode off, the Captain with the moustache in his wake, looking for Mrs. Kearney, who was locked by now in the bathroom, with one of the Sergeant pilots.

Louise smiled at Michael.

"Having a good time?" Michael asked.

"Charming," Louise said. "The General fell right on top of me when the bomb hit. I thought he was going to spend the summer there. Ready to go?"

"Ready," said Michael.

He took her hand and they went out.

"I raise you five hundred," the Hungarian was saying as the door closed behind them.

Outside there was a sullen smell of smoke in the air, foul and threatening. For a moment, Michael stopped, feeling his jaws and his nerves panicking again, and he nearly turned around and ran back inside. Then he controlled himself, and started down the dark, smoky street with Louise.

From St. James's Street came the thin tinkle of glass, and the heavy orange flicker of fire, spitting up through the smoke, and a new sound, thick and gurgling, that he had not heard before. They turned the corner and looked down toward the Palace. The street reflected the quivering orange fire in a million angles of broken glass. Down in front of the Palace, the fire shone back off a small lake of water. The gurgling was being made by ambulances and fire trucks pushing through the water in second gear. Without saying anything to each other, Michael and Louise walked swiftly, their shoes crackling on the glass, making a sound like people walking through a frozen meadow, toward the spot where the bomb had fallen.

A small car had been hit right in front of the Palace. It was lying against a wall, crushed and compressed, as though it had been put through a giant baling machine. There was no sign of the driver or any of the passengers, unless what an old man on the right-hand side of the street was carefully sweeping into a small pile, might be they. A woman's beret, dark blue and gay, rested, almost untouched by the catastrophe, a little to one side of the car.

The houses facing the Palace still stood, although their fronts had slipped down into the rubble. There was the familiar and sorrowful picture of rooms, ready for living, with tablecloths laid, and counterpanes turned back, and clocks still ticking the time, laid open to the eye of the night by the knife-like effect of the blast. It is what they are always striving to achieve

350

in the theatre, Michael thought, the removal of the fourth wall and a peep at the life inside.

No sounds came from the broken houses, and somehow Michael felt that very few people had been caught by the bomb. There were many deep air-raid shelters in the neighborhood, he comforted himself, and probably the inhabitants of the houses had been cautious.

Nobody seemed to be making any effort to rescue anybody who might still be in the blasted buildings. Firemen sloshed methodically through the pond of water, from the gushing, ruptured main. Air Raid Rescue people pushed desultorily and quietly at the more obvious bits of wreckage. That was all.

Against the wall of the Palace, where the sentry boxes had stood, and the sentries had marched and saluted in their absurd wooden-toy manner whenever they saw an officer half a block away, there was nothing now. The sentries, Michael knew, had not been permitted to leave their posts, and they had merely stood there, in their stiff, pompous, old-fashioned version of soldiers, and had accepted the whistle of the bomb, accepted the explosion, stiffly died as the windows evaporated behind them, and the old clock in the tower above them tore loose from its hinges and hung grayly out from its springs. While he, Michael, a hundred yards away, had been sitting with the whiskey in his hand, smiling, listening to the Hungarian describe The Guided Tour System of Democracy. And overhead, the desperate boy had crouched in the bucking plane, blinded by the searchlights, with London spinning crazily below him in an erupting glitter of explosions, with the Thames and the Houses of Parliament and Hyde Park Corner and Marble Arch swinging murderously around his head, and the flak ticking at the wings. The boy had crouched in the plane, peering shakily down, and had pressed, finally, whatever button the German Air Force pressed to kill Englishmen, and the bomb had come down, on the automobile and the girl with the beret and the houses that had stood there for a hundred years and on the two sentries whose organizations had been relieved from other duty and honored with the job of guarding the Palace where the Prince of Wales used to live and have his quiet, notorious parties. And if the boy in the plane above had touched the button a half second sooner, or a half second later, if the plane had not at that moment bucked to port in a sudden blast, if the searchlights hadn't blinded the pilot for a second earlier in the evening, if, if, if . . . then he, Michael would be lying in his own blood now in the wreck of the Canteen of the Allies, and the sentries would be alive, the girl with the beret alive, the houses standing, the clock running . . .

It was the most banal idea about a war, Michael knew, that *if* of fatality, but it was impossible not to think of it, impossible

351

not to think of the casual threads of accident on which we survive to face the next *if* that comes tomorrow.

"Come on, darling," Louise said. He could feel that she was shivering, and he was surprised, because she had always been so cool, so contained. "We're not doing any good here. Let's go home."

Silently, they turned and walked away. Behind them, the firemen had managed to reach some valve and the gushing from the broken main diminished, then stopped completely. The water in front of the Palace was calm and black.

A great many other things happened that day in the City of London.

A Major General who had just received the plans for the invasion of France pleaded for another division of infantry to be put on the beach in the first two days.

A Spitfire pilot who had completed two tours of duty and who had shot down six planes was grounded for drunkenness and shot himself in his mother's bedroom.

A new ballet was put into rehearsal in which the leading male dancer had to crawl on his stomach completely across the stage, symbolizing subconscious lust.

A girl in a top hat and long black silk stockings sang, "I'm going to get lit up when the lights go up again" in a musical comedy and was joined in the chorus by the audience, three-quarters of whom were Americans.

An ulcer finally broke through the stomach wall of a Service of Supply Major in Grosvenor Square who had been working sixteen hours a day, seven days a week, for two years. He had just picked up a memorandum, marked SECRET, on his desk, which notified him that a hundred and twenty tons of 105 millimeter ammunition, which had been ticketed for Southampton, had been lost due to the breaking apart in mid-ocean, in a mild squall, of a Liberty ship.

A B-17 pilot from Utah who had been listed as missing over Lorient three months before, arrived at Claridge's, smiling widely, speaking forty words of French, and asked for the royal suite. He made sixteen calls, using a small address book he had never allowed to leave his person, in the next twenty minutes.

A twenty-year-old farmer from Kansas spent eight hours in a cold pool learning how to swim under water so that he could blow up submerged obstacles off the coast of Europe the day of the invasion.

In the House of Commons, a question was asked of the Home Secretary, demanding an explanation of the fact that American soldiers accused of rape were tried and convicted by American courts-martial, and hanged, although there was no capital punishment for rape in British law, and the offense, which must be considered a civil one, was committed on British civilians on territory under the sovereignty of the King.

A Doctor of Philosophy from the University of Heidelberg, now a Private in His Majesty's Army, Corps of Pioneers, spent the day painting tarpaulins with a water-resistant shellac. At lunch time, speaking German, he quoted Kant and Spengler to a fellow-soldier and compared notes with a new arrival about the barracks at Dachau.

At noon, a maid in a boarding house in Chelsea noticed the smell of gas coming from a room and unlocked the door to find the naked bodies of an American Sergeant and a British girl, locked on the bed. They were both dead. When they went to bed they had left the gas heater on. The girl's husband was in India and the Sergeant's wife was in Montana. The American Army finally told the wife that her husband had died of a heart attack. He was twenty-one years old.

A Lieutenant in the Coastal Command had lunch at his club and drove down to his station, where he boarded his Liberator on a routine submarine patrol. The plane rose into the air, wheeled south toward the Bay of Biscay, and was never heard of again.

An Air Raid Rescue Warden dug a seven-year-old girl with black hair out of a caved-in cellar, where she had been trapped in a raid eight days before.

A Corporal in the American Army, on his way to lunch, saluted a hundred and eleven times on his passage across Grosvenor Square.

A Scotchman in a bomb-disposal squad reached carefully in between two crossed girders and slowly withdrew the fuse of a two-thousand-pound bomb that had failed to explode the night before. The bomb had been making a curious ticking noise for forty-five minutes.

An American poet, aged twenty-five, now a Sergeant in the Engineers, in London on a three-day pass, walked slowly through Westminster Abbey, and noticed that there was more room devoted to the remains of obscure nobility than to all the company of Keats, Byron, Shelley, et al., and reflected that if there were a Westminster Abbey in Washington, there would be more Goulds there than Whitmans, more Harrimans than Thoreaus.

A joke about the Americans, which ran, "What's wrong with Americans?" "Nothing. It's just that they're overpaid, overfed, overdressed, oversexed, and over here," was repeated twelve hundred times during the day.

The mother of three small children, whose father was at the moment crouched in a hole south of Anzio, being shot at by a German mortar crew, stood in a queue for an hour and three-quarters and returned home with a pound of boned haddock.

She looked at her children and considered killing them, but thought better of it, and made a stew of the fish, with one potato, and some soybean flour.

A committee of high-ranking officers of both Armies met to discuss making a motion picture about the invasion of Europe, in which the teamwork of all concerned was to be the main theme of the effort. The man representing the RAF quarreled with the man representing the British Ground Forces, the man representing the Eighth Air Force quarreled with the man representing the American Navy, the man representing the American Services of Supply grew furious with the British Captain who represented the Coastal Command, and it was resolved that the matter should be sent to a higher committee.

At noon, a squad of British enlisted men, clerks in the offices off Berkeley Square, could be seen practicing bayonet drill among the air-raid shelters and the wan trunks of dead trees, while other clerks sat on the cold benches and ate their lunch in the watery sunshine.

A British committee finished a carefully worded report to their Headquarters proving that American daylight bombing was wasteful and impractical.

The first jonquils appeared on barrows on street corners and shabby people in patched clothes stopped, with longing hearts, and bought the frail bunched blossoms and carried them self-consciously to their offices and their homes.

At the luncheon concert in the National Gallery, a trio played the works of Schubert, Walton and Bach.

Near Whitechapel a fence on which had been printed in large white letters, in 1942, Open the Second Front Now, was torn down for firewood.

In the Thames Estuary off the India docks, a Merchant Marine seaman from Seattle prayed for a raid that night, because his wife expected another child in two months, and he got a bonus for every raid on his ship while he was in port.

Also . . . four million souls went into offices and factories and warehouses and worked steadily and slowly and methodically, taking time out for tea at ten and four, at adding and subtracting, and mending and polishing, at assembling and stitching, carrying and sorting, typing and filing, making and losing. They did it all in a slow, sensible competent manner that irritated all the Americans who came into contact with them. Later they went home and some of them died in the night's raid, in exactly the same slow, dignified, sensible manner.

Four days after the opening of *Hamlet*, Michael was called into the orderly room of the Special Services Company to which he was attached for rations and quarters and told that he was ordered to report to the Infantry Replacement Depot at Litchfield. He was given two hours to pack his bags.

CHAPTER TWENTY-THREE

THE LANDING BARGE went around in a monotonous circle. The spray heaved in over the side, puddling on the slippery deck. The men crouched over their weapons, trying to keep them dry. The barges had been rolling a mile off the beach since three o'clock in the morning. It was seven-thirty now, and all conversation had long ago ceased. The preliminary barrage from the ships was almost over, and the simulated air attack. The smoke screen thrown across the cove by a low-flying Cub was even now settling on the water's edge. Everybody was wet, everybody was cold, everybody, except for the men who felt like throwing up, was hungry.

Noah was enjoying it.

Crouched in the bow of the barge, tenderly keeping dry the charges of TNT that were his especial care, feeling the salt spray of the North Sea batter against his helmet, breathing the sharp, wild, morning air, Noah was enjoying himself.

It was the final exercise for his regiment in their assault training. It was a full-dress rehearsal, complete with naval and air support and live ammunition, for the coast of Europe. For three weeks they had practiced in thirty-man teams, each team to a pillbox, riflemen, bazooka men, flame-throwers, detonation men. This was the last time before the real thing. And there was a three-day pass, waiting like a promise of Heaven, in the orderly room for Noah.

Burnecker was pale green from seasickness, his large farmer's hands gripping his rifle convulsively, as though there, at least, might be found something steady, something secure in a heaving world. He grinned weakly at Noah.

"Holy jumping mule," he said, "I am not a healthy man."

Noah smiled at him. He had grown to know Burnecker well in the last three weeks of working together. "It won't be long now," Noah said.

"How do you feel?" Burnecker asked.

"O.K.," said Noah.

"I'd trade you the mortgage on my father's eighty acres," Burnecker said, "for your stomach."

There was a confusion of amplified voices across the sliding water. The barge veered sharply and picked up speed as it headed for the beach. Noah crouched against the damp steel side, ready to jump when the ramp went down. Maybe, he thought, as the waves slapped with increasing force against the speeding hull, maybe there will be a cable from Hope when I get back to camp, saying it is all over. Then, later, he thought, I will sit back and tell my son, "The day you were born, I was landing on the coast of England with twenty pounds of dynamite." Noah grinned. It would have been better, of course, to have been with Hope while it was happening, but this really had its advantages. You were too occupied to worry very much. There was no anxious pacing of corridors, no smoking of too many cigarettes, no listening to the screams. It was selfish, of course, but it had its points.

The barge grated against the smooth beach and a second later the ramp went down. Noah leaped out, feeling his equipment banging heavily against his back and sides, feeling the cold water pouring in over his leggings. He raced for a small dune and flung himself down behind it. The other men lumbered out, spreading rapidly, ducking into holes and behind clumps of scrub grass. The riflemen opened up on the pillbox eighty yards away, on a small bluff overlooking the beach. The bangalore torpedo men crept carefully up to the barbed wire and set their fuses, then ran back. The bangalores exploded, adding the sharp smell of their explosion to the soft thick smell of the smoke that the plane had laid down.

Noah picked himself up, with Burnecker protecting him, and ran forward to a hole that lay near the wire. Burnecker fell in on top of him.

Burnecker was panting heavily. "Goodness," Burnecker said, "isn't dry land wonderful?"

They laughed at each other, then slowly poked their heads out of the hole. The men were working precisely, like a football team running through signals, advancing, as they had been taught, on the pale gray sides of the pillbox.

The bazooka went off again and again, in its rushing, noisy explosion, and large chunks of concrete flew up in the air from the pillbox.

"At times like this," Burnecker said, "I ask myself only one question. 'What are the Germans supposed to be doing while we go through all this?'"

Noah leaped out of the hole and dashed, crouching, holding his charges, through the opening in the wire. The bazooka spoke again and Noah threw himself to the sand, in case any of the concrete flew out toward him. Burnecker was lying beside him, panting heavily.

"And I used to think plowing was hard," Burnecker said.

"Come on, Farmboy," said Noah, "we're on our way." He stood up. Burnecker got off the ground, groaning.

They ran to the right and threw themselves behind a six-foot-high dune. The grass on top of the dune was snapping in the wet wind.

They watched the man with the flame-thrower carefully crawl towards the pillbox. The fire from the riflemen supporting them still whistled over their heads and ricocheted off the concrete.

If Hope could only see me now, thought Noah.

The man with the flame-thrower was in position now, and the other man with him turned the cock on the cylinders on his back. It was Donnelly who carried the enormous heavy cylinders. He had been picked because he was the strongest man in the platoon. Donnelly started the flame-thrower. The fire spurted out, whipping unevenly in the strong wind, smelling oily and heavy. Donnelly sprayed the slits of the pillbox in savage, arching bursts.

"All right, Noah," said Burnecker. "Do your act."

Noah leaped up and ran lightly and swiftly to windward of Donnelly, toward the pillbox. By now the men in the box were theoretically either dead, wounded, burned or stunned. Noah ran strongly, even in the deep sand. Everything seemed very clear to him, the chipped and blackened concrete, the dangerous narrow slits, the cliff rising dark green and steep behind the beach, against the streaked, gray sky. He felt strong, able to carry the heavy charges for miles. He breathed evenly and deeply as he ran, knowing exactly where to go, exactly what he was going to do. He was smiling as he reached the pillbox. Quickly and deftly he threw the satchel charge against the base of the wall. Then he poked the other charge on its long stick, into the ventilating hole. He was conscious as he worked that the eyes of all the men in the platoon were on him, performing expertly and well the final act in the ceremony. The fuses were spitting now, well-lit, and Noah turned and raced toward a foxhole thirty feet away. He threw himself in a long, bunched dive, into the hole, and ducked his head. For a moment there was silence on the beach, except for the hiss of the wind through the spikes of ocean grass. Then the explosions came, one on top of another. Chunks of concrete hurtled into the air and landed dully near him in the sand. He looked up. The pillbox was split open, smoking and black. Noah stood up. He smiled, rather proudly.

The Lieutenant who had been in charge of their training at the camp, and who had come along as an observer, was walking toward him.

"Roger," said the Lieutenant. "Good job."

Noah waved at Burnecker and Burnecker, standing now, leaning on his rifle, waved back.

There was a letter from Hope at Mail Call. Noah opened it solemnly, with slow hands.

"Darling," the letter read, "Nothing yet. I am ENORMOUS. There is a feeling here that the child will weigh a hundred and fifty pounds at birth. I eat all the time. I love you."

Noah read the letter three times, feeling adult and paternal. Then he folded it carefully and put it in his pocket, and went back to his tent to get ready for his three-day pass.

As he dug down in his barracks bag for a clean shirt, he felt secretly for the box he had hidden there. It was still there, wrapped in long johns. It was a box of twenty-five cigars. He had bought it in the United States and carried it across the ocean with him, for the day that was now almost upon him. He had lived so much of his life without ritual or ceremony, that the simple, rather foolish notion of signalizing the birth of an heir by handing out cigars had assumed solemn proportions in his mind. He had paid a great deal for the cigars in Newport News, Virginia, eight dollars and seventy-five cents, and the box had taken up precious room in his barracks bag, but he had never begrudged either the cost or the space. Somehow, more felt than thought, Noah dimly realized that the act of giving, the plain, clumsy symbol of celebration, would make him feel the real living presence of the child, three thousand miles away, would place the child and himself in his own mind and the minds of the men around him, in the proper normal relationship of father and son or father and daughter. Otherwise, in the ever-flowing stream of khaki, it would be so easy to make that day like every other day, that soldier like every other soldier . . . While the smoke still rose from the propitiatory offering, he would be more than a soldier, more than one of ten million, more than an exile, more than a rifle and a salute, more than a helmet and a dogtag . . . he would be a father, love's creative particularized link among the generations of men.

"Oh," said Burnecker, who was lying on his cot with his shoes off, but his overcoat still on, "look at that Ackerman! Sharp as Saturday night in a Mexican dance hall. Those girls in London will just fall over and lay down in the gutter when they see that haircomb."

Noah grinned, grateful to Burnecker for the familiar joke. How different this was from Florida. The closer they came to battle, the closer they got to the day when each man's life would depend upon every other man in the company, the more all differences fell away, the more connected and friendly they

358

all were. "I'm not going to London," he said, carefully knotting his tie.

"He has a duchess in Sussex," Burnecker said to Corporal Unger, who was cutting his toenails near the stove. "Very private."

"No duchess in Sussex, either," said Noah. He put on his blouse and buttoned it.

"Where you going then?"

"Dover," said Noah.

"Dover!" Burnecker sat up in surprise. "On a three-day pass?"

"Uhuh."

"The Germans keep lobbing shells into Dover," Burnecker said. "Are you sure you're going there?"

"Uhuh." Noah waved at them and went out of the tent. "See you Monday . . ."

Burnecker looked puzzledly after him. Then he shrugged. "That man's troubles," he said, "have unseated his reason." He lay down and in a minute and a half he was sleeping.

Noah slipped out of the clean, old, wood and brick hotel just as the sun was rising out of France.

He walked down the stone street toward the Channel. It had been a quiet night, with a thin fog. He had gone to the restaurant in the center of the town where a three-piece band had played and British soldiers and their girls had danced on the large floor. Noah had not danced. He had sat by himself, sipping unsweetened tea, smiling shyly when he caught a girl looking at him invitingly, and ducking his head. He liked to dance, but he had decided sternly that it would have been unseemly to be whirling around a floor with a girl in his arms at the very moment, perhaps, that his wife was at her crisis of birth and agony, and the first cry of his child was heard in the world.

He had gone back to the hotel early, passing the sign on the bandstand that read, "All Dancing Will Cease During Shelling."

He had locked himself in his cold, bare room and got into bed with a feeling of great luxury, alone, at ease, with no one to order him to do anything until Monday night. He had sat up in bed, writing a letter to Hope, remembering the hundreds of letters he had written her when he had first met her. "I am sitting up in bed," he wrote, "in a real bed, in a real hotel, my own man for three days, writing this, thinking of you. I cannot tell you where I am, because the Censor wouldn't like it, but I think I can safely tell you that there is a fog over the land tonight, that I have just come from a restaurant where a band was playing Among My Souvenirs, and where there was a sign

359

that read All Dancing Will Cease During Shelling. I think I can also tell you that I love you.

"I am very well and although they have worked us very hard for the last three weeks, I actually have gained four pounds. I will probably be so fat when I get home, neither you nor the child will recognize me.

"Please do not worry about it's being a girl. I will be delighted with a girl. Honestly. I have been giving great thought to the child's education," he wrote earnestly, bent over the pad in the flickering dim light, "and this is what I have decided. I do not like the new-fangled ideas in education that are inflicted upon children today. I have seen examples of what they do to unformed minds, and I would want to save our child from them. The idea of allowing a child to do whatever comes into its head, in order to permit free expression, seems to me to be absolutely nonsensical. It makes for spoiled, whining and disrespectful children," Noah wrote out of the depths of his twenty-three-year-old wisdom, "and is based, anyway, on a false notion. The world, certainly, will not permit any child, even ours, to behave completely according to its own desires, and to lead a child to believe that is the case is only to practice a cruel deception upon it. I am against nursery schools, too, and kindergartens, and I think we can teach the child all it has to know for the first eight years better than anyone else. I am also against forcing a child to read too early in life. I hope I do not sound too dogmatic, but we have never had the time to discuss this with each other and argue out any of the points and compromise on them.

"Please, darling, do not laugh at me for writing so solemnly about a poor little life that may not, at the moment I wrote this, have even begun. But this may be my last pass in a long time, and the last time I will be able to have the peace and quiet to think sensibly about this subject.

"I am certain, dearest," Noah wrote slowly and carefully, "that it will be a fine child, straight of limb, quick of mind, and that we shall love it very much. I promise to return to him and to you with a whole body and a whole heart. I know I shall, no matter what happens. I shall return to help with the diapers, to tell him stories at bedtime, to feed him spinach and teach him how to drink milk out of a glass, to take him out in the Park on Sundays and tell him the names of the animals in the zoo, to explain to him why he must not hit little girls and why he must love his mother as much as his father does.

"In your last letter you wrote that you were thinking of calling the child after my father if he was a boy. Please do not do that. I was not very fond of my father, although he undoubtedly had his good points, and I have been trying to run away from him all my life. Call him Jonathan, after your father, if you wish. I am a little frightened of your father, but I have admired him warmly ever since that Christmas morning in Vermont.

"I am not worried for you. I know you will be wonderful. Do not worry about me. Nothing can happen to me now.

Love,
Noah."

"P.S. I wrote a poem this evening before dinner. My first poem. It is a delayed reaction to assaulting fortified positions. Here it is. Don't show it to anyone. I'm ashamed.

> Beware the heart's sedition,
> It is not made for war:
> Fear the fragile tapping
> At the brazen door.

That's the first stanza. I'll write two more stanzas today and send them to you. Write me, darling, write me, write me, write me . . ."

He had folded the letter neatly and got out of bed and put it in his blouse pocket. Then he had put out the light and hurried back between the warm sheets.

There had been no shelling during the night. Around one in the morning the sirens had gone off, but only for some planes that had raided London and were on their way home and had crossed the coast ten miles to the west. No guns had been fired.

Noah touched the bulge of the letter under his coat as he walked down the street. He wondered if there was an American Army unit in town where he could have it censored. He always felt a twinge of distaste when he thought of the officers of his own company, whom he did not like, reading his letters to Hope.

The sun was up by now, burning under the slight mist. The houses shone palely, swimming up into the morning. Noah passed the neatly cleaned-out foundations where four houses had been knocked down by shellfire. Now, finally, he thought, as he passed the ruins, I am in a town that is at war.

The Channel lay out beneath him, gray and cold. He could not see the coast of France, through the thinning haze over the water. Three British torpedo boats, small and swift, were slicing into their concrete berths in the harbor. They had been out the night before, ranging the enemy coast, in a pale, blazing wake of foam, in a swirling confusion of swinging searchlights, streams of tracer bullets, underwater torpedo explosions that had sent black fountains of water three hundred feet in the air. Now they were coming in mildly, in the Sunday morning sunlight, at quarter-speed, looking playful and holiday-like, like speedboats at a summer resort.

A town at war, Noah repeated silently.

At the end of the street there was a bronze monument, dark and worn by the Channel winds. Noah read the inscription, which solemnly celebrated the British soldiers who had passed this spot on their way to France in the years between 1914 and 1918.

And again, in 1939, Noah thought, and on the way back, in 1940, from Dunkerque. What monument would a soldier read in Dover twenty years from now, what battles would they bring to his mind?

Noah kept walking. He had the town to himself. The road climbed up the famous cliffs out across the windswept meadows that reminded Noah, as so much of England did, of a park kept in good repair by a careful, loving, and not very imaginative gardener.

He walked swiftly, swinging his arms. Now, without the rifle, without the pack, without the helmet and canteen and bayonet scabbard, walking seemed like a light and effortless movement, a joyous, spontaneous expression of the body's health on a winter morning.

When he reached the top of the cliff, the mist had disappeared and the Channel sparkled playfully, blue and glittering all the way to France. In the distance stood the cliff of Calais. Noah stopped and stared across the water. France was amazingly near-by. As he watched he could almost imagine that he saw a truck, moving slowly, along a climbing road, past a church whose steeple rose into the washed air. Probably it would be an Army truck, he thought, and in it German soldiers. Probably on their way to church. It was a queer sensation, to look at enemy ground, even at this distance, and know that, in their glasses, they could probably see you, and all in a kind of trance-like, distance-born truce. Somehow, you could not help but feel that in a war, so long as you could see the enemy, or he you, killing should follow immediately. There was something artificial, spuriously arranged, about this peaceful observation of each other; it was an aspect of war that left you uneasy and dissatisfied. In a curious way, Noah thought, it would make it harder to kill them later.

He stood on the top of the cliff, regarding the doubtful, clear coast of Europe. The town of Calais, with its docks and spires and rooftops and bare trees rising into the wartime sky, lay still in its Sunday-morning quietness, just like the town of Dover below him. He wished Roger were here with him today. Roger would have had something to say, some obscure, significant point of information about the two linked towns, twins through history, sending fishing smacks, tourists, ambassadors,

362

soldiers, pirates, high explosive, back and forth at each other across the years. How sad that Roger had been sent to die among the palm trees and jungle moss of the Philippines. How much more fitting, if he had to die, if the bullet had reached him as he stormed the beach of the France he had loved so well, or been struck down riding into a country village near Paris, smiling, looking for the proprietor of the café he had drunk with all one summer—or if he had been in Italy when his death had reached him, fighting perhaps in the very fishing village through which he had passed up to Rome on his way from Naples in the autumn of 1936, recognizing the church, the city hall, the face of a girl, as he fell . . . Death, Noah realized, had its peculiar degrees of justness, and Roger's death had been low on that particular scale. *"You make time and you make love dandy, You make swell molasses candy, But, honey, are you makin' any money, That's all I want to know . . ."*

Later, Noah decided, after the war, he would come back to this place with Hope. *I stood here, in this exact spot, and it was absolutely quiet, and there was France, looking just the way it looks now. I don't know to this day exactly why I picked Dover for what might have been my last pass. I don't know . . . curiosity, maybe, a desire to see what it was like. A town at war, really at war, a look at the place where the enemy was . . . I'd been told so much about them, how they fought, what weapons they used, what horrors they'd committed—I wanted at least to see the place where they were. And, then sometimes there was shelling, and I'd never heard a gun fired in anger, as they used to say in the Army . . .*

No, Noah decided, we won't talk about the war at all. We'll walk here hand in hand, on a summer's day, and sit down next to each other on the cropped grass, and look out across the Channel and say, "Look, you can almost see the church steeple in France. Isn't it a lovely afternoon . . ."

The sound of an explosion shivered the quiet. Noah looked down at the harbor. A slow, lazy puff of smoke, small and toylike in the distance, was rising from the spot where the shell had hit among some warehouses. Then there was another explosion and another. The puffs of smoke blossomed in a random pattern throughout the roofs of the town. A chimney slowly crumbled, too faraway to make a sound, collapsing softly like bricks made out of candy. Seven times the explosions sounded. Then there was silence again. The town seemed to go back without an effort into its Sabbath sleep.

The Germans on the other side of the water, their malice satisfied or their anger cooled by the martial display, cleaned their guns and waited.

No answer came from the British guns. The dust clouds sent

363

swirling up by the shells subsided, and in five minutes it was almost impossible to believe that anything had happened.

Slowly, trying to fix in his mind the exact impression of what the explosions had looked and sounded like, Noah began to descend the hill into the town. It had all seemed so remote, so childishly spiteful, without plan . . . Is that it? he couldn't help thinking, as he braced himself against the grade, striding downwards, Is that what a war is like?

The town was awake by now. Two old ladies in black feathered bonnets, carrying prayer books in net-gloved hands, swept sedately toward church. A tall Marine Commando Lieutenant, with his arm in a white sling, rolled swiftly and debonairly past, beautifully uniformed, on a bicycle. A very small girl, held in tow by a church-bound aunt, looked up at Noah and offered, gravely, British childhood's ritualistic greeting to the American Army, "Any gum, Chum?"

"Harriet!" said the aunt coldly.

Noah grinned and shook his head at the small blonde creature being dragged off to worship.

A family group poured through a tall black door into the street, father, mother and a staggered ladder of children from the age of four to ten. The father held the hand of the smallest child. He had a round belly under decent broadcloth, and his face was sleepy and complacent under an ancient, wonderfully brushed hat. The mother circled the flock of children, like a collie dog, herding them down the street toward their prayers.

A very pretty girl with bare legs and a loose coat passed absent-mindedly through the group reading the Sunday *Times* as she walked.

A British Sergeant, with the standard British Sergeant's face, cool, reserved, stiff with authority and competence, walked rigidly on the other side of the street, his wife on his arm. His wife was young, and Noah could tell she was trying to live up to the portentous Manual-Of-Arms bearing of her husband. But her face kept breaking into smiling life as she looked sidewise at her husband, and the effect was incongruous and appealing, like a child with colored ribbons in her braids, mounted on a spry and shaggy Shetland pony, who has by accident strayed into a parade of armored vehicles.

"Good morning, good morning," the citizens of the town said on their assaulted thoroughfares. "Isn't it a lovely day? I hear they hit poor Mrs. Finchley's fishmarket again. Well, now isn't it nice to have your Albert back with you for the weekend? Isn't it nice that the fog has gone? You can see France today. We are going to go up after dinner and look. Yes, I heard from Sidney. Quite well, thank you, quite well, they took the last stitches out of the wound three weeks ago, and they re sending him to Calcutta on his convalescent leave . . . My Roberta has her American Sergeant down with her again this week-end and he brought a large can of that delicious American fruit salad and a whole carton of Chesterfields. A lovely boy, a lovely, lovely boy, and he says the permission ought to come through in about a month, now, you know how slow armies are, and they're to be married here, if it's before the invasion, I've already asked Reverend Redwine. Good morning, good morning, good morning . . ."

Noah stopped in front of the church. It was a squat, stone building, with a heavy, square tower. It looked as though the God who was addressed within it was a forbidding Old Testament God, Who laid the Law down squarely and with no frills or subtleties to the long generations of Channel-side worshipers; a Coast and Cliff God, a coldwater and storm God, long on justice and rationed in mercy. There was an air-raid shelter on the lawn, and rolls of zig-zagging barbed-wire fences near the rectory at the back, and menacing-looking concrete pyramids of tank blocks at the corner of the lawn, to stop the Germans who had never climbed the cliff as they had promised to do in 1940.

The service was already on, and they were singing a hymn to the accompaniment of an organ within. The soprano of women's and children's voices over the deeper rumble of the organ and the men, seemed surprisingly delicate and frivolous, coming from the angular, gray stone. On an impulse that he did not examine, Noah went in.

The congregation was small, and Noah sat down on one of the empty oak benches in the rear of the church. Many of the windows were broken, some patched with cardboard, others merely glittering edges of glass in heavy lead frames. The wind off the Channel, freighted with salt, gusted in through the holes, ruffling veils and Bible pages, flicking at the long white hair of the minister, who stood rather dreamily in the pulpit, rocking softly on his heels with the hymn, looking, with his thin, parchment face, and his blowing white hair, like an ancient pianist or astronomer, too deep in fugues or stars to remember to go to the barber.

Noah had never gone to synagogue. His father's overblown, rhetorical intimacy with religious literature had clouded over the idea of God in Noah's mind early in life. And he had never even spoken to a Chaplain, Jewish or Christian, in the Army. They had always seemed too bluff, too hearty, too soldierly and mundane, too much like any other Captain or Troop Commander, to offer spiritual comfort of any kind to Noah. He always felt that if he went to any one of them and cried, "Father, I have sinned," or "Father, I am afraid of Hell," they would

have clapped him on the back, quoted an Army regulation, an
sent him out to clean his rifle.

Noah hardly listened to the service. He stood with th
others, sat down with the others, listened, without bothering t
follow the words, to the pulsating sweet minors of the hymn:
and kept his eyes on the weary, delicate face of the minister
lit palely by the winter sea sun that drifted down through th
gaping windows above his head.

There was a final rustling among the congregation, a shift
ing of prayer books, a scuffling of feet, a *hush-hush* amon
the children, and the minister leaned reflectively on the pul
pit, his large, bleached hands gripping the polished dark woo
and began his sermon.

At first Noah did not follow the words. His mind seeme
to be in the state in which he often listened to music, not fol
lowing the melody exactly, or the unfolding development o
the composer's statements, but stirred by the abstract soun
into a separate stream of images of the mind's own-making
The minister had a low, old man's voice, gentle and intimate
lost for moments on end in the rush of wind from the broke
windows. It was a voice without professional passion or ex
hortation, a voice that seemed to address God and his congre
gation out of a fresh reflection, with no echoes of past devo
tion in it, a voice free of the lumber of the old sermons an
ceremony, a truly religious and unchurchly voice.

". . . love," the old man was saying, "is the word of Chris
and it admits of no divisions, no slyness of calculation, n
diversity of interpretation. We are told to love our neighbo
as ourself and our enemy as our brother, and the words an
the meaning are as plain as an iron weight in the scale i
which our actions are balanced.

"We are Channel-dwellers, but we do not dwell on the bank
of the Channel, we live among the sea moss and polished wreck:
among the waving salt ferns and bitter bones of the drowne
at the dark bottom, and above us roll the deep torrents o
man's hatred of man and God. Our tide now comes all from th
north and nourishes us on the polar juice of despair. We liv
among the guns and the brass sound of their speaking drown
out the soft voice of God, and only the wild crying of venge
ance can be heard above their thunder. We see our citie
crumble under the enemy's bombs, and we mourn for our chi
dren struck at their early tasks by the enemy's bullets, and w
strike back, cruelly and wildly, from the seabed of our hatre
at his cities and his children. The enemy is more savage tha
the tiger, hungrier than the shark, crueler than the wolf; i
honor and in defense of our moderate way of life, we stan
up to him and combat him, but in doing so we out-tiger him
out-shark the shark, over-wolf the wolf. Will we at the end o

366

all this then pretend to ourselves that the victory is ours? The thing we defend perishes from our victory as it would never perish from our defeat. Can we sit here, deep in our underwater hardness of heart, and think that our Sunday words swim up to God, after we have spent the week killing the innocent, dropping the bombs on the churches and the museums, burning the libraries, burying the children and the mothers in the jagged steel and broken concrete which is the special filth of our century?

"Do not boast to me in your newspapers of the thousands of tons of bombs you have let loose at random on the unhappy land of Germany, because I will tell you that you have let loose those bombs on me, on your church, on yourselves and on your God. Tell me, rather, how you have wept for the single German soldier you have been forced to kill as he stood before you armed and dangerous, and I will say, you are my defender and the defender of my church and my England.

"I see several soldiers among the congregation and I know they have a right to ask, What is love for a soldier? How does a soldier obey the word of Christ? How does a soldier love his enemy? I say it is this way—to kill sparingly and with a sense of sin and tragedy, sin that is yours equally with the sin of the man who falls at your hand. For was it not your indifference, your weakness of spirit, your greed, your deafness earlier in the day which armed him and drove him into the field to slay you? He struggled, he wept, he cried out to you, and you said, 'I hear nothing. The voice does not carry across the water.' Then, in his despair, he picked up the rifle, and, then, finally, you said, 'His voice is clear. Now let us kill him.'

"Do not," the old man said, his voice mild and growing weaker, "do not feel righteous in your heart because of this late and bloody attention you pay him. Kill, if you must, because in our weakness and in our error, we have found no other road to peace, but kill remorsefully, kill with a sense of sorrow, kill with economy for the immortal souls who leave this life in battle, carry mercy in your cartridge cases, forgiveness in your knapsacks, kill without revenge, because vengeance is not yours but the Lord's, kill, knowing that each life you spend makes your life that much the poorer.

"Come up, children, up from the Channel-bed cast off from the wrecks below, struggle up from the sea-fern jungle, nourish yourselves on a warmer current. Though we strive against butchers, let us not wet our hands in butchery. Let us not make ghosts of our enemies, let us rather make of them our brothers. If we carry the sword of God in our hands, as we boast, let us remember that it is a noble steel, let us not have it turn in our English hands into the slaughterer's busy knife."

The old man sighed and shivered a little, his hair blowing in the wind from the windows. He gazed abstractedly over the heads of the congregation, as though he had forgotten, in his old man's cluttered, almost dreaming way, that they were there. Then he smiled gently down at the half-empty pews.

He led the congregation in a prayer and a closing hymn, but Noah hardly heard. The minister's words had set up in him an excitement, a trembling tenderness toward the old man, toward the people around him, toward the soldiers standing beside their guns here and across the Channel, toward everything living and about to die. It filled him with a mysterious sense of hope. Logically, he did not agree with what the old man had said. Committed to killing, a target himself, knowing the confusion in design of such a war as he was fighting, he felt that it was almost impossible to be as strict and rigorous in attack as the old man desired, felt, too, that to attempt it would put too much of a burden on his own Army's shoulders, give the enemy too easy an advantage at a time when such an advantage might one day cost him his own life. Still, the minister's sermon filled him with hope. If, at such a time, in such a place, where the smoke from the last seven malicious shells had barely cleared, in a church already chipped and broken by war, among soldiers already wounded and civilians already bereft, if, at such a time, in such a place, there lived a man who could speak so passionately for brotherhood and mercy, and who could speak without fear of retribution or restriction, then, indeed, the world was not lost. Across the Channel, Noah knew, no man could raise his voice thus, and across the Channel were the men who were finally going to go down in defeat. The world was not going to fall into their hands, but into the hands of the people who sat nodding, a little sleepily, perhaps, a little dully, before their ancient preacher. So long, Noah thought, as such voices could be raised in the world, stern, illogical and loving, so long might his own child live in confidence and hope...

"Amen," said the minister.

"Amen," chorused the congregation.

Noah stood up slowly and went out. He stopped at the door and waited. Outside, a child with a bow and arrow was aiming at one of the tank blocks. He fired and missed, retrieved the arrow and took careful aim again.

The minister came to the door and stood there, shaking hands gravely with his parishioners as they filed past him to their rationed Sunday roasts. His hair blew more wildly than ever in the strong wind, and Noah saw that his hands shook badly. He looked very old and very frail.

Noah waited until all the congregation had scattered. Then, just as the minister was turning to go in, Noah went up to him.

"Sir," he said softly, not knowing exactly what he wanted to say, not being able to put into words the shimmering confusion of gratitude and hope that was shaking him, "Sir, I . . . I wanted to wait and . . . I'm sorry I can't say it better . . . thank you . . ."

The old man looked soberly at him. His eyes were dark, pouched in waxen wrinkles, farsighted and tragic. He nodded his head slowly and shook Noah's hand. His hand was dry and transparently fragile and Noah shook it very carefully.

"Ah, good," said the minister. "Thank you. It is to you young men that I speak, because it is you who have to make the decisions . . . Thank you." He peered curiously at Noah's uniform. "Ah . . ." he said politely, "Canadian?"

Noah couldn't help smiling. "No, Sir," he said, "American."

"American. Ah," said the old man, a little puzzled. "Ah, yes." Noah had the feeling that the old man had not quite digested the fact that America was in the war, that he had been told and forgotten a dozen times, that all uniforms seemed like the same drab blur to him. "Ah, welcome, welcome," the old man said warmly and vaguely. "Welcome, indeed. Ah," he said, suddenly glancing up at the windows of the church behind him, "we must get some new windows, it must have been a terrible draught inside."

"No, Sir," said Noah, and again he could not help smiling. "I didn't notice it at all."

"Good of you," said the minister, "good of you to say so. America?" Again that slight, polite note of puzzlement. "God bless you, Son, and return you safe to your home and your loved ones after the terrible days that lie ahead." He started in. Then, suddenly, he turned and came back. He stared almost harshly at Noah. "Tell me truthfully, Son," he said, and he sounded crisply alert, like a young, energetic man, "tell me, do you think I am a babbling old fool?" He gripped Noah's arms with surprising steadiness and strength.

"No, Sir," said Noah softly. "I think you are a great man."

The old man stared piercingly at Noah, as though he was hunting down any trace of mockery or patronage for his age and his old-fashioned, outmoded opinions in Noah's face. Then he seemed to be satisfied with what he saw. He took his hands away from Noah's arms and tried to smile, but his face trembled, his eyes clouded over.

"Son, Son," he whispered . . . He shook his head. "An old man," he said, "sometimes an old man hardly knows what world he is living in, whether he is speaking for the grave or the cradle . . . I look down into my congregation and I see faces that have been dead fifty years and for awhile I speak to them, until I remember. How old are you, Son?"

"Twenty-three, Sir," said Noah.

"Twenty-three," said the minister, reflectively, "twenty-

369

three." He put out his hand slowly and touched Noah's cheek. "A living face. Living. I will pray for your safety."

"Thank you, Sir," said Noah.

"Sir," said the minister. "Sir. I suppose they teach you that in the Army."

"Yes, Sir," said Noah.

"How ugly," the minister said. "Ah, God, how I hate armies." He blinked, and seemed to forget for a moment whom he was talking to. He looked around vaguely. "Come again, some Sunday," he said, his voice very tired, "perhaps we will have the windows back." He turned abruptly and shuffled in through the dark hole of the doorway.

When he got back to camp, Noah found a cable waiting for him. It had taken seven days to reach him. He opened it clumsily, feeling the blood jumping in his wrists and fingertips. *A boy*, he read, *six and a half pounds, I feel magnificent, I love you, love you. Hope.*

He walked dazedly out of the orderly room.

After supper, he distributed the cigars. He made a careful point of giving cigars to all the men whom he had fought back in Florida. Brailsford wasn't there, because he had been transferred back in the States, but all the rest of the men took them with a surprised, uneasy shyness, and they shook his hand with dumb, warm congratulation, as though they, too, shared the wonder, so far away, in the fine English rain, among the assembled instruments of destruction, of the state of fatherhood.

"A boy," said Donnelly, the Golden-Gloves heavyweight, the flame-thrower, shaking Noah's hand numb in his terrible, friendly fist, "a boy. What do you know about that? A boy! I hope the poor little son of a bitch never has to wear a uniform like his old man. Thank you," soberly sniffing the gift, "thanks a lot. This is a great cigar."

But at the last moment Noah could not bring himself to offer cigars to Sergeant Rickett or Captain Colclough. He gave three to Burnecker, instead. He smoked one himself, the first of his life, and went to sleep slightly dizzy, his head wavering in smoky, thick visions.

CHAPTER TWENTY-FOUR

THE DOOR OPENED and Gretchen Hardenburg stood there in a gray wrap.

"Yes," she said, opening the door only part way and peering out. "What is it?"

"Hello," Christian said, smiling. "I just arrived in Berlin."

Gretchen opened the door a little more widely and looked closely at him. After a perceptible moment, during which she looked at his shoulder boards, a faint light of recognition crossed her face. "Ah," she said. "The Sergeant. Welcome." She opened the door, but before Christian could kiss her, she extended her hand. They shook hands. Her hand was bony and seemed to be shaken by some slight, interior ague.

"For a moment," she apologized, "the light in the hall . . . And, you've changed." She stepped back and looked at him critically. "You've lost so much weight. And your color . . ."

"I had jaundice," Christian said shortly. He hated his color himself, and didn't like people to remark about it. This was not how he had imagined the first minute with Gretchen, caught at the door this way, in a sharp discussion of his unpleasant complexion. "Malaria and jaundice. That's how I got to Berlin. Sick leave. I just got off the train. This is the first place I've been . . ."

"How flattering," Gretchen said automatically, pushing her hair, which was uncombed, back from her face. "Very nice of you to have come."

"Aren't you going to ask me in?" Christian said. Begging again, he thought bitterly, as soon as I lay eyes on her.

"Oh, I'm so sorry." Gretchen laughed shrilly. "I was napping, and I suppose I'm still dazed. Of course, of course, come in . . ."

She closed the door behind him and put her hand familiarly on his arm, pressing it firmly. It may still be all right, Christian thought, as he went into the well-remembered room, maybe she was surprised in the beginning and now she's getting over it.

Once in the living room he made a move toward her, but she dipped away and lit a cigarette and sat down.

"Sit down, sit down," she said. "My pretty Sergeant. I often wondered what had happened to you."

"I wrote," Christian said, seating himself stiffly. "I wrote again and again. You never answered."

"Letters . . ." Gretchen made a face and waved her cigarette. "One simply doesn't have the time. I always mean to . . . And then, finally, I burn them, it is just impossible. I loved your letters, though, I really did, it was awful what they did to you in the Ukraine, wasn't it?"

"I was not in the Ukraine," Christian said soberly. "I was in Africa and Italy."

"Of course, of course," Gretchen said without embarrassment. "We're doing very well in Italy, aren't we, very well indeed. It is the one really bright spot."

371

Christian wondered how Italy could seem bright from any vantage point at all, but he did not speak. He watched Gretchen narrowly as she talked. She looked much older, especially in the wrinkled gray dressing gown, and her eyes were yellowed and pouchy, her hair dead, her movements, which before had been youthfully energetic, now neurotic, overcharged, quivering.

"I envy you being in Italy," she was saying. "Berlin is getting impossible. Impossible to keep warm, impossible to sleep at night, raids almost every night, impossible to get from place to place. I tried to get sent to Italy, merely to keep warm . . ." She laughed, and there was something whining in her laugh. "I really need a vacation," she rushed on. "You have no idea how hard we work back home, under what conditions. Often I tell the man who is the head of my bureau, if the soldiers had to fight under conditions like this, they would go on strike, I tell him to his face . . ."

Marvelous, thought Christian, she is boring me.

"Oh," said Gretchen, "I honestly do remember. My husband's company. That's it. The black lace. It was stolen last summer. You have no idea how dishonest people have become in Berlin, you have to watch every cleaning woman like a hawk . . ."

Garrulous, too, Christian thought, coldly making the additions to the damning account.

"I shouldn't talk like this to a soldier home from the front," Gretchen said. "All the newspapers keep saying how brave everyone is in Berlin, how they suffer without a word, but there'd be no use hiding anything from you, the minute you went out in the street you'd hear everyone complaining. Did you bring anything with you from Italy?"

"What?" Christian asked, puzzled.

"Something to eat," Gretchen said. "So many of the men come back with cheese or that wonderful Italian ham, and I thought perhaps you . . ." She smiled coquettishly at him and leaned forward, very intimately, her dressing gown falling open a little, revealing the sharp line of her breasts.

"No," said Christian shortly. "I didn't bring back anything except my jaundice."

He felt tired and a little lost. All his plans for the week in Berlin had been centered upon Gretchen, and now . . .

"It's not that we don't get enough to eat," Gretchen said officially, "but it's just that the variety . . ."

Oh, God, Christian mourned within him, here two minutes and we are discussing diet!

"Tell me," he said abruptly, "have you heard from your husband?"

"My husband," Gretchen said, checking herself, as though

she regretted giving up the subject of food. "Oh. He killed himself."

"What?"

"He killed himself," Gretchen said brightly. "With a pocket knife."

"It's not possible," Christian said, because it did not seem real that all that fierce, ordered energy, that intricate, cold, reasonable strength could have been self-destroyed. "He had so many plans . . ."

"I know about his plans," Gretchen said aggrievedly. "He wanted to come back here. He sent me his picture. How he ever got anyone to take a picture of that face I honestly don't know. He regained the sight of one eye and suddenly decided he wanted to come back and live with me. You have no idea of what he looked like." She shuddered visibly. "A man must be crazy to send his wife a picture like that. I would understand, he wrote, I would be strong enough. He was queer enough to begin with, but without a face . . . There are some limits, after all, even in a war. Horror has a proper place in life, he wrote, and we must all be able to bear it . . ."

"Yes," said Christian. "I remember."

"Oh," said Gretchen, "I suppose he told you honestly some of it, too."

"Yes," said Christian.

"Well," Gretchen said, petulantly, "I wrote him a most tactful letter. I worked on it for a whole evening. I suggested he would find it uncomfortable here, he would be better taken care of in an Army hospital, at least until they did something more with his face . . . although, to tell you the truth, there was nothing to be done, it was no face at all, things like that really shouldn't be permitted, but the letter was extremely tactful . . ."

"Have you the picture?" Christian asked suddenly.

Gretchen looked at him strangely. She pulled the wrap closer around her. "Yes," she said, "I have it."

"I can't understand," Gretchen said, standing up and going over to the desk against the far wall, "why anyone would want to look at it." She rummaged nervously through two of the desk drawers, then brought out a small photograph. She glanced at it briefly, then handed it to Christian. "There it is," she said. "As though there aren't enough things to frighten a person these days . . ."

Christian looked at the photograph. One bright, crooked eye stared coldly and imperiously out of the nameless wounded flesh, over the tight collar of the uniform.

"May I have this?" Christian asked.

"You people are getting queerer and queerer these days," Gretchen said shrilly. "Sometimes I have the feeling you all ought to be locked up, really I do."

"May I have it?" Christian repeated, staring down at it.

"I suppose so." Gretchen shrugged. "It doesn't do me any good."

"I was very attached to him," Christian said. "I owe a great deal to him. He taught me more than anyone else I ever knew. He was a giant, a true giant."

"Don't think, Sergeant," Gretchen said quickly, "that I wasn't fond of him. Because I was. Deeply fond of him. But I prefer remembering him like this . . ." She picked the silver-framed photograph of Hardenburg, handsome and stern in his cap, off the table and touched it sentimentally. "This was taken the first month we were married and I think he'd want me to remember him this way."

There was the turning of a key in the door, and Gretchen twitched nervously and tied the cord around her robe more tightly. "I'm afraid, Sergeant," she said hurriedly, "that you'll have to go now. I'm busy at the moment and . . ."

A large, heavy-framed woman in a black coat came into the room. She had iron-gray hair, brushed severely back from her forehead, and small, cold eyes behind steel glasses. She glanced once at Christian.

"Good evening, Gretchen," she said. "Aren't you dressed yet? You know, we're going out for dinner."

"I've had company," Gretchen said. "A Sergeant from my husband's old Company."

"Yes?" The woman's voice had a rising note of cold inquiry. She faced Christian heavily.

"Sergeant . . . Sergeant . . ." Gretchen's voice hesitated. "I'm terribly sorry, but I don't remember your name."

I would like to kill her, thought Christian, standing facing the middle-aged woman, the photograph of Hardenburg still in his hand. "Diestl," he said flatly. "Christian Diestl."

"Sergeant Diestl, Mademoiselle Giguet."

Christian nodded at the woman. She acknowledged the greeting with a brief downward flicker of her eyes.

"Mademoiselle Giguet is from Paris," Gretchen said nervously. "She is working for us in the Ministry. She is living with me until she can find an apartment. She's very important, aren't you, darling?" Gretchen giggled at the end of her sentence.

The woman ignored her. She began stripping her gloves off her square, powerful hands. "Forgive me," she said. "I must take a bath. Is there hot water?"

"Lukewarm," said Gretchen.

"Good enough." The square, heavy figure disappeared into the bedroom.

"She's very intellectual." Gretchen did not look at Christian. "You'd be amazed how they come to her for advice at the Ministry."

374

Christian picked up his cap. "I must go now," he said. "Thank you for the photograph. Good-bye."

"Good-bye," Gretchen said, pulling nervously at the collar of her wrap. "Just slam the door. The lock is automatic."

CHAPTER TWENTY-FIVE

"I SEE VISIONS," Behr was saying, as they walked slowly along the beach, toward their boots, their bare feet sinking into the cool sand. The sound of the waves, rolling mildly in from America three thousand miles away, made a springtime murmur in the still air. "I see visions of Germany one year from now." Behr stopped and lit a cigarette, his steady, workman's hands looking enormous around the frail tube of tobacco. "Ruins. Ruins everywhere. Twelve-year-old children using hand grenades to steal a kilo of flour. No young men on the streets, except the ones on crutches, because all the rest are in prison camps in Russia and France and England. Old women walking down the streets in potato sacking and suddenly dropping dead of hunger. No factories working, because they have all been bombed into the ground. No government, just military law, laid down by the Russians and the Americans. No schools, no homes, no future . . ."

Behr paused and stared out to sea. It was late afternoon, amazingly warm and tender for so early in the season on the Normandy coast. The sun was a pretty orange ball sinking peacefully into the water. The spike grass on the dunes barely moved in the quiet; the road, running in a black winding streamer along the beach, was empty and the pale stone farmhouses in the distance seemed to have been deserted a long time ago.

"No future," Behr repeated reflectively, staring out across the stretched barbed wire to the sea. "No future."

Behr was a Sergeant in Christian's new Company. He was a quiet, powerfully built man of about thirty, whose wife and two children had been killed in Berlin in January by the RAF. He had been wounded on the Russian Front in the autumn, although he refused to talk about it, and had only come to France a few weeks before Christian had arrived there after his leave in Berlin.

In the month that Christian had known him he had grown very fond of Behr. He had seemed to like Christian, too, and

375

they had begun to spend all their spare time together, on long walks through the budding countryside, and drinking the local Calvados and hard cider in the cafés of the village in which their battalion was based. They carried pistols in holsters at their belts when they went out because they were constantly being warned by superior officers about the activities of Maquis bands of Frenchmen. But there had been no incidents at all in that neighborhood, and Christian and Behr had agreed that the repeated warnings were merely symptoms of the growing nervousness and insecurity of the men higher up. So they wandered carelessly through the farmland and along the beaches, being polite to the French people they met, who seemed quite friendly, in their grave, reserved, country way.

What Christian liked best of all about Behr was his normality. Everyone else Christian had had anything to do with, ever since the bad night outside Alexandria, had seemed to be overwound, jumpy, bitter, hysterical, overtired . . . Behr was like the countryside, cool, self-contained, orderly, healthy, and Christian had felt himself relaxing, the snapping, malarial, artillery-worn nerves being soothed into a salutary calm.

When he had first been sent to the battalion in Normandy, Christian had been bitter. Enough, he'd thought, I've had enough. I can't do it any more. In Berlin he'd felt sick and old. He had spent his leave dozing sixteen, eighteen hours a day, in bed, not even getting up when the planes came over at night. Africa, he'd thought, Italy, the torn and never-quite-mended leg, the recurrent malaria, enough. What more do they want from me? And now, obviously, they wanted him to meet the Americans when they came onto the beaches. Too much, he thought, brimming with sick self-pity, they have no right to demand it of me. There must be millions of others who have barely been touched. Why not use them?

But then he'd got to know Behr, and the man's quiet unapprehensive strength had slowly cured him. In the peaceful, healthy month he had put on weight and regained his color. He hadn't had a single headache, and even his bad leg seemed to have made its final adjustment to its crooked tendons.

And now Behr was walking beside him on the cool sand of the beach, and was saying, disturbingly, "No future, no future. They keep telling us the Americans will never land in Europe. Nonsense. They are whistling to keep up their spirits among the tombstones. Only it will not be their tombstones, but ours. The Americans will land because they have made up their minds to land. I do not object to dying," Behr said, "but I object to dying uselessly. They will land, regardless of what you and I do, and they will go on into Germany, and they will meet the Russians there and when that happens Germany is finished, once and for all."

They walked in silence for awhile. Christian felt the sand come up between his bare toes and it reminded him of the time when he was a small boy and had run barefoot in the summer, and what with the memory and the pretty beach and the slow, majestic, happy afternoon, it was hard to be as sober and as thoughtful as Behr was asking him to be.

"I listen to them over the radio, from Berlin," Behr said, "boasting, inviting the Americans to try to come, hinting about secret weapons, predicting that any day now the Russians will be fighting the British and the Americans, and I could beat my head against the wall and weep. You know why I could weep? Not because they are lying, but because the lies are so weak, so barefaced, so contemptuous. That is the word—contemptuous. They sit back there and they say anything that comes into their heads because they despise us, they despise all Germans, the people in Berlin, they know we are fools and believe anything anybody chooses to tell us, because they know we are always ready to die for any nonsense they cook up in an odd fifteen minutes between lunch and the first drink in the afternoon.

"Listen," Behr said, "my father fought for four years in the last war. Poland, Russia, Italy, France. He was wounded three times and he died in 1926 from the effects of the gas he took into his lungs in 1918 in the Argonne Forest. Good God, we are so stupid they even get us to fight the same battles all over again, like a continuous showing in the movies! Same songs, same uniforms, same enemies, same defeats. Only new graves. And this time, too, the end will be different. Germans may never learn anything, but the others will learn this time. And it is different this time, and it is going to be much worse to lose. Last time it was a nice, simple, European-style war. Anyone could understand it, anyone could forgive it, because they'd all been fighting the same kind of war for a thousand years. It was a war within the same culture, one body of civilized Christian gentlemen fighting another body of civilized Christian gentlemen under the same general, predictable set of rules. When the war was over last time, my father marched back to Berlin with his regiment and the girls threw flowers at them along the roads. He took off his uniform and went back to his law office and started trying cases in the civil courts as though nothing had happened. Nobody is going to throw flowers at us this time." Behr said, "not even if there are any of us left to march back to Berlin.

"This time," he said, "this time it is not a simple, understandable war, within the same culture. This time it is an assault of the animal world upon the house of the human being. I don't know what you saw in Africa and Italy, but I know what I saw in Russia and Poland. We made a cemetery a thou-

377

sand miles long and a thousand miles wide. Men, women, children, Poles, Russians, Jews, it made no difference. It could not be compared to any human action. It could only be compared to a weasel in a henhouse. It was as though we felt that if we left anything alive in the East, it would one day bear witness against us and condemn us. And now," Behr said in his low, even voice, "and, now, after that, we have made the final mistake. We are losing the war. The animal is slowly being driven into his last corner, the human being is preparing his final punishment. And, now, what do you think will happen to us? I tell you, some nights I thank God my wife and my two children were killed, so that they will not have to live in Germany when this war is over. Sometimes," Behr said, staring out over the water, "I look out there and tell myself, 'Jump in! Try to swim! Swim to England, swim to America, swim five thousand miles, to get away from it.'"

They had reached their boots by now, and they stood over the heavy footgear, staring reflectively down at the dull black leather, as though the boots, hobnailed and blunt, were a symbol of their agony.

"But I cannot swim to America," Behr said. "I cannot swim to England. I must stay here. I am a German and what happens to Germany will happen to me, and that is why I am talking to you like this. You know," he said, "if you mention this to anyone, they will take me out the same night and shoot me . . ."

"I will not say a word," Christian said.

"I have been watching you for a month," said Behr, "watching and measuring. If I've made a mistake about you, if you're not the sort of man I think you are, it will mean my life. I would like to have taken more time, watching you, but we do not have so much more time . . ."

"Don't worry about me," Christian said.

"There is only one hope for us," Behr said, staring down at the boots in the sand. "One hope for Germany. We have to show the world that there are still human beings in Germany, not only animals. We have to show that it is possible for the human beings to act for themselves." Behr looked up from the boots and stared in his steady, healthy way at Christian and Christian knew the measuring process was still going on. He did not say anything. He was confused and he resented the necessity of listening to Behr, yet he was fascinated and knew that he had to listen.

"Nobody," said Behr, "not the English, not the Russians, not the Americans, will sign a peace with Germany while Hitler and his people are still in power, because human beings do not sign armistices with tigers. And if anything is to be saved in Germany, we must sign an armistice now, immediately. What

378

does that mean?" Behr asked like a lecturer. "That means that the Germans themselves must get the tigers out. Germans themselves must take the risk, must shed their blood to do it. We cannot wait for our enemies to defeat us and then give us a government as a gift, because then there will be nothing left to govern, and nobody who has the strength or the will to do it. It means that you and I must be ready to kill Germans to prove to the rest of the world that there is some hope for Germany." Again he stared at Christian. He is spiking me down, Christian thought resentfully, with one nail of confidence after another. Still, he could not stop Behr.

"Do not think," Behr continued, "that I am making this up myself, that I am alone. All through the Army, all through Germany, the plan is slowly being formed, people are slowly being recruited. I do not say we will succeed. I merely say that on one side there is certain death, certain ruin. On the other side . . ." He shrugged. "A little hope. Also," he went on, "there is only one kind of government that can save us, and if we do it ourselves, we can set up that government. If we wait for the enemy to do it for us, we'll have a half dozen little governments, all of them meaningless, all of them useless, all of them finally, no governments at all. 1920 will seem, then, like Utopia compared to 1950. If we do it ourselves, we can set up a Communist government, and overnight we will be the center of a Communist Europe, with every other nation on the Continent committed to feeding us, keeping us strong. There is no other form of government for us, no matter what the British and the Americans say, because keeping Germans from killing each other under what the Americans call democracy, for example, would be like trying to keep wolves from the sheepfold by the honor system. You don't keep a crumbling building standing by putting a new coat of bright paint on the outside; you have to go into its walls and foundations and put in iron girders to do it. The Americans are naïve and they have a lot of fat on their bones, and they can afford the luxury and the waste of democracy, and it has never occurred to an American that their system depends upon the warm layers of fat under their skin and not upon the pretty words they put in their books of law . . ."

What echo is this? thought Christian vaguely. When was this said before? Then he remembered the morning on the ski slope with Margaret Freemantle long ago, and his own voice saying the same words for another reason. How confusing and tiring it was, he thought, that we always reshuffle the same arguments so that we get the different answer we require from them.

". . . we can help right here," Behr was saying. "We have connections with many people in France. Frenchmen who are trying to kill us now. But, overnight, they would become our

379

most dependable allies. And the same thing in Poland, in Russia, in Norway, in Holland, everywhere. Overnight, we would present the Americans with a single, united Europe, with Germany at the center, and they would have to accept it, whether they liked it or not. Otherwise . . ." he shrugged. "Otherwise, merely pray that you get killed early in the game. Now," Behr said, "there are certain specific things that will have to be done right here. Can I tell my people that you will be willing to do them?"

Behr sat down suddenly in the sand and began putting on his socks. He moved with meticulous care, smoothing the wrinkles out of the socks and brushing the sand off them with detailed, unhurried movements of his hands.

Christian stared out to sea. He felt weary and baffled, weighed down by a thick, nagging anger at his friend. What choices you get to make these days! Christian thought resentfully. Between one death and another, between the rope and the rifle, the poison and the knife. If only I were fresh, he thought, if I had had a long, quiet, healthful vacation, if I had never been wounded, never been sick. Then it might be possible to look at this calmly and reasonably, say the correct word, put your hand out for the correct weapon . . .

"You'd better put your boots on," Behr said. "We have to get back. You don't have to give me an answer now. Think it over."

Think it over, Christian thought, grinning sourly, the patient thinking over the cancer in his belly, the condemned man thinking over his sentence, the target thinking over the bullet that is about to smash it.

"Listen," Behr looked up thoughtfully from the sand, a boot in his hand, "if you say anything about this to anyone, you will be found with a knife in your back one morning. No matter what happens to me. I like you very much, I honestly do, but I had to protect myself, and I told my people I was going to talk to you . . ."

Christian stared down at the calm, healthy, guileless face, like the face of the man who would have come to fix your radio before the war or the face of a traffic policeman helping two small children across a road on their way to school.

"I told you you don't have to worry," Christian said thickly. "I don't have to think anything over. I can tell you right now, I'll . . ."

Then there was the sound, and Christian automatically hurled himself to the sand. The bullets went in with short, whacking thuds, into the sand around his head, and he felt the strange, painless shock of the iron tearing his arm. He looked up. Fifty feet above him, with the engine suddenly roaring again after the long glide down out of the sky, the Spitfire was shivering through the air, the colors of the roundel gleaming on the wings and the tail assembly bright silver in the long rays of the sun. The plane climbed loudly out over the sea, and in a moment was a small, graceful shape, no larger than a gull, climbing over the sun, climbing into the green and purple of the clear, surprising spring afternoon, climbing to join another plane that was making a wide, sparkling arc over the ocean.

Then Christian looked at Behr. He was sitting erect, looking down thoughtfully at his hands, which were crossed on his belly. There was blood oozing slowly out between the fingers. Behr took his fingers away for a second. The blood spurted in uneven, jagged streams. Behr put his hands back, as though he were satisfied with the experiment.

He looked at Christian, and later, remembering the moment, Christian believed that Behr had been smiling gently then.

"This is going to hurt a great deal," Behr said in his calm, healthy way. "Can you get me back to a doctor?"

"They glided down," Christian said stupidly, gazing at the two twinkling disappearing specks in the sky. "The bastards had a few rounds of ammunition left before going home, and they couldn't bear the thought of wasting them . . ."

Behr tried to stand up. He got onto one knee, then slipped back again, to sit there in the sand once more, with the same thoughtful, remote expression on his face. "I can't move," he said. "Can you carry me?"

Christian went over to him and tried to lift him. Then he discovered that his right arm did not work. He looked at it, surprised, remembering all over again that he, too, had been hit. His sleeve was sodden with blood, and the arm was still numb, but already the wound seemed to be clotting in the cloth web of the sleeve. But he could not lift Behr with his one good arm. He got the man halfway up, and then, stopped, gasping, holding Behr under the armpit. Behr was making a curious, mechanical noise by this time, clicking and bubbling at the same time.

"I can't do it," Christian said.

"Put me down," Behr said. "Oh, please, Christ, put me down."

As gently as possible, Christian slid the wounded man back to the sand. Behr sat there, his legs stretched out, his hands back at the red leak in his middle, making his curious, bubbling, piston-like sound.

"I'll go get help," Christian said. "Somebody to carry you."

Behr tried to say something, but no words came from his mouth. He nodded. He still looked calm, relaxed, healthy, with his sturdy blond hair in a clean mat over his sunburned face. Christian sat down carefully and tried to put his boots on, but he could not manage it with his left hand. Finally he gave up. After patting Behr's shoulder with a false reassuring gesture, he started, at a heavy, slow, barefooted trot, toward the road.

When he was still about fifty meters from the road, he saw the two Frenchmen on the bicycles. They were going at a good clip, in their regular, tireless pumping rhythm, casting long, fantastic shadows across the marshy fields.

Christian stopped and shouted at them, waving his good hand. *"Mes amis! Camarades! Arrêtez!"* The two bicycles slowed down and Christian could see the two men peer doubtfully at him from under their caps. *"Blessé! Blessé!"* Christian shouted, waving toward Behr, a small, collapsed package now, near the edge of the gleaming sea. *"Aidez-moi! Aidez-moi!"*

The bicycles nearly stopped and Christian could see the two men turning inquiringly toward each other. Then they hunched lower over their handlebars and quickly gained speed. They passed quite close to Christian, twenty-five or thirty meters away. He got a good look at them, worn, brown, cold faces, expressionless and stony under the dark-blue caps. Then they were gone. They made a turn behind a high dune, which obscured the road for almost two kilometers on the other side of it, and then the road and the countryside all around Christian was empty, falling swiftly into the rich blue of twilight, with only the rim of the ocean still violent clear red.

Christian raised his arm, as though to wave at the two men, as though he could not believe that they were not still there, as though it were only a trick of his wound that had made him think they had merely pedaled away. He shook his head. Then he started to trot toward the cluster of houses he could barely see in the distance.

He had to stop after a minute, because he was panting heavily, and his arm had begun to bleed again. Then he heard the scream. He wheeled around and stared through the gathering darkness at the place where he had left Behr. There was a man crouching over Behr, and Behr was trying to crawl away in the sand, with a slow, dying movement. Then Behr screamed again, and the man who had been crouched over him took one long step and grabbed Behr by the collar and turned him over. Christian saw the gleam of a knife in the man's hand, a bright, sharp slice of light against the dull shining silver of the sea. Behr started to scream again, but never finished it.

Christian tore at the holster on his belt with his left hand, but it was a long time before he could get the pistol out. He saw the man put his knife away, and fumble at Behr's belt for the pistol. He got the pistol and stuck it in a pocket, then picked up Christian's boots, which were lying nearby. Christian took his pistol out and laboriously and clumsily got the safety off with his left hand. Then he began firing. He had never fired a pistol with his left hand before and the shots were very wild. But the Frenchman started to run toward the high dune. Christian lumbered down the beach toward Behr's quiet form, stopping from time to time to fire at the swiftly running Frenchman.

By the time Christian reached the spot where Behr was lying, stretched out, face up, arms spread wide, the man Christian had been chasing was on his bicycle, and, with the other man, was spurting out from behind the protection of the dune, down the black, bumpy road. Christian fired a last shot at them. It must have been close, because he saw the pair of boots drop from the handlebars of the second bicycle, as though the man had been frightened by the whistle of the bullet. The Frenchmen did not stop. They bent low over the handlebars of their bicycles and swept away into the lavender haze that was beginning to obscure the road, the pale sand of the beach, the rows of barbed wire, the small yellow signs with the skulls that said: Attention, Mines.

Then Christian looked down at his friend.

Behr was lying on his back, staring up at the sky, with the last crooked expression of terror on his face, the blood a sticky marsh under his chin, where the Frenchman had made the long, unnecessary slash with his knife. Christian gazed down at Behr stupidly, thinking: No, it is impossible, just five minutes ago he was sitting there, putting on his shoes, discussing the future of Germany like a professor of political science . . . The Englishman gliding down spitefully in the fighter plane, and the French farmer on his bicycle, carrying the hidden knife, had had their own notions of political science.

Christian looked up. The beach was pale and empty, the sea murmured into the sand in a small froth of quiet waves; the footprints on the sand were clearly marked. For a moment, Christian had a wild idea that there was something to be done, that if he did the single correct thing, the five minutes would vanish, the plane would not have swooped down, the two men on bicycles would not have passed by, Behr would even now be rising from the sand, healthy, reflective, whole, asking Christian to make a decision . . .

Christian shook his head. Ridiculous, he thought, the five minutes had existed, had passed; the careless, meaningless accidents had happened; the bright-eyed boy, going home to his pint of beer in a Devon pub after an afternoon of cruising over France, had spotted the two tiny figures on the sand; the sun-wrinkled farmer had irrevocably used the knife; the future of Germany would be decided with no further comment by Anton Behr, widower, late of Germany, late of Rostov, late coast-walker and philosopher.

Christian bent down. Slowly, panting heavily, he pulled first one boot then another from the feet of his friend. The bastards, he thought as he worked, at least they're not going to get these boots.

Then, carrying the boots, he scuffed heavily through the sand toward the road. He picked up his own boots, which the Frenchman had dropped. Then, carrying all four boots against his chest in the crook of his wounded arm, he plodded, barefoot, the road feeling smooth and cool under his soles, toward Battalion Headquarters five kilometers away.

With his arm in a sling, not hurting too much, Christian watched them bury Behr the next day. The whole company was out in parade dress, very solemn, with their boots polished and their rifles oiled. The Captain took the occasion to make a speech.

"I promise you men," the Captain said, standing erect, holding his belly in, ignoring the thick North-coast rain that was falling around him, "that this soldier will be avenged." The Captain had a high, scratchy voice, and spent most of his time in the farmhouse where he was billeted with a thick-legged Frenchwoman whom he had brought to Normandy with him from Dijon, where he had been stationed before. The Frenchwoman was pregnant now and made that an excuse to eat enormously five times a day.

"Avenged," the Captain repeated. "Avenged." The rain dripped down his visor and onto his nose. "The people of this area will learn that we are strong friends and terrible enemies, that the lives of you men are precious to me and to our Fuehrer. We are at this moment at the point of apprehending the murderer ..."

Christian thought dully of the English pilot, probably sitting this moment, because it was a wet day, unapprehended, in a snug corner of a tavern, with a girl, warming his beer between his hands, laughing in that infuriating, superior English way, as he described the crafty, profitable slide down the Norman sky the day before, to catch two barefooted Huns, out for their constitutional at sunset.

"We shall teach these people," the Captain thundered, "that these wanton acts of barbarism do not pay. We have extended the hand of friendship, and if in return we are faced with the assassin's knife, we shall know how to repay it. These acts of treachery and violence do not exist in themselves. The men who perform them are spurred on by their masters across the Channel. Beaten again and again on the battlefield, the savages, who call themselves English and American soldiers, hire others to fight like pickpockets and burglars. Never in the history of warfare," the Captain's voice went on, growing stronger

384

in the rain, "have nations violated the laws of humanity so completely as our enemies today. Bombs dropped on the innocent women and children of the Fatherland, knives planted in the throats of our fighting men in the dark of night by their hirelings in Europe. But," the Captain's voice rose to a scream, "it will avail them nothing! Nothing! I know what effect this has on me and on every other German. We grow stronger, we grow more bitter, our resolution increases to fury!"

Christian looked around him. The other men were standing sadly in the rain, their faces not resolute, not furious, mild, subtly frightened, a little bored. The battalion was a makeshift one, with many men who had been wounded on other fronts, and the latest culling of slightly older and slightly disabled civilians and a heavy sprinkling of eighteen-year-olds. Suddenly, Christian sympathized with the Captain. He was addressing an army that did not exist, that had been wiped out in a hundred battles. He was addressing the phantoms that these men should have been, the million men capable of fury who now lay quietly in their graves in Africa and Russia.

"But finally," the Captain was shouting, "they will have to come out of their holes. They will have to crawl out of their soft beds in England, they will have to stop depending upon their hired assassins, and they will have to come to meet us on the battlefield here like soldiers. I glory in that thought, I live for that day, I shout to them, 'Come, see what it is to fight the German like a soldier!' I face that day," the Captain said solemnly, "with iron confidence. I face it with love and devotion. And I know that each one of you feels the same identical fire."

Christian looked once more at the ranks of soldiers. They stood drearily, the rain soaking through their synthetic rubber capes, their boots sinking slowly into the French mud.

"This Sergeant," the Captain gestured dramatically to the open grave, "will not be with us in the flesh on the great day, but his spirit will be with us, buoying us up, crying to us to stand firm when we begin to falter."

The Captain wiped his face and then made place for the Chaplain, who rattled through the prayer. The Chaplain had a bad cold and wanted before it turned into pneumonia to get in from the rain.

The two men with spades came up and started shoveling in the dripping fresh mud piled to one side.

The Captain shouted an order, and marching erect, trying to keep his behind from waggling too much under his coat, he led his company out of the small cemetery, which had only eight other graves in it, through the stone main street of the village. There were no civilians on the street, and the shutters of all the houses were closed against the rain, the Germans, and the war.

The SS Lieutenant was very hearty. He had come over from Headquarters in a big staff car. He smoked little Cuban cigars one after another and had a bright, mechanical smile, like a beer salesman entering a rathskeller. There was also a smell of brandy about him. He sat back in the comfortable rear compartment of the car, with Christian beside him, as they sped along the beach road to the next little village, where a suspect was being detained for Christian to identify.

"You got a good look at the two men, Sergeant?" the SS Lieutenant said, nibbling at his cigar, smiling mechanically as he peered at Christian. "You could identify them easily?"

"Yes, Sir," said Christian.

"Good." The Lieutenant beamed at Christian. "This will be very simple. I like a simple case. Some of the others, the other investigators, grow melancholy when they are in an open-and-shut case. They like to pretend they are great detectives. They like to have everything complicated, obscure, so that they can show how brilliant they are. Not me. Oh no, not me." He beamed warmly at Christian. "Yes or no, this is the man, this is not the man, that is the way I like it. Leave the rest of it to the intellectuals. I was a machine operator in a leather-goods factory in Regensburg before the war, I do not pretend to be profound. I have a simple philosophy for dealing with the French. I am direct with them, and I expect them to be direct with me." He looked at his watch, "It is now three-thirty P.M. You will be back at your Company by five o'clock. I promise you. I make it fast. Yes or no. One way or another. Good-bye. Would you like a cigar?"

"No, Sir," said Christian.

"Other officers," said the Lieutenant, "would not sit in the back like this with a Sergeant, offering him cigars. Not me. I never forget that I worked in a leather-goods factory. That is one of the faults of the German Army. They all forget they ever were civilians or ever will be civilians again. They are all Caesars and Bismarcks. Not me. Plain, open and shut, you do business with me and I'll do business with you."

By the time the big car drove up to the town hall, in the basement of which the suspect was locked up, Christian had decided that the SS Lieutenant, whose name was Reichburger, was a complete idiot, and Christian would not have trusted him to conduct an investigation of a missing fountain pen.

The Lieutenant sprang out of the car and strode briskly and cheerfully into the ugly stone building, smiling his beer salesman's smile. Christian followed him into a bare, dirty-walled room, whose only adornment, besides a clerk and three peeling café chairs, was a caricature of Winston Churchill, naked, which was tacked on a piece of cardboard and used by the local SS headquarters detachment as a dart board.

"Sit down, sit down." The Lieutenant waved to a chair. "Might as well make yourself comfortable. After all, you must not forget, you have been recently wounded."

"Yes, Sir." Christian sat down. He was sorry he had told the Lieutenant he could recognize the two Frenchmen. He detested the Lieutenant and didn't want to have anything more to do with him.

"Have you been wounded before?" The Lieutenant smiled at him fondly.

"Yes," said Christian. "Once. Twice really. Once badly, in Africa. Then I was scratched in the head outside Paris in 1940."

"Wounded three times." The Lieutenant grew sober for a moment. "You are a lucky man. You will never be killed. Obviously, there is something watching over you. I do not look it, I know, but I am a fatalist. There are some men who are born to be merely wounded, others to be killed. Myself, I have not been touched so far. But I know I shall be killed before the war is over." He shrugged and smiled widely. "I am that type. So I enjoy myself. I live with a woman who is one of the best cooks in France, and on the side, she also has two sisters." He winked at Christian and chuckled. "The bullet will hit a well-satisfied man."

The door opened and an SS Private brought in a man in manacles. The man was tall and weather-beaten, and he was trying very hard to show that he was not afraid. He stood at the door, his hands locked behind him, and, by an obvious effort of the muscles of his face, wrestled a trembling look of disdain to his lips.

The Lieutenant smiled fondly at him. "Well," the Lieutenant said, in thick French, "we will not waste your time, Monsieur." He turned to Christian. "Is this one of the men, Sergeant?"

Christian peered at the Frenchman. The Frenchman took a deep breath, and stared back at Christian, his face a dumb combination of puzzlement and controlled hatred. Christian felt a small, violent tick of anger pulling at his brain. In this face, laid bare by stupidity and courage, there was the whole history of the cunning and malice and stubbornness of the French—the mocking silence in the trains when they rode in the same compartments with you, the derisive, scarcely stifled laughter when you walked out of a café in which there were two or more of them drinking at a corner table, the 1918 scrawled arrogantly on the church wall the very first night in Paris . . . The man scowled at Christian, and even in the sour grimace there was a hint of dry laughter at the corners of his mouth. It would be most satisfactory, Christian thought, to knock in those raw, yellow teeth with the butt of a rifle. He thought of Behr, so reasonable and decent, who had hoped to work with people like this. Now Behr was dead and this man was still alive, grinning and triumphant.

"Yes," Christian said. "That's the man."

"What?" the man said stupidly. "What? He's crazy."

The Lieutenant reached out with a swiftness that his rather chubby, soft body gave no evidence of possessing, and clubbed the heel of his hand across the man's chin. "My dear friend," the Lieutenant said, "you will speak only when spoken to." He stood above the Frenchman, who looked more puzzled than ever, and who kept working his lips over his teeth and sucking in the little trickles of blood from the bruised mouth. "Now," the Lieutenant said, in French, "this is established—yesterday afternoon you cut the throat of a German soldier on the beach six kilometers north of this village."

"Please," the Frenchman said dazedly.

"Now, it only remains to hear from you one more fact . . ." the Lieutenant paused. "The name of the man who was with you."

"Please," the man said. "I can prove I did not leave the village all afternoon."

"Of course," the Lieutenant said amiably, "you can prove anything, with a hundred signatures an hour. We are not interested."

"Please," said the Frenchman.

"We are only interested in one thing," said the Lieutenant. "The name of the man who was with you when you got off your bicycle to murder a helpless German soldier."

"Please," said the Frenchman. "I do not own a bicycle."

The Lieutenant nodded to the SS Private. The soldier tied the Frenchman into one of the chairs, not roughly.

"We are very direct," said the Lieutenant. "I have promised the Sergeant he will get back to his Company for dinner and I intend to keep my promise. I merely promise you that if you do not tell me, you will regret it later. Now . . ."

"I do not even own a bicycle," the Frenchman mumbled.

The Lieutenant went over to the desk and opened a drawer. He took out a pair of pliers and walked slowly, opening and closing the pliers, with a squeaking, homely sound, behind the chair in which the Frenchman was tied. The Lieutenant bent over briskly, and seized the Frenchman's right hand in one of his own. Then, quite briskly, and carelessly, with a sharp, professional jerk, he pulled out the fingernail of the man's thumb.

The scream had no connection with anything that Christian had ever heard before.

"As I told you," the Lieutenant said, standing behind the Frenchman, "I am very direct. We have a long war to fight, and I do not believe in wasting time."

"Please . . ." moaned the Frenchman.

The Lieutenant bent over again, and again there was the scream. The Lieutenant's face was quiet and almost bored, as though he were working the machine back at the leather-goods factory in Regensburg.

The Frenchman sagged forward against the ropes that bound him to the chair, but he was fully conscious.

"This is merely standard procedure, my friend," the Lieutenant said, coming around in front of the Frenchman, "merely to give you some idea that we are in earnest about this matter. Now, will you kindly give me the name of your friend?"

"I don't know, I don't know," the man moaned. The sweat was streaming off his face, and all expression had left it, save the reflection of pain.

As Christian watched, he could not help feeling a little weak, a little dizzy, and the screams seemed insupportable in the small, bare room, with the cartoon of Winston Churchill, naked and porcine, adorned with feathered darts in his private sections, on the wall.

"I am going to do something you won't believe," the Lieutenant was saying, speaking a little louder than ordinary, as though the Frenchman's agony had built a wall that was hard to pierce. "I told you I was a direct man, and I am going to prove it. I have no patience for slow examinations. I go from one step to another promptly. You may not believe this, as I said, when I tell you, but unless you name the man who was with you, I am going to tear out your right eye. Now, my friend, this minute, in the room, with my own hands."

Involuntarily, the Frenchman closed his eyes, and a low, gasping sigh crackled through his dry lips.

"No," he whispered. "It is a terrible mistake. I don't know." Then, with a crazy logic, "I do not even own a bicycle."

"Sergeant," the Lieutenant said to Christian, "there is no need for you to remain."

"Thank you, Sir," Christian said. His voice was not steady. He went out, closing the door carefully behind him, and leaned against the corridor wall. There was an SS Private with a rifle, standing expressionlessly near the door.

The scream, after thirty seconds, made the back of Christian's throat ache and seemed to be heard and collected in his lungs. He closed his eyes, pressing the back of his head against the wall.

He knew that things like this happened from time to time, but it seemed impossible that it could happen here, on a sunny afternoon, in a dusty, plain room, in a small, run-down village, across the street from a grocery shop in the window of which hung loops of sausage, in a room in which a cartoon of a fat man with a bare, ruddy behind was hanging ...

After a while the door opened and the Lieutenant came out.

389

He was smiling. "It worked," he said. "Direct. It is the best way. Stay here," he told Christian. "I will be back very soon." He disappeared into another room.

Christian and the other soldier leaned against the wall. The Private lit a cigarette, without offering one to Christian. He smoked, closing his eyes, as though he were trying to sleep, standing up, leaning against the cracked stone wall of the old town hall. Christian saw two soldiers come out of the room that the Lieutenant had entered, and start down the street. From behind the door against which he was leaning, Christian heard a whispering, sobbing, rising and falling, wordless praying noise.

Five minutes later, the two soldiers came into the town hall, with a small, round hatless bald man, whose eyes kept sweeping in an ecstasy of fear from side to side. The soldiers took him, holding his elbows, into the room in which the Lieutenant was waiting. A moment later one of the soldiers came out into the hall. "He wants you," the soldier said to Christian.

Christian walked slowly down the hall and into the other room. The little fat Frenchman was sitting on the floor, his head in his hands, weeping. There was a dark puddle around him, to show that his bladder had failed him in his hour of trouble. The Lieutenant was sitting at a desk, typing a letter. There was a clerk in the room, making out a payroll, and another soldier standing easily near the window, looking out at a young mother carrying a blonde child into the épicerie.

The Lieutenant looked up as Christian entered. He nodded in the direction of the Frenchman on the floor. "Is this the other one?" he asked. Christian stared at the Frenchman, sitting in the middle of his own water on the dusty wood floor.

"Yes," he said.

"Take him away," the Lieutenant said.

The soldier left the window and went over to the Frenchman, who was staring dazedly up at Christian. "I have never seen him," the man said, as the soldier grabbed his collar and pulled him limply to his feet. "As God is my judge, I have never seen this man before . . ."

The soldier dragged him out.

"Now," said the Lieutenant, smiling cheerfully, "that is finished. Now . . . the papers will go to the Colonel in the next half hour, and it will be out of my hands. Now . . . do you wish to go back to your Company immediately, or would you like to stay here tonight—we have a fine sergeant's mess—and see the execution tomorrow. It will be at six tomorrow morning. Whatever you say."

"I would like to stay," Christian said.

"Good," said the Lieutenant. "Sergeant Decher is next door. Go to him and tell him I sent you and that he's to make arrangements for you. I will see you here at five forty-five tomorrow morning." He turned back to his letter as Christian went out the door.

The execution was in the cellar of the town hall. There was a long, damp basement, lit by two bare, bright bulbs. The floor was made out of hard-packed earth and there were two stakes knocked into it near the wall at one end. There were two shallow coffins, made out of unpainted wood, that gleamed rawly in the harsh light, lying behind the stakes. The cellar was used as a prison, too, and other condemned men had written their final words to the living world in chalk and charcoal on the sweating walls.

"There is no God," Christian read, standing behind the six soldiers who were to do the shooting, and "Merde, Merde, Merde," and, "My name is Jacques. My father's name was Raoul. My mother's name was Clarisse. My sister's name was Simone. My uncle's name was Etienne. My son's name was . . ." The man had never finished that.

The two condemned men shuffled in, each between two soldiers. They moved as though their legs had not been used for a long time. When he saw the stakes, the smaller man made a low, whimpering sound, but the man with one eye, although he could not make the proper movements with his legs, tried to remember how to pull the muscles of his jaw to fashion an expression of scorn. He was almost successful, Christian noticed, as the soldiers quickly tied him to the stake.

The Sergeant in command of the squad gave the first order. His voice sounded strange, too parade-like and official for the shabby cellar.

"Never," the one-eyed man shouted from behind his bandage, "you will never . . ."

But the volley cut him short. The shots cut the small man's cords and he toppled forward. The Sergeant ran up hurriedly and put the coup de grâce in, first to the small man's head, then to the other man's. The smell of the powder for a moment obscured the other, damp, corrupt smells of the cellar.

The Lieutenant nodded to Christian. Christian followed him upstairs and out into the foggy gray light, his ears still ringing from the rifles.

The Lieutenant smiled faintly. "How did you like it?" he asked.

"All right," said Christian, evenly. "I didn't mind it."

"Excellent," said the Lieutenant. "Have you had your breakfast?"

"No."

"Come along with me," the Lieutenant said. "I have breakfast waiting. It's only five doors up."

They walked side by side, their footsteps muffled in the pearly fog off the ocean.

"The first one," the Lieutenant said, "the one with one eye, he didn't like the German Army at all, did he?"

"No, Sir," said Christian.

"We're well rid of him."

"Yes, Sir."

The Lieutenant stopped and faced Christian, smiling a little. "They weren't the men at all, were they?" he said.

Christian hesitated, but only for a moment. "Frankly, Sir," he said, "I am not sure."

The Lieutenant smiled more broadly. "You're an intelligent man," he said lightly. "The effect is the same. It proves to them that we are serious." He patted Christian on the shoulder. "Go around to the kitchen and tell Renée I told you she's to feed you well, the same breakfast she brings me. You speak French well enough for that, don't you?"

"Yes, Sir," Christian said.

"Good." The Lieutenant gave Christian's shoulder a final pat and went in through the large solid door in the gray house with the geranium pots at the windows and in the garden in front. Christian went around to the back door. He had a large breakfast, with eggs and sausage and real cream.

CHAPTER TWENTY-SIX

SMOKE from crashed and burned gliders stained the wet dawn sky to the east. There was small-arms fire all around the compass and more planes kept coming over, and more gliders, and everyone fired at them with all types of weapons, anti-aircraft cannon, machine guns, rifles, and Christian thought he remembered seeing Captain Penschwitz standing on a fence firing with a pistol at a glider that crashed right in front of the Company in a poplar tree and broke into flames, with men screaming in it, and leaping in veils of flame through the canvas sides to the ground.

It was very confusing, with everyone shooting at everyone else. It had been going on now for four hours, and Penschwitz had panicked and had marched the Company down a road toward the coast for three kilometers, where they had been fired upon, and had lost eight men, then marched the Company back, with men being picked off in the dark and straggling away into farmhouses. Then, at around seven in the morning, Penschwitz had been shot by a nervous sentry at an anti-aircraft battery, and the Company had melted away, until, in a momentary lull, behind the wall of a huge old Norman stone barn, among a herd of fat black and white cows who stared suspiciously at them, Christian counted the men around him and saw that there were only twelve left, and that there were no officers at all.

Wonderful, Christian thought grimly, staring back at the cows, five hours of war and no Company left. The war will be over by dinnertime if the rest of the Army is like this.

But, from the sound of it, the rest of the Army was in better shape. There was steady firing now, and it sounded organized, and the deep rumble of artillery in spaced series of shots.

Christian stared thoughtfully at the remnants of the Company. They were almost useless, he realized. One man had begun digging a hole for himself, and all the others were following suit. They were digging feverishly, at the base of the wall, in the soft barnyard earth, and already five or six of them were down to their hips, with the rich, dark-brown loam in loose piles around them.

Useless, Christian thought, useless. He had seen too many men in panic by now to have any illusions about this bunch. Compared to them, Heims and Richter and Dehn, back in Italy, had all been heroes of the first magnitude. For a moment he thought of slipping away on his own, finding a company that was doing some fighting, and joining them, leaving these cattle to their own devices. Then he thought better of it. They will fight today, he thought sourly, if I have to march them out across a field at the muzzle of a machine gun.

He went to the man nearest him. The man was bending over, wrestling with a root he had uncovered two feet down. Christian kicked him, hard, and the man fell face forward into the muck.

"Get out of your goddamn holes," Christian shouted. "You're not going to lie here waiting for the Americans to come and get you whenever they feel like it. Get out, get out!" He kicked the next man in line in the ribs. The man had never stopped digging, had not even seemed to hear Christian, and had dug the deepest hole in the barnyard. The man sighed and got out of the hole. He did not look at Christian.

"You," Christian said, "come with me. The rest of you stay here. Eat something. You're not going to have another chance to eat for a long time. I'll be right back."

He shoved the shoulder of the man he had kicked, and started toward the house, past the silent, white-faced men and the suspicious cows.

The back door was locked. Christian banged loudly on it

393

with his gun. The man with him, whose name, Christian finally remembered, was Buschfelder, shuddered at the noise. No good, Christian thought, looking at him, no good at all.

Christian banged on the door again, and there was the sound of a bolt being drawn. A moment later the door opened, and a small, fat old woman, in a faded green apron, was standing there. She had no teeth and her wrinkled lips were pulling dryly at each other.

"We are not responsible," the woman began.

Christian pushed past her and Buschfelder followed. He was an enormous, powerful-looking man, and he seemed to fill the kitchen, as he stood against the stove, with his rifle ready in his hand.

Christian looked around the room. It was blackened by smoke and age. Two large roaches were making their way across the cold stove. There was some butter, wrapped in cabbage leaves, on the windowsill, and a large loaf of bread on the table.

"Take the butter, and the bread," Christian told Buschfelder. Then he spoke in French to the woman. "I want all the alcohol you have in the house, Mother," he said. "Wine, Calvados, marc, whatever you have. And if you try to hold out one drop, we will burn the house down and slaughter all your cows."

The old woman was watching Buschfelder collect the butter, her lips trembling in protest. But she turned to Christian when he spoke to her. "This is barbarism," she said. "I shall report you to the Commandant. Our family is well known to him and my daughter works in his house . . ."

"All the liquor, Mother," Christian said harshly. "Fast!"

He waved his gun threateningly.

The woman went to a corner of the kitchen and lifted a trap door. "Alois," she called down, her voice echoing hollowly in the cellar below their feet, "it is the soldiers. They demand our Calvados. Bring it up. Bring it all up. They will kill the cows."

Christian grinned inwardly. He looked out the window. All the men were still there. There were two new ones with them, without guns, talking swiftly with large gestures, and the men grouped around them.

There was a clumping on the cellar steps and Alois climbed into the kitchen, carrying a two-liter jar. He was over sixty, and knotted and worn with years of Norman farming. At the moment, his large, misshapen brown hands were trembling on the jug.

"Here," he said. "My best apple. I deny you nothing."

"Good," Christian said, taking the Calvados. "I thank you."

"He thanks us," the old woman said bitterly. "But no talk of payment, none at all."

"Submit your bill," Christian said, grinning, enjoying the

scene suddenly, "to your friend, the Commandant. Come on, you," he touched Buschfelder.

Buschfelder went out the door. There was a new burst of small-arms fire, much closer, and the trembling roar of low-flying planes.

"What is it?" Alois peered out the door nervously. "Is it the invasion?"

"No," said Christian carrying the liquor out of the door. "Maneuvers."

"What will happen to our cows?" Alois called after him. "Where should we put our cows?"

Christian didn't answer the old man. He strode down to the barnyard wall and put the jug on the ground.

"Here," he said, "come and get some of this. Drink as much as you can now, and every other man fill his canteen with it. In ten minutes you will be ready to take on a regiment." He grinned at them, but they did not smile back. But one by one, they came up and drank and filled their canteens.

"Don't be bashful," Christian said. "This is on the Fatherland."

The two newcomers came up last. They drank eagerly. Their eyes were bloodshot and jumpy, and they spilled the liquor over their chins.

"What happened to you two?" Christian asked when they had put down the jug.

The two men looked at each other. They did not speak.

"They were two kilometers from here," said one of the other men, Stauch, who was standing next to Christian, biting greedily at a large chunk of butter he held in one hand, and sucking at his canteen full of Calvados to wash the butter down, "two kilometers, a whole battalion, and the battalion was surprised and they are the only ones left. American paratroopers. They don't take prisoners. They killed everyone. They are all drunk, too. They have tanks and heavy artillery . . ." Stauch's voice ran on, high and uneven, through the butter and the apple brandy. "Thousands of them. They are solid from here to the coast, and there is no organized resistance . . ."

The two survivors were nodding eagerly through all this, their eyes flickering back and forth from Christian's face to Stauch's.

"We are cut off here, too, they say," Stauch continued. "A runner broke through from Division Headquarters, and he said there was no one left there. They shot the General and knifed two Colonels . . ."

"Shut up," Christian said to Stauch. He turned to the two fugitives. "Get out of here," he said.

"But where . . ." asked one of the survivors. "The para-troopers are all over . . ."

"Get out of here," said Christian loudly, cursing the bad luck that had given these men five minutes with his squad. "If I can still see you in one minute I am going to have my men fire at you. And if I ever see you again, I am going to have you court-martialed and shot for deserters."

"Please, Sergeant."

"One minute," Christian said.

The two men looked around them wildly, then turned and started to trot away. Then they grew panicky and began to run. They were running frenziedly when they disappeared through the hedge of a neighboring field.

Christian took a long drink of the Calvados. It was raw and hot and burned ferociously as it went down his throat. But a moment later he was feeling confident and powerful, and as he peered through half-closed measuring eyes at the men of his squad, he thought, I will get you bastards to fight like a full company of Elite Guards.

"One more drink," he shouted. "One more before the party."

They all drank together. Then, in single file, walking in the ditch, alongside the thick hedge that bounded each field, they started, with Christian at the head, toward the sound of the firing to the east.

They went quickly for ten minutes, stopping only for a moment each time they came to the limit of a field or to the edge of one of the narrow, hedge-lined roads. Then Christian or one of the others would slide through the hedge, make sure the way was clear, and wave to the others. The men were behaving very well. The Calvados, Christian noticed with grim satisfaction, was working so far. The men were alert, tense but not panicky, and their fatigue had lifted. They responded quickly to orders, took risks promptly, and did not fire wildly, even when a machine gun from another field sent a burst into the trees over their heads.

If he could get them back to Regimental Headquarters inside an hour, Christian thought, if there still was a Regimental Headquarters, where they could be put into an organized group under the command of officers, with a definite plan of fighting, they might earn their keep today, after all.

Then they ran into bad luck. A machine gun, concealed in the ditch beneath the thick hedges in a corner of a field, opened fire. Before they could gain cover, two men were hit. One of the men, a small, middle-aged, sorrowful-looking fellow, had got it in the jaw, and the lower part of his face was a sickening mess, and he was making a lot of noise, trying not to drown in his own blood. Christian helped put a bandage on him, but the man was bleeding so badly there wasn't going to be much anyone could do for him.

"Just stay here," Christian told the two wounded men. "You're in good cover. We'll come back for you with help after we get to Regiment." He made himself sound bluff and confident, although he was certain he was not going to see either of these two men alive again.

The man with the wounded jaw made a wet, imploring noise, behind his soaking bandage, but Christian ignored it. He motioned to the others to get started, but they didn't move.

"Come on," Christian said. "The faster you move the better chance you have of getting through this. If you stand still, you'll catch it . . ."

"Listen, Sergeant," Stauch said, from his crouched position in the grassgrown ditch, "what's the sense in fooling ourselves? We're cut off, we haven't got a chance in the world, there's a whole damned American division here and we're in the middle of it. Besides, these men will die if they don't get help soon. I'll volunteer to go through this hedge with a white flag on my rifle and arrange the surrender . . ." He stopped lamely, refusing to face Christian.

Christian looked at the others. Their pale faces, peering wanly over the brink of the ditch, made it plain that the temporary fortitude they had gained from the jug had evaporated once and for all.

"The first man that goes through that hedge," he said quietly, "I guarantee to shoot myself. Any other suggestions?"

Nobody said anything.

"We are going to find Regiment," Christian said. "Stauch, you will lead the procession. I will be in the rear and I will be watching every single one of you. Keep in the ditches, on this side of the hedge. Keep low, and move fast. All right, start now."

Christian watched, his Schmeisser ready at his hip, as the ten men, one by one, began to crawl down the ditch. The man with the wounded jaw was still making the drowning, sorrowful noise as Christian passed him, but the sound was growing weaker and more irregular.

Twice they stopped and watched German tanks rumbling blindly down the road toward the beach, and that was reassuring. Once they saw a jeep with three Americans in it, skidding around the corner of a farmhouse. Christian could feel the trembling desire to run, to lie down, to weep, to die and get it over with, sweep through the men in front of him. They passed two dead cows, torn open by shells, lying feet up in the corner of a field, and a wild-eyed horse that galloped madly down the road, only to stop and gallop equally madly, its hooves making a muffled, urgent clatter on the damp clay. There were dead Germans and dead Americans strewn at random in the careless exposure of death, and it was impossible to tell from the manner in which they lay or the direction of their weapons what the lines had been or how the battle had gone. From time to time shells made their crushing, swift noise in the sky above their heads. In one field, in an almost mathematically spaced line, there were the bodies of five Americans whose parachutes had never opened. They had hit so hard they had driven into the ground, and their straps had burst and their equipment lay scattered around them as though ready for a kind of drunken inspection in a foreign army.

Then Christian saw Stauch, at the end of the ditch, thirty meters in front of him, waving cautiously. Christian ran, crouching over, past the other men. When he got to the end of the ditch, Stauch pointed through a small opening in the hedge. Twenty meters on the other side of the hedge there were two paratroopers out in the open, working to free another American who had been caught in a tree, and was hanging there, helplessly, swaying six feet from the ground. Christian fired two short bursts and the two men on the ground fell immediately. One of them moved and started to get up on one elbow. Christian fired again and the man fell over on his back and lay still.

The man in the tree yanked furiously at his cords, but he could not break free.

Christian could hear Stauch, crouched beside him, licking his lips noisily. Christian signaled to the first three men to follow him and the four of them went cautiously up to the man hanging from the tree, dangling over his two dead comrades.

Christian grinned up at the American. "How do you like France, Sammy?" Christian asked.

"Shit on you, Bud," said the paratrooper. He had a tough, athlete's face, with a broken nose and cold, tough eyes. But he stopped struggling with the traces and just hung there, staring at Christian. "I'll tell you, what, Kraut-face," the American said, "you cut me down and I'll accept your surrender."

Christian smiled at him. If only I had a few like him with me, today, Christian thought, instead of these worms . . .

He shot the paratrooper.

Christian patted the dead man's leg, with a gesture which he himself did not understand, part pity, part admiration, part mockery. Then he led the way back to the rest of the squad. Ah, Christian thought, if they are all like that, we are not going to do very well against them.

By ten o'clock in the morning they met up with a Colonel who was moving eastward with what was left of Regimental Headquarters. They had to fight twice before noon, but the Colonel knew his business, and they kept together and kept moving. The men of Christian's squad fought no better and no worse than the other men under the Colonel's command. Four of them were dead by nightfall, and Stauch had shot himself through the head when his leg was broken by a machine-gun bullet and he was told he was going to be left behind. But they fought decently, and none of them ever made a move to surrender, although the opportunities that first day were numerous.

CHAPTER TWENTY-SEVEN

"BACK IN TULSA, when I was in high school," Fahnstock was saying, between slow strokes of the hammer, "they called me Stud. From the time I was thirteen years old my prevailing interest in life was girls. If I could find me an English broad in town here, I wouldn't even mind this place." Reflectively he hammered out a nail from a weathered piece of lumber he was working on and threw the nail into the can next to him. Then he spat, a long, dark spurt of tobacco juice, from the cud that seemed to be permanently attached to the inside of his jaw.

Michael took out the pint bottle of gin from the back pocket of his fatigues and took a long gulp. He put the bottle away without offering Fahnstock a drink. Fahnstock, who got drunk every Saturday night, did not drink on weekdays before Retreat, and it was only ten o'clock in the morning now. Besides, Michael was tired of Fahnstock. They had been together for over two months now in the Replacement Center Casual Company. One day they worked on the lumber pile, taking nails out and straightening them, and the next day they worked on KP. The Mess Sergeant didn't like either of them, and for the last fifteen times he had put them on the dirtiest job in the kitchen, scrubbing the big greasy pots and cleaning the stoves after the day's cooking was over.

As far as Michael could tell, both he and Fahnstock, who was too stupid to do anything else, were going to spend the rest of the war and perhaps the rest of their lives alternating between the lumber pile and the kitchen. When this realization had sunk in, Michael had thought of desertion, but had compromised with gin. It was very dangerous, because the camp was run like a penal colony and men were constantly being sentenced to years in jail for smaller offenses than drunkenness on duty, but the dull, ameliorating effects of the steady flow of alcohol through his brain made it possible for Michael to continue to live, and he took the risk gladly.

He had written Colonel Pavone soon after he was put on the lumber pile, asking to be transferred, but there had been no answer from the Colonel, and Michael was too tired all the time now to bother to write again or to try any other avenues of escape.

"The best time I had in the Army," Fahnstock drawled, "was in Jefferson Barracks in St. Louis. I found three sisters in a bar. They worked in a brewery in St. Louis on different shifts. One was sixteen, one was fifteen, and one was fourteen. Hillbillies fresh out of the Ozark Mountains. They never owned a pair of stockings till they worked in the brewery for three months. I sure did regret it the day my orders came through for overseas."

"Listen," Michael said, pounding slowly on a nail, "will you please talk about something else?"

"I'm just trying to pass the time," Fahnstock said, aggrieved.

"Pass the time some other way," Michael said, feeling the gin, sour and strong, gripping the lining of his stomach.

They hammered at the splintery boards in silence.

A guard with a shotgun came by behind two prisoners who were rolling wheelbarrows full of lumber ends. The prisoners dumped the lumber onto the pile. They all moved with a dragging, deliberate slowness, as though there was nothing ahead of them in their whole lives that was important to do.

"Shake your ass," the guard said languidly, leaning on the shotgun. The prisoners paid no attention to him.

"Whitacre," said the guard, "whip out the bottle."

Michael looked glumly at him. The police, he thought, everywhere the same, collecting their blackmail for overlooking the breaking of the law. He took out the bottle and wiped the neck of it before handing it to the guard. He watched jealously as the guard took a deep swig.

"I only drink on holidays." The guard grinned as he handed back the bottle.

Michael put the bottle away. "What's this?" he asked. "Christmas?"

"Haven't you heard?"

"Heard what?"

"We hit the beach this morning. This is D Day, Brother, ain't you glad you're here?"

"How do you know?" Michael asked suspiciously.

"Eisenhower made a speech on the radio. I heard it," the guard said. "We're liberating the frigging frogs, he said."

"I knew somethin' was up yesterday," said one of the prisoners, a small, thoughtful-looking man who was in for thirty years because he had knocked out his Lieutenant in the orderly room. "They came to me and they offered to pardon me

400

and give me an honorable discharge if I would go back into the infantry."

"What did you say?" Fahnstock asked, interestedly.

"Screw, I said," said the prisoner. "An honorable discharge right into a military cemetery."

"Shut your goddamn mouth," said the guard languidly, "and pick up that wheelbarrow. Whitacre, one more drink, to celebrate D Day."

"I have nothing to celebrate," Michael said, trying to save his gin.

"Don't be ungrateful," said the guard. "You're here nice and dry and safe and you ain't laying on any beach with a hunk of shrapnel up your ass. You got plenty to celebrate." He held out his hand. Michael gave him the bottle.

"That gin," Michael said, "cost me two pounds a fifth."

The guard grinned. "You was gypped," he said. He drank deeply. The two prisoners looked at him thirstily and longingly. The guard gave Michael the bottle. Michael drank, because it was D Day. He felt the sweet wave of self-pity sweep alcoholically over him. He glared at the prisoners coldly as he put the bottle away.

"Well," said Fahnstock, "I guess old Roosevelt is finally satisfied today. He's gone and got himself a mess of Americans killed."

"I'll bet he jumped up out of his wheelchair," the guard said, "and is dancin' up and down on the White House floor."

"I heard," said Fahnstock, "the day he declared war on Germany, he had a big banquet in the White House with turkey and French wine, and after it they was all laying each other on the tables and desks."

Michael took a deep breath. "Germany declared war on the United States," he said. "I don't give a damn, but that's the way it happened."

"Whitacre is a Communist from New York," said Fahnstock to the guard. "He's crazy about Roosevelt."

"I'm not crazy about anybody," Michael said. "Only Germany declared war on us and so did Italy. Two days after Pearl Harbor."

"I'll leave it up to the boys," said Fahnstock. He turned to the guard and the prisoners. "Straighten out my friend," Fahnstock said.

"We started it," said the guard. "We declared war. I remember it as clear as day."

"Boys," Fahnstock appealed to two prisoners.

They both nodded. "We declared war on them," said the man who had been offered an honorable discharge if he would join the infantry.

"Roger," said the other prisoner, who had been in the Air

401

Forces before they caught him forging checks in Wales.

"There you are," said Fahnstock. "Four to one, Whitacre. The majority rules."

Michael glared drunkenly at Fahnstock. Suddenly it became intolerable to bear the pimply, leering, complacent face. Not today, Michael thought heavily, not on a day like this. "You ignorant, garbage-brained son of a bitch," Michael said clearly and wildly, "if you open your mouth once more I'll kill you."

Fahnstock moved his lips gently. Then he spat, a long, brownish, filthy spurt. The tobacco juice splashed on Michael's face. Michael leapt at Fahnstock and hit him in the jaw, twice. Fahnstock went down, but he was up in a moment, holding a heavy piece of two by four with three large nails sticking out of one end. He swung at Michael and Michael started to run. The guard and the prisoners stepped back to give the men room. They watched interestedly.

Fahnstock was very fast, despite his fat, and he got close enough to hit Michael's shoulder. Michael felt the sharp bite of the nails in his shoulder and wrenched away. He stopped and bent down and picked up a plank. Before he could straighten up, Fahnstock hit him on the side of the head. Michael felt the scraping, tearing passage of the nails across his cheekbone. Then he swung. He hit Fahnstock on the head and Fahnstock began to walk strangely, sideways, in a small half circle around Michael. Fahnstock swung again, but weakly, and Michael leapt out of the way easily, although it was getting difficult to judge distances correctly, because of the blood in his eye. He waited coldly, and just as Fahnstock raised his plank again, Michael stepped in, swinging his board sideways, like a baseball bat. The plank caught Fahnstock across the neck and jaw and he went down on his hands and knees. He stayed that way, peering dully at the thin dust on the bare ground around the lumber pile.

"All right," said the guard. "That was a nice little fight. You," he said to the prisoners, "sit the bastard up."

Both prisoners went over to Fahnstock and sat him up against a box. Fahnstock looked dully out across the sunny bare ground, his legs straight out in front of him. He was breathing heavily, but that was all.

Michael threw away his plank and got out his handkerchief. He put it to his face and looked curiously at the large red stain on it when he took it away from his face.

Wounded, he thought, grinning, wounded on D Day.

The guard saw an officer turn a corner of a barracks a hundred yards away and said hurriedly to the prisoners, "Come on, get moving." Then to Michael and Fahnstock, "Better get back to work. Here comes Smiling Jack."

The guard and the prisoners went off at a brisk clip, and

Michael stared at the approaching officer, who was called Smiling Jack because he never smiled at all.

Michael grabbed Fahnstock and pulled him to his feet. He put the hammer in Fahnstock's hand and automatically Fahnstock began to tap at the boards. Michael picked up some boards and ostentatiously carried them to the other end of the pile, where he put them down neatly.

He went back to Fahnstock and picked up his own hammer. Both men were making a busy noise when Smiling Jack came up to them. Court-martial, Michael was thinking, court-martial, five years, drunk on duty, fighting, insubordination, etc.

"What's going on here?" asked Smiling Jack.

Michael stopped hammering, and Fahnstock too. They turned and faced the Lieutenant.

"Nothing, Sir," Michael said, keeping his lips as tight as possible so that the Lieutenant couldn't smell his breath.

"Have you men been fighting?"

"No, Sir," said Fahnstock, united against the common enemy.

"How did you get that wound?" The Lieutenant gestured toward the three raw, bleeding lines across Michael's cheekbone.

"I slipped, Sir," said Michael blandly.

Smiling Jack's lip curled angrily and Michael knew he was thinking, They're all the same, they're all out to make fools of you, there isn't a word of truth in a single enlisted man in the whole goddamn Army.

"Fahnstock!" Smiling Jack said.

"Yes, Sir?"

"Is this man telling the truth?"

"Yes, Sir. He slipped."

Smiling Jack looked around helplessly and furiously. "If I find out you're lying . . ." He left the sentence threateningly in the air. "All right, Whitacre, finish up here. There're travel orders for you in the orderly room. You're being transferred. Go on and pick them up."

He glared once more at the two men and turned and stalked away, after exacting a salute.

Michael watched the retreating, frustrated back.

"You son of a bitch," said Fahnstock, "if I catch you again I'll razor-cut you."

"Nice to have known you," Michael said lightly. "Clean those pots nice and bright now."

He tossed away his hammer and strode lightly toward the orderly room, tapping his rear pocket to make sure the bottle wasn't showing.

With his orders in his pocket, later on, and a neat bandage on his cheek Michael packed his barracks bag. Colonel Pavone had come through, and Michael was to report to him in London immediately. As he packed, Michael sipped at his bottle, and planned, craftily, to take no chances, volunteer for nothing, take nothing seriously. Survive, he thought, survive; it is the only lesson I have learned so far.

He drove down to London in an Army truck the next morning. The people of the villages along the road cheered and made the V sign with their fingers because they thought every truck now was on its way to France, and Michael and the other soldiers in the truck waved back cynically, grinning and laughing.

They passed a British convoy near London, loaded with armed infantrymen. On the rear truck, there was a dourly chalked legend. "Don't cheer, Girls, We're British."

The British infantrymen did not even look up when the American truck sped by them.

CHAPTER TWENTY-EIGHT

A BATTLE EXISTS on many different levels. There is the purely moral level, at the Supreme Headquarters perhaps eighty miles away from the sound of the guns, where the filing cabinets have been dusted in the morning, where there is a sense of quiet and efficiency, where soldiers who never fire a gun and never have a shot fired at them, the high Generals, sit in their pressed uniforms and prepare statements to the effect that all has been done that is humanly possible, the rest being left to the judgment of God, Who has risen early, ostensibly, for this day's work, and is partially and critically regarding the ships, the men drowning in the water, the flight of high explosive, the accuracy of bombardiers, the skill of naval officers, the bodies being thrown into the air by mines, the swirl of tides against steel spikes at the water's edge, the loading of cannon in gun emplacements, and the building far back from the small violent fringe between the two armies, where the files have also been dusted that morning and the enemy Generals sit in different pressed uniforms, looking at very similar maps, reading very similar reports, matching their moral strength and intellectual ingenuity with their colleagues and antagonists a hundred miles away. In these places, in the rooms where the large maps with the acetate overlays and the red and black crayon markings are hung on the walls, the battle swiftly takes on an orderly and formal appearance. A plan is always in process of being worked out on the maps. If Plan I fails, Plan II is attempted. If Plan II is only partially successful, a pre-arranged modification of Plan III is instituted. The Generals have all studied from the same books at West Point and Spandau and Sandhurst, and many of them have written books themselves and read each other's works, and they all know what Caesar did in a somewhat similar situation and the mistake that Napoleon made in Italy and how Ludendorff failed to exploit a break in the line in 1915, and they all hope, on opposite sides of the English Channel, that the situation never gets to that decisive point where they will have to say the Yes or the No which may decide the fate of the battle, and perhaps the nation, and which takes the last trembling dram of courage out of a man, and which may leave him ruined and broken for the rest of his life, all his honors gone, his reputation empty, when he has said it. So they sit back in their offices, which are like the offices of General Motors or the offices of I. G. Farben in Frankfurt, with stenographers and typists and flirtations in the halls, and look at the maps and read the reports and pray that Plans I, II, and III will operate as everyone has said they will operate back on Grosvenor Square and the Wilhelmstrasse, with only small, not very important modifications that can be handled locally, by the men on the scene.

The men on the scene see the affair on a different level. They have not been questioned on the proper manner of isolating the battlefield. They have not been consulted on the length of the preliminary bombardment. Meteorologists have not instructed them on the rise and fall of the tides in the month of June or the probable incidence of storms. They have not been at the conferences in which was discussed the number of divisions it would be profitable to lose to reach a phase line one mile inland by 1600 hours. There are no filing cabinets on board the landing barges, no stenographers with whom to flirt, no maps in which their actions, multiplied by two million, become clear, organized, intelligent symbols, suitable for publicity releases and the tables of historians.

They see helmets, vomit, green water, shell geysers, smoke, crashing planes, blood plasma, submerged obstacles, guns, pale, senseless faces, a confused drowning mob of men running and falling, that seem to have no relation to any of the things they have been taught since they left their jobs and wives to put on the uniform of their country. To a General sitting before the maps eighty miles away, with echoes of Caesar and Clausewitz and Napoleon fleetingly swimming through his brain, matters are proceeding as planned, or almost as planned, but to the man on the scene everything is going wrong.

"Oh, God," sobs the man on the scene, when the shell hits the Landing Craft Infantry, H hour plus two, one mile out from shore, and the wounded begin to scream on the slippery decks, "Oh, God, it is all screwed up."

To the Generals eighty miles away, the reports on casualties are encouraging. To the man on the scene the casualties are never encouraging. When he is hit or when the man next to him is hit, when the ship fifty feet away explodes, when the Naval Ensign on the bridge is screaming in a high, girlish voice for his mother because he has nothing left below his belt, it can only appear to him that he has been involved in a terrible accident, and it is inconceivable at that moment to believe that there is a man eighty miles away who has foreseen that accident, encouraged it, made arrangements for it to happen, and who can report, after it has happened (although he must know about the shell, about the listing Landing Craft Infantry, about the wet decks and the screaming Ensign) that everything is going according to plan.

"Oh, God," sobs the man on the scene, watching the amphibious tanks sink under the waves, with perhaps one man swimming up out of the hatch, "Oh, God," he sobs, looking down at the queer, unattached leg lying beside his face and realizing it is his, "Oh, God," as the ramp goes down and the twelve men in front of him pile up in the cold two feet of water, with the machine-gun bullets inside them, "Oh, God," looking for the holes on the beach he has been told the Air Force was going to put there for him, and not finding them, and lying there face down, with the mortar shell dropping silently on top of him, "Oh, God," he sobs, seeing the friend he has loved since Fort Benning, Georgia, in 1940, blow up on a mine and hang across a barbed-wire fence with his back wide open from neck to hip, "Oh, God," sobs the man on the scene, "it is all screwed up."

The Landing Craft Infantry wallowed in the water until four o'clock in the afternoon. At noon a barge took off their wounded, all properly bandaged and transfused. Noah watched the swathed, blanketed men being swung over the side on stretchers, thinking, with a helpless touch of envy: They are going back, they are going back, in ten hours they will be in England, in ten days, they may be in the United States, what luck, they never had to fight at all.

But then, when the barge was only a hundred feet away, it was hit. There was a splash beside it, and nothing seemed to be happening for a moment. But then it slowly rolled over and the blankets and the bandages and the stretchers whirled in the choppy green water for a minute or two, and that was all. Donnelly had been one of the wounded, with a piece of shrapnel in his skull, and Noah looked for Donnelly in the froth and heavy cloudy water, but there was no sign of him. He never got a chance to use that flame-thrower, Noah thought dully. After all that practice.

Colclough was not to be seen. He was down below all day and Lieutenant Green and Lieutenant Sorenson were the only officers of the Company on deck. Lieutenant Green was a frail, girlish-looking man, and everybody had made fun of him all through training, because of his mincing walk and high voice. But he walked around on deck, among the wounded and the sick and the men who were sure they were going to die, and he was cheerful and competent and helped with the bandages and the blood transfusions, and kept telling everyone that the boat was not going to sink, the Navy was working on the engines, they would be in on the beach in fifteen minutes. He still walked in that silly, mincing way, and his voice was no lower and no more manly than usual, but Noah had the feeling that if Lieutenant Green, who had run a drygoods store in South Carolina before the war, had not been on board, half the Company would have jumped over the side by two in the afternoon.

It was impossible to tell how things were going on the beach. Burnecker even made a joke about it. All morning long he had kept saying, in a strange, rasping voice, holding violently onto Noah's arms, when the shells hit the water close to them, "We're going to get it today. We're going to get it today." But around noon he got hold of himself. He stopped vomiting and ate a K ration, complaining about the dryness of the cheese, and then he seemed to have either resigned himself or become more optimistic. When Noah peered out at the beach, on which shells were falling and men running and mines going up, and asked Burnecker, "How is it going?" Burnecker said, "I don't know. The boy hasn't delivered my copy of the New York *Times* yet." It wasn't much of a joke, but Noah laughed wildly at it and Burnecker grinned, pleased with the effect, and from then on, in the Company, long after they were deep in Germany, when anybody asked how things were going, he was liable to be told, "The boy hasn't delivered the New York *Times* yet."

The hours passed in a long, cold, gray daze for Noah, and much later, when he tried to remember how he had felt, while the boat was rolling helplessly, its decks slick with blood and sea water, and the shells hitting at random around him from time to time, he could only recall isolated insignificant impressions—Burnecker's joke, Lieutenant Green bent over, holding his helmet with weird fastidiousness for a wounded man to vomit in, the face of the Naval Lieutenant in command of the landing craft when he hung over the side to inspect the damage, red, angry, baffled, like a baseball player who has been victimized by a nearsighted umpire; Donnelly's face, after his head had been bandaged, its usual coarse, brutal lines all gone, now composed and serene in its unconsciousness, like a nun in the movies—Noah remembered these things and remembered looking a dozen times an hour to see if his satchel charges were still dry, and looking to see if the safety was on his rifle again and again, and forgetting two minutes later and looking again . . .

Fear came in waves, during which he could only crouch against the rail, helpless, holding his lips still, not thinking about anything. Then there were periods when he would feel above it all, as though it were not happening to him, as though this could never happen to him, and because it could not happen he could not be hurt, and if he could not be hurt there was nothing to be afraid of. Once he took out his wallet and gravely stared for a long time at the picture of Hope, smiling, holding a fat baby in her arms, the baby with its mouth wide open, yawning.

In the periods when he was not afraid, his mind seemed to run on without conscious direction from him, as though that part of him were bored with the day's activities and was amusing itself in recollections, like a schoolboy dreaming at his desk on a June day with the sun outside the window and the insects humming sleepily over the desks . . . Captain Colclough's speech in the staging area near Southampton a week before (was it only a week, in the sweet-smelling May woods, with the three good meals a day and the barrel of beer in the recreation tent, and the blossoms hanging over the tanks and cannon and the movies twice a day, *Madame Curie*, Greer Garson in a lady-like, well-dressed search for radium, Betty Grable's bare legs—doing God knows what for the morale of the infantry—flickering on the screen that flapped with each gust of wind in the tent, could it only be a week?) . . . "This is the showdown, Men . . ." (Captain Colclough used the word, "Men," twenty times in the speech.) "You're as well trained as any soldiers in the world. When you go onto that beach you're going to be better equipped, better trained, better prepared than the slimy bastards you're going to meet. Every advantage is going to be on your side. Now it is going to be a question of your guts against his. Men, you are going to go in there and kill the Kraut. That's all you're going to think about from this minute on, killing the bastards. Some of you are going to get hurt, Men, some of you are going to get killed. I'm not going to play it down or make it soft. Maybe a lot of you are going to get killed . . ." He spoke slowly, with satisfaction. "That's what you're in the Army for,

Men, that's why you're here, that's why you're going to be put on the beach. If you're not used to that idea yet, get used to it now. I'm not going to dress it up in patriotic speeches. Some of you are going to get killed, but you're going to kill a lot of Germans. If any man . . ." And here he found Noah and stared coldly at him, "If any man here thinks he is going to hold back, or shirk his duty in any way just to save his hide, let him remember that I am going to be along and I am going to see that everyone is going to do his share. This Company is going to be the best damned Company in the Division. I have made up my mind to it, Men. When this battle is over I expect to be promoted to Major. And you men are going to get that promotion for me. I've worked for you and now you are going to work for me. I have an idea the fat-asses in Special Service and Morale back in Washington wouldn't like this speech. I say, screw them. They've had their chance at you, and I haven't interfered. They've filled you full of those goddamn pamphlets and noble sentiments and ping-pong balls, and I've just laid back and let them have their fun. I've let 'em baby you and give you soft titty to suck and put talcum powder on your backsides and make you believe you're all going to live forever and the Army will take care of you like a mother. Now, they're finished, and you don't listen to anyone but me. And here's the gospel for you from now on, straight out of the shit-house—This Company is going to kill more Krauts than any other Company in the Division and I'm going to make Major by July fourth, and if that means we're going to have more casualties than anybody else, all I can say is: See the Chaplain, Boys, you didn't come to Europe to tour the monuments. Sergeant, dismiss the Company."

"AttenSHUN! Company, disMISS!"

Captain Colclough had not been seen all day. Perhaps he was below decks preparing another speech to signalize their arrival in France, perhaps he was dead. And Lieutenant Green, who had never made a speech in his life, was pouring sulfanilamide into wounds and covering the dead and grinning at the living and reminding them to keep the barrels of their rifles covered against the water that was spraying over the sides . . .

At four-thirty in the afternoon, the Navy finally got the engines working as Lieutenant Green had promised, and fifteen minutes later, the Landing Craft Infantry slid onto the beach. The beach looked busy and safe, with hundreds of men rushing back and forth, carrying ammunition boxes, piling rations, rolling wire, bringing back wounded, digging in for the night among the charred wrecks of barges and bulldozers and splintered fieldpieces. The sound of small-arms fire was quite distant by now, on the other side of the bluff that overlooked the beach. Occasionally a mine went off, and occasionally a shell struck the sand, but it was clear that, for the time being, the beach was secured.

Captain Colclough appeared on deck as the Landing Craft nosed into the shallow water. He had a pearl-handled forty-five in the fancy leather holster at his side. It was a gift from his wife, he had once told somebody in the Company, and he wore it dashingly, low on his thigh, like a sheriff on the cover of a Western magazine.

An Amphibious Engineer Corporal was waving the craft onto the crowded beach. He looked weary, but at ease, as though he had spent most of his life on the coast of France under shell and machine-gun fire.

The ramp went down on the side of the Landing Craft, and Colclough started to lead his Company ashore. Only one of the ramps worked. The other had been torn away when the boat was hit.

Colclough went to the end of the ramp. It led down into the soft sand, and when the waves came in it was under almost three feet of water. Colclough stopped, one foot in the air. Then he pushed back onto the ramp.

"This way, Captain," called the Engineer Corporal.

"There's a mine down there," Colclough said. "Get those men . . ." He pointed to the rest of the squad of Engineers, who were working with a bulldozer, making a road up across the dunes, ". . . to come over here and sweep this area."

"There's no mine, there, Captain," said the Corporal wearily.

"I said I saw a mine, Corporal," Colclough shouted.

The Naval Lieutenant who was in command of the vessel pushed his way down the ramp. "Captain," he said anxiously, "will you please get your men off this vessel? I've got to get away from here. I don't want to spend the night on this beach, and my engines aren't strong enough to pull a sick whore off a pisspot. We'll never get off if we hang around another ten minutes."

"There's a mine at the end of the ramp," Colclough said loudly.

"Captain," said the Engineer, "three Companies have come off barges right in this spot and nobody got blown up."

"I gave you a direct order," Colclough said. "Go over and get those men to come here and sweep this area."

"Yes, Sir," said the Engineer, shrugging. He went toward the bulldozer, past a row of sixteen corpses, laid out neatly, in blankets.

"If you don't get off this boat right away," the Naval Lieutenant said, "the United States Navy is going to lose one Landing Craft Infantry."

410

"Lieutenant," Colclough said coldly, "you pay attention to your business, and I'll pay attention to mine."

"If you're not off in ten minutes," the Lieutenant said, retreating up the ramp, "I am going to take you and your whole goddamned company out to sea. You'll have to join the Marines to see dry land again."

"This entire matter," said Colclough, "will be reported through proper channels, Lieutenant."

"Ten minutes," the Lieutenant shouted violently over his shoulder, making his way back to his shattered bridge.

"Captain," Lieutenant Green said, in his high voice, from halfway up the crowded ramp, where the men were lined up, peering doubtfully into the dirty green water, on which abandoned Mae Wests, wooden machine-gun ammunition boxes and cardboard K ration cartons were floating soddenly, "Captain," said Lieutenant Green, "I'll be glad to go ahead. As long as the Corporal said it was all right . . . Then the men can follow in my footsteps and . . ."

"I am not going to lose any of my men on this beach," Colclough said. "Stay where you are." He gave a slight, decisive hitch to the pearl-handled revolver that his wife had given him. The holster, Noah observed, had a little rawhide fringe on the bottom of it, like the holsters that come with cowboy suits little boys get at Christmas.

The Engineer Corporal was coming back across the beach now, with his Lieutenant. The Lieutenant was a tall, enormous man without a helmet. He was not carrying any weapons. With his windburned, red, sweating face and his huge, dirt-blackened hands hanging out of the sleeves of his rolled-back fatigues, he didn't look like a soldier, but like a foreman on a road gang back home.

"Come on, Captain," the Engineer Lieutenant said. "Come on ashore."

"There's a mine in here," Colclough said. "Get your men over here and sweep the area."

"There's no mine," said the Lieutenant.

"I say I saw a mine."

The men behind the Captain listened uneasily. Now that they were so close to the beach it was intolerable to remain on the craft on which they had suffered so much that day, and which still made a tempting target as it creaked and groaned with the swish of the rollers coming in off the sea. The beach, with its dunes and foxholes and piles of material, looked secure, institutional, homelike, as nothing that floated and was ruled by the Navy could look. They stood behind Colclough, staring at his back, hating him.

The Engineer Lieutenant started to open his mouth to say something to Colclough. Then he looked down and saw the pearl-handled revolver at the Captain's belt. He closed his mouth smiling a little. Then, expressionlessly, without a word, he walked into the water, with his shoes and leggings still on, and stamped heavily back and forth, up to the ramp and around it, not paying any attention to the waves that smashed at his thighs. He covered every inch of beach that might possibly have been crossed by any of the men, stamping expressionlessly up and down. Then, without saying another word to Colclough, he stamped back out of the water, his broad back bowed over a little from weariness, and walked heavily back to where his men were running the bulldozer over a huge chunk of concrete with an iron rail sticking out of it.

Colclough wheeled suddenly from his position at the bottom of the ramp, but none of the men was smiling. Then Colclough turned and stepped onto the soil of France, delicately, but with dignity, and one by one his Company followed him, through the cold sea water and the floating debris of the first day of the great battle for the continent of Europe.

The company did not fight at all the first day. They dug in and ate their supper K ration (veal loaf, biscuit, vitamin-crowded chocolate, all of it with the taste and texture of the factory in it, denser and more slippery than natural food can be), and cleaned their rifles and watched the new companies coming into the beach with the amused superiority of veterans for their jitteriness at the occasional shells and their exaggerated tenderness about mines. Colclough had gone off looking for Regiment, which was inland somewhere, although no one knew just where.

The night was dark, windy, wet and cold. The Germans sent over planes in the last twilight and the guns of the ships lying offshore and the anti-aircraft guns on the beach crowded the sky with flaming steel lines. The shrapnel dropped with soft, deadly plunks into the sand beside Noah, while he stared up helplessly, wondering if there ever was going to be a time when he would not be in danger of his life.

They were awakened at dawn, at which time Colclough returned from Regiment. He had got lost during the night and had wandered up and down the beach looking for the Company, until he had been shot at by a nervous Signal Corps sentry. Then he had decided that it was too dangerous to keep moving about and had dug himself a hole and bedded himself down until it was light enough, so that he would not be shot by his own men. He looked haggard and weary, but he shouted orders in rapid-fire succession and led the way up the bluff, with the Company spread out behind him.

Noah had a cold by then, and was sneezing and blowing his nose wetly. He was wearing long woolen underwear, two pairs of wool socks, a suit of OD's, a field jacket, and over it

412

all the chemically treated fatigues, which were stiff and wind-resistant, but even so he could feel his chilled bones grinding within his flesh as he made his way through the heavy sand past the smoke-blackened and ruptured German pillboxes and the dead gray uniforms, still unburied, and the torn German cannon, still maliciously pointed toward the beach.

Trucks and jeeps pulling trailers loaded with ammunition bumped and skidded past the Company, and a newly arrived tank platoon clanked up the rise, looking dangerous and invincible. MP's were waving traffic on, Engineers were building roads, a bulldozer was scraping out a runway for an airfield, jeep ambulances, with wounded on stretchers across the top, were sliding down the rutted road between the taped off minefields to the clearing stations in the lee of the bluff. In a wide field, pocketed with shell holes, Graves Registration troops were burying American dead. There was an air of orderly, energetic confusion about the entire scene that reminded Noah of the time when he was a small boy in Chicago and had watched the circus throwing up its tents and arranging its cages and living quarters.

When he got to the top of the bluff Noah turned around and looked at the beach, trying to fix it in his mind. Hope will want to know what it looked like, and her father, too, when I get back, Noah thought. Somehow, planning what he was going to tell them at some distant, beautiful, unwarlike day made it seem more uncertain to Noah that that day would arrive and he would be alive to celebrate it, dressed in soft flannels and a blue shirt, with a glass of beer in his hand, under a maple tree, perhaps, on a bright Sunday afternoon, boring his relatives, he thought with a grin, with the long-winded veterans' stories of the Great War.

The beach, strewn with the steel overflow of the factories of home, looked like a rummage basement in some store for giants. Close offshore, just beyond the old tramp steamers they were sinking now for a breakwater, destroyers were standing, firing over their heads at strong-points inland.

"That's the way to fight a war," Burnecker said beside Noah. "Real beds, coffee is being served below, Sir, you may fire when ready, Gridley. We would have joined the Navy, Ackerman, if we had as much brains as a jackrabbit."

"Come on, *move!*" It was Rickett, calling from behind them, the same, snarling, Sergeant's voice, which no sea voyage, no amount of killing, would ever change.

"My choice," Burnecker said, "for the man I would like most to be left alone with on a desert island."

They turned and plodded inland, leaving the coast behind them.

They marched for a half hour and then it became evident

413

that Colclough was lost again. He stopped the Company at a crossroad where two MP's were directing traffic from a deep hole they had dug to one side, with just their helmets and shoulders sticking out above ground level. Noah could see Colclough gesturing angrily and he could hear the violence in the Captain's voice as he yelled at the MP's, who were shaking their heads in ignorance. Then Colclough got out his map again and yelled at Lieutenant Green, who came up to help.

"Just our luck," Burnecker said wagging his head, "we got a Captain who couldn't find a plow in a ballroom."

"Get back," they heard Colclough shout at Green. "Get back where you belong. I know what I'm doing!"

He turned into a lane between high, gleaming green hedges, and the Company wound slowly after him. It was darker between the hedges, and somehow much quieter, although the guns were still going, and the men peered uneasily at the dense, intertwined leaves, made for ambush.

Nobody said anything. They trudged on both sides of the damp road, trying to hear a rustle, the click of a rifle bolt, a whisper of German, over the everlasting infantry squash-squash of their shoes, heavily scuffing in the thick clay of the lane.

Then the road opened up into a field and the sun broke through the clouds for awhile and they felt better. An old woman was grimly milking her cows in the middle of the field, attended by a young girl with bare feet. The old woman sat on a stool, next to her weathered farm wagon, between whose shafts stood a huge, shaggy horse. The old woman pulled slowly and defiantly at the teats of the smooth-shouldered, clean-looking cow. Overhead the shells came and went and occasionally, from what seemed like a very short distance, there was the excited rattle of machine guns, but the old woman never looked up. The girl with her was not more than sixteen years old, and was wearing a tattered green sweater. She had a red ribbon in her hair and she was interested in the soldiers.

"I think maybe I'll stop off right here," Burnecker said, "and help with the chores. Tell me how the war comes out, Ackerman."

"Keep moving, Soldier," said Noah. "Next war we'll all be in the Services of Supply."

"I love that girl," Burnecker said. "She reminds me of Iowa. Ackerman, do you know any French?"

"*A votre santé*," Noah said. "That's all I know."

"*A votre santé*," Burnecker shouted to the girl, grinning and waving his rifle, "*à votre santé*, Baby, and the same to your old lady."

The girl waved back at him, smiling.

"She's crazy about me," Burnecker said. "What did I say to her?"

"To your health."

"Hell," said Burnecker, "that's too formal. I want to tell her something intimate."

"*Je t'adore,*" said Noah, remembering it from some echo in his memory.

"What does that mean?"

"I adore you."

"That's more intimate," Burnecker said. He was near the end of the field now, and he turned and took off his helmet and bowed low, with a gallant sweep of the large metal pot. "Oh, Baby," he called thunderously, the helmet light and dashing in his huge, farmer's hand, his boyish, sunburned face grave and loving, "Oh, Baby, *je t'adore, je t'adore . . .*"

The girl smiled and waved again. "*Je t'adore, mon Americain,*" she called.

"This is the greatest country on the face of the earth," Burnecker said.

"Come on, Hot Pants," Rickett said, prodding him with a bony, sharp thumb.

"Wait for me," Burnecker howled across the green fields, across the backs of the cows so much like the cows in his native Iowa. "Wait for me, Baby, I don't know how to say it in French, wait for me, I'll be back . . ."

The old lady on the stool, without looking up, brought back her hand and smacked the girl across her buttocks, sharply. The stinging, mean sound carried to the end of the field. The girl looked down and began to cry. She ran around to the other side of the cart to hide her face.

Burnecker sighed. He put on his helmet and went through the break in the hedge to the next field.

Three hours later Colclough found Regiment and a half hour after that they were in contact with the German Army.

Six hours later, Colclough managed to get the Company surrounded.

The farmhouse, in which what was left of the Company defended itself, seemed almost to have been built for the purposes of siege. It had thick stone walls, narrow windows, a slate roof that would not catch fire, huge, rock-like timbers holding up the floors and ceilings, a pump in the kitchen, and a deep, safe cellar where the wounded could be put out of harm's way.

It could be depended upon to stand up for a long time even against artillery. So far the Germans had not used anything heavier than mortars on it, and the thirty-five men who had fallen back on the house felt, for the moment, fairly strong.

415

They fired from the windows, in hurried bursts at the momentarily seen figures among the hedges and the outhouses surrounding the main building.

In the cellar, in the light of a candle, lay four wounded and one dead, among the cider barrels. The French family whose farm this was, and who had retired to the cellar at the first shot, sat on boxes, staring silently down at the stricken men who had come so far to die in their basement. There was a man of fifty who limped from a wound he had received in the last war at the Marne, and his wife, a thin, lanky woman of his own age, and their two daughters, aged twelve and sixteen, both very ugly, and both numb with fear, who cowered between the doubtful protection of the barrels.

The Medics had all been lost earlier in the day and Lieutenant Green kept running down when he could find time to do what he could with first-aid dressings.

The farmer was not on good terms with his wife. "No," he said bitterly again and again. "Madame would not leave her boudoir, war or no war. Oh, no. Remain, she says, I will not leave my house to soldiers. Perhaps, Madame, you prefer this?"

Madame did not answer. She sat stolidly on her box, sipping at a cup of cider, looking down curiously at the faces of the wounded, beaded with cold sweat in the light of the candle.

When a machine gun that the Germans had trained on the living-room window on the first floor clattered away there was a sound of breaking glass and tumbling furniture above her head. She sipped her drink a little more quickly, but that was all.

"Women," said the farmer to the dead American at his feet. "Never listen to women. It is impossible to make them see that war is a serious matter."

On the ground floor the men had piled all the furniture against the windows, and were firing through loopholes and over cushions. Lieutenant Green shouted instructions at them from time to time, but no one paid any attention. When there was some movement to be seen through the hedges or in the clump of trees two hundred yards away, everyone on that side of the building fired, then fell back to the floor for safety.

In the dining room, at the head of a heavy oak table, Captain Colclough was sitting, his helmeted head bowed over on his hands, his pearl-handled pistol in its bright leather holster at his side. He was pale and he seemed to be sleeping. No one talked to him, and he talked to no one. Only once, when Lieutenant Green came in to see if he was still alive, he spoke. "I will need you to make out a deposition," he said. "I told Lieutenant Sorenson to maintain contact on our flank with L Company at all times. You were there when I gave him the order, you were there, weren't you?"

"Yes, Sir," said Lieutenant Green, in his high voice. "I heard you."

"We must get it down on paper," Colclough said, staring down at the worn oak table, "as soon as possible."

"Captain," said Lieutenant Green, "it's going to be dark in another hour, and if we're ever going to get out of here that's the time to try . . ."

But Captain Colclough had retired into his private dream at the farmer's dining-room table, and he did not speak, nor did he look up when Lieutenant Green spat on the carpet at his feet and walked back into the living room, where Corporal Fein had just been shot through the lungs.

Upstairs, in the bedroom of the master and mistress of the house, Rickett, Burnecker, and Noah covered a lane between the barn and the shed where a plow and a farm wagon were kept. There was a small wooden crucifix on the wall, and a stiff photograph of the farmer and his wife, rigid with responsibility on their wedding day. On another wall hung a framed poster from the French Line showing the liner *Normandie* cutting through a calm, bright blue sea.

There was a white embroidered spread on the lumpy four-poster bed, and little lace doilies on the bureau, and a china cat on the hearth.

What a place, Noah thought, as he put another clip in his rifle, to fight my first battle.

There was a prolonged burst of firing from outside. Rickett, who was standing next to one of the two windows, holding a Browning Automatic Rifle, flattened himself against the flowered wallpaper. The glass covering the *Normandie* shattered into a thousand pieces. The picture shivered on the wall, with a large hole at the water line of the great ship, but it did not fall.

Noah looked at the large, neatly made bed. He had an almost uncontrollable impulse to crawl under it. He even took a step toward it, from where he was crouched near the window. He was shivering. When he tried to move his hands, they made wide senseless circles, knocking over a small blue vase on a shawl-covered table in the center of the room.

If only he could get under the bed he would be safe. He would not die then. He could hide, in the dust on the splintery wood floor. There was no sense to this. Standing up to be shot in a tiny wallpapered room, with half the German Army all around him. It wasn't his fault he was there. He had not taken the road between the hedges, he had not lost contact with L Company, he had not neglected to halt and dig in where he

417

was supposed to, it could not be asked of him to stand at the window, next to Rickett and have his head blown in.

"Get over to that window!" Rickett was shouting, pointing wildly to the other window. "Get the hell over! The bathtards're coming in . . ."

Recklessly, Rickett was exposing himself at the window, firing in short, spraying bursts, from the hip, his arms and shoulders jerking with the recoil.

Now, thought Noah craftily, when he is not looking. I can crawl under the bed and nobody will know where I am.

Burnecker was at the other window, firing, shouting, "Noah! Noah!"

Noah took one last look at the bed. It was cool and neat and like home. The crucifix on the wall behind it suddenly leapt out from the wall, Christ in splinters, and tumbled on the bedspread.

Noah ran to the window and crouched beside Burnecker. He fired two shots blindly down into the lane. Then he looked. The gray figures were running with insane speed, crouched over, in a bunch, toward the house.

Oh, Noah thought, taking aim (the target in the center of the circle, remember, and resting on the top of the sight and even a blind man with rheumatism can't miss), oh, Noah thought, firing at the bunched figures, they shouldn't do that, they shouldn't come together like that. He fired again and again. Rickett was firing at the other window and Burnecker beside him, very deliberately, holding his breath, squeezing off. Noah heard a high, wailing scream and wondered where that was coming from. It was quite some time before he realized that it was coming from him. Then he stopped screaming.

There was a lot of firing from downstairs, too, and the gray figures kept falling and getting up and crawling and falling again. Three of the figures actually got close enough to throw hand grenades, but they missed the window and exploded harmlessly against the walls. Rickett got them all with the same burst of the gun.

The other gray figures seemed to glide to a stop. For a moment there was silence and the figures hung there, motionless, reflective, in the clayey barnyard. Then they turned and began running away.

Noah watched them with surprise. It had never occurred to him that they would not reach the house.

"Come on, come on!" Rickett was screaming. He was reloading feverishly. "Get the bathtards! Get 'em!"

Noah shook himself, then carefully aimed at a man who was running in a curious, clumsy, limping way, his gas-mask can banging on his hip and his rifle thrown away. Noah squinted, pulled the trigger gently, feeling the metal hot against the inside of his finger just as the man was turning behind the barn. The man fell in a long, sprawling slide. He did not move.

"That's it, Ackerman, that's it!" Rickett was at the window again, shouting hilariously. "That's the way to do it."

The lane was empty now, except for the gray figures that weren't moving any more.

"They've gone," Noah said stupidly. "They're not there now."

He felt a wet pressure on his cheek. Burnecker was kissing him. Burnecker was crying and laughing and kissing him.

"Get down," Rickett yelled, "get down from that window."

They ducked their heads. A second later they heard the whistle through the window. The bullets thudded into the wall below the *Normandie*.

Very nice of Rickett, Noah thought coolly, very surprising.

The door opened and Lieutenant Green came in. His eyes were granular and red and his jaw seemed to hang down with weariness. He sat on the bed, slowly, with a sigh, and put his hands between his legs. He wavered back and forth minutely, and, for a moment, Noah was afraid he was going to fall back onto the bed and go to sleep.

"We fixed 'em, Lieutenant," Rickett said, happily. "We gave 'em a good dose. Right up the old dog."

"Yes," said Lieutenant Green in his squeaky voice, "we did very well. Anybody hurt up here?"

"Not in thith room." Rickett grinned. "Thith is a rugged team up here."

"Morrison and Seeley got it in the other room," Green said wearily, "and Fein has one in the lungs downstairs."

Noah remembered Fein in the hospital ward in Florida, enormous, bullnecked, hard, saying, "After the war you can pick whatever company you please . . ."

"However . . ." Green said with sudden brightness, as though he were beginning a speech. "However . . ." Then he looked vaguely about the room. "Isn't that the *Normandie?*" he asked.

"Yes," said Noah, "it's the *Normandie*."

Green smiled foolishly. "I think I will sign up for a cruise," he said.

The men did not laugh.

"However," Green said, passing his hand across his eyes, "when it gets dark, we're going to make a break. We're almost out of ammunition downstairs, and if they try again, we're fried. French-fried with ketchup," he said vaguely. "You're on your own when it gets dark. Twos and threes, twos and threes," he chanted squeakily, "the Company will dissolve into twos and threes."

"Lieutenant," Rickett said, from the window, where he was

still peering out, with just a thin slice of his face exposed past the window-frame, "Lieutenant, is thith an order from Captain Colcough?"

"This is an order from Lieutenant Green," the Lieutenant said. He giggled. Then he caught himself and looked firm. "I have assumed command," he said formally. "Command."

"Is the Captain dead?" Rickett asked.

"Not exactly," said Green. He lay back suddenly on the white spread and closed his eyes. But he continued talking. "The Captain has retired for the season. He will be ready for next year's invasion." He giggled, lying, with his eyes closed, on the lumpy featherbed. Then, suddenly, he sprang up. "Did you hear anything?" he asked anxiously.

"No," said Rickett.

"Tanks," said Green. "If they bring up tanks before it gets dark, French-fried with ketchup."

"We have a bazooka and two shells in here," Rickett said.

"Don't make me laugh." Green turned and stared at the *Normandie.* "A friend of mine once took that boat," he said. "An insurance man from New Orleans, Louisiana. Got laid by three different women between Cherbourg and Ambrose Light. By all means," he said gravely, "by all means use the bazooka. That's what it's for, isn't it?" He got down on his hands and knees and crawled to the window. Slowly he lifted his head and peered out. "I can see fourteen dead Krauts," he said. "What do you think the live ones are planning now?" He shook his head sadly, then crawled away from the window. He had to hold onto Noah's leg to pull himself up to his feet. "The whole Company," he said wonderingly, "the whole Company is *fini.* One day. One day of combat. It doesn't seem possible, does it? You'd think someone would have done something about it, wouldn't you? When it gets dark, remember, you're on your own, try to get back to our own lines. Good luck."

He went downstairs. The men in the room looked at one another. "All right," Rickett said sourly, "you ain't hurt yet. Get up to those windows."

In the dining room downstairs, Jamison was standing in front of Captain Colclough and yelling. Jamison had been next to Seeley when he was hit in the eye. Jamison and Seeley were from the same town in Kentucky. They had been friends since they were boys, and had enlisted together.

"I'm not going to let you do it, you goddamn undertaker!" Jamison was yelling wildly to the Captain who still sat at the dark table with his head despairingly in his hands. Jamison had just heard that they were to leave Seeley in the cellar with the rest of the wounded, when they made the break at dark. "You got us in here, you get us out! All of us!"

Three other soldiers were in the room now, staring dully at Jamison and the Captain, but not interfering.

"Come on, you coffin-polishing son of a bitch," Jamison yelled, swaying slowly back and forth over the table, "don't just sit there. Get up and say something. You said plenty back in England, didn't you? You were a big man with a speech when nobody was shooting at you, weren't you, you bloody embalmer. Going to make Major by the Fourth of July! Major with the firecrackers. Take that goddamn toy gun off I can't stand that gun!"

Crazily, Jamison bent over and took the pearl-handled forty-five out of the holster and threw it into a corner. Then he ripped clumsily at the holster. He couldn't get it off. He took out his bayonet and cut it away with the belt with savage, inaccurate strokes. He threw the shiny holster on the floor and stamped on it. Captain Colclough did not move. The other soldiers continued to stand stupidly along the scroll-work oak buffet against the wall. "We were going to kill more Krauts than anybody else in the Division, weren't we, morgue-hound? That's what we came to Europe for, wasn't it? You were going to make sure that everybody did his share, weren't you? How many Germans have you killed today, you son of a bitch? Come on, come on, stand up, stand up!" Jamison grabbed Colclough and pulled him to his feet. Colclough continued to look dazedly down at the surface of the table. When Jamison stepped back, Colclough slid down to the floor and lay there. "Make a speech, Captain!" Jamison screamed, standing over him, prodding Colclough with his boot. "Make a speech now. Give us a lecture on how to lose a company a day in combat. Make a speech on how to leave the wounded for the Germans. Give us a speech on map-reading and military courtesy, I'm dying to hear it. Go on down to the cellar and give Seeley, a speech on first aid and tell him to see the Chaplain about the slug in his eye. Come on, give us a speech, tell us how a Major protects his flanks in an advance, tell us how well prepared we are, tell us how we're the best-equipped soldiers in the world!"

Lieutenant Green came in. "Get out of here, Jamison," Lieutenant Green said calmly. "All of you get back to your posts."

"I want the Captain to make a speech," Jamison said stubbornly. "Just a little speech for me and the boys downstairs."

"Jamison," Lieutenant Green said, his voice squeaky but armed with authority, "get back to your post. That's a direct order."

There was silence in the room. Outside, the German machine gun fired several bursts, and they could hear the bullets whining around the walls. Jamison fingered the catch of his rifle. "Behave yourself," Green said, like a schoolteacher to a class of children. "Go on out and behave yourself."

Jamison slowly turned and went out the door. The other three men followed him. Lieutenant Green looked down soberly at Captain Colclough, lying quietly, stretched out on his side, on the floor. Lieutenant Green did not offer to pick the Captain off the floor.

It was nearly dark when Noah saw the tank. It moved ponderously down the lane, the long snout of its gun poking blindly before it.

"Here it comes," Noah said, without moving, his eyes just over the windowsill.

The tank seemed to be momentarily stuck. Its treads spun, digging into the soft clay, and its machine guns waved erratically back and forth. It was the first German tank Noah had seen, and as he watched it he felt almost hypnotized. It was so large, so impregnable, so full of malice . . . Now, he felt, there is nothing to be done. He was despairing and relieved at the same time. Now, there was nothing more that could be done. The tank took everything out of his hands, all decisions, all responsibilities . . .

"Come on over here," Rickett said. "You. Ackerman."

Noah jumped over to the window where Rickett was standing, holding the bazooka. "I'm gahnta see," Rickett said, "if these gahdamn gadgets're worth a fart."

Noah crouched at the window, and Rickett put the barrel of the bazooka on his shoulder. Noah was exposed at the window, but he had a curious sensation of not caring. With the tank there, so close, in the lane, everybody in the house was equally exposed. He breathed evenly, and waited patiently while Rickett maneuvered the bazooka around on his shoulder.

"They got some riflemen waiting behind the tank," Noah said calmly. "About fifteen of them."

"They're in for a little thuprise," Rickett said. "Stand still."

"I am standing still," Noah said, irritated.

Rickett was fussing with the mechanism. The bazooka would have to throw about eighty yards to reach the tank, and Rickett was being very careful. "Don't fire," he told Burnecker at the other window. "Let's uth pretend we are not present up here." He chuckled. Noah was only mildly surprised at Rickett's chuckling.

The tank started again. It moved ponderously, disdaining to fire, as though there was an intelligence there that understood its paralyzing moral effect that hardly needed the overt act of explosion to win its purpose. After a few yards it stopped again. The Germans behind it crouched for protection close to its rear treads.

The machine gun farther off opened fire, spraying the whole side of the building loosely.

"For Christ's sake," Rickett said, "stand still."

Noah braced himself rigidly against the window frame. He was sure that he was going to be shot in a moment. His entire body from the waist up was fully exposed in the window. He stared down at the waving guns of the tank, obscure in the growing shadows of dusk in the lane.

Then Rickett fired. The bazooka shell moved very deliberately through the air. Then it exploded against the tank. Noah watched from the window, forgetting to get down. Nothing seemed to happen for a moment. Then the cannon swung heavily downwards, stopped, pointing at the ground. There was an explosion inside the tank, muffled and deep. Some wisps of smoke came up through the driver's slits and the edges of the hatch. Then there were many more explosions. The tank rocked and quivered where it stood. Then the explosions stopped. The tank still looked as dangerous and full of malice as before, but it did not move. Noah saw the infantrymen behind it running. They ran down the lane, with no one firing at them, and disappeared behind the edge of the shed.

"It works, Ah reckon," Rickett said. "Ah think we have shot ourselves a tank." He took the bazooka off Noah's shoulder and put it against the wall.

Noah continued to stare out at the lane. It was as though nothing had happened, as though the tank were a permanent part of the landscape that had been there for years.

"For Christ's sake, Noah," Burnecker was yelling, and then Noah realized that Burnecker had been shouting his name again and again, "get away from that window."

Suddenly, feeling in terrible danger, Noah jumped away from the window.

Rickett took his place at the window, holding his BAR again. "Nuts," Rickett was saying angrily, "we shouldn't ought to leave this here farm. We could stay here till Christmas. That fairy diaper salesman Green ain't got the guts of a turd-bug." He fired from the hip out into the lane. "Get back there," he muttered to himself. "Stay away from my tank."

Lieutenant Green came into the room. "Come on downstairs," he said. "It's getting dark. We're going to start out in a couple of minutes."

"I'll stay heah for a spell," Rickett said disdainfully, "jest to see that the Krauts keep a proper dithtance." He waved to Noah and Burnecker. "You-all go on ahead now and take off like a big-assed bird if they spot you."

Noah and Burnecker looked at each other. They wanted to say something to Rickett, standing scornfully at the window, the BAR loose in his big hands, but they didn't know what to say. Rickett didn't look at them as they went through the door and followed Lieutenant Green downstairs to the living room.

423

The living room smelled of sweat and gunpowder and there were hundreds of spent cartridges lying on the floor, crushed out of shape by the feet of the defenders. The living room looked more like a war than the bedroom upstairs. The furniture was piled on end against the windows and the wooden chairs were broken and splintered and the men were kneeling on the floor against the walls. In the twilit gloom Noah saw Colclough lying on the floor in the dining room. He was lying on his back, his arms rigid at his sides, his eyes staring unblinkingly at the ceiling. His nose was running, and from time to time he sniffed sharply, but that was the only sound from him. His sniffing made Noah remember that he had a cold, too, and he blew his nose on the sweaty khaki handkerchief he fished out of his back pocket.

It was very quiet in the living room. A single fly buzzed irritably around the room, and Riker swiped at it savagely twice with his helmet, but missed each time.

Noah sat down on the floor and took off his right legging and shoe. Very carefully he smoothed out his sock. It was very satisfactory to rub his foot gently with his fingers and pull the sock straight. The other men in the room watched him soberly as though he were performing an intricate and immensely interesting act. Noah put his shoe on. Then he put the legging back and laced it meticulously, blousing the trouser leg carefully over the top. He sneezed twice, loudly, and he saw Riker jump a little at the noise.

"God bless you," Burnecker said. He grinned at Noah and Noah grinned back. What a wonderful man, Noah thought.

"I can't tell you people what to do," Lieutenant Green said suddenly. He was crouching near the entrance to the dining room, and he spoke as though he had been preparing a speech in the silence, but then had been surprised at hearing his own voice coming out so abruptly. "I cannot tell you which is the best way to try to get back. Your guess is as good as mine. You'll see the flashes of the guns at night, and you'll hear them during the day, so you should have a good general idea of where our own people are. But maps won't do you any good, and you'd better keep off the roads as much as possible. The smaller the groups the better chance you'll have of getting back. I'm sorry it's worked out this way, but I'm afraid if we just sat here and waited, we'd all end up in the bag. This way, some of us are bound to get through." He sighed. "Maybe a lot of us," he said with transparent cheerfulness, "maybe most of us. The wounded're as comfortable as we can make them, and the French people downstairs are trying to take care of them. If anybody has any doubts," he said defensively, "he can go down and look for himself."

Nobody moved. From upstairs came the ripping, hurried

sound of a BAR. Rickett, thought Noah, standing there at the window.

"However . . ." Lieutenant Green said vaguely . . . "However . . . It's too bad. But you have to expect things like this. Things like this are bound to happen from time to time. I will try to take the Captain back with me. With me," he repeated, in his weary, thin voice. "If anybody wants to say something, let him say it now . . ."

Nobody wanted to say anything. Noah suddenly felt very sad.

"Well," said Lieutenant Green, "it's dark." He got up and went to the window, and looked out. "Yes," he said, "it's dark." He turned back to the men in the room. By now many of them were sitting on the floor, their backs against the walls, their heads drooped between their shoulders. They reminded Noah of a football team between halves, in a losing game.

"Well," said Lieutenant Green, "there's no sense in putting it off. Who wants to go first?"

Nobody moved. Nobody looked around.

"Be careful," Lieutenant Green said, "when you reach our own lines. Don't expose yourselves before you're absolutely sure they know you're Americans. You don't want to get shot by your own men. Who wants to go first?"

Nobody moved.

"My advice," said Lieutenant Green, "is to leave through the kitchen door. There's a shed back there that'll give you some cover and the hedge isn't more than thirty yards away. Understand, I am not giving any orders any more. It's entirely up to you. Somebody had better go now . . ."

Nobody moved. Intolerable, thought Noah, sitting on the floor, intolerable. He stood up. "All right," he said, because somebody had to say it. "Me." He sneezed.

Burnecker stood up. "I'm going," he said.

Riker stood up. "What the hell," he said.

Cowley and Demuth got up. Their shoes made a sliding sound on the stone floor. "Where's the goddamn kitchen?" Cowley said.

Riker, Cowley, Demuth, Noah thought. There was something about those names. Oh, he thought, we can fight all over again now.

"Enough," Green said. "Enough for the first batch."

The five men went into the kitchen. None of the other men looked up at them and nobody spoke. The trap door to the cellar was open in the kitchen floor. The light of the candle came up dimly through the dusty air, and the bubbling, groaning sound of Fein dying. Noah did not look down into the cellar. Lieutenant Green opened the kitchen door very carefully. It made a harsh, grating sound. The men held still for a moment.

425

From above there came the sound of the BAR. Rickett, Noah thought, fighting the war on his own hook.

The night air smelled damp and farmlike, with the sweet heavy smell of cows coming through the crack of the open door.

Noah muffled a sneeze in his hand. He looked around apologetically.

"Good luck," Lieutenant Green said. "Who's going?"

The men, bunched in the kitchen among the copper pans and the big milk containers, looked at the slight pale edge of night that showed between the door and the frame. Intolerable. Noah thought again, intolerable, we can't stand here like this. He pushed his way past Riker to the door.

He took a deep breath, thinking, I must not sneeze, I must not sneeze. Then he bent over and slid through the opening.

He made for the shed. He placed his feet very carefully and held his rifle in both his hands so that it wouldn't bang against anything. He kept his finger off the trigger because he could not remember whether the safety was off or not. He hoped the men behind him had the safeties on their rifles, so that if they stumbled they wouldn't shoot him.

His shoes made a sucking sound in the barnyard earth and he could feel his helmet straps slapping against his cheeks. The sound was flat and seemed very loud so close to his ears. When he got to the shadow of the shed in the deeper shadow of the night, he leaned against the cow-smelling wood and hooked the catch under his chin. One by one the thick shadows moved across the yard from the kitchen door. The breathing of the men all around him seemed immensely loud and labored. From inside the house, from the cellar, there was a long, high scream. Noah tensed against the shed wall as the scream echoed through the windless evening air, but nothing else happened.

Then he got down on his belly and started to crawl toward the hedge, which was outlined faintly against the sky. In the distance, far behind it, there was the small flicker of artillery.

There was a ditch alongside the hedge and Noah slid down into it and waited, trying to breathe lightly and regularly. The noise of the men coming after him seemed dangerously loud, but there was no way of signaling them to keep more quiet. One by one they slid in beside him. Grouped together like this, in the wet grass of the ditch, their combined breathing seemed to make a whistling announcement of their presence there. They didn't move. They lay in the ditch, piled against one another. Noah realized that each one was waiting for someone else to lead them on.

They want me to do it, Noah thought, resenting them. Why should it have to be me?

But he roused himself and peered through the hedge toward the artillery flashes. There was an open field on the other side. Dimly in the darkness, Noah could see shapes moving around, but he couldn't tell whether they were cattle or men. Anyway, it was impossible to get through the hedge here without making a racket. Noah touched the leg of the man nearest him, to indicate that he was moving, and wriggled down the ditch, alongside the hedge, away from the farmhouse. One by one, the men crawled after him.

Noah crawled slowly, stopping and listening every five yards, feeling the sweat soaking his body. The hedge was solid, murmuring slightly in an uneasy rustle of wind above him, and there was an occasional small scurry as a tiny animal flickered past in fright, and once there was the hollow drumming of wings from a tree as a disturbed bird rocketed up from the branches. Still there was no sign of the Germans.

Maybe, Noah was thinking as he crawled, smelling the loamy, decayed odor from the wet ditch, maybe we're going to make it.

Then he put his hand out and touched something hard. He remained rigid, motionless, except for his right hand, with which he made a slow, exploratory movement. It's round, he thought, it's made out of metal, it's . . . Then his hand felt something wet and sticky and Noah realized that it was a dead man in the ditch in front of him, and he had been feeling the man's helmet, then his face, and that the man had been hit in the face.

He backed up a little and turned his head.

"Burnecker," he whispered.

"What?" Burnecker's voice seemed to come from far away, and from a throat near strangling.

"In front of me," Noah whispered. "A stiff."

"What? I can't hear you."

"A stiff. A dead man," whispered Noah.

"Who is he?"

"Goddammit," Noah whispered, furious with Burnecker for being so dull. "How the hell do I know?" Then he nearly laughed, at the idiocy of the conversation carried on this way. "Pass the word back," Noah whispered.

"What?"

Noah hated Burnecker, deeply, bitterly. "Pass the word back," Noah said more loudly. "So they won't do anything foolish."

"O.K." said Burnecker, "O.K."

Noah could hear the dry rattle of the whispers going back and forth behind him.

"All right," Burnecker said finally. "They all got it."

Noah slowly crawled over the dead body. His hands rested

427

on the man's boots, and Noah realized suddenly that it was a German, because Americans didn't wear boots. He nearly stopped to tell the others what he had learned. He felt much better about it, knowing that the corpse was not one of theirs. Then he remembered that paratroopers wore boots, too, and it might be a paratrooper. Still crawling, he puzzled it out, and the mental effort kept him from being too tired or frightened. No, he decided, paratroopers have lace boots and these were not laced. A Kraut. One dead Kraut lying in a ditch. He should have realized by the shape of the helmet. Except that helmets were very much alike, and he'd never touched a German helmet before.

He came to the end of the field. The ditch and the hedge made a right angle and ran along the edge of the field. Cautiously Noah pushed his hand out ahead of him. There was a small break in the hedge, and a narrow road on the other side of it. They would have to cross the road eventually; they might as well do it now.

Noah turned back to Burnecker. "Listen," he whispered, "I'm going through the hedge here."

"O.K.," Burnecker whispered.

"There's a road on the other side."

"O.K."

Then there was the sound of men walking softly on the road, and the metallic jangling of equipment. Noah put his hand across Burnecker's mouth. They listened. It sounded like three or four men on the road and they were talking to one another as they walked slowly past. They were talking German. Noah listened, cocking his head tensely, as though, despite the fact that he could not understand a word of German, anything he could overhear would be of great value to him.

The Germans went past in a steady, easy pace, like sentries who would come back again very shortly. Their voices faded in the rustling night, but Noah could hear the sound of their boots for a long time.

Riker, Demuth and Cowley crawled up to where Noah was leaning against the side of the ditch.

"Let's get across the road," Noah whispered.

"The hell with it." Noah recognized Demuth's voice, hoarse now and trembling. "You want to go, go ahead. I'm staying here. Right in this here ditch."

"They'll pick you up in the morning. As soon as it gets light . . ." Noah said urgently, feeling illogically responsible for getting Demuth and the others across the road, because he had been leading them so far. "You can't stay here."

"No?" said Demuth. "Watch me. Anybody wants to get his ass shot off out there, go do it. Without me."

Then Noah understood that when Demuth had heard the

German voices, confident and open, on the other side of the hedge, he had given up. Demuth was out of the war. The despair or courage that had carried him the two hundred yards from the farmhouse had given out. Maybe he's right, Noah thought, maybe it is the sensible thing to do . . .

"Noah . . ." It was Burnecker's voice, controlled, anxious. "What're you going to do?"

"Me?" said Noah. Then, because he knew Burnecker was depending on him . . . "I'm going through the hedge," he whispered. "I don't think Demuth ought to stay here." He waited for one of the other men to whisper something to Demuth. Nobody whispered anything.

"O.K.," Noah said. He started through the hedge. He got through it quietly, with the wet branches flicking drops of water on his face. The road suddenly seemed very wide. It was badly rutted, too, and the rubber soles of his shoes slipped in the middle and he nearly fell. There was a soft jangle of metal as he lurched to right himself, but there was nothing else to do but go forward. He could see a break in the hedge where a tank had gone through and broken down the wiry boughs and sharp green leaves. The break was fifteen yards or so down the road, and he walked crouched over, near the edge of the road, feeling naked and exposed. He could hear the other men crouching behind him. He thought of Demuth, lying alone on the other side of the road, and he wondered how Demuth was feeling at that moment, solitary and full of surrender, waiting for the first light of dawn and the first German who looked as though he had heard of the Geneva Convention.

Far behind him he heard the clatter of the BAR. Rickett, who never surrendered anything, cursing and killing at the upstairs bedroom window.

Then a tommygun opened up. It sounded as though it was no more than twenty yards away, and the flashes were plain and savage in front of them. There were shouts in German, and other guns opened fire. Noah could hear the nervous whining of the bullets around his head as he ran, noisily and swiftly, to the opening in the hedge and hurled himself through it. He could hear the other men running behind him, their feet drumming wildly on the clay, and thrashing heavily through the stubborn barrier of the hedge. The firing grew in volume, and there were tracers from a hundred yards down the road, but the tracers were far over their heads. Somehow it gave Noah a sense of comfort and security, to see the wasted ammunition flaming through the branches of the trees.

He was out in a field now. He ran straight across the field, with the others after him. Tracers were crisscrossing in front of him aimlessly, and there were loud surprised shouts in German off to the left, but there didn't seem to be any really aimed fire anywhere near them. Noah could feel his breath soggy and burning in his lungs, and he seemed to be running with painful slowness. Mines, he remembered hazily, there are mines all over Normandy. Then he saw some moving figures loom in the darkness ahead of him and he nearly fired, on the run. But the figures made a low animal sound and he got a glimpse of horns rearing up to the sky. Then he was running among four or five cows, away from the firing, being jostled by the wet flanks, smelling the heavy milky odor. Then a cow was hit and went down. He stumbled over it and lay on the other side of it. The cow kicked convulsively and tried to get up, but couldn't manage it, and rolled over again. The other men fled past Noah, and Noah got up again and ran after them.

His lungs were sobbing again and it didn't seem possible that he could take another step. But he ran, standing straight up now, regardless of the bullets, because the biting, driving pain across his middle did not permit him to bend over any more.

He passed first one racing figure, then another and another. He could hear the other men's breath, sawing in their nostrils. Even as he ran he was surprised that he could move so fast, out-distance the others.

The thing was to get across the field to the other line of hedges, the other ditch, before the Germans turned a light on them . . .

But the Germans were not in any mood to light up any part of the country that night, and their fire diminished vaguely and sporadically. Noah trotted the last twenty yards to the line of hedge rising blackly against the sky, with trees rearing up at spaced intervals from the thick foliage. He threw himself to the ground. He lay there, panting, the air whistling crookedly into his lungs. One by one the other men threw themselves down beside him. They all lay there, face down, gripping the wet earth, fighting for breath, unable to speak. Above their heads there was a whining arch of tracers. Then the tracers suddenly veered and came down in the other corner of the field. There was a frantic bellowing and thumping of hooves from that end of the field and a shout in German, distant and angry, and the machine gunner stopped killing the cows.

Then there was silence, broken only by the dry gasping of the four men.

After a long while, Noah sat up. There, registered some distant, untouched, calculating part of his brain, I'm the first one again. Riker, Cowley, he thought with a remote childishness that had nothing to do with the sweaty, heaving man sitting bent over on the dark ground, Riker, Cowley, Demuth, Rickett, they'll have to apologize to me for the things they did in Florida . . .

"Well," Noah said coolly, "let's go on down to the PX."

One by one the men sat up. They looked around them. There was no sound and no movement in the darkness. From the farmhouse there was a snarling, challenging burst from Rickett's BAR, but it seemed to have no connection to them. There was an air raid going on far in the distance. The bright scratch of shells in the black sky and the occasional brief flare of an explosion looked like fireworks in an old silent picture. The Germans are raiding the beach, it must be the Germans, because we don't fly at night over here, thought Noah. He was pleased at the accurate, helpful way his mind was taking in impressions and interpreting them. All we have to do is keep moving in that direction, keep moving, that's all we have to do . . .

"Burnecker," Noah whispered crisply, as he stood up, "take hold of my belt with one hand, and Cowley, you hold Burnecker's, and Riker, you hold Cowley's, so we don't get lost."

Obediently, the men stood up and took hold of each other's belts. Then, in single file, with Noah in front, they started out through the darkness toward the long fiery pencil-lines on the horizon.

It was just at dawn that they saw the prisoners. It was light enough so that it was no longer necessary to hold onto each other's belts, and they were lying behind a hedge, getting ready to cross a narrow paved road, when they heard the steady, unmistakable shuffle of feet drawing near.

A moment later the column of about sixty Americans came into view. They were walking slowly, in a shambling careless way, with six Germans with tommyguns guarding them. They passed within ten feet of Noah. He looked closely at their faces. There was a mixture of shame and relief on the faces, and a kind of numbness, half involuntary, half deliberate. The men did not look at the guards or at each other, or at the surrounding countryside. They shuffled through the wet light in a kind of slow inner reflection, the irregular soft scuffing of their shoes the only sound accompanying them. They walked more easily than other soldiers, because they had no rifles, no packs, no equipment. Even as he watched, so close by, Noah felt the strangeness of seeing sixty Americans walking down a road in a kind of formation, with their hands in their pockets, unarmed and unburdened.

They passed and vanished down the road, the sound of their marching dying slowly among the dewy hedges.

Noah turned and looked at the men beside him. They were still looking, their heads lifted, at the spot where the prisoners

431

had disappeared. There was no expression on Burnecker's face or on Cowley's, just an overlay, a film, a fascination and interest. But Riker looked queer. Noah stared at him, and after a moment he realized that what he saw on Riker's face, in the red, pouched eyes, under the muddy stubble of his beard, was the same mixture of shame and relief that had been on all the faces that had passed.

"I'm going to tell you guys something," Riker said huskily, in a voice that was very different from his normal voice. "We're doing this all wrong." He did not look at Noah or the others, but continued to stare down the road. "We ain't got a chance like this, four of us all together. Only way is to divide up. One by one. One by one." He stopped. Nobody said anything.

Riker stared down the road. Faintly, half-heard, half-remembered, there was the shush-shush of the prisoners' marching. "It's a question of being sensible," Riker said hoarsely. "Four guys together're just a big fat target. One guy alone can really hide. I don't know what you're going to do, but I'm going my separate way." Riker waited for them to say something, but nobody spoke. They lay in the wet grass close to the hedge, no expression on their faces.

"Well," said Riker, "there's no time like the present." He straightened up. He hesitated for a moment. Then he climbed through the hedge. He stood at the edge of the road, still half bent over. He looked large and bear-like, with his thick arms hanging loosely down, his blackened, powerful hands near his knees. Then he started down the road in the direction in which the prisoners had gone.

Noah and the other two men watched him. As he walked, Riker grew more erect. There was something queer about him, Noah thought, and he tried to figure out what it was. Then, when Riker was fifty feet away, and walking more swiftly, more eagerly, Noah realized what it was. Riker was unarmed. Noah glanced down where Riker had been crouched. The Garand was lying on the grass, its muzzle carelessly jammed with dirt.

Noah looked up at Riker again. The big, shambling figure, with the helmet square on the head over the huge shoulders, was moving fast by now, almost running. As Riker reached the first turn in the road, his hands went up, tentatively. Then they froze firmly above his head, and that was the last Noah saw of Riker, trotting around the bend, with his hands high above his head.

"Cross off one rifleman," Burnecker said. He reached down to the Garand and automatically took out the clip and pulled the bolt to eject the cartridge in the chamber. He reached down and picked up the cartridge and put it in his pocket along with the clip.

432

Noah stood up and Burnecker followed him. Cowley hesitated. Then, with a sigh, he stood up, too.

Noah went through the hedge and crossed the road. The other two men came after him quickly.

From the distance, from the direction of the coast, the sound of the guns was a steady rumbling. At least, Noah thought, as he moved slowly and carefully along the hedge, at least the Army is still in France.

The barn and the house next to it seemed deserted. There were two dead cows lying with their feet up in the barnyard, beginning to swell, but the large gray stone building looked peaceful and safe as they peered at it above the rim of the ditch in which they were lying.

They were exhausted by now and moved, in their crawling, creeping, crouched-over progress, in a dull, dope-like stupor. Noah was sure that if they had to run, he could never manage it. They had seen Germans several times, and heard them often, and once Noah was sure two Germans on a motorcycle had glimpsed them as they hurled themselves down to the ground. But the Germans had merely slowed down a little, glanced their way, and had kept moving. It was hard to know whether it was fear or arrogant indifference on the part of the Germans which had kept them from coming after them.

Cowley was breathing very hard each time he moved, the air snoring into his nostrils, and he had fallen twice climbing fences. He had tried to throw away his rifle, too, and Noah and Burnecker had had to argue with him for ten minutes to make him agree not to leave it behind him. Burnecker had carried the rifle, along with his own, for a half hour, before Cowley had asked for it again.

They had to rest. They hadn't slept in two days and they had had nothing to eat since the day before, and the barn and the house looked promising.

"Take off your helmets and leave them here," Noah said. "Stand up straight. And walk slowly."

There was about fifty yards of open field to cross to the barn. If anyone happened to see them, they might be taken for Germans if they walked naturally. By now Noah was automatically making the decisions and giving the orders. The others obeyed without question.

They all stood up, and carrying their rifles slung over their shoulders, they walked as normally as possible toward the barn. The air of stillness and emptiness around the buildings was intensified by the sound of firing in the distance. The barn door was open, and they passed the odor of the dead cows and went in. Noah looked around. There was a ladder climbing through the dusty gloom to a hayloft above.

433

"Go on up," said Noah.

Cowley went first, taking a long time. Then Burnecker silently went after Cowley. Noah grabbed the rungs of the ladder and took a deep breath. He looked up. There were twelve rungs. He shook his head. The twelve rungs looked impossible. He started up, resting on each rung. The wood was splintery and old and the barn smell got heavier and dustier as he neared the top. He sneezed and nearly fell off. At the top he waited a long time, gathering strength to throw himself onto the floor of the loft. Burnecker knelt beside him and put his hands under Noah's armpits. He pulled, hard, and Noah threw himself upward and onto the hayloft floor, surprised and grateful for Burnecker's strength. He sat up and crawled over to the small window at the end of the loft. He looked out. From the height he could see some activity, trucks and small, quickly moving figures about five hundred yards away, but it all looked remote and undangerous.

There was a fire burning about a half mile off, too, a farmhouse slowly smoldering, but that, too, seemed normal and of no consequence. He turned away from the window, blinking his eyes. Burnecker and Cowley faced him inquisitively.

"We've found a home in the Army," Noah said. He grinned foolishly, feeling what he said had been clever and inspiring. "I don't know what you're going to do, but I'm going to get some sleep."

He put down his rifle carefully and stretched out on the floor. He closed his eyes, hearing Cowley and Burnecker making themselves comfortable. He fell asleep. Ten seconds later he woke up, feeling straw tickling his neck. He moved his head in a little, sharp jerk, as though he had forgotten how to control his muscles. Two shells landed near by, and he had a slight uncomfortable feeling that one of them ought to stand guard while the others slept, and he told himself that in another moment he was going to sit up and discuss it with Burnecker and Cowley. Then he fell asleep again.

It was nearly dark when he woke up. A strange heavy clatter was filling the barn, shaking the timbers and rattling the floors. For a long while Noah did not move. It was luxurious and sweet to lie on the wispy straw, smelling the dry fragrance of old harvests and departed farm animals, and not move, not think, not wonder what the noise was, not worry about being hungry or thirsty or far from home. He turned his head, Burnecker and Cowley were still sleeping. Cowley was snoring, but Burnecker slept quietly. His face, in the dimness of the twilit loft, was childish and relaxed. Noah could feel himself smiling tenderly at Burnecker's calm, trusting sleep. Then Noah remembered where he was and the noises outside began to make sense to him. There were heavy trucks going past and creaking wagons pulled by many horses.

Noah sat up slowly. He crawled over to the window and looked out. German trucks were going past, with men sitting silently on top of them, through a gap in the hedge to the next field. There, other trucks and wagons were being loaded with ammunition, and Noah realized that what he was looking at was a large ammunition dump, and that now, in the growing darkness, when they were safe from the Air Force, German artillery outfits were drawing their ammunition for the next day. He watched, squinting to pierce the haze and the darkness, while men hurriedly and silently swung the long, picnic-like baskets containing the 88 millimeter shells into the trucks and wagons. It was so strange to see so many horses, like visitors from older wars. It seemed old-fashioned and undangerous, all the big heavy patient animals, with men standing holding the reins at their heads.

My, he thought automatically, they would like to know about this dump back at Divisional Artillery. He searched through his pockets and found the stub of a pencil. He had used it on the landing craft, how many days ago was it, writing a letter to Hope. It had seemed then like a good way of forgetting where he was, forgetting the shells searching across the water for him, but he had not got far with the letter. *Dearest, I think of you all the time* (routine, flat, you'd think that at a moment like that you would write something more profound, come forth with some deep-hidden secret that never before had been expressed). *We are going into action very soon, or maybe you could say we were in action now, except it's hard to believe you could be sitting writing a letter to your wife in the middle of a battle* . . . Then he hadn't been able to write any more, because his hand began to jump, and he had to put the letter and the pencil away. He looked through his pockets for the letter now, but he couldn't find it. He got out his wallet and took out the picture of Hope and the baby. He turned it over. On the back, in Hope's handwriting, "Picture of worried mother and unworried child."

Noah stared out the window. On a direct line with the dump, perhaps a half mile away, there was a church steeple. Carefully he drew a tiny map, putting in the steeple and marking the distance. Five hundred yards to the west there was a cluster of four houses and he put that in. He looked at his map critically. It would do. If he ever got back to their own lines it would do. He watched the men methodically loading the straw baskets under the protecting trees, eight hundred yards from the church, five hundred yards from the four houses. There was an asphalt road on the other side of the field in which the dump was situated, and he put that in, being careful about the way the road curved. He slipped the picture into his wallet. With fresh interest, he peered out across the countryside. Some of the wagons and trucks were turning into a dirt road that crossed the asphalt road six hundred yards away. Noah lost sight of them behind a clump of trees, and they did not reappear on the other side of the trees. There must be a battery in there, he thought. Later on, he could go down and see for himself. That would make interesting news for Division, too.

He felt impatient now, and energetic. It was intolerable just to sit here with all this information in his pocket, while just five miles away, perhaps, the Division's guns were firing blindly and wastefully into empty fields. He moved away from the window and went over to where Burnecker and Cowley were sleeping. He bent over to wake Burnecker up, but then stopped himself. It would not be dark enough to leave the barn for another fifteen minutes. They might as well get the extra rest.

Noah crossed back to the window. A heavy wagon was rolling past just beneath him. A soldier was leading the team slowly, the horses' heads bobbing powerfully up and down. Two other soldiers were walking alongside, looking like farmers coming thoughtfully home from their fields after a day's work. They did not look up, but kept their eyes on the ground in front of them, as they walked beside the creaking wagon. One of the soldiers had his arm up, his hand resting on the side of the wagon for support.

The wagon creaked on toward the ammunition dump. Noah shook his head and went over and woke Burnecker and Cowley.

They were on the edge of a canal. It was not very wide, but there was no telling how deep it was, and the oily surface gleamed dangerously in the moonlight. They lay about ten yards back from the bank, behind some bushes, looking doubtfully across the rippling water. It was low tide and the bank on the other side showed dark and damp above the water. As nearly as they could tell, the night had nearly worn away and dawn would break very shortly.

Cowley had complained when Noah had led them close to the concealed battery, but he had stuck with them. "Goddammit," he had whispered bitterly, "this is a hell of a time to go chasing medals." But Burnecker had backed Noah, and Cowley had stuck.

But now, lying in the wet grass, looking across the silent band of water, Cowley said suddenly, "Not for me. I can't swim."

"I can't swim, either," said Burnecker.

A machine gun opened up from somewhere across the canal, and some tracers looped over their heads.

Noah sighed and closed his eyes. It was one of their own guns across the canal, because it was firing toward them, and it was so close, twenty yards of water, no more, and they couldn't swim . . . He could almost feel the photograph in his wallet, with the map on back of it, with the position of the dump, the battery, a small reserve tank park they had passed, all marked accurately on the back of the photograph, over Hope's handwriting. Twenty yards of water. It had been so long, it had taken so much out of him, if he didn't cross now, he would never make it, he might as well tear up the photograph and give himself up.

"It may not be very deep," Noah said. "The tide's out."

"I can't swim," Cowley said. His voice was stubborn and frightened.

"Burnecker," Noah said.

"I'll take a chance," Burnecker said slowly.

"Cowley . . ."

"I'll drown," Cowley whispered. "I had a dream before D Day. I drowned in the dream."

"I'll hold you," said Noah. "I can swim."

"I drowned," Cowley said. "I went under the water and drowned."

"They're just across that canal," said Noah. "Our own people."

"They'll shoot us," said Cowley. "They won't ask no questions, our own people, not our own people. They'll see us in the water and they'll spray us. And I can't swim, anyway."

Noah felt like yelling. Like going off away from Cowley, away from Burnecker, away from the canal, glinting in the moonlight, away from the random machine-gun tracers, and yelling madly at the top of his voice.

The machine gun clattered again. They all watched the tracers sail over their heads.

"That son of a bitch is nervous," Cowley said. "He won't ask no questions."

"Take off your clothes," Noah said, making his voice very calm. "All of them. In case it's deep." He started to unlace his shoes. He could tell from the sound on his right that Burnecker was beginning to undress, too.

"I'm not taking off anything," Cowley said. "I had enough of this."

"Cowley . . ." Noah began.

"I'm not talkin' to you no more. I had enough of you. I don't know what the hell you think you're doing, but I'm not doing it with you." Cowley's voice was rising hysterically. "I thought you was crazy back in Florida and I think you're even crazier now. I can't swim, I can't swim . . ." He was almost shouting now.

"Keep quiet," Noah said harshly. If he could have done it silently, he would have shot Cowley.

Cowley didn't say anything more. Noah could hear him breathing heavily in the darkness, but he didn't talk.

Methodically, Noah took off his leggings, his shoes, his jacket and trousers, the long wool underwear. He took off his shirt and pulled off the wool underwear top with the long sleeves. Then he put the shirt back on and buttoned it carefully, because his wallet was in it, with the map.

The night air curled bitterly around his bare legs. He began to shiver, long, deep spasms.

"Cowley," Noah whispered.

"Get out of here," Cowley said.

"I'm ready," Burnecker said. His voice was steady, emotionless.

Noah stood up. He started down the decline toward the canal. He heard the soft, crushing sound of Burnecker following him. The grass was very cold and slippery under his bare feet. He crouched over and moved swiftly. He did not wait when he got to the side of the canal. He dropped in, worried about the soft splash of his body. He slipped as he went in. His head went under the water and he swallowed a great draught of it. The thick, salty water made him gag, and made his head ache as it went up his nose. He scrambled around to get his feet under him and stood up, holding onto the bank. His head was above the water. Close to the bank, at least, it was only five feet deep.

He looked up. There was the pale blur of Burnecker's face, peering down at him. Then Burnecker slid in beside him.

"Hold my shoulder," Noah said. He felt the savage nervous grip of Burnecker's fingers through the wet wool of his shirt.

They started out across the canal. The bottom was slimy and Noah insanely worried about water snakes. There were mussels, too, and he had to hold himself back from crying out with pain when he stubbed his toe on the sharp edges. They walked steadily across, feeling with their feet for holes or a sudden deepening in the channel. The water was up to Noah's shoulders and he could feel the pull of the tide sweeping sluggishly in from the ocean.

The machine gun opened up and they stopped. But the bullets were far over their heads and to the right, the machine gunner aiming nervously in the general direction of the German Army. Step by step, they made their way toward the other side. Noah hoped Cowley was watching them, seeing that it could be done, that he could do it, that he didn't have to swim ... Then it got deeper. Noah had to swim, but Burnecker, who was a head taller than Noah, still had his mouth and nose out of the water, and he supported Noah, his arm and hand strong

438

under Noah's armpits. The other bank got closer and closer. It smelled rankly of salt mud and rotting shellfish, like the smell of fishing wharves back home. Still moving cautiously through the water, feeling their way, holding each other up, they peered at the bank for a place where they could climb up quickly and silently. The bank was steep ahead of them, and slippery.

"Not here," Noah whispered, "not here."

They reached the bank and rested, leaning against it.

"That dumb son of a bitch Cowley," Burnecker said.

Noah nodded, but he wasn't thinking of Cowley. He looked up and down the bank. The pull of the tide was getting stronger, gurgling against their shoulders. Noah tapped Burnecker and they started cautiously along the bank, going with the tide. The spasms of shivering were coming more violently now. Noah tried to jam his teeth together to keep his jaw steady. June, he repeated foolishly and silently deep in his brain, bathing on the French coast in the June moonlight, in the moonlight in June . . . He grinned idiotically. He had never been so cold before in his life. The bank was steep and greasy with sea moss and damp, and there was no sign that they would reach a place they could manage before it got light. Calmly, Noah thought of taking his hand from Burnecker's shoulder and floating into the middle of the canal and sinking quietly and peacefully there, once and for all . . .

"Here," Burnecker whispered.

Noah looked up. Part of the bank had crumbled away and there was a foothold there, rough and overgrown, with rounded rock edges jutting out of the dark clay.

Burnecker bent and put his hands under Noah's foot. There was a splashing, loud noise as he helped heave Noah up the bank. Noah lay for a second on the edge of the bank, panting and shivering, then he scrambled around and helped Burnecker up. An automatic weapon opened up close by and the bullets whistled past them. They ran, sliding and slipping in their bare feet, toward a rim of bushes thirty yards away. Other guns opened fire and Noah began to shout, "Stop it! Cut it out! Stop shooting! We're Americans. Company C!" he screamed, "Charley Company!"

They reached the bushes and dived down into the shelter behind them. From across the canal, the Germans were firing now, too, and flash followed flash, and Noah and Burnecker seemed to have been forgotten in the small battle they had awakened.

Five minutes later, abruptly, the firing stopped.

"I'm going to yell," Noah whispered. "Stay low."

"O.K.," Burnecker said quietly.

"Don't shoot," Noah called, not very loud, trying to keep

his voice steady. "Don't shoot. There are two of us here. Americans. C Company. Company C. Don't shoot."

He stopped. They lay hugging the earth, shivering, listening. Finally they heard the voice. "Get on up out o' theah," the voice called, thick with Georgia, "and keep yo' hands over yo' haid and fetch yo'selves over heah. Do it right quick, now, an' don't make any sudden moves . . ."

Noah tapped Burnecker. They both stood up and put their hands over their heads. Then they started walking toward the voice out of the depths of Georgia.

"Jesus Christ in the mawnin'!" the voice said, "they ain't got no more clothes on them than a plucked duck!"

Then Noah knew they were going to be all right.

A figure stood up from a gunpit, pointing a rifle at them. "Over this way, Soldier," the figure said.

Noah and Burnecker walked, their hands over their heads, toward the soldier looming up out of the ground. They stopped five feet away from him.

There was another man in the foxhole, still crouched down, with his rifle leveled at them.

"What the hell's goin' on out here?" he asked suspiciously.

"We got cut off," Noah said. "C Company. We've been three days getting back. Can we take our hands down now?"

"Look at their dogtags, Vernon," said the man in the hole.

The man with the Georgia accent carefully put his rifle down. "Stan' where you are and throw me yo' dogtags."

There was a familiar little jangle as first Noah, then Burnecker, threw their dogtags.

"Hand them down here, Vernon," said the man in the hole. "I'll look at them."

"You can't see anything," said Vernon. "It's as black as a mule's ass hole down there."

"Let me have them," said the man in the hole, reaching up. A moment later, there was a little scratching sound as the man bent over and lit his cigarette. He had it shielded and Noah could not see any light at all.

The wind was gaining in strength, and the wet shirt flapped around Noah's frozen body. He held himself tightly with his arms in an attempt to keep warm. The man in the foxhole took a maddeningly long time with the dogtags. Finally he looked up. "Name?" he said, pointing to Noah.

Noah told him his name.

"Serial number?"

Noah rattled off his serial number, trying not to stutter, although his jaws were stiff and salty.

"What's this H here on the dogtag?" the man asked suspiciously.

"Hebrew," said Noah.

"Hebrew?" asked the man from Georgia. "What the hell's that?"

"Jew," said Noah.

"Why don't they say so then?" said the man from Georgia aggrievedly.

"Listen," said Noah, "are you going to keep us here for the rest of the war? We're freezing."

"Come on in," said the man in the foxhole. "Make yourself at home. It'll be light in fifteen minutes and I'll take you on back to the Company CP. There's a ditch here behind me you can take cover in."

Noah and Burnecker went past the man in the foxhole. He threw them their dogtags and looked at them curiously.

"How was it back there?" he asked.

"Great," said Noah.

"More fun than a strawberry social," said Burnecker.

"I bet," said the man from Georgia.

"Listen," Noah said to Burnecker, "take this." He gave Burnecker his wallet. "The map's in there on the back of my wife's picture. If I'm not back here in fifteen minutes see that it gets to G2."

"Where you going?" Burnecker asked.

"I'm going to get Cowley," said Noah. He was a little surprised to hear himself say it. He hadn't thought about it or reasoned it out. Somehow, in the last three days he had become used to making decisions automatically, taking the responsibility for all the others, and now that he was safe the vision of Cowley crouched behind the bush on the other bank, forsaken because he thought the canal was too deep, had crowded into his mind.

"Where's this here Cowley?" asked the man from Georgia.

"Other side of the canal," said Burnecker.

"You must be mighty fond of Mr. Cowley," said the man from Georgia as he peered through the graying night across the canal.

"Crazy about him," said Noah. He wished the other men would refuse to let him go, but no one said anything.

"How long you figure to be gone?" asked the man in the foxhole.

"Fifteen minutes."

"Here," said the man, "here's fifteen minutes' worth of courage." He produced a bottle. It was muddy on the bottom from the cold slime the men had been standing in all night. Noah pulled out the cork and took a long deep drag. His eyes watered and his throat and chest burned intolerably and his stomach warmed up as though he had an electric heater there. "What the hell is that?" he asked, handing back the bottle.

"Native drink," said the man in the hole. "Apple, I think.

441

Good before crossing water." He handed the bottle to Burnecker, who drank slowly and carefully.

Burnecker put the bottle down. "You know," he said to Noah, "you don't have to go back for Cowley. He had his chance. You don't owe the son of a bitch anything. I wouldn't go. If I thought he had it coming to him, I'd go with you. He ain't got a goddamn thing coming to him, Noah."

"If I don't get back in fifteen minutes," Noah said, admiring the calm, logical, dispassionate way Burnecker's mind worked, "make sure that map gets back to G2."

"Sure," Burnecker said.

"I'll go on down the line here," said the man from Georgia, "and tell these trigger-happy Joe's not to shoot your ass when they see you."

"Thanks," Noah said, and started back toward the canal, the wet shirt tails flapping soggily around his bare legs, the alcohol rioting within him. At the bank of the canal he stopped. The tide was coming more strongly now, and the water was making a cold rustling noise against the banks. If he turned back now, he would be at the CP in a half hour, or in a hospital, perhaps, on a cot with blankets, with warm drinks, with nothing to do but sleep for days, for months . . . He had done everything he could do, more, nobody could accuse him of any lapse, he had come through and he'd brought Burnecker through and he'd made the map, and he hadn't given up when it would have been so easy to give up, and he'd taken every chance, and all Lieutenant Green had told them was get back to our own people any way you can, and even if he found Cowley, Cowley might refuse again to try the canal, and the canal was deeper now than it had been, with the tide coming in . . .

Noah wavered for a moment on the bank, kneeling, looking at the sliding water. Then he pushed himself over the bank and into the water.

He hadn't remembered that it was so cold. His chest seemed to cave in in the grip of the water. Then he took a deep breath and walked swiftly, losing his footing from time to time, toward the other bank. He reached the other bank, and started along it against the tide, trying to remember how far he and Burnecker had come, trying to remember what the spot on the bank that they had jumped off from had looked like. He walked slowly, feeling the cold water surge against his chest, stopping occasionally to see if he could hear anything. There was the sound of a single engine in the sky in the distance and desultory anti-aircraft fire, as the guns chased the last German flight before dawn back across the lines. But there was no sound in the immediate vicinity.

He came to a spot that looked familiar and pulled himself out slowly and painfully. He wriggled away from the canal toward a clump of bushes. He stopped five feet away from the bushes and whispered, "Cowley, Cowley." There was no answer. Somehow, Noah was sure that that was where they had left Cowley. He wriggled closer. "Cowley," he called more loudly. "Cowley . . ."

There was a rustle in the bushes. "Leave me alone," Cowley said.

Noah crawled toward the voice. Cowley's head appeared, a blurred shadow among the dark leaves. "I came back for you," Noah whispered. "Come on."

"Leave me alone," Cowley said.

"It's not deep," Noah said fiercely. "Goddamn you, it's not deep. You don't have to swim."

"Are you kidding me?" Cowley asked.

"Burnecker's there now. Come on. They're waiting for us. The pickets're all alerted, watching for us. Come on, before it gets light."

"You sure?" Cowley asked suspiciously.

"I'm sure."

"The hell with it," said Cowley. "I'm not going."

Without a word, Noah started back toward the bank. Then he heard the rustling behind him and he knew Cowley was following him. At the edge of the canal, Cowley nearly changed his mind again. Noah didn't say anything to him, but merely slid back into the water. This time the water did not seem cold at all. I must be getting numb, Noah thought. Cowley fell in with a splash. Noah gripped him to keep him from floundering around. He could feel the man trembling through the heavy, soggy clothes.

"Hold onto me," Noah said, "and keep quiet."

They started across the canal. Now everything seemed to go very fast. It all was familiar and routine and Noah was almost careless as he made his way swiftly toward the opposite bank.

"Oh, Mother," Cowley kept muttering to himself, his voice shrill and nervous, "oh, Mother, Mother, Mother." But he stuck close behind Noah, and even in the deep part, he kept going steadily. When they reached the other bank, Noah did not stop. He turned and pushed against the tide, searching for the broken part of the bank up which he and Burnecker had gone before.

He reached it long before he expected to. "Here," he said, turning. "Let me help you up."

"Mother," Cowley said, "oh, Mother."

Shoving and pushing, Noah managed to get Cowley started up the bank. Cowley was heavy and clumsy and he knocked a stone out of place that fell with a loud splash. But he got one knee up to the top of the bank and started to get his other leg up. Then there was a short burst of gunfire.

Cowley stood up crazily and waved his arms around. He tried to lunge forward, but he whirled and fell back. His shoe hit Noah a heavy, stunning blow along the head. Cowley screamed once. Then he crashed into the water. He never came up. Noah stood under the bank, dazedly watching the spot where Cowley had disappeared. He took a step in that direction, but he couldn't see anything and he felt his knees begin to go. He lurched back to the bank. Then, slowly, numbly, he crawled up. He had a dream he was going to drown, Noah thought stupidly, he had a dream.

He was shaking uncontrollably when he reached the top of the bank. He was still shaking when Burnecker and the man from Georgia picked him up and ran with him, away from the canal.

A half hour later, dressed in a uniform three sizes too large for him that had been taken from a dead man outside the Company CP, Noah was standing in front of the Division G2. The G2 was a gray-haired round little Lieutenant Colonel with purple dye all over his face, staining his skin and grizzled beard. The G2 had impetigo and was trying to cure it while doing everything else that was expected of him.

Division CP was in a sandbagged shed and there were men sleeping everywhere on the dirt floor. It still wasn't light enough to work by and the G2 had to peer at the map Noah had drawn by the light of a candle, because all the generators and electrical equipment of Headquarters had been sunk on the way in to the beach.

Burnecker was standing dreamily beside Noah, his eyes almost closed.

"Good," the G2 was saying, nodding his head again and again, back and forth, "good, very good." But Noah hardly remembered what the man was talking about. He only knew that he felt very sad, but it was hard to remember just why he felt that way.

"Very good, boys," the man with the purple face was saying kindly. He seemed to be smiling at them. "Above and beyond the . . . There'll be a medal in this for you boys. I'll get this right over to Corps Artillery. Come around this afternoon and I'll tell you how it came out."

Noah wondered dimly why he had a purple face and what he was talking about.

"I would like the photograph back," he said clearly. "My wife and my son."

"Yes, of course," the man smiled even more widely, yellow, old teeth surrounded by purple and gray beard. "This afternoon, when you come back. C Company is being re-formed. We've got back about forty men, counting you two. Evans,"

444

he called to a soldier who seemed to be sleeping standing up against the shed wall, "take these two men to C Company. Don't worry," he said, grinning at Noah, "you won't have to walk far. They're only in the next field." He bent over the map again, nodding and saying, "Good, very good." Evans came over and led Burnecker and Noah out of the shed and through the morning mist to the next field.

The first man they saw was Lieutenant Green, who took one look at them and said, "There are some blankets over there. Roll up and go to sleep. I'll ask you questions later."

On the way over to the blankets they passed Shields, the Company Clerk, who had already set up a small desk for himself, made out of two ration boxes, in a ditch under the trees along the edge of the field. "Hey," Shields said, "we got some mail for you. The first delivery. I nearly sent it back. I thought you guys were missing."

He dug around in a barracks bag and brought out some envelopes. There was a brown Manila envelope for Noah, addressed in Hope's handwriting. Noah took it and put it inside the dead man's shirt he was wearing and picked up three blankets. He and Burnecker walked slowly to a spot under a tree and unrolled the blankets. They sat down heavily and took off the boots that had been given them. Noah opened the Manila envelope. A small magazine fell out. He blinked and started to read Hope's letter.

"Dearest," she wrote, "I suppose I ought to explain about the magazine right off. The poem you sent me, the one you wrote in England, seemed too nice to hold just for myself, and I took the liberty of sending it . . ."

Noah picked up the magazine. On the cover he saw his name. He opened the magazine and peered heavily through the pages. Then he saw his name again and the neat, small lines of verse.

"Beware the heart's sedition," he read, "It is not made for war . . ."

"Hey," he said, "hey, Burnecker."

"Yes?" Burnecker had tried to read his mail, but had given up, and was lying on his back under the blankets, staring up at the sky. "What do you want?"

"Hey Burnecker," Noah said, "I got a poem in a magazine. Want to read it?"

There was a long pause, then Burnecker sat up.

"Of course," he said. "Hand it over."

Noah gave Burnecker the magazine, folded back to his poem. He watched Burnecker's face intently as his friend read the poem. Burnecker was a slow reader and moved his lips as he read. Once or twice he closed his eyes and his head rocked a little, but he finished the poem.

"It's great," Burnecker said. He handed the magazine to Noah, seated on the blanket beside him.

"Are you on the level?" Noah asked.

"It's a great poem," Burnecker said gravely. He nodded for emphasis. Then he lay back.

Noah looked at his name in print, but the other writing was too small for his eyes at the moment. He put the magazine inside the dead man's shirt again and lay back under the warm blankets.

Just before he closed his eyes he saw Rickett. Rickett was standing over him and Rickett was shaved clean and had on a fresh uniform. "Oh, Christ," Rickett said, off in the distance high above Noah, "oh, Christ, we still got the Jew."

Noah closed his eyes. He knew that later on what Rickett had said would make a great difference in his life, but at the moment all he wanted to do was sleep.

CHAPTER TWENTY-NINE

THERE WAS a sign on the side of the road that said "You Are Under Observed Shellfire for the Next One Thousand Yards. Keep an Interval of Seventy-five Yards."

Michael glanced sideways at Colonel Pavone. But Pavone, in the front seat of the jeep, was reading a paper-covered mystery story he had picked up in a staging area in England while they were waiting to cross the Channel. Pavone was the only man Michael had ever seen who could read in a moving jeep.

Michael stepped on the accelerator and the jeep spurted swiftly down the empty road. On the right there was a bombed-out airdrome, with the skeletons of German planes lying about. There was a strip of smoke farther off in front, lying in neat folds over the wheatfields in the bright summer afternoon air. The jeep bounced rapidly over the macadam road to the shelter of a clump of trees, and over a little rise, and the thousand observed yards were crossed.

Michael sighed a little, to himself, and drove more slowly. There was a loud, erratic growling of big guns ahead of them, from the city of Caen, that the British had taken the day before. Just what Colonel Pavone wanted to do in Caen, Michael didn't know. In his job as a roving Civil Affairs officer, Pavone had orders which permitted him to wander from one end of the front to another, and with Michael driving him, he visited all over Normandy, like a rather sleepy, good-humored tourist, looking at everything, when he wasn't reading, nodding brightly to the men who were fighting at each particular spot, talking in rapid, Parisian French to the natives, occasionally jotting down notes on scraps of paper. At night Pavone would retire to the deep dugout in the field near Carentan, and type out reports by himself, and send them on some place, but Michael never saw them, and never knew exactly where they were going.

"This book stinks," Pavone said. He tossed it into the back of the jeep. "A man has to be an idiot to read mystery stories." He looked around him, with his perky, clown's grimace. "Are we close?" he asked.

A battery concealed behind a row of farmhouses opened fire. The noise, so near, seemed to vibrate the windshield and Michael had, once again, the expanding, tickling concussion feeling low down in his stomach, that he never seemed to get over when a gun went off nearby.

"Close enough," Michael said grimly.

Pavone chuckled. "The first hundred wounds are the hardest," he said.

The son of a bitch, Michael thought, one day he is going to get me killed.

A British ambulance passed them, fast, going back, loaded, bumping cruelly on the rough road. Michael thought for a moment of the wounded in back, gasping as they rolled on the stretchers.

On one side of the road was a burned-out British tank, blackened and gaping, and there was a smell of the dead from it. Every new place you approached, every newly taken town which represented a victory on the maps and over the BBC, had the same smell, sweet, rotting, unvictorious. Michael wished vaguely, as he drove, feeling his nose burn in the strong sun, squinting through his dusty goggles, that he was back on the lumber pile in England.

They came over the brow of a hill. Ahead of them stretched the city of Caen. The British had been trying to take it for a month, and after looking at it for a moment, you wondered why they had been so anxious. Walls were standing, but few houses. Block after block of closely packed stone buildings had been battered and knocked down, and it was the same as far as the eye could reach. Tripe à la mode de Caen, Michael remembered from the menus of French restaurants in New York, and the University of Caen, from a course in Medieval History. British heavy mortars were firing from the jumbled books of the University library at the moment, and Canadian soldiers were crouched over machine guns in the kitchens where the tripe had at other times been so deftly prepared.

They were in the outskirts of the town by now, winding in

447

and out of stone rubble. Pavone signaled Michael to stop, and Michael drew the jeep up along a heavy stone convent wall that ran beside the roadside ditch. There were some Canadians in the ditch and they looked at the Americans curiously.

We ought to wear British helmets, Michael thought nervously. These damn things must look just like German helmets to the British. They'll shoot first and examine our papers later.

"How're things?" Pavone was out of the jeep and standing over the ditch, talking to the soldiers there.

"Bloody awful," said one of the Canadians, a small, dark, Italian-looking man. He stood up in the ditch and grinned. "You going into the town, Colonel?"

"Maybe."

"There are snipers all over the place," said the Canadian. There was the whistle of an incoming shell and the Canadians dived into the ditch again. Michael ducked, but he could not get out of the jeep fast enough, anyway, so he merely covered his face jerkily with his hands. There was no explosion. Dud, Michael's mind registered dully, the brave workers of Warsaw and Prague, filling the casings with sand and putting heroic notes among the steel scraps, "Salute from the anti-fascist munitions workers of Skoda." Or was that a romantic story from the newspapers and the OWI, too, and would the shell explode six hours later when everyone had forgotten about it?

"Every three minutes," the Canadian said bitterly, standing up in the ditch. "We're back here on rest and every three bleeding minutes we got to hit the ground. That's the British Army's notion of a rest area!" He spat.

"Are there mines?" Pavone asked.

"Sure there're mines," the Canadian said aggressively. "Why shouldn't there be mines? Where do you think you are, Yankee Stadium?"

He had an accent that would have sounded natural in Brooklyn. "Where you from, Soldier?" Pavone asked.

"Toronto," said the soldier. "The next man that tries to get me out of Toronto is going to get a Ford axle across his ears."

There was the whistle again, and again Michael was too slow to get out of the jeep. The Canadian disappeared magically. Pavone merely leaned negligently against the jeep. This time the shell exploded, but it must have been a hundred yards away, because nothing came their way at all. Two guns on the other side of the convent wall fired rapidly again and again, answering.

The Canadian raised himself out of the ditch again. "Rest area," he said venomously. "I should have joined the bloody American Army. You don't see any Englishmen around here, do you?" He glared at the broken street and the smashed buildings with hatred flaring from his clouded eyes. "Only Canadians. When it's tough, hand it to Canada. There isn't an Englishman who's got further than the whorehouse in Bayeau."

"Now . . ." Pavone began, grinning at this wild inaccuracy.

"Don't argue with me, Colonel, don't argue with me," the man from Toronto said loudly. "I'm too nervous to argue."

"All right," Pavone said, smiling, pushing his helmet back, so that it looked like an unmilitary chamber pot over his bushy, burlesque eyebrows. "I won't argue with you. I'll see you later."

"If you don't get shot," said the Canadian, "and if I don't desert in the meantime."

Pavone waved to him. "Mike," he said, "I'll drive now. You sit up in back, and keep your eyes open."

Michael climbed in back and sat high up on the folded-down jeep top, so that he could fire more easily in all directions. Pavone took the wheel. Pavone always took the most responsible and dangerous position at moments like this.

Pavone waved once more to the Canadian, who didn't wave back. The jeep growled down the road into town.

Michael blew at the dust in the carbine chamber and took it off safety. He sat with the carbine over his knees and peered ahead of him as Pavone slowly drove down the battered street among the ruins.

Again and again British batteries hidden among the ruins spoke up in fierce, rolling succession. Pavone had to snake in and out to avoid piles of building bricks and stones that blocked the road.

Michael scanned the windows of the still-standing houses. Suddenly it seemed that Caen was composed of windows, with blinds drawn, that miraculously had survived the bombings, the tank fights, the artillery of the Germans and the British. Michael felt naked and insanely vulnerable sitting up so high, going down the empty, broken street, among all the windows, behind any one of which a German sniper might be hiding, babying his rifle, with the fine telescopic lenses, smiling quietly to himself as he waited for the open, foolish jeep to come just a little closer . . .

I wouldn't mind being killed, Michael told himself unhappily, suddenly twisting because he thought he heard a window opening behind him. I wouldn't mind being killed in a battle, in a battle in which I was fighting, but like this, sightseeing with an idiotic ex-circus gambler . . . Then he knew he was lying to himself. He would mind getting killed, no matter what. There didn't seem to be much sense to getting killed. The war went on at its own slow, deliberate pace, and if he got himself killed it would make no difference one way or another to anyone but himself, and to his family, perhaps. Whether he was dead or not, at exactly the same moment of the twentieth century the armies would move, the machines in which the real fighting finally took place would destroy each other, the surrender would be signed . . . Survive, he remembered desperately from the lumber pile, survive, survive . . .

The batteries crashed all around him. It was hard to imagine the organization, the men telephoning, jotting down numbers on maps, correcting ranges, fiddling with the delicate enormous mechanisms that raised a gun so that it would fire five miles this minute and seven the next, all going on unseen among the cellars of the old town of Caen, and behind ancient garden walls and in the living rooms of Frenchmen who had been plumbers and meatpackers before this and were now dead. How large was Caen, how many people had lived in it, was it like Buffalo, Jersey City, Pasadena?

The jeep went slowly on, with Pavone looking interestedly around him, and Michael feeling increasingly naked in back.

They turned a corner and came to a street of three-story houses which had been badly mauled. Cascades of rubble swept down from the back walls of the houses to the street and there were men and women patiently bent over, high in the ruins, like berry pickers, taking a rag here, a lamp there, a pair of stockings, a cooking pot, out of the thick pile of rubbish which had been their homes, oblivious to the English guns around them, oblivious to the snipers, oblivious to the German guns across the river that were shelling the town, oblivious to everything except that these were their homes and in these torrents of stone and lumber were their possessions, slowly accumulated in the course of their lives.

On the street were wheelbarrows and baby carriages. The gleaners gathered up armloads high in the pile and slid down, balancing their dusty treasures, and put them neatly in the small conveyances. Then, without looking at the Americans who were passing them, or at the occasional Canadian jeep or ambulance that ground by, they would climb methodically up the static torrent and begin digging all over again for some remembered and broken treasure.

As the jeep passed these patient harvesters, Michael forgot for a moment that he might be shot in the small, tender part between his shoulder blades that always seemed ready and about to receive a bullet, or in the throbbing part just under his rib cage where he knew he would be hit if he were hit in front at all. He wanted to stand up and make a speech to the Frenchmen searching the ruins of their homes. "Leave," he wanted to shout, "flee the town. Nothing you find there is worth being killed for. Those sounds you hear are shells bursting. And when a shell bursts the steel makes no distinction between uniform and flesh, civilians and military. Come back later, when the war has gone by. Your treasures are safe, because no one wants them or can use them."

But he said nothing, and the jeep slowly went down the street on which, in a tenacious fever of possession, the inhabitants dug high up for silver-framed pictures of grandmothers, for colanders and carving knives, for embroidered bedspreads that had been white before the shells had hit them.

They came into a wide square, deserted now, and open at one end because all the buildings had been leveled completely there. The Orne River was on the other side. Beyond that, Michael knew, the Germans had their lines, and he knew that somewhere across the river there were enemy eyes peering at the slow-moving jeep. He knew that Pavone understood that too, but Pavone did not increase his speed. What the hell is the bastard proving, Michael thought, and why doesn't he go prove it by himself?

But no one fired at them, and they went on.

Everything seemed very quiet, even though the guns kept firing quite regularly. The noise of the jeep engine, so familiar after all the days of traveling through the dust and among the convoys and between the shellbursts, no longer made any particular claim on the eardrums. Michael listened carefully for a rustle, a squeak, the turning of a doorknob, the click of a riflebolt, anywhere around him in the dead and broken streets of the old city, and he was sure he would be able to hear such a noise, even if it came at the exact moment that a whole regiment of artillery opened fire within a radius of a hundred yards.

Pavone wound slowly about the city in and out of the strong summer sunlight and the purple French shadows that Michael had known from the paintings of Cezanne and Renoir and Pissarro long before he had ever set foot on the soil of France. Pavone stopped the jeep to look at a street sign that, untouched and municipally proud, named two streets that no longer existed. Pavone moved in a slow, interested way, and Michael divided his time between staring at the thick, healthy, brown neck under the helmet and at the gaping gray sides of the stone buildings from which at any moment his death might arrive.

Pavone started the jeep again and drove thoughtfully down what had once been a main thoroughfare. "I came here for a week-end in 1938," Pavone said, looking back, "with a friend of mine who produced movies, and two girls from one of his companies." He shook his head reflectively. "We had a very nice week-end. My friend, his name was Jules, was killed right away in 1940." Pavone peered at the jagged shopfronts. "I can't recognize a single street."

Fantastic, Michael thought, he is risking my life for the memory of a week-end with two bit players and a dead producer six years ago.

They turned into a street in which there was considerable

451

activity. There were trucks drawn up alongside a church and three or four young Frenchmen with FFI armbands patrolling along an iron fence and some Canadians helping wounded civilians into one of the trucks. Pavone stopped the jeep in a little square in front of the church. The pavement was piled high with old valises, wicker hampers, carpet-bags, net market sacks stuffed with linen, sheets and blankets in which were rolled an assortment of household belongings.

A young girl in a light-blue dress, very clean and starched, went by on a bicycle. She was very pretty, with lively blue-black hair piled over the bright dress. Michael looked at her curiously. She stared at him coldly, hatred and contempt very plain in her face. She is blaming me, Michael thought, for the bombings, for the fact that her house is down, her father dead perhaps, her lover God knows where. The girl flashed on, her pretty skirt billowing past the ambulance and the shell-marked stone. Michael would have liked to follow her, talk to her, convince her . . . Convince her of what? That he was not just an iron-hearted, leering soldier, admiring pretty legs even in the death of a city, that he understood her tragedy, that she must not judge him so swiftly, in the flashing of an eye, must have mercy in her heart for him, and understanding, just as she must expect mercy and understanding in return . . .

The girl disappeared.

"Let's go in," said Pavone.

The inside of the church was very dark after the brilliant sunlight outside. Michael smelled it first. Mixed with the slight, rich odor of old candles and incense burned in centuries of devotion, there was a smell of barnyard and the sick smell of age and medicine and dying.

He blinked, standing at the door, and listened to the scuffle of children's feet on the great stone floor, now strewn with straw. High overhead there was a large, gaping shell hole. The sunlight streamed down through it, like a powerful amber searchlight, piercing the religious gloom.

Then, as his eyes grew accustomed to the darkness, he saw that the church was very crowded. The inhabitants of the city, or those who had not fled and not yet died, had assembled here, numbly looking for protection under God, waiting to be taken away behind the lines. The first impression was that he was in a gigantic religious home for the aged. Stretched out on the floor on litters and on blankets and on straw heaps were what seemed like dozens of wrinkled, almost-evaporated, yellow-faced, fragile octogenarians. They rubbed their translucent hands numbly over their throats; they pushed feebly at blanket ends; they mumbled with animal squeaky sounds; they stared, hot-eyed and dying, at the men who stood over them; they wet the floor because they were too old to move and too

452

far gone to care; they scratched at grimy bandages that covered wounds they had received in the young men's war that had raged in their city for a month; they were dying of cancer, tuberculosis, hardening of the arteries, nephritis, gangrene, malnourishment, senility; and the common smell of their disease and their helplessness and their age, collected together like this in the once-shelled church, made Michael gasp a little as he regarded them, lit here and there in a mellow and holy beam of sunlight, dancing with dust motes and shimmering over the wasted, fiercely hating faces. Among them, between the straw paillasses and the stained litters, between the cancer cases and the old men with broken hips who had been bedridden for five years before the British came, between the old women whose great grandchildren had already been killed at Sedan and Lake Chad and Oran, among them ran the children, playing, weaving in and out, swiftly and gaily shining for a moment in the golden beam from the German shell hole, then darting like glittering water flies into the rich pools of purple shadow, the high tinkle of their laughter skimming over the heads of the gravebound ancients on the stone floor.

This was the war, Michael thought, this was finally the war. No captains hoarsely shouting among the guns, no men flinging themselves on bayonets for great causes, no communiqués or promotions, merely the very old, the brittle-boned, toothless, bleached, deaf, suffering, sexless very old, gathered from the ill-smelling corners among the ruins and put carelessly down on a stone floor to wet themselves and die among the flashing feet of children playing tag, while the guns spoke outside in their own energetic afternoon rhetoric full of windy meanings, echoing slogans that seemed great truths three thousand miles away. The very old lay, outside the reach of all slogans, moaning their dumb animal moans among the dancing feet of the children, waiting for a Quartermaster Captain to wheedle an extra three trucks away from carrying ammunition for a couple of days, so that they could be transported with all their accumulated agonies, to another broken town, and put down and forgotten where they would not interfere with the fighting.

"Well, Colonel," Michael said, "what has Civil Affairs to say about this?"

Pavone smiled gently at Michael and touched his arm softly, as though he realized, out of his greater age and deeper experience, that Michael felt somehow guilty for this and must be forgiven for his sharpness because of it. "I think," he began, "we had better get out of here. The British got this, let them worry about it . . ."

Two children came up to Pavone, and stood in front of him. One was a tiny, frail four-year-old girl, with large, shy eyes.

453

She held onto the hand of her brother, two or three years older than she, but even more shy.

"Please," the little girl said, in French, "may we have some sardines?"

"No, no!" The little boy pulled his hand away from hers angrily and slapped her harshly on the wrist. "Not sardines. Not from these. Biscuits from these. It was the others who gave sardines."

Pavone grinned at Michael, then bent down and gently hugged the little girl, to whom the difference between Fascism and Democracy was merely that from one children might expect sardines and from the other hardtack. The little one fought back tears. "Of course," he said in French. "Of course." He turned to Michael. "Mike," he said, "go get a K ration."

Michael went outside, grateful for the sunlight and the fresh smell, and picked up a K ration from the jeep. Back in the church he looked for Pavone. As he stood there, the cardboard box in his hand, a seven-year-old boy, with a wild mop of hair and a tough grin, skidded up to him and said pleadingly and at the same time impudently, "Cigarette, cigarette for Papa?"

Michael reached into his pocket. But a thick-set woman of about sixty bustled over to the little boy and grabbed his shoulders. "No," she said to Michael. "No. Do not give it to him." She turned on the boy with grandmotherly indignation. "No!" she said angrily. "Do you wish to stunt your growth?"

A shell landed in the next street and Michael did not hear the boy's reply. He wriggled out of his grandmother's grasp and danced away between the aisles of old men and women.

The grandmother shook her head. "Wild," she told Michael, "these days they are impossibly wild." She bowed gravely and moved off.

Michael saw Pavone, squatting, talking to the girl and her brother. Michael went over to Pavone, smiling a little. Pavone gave the little girl the K ration and kissed her gently on her forehead. The two children backed away gravely and slipped off to a niche on the other side of the church, where they could open their treasure and sample it in peace.

Michael and Pavone went outside. At the door of the church Michael could not help turning around and taking a last look at the high-vaulted, evil-smelling, lavender-shadowed interior. An old man, lying near the door, was waving one hand feebly in the air and no one was paying any attention to him; and far off, infinitesimal and frail at the other side of the church, the two children, the boy and the girl, were crouched over the K ration box, alternating at nibbling at the chocolate bar they had found there.

Outside, they climbed silently into the jeep, with Pavone at the wheel again. Standing next to the jeep was a squat, sixty-year-old Frenchman, dressed in a blue denim jacket and ragged, baggy pants, patched twenty times. He saluted Pavone and Michael, in a quivering French military salute. Pavone saluted the old man, who had a bristling yellowed moustache and who looked a little like Clemenceau, a large, fierce head under his workingman's cap.

The Frenchman went around to Pavone and shook his hand, then shook Michael's hand. "Americans," he said, in slow English. "Liberty, fraternity, equality."

Oh, God, Michael thought sourly, a patriot. After the church, he was not in the mood for patriots.

"I was in America seven times," said the old man, in French. "I once used to speak English like a native. But I have forgotten it all."

A shell landed in the next street and Michael wished Pavone would start. But Pavone leaned easily over the wheel, listening to the Frenchman.

"I was a sailor," said the Frenchman. "Merchant Marine. I visited the cities of New York, Brooklyn, New Orleans, Baltimore, San Francisco, Seattle, North Carolina. I still can read English fluently."

He wavered back and forth a little as he spoke and Michael decided that he was drunk. He had a strange yellow look in his eyes and his mouth quivered under his wet and drooping moustache.

"In the first war," the Frenchman went on, "I was torpedoed off Bordeaux. I spent six hours in the waters of the Atlantic Ocean." He nodded briskly, looking more drunk than ever.

Michael shuffled his feet impatiently, hoping to show Pavone that he thought they ought to get out of there. Pavone did not move. He listened interestedly to the Frenchman, who was patting the jeep fondly, as though it were a fine, proud horse.

"In the last war," said the Frenchman, "I volunteered for the Merchant Marine again." Michael had heard this before. Frenchmen describing the battles of 1940, the fall of France, as the last war. This makes the third one, then, Michael computed automatically. Too many, even for Europeans. "I was too old, they told me at the bureau," the Frenchman went on angrily, stroking the jeep hood, "they would call me if affairs became desperate." He laughed sardonically. "Affairs never became desperate enough for the young men at the bureau. They never called me." He looked vaguely around him, at the sunlit church and the piles of shabby luggage in front of it, and the rubble-strewn square and bombed-out homes. "My son, however, was in the Navy. He was killed at Oran, by the British. Oran, in Africa. I hold no ill will. A war is a war."

Pavone touched the man's arm delicately in sympathy.

"He was my only son," the Frenchman went on, calmly. "I used to describe to him the cities of San Francisco and New York when he was a small boy." The Frenchman suddenly rolled up his left sleeve. There was something tattooed on his forearm. "Observe," he said. Michael leaned forward. On the old, powerful arm, over the bulging muscle, there was a green, tattooed picture of the Woolworth Building, rearing up above romantic clouds. "The Woolworth Building, in the city of New York," said the ex-seaman proudly. "I was immensely impressed."

Michael leaned back and made a small tapping noise with his foot to try to get Pavone to move. Pavone did not move.

"A beautiful representation," said Pavone warmly to the Frenchman.

The Frenchman nodded and rolled down his sleeve.

"I am enchanted that you finally came," said the Frenchman, "the Americans."

"Thank you," said Pavone.

"When the first American planes flew over, even though they dropped bombs on us, I stood up on my roof and waved. And now you are here, in person. I also understand," he said delicately, "why you took so long in coming."

"Thank you," said Pavone again.

"A war is not a matter of minutes, no matter what some people say. And each war takes longer than the one before it. It is the simple arithmetic of history." The Frenchman nodded vigorously in emphasis. "I do not deny it was not pleasant waiting. You have no idea what the Germans are like, to live under day after day." The Frenchman whipped out an old, tattered leather wallet and flipped it open. "All during the occupation, from the first day, I carried this." He showed the wallet to Pavone and Michael bent forward to look at it. There was a waded piece of tricolor bunting from a penny flag under the yellow celluloid cover in the wallet. "If they had found it on me," the Frenchman said, regarding the sleazy muslin, "they would have killed me. But I carried it, four years."

He sighed, and put the wallet away.

"I have just come back from the front," he announced. "Someone told me, on the bridge across the river, in the middle, between the British and the Germans, there is an old woman lying. Go and see if it is your wife. I went and looked." He paused and stared up at the damaged church steeple. "It was my wife."

He stood in silence, stroking the jeep. Neither Pavone nor Michael said anything. "Forty years," the Frenchman said. "We were married forty years. We had our ups and downs. We lived on the other side of the river. I suppose she forgot a parrot or a hen and decided she must go look for it and the

456

Germans machine-gunned her. Machine gun for a sixty-year-old woman. They are inconceivable, the Germans. She is lying there, with her dress up over her legs and her head down. The Canadians wouldn't let me go out to get her. I will have to wait until the battle is over, they told me. She has on her good dress." He began to cry. The tears ran into his moustache, and he swallowed them wetly. "Forty years. I saw her a half hour ago." He took out his wallet again, crying. "Even so," he said fiercely, "even so . . ." He opened the wallet and kissed the tricolor bunting under its celluloid cover, kissed it passionately, insanely. "Even so."

He shook his head and put the wallet away. He patted the jeep once more. He moved off down the street, vaguely, past the torn iron of the shopfronts and the carelessly piled stones, moved off without saluting or saying good-bye.

Michael looked after him, feeling his face rigid and aching.

Pavone sighed and started the jeep. They drove slowly toward the outskirts of town. Michael still watched the windows, but without fear, somehow confident that there would be no snipers now.

They passed the convent wall, but the boy from Toronto was gone. Pavone stepped hard on the accelerator and they sped out of town. It was lucky they had not stopped before the convent, because they hadn't gone three hundred yards when they heard the explosion behind them. There was a whirling cloud of dust squarely in the road where they had been.

Pavone turned to look, too. Michael and he glanced at each other. They did not smile and they did not speak. Pavone turned back and hunched over the wheel.

They crossed the marked thousand yards, where the road was under observed shellfire, without incident. Pavone stopped the jeep and signaled for Michael to come up and take the wheel.

As he climbed over the seat Michael halted and looked back. There was no sign that a city, ruined or unruined, lay over the horizon.

He started the jeep, feeling better to be at the wheel, and they drove slowly without speaking through the yellow afternoon sun toward the American lines.

A half mile farther on they saw troops coming up on both sides of the road, in single file, and they heard a strange, skirling noise. A moment later they saw that it was a battalion of infantry, Scotch-Canadian, each company led by a bagpiper, walking slowly toward a road that led off into wheatfields to the left. Other troops could be seen, just their heads and weapons showing above the wheat, marching slowly down toward the river.

457

The noise of the bagpipes sounded wild and comic and pathetic in the open, deserted country. Michael drove very slowly toward the approaching troops. They were walking heavily, sweating dark stains into their heavy battle dress, loaded down with grenades and bandoliers and boxes of machine-gun ammunition. In front of the first Company, just behind the bagpiper, strode the Commanding Officer, a large-red-faced young Captain, with a swooping red moustache. He carried a small swagger stick and he stepped out strongly in front of his troops, as though the crying, thin music of the pipes were a joyous march.

The officer grinned when he saw the jeep, and waved his swagger stick. Michael looked past him to the men. Their faces were strained under the sweat, and no one was smiling. Their battle dress and equipment were fresh and neat and Michael knew that these men were going into their first battle. They walked silently, already weary, already overburdened, with a blank, wrenched look on their crimson faces, as though they were listening to something, not to the pipes or to the distant rumble of the guns, or the weary scuffle of their boots on the road, but to some inner debate, deep within them, that reached them thinly and to which they had to pay close attention if they wished to catch its meaning.

But as the jeep came abreast of the officer he grinned widely, a twenty-year-old athlete's, white-toothed grin under the ludicrous and charming moustache, and boomed out, in a voice that could be heard for a hundred yards, although the jeep was only five feet from him, "Lovely day, isn't it?"

"Good luck," Pavone said, in the simple, not overloud, well-modulated tone of the man who is going back from the fighting and can now control his voice, "good luck to you all. Captain."

The Captain waved his stick again, in a jerky, friendly gesture, and the jeep slowly rolled past the rest of the Company, brought up at the rear by the Medic, with the red crosses on his helmet, and a young, listening, thoughtful look on his face, and the aid kits in his hands.

The music of the bagpipes died down into fragile, gull-like echoes as the Company turned off into the wheatfield and wound deeper and deeper into it, like armed men marching purposefully and regretfully into a rustling, golden sea.

Michael woke up, listening to the growing mutter of the guns. He was depressed. He smelled the damp, loamy odor of the foxhole in which he slept, and the acid, dusty smell of the pup-tent dark over his head. He lay rigid, in the complete darkness, too tired to move, warm under the blankets, listening to the sound of guns that was coming closer each moment. The usual air raid, he thought, hating the Germans, every goddamn night.

The sound of the guns was very close now and there was the soft deadly hiss of shrapnel falling near by and the plump, solid sounds as the steel fragments hit the earth. Michael reached in back of him and got his helmet and put it over his groin. He pulled his barracks bag, which was lying next to him in the hole, stuffed with extra longjohns and pants and shirts, and rolled it on top of him, on his belly and chest. Then he crossed his arms over his head, covering his face with the warm smell of his flesh and the sweaty smell of the long sleeves of the wool underwear. Now, he thought, as this nightly routine which he had worked out in the weeks in Normandy was completed, now they can hit me. He had figured out the various parts of himself which were most vulnerable and most precious, and they were protected. If he got hit in the legs or arms it would not be so serious.

He lay there, in the complete darkness, listening to the roaring and whistling above his head. He began to feel cozy and protected in the deep hole in which he slept. The inside of the hole was lined with stiff canvas cut from a crashed glider, and he had put down as a ground cloth a luminescent silk signaling panel that gave an air of Oriental luxury to the neat underground establishment.

Michael wondered what time it was, but he was too tired to try to find his flashlight and look at his watch. From three to five in the morning he was to be on guard duty and he wondered dully whether it was worth while to try to go to sleep again.

The raid went on. The planes must be very low, he thought, they're firing machine guns at them. He listened to the machine guns and to the patient roar of the planes above. How many air raids had he been in? Twenty? Thirty? The Luftwaffe had tried to kill him thirty times, in a general, impersonal way, and had failed.

He played with the idea of being hit. A nice, eight-inch gash in the fleshy part of the leg. With a nice little fracture of the thigh bone thrown in. Michael thought of himself hobbling bravely up the ramp of Grand Central Station in New York, fully equipped with Purple Heart, crutches, and discharge papers.

He moved a little under his blankets, and the barracks bag shifted slightly on top of him, in a warm, almost living movement. It was almost like having a girl lying on top of him. Suddenly he wanted a girl fiercely, imperiously. He thought of the girls he had made love to, and the places it had happened. His first girl, Louise, sixteen years old, but knowing exactly what she wanted. On a Saturday night, when her parents were out playing bridge three blocks away. Her schoolbooks on the desk next to the bed and the fearful listening for the key in the front door all the time. The other girls by the name of Louise. Somehow, he had seemed to know a great many girls by the name of Louise. The Warner Brothers starlet in Hollywood, who had lived with three other girls in the Valley, the cashier in the restaurant on 60th Street in New York, Louise in London, during the air raids, with the electric heater making the warm red glow in the room. He loved all the Louises now, and all the Marys and Margarets, and he moved heart-brokenly on the hard ground thinking of the way they chuckled and the smooth skin of their shoulders and legs and the things they said when he made love to them.

He thought of all the girls he might have had, whom, for one reason or another, he had abstained from. Helen, ten years ago, tall and blonde, who had significantly touched knees with him in a restaurant and who had whispered to him when her husband had gone to get a cigar. But her husband had been Michael's best friend in college, and Michael, half-shocked, half-noble, had pulled away. He thought of the tall, full body of his friend's wife, and moved agonizedly in the dark. Florence, who had come to him with a letter from his mother, because she wanted to go into the theatre. Florence had been very young and awkwardly blunt. Michael had discovered she was a virgin, and had felt, sentimentally, that it was not just that a virgin should give herself so casually to a man who did not love her and would never love her. He thought of the slender, slightly awkward girl from his home town, and twitched sorrowfully under the barracks bag.

Then, the modern dancer with the pianist husband, who had pretended to be drunk and had fallen into his lap at that party on 23rd Street, but Michael had been occupied then with a schoolteacher from New Rochelle. And the girl from Louisiana, who had three enormous brothers, of whom Michael was frankly afraid; and the woman who had looked back with calm invitation on 11th Street, on the winter night in the Village, and the wide-hipped young nurse from Halifax the time his brother broke his leg, and . . .

Michael thought despairingly of all the fair, offered, declined flesh, and gritted his teeth under the wet canvas, mourning for the insane fastidiousness of days gone by. Ignorant, he thought, oh, you ignorant, pompous bastard!

And then the girls he *had* gone to bed with, and then neglected—Katherine, Rachel, Faith, Elizabeth—all the dear hours of lightly lost pleasure, never to be found again. He moaned miserably and seized the barracks bag with clutching, furious anger.

Still, he comforted himself, finally, there had been quite a few he hadn't declined. In fact, when you looked back on it this way, you were ashamed there were so many others, but you were glad that you hadn't been ashamed then, and had not let it stand in your way.

Still, when he got back, if he got back, he was going to change. That part of his life was over. Now he wanted an orderly, decent, well-run, faithful, valuable life. Margaret. He had avoided thinking about Margaret for a long time. Now, in the damp, rough hole in the ground, with the shrapnel raining softly down, he couldn't help but think about her. Tomorrow, he decided, I will write her. I don't give a damn what she's doing now. When I get back, we must get married. He convinced himself swiftly that Margaret would swing back to her old affection for him, marry him, they would take a sunny apartment downtown, have children, and he would work hard, stop wasting his life. Perhaps get out of the theatre. He probably wasn't going to amount to a hell of a lot in the theatre, if he hadn't yet. Perhaps politics. Maybe he had a talent for it. Finally do something useful, useful for himself, for the poor devils dying on the crust of the front lines tonight, for the old men and women lying on the straw in the church at Caen, for the despairing Canadian, the moustached Captain behind the bagpipes who had roared, "Lovely day, isn't it?", for the little girl who had asked for sardines . . . Maybe a world in which the common element was not death, a world in which you did not live among the growing cemeteries, a world not governed finally by the Graves Registration Sergeant.

Still, if you wanted to be listened to later, you had to earn that right. You could not merely spend the war being a chauffeur for a Civil Affairs Colonel. Only the men who had come back from the frightful, sickening crust out in front of him would be able to speak with authority, with a sense that they had really paid for their opinions and owned them, irrevocably, once and for all . . .

Must ask Pavone tomorrow, Michael thought drowsily, to have me transferred, must ask. And must write Margaret, she must know, she must prepare . . .

The guns stopped outside and the planes droned back toward the German lines. Michael slipped the barracks bag off his chest and rolled the helmet away from his groin. Ah, God, he thought, ah, God, how long is this going to last?

Then the guard he was to relieve poked his head into the tent and pulled Michael's toe under the blankets.

"On your feet, Whitacre," said the guard. "You're going for a walk."

"O.K., O.K.," Michael said, pushing back the blankets. He shivered and hurriedly put on his shoes. He put on his field jacket and picked up his carbine, and, shivering badly, stepped out into the night. It had clouded over and a fine drizzle was falling. Michael reached into the tent and got out his raincoat and put it on. Then he went over to the guard, who was leaning against a jeep, talking to another sentry, and said, "All right, go on back to sleep."

He stood leaning against the jeep, next to the other guard, shivering, feeling the drizzle filtering in under his collar and rolling down his face, peering out into the cold wet darkness, remembering all the women he had thought about during the raid, remembering Margaret, and trying to compose a letter, a letter so moving, so tender and heartbreaking and true and loving, that she would see how much they needed each other and would be waiting for him when he got back to the sorrowful, chaotic world of America after the war.

"Hey, Whitacre," it was the other sentry, Private Leroy Keane, who had already been on duty for an hour, "do you have anything to drink?"

"No," said Michael. He was not fond of Keane, who was garrulous and a scrounger, and who had, to boot, the reputation of being an unlucky man to be with, because the first time he had left camp in Normandy, his jeep had been strafed and two of the men in it had been wounded, and one killed, although Keane had not been touched. "Sorry." Michael moved away a little.

"Have you got any aspirin?" Keane asked. "I got a terrible headache."

"Wait a minute." Michael went back to his pup-tent and brought back a small tin of aspirin. He gave the tin to Keane. Keane took six of them and tossed them into his mouth. Michael watched, feeling his own mouth curl in distaste.

"Don't you use water?" Michael asked.

"What for?" asked Keane. He was a large, bony man of about thirty, whose older brother had won the Congressional Medal of Honor in the last war, and Keane, trying to live up to the glory of the family, put on a very tough front.

Keane gave Michael the aspirin box. "What a headache," Keane said. "From constipation. I haven't been able to move my bowels for five days."

I haven't heard anybody use that expression, Michael thought, since Fort Dix. He walked slowly beside the line of pup-tents along the edge of the field, hoping Keane wouldn't follow him. But there was the clumsy scuffle of Keane's boots in the grass beside him and Michael knew there was no escaping the man.

"I used to have a perfect digestion," Keane said mournfully. "But then I got married."

They walked in silence to the end of the row of pup-tents

462

and the officers' latrine. Then they turned and started back.

"My wife stifled me," said Keane. "Also, she insisted on having three children, right away. You wouldn't believe it, that a woman who wanted children like that was frigid, but my wife is frigid. She can't bear to have me touch her. I got constipated six weeks after the wedding day and I haven't had a healthy day since then. Are you married, Whitacre?"

"Divorced."

"If I could afford it," Keane said, "I would get divorced. She's ruined my life. I wanted to be a writer. Do you know many writers?"

"A few."

"Not with three children, though, that's a cinch." Keane's voice was bitter in the darkness. "She trapped me from the beginning. And when the war began, you don't know what a job I had getting her to allow me to enlist. A man from a family like mine, with my brother's record . . . Did I ever tell you how he won the medal?"

"Yes," said Michael.

"Killed eleven Germans in one morning. Eleven Germans," Keane said, his voice musical with regret and wonder. "I wanted to join the paratroopers, and my wife threw a fit of hysterics. It all goes together, frigidity, lack of respect, fear, hysteria. Now look what I'm doing. Pavone hates me. He never takes me out with him on his trips. You were at the front today, weren't you?"

"Yes."

"You know what I was doing?" asked the brother of the Medal-of-Honor winner bitterly. "I was sitting here typing up rosters. Five copies apiece. Promotions, medical records, allowances. I'm really glad my brother isn't alive, I really am."

They walked slowly, in the rain, the water dripping from their helmets, the muzzles of their carbines held low, pointing groundward, to keep the wet out.

"I'll tell you something," Keane said. "A couple of weeks ago, when the Germans nearly broke through here, and there was talk about our being set up as part of a defensive line, I'll admit to you, I was praying they would break through. Praying. So we would have to fight."

"You're a goddamn fool," Michael said.

"I could be a great soldier," Keane said harshly, belching. "Great. I know it. Look at my brother. We were full brothers, even if he was twenty years older than me. Pavone knows it. That's why he takes a perverted pleasure in keeping me back here at a typewriter, while he takes other people out with him."

"It would serve you damned well right," Michael said, "if you got a bullet in your head."

"I wouldn't care," Keane said flatly. "I wouldn't give a damn. If I get killed, don't give my regards to anyone."

Michael tried to see Keane's face, but it was impossible in the dark. He felt a wave of pity for the constipated, brother-and-hero-haunted man with the frigid wife.

"I should have gone to OCS," Keane went on. "I would have made a great officer. I'd have my own company by now, and I guarantee I'd have the Silver Star . . ." His voice went on, mad, grating, sick, as they walked side by side under the dripping trees. "I know myself. I'd have been a gallant officer."

Michael couldn't help smiling at the phrase. Somehow, in this war, you never heard that word, except in the rhetoric of the communiqués and citations. Gallant was not a word for this particular war, and only a man like Keane would use it so warmly, believing in the word, believing that it had reality and meaning.

"Gallant," Keane repeated firmly. "I'd show my wife. I'd go back to London with the ribbons on me and I'd cut a path a mile wide through the women there. I never had any luck there before because I was a Private."

Michael grinned, thinking of all the Privates who had done spectacularly well among the English ladies, knowing that Keane could arrive any place, with all the ribbons in the world, and stars on his shoulders, and find only frigid women at all bars, in all bedrooms.

"My wife knew it," Keane complained. "That's why she persuaded me not to become an officer. She had it figured out, and then when I saw what she'd done to me, it was too late, I was overseas."

Michael was beginning to enjoy himself, and he had a cruel sense of gratitude to the man beside him, for taking his mind off his own problems.

"What's your wife like?" he asked maliciously.

"I'll show you her picture tomorrow. Pretty," Keane said. "Very well formed. She looks like the most affectionate woman in the world, always smiling and lively when anybody else is around. But let the door close, let us be alone, and it is like the middle of a glacier. They trick you," Keane mourned in the wet darkness, "they trick you, they trick you before you know what's happening . . . Also," he went on, pouring it out, "she takes all my money. And it's awful here, because I just sit around and I remember all the things she did to me, and I could go crazy. If I was in combat I could forget. Listen, Whitacre," Keane said passionately, "you're in good with Pavone, he likes you, talk to him for me, will you?"

"What do you want me to say?"

"Either let him transfer me out to the infantry," said Keane, and Michael's mind registered, This one, too, and for what reasons! "or," Keane went on, "let him take me with him when he leaves camp. I'm the sort of man he needs. I'm not afraid of being killed, I have nerves of steel. When the jeep was strafed and the other men were hit, I just watched them as coolly as if I was sitting in a movie looking at it on the screen. That's the sort of man Pavone needs with him ..."

I wonder, Michael thought.

"Will you talk to him?" Keane pleaded. "Will you? Every time I start to talk to him, he says, 'Private Keane, are those lists typed yet?' And he laughs at me. I can see him laughing at me," Keane said wildly. "It gives him a distorted pleasure to think that he has the brother of Gordon Keane sitting back in the Communication Zone, typing rosters. Whitacre, you've got to talk to him for me. The war will be over and I will never be in a single battle if someone doesn't help me!"

"O.K.," Michael said. "I'll talk to him." Then, harshly and cruelly, because Keane was the kind of man who invited cruelty from everyone he spoke to, "Let me tell you, though, if you ever get into a battle, I hope to God you're no place near me."

"Thanks, Boy, thanks a lot," Keane said heartily. "Gee, Boy, it's great of you to talk to Pavone about me. I'll remember you for this, Boy, I really will."

Michael strode off ahead of Keane and for awhile Keane took the hint and stayed behind and they did not talk. But near the end of the hour, just before Keane was due to go in, he caught up with Michael, and said, reflectively, as though he had been thinking about it for a long time, "I think I'll go on sick call tomorrow and get some Epsom salts. Just one good bowel movement and it may start it, I may be a new man from then on."

"You have my heartiest best wishes," Michael said gravely.

"You won't forget about talking to Pavone now, will you?"

"I won't forget. I will personally suggest," Michael said, "that you should be dropped by parachute on General Rommel's Headquarters."

"It may be funny to you," Keane said aggrievedly, "but if you came from a family like mine, with something like that to live up to ..."

"I'll talk to Pavone," Michael said. "Wake Stellevato up and turn in. I'll see you in the morning."

"It was a great relief," said Keane, "to be able to talk to someone like this. Thanks, Boy."

Michael watched the brother of the dead Medal-of-Honor winner walk heavily off toward the tent near the end of the line where Stellevato slept.

Stellevato was a short, small-boned Italian, nineteen years old, with a soft dark face, like a plush sofa cushion. He came from Boston, where he had been an iceman, and his speech was a mixture of liquid Italian sounds and the harsh long a's of the streets adjoining the Charles River. When he served as a sentry, he stood in one place, leaning against a jeep hood, and nothing could make him move. He had been in the infantry in the States and he had developed such a profound distaste for walking that now he even got into his jeep to ride the fifty yards to the latrine. Back in England he had fought the entire Medical Corps in a stubborn, clever battle to convince the Army that his arches were bad and that he was not fit to serve any longer on foot. It was his great triumph of the war, one that he remembered more dearly than anything else that had happened since Pearl Harbor, that he had finally prevailed and had been assigned to Pavone as a driver. Michael was very fond of him and when they were on duty together like this they both stood lounging against the jeep hood, smoking surreptitiously, exchanging confidences, Michael digging into his mind to remember random meetings with movie stars whom Stellevato admired hungrily, and Stellevato describing in detail the ice-and-coal route in Boston, and the life of the Stellevato family, father, mother, and three sons in the apartment on Salem Street.

"I was havin' a dream," Stellevato said, slouched into his raincoat, with all the buttons torn off, a squat, unsoldierly silhouette with a carelessly held weapon angling off its shoulder, "a dream about the United States when that son of a bitch Keane woke me up. That Keane," Stellevato said angrily, "there's somethin' wrong with him. He comes over and smacks me across the shins like a cop kickin' a bum off a park bench, and he makes a helluva racket, he keeps sayin', loud enough to wake up the whole Army, 'Wake up, Boy, it's rainin' out and you got some walkin' to do, come on, wake up, Boy, you got to walk in the cold, cold rain.' " Stellevato shook his head aggrievedly. "He don't have to tell me. I can see it's rainin'. He enjoys makin' people miserable, that feller. And this dream I was havin', I didn't want it to break off in the middle . . ." Stellevato's voice grew remote and soft. "I was on the truck with my old man. It was a sunny day in the summertime and my old man was sitting on the seat next to me, sort of sleeping and smoking one of those crooked little black cigars, Italo Balbo cigars, maybe you know them?"

"Yes," said Michael gravely. "Five for ten cents."

"Italo Balbo," said Stellevato, "he's the one who flew from Italy. He was a big hero to the Italians a long time ago and they named a cigar after him."

"I heard of him," said Michael. "He got killed in Africa."

"He did? I ought to write it to my old man. He can't read, but my girl, Angelina, comes over and reads the letters to him and my old lady. Well, he was smokin' one of these cigars," Stellevato's voice fell back into the soft Boston summertime of the dream, "and we was goin' slow because we had to stop at every other house, and he woke up and he said, 'Nikki, take twenty-fi' cents' worth up to Mrs. Schwartz today, but tell her she gotta pay cash.' I could hear his voice just like I was back on the truck behind the wheel," Stellevato murmured. "So I got off the truck and I picked up the ice, and I went up the stairs to Mrs. Schwartz, and my father yelled after me, 'Nikki, come on ri' down. Don't you stay up there with that Mrs. Schwartz.' He was always yelling things like that at me, and then he would go off to sleep and he wouldn't know if I stayed up there for the matinee and evening performance. Mrs. Schwartz opened the door, we had all kinds of customers in that neighborhood, Italian, Irish, Polack, Jewish, I was very popular with everybody, and you'd be surprised all the whiskey and coffee cake and noodle soup I got in a day's work on that route. Mrs. Schwartz opened the door, a nice fat blonde woman, and she patted my cheek and she said, 'Nikki, it's a hot day, stay and I'll give you a glass of beer,' but I said, 'My father is waiting downstairs and he's wide awake,' so she said come back at four o'clock, and she gave me the twenty-five cents and I went downstairs and my father looked sore, and he said, 'Nikki, you gotta make up your mind, are you a businessman or are you the farmer's prize bull?' But then he laughed and said, 'As long as you got the twenty-fi' cents, O.K.' Then somehow, everybody was in the truck, the whole family, like on Sunday, and my girl Angelina, and her mother, and we were comin' home from the beach, and I was just holding Angelina's hand, she never lets me do anything else, because we're going to get married, but her old lady is a different story, and we were sitting down at the table, everybody was there, my two brothers, the one that's in Guadalcanal and the one that's in Iceland, and my old man pouring a bottle of wine he made and my old lady bringing a big plate of spaghetti . . . And that's when that son of a bitch Keane hit me across the shins . . ."

Stellevato fell silent for a moment. "I really wanted to come to the end of that dream," he said softly, and then Michael knew that he was weeping.

Tactfully, Michael said nothing.

"We had two General Motors trucks. Painted yellow," Stellevato said, his voice echoing with homesickness for the yellow trucks, for his father, for the streets of Boston, for the weather of Massachusetts, for the flesh of Mrs. Schwartz, and the touch of his fiancée's hand, for the wine of his home and the clamor of his brothers' voices over the Sunday-night spaghetti. "We was expanding. My father started out with a eighteen-year-old horse and a secondhand wagon when he arrived from Italy, and by the time the war began we had two trucks and we were thinking of buying another one and hiring a man to run it. Then me and my brothers were drafted and we had to sell the trucks and my old man went and got another horse, because he can't read or write and he can't run a truck. My girl writes he loves the horse, it's a spotted one, very young, only seven years old, but it's no General Motors truck. We were really doing all right. Right on my route I had fourteen different women I could visit any time I wanted to between the hours of nine in the morning and four in the afternoon. I'll bet, Mike," Stellevato said, his voice youthfully proud, "you never had anything like that in Hollywood."

"Never, Nikki," said Michael gravely. "There was never anything like that in Hollywood."

"When I get back, though," Stellevato said soberly, "that's all changed. I'm going to marry Angelina or somebody else if Angelina's changed her mind, and I'm going to raise some kids, and it's going to be one woman for me and that's all, and if I ever catch her cheating, I'll put the ice forks through her skull . . ."

I must write this to Margaret, Michael thought, the fourteen women on one route all forsworn and the single love firmly established in the war-weary heart.

Michael heard the sound of a man climbing out of his tent near by. He saw a shadowy figure approaching.

"Who's there?" he asked.

"Pavone," a voice said in the darkness, then, as a hurried afterthought, "Colonel Pavone."

Pavone came up to Michael and Stellevato. "Who's on?" he asked.

"Stellevato and Whitacre," said Michael.

"Hello, Nikki," said Pavone. "Having a good time?"

"Great, Colonel." Stellevato's voice was warm and pleased. He was very fond of Pavone, who treated him more as a mascot than as a soldier, and who occasionally traded dirty jokes and stories of the old country in Italian with him.

"Whitacre," said Pavone, "are you all right?"

"Dandy," said Michael. In the rainy darkness there was a sense of friendliness and relaxation that never could exist between the Colonel and the enlisted men in the full light of day.

"Good," said Pavone. His voice was tired and reflective as he leaned against the jeep hood beside them. Carelessly, he lit a cigarette, not hiding the match, his eyebrows shining dark and heavy in the sudden small flare.

"You come out to relieve me, Colonel?" Stellevato asked.

"Not exactly, Nikki. You sleep too much anyway. You'll never amount to anything if you sleep all the time."

"I don't want to amount to anything," Stellevato said. "I just want to get back to my ice route."

"If I had a route like that," said Michael, "I'd want to get back to it, too."

"Did he tell you those lies about the fourteen women, too?" Pavone asked.

"I swear to God," Stellevato said.

"I never knew an Italian who told the truth about women," said Pavone. "If you ask me, Nikki's a virgin."

"I'll show you some of the letters they write me," Stellevato said, his tone injured.

"Colonel," Michael said, emboldened by the darkness and the joking, "I'd like to talk to you for a minute. That is, if you're not going back to bed."

"I can't sleep," said Pavone. "Sure. Come on, let's take a walk." He and Michael took two or three steps together. Pavone stopped and called to Stellevato, "Watch out for paratroopers and husbands, Nikki."

He took Michael's arm lightly as they walked away from the jeep. "You know something," he said softly, "I believe Nikki's telling the absolute truth about that ice route." He chuckled. Then his voice grew more serious. "What's on your mind, Michael?"

"I wanted to ask a favor." Michael hesitated. Here, again, he thought irritably, the endless necessity of decision. "I want you to have me transferred to a combat unit."

Pavone walked quietly for a moment. "What is it?" he asked. "Brooding?"

"Maybe," said Michael, "maybe. The church today, the Canadians . . . I don't know. I began to remember what I was in the war for."

"You know what you're in the war for?" Pavone laughed dryly. "Lucky man." They walked ten paces in silence. "When I was Nikki's age," he said, finally, surprisingly, "a woman gave me the worst time of my life."

Michael bit his lips, annoyed at the manner in which Pavone had ignored him.

"Tonight, lying there in my tent, during the air raid, I kept remembering it," Pavone said reflectively. "That's why I couldn't sleep. I was nineteen years old and I was running a burlesque theatre in New York. I was making three hundred dollars a week and I kept a girl in an apartment on Central Park South. A beautiful girl . . ." In Pavone's voice, soft and full of memory and longing, the beauty of the girl in the apartment on Central Park South so many years before was sorrowfully celebrated. "I was crazy about her. I spent all my money on her, and I used to think about her all day long. When you're nineteen years old and as funny-looking as I am, your gratitude can unhinge your mind. You don't see the plainest thing that every elevator operator and colored maid understands the first time they clap eyes on you and the girl together. She had a friend. A girl from Minneapolis who worked in the same night club. I used to take them both out to dinner almost every night. They used to make me feel like a big man, laughing at my jokes, giving me silly presents they'd buy for me . . . Shaking their heads and worrying about my drinking too much and smoking too many cigars. Two women like that can make you feel more important than the President of the United States. At the age of nineteen, I thought I was one of the most promising and unique specimens ever to show up on Manhattan Island. Then one afternoon, I came home early and I found them in bed together." Pavone stopped and pulled thoughtfully at a loose piece of canvas on a weapons carrier that was parked under a tree. "I'll never forget the way they looked at me when I came into the room. Cold, wild, despising me . . . Then my girl giggled. I remember the first thing that came into my head, 'They're laughing at me because I'm a Wop.' I went after them. I beat them till I couldn't raise my hands any more. They tried to run away from me, but they never opened their mouths. They didn't scream or beg or anything, they just kept running around the apartment, naked, falling, not making a sound, until I quit and left. When I went downstairs into the street I was sure everyone knew all about me, everyone in the city, that I was a fool, that I was no good as a man . . . I couldn't stand it. I went down to the office of the French Line and I got passage on the *Champlain* for the next day. I stayed drunk all the way over and I arrived in Paris with forty dollars to my name . . . I've been running away from that bedroom ever since . . . God," he said, looking up at the dark, rainy sky, "twenty years later, in a hole in the ground, in the middle of an air raid, I wake up feeling myself blush from head to toe, thinking about it. Thanks for listening to me," Pavone said brusquely. "If it's dark enough, or I'm drunk enough, I can tell the story. It helps considerably. I'm going back to bed."

"Colonel," Michael began, "I started to ask you a favor."

"What?" Pavone stopped and turned back to Michael.

"I want to ask you to transfer me to a combat outfit," Michael said, feeling silly at the heroics of his request.

Pavone chuckled sourly. "What bedroom are *you* running from?" he asked.

"It isn't anything like that," Michael said, encouraged by the darkness. "It's just that I feel I have to be of use . . ."

"What egotism," Pavone said, and Michael was surprised by the loathing in his voice. "Christ, I hate intellectual soldiers! You think all the Army has to do these days is make sure you

470

can make the proper sacrifice to satisfy your jerky little consciences! Not happy in the service?" he inquired harshly. "You don't think driving a jeep is dignified enough for a college graduate? You won't be content until you get a bullet in your balls. The Army isn't interested in your problems, Mr. Whitacre. The Army'll use you when it needs you, don't you worry. Maybe for only one minute in four years, but it'll use you. And maybe you'll have to die in that minute, but meanwhile don't come around with your goddamn cocktail-party conscience, asking me to give you a cross to climb on. I'm busy running an outfit and I can't take the time or the effort to put up crosses for half-baked PFC's from Harvard."

"I didn't go to Harvard," Michael said absurdly.

"Never mention that transfer to me again, Soldier," Pavone said. "Good night."

"Yes, Sir," Michael said. "Thank you, Sir."

Pavone turned and strode off in the darkness toward his puptent, his shoes making a sliding wet sound on the grass.

The son of a bitch, Michael thought bruisedly, it just shows you can't trust an officer. Slowly he trudged past the line of pup-tents, obscure shadows in the wet night. He felt embarrassed and hurt. No part of a war ever turned out to be anything like what you expected it to be. He stopped at his own tent and reached in and took out the bottle of Calvados he had been hoarding. He took a long drink, the raw alcohol knotting and burning in his chest. I'll probably die, Michael thought, of an ulcer of the duodenum, in a field hospital near Cherbourg. I'll be buried in the same cemetery with the men of the First Division and the Twenty-ninth who died taking pillboxes and broken ancient towns, and the French will come out on Sunday and put flowers on my grave in sorrowful gratitude. He took another drink, emptying the bottle, and placed the bottle back under the canvas.

He walked thoughtfully down the line. Everybody is in flight, he thought dreamily, through the Calvados, in flight from Lesbians, in flight from the Italians and the Jews who were their parents, in flight from frigid wives and brothers who won the Congressional Medal of Honor, in flight from the infantry and regret, in flight from conscience and misspent lives. The Germans five miles away, too, it would be interesting to know what they were in flight from. Two armies in despairing flight toward each other, fleeing the dreadful memories of peace.

Ah, God, Michael thought, watching the first charcoal of dawn smudge the sky over the German Army, ah, God, how wonderful it would be to be killed today.

471

AT NINE O'CLOCK the planes started to come over. B-17's, B-24's, Mitchells, Marauders. Noah had never seen so many planes in his whole life. It was like the Air Forces in the recruiting posters, deliberate, orderly, shining in a bright-blue summer sky, aluminum tribute to the inexhaustible energy and cunning of the factories of America. Noah stood up in the hole he had been living in for the past week with Burnecker and watched the smooth formations with interest.

"It's about time," Burnecker said sourly. "The stinking Air Force. They should've been here three days ago."

Noah watched without saying anything, as flak from the German guns began to bloom in black puffs among the glistening shapes so high above the lines. Here and there a plane was hit and wavered out of formation. Some of the stricken planes turned and glided down the sky, trailing smoke, making for friendly fields behind them, but others exploded in silent bursts of fire, pale against the bright sky, and hurtled down the many thousands of feet in disintegrating balls of smoke and flame. Parachutes gleamed here and there and swung deliberately over the battlefield, white silk parasols for a sunny, summer, French morning.

Burnecker was right. The attack was to have started three days before. But the weather had been bad. Yesterday the Air Forces had sent some planes over, but the clouds had closed in and after an opening bombardment, the planes had gone back and the infantry had clung to its holes. But this morning, there was no doubt about it.

"It's sunny enough today," Burnecker said, "to kill the whole German Army from 30,000 feet."

At eleven o'clock, after the Air Forces had theoretically destroyed or demoralized all the opposition in front of the massed American troops on the ground, the infantry was to move, open a hole for the armor, and keep it open for the rolling fresh divisions which would pierce deep into the German rear. Lieutenant Green, who was now in command of the Company, had explained it all very clearly to them. While the men had on the surface kept a cool skepticism about this neat arrangement, it was impossible now, watching the terrible precision of the huge aircraft above them, not to feel that this was going to be easy.

Good, Noah thought, it is going to be a parade. Ever since his return from the days behind the enemy lines, he had kept to himself as much as he could, remaining reticent, trying, in the days of rest which had been permitted him, and the more or less uneventful hours in the line, to develop a new attitude, a philosophy of aloof detachment, to protect him once and for all from the hatred of Rickett and whichever other men in the Company felt as Rickett did about him. In a way, as he watched the planes roar above him, and heard the thunder of their bombs out in front of him, he was grateful to Rickett. Rickett had absolved him from the necessity of proving himself, because he had demonstrated that no matter what Noah did, if he took Paris singlehanded, if he killed an SS brigade in a day, Rickett would not accept him.

Now, Noah decided, nothing is up to me. I travel with the tide. No faster, no slower, no better, no worse. If they want to advance, I will advance, if they want to run, I'll run. Standing in the damp hole, behind the everlasting green hedge, listening to the wild grumbling of the bombs and the shriek of the artillery over his head, he felt strangely at peace with his new decision. It was a gloomy and hopeless peace, and it came only from the most bitter defeat of his dearest hopes, but it was soothing, relaxing, and, in a sour way, held promise of survival in it.

He watched the planes with interest.

Abstractly, squinting out in front of him through the hedge toward the enemy's lines, shaking his head a little to clear his ears of the shock of the percussion of the bombs, he felt sorry for the Germans behind the bloody imaginary fall line of the Air Forces. On the ground himself, armed with a weapon that carried a two-ounce projectile a pitiful thousand yards, he felt a common hatred for the impersonal killers above him, a double self-pity for those helpless men cowering in holes, blasted and sought out by the machine age with thousand-pound explosives hurled from the impregnable distance of five miles. He looked at Burnecker beside him and he could tell from the pained grimace on the thin young face that something of the same thoughts were passing through his friend's brain.

"God," Burnecker whispered, "why don't they stop? That's enough, that's enough. What do they want to do, make mince pie?"

By now, the German anti-aircraft guns had been silenced and the planes wheeled calmly overhead, as safely as though they were conducting maneuvers over Wright Field.

Then there was a whistling around him, a roaring and upheaval of the green earth. Burnecker grabbed him and dragged him down into the hole. They crouched together, as far down as they could get, their legs jumbled together, their helmets touching, as bomb after bomb hit around them, deafening them, covering them with a pelting shower of earth, stones and broken twigs.

"Oh, the bastards," Burnecker was saying, "oh, the murdering Air Force bastards."

They heard screams on all sides of them and the cries of the wounded. But it was impossible to get out of the hole while the bombs poured down in a rattling, closely spaced barrage. Overhead, Noah could hear the steady, droning, business-like roar of the planes, untouched, untouchable, going calmly about their business, the men in them confident of their skill, pleased, no doubt, for the time being, with the results they imagined they were achieving.

"Oh, the miserable, easy-living, extra-pay murderers," Burnecker was saying. "They won't leave one of us alive."

This will be the final thing the Army will do to me, Noah thought, it will kill me itself. It won't trust the Germans to do the job. They just mustn't tell Hope how it happened. She mustn't ever know the Americans did it to me . . .

"Flying pay!" Burnecker was shouting by now, in between explosions, his voice wild with hatred. "Everybody's a Sergeant, everybody a Colonel! The Norden bombsight! The wonder of modern science! We should've expected it! Christ, they even bombed Switzerland one day! Precision bombing! The bastards can't even tell one country from another, how the hell can you expect them to tell one army from the next!"

He was shouting it directly into Noah's face, four inches away, spraying saliva over Noah in his rage. Noah knew that Burnecker was shouting and carrying on like this to keep them both sane, both low in the hole, both clutching onto a last hope and shred of life.

"They don't care," Burnecker shouted. "They don't care who the hell they hit. They got a standing order to drop a hundred tons of bombs a day. They don't care if they drop it on their own mothers! The goddamn navigator probably went out and got clap last night and he's a little jittery this morning and wants to get back to sick call early, so he pushed the button a couple of minutes in advance. What the hell, it's another mission, no matter what. Only five more to go, he'll be back home in another month, anyway . . . I swear to God, the next guy I see with wings on his chest I'm going to go up and kill him with my bare hands. I swear to God . . ."

Then, miraculously, the bombing stopped. The noise of engines still continued above them, but somehow, a correction had been made, and the planes were moving on to other targets.

Burnecker slowly stood up and looked out. "Oh, God," he said brokenly, at what he saw.

Trembling, feeling his knees weak beneath him, Noah began to stand, too. But Burnecker pushed him down.

"Stay down," Burnecker said harshly. "Let the Medics clean 'em up. They're mostly replacements anyway. Stay where you are." He pushed Noah forcibly back and down. "I bet those bloody idiots'll come back and start dropping things on us again right away. Don't get caught out in the open. Noah . . ." He bent beside Noah and gripped Noah's arms passionately with fierce hands. "Noah, we have to stay together. You and me. All the time. We're lucky for each other. We take care of each other. Nothing'll ever happen to either of us if we hang onto each other. The whole damn Company'll die, but you and me, we'll come out . . . we'll come out . . ."

He shook Noah violently. His eyes were wild, his mouth was working, his voice was hoarse with the intensity of his belief, tested now so many times, on the water of the Channel, in the besieged stone farmhouse, in the sliding salt tide of the canal on the night that Cowley had drowned.

"You got to promise me, Noah," Burnecker whispered, "we don't let them break us up. Never! No matter how hard they try! Promise me!"

Noah began to cry, the tears rolling down his cheeks softly and helplessly at his friend's need and mystic faith. "Sure, Johnny," he said. "You bet, Johnny." And for a moment, he believed, along with Burnecker, that they had been given a sign, that they would survive whatever lay ahead of them, if somehow they clung to each other.

Twenty minutes later what was left of the Company got up from the line of foxholes and advanced to the positions from which they had withdrawn to give the planes a margin for error. Then they broke through the hedge and started across the bomb-marked field toward where the Germans were theoretically all dead or demoralized.

The men walked slowly, in a thin, thoughtful line across the cropped pasture grass, holding their rifles and tommyguns at their hips. Is this the whole Company, Noah thought with dull surprise, is this all that's left? All the replacements who had been put in the week before, and who had never fired a shot, were they already gone?

In the next field, Noah could see another thin line of men, walking with the same slow, weary thoughtfulness toward an embankment with a ditch at its bottom that made a sharp traversing line across the green landscape. Artillery was still going over their heads, but there was no small-arms fire to be heard. The planes had gone back to England, leaving the ground littered with shining silver bits of tinsel that they had dropped to confuse the enemy's radar equipment. The sun caught the strips of brightness in sparkling pinpoints among the rich green of the grass, attracting Noah's eye again and again as he walked side by side, close to Johnny Burnecker.

It seemed to take the line a long time to get to the cover of the embankment, but finally they were there. Automatically, without a signal, the men threw themselves into the small ditch, against the safe grassy slope of the shielding embankment, although there still hadn't been a shot fired at them. They lay there, as though this had been a dear objective and they had fought for days to reach it.

"Off your ass!" It was Rickett's voice, the same tone, the same vocabulary, whether he was snarling at a man to clean a latrine in Florida or charge a machine-gun post in Normandy. "The war ain't over. Get up over that there ditch."

Noah and Burnecker lay slyly, with heads averted, against the soft sloping grass, pretending that Rickett was not there, that Rickett was not alive.

Three or four of the replacements stood up, with a jangle of equipment, and started climbing heavily up. Rickett followed them and stood at the top shouting down at the rest of the men. "Come on, off your ass, off your ass . . ."

Regretfully, Noah and Burnecker stood up and clambered up the slippery six feet. The rest of the men around them slowly were doing the same thing. Burnecker, who reached the top first, helped Noah. They stood for a moment, peering ahead of them. A long field, dotted with blown-up cows, stretched ahead of them toward a row of hedges, spaced with trees, in the distance. It still seemed very quiet. The three or four replacements who had been the first to climb up were tentatively walking out ahead, and Rickett was still snarling away.

As he took the first few steps across the quiet field, following the other men, Noah hated Rickett more fiercely than he ever had before.

Then, without warning, the machine guns started. There were the high screams of thousands of bullets around him, and men falling, before he heard the distant mechanical rattling sound of the guns themselves.

The line hesitated for a moment, the men staring bewilderedly at the enigmatic hedge from which the fire came.

"Come on! Come on!" Rickett's voice yelled crazily over the noise of the guns. "Keep moving!"

But half the men were down by now. Noah grabbed Burnecker's arm, and they turned and raced, crouching low, the few yards back to the edge of the embankment. They flung themselves down, sobbing for breath, into the green safety of the ditch. One by one the other men came tumbling back over the edge to crash, sobbing and exhausted, into the ditch. Rickett appeared on the brink, swaying crazily, waving his arms around, shouting something thickly through an arching spurt of blood that seemed to come from his throat. He was hit again and slid face down on top of Noah. Noah could feel the hot wetness of the Sergeant's blood on his face. He pulled back, although Rickett was clinging to him, his hands around Noah's shoulders, gripping into the pack-harness on his back.

"Oh, you bathtards!" Rickett said distinctly, "oh, you bathtards." Then he relaxed and slithered into the ditch at Noah's feet.

"Dead," Burnecker said. "The son of a bitch is finally dead."

Burnecker pulled Rickett's body to one side while Noah slowly tried to wipe the blood off his face.

The firing stopped and it was quiet again, except for shouts from the wounded out in the field. When a man raised his head carefully to look over the embankment to see what could be done, the guns started again, and the grass on the edge of the embankment snapped and slashed through the air as the bullets cut through it. The remnants of the Company lay exhausted, then, along the ditch.

"The Air Force," Burnecker said coldly. "All opposition was going to be wiped out. Destroyed or demoralized. They're pretty demoralized, aren't they? The next soldier I see with wings, I swear to God . . ."

The men lay silently, breathing more normally now, waiting for someone else to do something with the war.

After awhile Lieutenant Green showed up. Noah could hear the high, girlish voice as Lieutenant Green came hurrying along the ditch, imploring the men to move. ". . . impossible," Lieutenant Green was screaming. "Get up there. You've got to keep moving. Keep moving. You can't just stay here. The second platoon is sending a party out on the left to get those machine guns, but we have to keep them pinned down from here. Come on, get up, get up . . ."

There was a shrill, hopeless note in Lieutenant Green's voice, and the men didn't even look at him. They turned their faces into the soft grass of the slope, ignoring the Lieutenant.

Suddenly, Lieutenant Green clambered up the side of the embankment himself. He stood on top, calling out, imploring, but none of the men moved. Noah watched Lieutenant Green with interest, waiting for him to die. The machine guns started up again, but Green kept jumping around wildly, like a maniac, shouting incoherently, "It's easy. There's nothing to it. Come on . . ."

Finally Green jumped down again and walked away from the ditch, back across the open field. The guns died down again and everybody was pleased the Lieutenant had left.

This is the system, Noah thought craftily. I'll live forever. Just do whatever everybody else is doing. What can they do to me if I just stay here?

On both sides of them there were the heavy sounds of battle, but they couldn't see anything, and there was no way of telling how things were going. But the ditch remained safe and quiet. The Germans couldn't reach them in the ditch, and the men had no desire to do any harm to the Germans from the ditch. There was a pleasant, warming sense of secure permanence about the arrangement. At some future time, the Germans might withdraw or be encircled from somewhere else, and then there would be time to think about getting up and moving on. Not before.

Burnecker took out his K ration and opened it up. "Veal loaf," Burnecker said flatly, eating slabs of it off his knife. "Who the hell ever invented veal loaf?" He threw the little bag of synthetic lemonade powder away. "Not if I was dying of thirst," he said.

Noah didn't feel like eating. From time to time he stared at Rickett, lying dead five feet away from him. Rickett's eyes were wide open and there was a bloody grimace of anger and command on his face. His throat was badly torn open under the raw mouth. Noah tried to make himself be pleased with the sight of his dead enemy, but he found it was impossible. Rickett, by the act of dying, had changed from the brutal Sergeant, the vicious bully, the foul-mouthed killer, and had become another dead American, a lost friend, a vanished ally . . .

Noah shook his head and turned away from staring at Rickett.

Lieutenant Green was coming along the ditch again, and with him was a tall man, who walked slowly, peering thoughtfully at the resting, stubborn men in the ditch. When Green and the other man got closer, Burnecker said, "Holy God, two stars."

Noah sat up and stared. He had never been this close to a Major General in all his months in the Army.

"General Emerson," Burnecker whispered nervously. "What the hell is he doing here? Why doesn't he go home?"

Suddenly, with sharp agility, the General leaped up the side of the embankment and stood at the top, in full view of the Germans. He walked slowly along the edge, talking down at the men in the ditch, who stared up at him numbly. He had a pistol in a holster, and he carried a short swagger stick under one arm.

Impossible, Noah thought, it must be somebody dressed up like a General. Green is playing a trick on us.

The machine guns were going again, but the General did not change the tempo of his movements. He walked smoothly and easily, like a trained athlete, talking down into the ditch as he crossed in front of the men.

"All right, Boys," Noah heard him say as he approached, and the voice was calm, friendly, not loud. "Up we go now, Boys. We can't stay here all day. Up we go. We're holding up the whole line here and we've got to move now. Just up to the next row of hedges, Boys, that's all I'm asking of you. Come on, Son, you can't stay down there . . ."

As he watched, Noah saw the General's left hand jerk, and blood begin to drop down from the wrist. There was just the slightest twist of the General's mouth, and then he continued talking in the same quiet, but somehow piercing tone, grasping the swagger stick more tightly. He stopped in front of Noah and Burnecker. "All right, Boys," he was saying kindly, "just walk on up here . . ."

Noah stared at him. The General's face was long and sad and handsome, the kind of face you might expect to see on a scientist or a doctor, thin, intellectual, quiet. Looking at his face confused Noah, made him feel as though the Army had fooled him all along. Looking at the sorrowful, courageous face, he suddenly felt that it was intolerable that he, Noah, could refuse a man like that anything.

He moved and, at the same moment, he felt Burnecker move beside him. A little dry, appreciative smile momentarily wrinkled the General's mouth. "That's it, Boys," he said. He patted Noah's shoulder. Noah and Burnecker ran forward fifteen yards and dropped into a hole for cover.

Noah looked back. The General was still standing on the brink of the ditch, although the fire was very heavy by now, and men all along the line were leaping up and advancing in short bursts across the field.

Generals, he thought hazily, as he turned back toward the enemy, he had never known what Generals were for, before this . . .

He and Burnecker leaped out of their hole, just as two more men dived into it. The Company, or the half Company that was left, was moving at last.

Twenty minutes later they had reached the line of hedge from which the enemy machine guns had been firing. Mortars had finally found the range and had destroyed one of the nests in a corner of the field, and the other sections had pulled out before Noah and the Company reached them.

Wearily, Noah kneeled by the side of the cleverly concealed, heavily sandbagged position, now blown apart to reveal three Germans dead at their torn gun. One of the Germans was still kneeling behind it. Burnecker reached down with his boot and shoved at the kneeling dead man. The German rocked gently, then fell over on his side.

Noah turned away and drank a little water from his canteen. His throat was brassy with thirst. He hadn't fired his rifle all day, but his arms and shoulders ached as though he had caught the recoil a hundred times.

He looked out through the hedge. Three hundred yards away, across the usual field of bombholes and dead cows, was another thick hedge, and machine-gun fire was coming from there. He sighed as he saw Lieutenant Green walking toward him, urging the men out once more. He wondered hazily what had happened to the General. Then he and Burnecker started out again.

Noah was hit in the first ten feet, and Burnecker dragged him back behind the safety of the hedge.

An aid man came up with surprising speed. Noah had lost a great deal of blood very quickly and he felt cold and remote and the aid man's face swam above him dreamily. The aid man was a little Greek with crossed eyes and a dapper moustache, and the strange dark eyes and the thin moustache floated independently in the air as the aid man gave him a transfusion, with Burnecker helping. Shock, Noah remembered fuzzily. In the last war a man would be hit and feel perfectly all right and ask for a cigarette, it had been in a magazine somewhere, and ten minutes later he would be dead. But it was different in this war. This was a high-class, up-to-the-minute type of war, with blood to spare. The cockeyed Greek aid man gave him some morphine, too. That was very thoughtful of him, above and beyond the call of the Medical Corps . . . Strange, to be so fond of a crosseyed man who used to be a short-order cook in a diner in Scranton, Pennsylvania. Ham and eggs, hamburger, canned soup. Now it was canned blood. His name was Markos. Ackerman, out of Odessa, and Markos, out of Athens, linked by a tube of preserved blood somewhere near the reduced city of St. Lô, in the province of Normandy, on a summer's day, with an Iowa farmer named Burnecker crouched beside them, weeping, weeping . . .

"Noah, Noah," the boy from Iowa was sobbing, "how do you feel? Are you all right?"

Noah thought he was smiling up at Johnny Burnecker, but after awhile he realized nothing much was happening on his face, no matter how hard he tried to move it. And it was getting terribly cold, very cold for summer, very cold for noon, very cold for France, very cold for July and a young man . . .

"Johnny," he managed to whisper. "Don't worry, Johnny. Take care of yourself. I'll be back, Johnny, honest, I'll be back . . ."

The war had turned out funny. No more snarling and cursing. No more Rickett, because Rickett had died in his arms, covering him with Sergeant's blood. Now it was the soft-voiced, soft-handed, crosseyed little short-order cook, as gentle as Christ, a cockeyed, thin-moustached Christ with a strange Greek name, and it was the thin, sorrowful face of the General, who earned his pay by walking out into gunfire with a little stick in his hand, a General with a face full of tragedy and authority, whom you could not refuse anything; and it was the racked sobbing of his brother Johnny Burnecker, whom he had promised never to desert because they were lucky for each other, they would live, though the whole Company died, as of course they would, because there were so many hedges across so many fields that still lay ahead of all of them. The Army had changed, was changing, swiftly, softly, in a roaring mist of tubes and tourniquets, morphine and tears.

They lifted Noah onto a stretcher and started carrying him back. Noah raised his head. Seated on the ground, with his helmet off, abandoned to grief, sat Johnny Burnecker, weeping for his friend. Noah tried to call out to him, to assure him that all in the end would turn out well, but no sound came from his throat. He dropped his head and closed his eyes, as he was borne away, because he could not bear to see his deserted friend any more.

CHAPTER THIRTY-ONE

THE DEAD HORSES were beginning to bloat and smell in the strong summer sun. The odor mingled with the acrid, medicinal smell of the ruptured ambulance convoy that lay, a jumble of overturned wagons, spilled pungent powders, scattered heaps of papers, torn and useless red crosses, along the road. The dead and the wounded had been removed, but otherwise the convoy remained, curving up the long hill, just as it had been left after the strafing and dive-bombing Americans had passed over it.

Christian went by it slowly, on foot, still carrying his Schmeisser, in a straggling group of perhaps twenty men, none of whom was known to him. He had picked them up early in the morning, after he had become separated from the hastily organized platoon with which he had been posted three days before. The platoon, he was sure, had deserted to the Americans during the night. Christian felt a somber sense of relief that he was no longer responsible for them or their actions.

Looking at the dead convoy, sadly marked with the red

crosses that had done no good at all, he was overwhelmed with a sense of anger and despair. Anger at the swooping, 400-mile-an-hour young Americans who had come upon the slow-moving wagons toiling up the hill with their load of broken and dying men and had, in the wanton fury of destruction, roweled it with their machine guns and rockets.

The men around him, he could tell from glancing at them, did not share his anger. All that was left was their despair. They were past anger, as they trudged, gravel-eyed and exhausted, under heavy packs, some of them with no weapons, past the ruins of the convoy, past the growing smell of the horses. They dragged slowly eastward, keeping their eyes with dull wariness on the dangerous clear sky above them, moving like a dying beast, without reason or hope, toward the final cool, sheltered place where they might lie down and die. Some of them, with crazy miserliness, through all the welter of retreat and death, still carried loot with them. One man held a violin in his hand, stolen from what music-lover's living room no one would ever know. A pair of silver candlesticks jutted out of another man's pack, mute and stubborn evidence that this soldier, even in this agony, had faith in a future of dinners, table-linen, food, soft lights. A huge, red-eyed man without a helmet, whose long shock of blond hair was crusted with dust, carried in his pack a dozen wooden containers of Camembert cheese. When he passed Christian, because he was a powerful man and walked with dogged swiftness, the ripe, fermenting aroma of the melting cheese made a sick marriage with the smell of the convoy.

At the head of the convoy was a wagon on which was mounted an 88 millimeter anti-aircraft cannon. The horses were dead in the traces, in wild attitudes of gallop and fear, and there was blood all over the gun and its mounting. The German Army, Christian thought dully, as he went past, horses against airplanes. At least, in Africa, when he retreated, he had retreated with the aid of engines. He remembered the motorcycle and Hardenburg, the Italian staff car, the hospital plane that had crossed the Mediterranean with him, carrying him to Italy. It seemed to be the fate of the German Army, as a war went on, to go back to more and more primitive methods of fighting. Ersatz. Ersatz gasoline, ersatz coffee, ersatz blood, ersatz soldiers . . .

He seemed to have been retreating all his life. He had no memory any more of ever advancing any place. Retreat was the condition, the general weather of existence. Going back, going back, always hurt, always exhausted, always with the smell of German dead in his nostrils, always with enemy planes flickering behind his back, their guns dancing brightly

482

in their wings, their pilots grinning because they were safe and they were killing hundreds of men a minute.

There was a loud blowing of a horn behind him, and Christian scrambled to one side. A small, closed car sped past, its wheels sending a fine cloud of dust over him. Christian got a glimpse of clean-shaven faces, a man smoking a cigar . . .

Then somebody was shouting, and there was the howl of engines above him. Christian lumbered away from the road and dove into one of the carefully spaced holes that had thoughtfully been provided by the German Army along many of the roads of France for the use of its troops at moments like this. He crouched deep in the damp earth, covering his head, not daring to look up, listening to the returning whine of the engines, and the savage tearing sound of the guns. After two passes, the planes moved off. Christian stood up. He climbed out of the hole. None of the men he had been walking with had been touched, but the little sedan was overturned, against a tree, and it was burning. Two of the men who had been in it had been thrown clear, and were lying very still in the center of the road. The other two men were burning in a welter of spilled gasoline, torn rubber and whipcord upholstery.

Christian walked slowly up to where the two men were lying face down on the road. He did not have to touch them to see that they were dead.

"Officers," said a voice behind him. "They wanted to ride." The man behind him spat.

The other men walked past the two dead forms and the burning car. For a moment Christian thought of ordering some of the men to help him move the bodies, but it would have meant an argument, and at the moment, it did not seem very important whether two bodies, more or less, were put to one side or not.

Christian slowly started eastward once more, feeling his bad leg shiver beneath him. He blew his nose and spat again and again to try to get the smell and the taste of the dead horses and the spilled medicine out of his mouth and throat.

The next morning he had a stroke of luck. He had pulled away from the other men during the night and had marched slowly on to the outskirts of a village, which lay across his path in the moonlight, dark, empty, seemingly lifeless. He had decided not to try to get through it by himself, at night, since it was all too possible that the inhabitants, seeing a lone soldier wandering past in the dark, might pick him off, rob him of his gun, boots and uniform, and throw him behind a hedge to rot. So he had camped under a tree, eaten sparingly of his emergency ration, and slept until dawn.

Then he had hurried through the town, almost trotting down

the cobbled road, past the gray church, the inevitable statue of victory with palms and bayonets in front of the town hall, the shuttered shops. No one was stirring. The French seemed to have vanished from the face of the land as the Germans retreated through it. Even the dogs and the cats seemed to understand that it was safer for them to hide until the bitter tide of defeated soldiers passed over them.

It was on the other side of town that his luck changed. He was hurrying, because he was still in sight of the walls of the last row of houses, and his breath was coming hoarsely into his lungs, when he saw, coming around a bend in the road ahead of him, a figure on a bicycle.

Christian stopped. Whoever it was on the bicycle was in a hurry. He kept his head down and pedaled swiftly toward where Christian was standing.

Christian moved to the middle of the road and waited. He saw that it was a young boy, perhaps fifteen or sixteen years old, capless, dressed in a blue shirt and old French Army pants, racing bumpily through the cool, misty dawn light between the still rows of poplars on each side of the road, casting a soft, elongated shadow of legs and wheels on the road in front of him.

The boy saw Christian when he was only thirty yards away. He stopped suddenly.

"Come here," Christian shouted hoarsely, in German, forgetting his French. "Walk over here."

He started toward the boy. For a moment the two of them stared at each other. The boy was very pale, with curly black hair and dark, frightened eyes. With a swift, animal-like movement, the boy picked up the front wheel of the bicycle and whirled it around. He was running with the bicycle before Christian could unsling his gun. The boy jumped onto the bicycle. Bent over, with his blue shirt filling with wind behind him, he pedaled furiously back along the road, away from Christian.

Without thinking, Christian opened fire. He caught the boy with the second burst. The bicycle careened off into the ditch alongside the road. The boy went sliding across the road to the other side, and lay there without moving.

Christian lumbered quickly along the uneven road, his boots making a thick thudding sound in the silent morning. He bent over the bicycle and picked it up. He rolled it back and forth. It was unharmed. Then he looked at the boy. The boy's head was twisted toward him, very pale and unmarked under the curly hair. There was a light blond fuzz of moustache under the slender nose. A red stain slowly spread across the back of the faded blue shirt. Christian made a movement toward the boy, but thought better of it. They'd have been bound to hear the shooting in the village, and if they found him there, fiddling over a dying child, they'd make short work of him.

Christian swung himself up on the bicycle and started east. After the weary days of walking, the ground seemed to spin past beneath him with charming swiftness and ease. His legs felt light; the dawning breeze against his cheeks was soft and cool; the light dewy green of the foliage on both sides of the road was pleasing to the eye. Now, he thought, it needn't only be officers who ride.

The roads of France seemed to have been made for bicyclists, not too rough, with the paving in fair condition, and no high hills to slow a man down. Why, it was easily possible for a man to do two hundred kilometers a day, easily . . .

He felt youthful, strong, and for the first time since he had seen the first glider coming down out of the coastal sky that bad morning so long ago, he began to feel as though there was some hope for him. After a half hour, as he was gliding down a gentle slope between two fields of half-grown wheat, pale yellow in the morning sun, he found himself whistling, a vacation-like, holiday-like, tuneless, heart-free merry sound, rising gay and uninstructed in his throat.

All that day, he fled east along the road to Paris. He passed groups of men, walking, moving slowly in overloaded farm wagons stubbornly loaded with pictures and furniture and barrels of cider. He had passed refugees before in France, a long time ago, but it had been more natural then, because they were mostly women, children and old men, and you knew they had some reason to hold onto mattresses and kitchen pots and odds and ends of furniture because they hoped to set up domestic lives somewhere else. But it was strange to see a German Army trudging along this way, young men with guns and uniforms, who could only hope either finally to be reformed on some line by some miracle and turned around to fight—or to fall into the hands of the Americans who, it was rumored, were closing in on them from all directions. In either case, framed paintings from Norman châteaux and cloisonné lamps would do them a minimum amount of good. With set faces, past all reasonableness, the defeated men streamed slowly toward Paris on the summer roads, officerless, without formations or discipline, abandoned to the tanks and the planes of the Americans who were following them. Occasionally a wheezing French bus, with a charcoal furnace, would drag past, loaded down with dusty soldiers, who would have to get out on the hills to push. Once in awhile an officer could be seen, but he would keep his mouth shut, look as lost and deserted as any of the others.

And, meanwhile, the country, in the full bloom of summer, with the geraniums high and pink and red along the farmers' walls, was shining and lovely in the long perfect days.

By evening, Christian was exhausted. He hadn't ridden a bicycle for years, and in the first hour or two he had gone too fast. Also, twice during the day, shots had been fired at him, and he had heard the bullets snipping by, past his head, and had driven himself frantically out of danger. The bicycle was wavering almost uncontrollably all over the road as he slowly pushed into the square of quite a fair-sized town at sunset. He was pleased, dully, to see that the square was full of soldiers, sitting in the cafés, lying exhausted and asleep on the stone benches in front of the town hall, tinkering hopelessly with broken-down 1925 Citroëns in an attempt to get them to move just a few more kilometers. Here, for a few moments, at least, he could be safe.

He dismounted from the bicycle, which by now was a kind of slippery enemy, raw-boned and malicious, a French machine with a sly intelligence of its own, which seemed to drag on his last strength with tenacious and murderous purpose, and which had almost thrown him four or five times on mild curves and hidden bumps in the road.

He walked stiffly beside the bicycle, his legs rigid and weak. The other men sitting and lying in the square glanced stonily at him for a moment, without interest or connection, then dropped their eyes with bleak indifference. He clutched the bicycle tightly, feeling that any one of these weary, foreign-looking, cold-eyed men would gladly murder him for the two wheels and the worn saddle if they could.

He would have liked to lie down and sleep for a few hours, but he didn't dare. Since the two shots on the road, he refused to take the risk of stopping any place, even in the most remote and quiet spot, by himself. The only safety from the lurking French now was either in speed or numbers. And he could not lie down here, in town, among the other men, because he knew that when he awoke, the bicycle would be gone. He knew that he, himself, would have leaped at the chance to steal the machine from any sleeping comrade, even from General Rommel, himself, and there was no reason to suppose the other footsore and bloody-minded gentlemen in the town square would be more fastidious.

A drink, he thought, a drink will give me a breathing spell, a drink will keep me going.

He walked stiffly through the open door of a café, wheeling the bicycle at his side. There were some soldiers sitting in the back of the room and they looked at him briefly and without surprise, as though it was the most natural thing in the world for German Sergeants to enter cafés wheeling bicycles, or leading horses, or at the controls of armored cars. Christian carefully put the bicycle against the wall and placed a chair against the back wheel. Then he sat down slowly in the chair. He gestured to the old man behind the bar. "Cognac," he said. "A double cognac."

Christian looked around the shadowy room. There were the usual signs in French and German, with the rules for the sale of alcohol on them, and the legend that only apéritifs would be sold on Tuesdays and Thursdays. This was a Thursday, Christian remembered hazily, but the special nature of this particular Thursday might be said to countermand even the regulations of a Minister of the French Government at Vichy. At any rate, the Minister who had delivered himself of the regulation was no doubt running as fast as he could at the moment and would probably be grateful for a little cognac himself. The only law anyone could be expected to observe on the evening of this summer day was the law of flight, the only authority the guns of the First and Third American Armies, not yet heard in this part of the country, but already felt, already exercising a premature and dreadful sovereignty.

The old Frenchman shuffled over with a small glass of brandy. The old man had a beard like a Jewish prophet and his teeth smelled terribly of decay, Christian noticed irritably. Was there no escaping, even in this cool dark place, the odors of ferment and mortality, the scent of dying bone and turning flesh?

"Fifty francs," said the old man, leaning horribly over Christian, his hand still cautiously on the glass.

For a moment Christian thought of arguing with the old thief about the overcharge. The French, he thought, making a good thing out of victory and defeat, advance and retreat, friend and enemy. God, he thought sourly, let the Americans have them for awhile, see how happy *they'll* be about it. He tossed the fifty francs, worn scraps of paper printed by the German Army, on the table. He would have little use for francs, soon, anyway, and he grinned within himself at the thought of the old man trying to collect on the printed, flimsy German promise from the new conquerors.

Methodically, the old man put the paper away, and dragged himself back, past the outstretched legs of the other soldiers, to his position behind the bar. Christian toyed with his glass, not drinking yet, content for the moment merely to sit, with his aching legs resting, his shoulders heavily comfortable against the wooden back of the chair. He glanced idly at the other men in the bar. It was too dark to see their faces clearly, and they were not talking or making a sound, merely sitting in attitudes of exhaustion and contemplation, sipping slowly at their drinks, as though they did not expect to be able to drink much longer, and wished to hold the memory of the alcohol, the sense of its sharpness against their tongues, as long as possible now.

Hazily, Christian remembered that other bar in Rennes, long ago, and the group of soldiers with their tunics unbuttoned, loud and boisterous and rich, drinking cheap champagne. No one was drinking champagne now, and no one was loud, and if anyone talked, he spoke in a single low phrase and was answered in a monosyllable. Yes. No. Will we die tomorrow? What will the Americans do to us? Is the road to Rennes passable? Did you hear what happened to the Panzer Lehr Division? What does the BBC say? Is it over yet? Is it over? Dimly, toying with his glass, Christian wondered whatever had happened in the long years to the Private in the Pioneers he had turned in for insubordination and improper conduct. Confined to barracks for a month. Christian smiled weakly, leaning back against his bicycle. How wonderful it would be to be confined to barracks for a month. Confine the First American Army to barracks for a month, confine the Eighth Air Force, confine all Austrians in the German Army, for improper conduct . . .

He sipped gently at the cognac. It was raw and probably not even cognac. Probably made three days ago and doctored with plain spirits. The French, the miserable French. He looked at the old man behind the bar, hating him. He knew that the old man had been dragged out of doddering retirement for this week's work. Probably, a sturdy fat merchant and his plump, sweaty wife owned this place, and had run it until now. But when they saw how things were going, had seen the first scum of the German tide racing through the town, they had resuscitated the old man and put him behind the bar, feeling that even the Germans would not take out their venom on such a poor, outdated specimen. Probably the owner and his wife were tucked away somewhere in a safe attic, eating a veal steak and a salad, with a strong bottle of wine, or they were climbing into bed with each other in a sweaty, garlicky embrace. (Remember Corinne in Rennes, the cowy flesh and the milkmaid's hands, and the coarse dyed ropes of hair.) The owner and his wife, chubbily linked in a warm featherbed, were probably chuckling at this moment at the thought of the drained soldiers paying fantastic prices to Papa in their dirty estaminet, and at the dead Germans all along the road, and at the Americans rushing toward the town, eager to pay even higher prices for their wretched raw alcohol.

He stared at the old man. The old man stared back, his little pebbles of eyes black and insolent, secure and defiant in the rotting, ancient face. Old man with thousands of printed, useless francs in his pockets, old man with bad teeth, old man who felt he would outlive half the young men sitting silently in his daughter's establishment, old man roaring within him at the thought of what dire handling lay ahead for these almost-

488

captured and almost-dead foreigners huddled around the stained tables in the dusk.

"Monsieur wishes . . . ?" the old man said in his high wheezy voice that sounded as though he were listening to a joke no one else in the room had heard.

"Monsieur wishes nothing," Christian said. The trouble was, they had been too lenient with the French. There were enemies and there were friends, and there was nothing in between. You loved or you killed, and anything else you did was politics, corruption and weakness, and finally you paid for it. Hardenburg, faceless on Capri, in the room with the armored Burn, had understood, but the politicians hadn't.

The old man veiled his eyes. Yellow, wrinkled lids, like dirty old paper, hooded down over the black, mocking pebbles of his pupils. He turned away and Christian felt that somehow the old man had won a bloody victory over him.

He drank his cognac. The alcohol was beginning to have an effect on him. He felt at once sleepy and powerful, like a giant in a dream, capable of slow, terrible movements, and enormous, semi-conscious blows.

"Finish your drink, Sergeant." It was a low, remembered voice, and Christian looked up, squinting through the increasing evening haze at the figure standing before his table.

"What?" he asked stupidly.

"I want to talk to you, Sergeant." Whoever it was, was smiling.

Christian shook his head and opened his eyes very wide. Then he recognized the man. It was Brandt, in an officer's uniform, standing over him, dusty, thin, capless, but Brandt, and smiling.

"Brandt . . ."

"Sssh." Brandt put his hand on Christian's arm. "Finish your drink and come on outside."

Brandt turned and went outside. Christian saw him there, standing against the café window, with his back to it, and a ragged column of labor troops trudging past him. Christian gulped down the rest of the cognac and stood up. The old man was watching him again. Christian pushed the chair away and carefully grabbed hold of the handlebars of the bicycle and wheeled it toward the door. He could not resist turning at the door for one last encounter with the pebbly, French, 1870, mocking, Verdun and Marne-like eyes of the antique bartender. The old man was standing in front of a poster, printed in French but inspired by the Germans, of a snail horned with one American flag and one British flag, creeping slowly up the Italian peninsula. The words on the poster ironically pointed out that even a snail would have reached Rome by now . . . The final insolence, Christian felt. Probably the old man had put the poster up this very week, straight-faced and cackling, so that every fleeing German who came by could look and suffer.

"I hope," the old man wheezed, in that voice that sounded like laughter heard among rocking chairs in a home for the aged, "that Monsieur enjoyed his drink."

The French, Christian thought furiously, they will beat us all yet.

He went out and joined Brandt.

"Walk with me," Brandt said softly. "Walk slowly around the square. I don't want anyone to hear what I am going to say to you."

He started along the narrow sidewalk, along the shuttered row of shops. Christian noticed with surprise that Brandt looked considerably older than when last they met, that there was considerable gray at the photographer's temples, and heavy lines around his eyes and mouth, and that he was very thin.

"I saw you come in," Brandt said, "and I couldn't believe my eyes. I watched you for five minutes to make sure it was you. What in God's name have they done to you?"

Christian shrugged, a little angry at Brandt, who, after all, didn't look magnificently healthy himself. "They moved me around a little," Christian said. "Here and there. What are you doing here?"

"They assigned me to Normandy," Brandt said. "Pictures of the invasion, pictures of captured American troops, atrocity pictures of French women and children dead from American bombing. The usual thing. Keep walking. Don't stop. If you settle down any place, some damned officer is liable to come over and ask for your papers and try to assign you to a unit. There are just enough busybodies around to make it unpleasant."

They walked methodically along the side of the square, like soldiers with orders and destinations. The gray stone of the buildings was purple now in the sunset, and the lounging and restless men looked hazy and evening-colored against the cobblestones and the shuttered windows.

"Listen," Brandt said, "what do you intend to do?"

Christian chuckled. He was surprised to hear the dry sound come out of his throat. For some reason, after the many days of running, dictated only by the threat of the onrushing Americans, the thought that it was possible for him to have any intentions of his own had struck him as amusing.

"What're you laughing at?" Brandt looked at him suspicously, and Christian arranged his face, because he had the feeling that if he antagonized Brandt, Brandt would withhold valuable information from him.

"Nothing," Christian said. "Honestly, nothing. I'm just a little tired. I have just won the cross-country nine-day all-European bicycle race, and I'm not exactly in control of myself. I'll be all right."

"Well?" Brandt asked querulously. Christian could tell from the timbre of the photographer's voice that he was very near the thin edge of breaking, himself. "Well, what *do* you intend to do?"

"Bicycle back to Berlin," Christian said. "I expect to equal the existing record."

"Don't joke, for the love of Christ," Brandt said.

"I love pedaling through the historic French countryside," Christian said light-headedly, "conversing with the historic natives in their native costumes of hand-grenades and Sten guns, but if something better came up, I might be interested . . ."

"Listen," Brandt said, "I have a two-seater English car in a farmer's barn one mile from here . . ."

Christian became very cool and all tendency to chuckle left him.

"Keep moving!" Brandt snapped, under his breath. "I told you not to stop. I want to get back to Paris. My idiotic driver quit last night. We were strafed yesterday and he got hysterical. He started toward the American lines around midnight."

"Well . . . ?" Christian asked, trying to seem very keen and understanding. "Why've you been hanging around here all day?"

"I can't drive," Brandt said bitterly. "Imagine that, I never learned how to drive a car!"

This time Christian couldn't keep his laughter down. "Oh, my God," he said, "the modern industrial man!"

"It isn't so funny," said Brandt. "I'm too highly strung to learn how. I tried once, in 1935, and I nearly killed myself."

What a century, Christian thought deliciously, enjoying this sudden advantage over a man who had before this done so well out of the war, what a century to pick to be too highly strung! "Why didn't you get one of these fellows . . ." Christian gestured toward the men lounging on the town hall steps, "to drive you?"

"I don't trust them," Brandt said darkly, with a paranoiac glance around him. "If I told you half the stories I've heard about officers being killed by their own troops in the last few days . . . I've been sitting in this damned little town for nearly twenty-four hours, trying to figure out what to do, trying to find a face I really could trust. But they all travel in groups, they all have comrades, and there're only two places in the car. And, who knows, by tomorrow the Americans might be here, or the road to Paris will be closed . . . Christian, I confess to you, when I saw your face in that café, I had to hold onto myself to keep from crying. Listen . . ." Brandt grabbed his arm anxiously. "There's nobody with you? You're alone, aren't you?"

"Don't worry," Christian said. "I'm alone."

Suddenly Brandt stopped. He wiped his face nervously, "It never occurred to me," he whispered. "Can *you* drive?"

The bare anguish plain on Brandt's face as he asked the simple, foolish question that at this moment, at the time of the crumbling of an army, had become the focal point and tragedy of his life, made Christian feel grotesquely and protectively full of pity for the thin, aging ex-artist. "Don't worry, comrade." Christian patted Brandt's shoulder soothingly. "I can drive."

"Thank God," Brandt sighed. "Will you come with me?"

Christian felt a little weak and giddy. Safety was being offered here, speed, home, life . . . "Try and stop me," he said. They grinned weakly like two drowning men, who somehow have contrived, by helping each other, to reach shore.

"Let's start right away," Brandt said.

"Wait," said Christian. "I want to give this bicycle to someone else. Let someone else have a chance to get away . . ." He peered at the shadowy figures stirring around the town hall, trying to devise some innocent way of choosing the lucky man to survive.

"No." Brandt pulled Christian back toward him. "We can use the bicycle. The Frenchman at the farm will give us all the food we can carry for that bicycle."

Christian hesitated, but only for a second. "Of course," he said evenly. "What could I have been thinking of?"

With Brandt looking back nervously over his shoulder to make certain they were not being followed, and Christian wheeling the bicycle, they walked out of town, back over the road Christian had traversed just a half hour before. At the first intersection, where a dusty dirt road slid out into the main highway between banks of flowering hawthorn bushes, fragrant and heavy in the still evening air, they turned off. After walking for fifteen minutes, they reached the comfortable, geranium-bordered farmhouse and the large stone barn in which, under a pile of hay, Brandt had hidden the two-seater.

Brandt had been right about the bicycle. When, under the first stars of evening, they started out along the narrow dirt road leading from the farmhouse, they had with them two hams, a large can of milk, half a huge cheese, a liter of Calvados and two of cider, a half dozen thick loaves of coarse brown bread and a whole basketful of eggs that the farmer's wife had hard-boiled for them while they were taking the hay off the small car. The bicycle had proved most useful.

492

With his stomach full, relaxed behind the wheel of the small, humming, beautifully conditioned car, riding past the pale glow of the hawthorns into the main road in the moonlit evening, Christian smiled gently to himself. Meeting the boy in the blue shirt on the empty road early that morning, he reflected, had proved considerably more profitable than he had expected.

They drove back through the town without stopping. Some-one shouted at them as they sped through the square, but whether it was a command to halt or an appeal for a ride or a curse because they were going too fast and were endangering the men on foot, they never found out, because Christian ac-celerated as much as he dared. A moment later, they were sliding out on the dim ribbon of road that stretched ahead of them across the moonlit countryside toward the city of Paris two hundred kilometers away.

"Germany is finished," Brandt was saying, his voice thin and weary, but loud, to be heard against the rush of night wind that piled across the open car as they went at the same steady pace across the sleeping countryside. "Only a lunatic wouldn't know it. Look at what's happening. Collapse. Nobody gives a damn. A million men left to wander around the best way they know how. A million men, almost without officers, without food, plans, ammunition, left to be picked up by the Americans when they have time. Or massacred, if they're foolish enough to make a stand any place. Germany can't support an army any more. Maybe, somewhere, they'll collect some troops and draw a line, but it will only be a gesture. A temporary, blood-thirsty gesture. A sick, romantic Viking funeral. Clausewitz and Wagner, the General Staff and Siegfried, combined for a graveyard theatrical effect. I'm as much of a patriot as the next man, and God knows, I've served Germany the best way I knew how, in Italy, in Russia, here in France . . . But I'm too civilized for what they're doing to us now. I don't believe in the Vikings. I'm not interested in burning on Goebbels' pyre. The difference between a civilized human being and a wild beast is that a human being knows when he is lost, and takes steps to save himself . . . Listen, when it looked as though the war was about to start, I had my application in to become a citizen of the French Republic, but I gave it up. Germany needed me," Brandt went on, earnestly, convincing himself as much as the man in the seat beside him, of his honesty, his rectitude, his good sense, "and I delivered myself. I did what I could. God, the pictures I've taken. And what I've gone through to get them! But there are no more pictures left to be taken. Nobody to print them, nobody to believe them or be touched by them if they are printed. I traded my camera to that farmer back there for ten liters of gasoline. The war is no longer a subject for photographers because there is no war left to photograph. Only the mopping-up process. Leave that to the American photographers. It is ridiculous for the people who are being mopped up to record the process on film. Nobody can expect it of them. Listen, when a soldier joins an army, any army, there is a kind of basic contract the army makes with him. The contract is that while the army may ask him to die, it will not knowingly ask him to throw his life away. Unless the government is asking for peace this minute, and there are no signs that this is happening, they are violating that contract with me, and with every other soldier in France. We don't owe them anything. Not a thing."

"What are you telling me all this for?" Christian asked, keeping his eyes on the pale road ahead of him, thinking, warily: He has a plan, but I will not commit myself to him yet.

"Because when I get to Paris," Brandt said slowly, "I am going to desert."

They drove in silence for a full minute.

"It is not the correct way to put it," said Brandt. "It is not I who am deserting. It is the Army which has deserted me. I intend to make it official."

Desert. The word trembled in Christian's ear. The Americans had dropped leaflets and safe-conducts on him, urging him to desert, telling him, long before this, that the war was lost, that he would be treated well . . . There were stories of men who had been caught by the Army in the attempt, hung to trees in batches of six, whose families back in Germany had been shot . . . Brandt had no family, and was a freer agent than most. Of course, in confusion like this, who would know who had deserted, who had died, who had been captured while fighting heroically? A long time later, perhaps in 1960, perhaps never, some rumor might come out, but it was impossible to worry about that now.

"Why do you have to go to Paris to desert?" Christian asked, remembering the leaflets. "Why don't you go to the other way and find the first American unit and give yourself up?"

"I thought of that," Brandt said. "Don't think I didn't. But it's too dangerous. Troops in the field aren't dependable. They may be hot-headed, maybe one of their comrades was killed twenty minutes before by a sniper, maybe they're in a hurry, maybe they are Jews with relatives in Büchenwald, how can you tell? And then, in the country like this, there'd be a good chance you'd never reach the Americans. Every damned Frenchman between here and Cherbourg has a gun by now, and is dying to kill one German for the record before it's too late. Oh, no. I want to desert, not die, my friend."

A thoughtful man, Christian thought admiringly, a man who

figured things out reasonably in advance. It was no wonder Brandt had done so well in the Army, had taken just the kind of pictures he knew would be liked by the Propaganda Ministry, had got the fat job in Paris on the magazine, had been billeted for so long in the fancy apartment in Paris, had eaten well, dressed well, whored well.

"Listen," Brandt said, "You know my friend, Simone . . ."

"Are you still connected with her?" Christian asked, surprised. Brandt had been living with Simone as far back as 1940. Christian had met her with Brandt on his first leave in Paris. They had gone out together and Simone had even brought along a friend—what was her name?—Françoise, but Françoise had been as cold as ice, and had made no bones about the fact that she was not fond of Germans. Brandt had been lucky in this war. Dressed in the uniform of the conquering army, but almost a citizen of France, speaking French so well, he had made the best of the two possible worlds.

"Of course, I'm still connected with Simone," Brandt said. "Why not?"

"I don't know." Christian smiled. "Don't get angry. It's just that it's been so long . . . four years . . . in a war . . ." Somehow, although Simone had been very pretty, Christian had always imagined Brandt, with all his opportunities, as soaring beautifully from one dazzling woman to another through the years.

"We intend to marry," Brandt said firmly, "as soon as this damned thing is over."

"Of course," said Christian, slowing down as they passed a column of men, in single file, trudging silently along the road's edge, the moonlight glinting on the metal of their weapons. "Of course. Why not?" Brandt, he thought enviously, lucky, sensible Brandt, unwounded, with a nice war behind him, and a cozy, warm future ahead of him, all planned out.

"I'm going to go straight to her house," Brandt said, "and take off this uniform and put on civilian clothes. And I'm going to stay right there until the Americans arrive. Then, after the first excitement, Simone will go to the American Military Police and tell them about me, that I am a German officer who is anxious to give himself up. The Americans are most correct. They treat prisoners like gentlemen, and the war will be over soon, and they will free me, and I will marry Simone and go back to my painting . . ."

Lucky Brandt, Christian thought, everything ingeniously arranged, wife, career, everything . . .

"Listen, Christian," Brandt said earnestly, "this will work for you, too."

"What?" Christian asked, grinning. "Does Simone want to marry me, too?"

"Don't joke," Brandt said. "She's got a big apartment, two

495

bedrooms. You can stay there, too. You're too good to sink in this swamp of a war . . ." Brandt waved his hand stiffly to take in the reeling men on the road, the death in the sky, the downfall of states. "You've done enough. You've done your share. More than your share. This is the time when every man who is not a fool must take care of himself." Brandt put his hand on Christian's arm softly, imploringly. "I'll tell you something, Christian," he said. "Ever since that first day, on the road to Paris, I've looked up to you, I've worried about you, I've felt that if there was one man I could pick to come out of this alive and well, you would be that man. We're going to need men like you when this is over. You owe it to your country, even if you don't feel you owe it to yourself. Christian . . . Will you stay with me?"

"Maybe," said Christian slowly. "Maybe I will." He shook his head to throw off the weariness and sleep from his eyes and maneuvered around a stalled armored car that lay across the road, with three men working feverishly on it in the frail light of shaded flashlights. "Maybe I will. But first, we have to try to get through to Paris. Then we can begin worrying about what we'll do after that . . ."

"We'll get through," Brandt said calmly. "I am sure of it. Now I am absolutely sure of it."

They arrived in Paris the next night. There was very little traffic on the streets. It was as dark as ever, but it didn't look any different than it had the other times that Christian had come back to it, in the days before the invasion. German staff cars still whipped about the streets; there were fitful gleams of light as café doors swung open, and bursts of laughter from strolling soldiers. And the girls, Christian noticed, as they swung across the Place de l'Opera, were still there, calling out to the shadowy, passing uniforms. The world of commerce, Christian thought grimly, continuing whether the enemy was a thousand kilometers away or just outside town, whether the Americans were in Algiers or Alençon . . .

Brandt was very tense now. He sat on the edge of the seat, breathing sharply, directing Christian through the jumbled maze of blacked-out streets. Christian remembered the other time he and Brandt had rolled down these boulevards, with Sergeant Himmler pointing out places of interest like a professional guide, and Hardenburg in the front seat. Himmler, full of jokes, and now a curious collection of bones on the sandy hill in the desert; Hardenburg, a suicide in Italy . . . But Brandt and he still alive, softly driving over the same pavements, smelling the same, sour, ancient aroma of the old city, passing the same monuments along the everlasting river . . .

"Here," Brandt whispered. "Stop here."

Christian put on the brakes and turned off the motor. He felt very tired. They were in front of a garage, a garage with a big blank door, and a steep incline of cement. "Wait for me," Brandt said, climbing hurriedly out of the car. Brandt knocked on a door to one side of the incline. In a moment the door opened, and Brandt disappeared inside. (Remember Himmler disappearing inside the brothel door, and the Moorish hangings and the cold bottles of champagne and the smile on the dark girl's red mouth. "A curious taste," the red mouth had said mockingly, "a curious taste, wouldn't you say?" And Brandt's curt answer . . . "We are a curious people. You will discover that. Attend to your business." And the green silk dress in Himmler's hands, and the 1918 on the scrawled wall.) The French, Christian repeated dully in some deep chamber of his mind, they will beat us all, yet.

There was a grinding noise and the blank door of the garage swung open. A light shone dimly at the top of the incline, a gloomy yellow dab in the depths of the building. Brandt came out hurriedly. He looked up and down the empty street.

"Drive in," he whispered to Christian. "Fast."

Christian started the motor and swung the little car up the incline toward the light. Behind him he heard the garage door closing. He drove carefully up the narrow passageway and stopped at the top. He looked around. In the dim light he saw the shapes of three or four other cars, covered with tarpaulins.

"All right." It was Brandt's voice behind him. "This is where we get off."

Christian killed the motor and got out. Brandt and another man were coming toward him. The other man was small and fat and was wearing a homburg hat, half-comic, half-sinister at this moment in this shaded place.

The man in the homburg hat walked slowly around the car, touching it tentatively from time to time. "Good enough," he said in French. He turned and disappeared into a small office to one side, from which came a meager glow of light from a hidden lamp.

"Listen," Brandt said. "I've sold them the car. Seventy-five thousand francs." He waved the notes in front of Christian. Christian couldn't see them very well, but he heard the dry rustle of the paper. "They'll be very useful in the next few weeks. Let's get our things out. We'll walk from here."

Seventy-five thousand francs, Christian thought admiringly, as he helped Brandt unload the bread, the hams, the cheese, the Calvados. This man cannot be defeated by anything! He has friends and commercial acquaintances all over the world, ready to spring to his assistance at any moment.

The man in the homburg hat came back with two burlap sacks. Christian and Brandt stowed all their belongings into them. The Frenchman did not offer to help, but stood outside the shine of the one small light, obscure, watching, expressionless. When the packing was finished, the Frenchman led the way down a half-flight of steps and unlocked a door. "*Au revoir*, Monsieur Brandt," he said, his voice flat. "Enjoy yourself in Paris." There was a subtle overtone of warning and mockery in the Frenchman's voice. Christian would have liked to seize him and drag him under a light to get a good look at him. But as he hesitated, Brandt pulled nervously at his arm. He allowed himself to be guided into the street. The door closed behind them, and he heard the quiet clicking of the lock.

"This way," Brandt said, and started off, the sack of loot over his shoulder. "We don't have far to go." Christian followed him down the dark street. Later on, he decided he would question Brandt about the Frenchman in the homburg hat and what he might be expected to do with the little car. But he was too tired now, and Brandt was hurrying ahead of him, anyway, walking swiftly and silently toward his girl's house.

Two minutes later Brandt stopped at the doorway of a four-story house, its shaded window blind against the street. Brandt rang the bell. They had not passed anyone.

It was a long time before the door opened, and then only a crack. Brandt whispered into the crack and Christian heard an old woman's voice, at first querulous, then warm and welcoming as Brandt established his identity. There was the small rattling of a chain and the door swung wide. Christian followed Brandt up the steps, past the muffled figure of the concierge. Brandt, Christian thought, the man who knows precisely on which doors to knock, and what to say to get them open. Someone pushed a button and the lights on the stairway went up. Christian saw that it was quite a respectable building, with marble steps, clean, bourgeois, a place where vice-presidents might live, and superior clerks in government offices.

The lights went out after twenty seconds. They climbed in darkness. Christian's Schmeisser, slung on his shoulder, banged against the wall with an iron sound. "Quiet!" Brandt whispered harshly. "Be careful." He pushed the button on the next landing and the lights went on for another twenty seconds, in the thrifty French style.

They climbed to the top floor and Brandt knocked on a door gently. This door opened quickly, almost as though whoever lived in the apartment had been waiting eagerly for the signal. A beam of light flooded into the hallway, and Christian saw the figure of a woman in a long robe. Then the woman threw herself into Brandt's arms. She began to sob, brokenly, saying "You're here, oh *chéri*, you're here . . . you're here."

Christian stood awkwardly against the wall, holding onto the butt of his gun so it wouldn't rattle, watching the two people embrace. It was a domestic, husband-and-wife embrace, more relief than passion, plain, unbeautiful, tearful, touching, profoundly private, and Christian wished he didn't have to be present to witness it.

Finally, half-sobbing, half-laughing, Simone broke away, pushing back her straight long hair with one hand, and with the other still clutching Brandt's arm, as though to reassure herself that he was real and to make certain that he would not vanish in the next minute.

"Now," she said, and Christian remembered her light, soft voice very well, "now, we have time to be polite." She turned to Christian.

"You remember Diestl, don't you?" Brandt said.

"Of course, of course." She put out her hand impulsively. Christian shook it. "I am so glad to see you. We have talked about you so often . . . Come in, come in . . . You can't stand out in the hall all night."

They stepped into the apartment and Simone locked the door behind them, the sound homelike and secure. Brandt and Christian followed her into the living room. Standing before the drawn curtains in front of a window was a woman in a quilted robe, her face in shadow, outside the light of the single lamp on the table near the couch.

"Put your things down, oh, you'll want to wash, oh, you must be starving," Simone was saying in a babble of wifely consideration, "we have some wine, we must open a bottle of wine to celebrate . . . Oh, Françoise, see who's here, isn't it wonderful?"

Françoise, Christian remembered, the German-hater, that's who it is. He watched Françoise warily as she came out from her place near the window and shook hands with Brandt.

"I am so glad to see you," Françoise said.

She was even prettier than Christian remembered, a tall woman, with piled chestnut hair and a long, fine nose over a controlled mouth. She turned to Christian, smiling and extending her hand. "Welcome, Sergeant Diestl," Françoise said. She pressed his hand warmly.

"Oh," said Christian carefully, "you remember me."

"Of course," said Françoise, staring directly at him. "I have thought of you again and again."

Greenish, hidden eyes, Christian thought troubledly, what is she smiling at, what does she mean by saying she thought of me again and again?

"Françoise moved in with me last month, *chéri*," Simone said to Brandt. "Her apartment was requisitioned. Your Army." She made a charming little face at Brandt and Brandt chuckled and kissed her. Her hands lingered for a moment on his shoulders before she pulled away. Christian noticed that she looked much older. She was still small and trim, but there were fine, anxious wrinkles around her eyes, and her skin looked dry and lifeless.

"Do you plan to stay long?" Françoise asked.

There was a moment of hesitation. Then Christian said, stolidly, "Our plans are not definite at the moment, we . . ."

He heard Brandt laughing and stopped. The laughter was high, near hysteria, a combination of relief and amusement. "Christian," Brandt said, "stop being so damned correct. We plan to stay to the end of the war."

Then Simone broke down. She sat on the edge of the couch and Brandt had to comfort her. Christian caught Françoise's eye for a flicker and observed what he thought was cool amusement there, before Françoise politely turned away and strolled back to her window.

"Go," Simone was saying. "This is ridiculous. I don't know why I'm crying. Ridiculous. I am getting like my mother, cry because she's happy, cry because she's sad, cry because it's sunny, cry because it's beginning to rain. Go. Go in and wash up, and when you come back, I shall be as sensible as you can imagine, and I'll have a beautiful supper all fixed for you. Go. Don't look at me with my eyes like this. Go ahead."

Brandt was grinning, a foolish, homecoming, childish grin, incongruous on his thin, lined, intelligent face, now grimed with the dust of the long march from Normandy.

"Come on, Christian," said Brandt, "let's get the dirt off our faces."

Together they went into the bathroom. Françoise, Christian noticed, did not look at them as they left the room.

In the bathroom, with the water running (all cold because of the fuel situation), Brandt spoke through the soapsuds, while Christian arranged his dark hair, wet with water, with someone's comb. "There is something about that woman," Brandt was saying, "something I have never found in anyone else. I . . . I accept everything about her. It's funny, with other women, I was too critical. They were too thin, they were too vain, they were a little silly . . . Two, three weeks, and I couldn't stand them any more. But with Simone . . . I know she is a little sentimental, I know she is getting older, there are wrinkles . . . And . . ." He grinned soapily, "I love it. She is not so smart. I love it. She has a tendency to weep. I love it." Then he spoke very seriously. "It is the one good thing I have gotten from the war." Then, as though ashamed at having talked so frankly, he turned the water on full blast and vigorously rinsed the soap off his face and neck. He was stripped to the waist, and Christian noticed with amused pity how his friend's bones jutted out of his skin, like a small boy's, how frail his arms were. What a lover,

Christian thought, what a soldier, how had he ever managed to survive four years of war?

Brandt stood up and toweled his face. "Christian," he said seriously, through the muffling cloth, "you're going to stay with me, aren't you?"

"First," Christian began, keeping his voice low, so that the rushing water from the tap obscured it, "what about that other one?"

"Françoise?" Brandt waved his hand. "Don't worry about her. There's plenty of room. You can sleep on the couch. Or . . ." He grinned. "Come to an understanding with her. Then you wouldn't have to sleep on the couch."

"I'm not worried about the overcrowding," Christian said.

Brandt reached over to turn the water off. "Leave it on," Christian said sharply, holding Brandt's hand.

"What's the matter with you?" Brandt asked, puzzled.

"She doesn't like Germans, that one," Christian said. "She can make a lot of trouble."

"Nonsense." With a quick movement, Brandt snapped the water off. "I know her. I guarantee that lady. She'll grow very fond of you. Now, listen to me, promise you'll stay . . ."

"All right," Christian said slowly. "I'll stay." He could see Brandt's eyes glistening. Brandt's hand, as it patted Christian's bare shoulder, was trembling a little.

"We're safe, Christian," Brandt whispered. "Finally, we're safe . . ."

He turned and awkwardly put on his shirt and went out into the other room. Christian put his shirt on slowly, buttoning it carefully, looking at himself in the mirror, studying the haggard eyes, the ridged lines on his cheeks, the topography of fear and grief and exhaustion that was obscurely and invincibly marked there. He leaned close to the mirror and stared at his hair. There was a sanding of gray, heavy at the temples, glistening in little pale tips on top. God, he thought, I never saw that before. I'm getting old, old . . . He braced himself fiercely, hating the wave of self-pity that for a moment he had allowed to flood through him, and walked stiffly out into the living room.

The living room was cozy, with the one shaded lamp disseminating a dull rosy glow over the modern blond wood, over the pale red rug and the flowered drapes and the empty glasses and over the long, reclining figure of Françoise on the soft couch.

Brandt and Simone had gone to bed, holding hands domestically as they had gone down the hallway. After eating, after telling a jumbled, inaccurate account of the last few days, Brandt had nearly fallen asleep in his chair and Simone had fondly pulled him up by his hands and led him away, smiling in an almost motherly way at Christian and Françoise left together in the shadowy room.

"The war is over," Brandt had mumbled in farewell, "the war is over, boys, and now I am going to sleep. Farewell, Lieutenant Brandt, of the Army of the Third Reich," he had said with sleepy oratory, "farewell, soldier. Tomorrow once more the decadent painter of non-objective pictures awakens in his civilian bed, next to his wife." He had pointed in a limp, gentle way at Françoise. "Be good to my friend. Love him well. He is the best of the best. Strong, delicate, tested in the fire, the hope of the new Europe, if there will be a new Europe and if there is any hope for it. Love him well."

Shaking her head fondly, saying, "The drink has gone to the man's tongue," Simone had pushed him gently toward the bedroom.

"Good night," they had heard Brandt's mumbled valedictory in the hallway, "good night, my good dear friends . . ."

Then the door had closed and there had been silence in the small, feminine room, with its pale wood and its dark, night-time mirrors, its soft-colored cushions, and its silver-framed photograph of Brandt taken in beret and Basque shirt before the war.

Christian looked over at Françoise. She was staring up at the ceiling, her hands behind her head, sunk in the cushions, half her face in shadow. Her body, under the quilted blue robe, was absolutely still. Occasionally, in a lazy, small movement, she pointed the toes of one foot, encased in a satin, flat-heeled slipper, toward the end of the couch, then flipped the foot back into its original position. Vaguely, Christian remembered another quilted robe. Red, deep red, on Gretchen Hardenburg, the first time he had seen her at the door of the massive apartment in Berlin. He wondered what Mrs. Hardenburg was doing now, whether the building was still standing, whether she was alive, whether she still went around with the gray-haired Frenchwoman . . .

"A tired soldier," Françoise murmured from the depths of the couch, "a very tired soldier, our Lieutenant Brandt."

"Yes," said Christian, watching her carefully.

"He's had a hard time, hasn't he?" Françoise moved her toes. "It hasn't been pleasant, the last few weeks, has it?"

"No, not very."

"The Americans," said Françoise, in a flat, innocent voice, "they're very strong, very fresh, aren't they?"

"You might say that."

"The papers here," Françoise shifted her weight gently and the long lines rearranged themselves in silvery shadows under the robe, "keep saying it is all going according to plan. The Americans are being cleverly contained, there will be a sur-

prising counterattack." The tone of lazy amusement in Françoise's voice was very clear. "The papers are very reassuring.
Mr. Brandt ought to read them more often." She chuckled
softly. The chuckle would have seemed sensual and inviting,
Christian realized, if they had been talking on a different subject. "Mr. Brandt," Françoise, said gently, "is not of the opinion that the Americans will be contained. And a counter-attack
would be really surprising to him, wouldn't it?"

"I imagine so," Christian said, sparring, wondering: What
is this woman up to?

"How about you?" She spoke abstractedly, not really to
Christian, but into the warm, dusky air.

"Perhaps I share Brandt's opinion," Christian said.

"You're very tired, too, aren't you?" Françoise sat up and
stared at him, her lips straight and quite sympathetic, but her
heavy-lidded green eyes contracted in what seemed to Christian to be a hidden smile. "You probably want to go to sleep,
too."

"Not right now," said Christian. Suddenly he couldn't bear
the thought of this long-limbed, green-eyed, mocking woman
leaving him. "I've been a lot more tired than this in my time."

"Oh," said Françoise lying back again, "oh, what an excellent soldier. Stoical, inexhaustible. How can an army lose a
war when it still has troops like that?"

Christian stared at her, hating her. She turned her head in a
sleepy movement on the cushions, to look at him. The long
muscles under the pale skin of her throat made a delicate new
pattern of flesh and shadows in the lamplight. Finally, Christian
knew, staring at her, he would have to kiss that place where
the skin swept in an ivory, trembling, living sheet from the
base of her throat to the half-exposed shoulder.

"I knew a boy like you long ago," Françoise said, not smiling now, looking directly at him. "A Frenchman. Strong. Uncomplaining. A resolute patriot. I liked him very much, I must
say." The deep voice murmured in his ears. "He died in '40.
In another retreat. Do you expect to die, Sergeant?"

"No," said Christian, slowly. "I do not expect to die."

"Good." Françoise's full lips murmured into a small smile.
"The best of the best, according to your friend. The hope of
the new Europe. Do you consider yourself the hope of the new
Europe, Sergeant?"

"Brandt was drunk."

"Was he? Possibly. Are you sure you don't want to go to
sleep?"

"I'm sure."

"You do look very tired, you know."

"I do not wish to go to sleep."

Françoise nodded gently. "The ever-waking Sergeant. Does

not wish to go to sleep. Prefers to remain awake, at great personal sacrifice, and entertain a lonely French lady who is at a loose end until the Americans enter Paris . . ." She put her hand, palm upward, over her eyes, the loose sleeve falling back from the slender wrist and the long, sharp-nailed fingers. "Tomorrow," she said, "we will enter your name for the Legion of Honor, second class, service to the French nation."

"Enough," Christian said, without moving from his chair. "Stop making fun of me."

"Nothing," said Françoise flatly, "could be further from my mind. Tell me, Sergeant, as a military man, how long do you think it will be before the Americans get here?"

"Two weeks," said Christian. "A month."

"Oh," Françoise said, "we are in for an interesting time, aren't we?"

"Yes."

"Shall I tell you something, Sergeant?"

"What?"

"I have remembered our little dinner party again and again. '40? '41?"

" '40."

"I wore a white dress. You looked very handsome. Tall, straight, intelligent, conquering, shining in your uniform, the young god of mechanized warfare." She chuckled.

"You are making fun of me again," Christian said. "It is not pleasant."

"I was very much impressed with you." She waved her hand, as though to stop a contradiction that Christian had no idea of voicing. "Honestly, I was. I was very cold to you, wasn't I?" Again the small, remembering chuckle. "You have no idea how difficult it was for me to manage it. I am far from impervious, Sergeant, to the attractions of young men. And you were so beautiful, Sergeant . . ." The sleepy, hypnotic voice whispering musically in the darkened, civilized room, seemed remote, unreal. "So ripe with conquest, so arrogant, so beautiful. It took all my enormous powers of self-control. You are less arrogant, now, aren't you, Sergeant?"

"Yes," said Christian, feeling himself between sleeping and waking, rhythmically adrift on a soft, perfumed, subtly dangerous tide. "Not arrogant at all any more."

"You're very tired now," the woman murmured. "A little gray. And I noticed that you limp a bit, too. In '40 it did not seem you could ever grow tired. You might die, then, I thought, in one glorious burst of fire, but never weary, never . . . You are very different now, Sergeant, very different. By ordinary standards, one would never say you were beautiful now, with your limp and your graying hair and your thin face . . . But I'm going to tell you something, Sergeant. I am a woman of peculiar tastes. Your uniform is no longer shining. Your face is gray. No one would ever believe that there is a resemblance in you to the young god of mechanized warfare . . ." A final hint of soft laughter echoed in her voice. "But I find you much more attractive tonight, Sergeant, infinitely more . . ."

She stopped speaking, her opium-like voice dying among the shadows of the cushioned couch.

Christian stood up. He went over and stared at her for a moment. She looked up at him, her eyes wide, smiling with candor.

He knelt swiftly and kissed her.

He lay beside her in the dark bed. The curtains on the window were open, blowing gently in the summer night wind. A pale silvery wash of moonlight draped and made soft the outlines of the bureau, the vanity table, the chairs with his clothes thrown over them.

It had been a passionate, knowing, drowning experience, a sensual milestone in his journey among women, an unreticent flood of desire which had swept away all the hours of flight, all memory of the smells of the broken ambulance convoy, all memory of the marching, the dying French boy, the hateful bicycle, the sandy-eyed groping retreat along the crowded roads in the little stolen automobile. All war had vanished here in the soft bed and the moonlit room. For the first time since his arrival in France so many years ago, and so late in the game, Christian realized, the promise which he had once believed in and finally forgotten, the promise of magnificent and accomplished women, had been fulfilled.

The German-hater . . . He grinned and turned his head. Her hair tumbled in a dark, fragrant mass on the pillow, Françoise was lying beside him, touching his skin lightly with the tips of her fingers, her eyes once more mysterious in the wavering pale light.

She smiled slowly. "See," she said, "you weren't so terribly tired, after all, were you?"

They chuckled together. He moved his head and kissed the smooth, silvery sheet of skin where her throat joined her shoulder, drowsily submerged in the mingled textures of skin and hair, swimming hazily in the living double fragrance of hair and skin.

"There is something to be said," Françoise whispered, "for all retreats."

Through the open window came the sound of soldiers marching, hobnails making a remote military rhythmic clatter, pleasant and meaningless heard this way in a hidden room through the tangled perfumed strands of his mistress' hair.

"I knew it, as soon as I saw you," Françoise said. "The first time, long ago, that it could be like this. Formidable. I could tell."

"Why did you wait so long?" Christian pulled back gently, turning, looking up at the pattern the moonlight, reflected from a mirror, made on the ceiling. "God, the time we've wasted. Why didn't you do this then?"

"I was not making love to Germans, then," Françoise said coolly. "I did not think it was admirable to surrender *everything* in the country to the conqueror. You may not believe this, and I don't care whether you do or not, but you are the first German I have permitted to touch me."

"I believe you," Christian said. And he did, because whatever else her faults might be, dishonesty was certainly not one of them.

"Don't think it was easy," Françoise said. "I am not a nun."

"Oh, no," said Christian gravely. "I will put that in writing." Françoise did not laugh. "You were not the only one," she said. "So many magnificent young men, such a pleasant variety of young men . . . But, not one of them, not one . . . The conquerors did not get anything . . . Not until tonight . . ."

Christian hesitated, vaguely troubled. "Why," he asked, "why have you changed now?"

"Oh, it's all right now." Françoise laughed, a sly, sleepy, satisfied, womanly laugh. "It's perfectly all right now. You're not a conqueror any more, darling, you're a refugee . . ." She twisted over to him and kissed him. "Now," she said, "it is time to sleep. . . ."

She moved over to her side of the bed. Lying flat on her back, with her arms chastely at her side, her long body sweepingly outlined under the white blur of the sheet, she dropped off to slumber. Her breath came in an even, healthy rhythm in the quiet room.

Christian did not sleep. He lay uncomfortably, with growing rigidity, listening to the breathing of the woman beside him, staring at the moon and mirror-flecked ceiling. Outside, there was the noise of the hobnailed patrol again, increasing and receding on the silent pavement. It did not sound remote any more, or pleasant, or meaningless.

Refugee, Christian remembered, and remembered the low, mocking laugh that accompanied it. He turned his head a little and looked at Françoise. Even as she slept, he imagined seeing a tiny, superior, victorious smile at the corner of the long, passionate mouth. Christian Diestl, the non-conquering refugee, finally given the franchise of the Parisienne's bed. The French, he remembered, they will beat us all yet. And, what's worse, they know it.

With growing rage, staring at the long, beautiful face on the pillow beside him, he felt used, seduced, and for what an ironic and superior purpose! And Brandt, drunk and hopeful and exhausted in the next room, caught by another trap, with the trademark, "Made in France," also on it.

Lying there he began to hate Brandt for being so willingly trapped. Christian thought of all the men he had touched and who had died. Hardenburg, Kraus, Behr, the brave, hopeless little Frenchman on the road to Paris, the boy on the bicycle, the farmer in the town-hall cellar next to the open yellow coffin, the men in his platoon in Normandy, the American firing up, half-naked and crazily courageous, from the mined bridge in Italy. It is unjust, he thought, for the soft ones to survive where the hard ones die. Brandt, with his civilian cunning, luxurious in the silk Parisian bed, was a sick rebuke to them all. There were too many men, as it was, who knew on which doors to knock and what to say when they were opened. The good had fallen, should the weak now luxuriate? Death was the best cure for luxury, and easily applied. Better friends than Brandt had died beside him for four years; should Brandt be left alive to suck on Hardenburg's bones? The end justifies the means—and after the geometric slaughter, was the end to be Civilian Brandt, after three or four easy months in an American stockade, returning to his soft French wife, painting his silly, piddling pictures, apologizing for the next twenty years to the victors for the hard, dead men he had betrayed? Death had been in Christian's touch from the beginning—now, at the end, out of a sentimental notion of friendship, was he to spare only the least deserving? Was that all he had learned in four years of killing?

Suddenly it was intolerable to think of Brandt snoring softly in the next room, intolerable for himself to remain in bed next to the handsome woman who had used him so comfortably and mercilessly. He slid noiselessly onto the floor and walked barefooted and naked over to the window. He stared out over the roofs of the sleeping city, the chimneys shining under the moon, the pale streets winding away narrowly with their memories of other centuries, the river shining under its bridges in the distance. He could hear the patrol from the window, faint and brave across the still dark air, and he got a glimpse of it as it crossed an intersection. Five men walking deliberately and cautiously down the night-time streets of the enemy, vulnerable, stolid, pathetic, friends . . .

Swiftly and soundlessly, Christian dressed himself. Françoise stirred once, threw her arm out languidly toward the other side of the bed, but she did not awake. Her arm looked white and snakelike stretched into the warm emptiness beside her.

With his boots in his hand, Christian padded over to the door. He opened the door gently, without noise. Standing there, he looked back for a last moment. Françoise was lying as he had left her, one arm extended in dreamlike satiety and invitation to her conquered lover. On her face Christian imagined he saw a new, satisfied smile of sensuality and victory.

Christian stole through the door and closed it softly behind him.

Fifteen minutes later he was standing before the desk of a Colonel in the SS. In the sleeping city, the SS offices did not sleep. The rooms were brilliantly lighted, men came and went in an endless bustle, there was the clatter of typewriters and teletype machines, and it had the unreal, hectic air of a factory going full blast during an overtime night-shift.

The Colonel behind the desk was wide awake. He was short and he wore heavy horn-rimmed glasses, but there was no air of clerkishness about him. He had a thin gash for a mouth, and his magnified pale eyes were coldly probing behind their glasses. He held himself like a weapon always in readiness to strike.

"Very good, Sergeant," the Colonel was saying. "You will go with Lieutenant von Schlain and point out the house and identify the deserter and the women who are hiding him."

"Yes, Sir," said Christian.

"You are right in supposing that your organization no longer exists as a military unit," the Colonel said dispassionately. "It was overrun and destroyed five days ago. You have displayed considerable courage and ingenuity in saving yourself . . ." Christian could not tell whether the Colonel was being ironic or not, and he felt a twinge of uneasiness. The Colonel, he realized, made a technique out of making other people uneasy, but there was always the chance this was something special. "I shall have orders made out for you," the Colonel went on, his eyes glinting behind the thick lenses, "to be returned to Germany for a short leave, and assigned to a new unit there. In a very short time, Sergeant," the Colonel said, without expression in his voice, "we will need men like you on the soil of the Fatherland. That is all. Heil Hitler."

Christian saluted and went out of the room with Lieutenant von Schlain, who also wore glasses.

In the small car with Lieutenant von Schlain, which preceded the open truck with the soldiers, Christian asked, "What will happen to him?"

"Oh," said von Schlain, yawning, taking off his glasses, "we'll shoot him tomorrow. We shoot a dozen deserters a day, and now, with the retreat, business will be better than ever." He put his glasses back and peered out. "Is this the street?"

"This is the street," Christian said. "Stop here."

The small car stopped in front of the well-remembered door. The truck clanged to a halt behind it and the soldiers jumped out.

"No need for you to go up with us," von Schlain said. "Might make it unpleasant. Just tell me which floor and which door and I'll handle it in no time."

"Top floor," said Christian, "the first door to the right of the stairway."

"Good," said von Schlain. He had a lordly, disdainful way of speaking, as though he felt that the Army was making poor use of his great talents, and he wished the world to understand that immediately. He gestured languidly to the four soldiers who had come in the truck, and went up the steps and rang the bell very loudly.

Standing on the curb, leaning against the car in which he had come from SS Headquarters, Christian could hear the bell wailing mournfully away in the concierge's quarters deep in the sleeping fastnesses of the house. Von Schlain never took his finger off the bell, and the ringing persisted in a hollow, nervous crescendo. Christian lit a cigarette and pulled at it hard. They'll hear it upstairs, he thought. That von Schlain is an idiot.

Finally there was a clanking at the door and Christian heard the irritable, sleepy voice of the concierge. Von Schlain barked at her in rapid French and the door swung open. Von Schlain and the four soldiers went in and the door closed behind them.

Christian paced slowly up and down alongside the car, puffing on the cigarette. Dawn was beginning to break and a pearly light, mingled with secret blues and silvery lavenders, was drifting across the streets and buildings of Paris. It was very beautiful and Christian hated it. Soon, that day perhaps, he would leave Paris, and probably never see it again in his whole life, and he was glad. Leave it to the French, to the supple, cheating, everlastingly victorious French . . . He was well rid of it. It looked like a fair meadow and it turned out to be slippery swampland. It seemed full of beauty and promise and it turned out to be a sordid trap, well-baited and fatal to a man's dignity and honor. Deceptively soft, it blunted all weapons that attacked it. Deceptively gay, it lured its conquerors into a bottomless melancholy. Long ago, the Medical Corps had been right. The cynical men of science had supplied the Army with the only proper equipment for the conquest of Paris . . . three tubes of Salvarsan . . .

The door was flung open and Brandt, with a civilian coat thrown over pajamas, came out between two soldiers. Right after him came Françoise and Simone, in robes and slippers. Simone was sobbing, in a childish, strangled, tearing convulsion, but Françoise looked out at the soldiers with calm derision.

Christian stared at Brandt, who looked painfully back at him in the half-light. There was no expression on Brandt's face, snatched out of its deep, secure sleep, only dull exhaustion. Christian hated the lined, over-delicate, compromising, losing

509

face. Why, he thought with surprise, he doesn't even look like a German!

"That's the man," Christian said to von Schlain, "and those're the two women."

The soldiers pushed Brandt up into the truck, and rather gently lifted Simone, now lost in a tangled wet marsh of tears. Helplessly, Simone, once she was in the truck, stretched out her hand toward Brandt. Christian despised Brandt for the soft, tragic way in which, without shame, in front of the comrades he would have deserted, he put out his hand to take Simone's and carry it up to his cheek.

Françoise refused to allow the soldiers to help her climb into the truck. She stared for a moment with harsh intensity at Christian, then shook her head gently in a gesture of numb bewilderment, and climbed heavily up by herself.

There, Christian thought, watching her, there, you see, it is not all over yet. Even now, there are still some victories to be won—

The truck started down the street. Christian got into the small car with Lieutenant von Schlain and followed it through the lavender streets of dawning Paris toward SS Headquarters.

CHAPTER THIRTY-TWO

THERE WAS something wrong about the town. There were no flags hanging out of the windows, as there had been in all the towns along the way from Coutances. There were no improvised signs welcoming the Americans, and two Frenchmen who saw the jeep ducked into houses when Michael called to them.

"Stop the jeep," Michael said to Stellevato. "There's something fishy here."

They were on the outskirts of the town, at a wide intersection of roads. The roads, stretching bleakly away in the gray morning, were cold and empty. There was no movement to be seen anywhere, just the shuttered windows of the stone houses, and the vacant roads with nothing stirring on them. After the crowded month, in which almost every road in France had seemed to be jammed with tanks and half-tracks and gasoline trucks and artillery pieces and marching men, in which every town had been crowded with cheering Frenchmen and women in their brightest clothes, waving flags hidden through all the years of the Occupation, and singing the Marseillaise, there was something threatening and baleful about the dead silence around them.

"What's the matter, Bo?" Keane said from the back seat. "Did we get on the wrong train?"

"I don't know," Michael said, annoyed at Keane. Pavone had told him to pick up Keane three days ago and bring him along, and Keane had spent the three days in mournful chatter about how timidly the war was being run, and how his wife kept writing him that the money she was getting was not enough to keep a family alive with prices going up the way they were back home. By now, the prices of chopped meat, butter, bread and children's shoes were indelibly engraved in Michael's brain, thanks to Keane. In 1970, if somebody asks me how much hamburger cost in the summer of 1944, Michael thought irritably, I'll answer, sixty-five cents a pound, without thinking for a second.

He got out the map and opened it on his knees. Behind him he heard Keane snapping the safety off his carbine. A cowboy, Michael thought, staring at the map, a brainless, bloodthirsty cowboy . . .

Stellevato, slouched in the front seat beside him, smoking a cigarette, his helmet tipped far back on his head, said, "Do you know what I could use now? One bottle of wine and one French dame." Stellevato was either too young, too brave, or too stupid to be affected by the autumnal, dangerous morning, and by the unusual, unliberated aspect of the buildings in front of them.

"This is the place, all right," Michael said, "but it certainly doesn't look good to me." Four days before, Pavone had sent him back to Twelfth Army Group with a bagful of reports on a dozen towns they had inspected, reports on the public-utility situations, the food reserves, the number of denunciations of the incumbent civil officials, that had been made by the local people. After that, he had ordered Michael to report back to him at the Infantry Division's Headquarters, but the G3 there had told Michael that Pavone had left the day before, leaving instructions for Michael to meet him in this town the next morning. A combined armored and mechanized task force was to have reached the town by ten hundred hours and Pavone was to be with them.

It was eleven o'clock now, and aside from a small sign that read "Water Point," in English, with an arrow, there was no hint that any Americans had been here since 1919.

"Come on, Bo," Keane said. "What're we waiting for? I want to see Paris."

"We don't have Paris," Michael said, putting the map away, and trying to make some sense out of the empty streets before him.

"I heard over the BBC this morning," Keane said, "that the Germans've asked for an armistice in Paris."

"Well, they haven't asked me," Michael said, sorry that Pavone wasn't with him at this moment to take on the burden of responsibility. The last three days had been pleasant, riding around the celebrating French countryside as commander of his own movements, with no one to order him about. But there was no celebrating going on here this morning, that was certain, and he had an uneasy sensation that if he guessed wrong in the next fifteen minutes, they might all be dead by noon.

"The hell with it." Michael nudged Stellevato. "Let's see what's happening at the Water Point."

Stellevato started the jeep and they went slowly down a side street toward a bridge they could see in the distance, crossing a small stream. There was another sign there, and a big canvas tank and pumping apparatus. For a moment, Michael thought that the Water Point, along with the rest of the town, was deserted, but he saw a helmet sticking cautiously up from a foxhole covered with branches.

"We heard the motor," said the soldier under the helmet. He was pale and weary-eyed, young and, as far as Michael could tell, frightened. Another soldier stood up next to him and came over to the jeep.

"What's going on here?" Michael asked.

"You tell us," said the first soldier.

"Did a task force go through here at ten o'clock this morning?"

"Nothing's been through here," the second soldier volunteered. He was a pudgy little man, nearly forty, who needed a shave badly, and he spoke with a hint of a Swedish singsong in his voice. "Fourth Armored Headquarters went through last night and dropped us off here and turned south. Since then it's been mighty lonesome. There was some shooting near dawn from the middle of the town . . ."

"What was it?" Michael asked.

"Don't ask me, Brother," said the pudgy man. "They put me here to pump water out of this creek, not conduct private investigations. These woods're full of Krauts and they shoot the Frogs and the Frogs shoot them. Me, I'm waiting for reinforcements."

"Let's go into the middle of the town and look around," Keane said eagerly.

"Will you shut up?" Michael swung around and spoke as sharply as he could to Keane. Keane, behind his thick glasses, grinned unhappily.

"Me and my buddy here," the pudgy soldier said, "have been debating whether maybe we ought to pull out altogether. We ain't doing anybody any good sitting here like ducks on a pond.

512

A Frog came by this morning, he spoke some English, and he said there was 800 Krauts with three tanks on the other side of town, and they was going to come in here and take the town some time this morning."

"Happy days," Michael said. That was why there had been no flags.

"Eight hundred Krauts," Stellevato said. "Let's go home."

"Do you think it's safe here?" the pale-faced young soldier asked Michael.

"Just like your own living room," said Michael. "How the hell would I know?"

"I was just asking a question," the young soldier said reproachfully.

"I don't like it," said the man with the Swedish accent, peering down the street. "I don't like it one bit. They got no right leaving us like this, all by ourselves, sitting next to this goddamn creek."

"Nikki," Michael said to Stellevato. "Turn the jeep around and leave it on the road, so we can get away from here fast if we have to."

"What's the matter?" Keane asked, leaning toward Michael. "Got your wind up?"

"Listen, General Patton," Michael said, trying to keep the annoyance out of his voice, "when we need a hero, we'll call on you. Nikki, turn that jeep around."

"I wish I was home," Stellevato said. But he got into the jeep and turned it around. He unhooked his tommygun from under the windshield and blew vaguely on it. It was coated with dust.

"What're we going to do, Bo?" Keane asked. His big blotched hands moved eagerly on his carbine. Michael looked at him with distaste. Is it possible, Michael thought, that his brother won the Congressional Medal of Honor out of sheer stupidity?

"We're going to sit ourselves down here for awhile," Michael said, "and wait."

"For what?" Keane demanded.

"For Colonel Pavone."

"What if he doesn't show up?" Keane persisted.

"Then we'll make another decision. This is a lucky day for me," Michael said crisply. "I bet I'm good for three decisions before sunset."

"I think we ought to say the hell with Pavone," said Keane, "and move right in on Paris. The BBC says . . ."

"I know what the BBC says," Michael said, "and I know what you say, and I say we're going to sit here and wait."

He walked away from Keane and sat down on the grass, leaning against a low stone wall that ran alongside the stream.

The two Armored Division soldiers looked at him doubtfully, then went back into their foxhole, pulling the branches cautiously over their heads. Stellevato leaned his tommygun against the wall and lay down and went to sleep. He lay straight out, with his hands over his eyes. He looked dead.

Keane sat on a stone and took out a pad of paper and a pencil and began writing a letter to his wife. He sent his wife a detailed account of everything he did, including the most horrible descriptions of the dead and wounded. "I want her to see what the world is going through," he had said soberly. "If she understands what we are going through, it may improve her outlook on life."

Michael stared past the helmeted head of the man who, at this distance, was attempting to improve the outlook on life of his frigid wife three thousand miles away. On the other side of Keane, the unscarred old walls of the town, and the shuttered, unbannered windows, held their enigmatic secret.

Michael closed his eyes. Someone ought to write me a letter, he thought, to make me understand what I am going through. The last month had been so crowded with experience, of such a wildly diversified kind, that he felt he would need years to sift it, classify it, search out its meaning. Somewhere, he felt, in the confusion of strafing and capturing and bumping in dusty convoys through the hot French summer, somewhere in the waving of hands and girls' kisses and sniping and burning, there was a significant and lasting meaning. Out of this month of jubilation, upheaval and death, a man, he felt, should have been able to emerge with a key, a key to wars and oppression, a key to unlock the meaning of Europe and America.

Ever since Pavone had so savagely put him in his place that night on sentry duty back in Normandy, Michael had almost given up any hope of being useful in the war. Now, he felt, in lieu of that, I should at least *understand* it . . .

But nothing fell into generalities in his brain, he could not say, "Americans are thus and so and therefore they are winning," or "It is the nature of the French to behave in this fashion," or "What is wrong with the Germans is this particular misconception . . ."

All the violence, all the shouting, ran together in his brain, in a turbulent, confused, many-threaded drama, a drama which endlessly revolved through his mind, kept him from sleeping, even in these days of heat and exhaustion, a drama which he never could shake, even at a time like this, when his life perhaps was silently being jeopardized in this quiet, gray, lifeless village on the road to Paris.

The hush-hush of the water going by between its banks mingled with the soft, busy scratching of Keane's pencil. With his eyes closed, leaning against the stone wall, drowsy from all the lost hours of sleep, but not surrendering to sleep, Michael sifted through the furious events of the month just passed ...

The names ... The names of the sunlit towns, like a paragraph out of Proust: Marigny, Coutances, St. Jean le Thomas, Avranches, Pontorson, stretching away into the seaside summer in the magic country where Normandy and Brittany blended in a silvery green haze of pleasure and legend. What would the ailing Frenchman in the cork-lined room have said about his beloved Maritime Provinces during the bright and deadly August of 1944? What observations would he have made, in his shimmering, tidal sentences, about the changes in architecture of the 105's and the dive-bombers had brought about in the fourteenth-century churches; what would have been his reaction to the dead horses in the ditches under the hawthorn bushes and the burned-out tanks with their curious smell of metal and flesh; what elegant, subtle and despairing things would M. de Charlus and Mme. de Guermantes have had to say about the new travelers on the old roads past Mont St. Michel?

"I have been walking for five days now," the young Middle Western voice had said next to the jeep, "and I ain't fired a shot yet. But don't get me wrong, I ain't complaining. Hell, I'll *walk* them to death, if that's what they want ..."

And the sour-faced aging Captain in Chartres, leaning against the side of a Sherman tank across the square from the cathedral, saying, "I don't see what people've been raving all these years about this country for. Jesus Christ on the mountain, there ain't nothing here we can't make better in California ..."

And the chocolate-colored dwarf with a red fez dancing among the Engineers with minesweepers, at a crossroads, entertaining the waiting tankmen, who cheered him on and got him drunk with Calvados they had taken as gifts from the people along the road that morning.

And the two drunken old men, weaving down the shattered street, with little bouquets of pansies and geraniums in their hands, who had given the bouquets to Pavone and Michael, and had saluted and welcomed the American Army to their village, although they would like to ask one question: Why it was on July fourth, with not a single German in the town, the American Army had seen fit to come over and bomb the place to rubble in thirty minutes?

And the German Lieutenant in the First Division prisoner-of-war cage who, in exchange for a clean pair of socks, had pointed out on the map the exact location of his battery of 88's, to the Jewish refugee from Dresden who was now a Sergeant in the MP's.

515

And the grave French farmer who had worked all one morning weaving an enormous "Welcome USA" in roses in his hedge along the road to cheer the soldiers on their way; and the other farmers and their women who had covered a dead American along the road with banks of flowers from their gardens, roses, phlox, peonies, iris, making death on that summer morning seem for a moment gay and charming and touching as the infantry walked past, circling gently around the bright mound of blossoms.

And the thousands of German prisoners and the terrible feeling that you got looking at their faces that there was nothing there to indicate that these were the people who had torn Europe from its roots, murdered thirty million people, burned populations in gas-ovens, hanged and crushed and tortured through three thousand miles of agony. There was nothing in their faces but weariness and fear, and you knew, being honest with yourself, that if they were dressed in OD's, they would all look as though they came from Cincinnati.

And the funeral of the FFI man in that little town—what was its name?—near St. Malo, with the artillery going off all around it, and the procession winding behind the black plumed horses and the rickety hearse up the hill to the cemetery, and all the people of the town in their best clothes, shuffling along in the dust, to shake the hands of the murdered man's relatives who stood at the gate in a solemn reception line. And the young priest, who had helped officiate at the funeral services in the church, who answered, when Michael asked him who the dead man was, "I don't know, my friend. I'm from another town."

And the carpenter in Granville, who had been born in Canada and had worked on the German coastal fortifications, who had shaken his head and said, "It makes no difference now, Friend. You've come too late. 1942, 1943, I'd've shaken your hand and greeted you gladly. Now . . ." He had shrugged. "Too late, Friend, too late . . ."

And the fifteen-year-old boy in Cherbourg who had been furious with the Americans. "They are fools," he had said hotly. "They take up with exactly the same girls who lived with the Germans! Democrats! Pah! I give you democrats like that! I, myself," the boy boasted, "have shaved the hair off five girls in the neighborhood for being German whores. And I did it when it was dangerous, long before the invasion. And I'll do it again, oh, yes, I'll do it again . . ."

And the brothel with the girls dressed in short skirts, and the Madam at the counter, taking the money from the line of soldiers, and giving them a towel and an infinitesimal piece of soap, saying, "Be gentle to the little girl, my dear, remember to be gentle." And the soldiers going up to the rooms, still carrying their M-1's and their tommyguns . . .

Stellevato was snoring, and the noise of Keane's pencil went on steadily. There was no sound from the gray village around them and Michael stood up and went over to the little bridge and stared down at the dark-brown water eddying gently below. If the 800 Germans were going to put in an attack, he wished they'd do it fast. Or even better, if the task force would only show up, and Pavone with it. A war was more bearable when you were surrounded by hundreds of other men and all responsibility was out of your hands, and you knew that trained minds somewhere were busy with your problem. Here, on the old, mossy bridge over the nameless, dark stream in a forgotten, silent town, you had the feeling that you had been deserted, that no one would care if the 800 Germans came down and shot you, no one would care whether you fought them, surrendered to them, or ran from them. . . . It is almost like civilian life, Michael thought with a grin, nobody gives a damn whether you live or die . . .

I'll give Pavone and that task force another thirty minutes, Michael decided, then I'll pull out. Go back and find an American Army to attach myself to.

He stared uneasily up at the sky. It was too bad it was so gray and threatening. There was something ominous about the swollen low clouds. All the rest of the time had been so sunny. The sun had brought you a feeling of luck, so that when you had been sniped at, you felt that it was normal that they'd missed you, when you'd been strafed on the road outside Avranches and jumped into the ditch on top of the dead Armored Division Corporal, you were sure they weren't going to hit you, and they hadn't . . . And when the Regimental CP outside St. Malo had been shelled, and the visiting General had started yelling, in the room full of tense, red-eyed men at telephones, "What the hell is that son of a bitch in the Cub doing? Why doesn't he spot that gun? Call him and ask him to locate the bastard!", even then, with the house rocking from the shells and the men outside crouched in their holes, you felt that you were going to come out all right . . .

Today, somehow, seemed different. It was not sunny, and he didn't feel lucky today. . . .

The hilarious sunny march seemed over. The little girl singing the Marseillaise in the bar at Saint James, the spontaneous bursting parade of the inhabitants of the little town of Miniac when the first infantrymen came through, the free bottles of brandy in Rennes, the nuns and the little children lined up alongside the road near Le Mans, the troop of serious-faced boy scouts marching on their Sunday hike near Alençon, alongside the armored columns, the family parties bathing stubbornly along the banks of the Vilaine in the sunny weather, the V signs, the banners, the proud-faced FFI men with their prisoners—all seemed vanished, belonging to another age. Today seemed like the beginning of a new time, a gray time, without luck . . .

"The hell with it," Michael said, turning to Keane. "Let's get into the middle of town and see if anything's happening there."

Keane grinned bleakly. "O.K., Bo," he said, putting away the pad he was writing on. "You know me. I'll go anywhere."

The son of a bitch, Michael thought, I bet he would. Michael went over to Stellevato, and bent over and tapped on Stellevato's helmet. Stellevato moaned softly, lost in some warm, immoral iceman's dream. "Lea' me alone," Stellevato mumbled.

"Come on, come on!" Michael tapped more impatiently on the helmet. "We're going to go win the war."

The two Armored Division soldiers came out of their hole.

"You leaving us here alone?" the pudgy man said accusingly.

"Two of the best-trained, best-fed, best-equipped soldiers in the world," Michael said, "ought to be able to handle 800 Krauts any day in the week."

"You're full of jokes, ain't you?" the pudgy man said aggrievedly. "Leaving us alone like this."

Michael climbed into the jeep. "Don't worry," he said, "we're just going to take a look around the town. We'll notify you if you're missing anything."

"Full of jokes," the pudgy man was repeating, looking mournfully at his partner, as Stellevato slowly drove across the bridge.

The town square, when they rolled cautiously into it, with their fingers on the triggers of their carbines, seemed completely deserted. The windows of the shops were covered with their tin shutters, the doors of the church were closed, the hotel looked as though no one had gone in or out for weeks. Michael could feel a muscle in his cheek begin to pull nervously as he stared around him. Even Keane, in the back seat, was quiet.

"Well?" Stellevato whispered. "Now what?"

"Stop here," Michael said.

Stellevato put on the brakes and they stopped in the middle of the cobbled square.

There was a loud, swinging noise. Michael jumped around, bringing his carbine up. The doors of the hotel had opened and a crowd of people was pouring out. Many of them were armed, some of them with Sten guns, others with hand grenades stuck in their belts, and there were some women among them, their scarves making bright bobbing bits of color among the caps and dark heads of the men.

"Frogs," Keane said from the back seat, "with the keys of the city."

In a moment the jeep was surrounded, but there was no air of celebration about the group. They looked serious and frightened. A man in knickers, with a Red Cross band on his arm, had a bloody bandage around his head.

"What's going on here?" Michael asked in French.

"We were expecting the Germans," said one of the women, a small, chubby, shapeless middle-aged creature in a man's sweater and men's work boots. She spoke in English, with an Irish accent, and for a moment Michael had the feeling that some elaborate, dangerous practical joke was being played on him. "How did you get through?"

"We just rode into town," Michael said irritably, annoyed unreasonably at these people for being so timid. "What's the matter, here?"

"There are 800 Germans on the other side of town," said the man with the red cross on his arm.

"And three tanks," Michael said. "We know all about that. Have there been any American convoys going through here this morning?"

"A German truck went through here this morning," the woman said. "They shot André Fouret. Seven-thirty this morning. Since then, nothing."

"Are you going to Paris?" asked the Red Cross man. He had no cap, and his hair was long and blond over the stained bandage. He was wearing short socks and his legs were bare, sticking out of the baggy knickers. Michael looked at him, thinking: This man is made up for something, these can't be real clothes. "Tell me," the man said, eagerly, leaning into the jeep, "are you going to Paris?"

"Eventually," Michael said.

"Follow me," the Red Cross man said. "I have a motorcycle. I have just come from there. It will only take an hour."

"What about the 800 Germans and the three tanks?" Michael asked, certain this man was somehow trying to trap him.

"I go by back roads," said the Red Cross man. "I was only fired on twice. I know where all the mines are. You have three guns. We need every gun we can find in Paris. We have been fighting for three days and we need help . . ."

The other people standing around the jeep nodded soberly and talked to one another in French too rapid for Michael to follow.

"Wait a minute, wait a minute." Michael took the arm of the woman who spoke English. "Let's get this straight. Now, Madame . . ."

"My name is Dumoulin. I am an Irish citizen," the woman said loudly and aggressively, "but I have lived in this town for

519

thirty years. Now, tell me, young man, do you propose to protect us?"

Michael shook his head numbly. "I shall do everything in my power, Madam," he said, feeling: This war has got completely out of hand.

"You have ammunition, too," said the man with the Red Cross armband, peering hungrily into the back of the jeep where there was a jumble of boxes and bedrolls. "Excellent, excellent. You will have no trouble, if you follow me. Just put on an armband like this, and I will be very surprised if they shoot at you."

"Let Paris take care of itself," Mrs. Dumoulin snapped. "We have our own problem of the 800 Germans."

"One at a time, please," Michael said, spreading his hands out dazedly, thinking: This is one situation they never told me about at Fort Benning. "First, I'd like to hear if anyone actually *saw* the Germans."

"Jacqueline!" said Mrs. Dumoulin loudly. "Tell the young man."

"Speak slowly, please," Michael said. "My French leaves a great deal to be desired."

"I live one kilometer outside town," said Jacqueline, a squat girl with all her front teeth missing, "and last night a Boche tank stopped and a Lieutenant got out and demanded butter and cheese and bread. He said he would give us some advice, not to welcome the Americans, because the Americans were just going to pass through the town and leave us alone. Then the Germans were coming back. And anybody who had welcomed the Americans would be shot and he had 800 men waiting with him. And he was right," Jacqueline said excitedly. "The Americans came and one hour later they were gone and we'll all be lucky if the Germans don't burn the whole town down by evening . . ."

"Disgraceful," said Mrs. Dumoulin firmly. "The American Army ought to be ashamed of itself. Either they should come and stay or they should not come at all. I demand protection."

"It is criminal," said the man with the Red Cross armband, "leaving the workers of Paris to be shot down like dogs without ammunition, while they sit here with three guns and hundreds of cartridges."

"Ladies and gentlemen," Michael stood up and spoke in a loud, oratorical voice, "I wish to state that . . ."

"Attention! Attention!" It was a woman's shrill cry from the edge of the crowd.

Michael swung around. Coming at a fair rate of speed into the square, was an open car. In it two men were standing with their hands above their heads. They were dressed in field gray.

The people around the jeep stood for a moment in surprised silence.

"Boches!" someone shouted. "They wish to surrender."

Then, suddenly, when the car was almost abreast of the jeep, the two men with their hands in the air dived down into the body of the car and the car spurted ahead. Out of the back of it a figure loomed up and there was the ugly high sound of a machine pistol and screams from people who were hit. Michael stared stupidly at the careening car. Then he fumbled at his feet for his carbine. The safety was on, and it seemed to take hours to get it off.

From behind him there was the sharp, beating rhythm of a carbine. The driver of the car suddenly threw up his hands and the car hit the curb, wobbled, turned and crashed into the épicerie on the corner. There was a cymbal-like sound as the tin shutter came down, and the splintering of the window behind it. The car slowly fell on its side and two figures sprawled out.

Michael got the safety catch off his carbine. Stellevato was still sitting, his hands on the wheel, frozen in surprise. "What happened?" Stellevato whispered angrily. "What the hell's going on here?"

Michael turned. Keane was standing up behind him, his carbine in his hand, grinning bleakly at the broken Germans. There was the acrid smell of burned powder. "That'll teach them," Keane said, his yellowish teeth bared with pleasure.

Michael sighed, then looked around him. The Frenchmen were getting slowly and warily to their feet, their eyes on the wreck. Two figures lay in contorted heaps on the cobblestones. One of them, Michael noticed, was Jacqueline. Her dress was high over her knees. Her thighs were thick and yellowish. Mrs. Dumoulin was bending over her. A woman was weeping somewhere.

Michael got out of the jeep, and Keane followed him. They walked carefully across the square, their guns ready, to the overturned car.

Keane, Michael thought bitterly, his eyes on the two gray figures sprawled head down on the pavement, it had to be Keane. Faster than I, more dependable, while I was still fiddling with the catch. The Germans could've been in Paris by the time I got ready to shoot them . . .

There had been four men in the car, Michael saw, three of them officers. The driver, a Private, was still alive, with blood bubbling unevenly between his lips. He was trying to crawl away, on his hands and knees, with stubborn persistence, when Michael got to him. He saw Michael's shoes and stopped trying to crawl. Keane looked at the three officers.

"Dead," he reported, smiling his sick, humorless smile. "All three of them. We ought to get a Bronze Star, at least. Get Pavone to write it up for us. How about that one?" Keane indicated, with his toe, the wounded driver.

"He's not very healthy," Michael said. He bent down and touched the man's shoulder gently. "Do you speak French?" he asked.

The man looked up. He was very young, eighteen or nineteen, and the froth of blood on his caked lips, and the long lines of pain cutting down from his eyes, made him look animal-like and pathetic. He nodded. The effort of moving his head brought a spasm of pain to his lips. A gob of blood dripped down to Michael's shoes.

"Do not move," Michael said slowly, bent over, speaking softly into the boy's ear. "We'll try to help you."

The boy gently let himself down to the pavement. Then he slowly rolled over. He lay there, staring up through pain-torn eyes at Michael.

By now the Frenchmen were grouped around the wrecked car. The man with the Red Cross armband had two machine pistols. "Wonderful," he was saying happily, "wonderful. These will be most welcome in Paris." He came over to the wounded boy and briskly yanked the pistol out of the boy's holster. "Good," he said, "we have 38 caliber ammunition for this."

The wounded boy stared dumbly up at the red cross on the Frenchman's arm. "Doctor," he said slowly, "Doctor. Help me."

"Oh," said the Frenchman gaily, touching the red cross, "it is just a disguise. Just for getting past your friends on the road. I am not a doctor. You will have to find someone else to help you, old man . . ." He took his treasures off to one side and began to inspect them minutely for damage.

"Don't waste any time on the pig." It was the voice of Mrs. Dumoulin, stony and cold. "Put him out of his misery."

Michael stared disbelievingly at her. She was standing at the wounded boy's head, her arms crossed on her chubby bosom, speaking, Michael could tell from their harsh faces, for the men and women grouped behind her.

"Now, wait a minute," Michael said. "This man is our prisoner and we don't shoot prisoners in our Army."

"Doctor," said the boy on the cobbles.

"Kill him," said someone from behind Mrs. Dumoulin.

"If the American doesn't want to waste ammunition," another voice said, "I'll do it with a stone."

"What's the matter with you people?" Michael shouted. "What are you, animals?" He spoke in French so that they could all understand, and it was very difficult to translate his anger and disgust in his high-school accent. He stared at Mrs. Dumoulin. Inconceivable, he thought, a plump little housewife;

522

an Irish lady improbably in the middle of the Frenchmen's war, violent for blood, outside the claims of pity. "He's wounded, he can't do you any harm," Michael went on, furious at his slow searching for words. "What's the sense in it?"

"Go," Mrs. Dumoulin said coldly, "go look at Jacqueline over there. Go see Monsieur Alexandre, that's the other one, lying there, with a bullet in his lung . . . Maybe you'll understand a little better."

"Three of them are dead," Michael pleaded with Mrs. Dumoulin. "Isn't that enough?"

"It is not enough!" The woman's face was pale and furious, her dark, almost purple eyes set maniacally in her head. "Maybe it's enough for you, young man. You haven't lived here under them for four years! You haven't seen your sons taken away and killed! Jacqueline was not your neighbor. You're an American. It's easy for you to be humane. It is not so easy for us!" She was screaming wildly by now, shaking her fists under Michael's nose. "We are not Americans and we do not wish to be humane. We wish to kill him. Turn your back if you're so soft. We'll do it. You'll keep your pretty little American conscience clean . . ."

"Doctor," the boy on the pavement moaned.

"Please . . ." Michael said, appealing to the locked faces of the townspeople behind Mrs. Dumoulin, feeling guilty that he, a stranger, a stranger who loved them, loved their country, their courage, their suffering, dared to oppose them on a profound matter like this on the streets of their own town . . . "Please," he said, feeling confusedly that perhaps she was right, perhaps it was his usual softness, his wavering, unheroic indecision that was making him argue like this. "It is impossible to take a wounded man's life like this, no matter what . . ."

There was a shot behind him. Michael wheeled. Keane was standing above the German's head, his finger on the trigger of his carbine, that sick, crooked smile on his face. The German was still now. All the townspeople stared quietly and with almost demure good manners at the two Americans.

"What the hell," Keane said, grinning, "he was croaking anyway. Might as well please the lady." Keane slung the carbine over his shoulder.

"Good," said Mrs. Dumoulin flatly. "Good. Thank you very much." She turned, and the little group behind her parted so that she could walk through it. Michael watched her, a small, plump, almost comic figure, marked by childbearing and laundering and endless hours in the kitchen, rolling solidly from side to side, as she crossed the gray square to the place where the ugly farm girl lay, her skirts up, now once and for all relieved of her ugliness and her labors.

One by one, the Frenchmen wandered off, politely leaving

the two American soldiers alone over the body of the dead boy. Michael watched them carry the man with the bullet in his lungs into the hotel. Then he turned to Keane. Keane was bent over the dead boy, going through his pockets. Keane came up with a wallet. He opened the wallet and took out a folded card.

"His paybook," Keane said. "His name is Joachim Ritter. He's nineteen years old. He hasn't been paid for three months." Keane grinned at Michael. "Just like the American Army." He groped inside the wallet and brought forth a photograph. "Joachim and his girl," Keane extended the photograph. "Take a look. Juicy little piece of tail."

Dumbly, Michael looked at the photograph. A thin, living boy in an amusement park peered out at him, and next to him a plump blonde girl with her young man's military cap perched saucily on her short blonde hair. There was something scrawled in ink across the face of the photograph. It was in German.

"Forever in your arms, Elsa," Keane said. "That's what it says. In German. I'm going to send it back to my wife to hold for me. It will make an interesting souvenir."

Michael's hands trembled on the glossy bit of amusement-park paper. He nearly tore it up. He hated Keane, hated the thought of the long-faced, yellow-toothed man fingering happily over the picture later in the century, back in the United States, remembering this morning with pleasure. But he knew he had no right to tear up the photograph. As much as he hated the man, Michael realized, Keane had earned his souvenir. When Michael had faltered and fumbled, Keane had behaved like a soldier. Without hesitation or fear, he had mastered the emergency, brought the enemy down when everyone else around him had been frozen and surprised. As for the killing of the wounded boy, Michael thought wearily, Keane had probably done the correct thing. There was nothing much they could have done with the German, and they'd have had to leave him, and the townspeople would have brained him as soon as Michael left. Keane, in his sour, sadistic way, had acted out the will of the people whom they had, after all, come to Europe to serve. By the single shot, Keane had given the bereaved and threatened inhabitants of the town a sense that justice had been done, a sense that, on this morning at least, the injuries they had suffered for so long had been paid for in a fitting coin. I should be pleased, Michael thought bitterly, that Keane was along with us. I could never have done it, and it probably had to be done . . .

Michael started back toward where Stellevato was standing next to the jeep. He felt sick and weary. This is what we're here for, he thought heavily, this is what it's all been for, to kill Germans. I should be light-hearted, triumphant . . .

He did not feel triumphant. Inadequate, he thought bruisedly, Michael Whitacre, the inadequate man, the doubtful civilian, the non-killing soldier. The girls' kisses on the road, the
roses in the hedge, the free brandy had not been for him, because he could not earn it . . . Keane, who could grin as he put a
bullet through a dying boy's head at his feet, carefully folding
away a foreign photograph in his wallet for a souvenir, was
the man these Europeans had really celebrated on the sunny
march from the coast . . . Keane was the victorious, adequate,
liberating American, fit for this month of vengeance . . .

The man with the Red Cross armband came roaring past on
his motorcycle. He waved gaily, because he had two new guns
and a hundred rounds of ammunition to take to his friends behind the improvised barricades of Paris. Michael did not turn
to watch him as the bare legs, the absurd knickers, the stained
bandage, bumped swiftly past the overturned car and disappeared in the direction of the 800 Germans, the mined crossroads, the capital of France.

"Holy man," Stellevato said, his soft Italian voice still husky,
"what a morning. You all right?"

"Fine," Michael said flatly. "I'm just fine."

"Nikki," Keane said, "don't you want to go over and take
a look at the Krauts?"

"No," Stellevato said. "Leave them to the undertakers."

"You might pick up a nice souvenir," Keane said, "to send
home to your folks from France."

"My folks don't want any souvenirs," Stellevato said. "The
only souvenir they want from France is me."

"Look at this." Keane took out the photograph again and
shoved it in front of Stellevato's nose. "His name was Joachim
Ritter."

Stellevato slowly took the photograph and stared at it. "Poor
girl," Stellevato said softly. "Poor little blonde girl."

Michael wanted to take Stellevato in his arms and embrace
him.

Stellevato gave the photograph back to Keane. "I think we
ought to go back to the Water Point," Stellevato said, "and tell
the boys there what happened. They must've heard the shooting and they're probably scared out of their boots."

Michael started to climb into the jeep. He stopped. There
was a jeep coming slowly down the main street. He heard
Keane throw a cartridge into the chamber of his carbine.

"Cut it out," Michael said sharply. "It's one of ours."

The jeep drew slowly up beside them and Michael saw that
it was Kramer and Morrison, who had been with Pavone three
days before. The townspeople who were grouped on the steps
of the hotel stared down at the new arrivals stonily.

"Hiya, Boys," Morrison said. "Enjoying yourself?"

"It's been great, Bo," Keane said heartily.

"What happened there?" Kramer gestured incredulously toward the dead Germans and the overturned car. "A traffic accident?"

"I shot them," Keane said loudly, grinning. "Perfect score for the day."

"Is he kidding?" Kramer asked Michael.

"He's not kidding," Michael said. "They're all his."

"Jee-sus!" Kramer said, looking with new respect at Keane, who had been the butt of the organization ever since its arrival in Normandy. "Old big-mouth Keane . . . What do you know?"

"Civil Affairs," Morrison said. "This is a hell of a thing for a Civil Affairs outfit to get mixed up in."

"Where's Pavone?" Michael asked. "Is he coming here this morning?"

Morrison and Kramer kept staring at the dead Germans. Like most of the outfit, they had seen no fighting in all the time they had been in France, and they were frankly impressed. "The plans've been changed," Kramer said. "The task force ain't coming through here. Pavone sent us to get you. He's at a town called Rambouillet. It's only an hour from here. Everybody's waiting for a Frog division to lead the parade into Paris. We know the roads. Nikki, you follow us."

Stellevato looked inquiringly at Michael. Michael felt numb, relieved a little that the necessity for making decisions was now out of his hands. "O.K., Nikki," Michael said, "let's get started."

"This looks like a pretty hot little town," Kramer said. "You think those Frogs'd knock up a meal for us?"

"I'm dying for a steak," Morrison said. "With French fried potatoes."

Suddenly the thought of remaining any longer in the town, under the cold measuring eyes of the townspeople, with the German dead sprawled in front of the épicerie, was intolerable to Michael. "Let's get back to Pavone," he said. "He may need us."

"If there's one thing that gets on my nerves, it's PFC's," Morrison said. "Whitacre, your rank is too big for you." But he turned the jeep around.

Stellevato turned their jeep and started to follow Morrison. Michael sat stiffly in the front seat. He avoided looking at the hotel steps where Mrs. Dumoulin was standing in front of her neighbors.

"Monsieur!" It was Mrs. Dumoulin's voice, loud and commanding. "Monsieur!"

Michael sighed. "Hold it," he told Stellevato.

Stellevato stopped the jeep and honked the horn at Morrison. Morrison stopped too.

Mrs. Dumoulin, followed by the others, came across from

the hotel steps. She stood next to Michael, surrounded by the weary, work-worn farmers and merchants in their clumsy, frayed clothing.

"Monsieur," Mrs. Dumoulin said, with her arms crossed again on her full, shapeless breast, her tattered sweater flapping a little in the wind around her broad hips, "do you intend to leave?"

"Yes, Madam," Michael said quietly. "We have orders."

"What about the 800 Germans?" Mrs. Dumoulin asked, her voice savagely controlled.

"I doubt that they will come back," Michael said.

"You doubt that they will come back," Mrs. Dumoulin mimicked him. "What if they don't know about your doubts, Monsieur? What if they *do* come back?"

"I'm sorry, Madam," Michael said wearily. "We have to go. And if they did come back, what good would five Americans be to you?"

"You are deserting us," Mrs. Dumoulin said loudly. "They will come back and see the four dead ones over there and they will kill every man, woman and child in town. You can't do that? You can't behave like that! You must stay here and protect us!"

Michael looked wearily at the two jeeploads of soldiers—Stellevato, Keane, Morrison, Kramer, himself—stalled in the ugly little square. Keane was the only one who had ever fired a shot in anger, and he might be considered to have done his share for the day. Lord, Michael thought, turning regretfully back to Mrs. Dumoulin, who stood there like the fierce, prodding, squat incarnation of complex duty, Lord, what protection you would get against that phantom German battalion from these five warriors! "Madam," Michael said, "it's no good. There's nothing we can do about it. We are not the American Army. We go where we are told and we do what we are ordered to do." He stared past Mrs. Dumoulin at the anxious, accusing faces of the townspeople, trying to reach them with his good intentions, his pity, his helplessness. But there was no answering glow in the frightened faces of the men and women who were certain that they were being left to die that day in the ruins of their homes. "Forgive me, Madam," Michael said, almost sobbing, "I can't help . . ."

"You had no right to come," Mrs. Dumoulin said, suddenly quiet, "unless you were prepared to stay. The tanks last night, you this morning. War or no war, Americans or no Americans, you have no right to treat human beings like this . . ."

"Nikki," Michael said thickly, "let's get out of here! Fast!"

"It is dirty," Mrs. Dumoulin was saying, speaking for the racked men and women behind her as Stellevato drove the jeep away, "it is too dirty, it is not civilized . . ."

Michael could not hear the end of her sentence, and he did not look back as they drove swiftly out of town, following Kramer and Morrison, in the direction of Colonel Pavone.

There were champagne bottles all over the table, catching the light of the hundreds of candles which were the only illumination in the night club. The room was very crowded. Uniforms of a dozen nations mingled with gay print dresses, bare arms, high-piled gleaming hair. Everybody seemed to be talking at once. The liberation of Paris the day before and the parade that afternoon, with the attendant interesting sniping from the rooftops, had liberated an enormous flood of conversation, most of which had to be shouted loudly to be heard over the three-piece band in the corner, which was playing, very loudly, "Shuffle Off to Buffalo."

Pavone was sitting across from Michael, smiling widely, a cigar in his mouth, his arm lightly around a bleached lady with long false eyelashes. Occasionally he waved his cigar in pleasant salute to Michael, who was flanked by the correspondent, Ahearn, the man who was making a study of fear for *Collier's*, and a middle-aged, beautifully dressed pilot in the French Air Force.

There were two other American correspondents at the table, a little drunk. They were speaking gravely to each other in clipped, high-ranking tones.

"General," the first correspondent said, "I have reached the river. What are my orders?"

"Cross that goddamn river."

"I can't, Sir. There are eight armored divisions on the other side."

"You're relieved. If you can't cross that river, I'm going to find me somebody who can."

"Where you from, Bud?" the first correspondent said.

"East St. Louis."

"Shake."

They shook hands.

"You're relieved," said the second correspondent.

They emptied their glasses and peered gravely at the dancers.

"Oh," said the French pilot, who had completed three tours of duty with the RAF, and had arrived in Paris on some obscure liaison job with the 2nd French Armored Division, "oh, those were the days." He was talking about 1928, in New York City, when he had visited America and had been attached to a brokerage firm in Wall Street, in a lordly and not very serious way. "I had an apartment on Park Avenue," the pilot said, smiling fondly, "and every Thursday I gave a cocktail party for my men friends. There was only one rule. Each man had to

528

bring a girl who had never been there before. My God," the pilot said, "the hundreds of girls you got to know that way!" He shook his head in wonder at the beautiful days of his youth during the boom. "And, late at night, we would go to Harlem. Those dark girls and that music! The soul shivers, remembering!" He drank his ninth glass of champagne and beamed at Michael. "I knew 135th Street better than I knew the Place Vendôme. After the war, I go back. Perhaps," he said thoughtfully, "perhaps I will rent myself an apartment on 135th Street."

A dark woman with a black lace shawl drifted over from another table and kissed the pilot. "My dear Lieutenant," the dark lady said, "I am so happy to see a French officer."

The pilot stood up and bowed sedately and asked the dark lady if she wished to dance. The lady melted into his arms and they inched out onto the tiny, crowded dance floor. The band was playing a rhumba now and the pilot, elegant in his blue uniform, dancing like a Cuban, wove in and out with a serious and exalted expression on his face.

"Whitacre," Pavone said, across the table, "you're a fool if you ever leave this city."

"I agree with you, Colonel," Michael said. "When the war is over, I'm going to ask them to discharge me on the Champs Elysées." And, for the moment, he meant it. From the second, when, from among the rolling troop-filled trucks, he had seen the spire of the Eiffel Tower rising above the roofs of Paris, he had felt that he had finally arrived at his true home. Caught in the riotous confusion of kissing and handshaking and gratitude, hungrily reading the names of the streets which had haunted his brain ever since he was a boy, "Rue de Rivoli," "Place de l'Opera," "Boulevard des Capucines," he had felt washed of all guilt and all despair. Even the occasional outbursts of fighting, among the gardens and the monuments, when the remaining Germans had fired away their ammunition before surrendering, had seemed like a pleasant and fitting introduction to the great city. And the spilled blood on the streets, and the wounded and dying men being hurried away on stained stretchers by the FFI red-cross women, had added the dramatically necessary, proper note of poignance and suffering to the great act of liberation.

He would never be able to remember, he knew, what it had been like, exactly. He would only remember the cloud of kisses, the rouge on his shirt, the tears, the embraces, the feeling that he was enormous, invulnerable, and loved.

"Hey, you," said the first correspondent.

"Yes, Sir," said the second correspondent.

"Which way is Second Armored Headquarters?"

"I don't know, Sir. I just arrived from Camp Shanks."

"You're relieved."

"Yes, Sir."

They drank solemnly.

"I remember," Ahearn was saying next to him, "that the last time I saw you I questioned you on the subject of fear."

"Yes," Michael said, looking agreeably at the sunburned red face, and the serious gray eyes, "I believe you did. How's the market on fear these days among the editors?"

"I decided to put off writing it," Ahearn said earnestly. "It's been overdone. It's the result of the writers after the last war, plus the psychoanalysts. Fear has been made respectable and it's been done to death. It's a civilian concept. Soldiers really don't worry as much about it as the novelists would have you believe. In fact, the whole picture of war as an unbearable experience is a false one. I've watched carefully, keeping my mind open. War is enjoyable, and it is enjoyed by and large by almost every man in it. It is a normal and satisfactory experience. What is the thing that has struck you most strongly in the last month in France?"

"Well," Michael began, "it's . . ."

"Hilarity," Ahearn said. "A wild sensation of holiday. Laughter. We have moved three hundred miles through an enemy army on a tide of laughter. I plan to write it for *Collier's*."

"Good," Michael said gravely. "I shall look forward to it."

"The only man who has ever written accurately about a battle," said Ahearn, leaning over so that his face was just six inches from Michael's, "was Stendhal. In fact, the only three writers who have ever been worth reading twice in the whole history of literature, were Stendhal, Villon and Flaubert."

"The war will end in thirty days," a very handsome British correspondent on the other side of the table was saying, "and I regret it. There are a lot of Germans who must be killed, and if the war continues we will do the work in hot blood. If the war ends, they will still have to be killed, but in cold blood, and I'm afraid we, the British and the Americans, will flinch from the job. And we will leave a powerful generation of enemies in the center of Europe. Personally, I pray for a terrible reverse of our fortunes . . ."

"Oh, sweet and lovely, lady be good," the trumpet player was singing in accented English, "oh, lady be good to me . . ."

"Stendhal caught the unexpected and insane and humorous aspect of war," Ahearn said. "Do you remember in his journal, his description of the Colonel who rallied his men during the Russian campaign?"

"I'm afraid not," Michael said.

"What's the situation?" asked the first correspondent.

"We are surrounded by two full divisions."

"You're relieved," said the first correspondent. "If you can't cross that river, I'm going to find me somebody who can."

They drank.

"You look like a nice, lonesome soldier." It was a tall, dark-haired girl in a flowered dress whom Michael had smiled at across the room fifteen minutes before. She was standing, bent over the table, her hand on Michael's. Her dress was cut low, and Michael noticed the pleasant firm olive sweep of her bosom so close to his eyes. "Wouldn't you like to dance with a grateful lady?"

Michael smiled at her. "In five minutes," he said, "when my head is cleared."

"Good." The girl nodded, smiling invitingly. "You know where I'm sitting..."

"Yes, I certainly do," Michael said. He watched the girl slip through the dancers in a sinuous flowery movement. Nice, he thought, very nice for later. I should really make love to a Parisienne to make official our entry into Paris.

"There are volumes to be written," Ahearn said, "about the question of men and women in wartime."

"I'm sure there are," Michael said. The girl sat down at her table and smiled across at him.

"Relations are healthy and free, with a romantic undertone of haste and tragedy," said Ahearn. "Take my case, for example. I have a wife and two children in Detroit. Frankly, while I admire my wife immensely, I find I am now bored with the idea of her. She is a small, plain woman, and her hair is thinning. In London, I have been living with a voluptuous girl of nineteen who works in the Ministry of Supply. She has lived through the war, she understands things that I have gone through, I am very happy with her . . . How can I be honest and say I would like to return to Detroit?"

"Everyone," said Michael politely, "has his own particular problems."

There were shouts from the other end of the room, and four young men with FFI armbands and rifles pushed their way through the dancers, dragging another young man whose face was bleeding from a long gash over his eyes. "Liars!" the bloody young man was shouting. "You're all liars! I am no more of a collaborationist than anybody in this room!"

One of the FFI men hit the prisoner on the back of the neck. The young man's head sagged forward and he was quiet. The blood made a thin arc to the dance floor. The four FFI men dragged him up the steps past the candles in their glass holders on the maroon walls. The orchestra played louder than before.

"Barbarians!" It was a woman's voice, speaking in English. A lady of forty was sitting in the seat that the French pilot had vacated next to Michael. She had long, dark-red fingernails and an elegant simple black dress, and she was still very handsome. "They all ought to be arrested. Just looking for an excuse to stir up mischief. I am going to suggest to the American Army that they disarm them all." Her accent was plainly American and both Ahearn and Michael stared at her puzzledly. She nodded briskly to Ahearn, and more coolly to Michael, after swiftly noting that he was not an officer. "My name is Mabel Kasper," she said, "and don't look so surprised. I'm from Schenectady."

"We are delighted, Mabel," Ahearn said gallantly, bowing without rising.

"I know what I'm talking about," the lady from Schenectady said feverishly, obviously three or four drinks past cold sobriety. "I've lived in Paris for twelve years. Oh, the things I've suffered. You're a correspondent—the stories I could tell you about what it was like under the Germans. . . ."

"I would be delighted to hear," Ahearn began.

"The food, the rationing," Mabel Kasper said, pouring a large glass full of champagne and drinking half of it in one gulp. "The Germans requisitioned my apartment, and they only gave me fifteen days to move my furniture. Luckily, I found another apartment, a Jewish couple's, the man is dead now, but this afternoon, imagine that, the second day of liberation, the woman was around asking me to give it back to her. And there wasn't a stick of furniture in it when I moved in, I was damn careful to have affidavits made, I knew this would happen. I have already spoken to Colonel Harvey, of our Army, he's been most reassuring. Do you know Colonel Harvey?"

"I'm afraid not," Ahearn said.

"These are going to be hard days ahead of us in France." Mabel Kasper finished the glass of champagne. "The scum are in the saddle. Hoodlums, parading around with their guns."

"Do you mean the FFI?" Michael asked.

"I mean the FFI," said Mabel Kasper.

"But they've done all the fighting in the underground," said Michael, trying to puzzle out what this woman was driving at through all the noise.

"The underground!" Mabel Kasper snorted in a genteel, annoyed way. "I'm so tired of the underground. All the loafers, all the agitators, all the ne'er-do-wells, who had no families to worry about, no property, no jobs . . . The respectable people were too busy, and now we'll all pay for it unless you help us." She poured herself another glass of champagne and leaned toward Michael. "You've liberated us from the Germans, now you must liberate us from the French and the Russians." She drained her glass and stood up. "A word to the wise," she said, nodding gravely.

Michael watched her walk along the jumbled line of tables, in her simple, handsome black dress. "Lord," he said softly, "and out of Schenectady, too."

"A war," Ahearn said soberly, "as I was saying, is full of confusing elements."

"What's the situation?" the first correspondent asked.

"My left flank has been turned," said the second correspondent. "My right flank is crumbling, my center has been driven back. I shall attack."

"You're relieved," said the first correspondent.

"After the war," the handsome British correspondent was saying, "I am going to buy a house outside Biarritz, and just stay there. I can't stand English food. When I am forced to go to London, I'll pack a hamper and take a plane for a weekend, eating in my hotel room . . ."

"This wine," said a public-relations officer with a brand-new, shining shoulder holster, at the other end of the table, "is not mature."

"If there is any hope in the future," Michael heard Pavone lecturing two young American infantry officers who were AWOL from their Division for the night, "it is in France. It is not enough for Americans to fight for France, they must understand it, stabilize it, be patient with it. That is not easy, because the French are the most annoying people in the whole world. They are annoying because they are chauvinistic, scornful, reasonable, independent, and great. If I were the President of the United States, I would send every young American to France for two years instead of to college. The boys would learn about food and art, and the girls would learn about sex, and in fifty years you would have Utopia on the banks of the Mississippi . . ."

Across the room, the girl in the flowered dress, who had been watching Michael intently, smiled broadly and nodded when she caught Michael's eye.

"The irrational element in war," Ahearn said, "is the one that has been missing from all our literature. Let me remind you once more of the Colonel in Stendhal . . ."

"What did the Colonel in Stendhal say?" Michael asked dreamily, happily floating in the haze of champagne, smoke, perfume, candlelight, lust . . .

"His men were demoralized," Ahearn said sternly, his tone now martial and commanding, "and they were on the verge of running under a Russian attack. The Colonel swore at them, waved his sword, and shouted, 'My ass-hole is as round as an apple, follow me!' And they followed him and routed the Russians. Irrational," Ahearn said professorially, "a perfect non-sequitur, but it touched some obscure spring of patriotism and resistance in the hearts of the soldiers, and they won the day."

"Ah," said Michael regretfully, "there are no Colonels like that today."

A drunken British Captain was singing, very loudly, "We're going to hang our washing on the Siegfried Line," his voice bellowing strongly, drowning out the music of the orchestra. Immediately, other voices took up the song. The orchestra gave in and stopped the dance tune they were playing and began to accompany the singers. The drunken Captain, a huge, red-faced man, with glaring teeth, grabbed a girl and began to dance around the room among the tables. Other couples jumped up and attached themselves to the line, weaving slowly and loudly between the paper tablecloths and the wine buckets. In a minute, the line was twenty couples long, chanting, their heads thrown back, each person's hands on the waist of the dancer ahead of him, like a triumphant snake dance in college after a football game, except that it was all enclosed in a low-ceilinged, candle-lit room, and the singing was deafening.

"Agreeable," Ahearn said, "but too normal to be interesting, from a literary point of view. After all, after a victory like this, it is only to be expected that the liberators and the liberated sing and dance. But what a thing it would have been to be in the Czar's palace in Sevastopol when the young cadets filled the swimming pool with champagne from the Czar's cellar and tossed naked ballet girls by the dozen into the foam, while waiting for the arrival of the Red Army which would execute them all! Excuse me," Ahearn said gravely, standing up, "I must join this."

He wriggled out onto the floor and put his hands on the waist of the Schenectady-born Mabel Kasper, who was swaying her simple taffeta hips and singing loudly at the end of the line.

The girl in the flowered dress was standing in front of the table, looking at Michael, smiling through the clamor. "Now?" she asked softly, putting out her hand.

"Now," Michael said. He stood up and took her hand. They hitched onto the line, the girl in front of Michael, her hips living and slender under the frail silk of her gown.

By now everybody in the room was in the line, spiraling in a roaring, silk and uniformed line, over the dance floor, in front of the blaring band, among the tables. "We're gonna hang out the washing on the Siegfried Line," they sang. "Have you any dirty washing, Mother dear?"

Michael sang with the loudest of them, his voice hoarse and happy in his ears, holding tight to the desirable slim waist of the girl who had sought him out of all the victorious young

534

men in the celebrating city. Lost on a clangorous tide of music, shouting the crude, triumphant words, remembering with what savage irony the Germans had thrown those words back in the teeth of the British who had first sung them in 1939, Michael felt that on this night all men were his friends, all women his lovers, all cities his own, all victories deserved, all life imperishable...

"We're gonna hang out the washing on the Siegfried Line," the blended voices sang among the candles, "if the Siegfried Line's still there," and Michael knew that he had lived for this moment, had crossed the ocean for it, carried a rifle for it, escaped death for it.

The song ended. The girl in the flowered dress turned and kissed him, melting into him, clutching him, making him dizzy with the smell of wine and heliotrope perfume, as the other people around him sang, like all the gay, jubilating ghosts at every New Year's party that had ever been held, the sentimental and haunting words of "Auld Lang Syne."

The middle-aged pilot from Park Avenue, who had given the ingenious parties in 1928, and who had gone to Harlem late at night, and who had flown three complete tours in the Lorraine Squadron, and whose friends had all died through the years, and who now was finally back in Paris, was weeping as he sang, the tears unashamedly and openly streaming down his handsome, worn face... "should old acquaintance be forgot," he sang, his arm around Pavone's shoulders, already hungry and nostalgic for this great and fleeting night of hope and joy, "and never brought to mind...?"

The girl kissed Michael ever more fiercely. He closed his eyes and rocked gently with her, the nameless gift of the free city, locked in his arms...

Fifteen minutes later, when Michael, carrying his carbine, and the girl in the flowered dress and Pavone and his bleached lady were walking along the dark Champs Elysées, in the direction of the Arch, near where Michael's girl lived, the Germans came over, bombing the city. There was a truck parked under a tree, and Michael and Pavone decided to wait there, sitting on the bumper, under the moral protection of the summer foliage above their heads.

Two minutes later, Pavone was dead, and Michael was lying on the tarry-smelling pavement, very conscious, but curiously unable to move his legs below the hips.

Voices came from far away and Michael wondered whatever had happened to the girl in the silk dress, and tried to puzzle out how it had happened, because all the firing had seemed to be on the other side of the river, and he hadn't heard any bombs dropping...

Then he remembered the sudden dark shape roaring across

the intersection . . . A traffic accident . . . He chuckled remotely to himself. Beware French drivers, all his traveling friends had always said.

He couldn't move his legs and the light of the torch on Pavone's face made it seem very pale, as though he had been dead forever, and there was an American voice saying, "Hey, look at this, an American, and he's dead. Hey, look, it's a Colonel. What do you know . . . ? He looks just like a GI."

Michael started to say something clear and definitive about his friend, Colonel Pavone, but it never quite formed on his tongue. When they picked Michael up, although they did it very gently, considering the dark and the confusion and the weeping women, he dropped steeply into unconsciousness . . .

CHAPTER THIRTY-THREE

THE REPLACEMENT DEPOT was on a sodden plain near Paris, a sprawling collection of tents and old German barracks, still with the highly colored paintings of large German youths and smiling old men drinking out of steins, and bare-legged farm-girls like Percheron horses on the walls, under the swastika and eagle. Many Americans, to show that they had passed through this hallowed spot, had written their names on the painted walls, and legends like, "Sgt. Joe Zachary, Kansas City, Missouri" and "Meyer Greenberg, PFC, Brooklyn, USA" were everywhere in evidence.

In the November mud, the thousands of men, waiting in the camp to be sent up to divisions to make up combat losses, milled slowly about, in a restrained, quiet manner that was very different, Michael thought, from the usual boisterous and loudly complaining habits of any other American soldiers he had ever seen. This camp, Michael thought, standing at the entrance to the tent in which he was quartered, peering out into the dull drizzle, and the men in the wet raincoats moving aimlessly and restlessly about on the long, thick streets, is not really human. The only thing it can be compared to is the stockyards at Chicago, with the beasts caught in the corrals, uneasily aware that doom is near, sniffing the scent of the waiting slaughter house.

"The infantry!" Young Speer was saying bitterly inside the tent. "They send me to Harvard for two years and I'm supposed to be an officer when I come out, and then they change their minds and stop the whole damn thing! A Private in the infantry, after two years at Harvard! What an Army!"

"It's tough," Krenek, on the next bed, said sympathetically. "There's no doubt about it, this Army is in a terrible mess. It all depends who you know."

"I know plenty of people," Speer said sharply. "How do you think I got into Harvard? But they couldn't help when the transfer came through. My mother nearly died."

"Gee," Krenek said gently, "it must of been a real disappointment to everyone concerned."

Michael grinned sourly and turned back to look at Krenek, to see if he was making fun of the young man from Harvard. Krenek was a machine gunner from the First Division, who had been wounded in Sicily and then again on D Day, and was now going up for his third time around. But Krenek, who was a small, wiry, dark-faced boy from the slums of Chicago, was honestly sorry for the young lordling from Boston.

"Ah," said Michael, "maybe the war will be over tomorrow."

"You got any private information?" Krenek asked.

"No," Michael said, "but in *Stars and Stripes* it says the Russians are advancing fifty miles a day . . ."

"Oh, the Russians," Krenek shook his head. "I wouldn't depend too much on the Russians winning any war for us. It's going to take the First Division, finally, to go into Berlin and finish it."

"You going to try to get sent back to the First Division?" Michael asked.

"God, no," said Krenek, shaking his head mildly, looking up from the M1, which he was cleaning on his cot. "I want to come out of this war alive. The First Division is too good and everybody knows it. It's too famous. The publicity is murderous. Is there a tough beach to hit, is there a hill to take, is there an attack to lead, they call on the old Red One. You might just as well put a bullet right here between the eyes as join the First Division. I want to be sent to a nice, mediocre division that no one has ever heard of, that hasn't taken a town since Pearl Harbor. You join the First Division, the best you can hope for is a wound. I was Purple-Hearted twice and each time all the guys in my platoon congratulated me. They always give the First Division the best Generals in the Army, always fighting, ain't afraid of nothing, and that's Good night, Happy, for the enlisted man. I came through this far, my motto now is, Let the other fellow in on the glory." He went back carefully to cleaning the oily parts of the M1.

"What's it like?" Speer asked nervously. He was a nice-looking blond boy, with wavy hair and mild blue eyes, and you got a vision, looking at him, of a long line of governesses and aunts and related women who took him to hear Koussevitsky on Saturday afternoons. "What's it like in the infantry?"

"What's it like in the infantry," Krenek sang, "You walk, walk, walk . . ."

"No, I mean seriously," Speer said. "What do they do, just take you up there and leave you out there to fight right away?"

"If you want to know, do they do it gradual," Krenek said, "they don't do it gradual. Anyway, not in the old Red One."

"How about you?" Speer asked Michael. "Which division were you in?"

Michael went over to his cot and sat down heavily. "I wasn't in any division. I was in Civil Affairs."

"Civil Affairs," Speer said. "That's what they should have put me in."

"Civil Affairs?" Krenek said, surprised. "How the hell could you get a Purple Heart in Civil Affairs?"

"I was run over by a French taxicab in the city of Paris, Michael said, "and my left leg was broken."

"You'd never get a Purple Heart in the First for anything like that," Krenek said proudly.

"I was in a ward with twenty other guys," Michael said, "and one morning a Colonel came in and he handed them out to everybody."

"Five points," Krenek said, "toward graduation. Some day, you're liable to be mighty grateful to that busted leg."

"My heavens," Speer said, "what a classification system—putting a man with a broken leg in the infantry."

"It isn't broken now," Michael said mildly. "It works. It is cosmetically unsatisfactory, according to the doctors, but it is guaranteed to work, especially in dry weather."

"Even so," Speer went on, "why don't you go back to your Civil Affairs unit?"

"Sergeant or below," Krenek chanted, "they do not bother to send you back to your original organization. Sergeant or below, you are an interchangeable part."

"Thanks, Krenek," Michael said soberly. "That's the nicest thing anybody has said about me in nine months."

"What's your Army Specialty number?" Krenek asked.

"745," Michael said.

"745," said Krenek. "Basic rifleman. That is some specialty. An interchangeable part. We are all interchangeable parts."

Michael could see Speer's soft, pleasant young mouth twisting a little in nervousness and distaste. Speer obviously did not like the concept of himself as an interchangeable part. It did not fit in with the picture of himself which had been built up by the rosy years among the governesses and the Harvard classrooms.

"There must be some divisions that're better to be a replacement in than others," Speer persisted, working on his problem.

"It is possible to get killed," Krenek said wisely, "in any division in the American Army."

"I mean," said Speer, "a division where they break a man in gently. Not all at once, I mean."

"That must of been some course they gave you at Harvard College, feller," Krenek said, bending over his rifle. "They must of told you some pretty rich stories about the service."

"Papuga!" Speer turned to the other man in the tent, who had been lying straight out on his cot in silence, his eyes open, staring unblinkingly up at the damp, sloping canvas above his head. "Papuga, what division were you in?"

Papuga did not turn his head. He continued to stare reflectively at the canvas. "I was in the anti-aircraft," Papuga said, in a flat, remote voice.

Papuga was a fat man of about thirty-five, with a sallow, pock-marked face and long dry black hair. He lay on his cot all day long, and Michael had noticed that he often skipped meals. On all Papuga's clothes there were the faded marks where Staff Sergeant's stripes had been ripped off. Papuga never joined in the conversations in the tent, and with his dark, day-long staring into space, and his habit of not eating, and the signs of his broken rank on his sleeve, he was something of a mystery to the other men.

"The anti-aircraft," Krenek said, nodding judiciously. "Now, there's a nice assignment."

"What're you doing here?" Speer wanted to know. Speer was looking for comfort on this wet, November plain, with the smell of the slaughterhouse in his nostrils, and he would take it away from any of the veterans around him. "Why didn't you stay in the anti-aircraft?"

"One day," Papuga said, without looking at Speer, "I shot down three P-47's."

There was silence in the tent. Uncomfortably, Michael wished Papuga wouldn't say anything else.

"I was on a 40 mm gun," Papuga said after awhile, in his flat, automatic-sounding voice. "Our battery was guarding a P-47 airstrip. It was nearly dark, and the Germans had a habit of sending planes over to strafe us just at that time. I hadn't had a day off for two months, and I never sleep good, anyway, and I'd just got a letter from my wife, she told me she was having a baby, only I hadn't been home in two years . . ."

Michael closed his eyes, hoping that Papuga would stop. But there was an accumulated mass of agony in Papuga that had been simmering in silence all this time. Now that he had started, he didn't seem to be able to stop.

"I was not in good shape," Papuga said, "and a buddy of mine gave me half a bottle of marc, that's a French drink that the farmers make, it's like plain alcohol, it bites the back of your throat like a trap. I drank all of it by myself, and when some planes started to come in low, and somebody began to yell, I must of got a little confused. It was almost dark, understand, and the Germans had a habit of . . ." He stopped and sighed and passed his hand across his eyes slowly. "I turned the gun on them, I'm a good gunner, and then the other guns started in on them, too. I'll tell you something, the third one, I saw the stripes on the underside of the wings, I saw the star and the bar, but somehow I couldn't stop. He flew right over me, real slow, with his flaps down, trying to land, I couldn't explain it, I couldn't stop . . ." Papuga took his hand away from his eyes. "Two of them burned," he said flatly, "and the other one crashed and turned over. Ten minutes later, the Colonel in command of the Group came over to me, he was just a young feller, you know those Air Force Colonels, he got the Congressional Medal for something while we were still in England. He came up to me and he smelled my breath and I thought he was going to shoot me right there and then, and to tell the truth, I don't blame that Colonel, I don't hold nothing against him."

Krenek slipped the bolt of the M1 into place with a sharp snapping noise.

"But he didn't shoot me," Papuga said dully. "He took me out to the field where the planes were, and he made me look at what was left of the two guys that burned, and he made me help carry the other one, the one that turned over, back to the doctor's tent, only he was dead anyway."

Speer was making a nervous, sucking sound with his tongue, and Michael was sorry the boy had had to hear this. It would do him no good, in the approaching time when they would put him, not gradually, into the line in front of the Siegfried fortifications.

"They held me for court-martial, and the Colonel said he was going to have them hang me," Papuga said, "and, like I said, I didn't blame that Colonel for a minute, he was just a young feller, anyway. But after awhile, they came to me and they said, 'Papuga, we will give you a chance, we will dispense with the court-martial, we will put you in the infantry,' and I said, 'Anything you say.' They took off my stripes and the day before I came up here the Colonel came to me and he said, 'I hope they shoot your balls off in the infantry the first day.' "

Papuga stopped talking. He stared flatly and expressionlessly up at the canvas above his head.

"I hope," said Krenek, "they don't put you in the First."

"They can put me anywhere they like," Papuga said. "It don't make no difference to me."

A whistle blew outside. They all got up and put on their

raincoats and helmet liners and went out to stand the Retreat formation.

There was a big new batch of replacements that had just come over from the States. The swollen, oversize, casual company stood in the drizzle, the mud thick on their boots, answering to their names, and the Sergeant said, "Sir, L Company all present and accounted for," and the Captain took the salute and walked away to supper.

The Sergeant did not dismiss the Company. He strolled back and forth in front of the first line, peering out at the dripping men standing in the mud. The rumor was that the Sergeant had been a chorus boy before the war. He was a slender, athletic-looking man, with a pale, sharp face. He wore the good-conduct ribbon and the American defense ribbon and the European Theatre ribbon, with no campaign stars.

"I have a couple of things to say to you guys," the Sergeant began, "before you go slop up your supper."

A slight, almost inaudible sigh rustled through the ranks. By this stage of the war everyone knew that there was nothing a Sergeant could say that could be listened to with pleasure.

"We had a little trouble here the last few days," the Sergeant said, nastily. "We are close to Paris and some of the boys got the notion it would be nice to slip off for a couple of nights and get laid. In case any of you boys're entertaining the same idea, let me tell you they never got to Paris, they never got laid, and they are already way up front in Germany and I will give any man here odds of five to one they never come back." The Sergeant walked meditatively, looking down at the ground, his hands in his pockets. He walks like a dancer, quite graceful, Michael thought, and he looks like a very good soldier, the neat, dashing way he wears his clothes . . . "For your information," the Sergeant began again in a low, mild voice, "Paris is out of bounds to all GI's from this camp, and there are MP's on every road and every entrance leading into it, and they are looking at everybody's papers, very careful. Very, very careful."

Michael remembered the two men with full packs pacing slowly back and forth in front of the orderly room at Dix, in payment for going to Trenton for a couple of beers. The long continuing struggle of the Army, the sullen attempts by the caged animals to get free for an hour, a day, for a beer, a girl, and the sullen punishments in return.

"The Army is very lenient over here," the Sergeant said. "There are no courts-martial for being AWOL like in the States. Nothing is put on your record. Nothing to stop you from getting an honorable discharge, if you live that long. All we do is, we catch you and we look up the requests for replacements, and we see, 'Ah, the Twenty-ninth Division is having the heaviest casualties this month' and I personally make out your orders and send you there."

"That son of a bitch is a Peruvian," a voice whispered behind Michael. "I heard about him. Would you believe it, not even a citizen, a Peruvian, and he's talking to us like that!"

Michael looked with new interest at the Sergeant. It was true that he was dark and foreign-looking. Michael had never seen a Peruvian before, and for a moment he was mildly amused at the thought of standing here in the French rain being lectured to by a Peruvian Master Sergeant who had been a chorus boy before the war. Democracy, he thought appreciatively, how inscrutable are your works . . .

"I have been handling replacements for a long time," the Sergeant was saying. "I've seen fifty, maybe seventy thousand GI's go through this depot, and I know what's going on in your minds. You been reading the newspapers and listening to the speeches, and everybody keeps saying, 'Our brave fighting boys, the heroes in khaki,' and you feel, as long as you are heroes you can do whatever you damn well please, go AWOL into Paris, get drunk, pick up the clap from a French whore for 500 francs outside the Red Cross club. I'm going to tell you something, boys. Forget what you read in the newspapers. That's for civilians. Not for you. That's for guys making four dollars an hour in the airplane factories, that's for the air-raid wardens in Minneapolis with a bottle of Budweiser in one hand, and some dogface's loving wife in the other. You ain't heroes, Boys. You're culls. Culls. That's why you're here. You're the people nobody else wanted. You're the guys who can't type or fix a radio or add up a column of figures. You're the guys nobody would have in an office, you're the guys nobody could find any use for back in the States. You're the frig-ups of the Army, and I'm the boy who knows it. I don't read the papers. They heaved a sigh of relief back in Washington and it was on the boat for you, and nobody cares do you come home or don't you come home. You're replacements. And there's nothing lower in this Army than a replacement, unless it's another replacement. Every day they bury a thousand like you, and the guys like me, who never frigged up, go over the lists and send up a thousand more. That's how it is in this camp, Boys, and I'm telling it to you for your own good, so you know where you stand. There's a lot of new boys in camp tonight, with the beer from the Kilmer PX still wet on their lips, and I want to put things straight for them. So don't get any fancy ideas in your head about Paris, Boys, it won't work. Go back to your tents and clean your rifles nice and neat and write your final instructions home to the folks. So forget about Paris, Boys.

Come back in 1950. Maybe it will not be out of bounds for GI's then."

The men stood rigidly, in silence. The Sergeant stopped his pacing. He smiled grimly at the ranks, his jaws creasing in razored lines under his soft garrison cap with the cellophane rain-covering over it, like an officer's.

"Thanks for listening, Boys," the Sergeant said. "Now we all know where we stand. Dis-miss!"

The Sergeant walked springily down the Company street as the lines dissolved into confusion.

"I'm going to write to my mother," Speer said, angrily, next to Michael, as they walked toward their tent to pick up their mess kits. "She knows the Senator from Massachusetts."

"By all means," Michael said politely. "Do that."

"Whitacre . . ."

Michael turned around. A small, half-familiar figure, almost lost in a raincoat, was standing there. Michael moved closer. Through the dusk, he could make out a battered face, a split eyebrow, a full, wide mouth, now curved in a small smile.

"Ackerman!" Michael said. They shook hands.

"I didn't know whether you'd remember me or not," Noah said. His voice was low and even and sounded much older than Michael remembered. The face, in the half-light, was very thin and had a new, mature sense of repose.

"Lord," Michael said, delighted, in this strange mass of men, to come across a face that he knew, a man with whom once he had been friendly, feeling as though somehow, by great luck, in a sea of enemies, he had found an ally. "Lord, I'm glad to see you."

"Going to chow?" Ackerman asked. He was carrying his mess kit.

"Yes." Michael took Ackerman's arm. It seemed surprisingly wasted and fragile under the slippery material of the raincoat. "I just have to get my mess kit. Hang onto me."

"Sure," Noah said. He smiled gravely, and they walked side by side toward Michael's tent. "That was a real little dandy of a speech," Noah said, "wasn't it?"

"Great for the morale," said Michael. "I feel like wiping out a German machine-gun nest before chow."

Noah smiled softly. "The Army," he said. "They sure love to make speeches to you in the Army."

"It's an irresistible temptation," Michael said. "Five hundred men lined up, not allowed to leave or talk back . . . Under the circumstances, I think I'd be tempted myself."

"What would you say?" Noah asked.

Michael thought for a moment. "God help us," he said soberly. "I'd say, 'God help every man, woman and child alive today.' "

He ducked into his tent and came out with his mess kit. Then they walked slowly over to the long line outside the mess hall.

When Noah took off his raincoat in the mess hall, Michael saw the Silver Star over his breastpocket, and for a moment he felt the old twinge of guilt. He didn't get that by being hit by a taxicab, Michael thought. Little Noah Ackerman, who started out with me, who had so much reason to quit, but who obviously hadn't quit ...

"General Montgomery pinned it on," Noah said, noticing Michael staring at the decoration. "On me and my friend Johnny Burnecker. In Normandy. They sent us to the supply dump to get brand-new uniforms. Patton was there and Eisenhower. There was a very nice G2 in Division Headquarters, and he pushed it through for us. It was on the Fourth of July. Some kind of British-American good will demonstration." Noah grinned. "General Montgomery demonstrated his good will to me, with the Silver Star. Five points toward discharge."

They sat at the crowded table, in the big hall, eating warmed-up C rations, vegetable hash, and thin coffee.

"Isn't it a shame," asked Krenek, lower down at the table, "how the civilians are deprived of all their porterhouse steaks for the Armed Forces?"

Nobody laughed at the ancient joke, which had served Krenek as table conversation in Louisiana, Feriana, Palermo ...

Michael ate with pleasure, going back over the years with Noah, filling the gaps between Florida and the Replacement Depot. He looked gravely at the photograph of Noah's son ("Twelve points," Noah said, "he has seven teeth.") and heard about the deaths of Cowley, Donnelly, Rickett, and the break-up of Captain Colclough. He felt a surprising family-like wave of nostalgia for the old Company which he had been so happy to leave in Florida.

Noah was very different. He didn't seem nervous. Although he was terribly frail now, and coughed considerably, he seemed to have found some inner balance, a thoughtful, quiet maturity which made Michael feel that Noah somehow was much older than he. Noah talked gently, without bitterness, with none of his old intense, scarcely controlled violence, and Michael felt that if Noah survived the war he would be immensely better equipped for the years that came after than he, Michael, would be.

They cleaned their mess kits and, luxuriously smoking nickel cigars from their rations, they strolled through the sharp, dark evening, toward Noah's tent, their mess kits jangling musically at their sides.

544

There was a movie in camp, a 16 mm version of Rita Hayworth in *Cover Girl,* and all the men who were billeted in the same tent with Noah were surrendering themselves to its technicolor delights. Michael and Noah sat on Noah's cot in the empty tent, puffing at their cigars, watching the blue smoke spiral softly up through the chilled air.

"I'm pulling out of here tomorrow," Noah said.

"Oh," Michael said, feeling suddenly bereaved, feeling that it was unjust for the Army to throw friends together like this, only to tear them apart twelve hours later. "Your name on the roster?"

"No," said Noah quietly. "I'm just pulling out."

Michael puffed carefully at his cigar. "AWOL?" he asked.

"Yes."

God, Michael thought, remembering the time Noah had spent in prison, hasn't he had enough of that? "Paris?" he asked.

"No. I'm not interested in Paris." Noah bent over and took two packs of letters, carefully done up in string, from his barracks bag. He put one pack, the envelopes scrawled unmistakably in a woman's handwriting, on the bed. "Those are from my wife," Noah said flatly. "She writes me every day. This pack . . ." He waved the other bunch of letters gently. "From Johnny Burnecker. He writes me every time he has a minute off. And every letter ends, 'You have to come back here.' "

"Oh," Michael said, trying to recall Johnny Burnecker, remembering an impression of a tall, raw-boned boy with a girlish complexion and blond hair.

"He's got a fixation, Johnny," Noah said. "He thinks if I come back and stay with him, we'll both come through the war all right. He's a wonderful man. He's the best man I ever met in my whole life. I've got to get back to him."

"Why do you have to go AWOL?" Michael asked. "Why don't you go into the orderly room and ask them to send you back to your old Company?"

"I did," Noah said. "That Peruvian. He told me to get my ass the hell out of there, he was too busy, he wasn't any goddamn placement bureau, I'd go where they sent me." Noah played slowly with the pack of Burnecker's letters. They made a dry, rustling sound in his hands. "I shaved and pressed my uniform, and I made sure I was wearing my Silver Star. It didn't impress him. So I'm taking off after breakfast tomorrow."

"You'll get into a mess of trouble," Michael said.

"Nah." Noah shook his head. "People do it every day. Just yesterday a Captain in the Fourth did it. He couldn't bear hanging around any more. He just took a musette bag. The guys picked up all the other gear he left and sold it to the French. As long as you don't try to make Paris, the MP's don't bother you, if you're heading toward the front. And Lieutenant Green, I hear he's Captain now, is in command of C Company, and he's a wonderful fellow. He'll straighten it out for me. He'll be glad to see me."

"Do you know where they are?" Michael asked.

"I'll find out," Noah said. "That won't be hard."

"Aren't you afraid of getting into any more trouble?" Michael asked. "After all that stuff in the States?"

Noah grinned softly. "Brother," he said, "after Normandy, anything the United States Army might do to me couldn't look like trouble."

"You're sticking your neck out," Michael said.

Noah shrugged. "As soon as I found out in the hospital that I wasn't going to die," he said, "I wrote Johnny Burnecker I'd be back. He expects me." There was a note of quiet finality in Noah's voice that admitted no further questioning.

"Happy landing," Michael said. "Give my regards to the boys."

"Why don't you come with me?"

"What?"

"Come along with me," Noah repeated. "You'll have a lot better chance of coming out of the war alive if you go into a company where you have friends. You have no objections to coming out of the war alive, have you?"

"No," Michael smiled weakly. "Not really." He did not tell Noah of the times when it hadn't seemed to make much difference to him whether he survived or not, some of the rainy, weary nights in Normandy when he had felt so useless, when the war had seemed to be only a growing cemetery, whose only purpose seemed the creation of new dead; or the bleak days in the hospital in England, surrounded by the mangled product of the French battlefields, at the mercy of the efficient, callous doctors and nurses, who would not even give him a twenty-four-hour pass to visit London, to whom he had never been a human being in need of comfort and relief, but merely a poorly mending leg that had to be whipped back into a facsimile of health so that its owner could be sent back as soon as possible to the front. "No," Michael said, "I don't really mind the idea of being alive at the end of the war. Although to tell you the truth, I have a feeling, five years after the war is over, we're all liable to look back with regret to every bullet that missed us."

"Not me," said Noah fiercely. "Not me. I'm never going to feel that."

"Sure," Michael said, feeling guilty. "I'm sorry I said it."

"You go up as a replacement," said Noah, "and your chances are awful. The men who are there are all friends, they feel responsible for each other, they'll do anything to save each

546

other. That means every dirty, dangerous job they hand right over to the replacements. The Sergeants don't even bother to learn your name. They don't want to know anything about you. They just trade you in for their friends and wait for the next batch of replacements. You go into a new Company, all by yourself, and you'll be on every patrol, you'll be the point of every attack. If you ever get stuck out some place, and it's a question of saving you or saving one of the old boys, what do you think they'll do?"

Noah was speaking passionately, his dark eyes steady and intense on Michael's face, and Michael was touched by the boy's solicitude. After all, Michael remembered, I did damn little for him in his trouble in Florida, and I was no great comfort to his wife back in New York. He wondered if that frail dark girl had any notion of what her husband was saying now on the wet plain outside Paris, any notion of what subterranean, desperate reasoning a man went through in this cold foreign autumn so that he could one day come back and touch her hand, pick up his son in his arms . . . What did they know about the war back in America, what did the correspondents have to say about the replacement depots in their signed pieces on the front pages of the newspapers?

"You've got to have friends," Noah was saying fiercely. "You can't let them send you any place where you don't have friends to protect you . . ."

"Yes," Michael said gently, putting out his hand and touching the boy's wasted arm, "I'll go with you."

But he didn't say it because he felt that he was the one who needed friends.

CHAPTER THIRTY-FOUR

A CHAPLAIN in a jeep picked them up on the other side of Château-Thierry. It was a gray day and the old monuments among the cemeteries and the rusting wire of another war looked bleak and ill-tended.

The Chaplain was quite a young man, with a Southern accent, and very talkative. He was attached to a P-51 fighter group and was going up to Reims to testify as a character witness for a pilot who was being court-martialed there.

"Poor young feller," the Chaplain said, "nicest boy you could hope to meet. Has a darn nice record too, twenty-two missions already, one certain and two probables, and even though the Colonel personally asked me not to testify, I believe it's my Christian duty to go up there and say my piece in court."

"What is he up for?" Michael said.

"He committed a nuisance at a Red Cross dance," the Chaplain said. "He pissed on the floor in the middle of a number."

Michael grinned.

"Conduct unbecoming an officer, the Colonel says," said the Chaplain, looking around dangerously from the wheel. "The boy was a little drunk and I don't know what-all was passing through his mind. I am taking a real personal interest in the case. I have had a long correspondence with the officer who is conducting the defense, a very smart Episcopalian boy who was a lawyer in Portland before the war. Yes, Sir. And the Colonel is not going to stop me from saying what I have to say, and he knows it. Why," the Chaplain said indignantly, "Colonel Button is the last man in the world to persecute a man on a charge like that. I'm going to tell the Court about the Colonel's activity at a dance in Dallas, right at home, in the heart of the United States of America, surrounded by American women. You may not believe it, but Colonel Button, in full uniform, pissed into a potted rubber plant in the ballroom of a downtown hotel, and I saw it with my own eyes. Only he was a high-ranking officer, and we all hushed it up. But it's going to come out now, it really is."

It started to rain. Curtains of water sifted down over the ancient earthworks and the rotting wooden posts that had supported the wire in 1917. The Chaplain slowed down, peering through the clouded windshield. Noah, who was sitting in the front seat, worked the manual wiper to clear the glass. They passed a little fenced-off plot next to the road where ten Frenchmen had been buried on the retreat in 1940. There were faded artificial flowers on some of the graves, and a little statue of a saint in a glass case on a gray wood pedestal. Michael looked away from the Chaplain, thinking vaguely of the overlapping quality of wars.

The Chaplain stopped the jeep abruptly, and backed it down the road toward the little French cemetery.

"That will make a very interesting photograph for my album," the Chaplain said. "Would you boys mind posing in front of it?"

Michael and Noah climbed out and stood in front of the neat little plot. "Pierre Sorel," Michael read on one of the crosses, *Soldat, première class, né 1921 mort 1940.*" The artificial leaves of laurel and the dark memorial ribbon around them had run together in streaks of green and black in the long rains and the warm sun of the years between 1940 and 1944.

"I have more than a thousand photographs I've taken since the war began," said the Chaplain, busily working on a shiny Leica camera. "It will make a valuable record. A little to the left, please, Boys. There, that's it." There was a click from the camera. "This is a wonderful little camera," the Chaplain said proudly. "Takes pictures in any light. I bought it for two cartons of cigarettes from a Kraut prisoner. Only the Krauts know how to make good cameras, really. They have the patience we lack. Now, you boys give me the address of your families back in the States, and I'll make up two extra prints, and send them back to show the folks how healthy you are."

Noah gave the Chaplain Hope's address in care of her father in Vermont. The Chaplain carefully wrote it down in a pocket notebook with a black leather cover and a cross on it.

"Never mind about me," Michael said, feeling that he didn't want his mother and father to see a photograph of him, thin and worn, in his ill-fitting uniform, standing in the rain before the ten-grave roadside cemetery of the lost young Frenchmen. "I don't like to bother you, Sir."

"Nonsense, Boy," said the Chaplain. "There must be somebody who'd be right happy with your picture. You'd be surprised, all the nice letters I get from folks whose boys' pictures I send them. You're a smart, handsome young feller, there must be a girl who would like to put your picture on her bedtable."

Michael thought for a moment. "Miss Margaret Freemantle," he said, "26 West 10th Street, New York City. It's just what she needs for her bedtable."

While the Chaplain scratched away in his notebook, Michael thought of Margaret receiving the photograph and the note from the Chaplain on the quiet, pleasant street in New York. Maybe now, he thought, she'll write . . . Although what she'll have to say to me, and what I might possibly answer, I certainly don't know. Love, from France, a million years later. Signed, Your interchangeable lover, Michael Whitacre, Army Specialty Number 745, from the grave of Pierre Sorel, *né 1921, mort 1940*, in the rain. Having a wonderful time, wish you were . . .

They got into the jeep again and the Chaplain drove carefully along the narrow, high-backed, slippery road with the marks of tank treads and a million heavy army wheels on it.

"Vermont," the Chaplain said pleasantly to Noah, "that's a pretty quiet section of the country for a young feller, isn't it?"

"I'm not going to live there," Noah said, "after the war. I'm going to move to Iowa."

"Why don't you come to Texas?" the Chaplain said hospitably. "Room for a man to breathe there. You got folks in Iowa?"

"You might say that," Noah nodded. "A buddy of mine. Boy by the name of Johnny Burnecker. His mother's found a house we can have for forty dollars a month, and his uncle owns a newspaper and he's going to take me on when I get back. It's all arranged."

"Newspaperman, eh?" the Chaplain nodded sagely. "That's the lively life. Rolling in money, too."

"Not this newspaper," Noah said. "It comes out once a week. It has a circulation of 8,200."

"Well, it's a start," said the Chaplain agreeably. "A springboard to bigger things in the city."

"I don't want a springboard," said Noah quietly. "I don't want to live in a city. I haven't got any ambition. I just want to sit in a small town in Iowa for the rest of my life, with my wife and my son, and my friend, Johnny Burnecker. When I get the itch to travel, I'll walk down to the post office."

"Oh, you'll get tired of it," the Chaplain said. "Now that you've seen the world, a small town will seem pretty dull."

"No, I won't," said Noah, very firmly, working the manual wiper with a decisive flick of his arm. "I won't ever get tired of it."

"Well, you're different from me, then." The Chaplain chuckled. "I come from a small town and I'm tired in advance. Though, to tell the truth, I don't think I'll have anybody much waiting for me at home." He clucked sympathetically to himself. "I have no children, and my wife said, when the war began, and I felt I had the call to join up, 'Ashton,' she said, 'you have got to make your choice, it is either the Corps of Chaplains or your wife. I am not going to sit home by myself for five years, thinking of you traveling around the world, loose as a hummingbird, picking up with God knows what kind of women. Ashton,' she said, 'you don't fool me, not for a minute.' I told her she was unreasonable, but she's a stubborn woman. The day I come home I bet she starts proceedings for a divorce. I had quite a decision to make, I can tell you that. Oh, well," he sighed philosophically, "it hasn't been so bad. There's a very nice little nurse in the 12th General, and I have managed to assuage my sorrows." He grinned. "Between my nurse and my photography, I find I hardly think of my wife at all. As long as I have a woman to soothe me in my hours of despair, and enough film to take my pictures, I can face whatever comes . . ."

"Where *do* you get all that film?" Michael asked, thinking of the thousand pictures for the album, and knowing how difficult it was to get even one roll a month out of any PX.

The Chaplain made a sly face and put his finger along his

nose. "I had some trouble for awhile, but I have it taped now, as our English friends say. Oh, yes, it's taped now. It's the best film in the world. When the boys come in from their missions, I get the Engineering Officer of the Group to let me clip off the unexposed ends in the gun cameras. You'd be surprised how much film you can accumulate that way. The last Engineering Officer was beginning to get very stuffy about it, and he was on the verge of complaining to the Colonel that I was stealing government property, and I couldn't make him see the light . . ." The Chaplain smiled reflectively. "But I have no trouble any more," he said.

"How did it work out?" Michael asked.

"The Engineering Officer went on a mission. He was a good flier, oh, he was a crackerjack flier," the Chaplain said enthusiastically, "and he shot down a Messerschmitt, and when he came back to the field he buzzed the radio tower to celebrate. Well, the poor boy miscalculated by two feet, and we had to sweep him together from all four quarters of the field. I tell you, I gave that boy one of the best funerals anybody has ever had from the Corps of Chaplains in the Army of the United States. A real, full-sized, eloquent funeral . . ." The Chaplain grinned slyly. "Now I get all the film I want," he said.

Michael blinked, wondering if the Chaplain had been drinking, but he drove the jeep with easy competence, as sober as a judge. The Army, Michael thought dazedly, everybody makes his own arrangements with it . . .

A figure stepped out from under the protection of a tree and waved to them, and the Chaplain slowed to a halt. An Air Forces Lieutenant was standing there, wet, dressed in a Navy jacket, carrying one of those machine pistols with a collapsible stock. "Going to Reims?" the Lieutenant asked.

"Hop in, Boy," said the Chaplain heartily, "get right on in there in the back. The Chaplain's jeep stops for everybody on all roads."

The Lieutenant climbed in beside Michael and the jeep rolled on through the thick rain. Michael looked sidelong at the Lieutenant. He was very young, and he moved slowly and wearily, and his clothes didn't fit him. The Lieutenant noticed that Michael was staring at him.

"I bet you wonder what I'm doing here," the Lieutenant said.

"Oh, no," said Michael hastily, not wishing to get into that conversational department. "Not at all."

"I'm having a hell of a time," the Lieutenant said, "trying to locate my glider group."

Michael wondered how you could lose a whole group of gliders, especially on the ground, but he didn't inquire further.

"I was on the Arnhem thing," the Lieutenant said, "and I was shot down inside the German lines in Holland."

"The British," said the Chaplain crisply, "screwed the whole thing, as usual."

"Did they?" the Lieutenant said wearily. "I haven't read the papers."

"What happened?" Michael asked. Somehow it was hard to imagine this pale, gentle-faced boy being shot down out of a glider behind the enemy lines.

"It's the third mission I've been on," the Lieutenant said. "The Sicily drop, the Normandy drop, and this one. They promised us it would be our last one." He grinned weakly. "As far as I'm concerned, they were damn near right." He shrugged. "Though I don't believe them. They'll have us dropping into Japan before it's over." He shivered in his wet, outsize clothes. "I'm not eager," he said, "I'm far from eager. I used to think I was one hell of a brave, hundred-mission pilot, but I'm not. The first time I saw flak off my wing, I couldn't bear to watch. I turned my head away and flew by touch, and I told myself, 'Francis O'Brien, you are not a fighting man.'"

"Francis O'Brien," said the Chaplain. "Are you a Roman Catholic?"

"I am, Sir," said the glider pilot.

"I would like your opinion on this," the Chaplain said, hunched over the wheel. "I found a little foot-pedal organ in a church in Normandy that our artillery had beat up quite a bit, and I had it transferred to the field for my Sunday services, and I advertised for an organist. The only organist in the Group turned out to be a Tech Sergeant who was an armorer. He was an Italian, a Roman Catholic, but he played the organ like Horowitz plays the piano. I got a colored boy to pump the organ for him and the first Sunday we had the most satisfactory service I ever conducted. Even the Colonel came and sang the hymns like a bullfrog in spring, and everybody was real pleased with the innovation. Well, Sir, the next Sunday, the Italian didn't show up, and when I searched him out that afternoon and asked him what was the matter, he said he'd questioned his conscience and he couldn't see his way clear to playing songs for the religious rituals of heathen. Now, Francis O'Brien, you're a Roman Catholic and an officer, do you think that Tech Sergeant was displaying a proper Christian spirit?"

The glider pilot sighed gently. It was obvious that he did not think that he was in the proper condition to make considered judgments on grave matters of doctrine at the moment. "Well, Sir," he said, "it is up to the individual conscience..."

"Would you have played the organ for me?" the Chaplain asked accusingly.

"I would, Sir," said the glider pilot.

"Do you play the organ?"

"No, Sir," said the glider pilot.

"There you are," said the Chaplain darkly. "That Wop was the only one in the Group who could. I've conducted my services ever since without music."

They drove in silence for a long time between the vineyards and the signs of old wars in the gray rain.

"Lieutenant O'Brien," Michael said, fascinated by the pale, gentle boy, "you don't have to tell me if you don't want, but how did you get out of Holland?"

"I don't mind telling," said O'Brien. "The right wing was tearing away and I signaled the tow plane I was breaking off. I came down in a field, pretty hard, and by the time I got out of the glider all the men I was carrying had scattered, because there was machinegun fire coming in at us from a bunch of farmhouses about a thousand yards away. I ran as far as I could and I took off my wings and threw them away, because people're liable to get very mad at the Air Force when they catch them. You know, all the bombing, all the mistakes, all the civilians that get killed by accident, it doesn't do any good to be caught with wings. I laid in a ditch for three days, and then a farmer came up and gave me something to eat. That night he led me through the lines to a British reconnaissance outfit. They sent me back and I hitched a ride on an American destroyer. That's where I got this jacket. The destroyer mooched around all over the Channel for two weeks. Lord, I've never been so sick in my life. Finally they landed me at Southampton, and I hitched a ride to where I'd left my Group. But they'd pulled out a week before, they'd come to France. They'd reported me missing, and God knows what my mother was going through, and all my things'd been sent back to the States. Nobody was much interested in giving me orders. A glider pilot seems to be a big nuisance to everybody when there's no drop scheduled, and nobody seemed to have the authority to pay me or issue me orders or anything, and nobody gave a damn." O'Brien chuckled softly, without malice. "I heard the Group was over here, near Reims, so I hitched a ride back to Cherbourg in a Liberty ship that was carrying ammunition and ten-in-one rations. I took two days off in Paris, on my own, except that a Second Lieutenant who hasn't been paid in a couple of months might as well be dead as be in Paris, and here I am . . ."

"A war," the Chaplain said officially, "is a very complex problem."

"I'm not complaining, Sir," O'Brien said hastily, "honest, I'm not. As long as I don't have to make any more drops, I'm as happy as can be. As long as I know I'm finally going back to my diaper service in Green Bay, they can push me around all they want."

"Your what?" Michael asked dully.

"My diaper service," O'Brien said shyly, smiling a little. "My brother and I have a dandy little business, two trucks. My brother's taking care of it, only he writes it's getting impossible to get hold of cotton materials of any kind. The last five letters I wrote before the drop, I was writing to cotton mills in the States to see if they had any material they could spare . . ."

The heroes, Michael thought humbly, as they entered the outskirts of Reims, come in all sizes.

There were MP's on the corners and a whole batch of official cars near the Cathedral. Michael could see Noah tensing in the front seat at the prospect of being dumped out in the middle of this rear-echelon bustle. Still, Michael couldn't help staring with interest at the sandbagged Cathedral, with its stained glass removed for safekeeping. Dimly he remembered, when he was a little boy in grade school in Ohio, he had donated ten cents to rebuilding this Cathedral, so piteously damaged in the last war. Staring at the soaring pile now from the Chaplain's jeep, he was pleased to find that his investment hadn't been wasted.

The jeep stopped in front of Communications Zone Headquarters. "Now you get out here, Lieutenant," the Chaplain said, "and go in there and demand transportation back to your Group, no matter where they are. Raise your voice nice and loud. And if they won't give you any satisfaction, you wait for me right here. I'll be back in fifteen minutes and I'll go in and threaten to write Washington if they don't treat you good."

O'Brien got out. He stood, looking, puzzled and frightened, at the shabby row of buildings, obviously lost and doubtful of Army channels.

"I have an even better idea," the Chaplain said. "We passed a café two blocks back. You're wet and cold. Go in and get yourself a double cognac and fortify your nerves. I'll meet you there. I remember the name . . . Aux Bons Amis."

"Thanks," O'Brien said uncertainly. "But if it's all the same to you, I'll meet you here."

The Chaplain peered across Noah at the Lieutenant. Then he stuck his hand in his pocket and came up with a five-hundred-franc note. "Here," he said, giving it to O'Brien. "I forgot you weren't paid."

O'Brien's face broke into an embarrassed smile as he took the money. "Thanks," he said. "Thanks." He waved and started back to the café, two blocks away.

"Now," said the Chaplain briskly, starting the jeep, "we'll get you two jailbirds away from these MP's."

"What?" Michael asked stupidly.

"AWOL," the Chaplain said. "Plain as the noses on your face. Come on, lad, wipe that windshield."

Grinning, Noah and Michael drove through the grim old town. They passed six MP's on the way, one of whom saluted the jeep as it slithered along the wet streets. Gravely, Michael returned the salute.

CHAPTER THIRTY-FIVE

THE CLOSER THEY GOT to the front, Michael noticed, the nicer people got. When they finally began to hear the enduring rumble of the guns, disputing over the autumnal German fields, everyone seemed to speak in a low, considerate voice, everyone was glad to feed you, put you up for the night, share his liquor with you, show you his wife's picture and politely ask to see the pictures of your own family. It was as though, in moving into the zone of thunder, you had moved out of the selfishness, the nervous mistrust, the twentieth-century bad manners in which, until that time, you had always lived, believing that the human race had forever behaved that way.

They were given rides by everyone . . . a Graves Registration Lieutenant who explained professionally how his team went through the pockets of the dead men, making two piles of the belongings they found there. One pile, consisting of letters from home, and pocket Bibles, and decorations, to be sent to the grieving family, the other pile consisting of such standard soldiers' gear as dice, playing cards, condoms, pictures of nude women, and frank letters from girls in England with references to delightful nights in the hayfields near Salisbury or on Clarges Street, which might serve to impair the memory of the deceased heroes, to be destroyed. Also, the Graves Registration Lieutenant, who had been a clerk in the ladies' shoe department of Magnin's, in San Francisco, before the war, discussed the difficulties his unit had in collecting and identifying the scraps of men who had met with the disintegrating fury of modern war. "Let me give you a tip," said the Graves Registration Lieutenant, "carry one of your dogtags in your watch pocket. In an explosion your neck is liable to be blown right away, and your identification chain right along with it. But nine times out of ten, your pants will stay on, and we'll find your tag and we'll make a correct notification."

"Thanks," said Michael. When he and Noah got out of the

jeep, they were picked up by an MP Captain, who saw immediately that they were AWOL and offered to take them into his Company, making all the proper arrangements through channels, because he was understaffed.

They even got a ride in a General's command car, a two-star General whose Division was resting for five days behind the lines. The General, who was a fatherly-looking man with a crew haircut and a comfortable paunch, and the kind of complexion you see in the blood-temperature rooms in which modern hospitals keep newly born children, asked his questions kindly but shrewdly. "Where you from, Boys? What outfit you heading for?"

Michael, who had an old distrust of rank, frantically searched in his mind for an innocent answer, but Noah answered promptly. "We're deserters, Sir, we're deserting from a repple depple to our old outfit. We have to get back to our old Company."

The General had nodded understandingly, and had glanced approvingly at Noah's decoration. "Tell you what, Boys," he said, in the tone of a furniture salesman softly advertising a bargain in bridge lamps, "we're a little depleted ourselves, in my Division. Why don't you just stop off and see how you like it? I'll do the necessary paper work personally."

Michael had grinned at this vision of a new, more flexible, accommodating Army. "No, thank you, Sir," Noah said firmly. "I've made a solemn promise to the boys to come back there."

The General had nodded again. "I know how you feel," he said. "I was in the old Rainbow in 1918, and I raised heaven and hell to get back after I was hurt. Anyway, you can stop off for dinner. This is Sunday and I do believe we're having chicken for dinner at the Headquarters mess."

As the noise of the guns among the distant ridges grew nearer and nearer, Michael had the feeling that now, finally, he was going to find that gentle citizenship, that openness of heart, that million-throated, inarticulate yea-saying of which he had dreamed before he went into the Army and which, so far, had eluded him. Somewhere just ahead of him, he felt, under the constant trembling of the artillery among the hills, he was going to find that America he had never known on its own continent, a tortured and dying America, but an America of friends and neighbors, an America in which a man could finally put away his over-civilized doubts, his book-soured cynicism, his realistic despair, and humbly and gratefully lose himself . . . Noah, going back to his friend Johnny Burnecker, had already found that country, and it was plain in the quiet, assured way he spoke to Sergeants and to Generals alike. The exiles, living in mud and fear of death, had, in one way at least, found a better home than those from which they had been driven, a blood-spattered Utopia, now on the fringe of German soil, where no

556

man was rich and none poor, a shell-burst democracy where all living was a community enterprise, where all food was distributed according to need and not according to pocket, where light, heat, lodging, transportation, medical attention, and funeral benefits were at the cost of the government and available with absolute impartiality to white and black, Jew and Gentile, worker and owner, where the means of production, in this case M1's, 30 caliber machine guns, 90's, 105's, 204's, mortars, bazookas, were in the hands of the masses; that ultimate Christian socialism in which all worked for the common good and the only leisure class were the dead.

Captain Green's CP was in a small farmhouse, with a steeply slanting roof, that looked like the medieval homes in colored cartoons in fairy stories in the movies. It had been hit only once, and the hole had been boarded up with a door torn off from a bedroom entrance inside the house. There were two jeeps parked close against the wall, on the side from the enemy, and two soldiers with matted beards were sleeping in the jeeps, wrapped in blankets, their helmets tipped down over their noses. The rumble of the guns was much stronger here, most of it going out, with a high, diminishing whistle. The wind was raw, the trees bare, the roads and fields muddy, and aside from the two sleeping men in the jeeps there was no one else to be seen. It looked, Michael thought, like any farm in November, with the land given over to the elements, and the farmer taking long naps inside, dreaming about the spring to come.

It was amazing to think that they had defied the Army, crossed half of France, making their way arrow-like and dedicated through the complex traffic of guns and troops and supply trucks on the roads, to arrive at this quiet, rundown, undangerous-looking place. Army Headquarters, Corps Headquarters, Division, Regiment, Battalion, CP Company C, called Cornwall forward, the chain of command. They had gone down the chain of command like sailors down a knotted rope, and now that they were finally there, Michael hesitated, looking at the door, wondering if perhaps they hadn't been foolish, perhaps they were going to get into more trouble than it was worth . . . In that most formal of all institutions, the Army, they had behaved, Michael realized uneasily, with alarming informality, and the penalities for such things were undoubtedly clearly specified in the Articles of War.

But Noah did not seem to be bothered by any such reflections. He had walked the last three miles at a blistering, eager pace, through all the mud. There was a tense, trembling smile on his lips as he threw the door open and went in. Slowly, Michael followed him.

Captain Green was talking over the handset, his back to the door. "My Company front is a joke, Sir," he was saying.

"You could drive a milk wagon any place through us, we're stretched so thin. We need at least forty replacements right away. Over." Michael could hear the thin voice of Battalion, over the wire, angry and abrupt. Green flipped the lever on the handset and said, "Yes, Sir, I understand we will get the replacements when the goddamn Corps sees fit to send them down. Meanwhile," he said, "if the Krauts attack, they can go through us like Epsom salts through an eel. What should I do if they put in an attack? Over." He listened again, Michael heard two crisp sounds over the wire. "Yes, Sir," said Green, "I understand. That is all, Sir." He hung up the phone and turned to a Corporal who was sitting at an improvised desk. "Do you know what the Major told me?" he asked aggrievedly. "He said if we were attacked, I should notify him. A humorist! We're a new branch of the Army, notification troops!" He turned wearily to Noah and Michael. "Yes?"

Noah didn't say anything. Green peered at him, then smiled wearily and put out his hand. "Ackerman," he said, as they shook hands, "I thought you'd be a civilian by now."

"No, Sir," said Noah. "I'm not a civilian. You remember Whitacre, don't you?"

Green peered at Michael. "Indeed I do," he said in his almost effeminate, high, pleasant voice. "From Florida. What sins have you committed to be returned to C Company?"

He shook Michael's hand, too.

"We haven't been returned, Sir," Noah said. "We're AWOL from a replacement center."

"Excellent," said Green, grinning. "Don't give it another thought. Very good of you, very good of you indeed. I'll straighten it out in no time. Though why anyone should be anxious to come back to this miserable Company, I won't inquire. You boys now constitute my reinforcements for the week . . ." It was plain that he was touched and pleased. He kept patting Noah's arm in a warm, almost motherly gesture.

"Sir," Noah said, "is Johnny Burnecker around?" Noah was trying to keep his voice level and casual, but he was not having much success with it.

Green turned away and the Corporal at the table drummed slowly with his fingertips on the wood. It's going to be awful, Michael realized, the next ten minutes are going to be very bad.

"I forgot for the moment," Green said flatly, "how close you and Burnecker were."

"Yes, Sir," said Noah.

"He made Sergeant, you know," Green said. "Staff Sergeant. Platoon leader, way back in September. He is a hell of a fine soldier, Johnny Burnecker."

"Yes, Sir," Noah said.

"He was hit last night, Noah," Green said. "One freak shell. He was the only casualty we've had in the Company in five days."

"Is he dead, Sir?" Noah asked.

"No."

Michael saw Noah's hands, which had been clenched into fists along his trousers seams, slowly relax.

"No," Green said, "he isn't dead. We sent him back right after it happened."

"Sir," Noah asked eagerly, "could I ask you a favor, a big favor?"

"What is it?"

"Could you give me a pass to go back and see if I can talk to him?"

"He might have been sent back to a field hospital by now," Green said gently.

"I have to see him, Captain," Noah said, speaking very quickly. "It's terribly important. You don't know how important it is. The field hospital's only fifteen miles back. We saw it. We passed it on the way up. It won't take more than a couple of hours. I won't hang around long. Honest, I won't. I'll come right back. I'll be back by tonight. I just want to talk to him for fifteen minutes. It might make a big difference to him, Captain . . ."

"All right," Green said. He sat down and scribbled on a sheet of paper. "Here's a pass. Go outside and tell Berenson I said he was to drive you."

"Thanks," Noah said, his voice almost inaudible in the bare room. "Thanks, Captain."

"No side expeditions," Green said, staring at the cellophane-covered sector map, symboled in crayon on the wall. "We need that jeep tonight."

"No side expeditions," Noah said. "I promise." He started toward the door, then stopped. "Captain," he said.

"Yes?"

"Is he hurt bad?"

"Very bad, Noah," Green said wearily. "Very, very bad."

Noah arranged his face neatly and coldly, and went out, with the pass in his hand. A moment later, Michael heard the jeep starting up, and moving through the mud, making a chugging, motor-boat kind of noise into the distance.

"Whitacre," Green said, "you can hang around here until he gets back."

"Thank you, Sir," Michael said.

Green peered sharply at him. "What kind of soldier have you turned out to be, Whitacre?" he asked.

Michael thought for a moment. "Miserable, Sir," he said.

Green smiled palely, looking, more than ever, like a clerk

after a long day at the counter in the Christmas rush. "I'll keep that in mind," he said. He lit a cigarette and went over to the door and opened it. He stood there, framed against the gray, washed-out colors of the autumnal countryside. From afar, now that the door was open, could be heard the faint chugging of a jeep. "Ah," Green said, "I shouldn't've let him go. What's the sense in a soldier going to watch his friends die when he doesn't have to?"

He closed the door and went back and sat down. The phone rang and he picked it up languidly. Michael heard the sharp voice of Battalion. "No, Sir," Green said, speaking as though on the brink of sleep. "There has been no small-arms fire since 700 hours. I will keep you informed." He hung up the handset and sat silently, staring at the patterns his cigarette smoke was making before the terrain map on the wall.

It was long after dark when Noah got back. It had been a quiet day, with no patrols out. Overhead, the artillery came and went, but it seemed to have very little relation to the men of C Company who occasionally drifted into the CP to report to Captain Green. Michael had dozed all afternoon in a corner, considering this new, languid, relaxed aspect of the war, so different from the constant fighting in Normandy, and the wild rush after the break through. This was the slow movement, he thought sleepily, with the melody, such as it was, being carried by other instruments. The main problems, he saw, were keeping warm, keeping clean and keeping fed, and Captain Green's big concern all day had seemed to be the growing incidence of trenchfoot in his command.

Michael remembered with wonder all the huge bustle and movement of men and vehicles he had seen on his way up to the front, all those thousands of men, all those busy officers, all those jeeps and trucks and railroad cars busily rattling around just to keep these few, forlorn, sleepy-eyed, slow-moving soldiers rooted and secure on this forgotten strip of line. Everywhere else in the Army, Michael realized, thinking of Green demanding forty replacements, there had always been two or three men for every job; in the supply rooms, in the offices, in the Special Services departments, in the hospitals, on the convoys. Only here, in the face of the enemy, were the numbers sparse. Only here, in the dreary autumn weather, among the damp and slit-trenches, did it seem as though the Army were representing a decimated, impoverished nation of beggars. One-third of the nation, he dimly remembered the President saying long ago, ill-housed, ill-nourished. The Army here, by some curious trick of distribution, seemed to be representing only that third of America . . .

Michael heard the jeep coming up through the darkness outside. The windows were covered with blankets to show no light, and a blanket hung over the doorway. The door swung open and Noah came in slowly, followed by Berenson. The blanket flickered in the light of the electric lantern, blowing in the raw gust of night air.

Noah closed the door behind him. He leaned wearily against the wall. Green looked up at him.

"Well?" Green asked gently. "Did you see him, Noah?"

"I saw him." Noah's voice was exhausted and hoarse.

"Where was he?"

"At the field hospital."

"Are they going to move him back?" Green asked.

"No, Sir," Noah said. "They're not going to move him back."

Berenson clattered over to one corner of the room and got out a K ration from his pack. He ripped open the cardboard loudly, and tore the paper around the biscuits. He ate noisily, his teeth making a crackling sound on the hard biscuit.

"Is he still alive?" Green spoke softly and hesitantly.

"Yes, Sir," said Noah, "he's still alive."

Green sighed, seeing that Noah did not wish to speak further. "O. K." he said. "Take it easy. I'll send you and Whitacre over to the second platoon tomorrow morning. Get a good night's rest."

"Thank you, Sir," said Noah. "Thanks for the use of the jeep."

"Yeah," said Green. He bent over a report he was working on.

Noah looked dazedly around the room. Suddenly he went to the door and walked out. Michael stood up. Noah hadn't even looked at him since his return. Michael followed Noah out into the raw, black night. He sensed rather than saw Noah, leaning against the farmhouse wall, his clothes rustling a little in the gusts of wind.

"Noah . . ."

"Yes?" The voice told nothing. Even, exhausted, emotionless. "Michael . . ."

They stood in silence, staring at the bright, distant flicker on the horizon, where the guns were busy, like the nightshift in a factory.

"He looked all right," Noah said finally, in a whisper. "At least his face was all right. And somebody had shaved him this morning, he'd asked for a shave. He got hit in the back. The doctor warned me he was liable to act queer, but when he saw me, he recognized me. He smiled. He cried . . . He cried once before, you know, when I got hurt . . ."

"I know," Michael said. "You told me."

"He asked me all sorts of questions. How they treated me in the hospital, if they give you any convalescent leave, whether I'd been to Paris, if I had any new pictures of my kid. I showed him the picture of the kid that I got from Hope a month ago, the one on the lawn, and he said it was a fine-looking kid, it didn't look like me at all. He said he'd heard from his mother. It was all arranged for that house back in his town, forty dollars a month. And his mother knew where she could get a Kelvinator second-hand . . . He could only move his head. He was paralyzed completely from the shoulders down."

They stood in silence, watching the flicker of the guns, listening to the uneven rumble carried fitfully by the gusty November wind.

"They were crowded in the hospital," Noah said. "There was a Second Lieutenant in the next cot. From Kentucky. He'd had his heel blown off by a mine. He was very pleased, the Lieutenant said. He was getting tired of being the first man to poke his head over every hill in France and Germany to be shot at."

Silence again.

"I've had two friends in my whole life," Noah said. "Two real friends. A man called Roger Cannon, he used to sing a song, 'You make time and you make love dandy, You make swell molasses candy, But, honey, are you makin' any money, That's all I want to know . . .'" Noah moved slowly in the cold mud, rubbing against the wall with a small, scraping sound. "He got killed in the Philippines. My other friend was Johnny Burnecker. A lot of people have dozens of friends. They make them easy and they hold onto them. Not me. It's my fault and I realize it. I don't have a hell of a lot to offer . . ."

There was a bright flash in the distance and a fire sprang up, surprising and troubling in the blacked-out countryside, where people on your own side would fire at you if you struck a match after dark because it exposed your position to the enemy.

"I sat there, holding Johnny Burnecker's hand," Noah's voice went on evenly. "Then, after about fifteen minutes he began to look at me very queerly. 'Get out of here,' he said, 'I'm not going to let you murder me.' I tried to quiet him, but he kept yelling that I'd been sent to murder him, that I'd stayed away while he was healthy and could take care of himself, but now that he was paralyzed, I was going to choke him when nobody was looking. He said he knew all about me, he'd kept his eye on me from the beginning, and I'd deserted him when he needed me, and now I was going to kill him. He yelled that I had a knife on me. And the other wounded began to yell too, and I couldn't get him quiet. Finally, a doctor came and made me leave. As I went out of the tent, I could hear Johnny Burnecker yelling for them not to let me come near him with my knife." For a moment, Noah's voice stopped. Michael kept his eyes on the distant flare of the German farm going up in flames. Vaguely he thought of the featherbeds, the table linen, the crockery, the photograph albums, the copy of *Mein Kampf*, the kitchen tables, the beer steins, being brightly eaten away there in the darkness.

"The doctor was very nice," Noah's voice took up in the darkness. "He was a pretty old man from Tucson. He'd been a specialist in tuberculosis before the war, he told me. He told me what was the matter with Johnny, and for me not to take what Johnny said to heart. Johnny's spine had been broken by the shell, and his nervous system had degenerated, the doctor said, and there was nothing to be done for him. The nervous system had degenerated," Noah said, horribly fascinated by the word, "and it would get worse and worse until he died. Paranoia, the doctor said, from a normal boy to an advanced case of paranoia in one day. Delusions of grandeur, the doctor said, and manias of persecution. It might take him another three days to die, the doctor said, and he would finally be completely crazy. . . . That's why they weren't even bothering to send him back to a general hospital. Before I left, I looked in the tent again. I thought maybe he would be having a quiet period. The doctor said that was still possible. But when he saw me, he began to yell I was trying to kill him again . . ."

Michael and Noah stood side by side, leaning against the flaking, damp, cold stone wall of the CP, behind which Captain Green was worrying about trenchfoot. In the distance, the fire was growing brighter, as it took hold more strongly on the timbers and heirlooms of the German farmer's home.

"I told you about the feeling Johnny Burnecker had about us," said Noah. "How if we stayed together nothing would happen to us . . ."

"Yes," said Michael.

"We went through so much together," said Noah. "We were cut off, you know, and we got through, and we weren't hurt when the LCI we were on was hit on D Day . . ."

"Yes," said Michael.

"If I hadn't been so slow," Noah said, "if I'd got up here one day earlier, Johnny Burnecker would have come out of this war alive."

"Don't be silly," Michael said sharply, feeling: Now this is finally too much of a burden for this boy to carry.

"I'm not silly," Noah said calmly. "I didn't act quickly enough. I took my time. I hung around that replacement depot five days. I went and talked to that Peruvian. I knew he wouldn't do what I wanted, but I was lazy, I just hung around."

"Noah, don't talk like that!"

"And we took too long on the trip up," Noah continued,

disregarding Michael. "We stopped at night, and we wasted a whole afternoon on that chicken dinner that General arranged for us. I let Johnny Burnecker die for a chicken dinner."

"Shut up!" Michael shouted thickly. He grabbed Noah and shook him hard. "Shut up! You're talking like a maniac! Don't ever let me hear you say anything like that again!"

"Let me go," Noah said calmly. "Keep your hands off me. Excuse me. There's no reason why you should have to listen to my troubles. I realize that."

Slowly Michael relinquished his grip. Once again, he felt, I have failed this battered boy . . .

Noah hunched into his clothes. "It's cold out here," he said pleasantly. "Let's go inside."

Michael followed him into the CP.

The next morning Green assigned them to their old platoon, the one they had been in together in Florida. There were still three men left out of the forty who had been in the original platoon, and they welcomed Michael and Noah with heartwarming cordiality. They were very delicate when they spoke of Johnny Burnecker in front of Noah.

CHAPTER THIRTY-SIX

"So THEY ASKED this GI, what would you do if they sent you home," Pfeiffer was saying. He and Noah and Michael were squatting on a half-submerged log against a low stone wall, their meat balls, spaghetti and canned peaches in rich combination on their mess kits. It was the first warm food they'd had in three days, and everyone was very pleased with the cooks who had got the field kitchen so close up. The line of men, spaced ten yards apart so that if a shell came it would only hit a few of them at one time, wound through a copse of bare, artillery-marked beeches. The line moved swiftly as the cooks hurriedly dished out the food. "What would you do if they sent you home?" Pfeiffer repeated, through the thick mash in his mouth. "The GI thought for a minute . . . Have you heard this one?" Pfeiffer asked.

"No," Michael said politely to Pfeiffer.

Pfeiffer nodded, pleased. "First, the GI said, I'd take off my shoes. Second, I'd lay my wife. Third, I'd take off my pack."

Pfeiffer roared at his joke. He stopped suddenly. "You sure you haven't heard it before?"

"Honest," said Michael. Witty table conversation, he thought, in the heart of European civilization. The guests included a smattering of representatives of the arts and military men on a brief holiday (one hour and a half) from their pressing duties at the front. PFC Pfeiffer, well known in Kansas bookmaking circles, and with a local celebrity among the general courts-martial of the region, entertained with reflections on post-war problems. One of the luncheon guests, representing our national theatre in Western Europe, dabbled at his canned peach, a delicacy of the country, and remarked to himself that Private Anacreon of Macedonia, during Philip's campaign in Persia, undoubtedly heard a similar story outside Bagdad, that Caius Publius, centurion in Caesar's Army, told somewhat the same enlightening tale two days after landing in Britain, that Julian Saint-Crique, Adjutant in the corps of Murat, drew extensive laughter from his comrades with a literal translation of the epigram the day before Austerlitz. It was not unknown, the thoughtful student of history reflected, looking doubtfully at his mud-encased shoe packs, and wondering if his toes had begun to rot yet, to Warrant Officer Robinson of the Welsh Rifles at Ypres, or to Feldwebel Fugelheimer at Tannenberg, or to Sergeant Vincent O'Flaherty of the First Marines, pausing for a moment of refreshment on the road into the Argonne Forest.

"That's a hell of a funny story," Michael said.

"I thought you'd like it," Pfeiffer said with satisfaction, wiping up the last thick juice of the meat balls, spaghetti and peach syrup. "What the hell, you have to laugh every once in a while."

Pfeiffer industriously scrubbed his mess kit with a stone and a piece of the toilet paper he always carried in his pocket. He got up and wandered over to the crap game that was going on behind a blackened chimney that was all that was left of a farmhouse that had survived three wars before this. There were three soldiers, a Lieutenant and two Sergeants, from a Communications Zone Signal Corps message center, who had somehow arrived here in a jeep on a tourist visit. They were shooting craps, and they seemed to have a lot of money which would do more good in the pockets of the infantry.

Michael lit a cigarette, relaxing. He wiggled his toes automatically, to make certain he could still feel them, and enjoyed the sense of having eaten well, and being out of danger for an hour. "When we get back to the States," Michael said to Noah, "I will take you and your wife out for a steak dinner. I know a place on Third Avenue, on the second floor. You eat your meal and watch the L pass by at dish level. The steaks are as thick as your fist, we'll have it very rare . . ."

"Hope doesn't like it very rare," Noah said, seriously.

"She will have it any way she wants it," Michael said. "Antipasto first, then these steaks, charred on the outside and they sigh when you touch a butter knife to them, and you get spaghetti and green salad and red California wine, and after that, cake soaked in rum and *café espresso,* that's very black, with lemon peel. The first night we get home. On me. You can bring your son, too if you want, we'll put him in a high chair."

Noah smiled, "We'll leave him home that night," he said.

Michael was gratified at the smile. Noah had smiled very seldom in the three months since they had returned to the Company. He had spoken little, smiled little. In his taciturn way, he had attached himself to Michael, watched out for him with critical, veteran eyes, protected him by word and example, even when it had been a full-time job trying to keep himself alive, even in December, when it had been so bad, when the Company had been loaded on trucks and had been thrown in hurriedly against the German tanks that had suddenly materialized out of the supposedly exhausted Army in front of them. The Battle of the Bulge, it was now called, and it was in the past, and the one thing Michael really would remember from it for the rest of his life was crouching in a hole, which Noah had made him dig two feet deeper, although Michael had been weary and annoyed at what he considered Noah's finickiness . . . The German tank looming up on the bare field, coming at them, and all the bazooka ammunition gone, and the anti-tank gun on the half-track behind them burning, and nothing to do but duck down deep . . . The driver of the tank had seen Michael ducking in and had driven up and tried to run him over, because they couldn't reach him with their guns. The interminable minute, with the roaring seventy-ton machine over his head, and the tread spinning, sending a heavy shower of dirt and stones down on his helmet and his back, and his own voice screaming soundlessly in the thundering darkness . . . As you looked back on it, it seemed like the sort of thing men bucking for Section Eights reported as nightmares to the psychoanalysts in the Medical Corps. It did not seem possible that it ever could really happen to you, a man over thirty who had had his own well-ordered apartment in New York City, who had eaten in so many good restaurants, who had five good soft tweed suits hanging in the closet, who had driven slowly up Fifth Avenue in a convertible car, with the top down, and the sun shining on his face . . . And, having happened, it did not seem possible that you could live through it, that the churning, spiked steel tread one foot above your head could let you survive, that the man to whom this final, hellish thing had happened, could ever come back to a moment in which he could even think about such things as steaks and wine and Fifth Avenue. The tank, impersonally seeking his life in the hole that he had been forced by his friend to dig deep enough to protect him, had seemed to cut the bridge back to civilian existence. There was a gap there now, a dark ravine spanned only by hallucinations. Looking back on it now, remembering the lumbering withdrawal of the machine across the field, with shellbursts tossing up spouts of dirt around it, he realized that that was the moment he had finally become a soldier. Until then, he had merely been a man in uniform, on temporary duty from another life ...

The Battle of the Bulge, they now called it in *Stars and Stripes*, and many men had been killed in it, and Liége and Antwerp had been threatened, and there were accounts of how magnificently the Army had reacted, and some unpleasantness about Montgomery, who was not now as full of British-American good will as he had been on July Fourth, when he had pinned the Silver Star on Noah ... The Battle of the Bulge, another bronze campaign star, five points toward discharge. All he remembered was Noah standing over him, saying crisply and unpleasantly, "I don't care how tired you are, dig two feet deeper," and the whirling, roaring tread over his muddy helmet.

Michael looked over at Noah. Noah was sleeping now, sitting up, leaning against the stone wall. Only when he slept did his face look young. He had a very light beard, blondish and sparse, as compared with Michael's thick black mat, which made Michael look like a hobo who had been riding the rods from Vancouver to Miami. Noah's eyes, which, when he was awake, stared out with a dark, elderly tenacity, were closed now. Michael noticed for the first time that his friend had soft, upcurling eyelashes, full and blond at the tips, giving the upper part of his face a gentle appearance. Michael felt a wave of gratitude and pity for the sleeping boy, muffled now in his heavy, stained overcoat, his wool-gloved fingertips just touching the barrel of his rifle. ... Looking at him now, this way, Michael realized at what cost this frail boy maintained his attitude of grave competence, made his intelligent, dangerous, soldierly decisions, fought tenaciously and cautiously, with a manual-like correctness, to remain alive in this country and this time when death came so casually to so many of the men around him. The blond lash-tips fluttered softly on the fist-broken face, and Michael thought of the times Noah's wife must have stared, with sorrowful tenderness and amusement, at the incongruous, girlish ornament. How old was he? Twenty-two, twenty-four? Husband, father, military man ... Two friends, and both lost ... Needing friends as other men needed air and, out of that need, worrying desperately, in the middle of his own agony, how to keep the clumsy, aging soldier called Whitacre alive, who, left to his own blundering, ill-trained devices would most certainly have walked over a mine by now, or silhouetted himself against a ridge to a sniper, or out of laziness and inexperience, been mangled by a tank in a too-shallow hole . . . Steaks and red California wine across the gap spanned only by hallucinations, the first night home, on me . . . It was impossible, and it must happen. Michael closed his eyes, feeling an immense, sorrowing responsibility.

From the crap game the voices floated over. "I'll fade a thousand francs. The point is nine . . ."

Michael opened his eyes and stood up quietly and, carrying his rifle, went over to watch.

Pfeiffer was shooting and he was doing well. He had a pile of paper crushed in his hand. The Services of Supply Lieutenant wasn't playing, but the two Sergeants were. The Lieutenant was wearing a beautiful officer's coat, brindle-colored and full. The last time he had been in New York, Michael had seen such a coat in the window of Abercrombie and Fitch. All three men were wearing parachute boots, although it was plain that they had never jumped from anything higher than a barstool. They were all large, tall men, clean shaven, well dressed, and fresh looking, and the bearded infantrymen with whom they were playing looked like neglected and rickety specimens of an inferior race.

The visitors talked loudly and confidently, and moved with energy, in contrast to the weary, mumbling, laconic behavior of the men who had dropped out of the line to have their first warm meal in three days. If you were going to pick soldiers for a crack regiment, a regiment to seize towns and hold bridge-heads and engage armor, you certainly would not hesitate to choose these three handsome, lively fellows, Michael thought. The Army, of course, had worked things out somewhat differently. These bluff-voiced, well-muscled men worked in a snug office fifty miles back, typing out forms, and shoveling coal into the rosy iron stove in the middle of the room to keep out the wintry chill. Michael remembered the little speech Sergeant Houlihan, of the second platoon, always made when he greeted the replacements . . . "Ah," Houlihan would say, "why is it the infantry always gets the 4F's? Why is it the Quartermasters always get the weight-lifters, the shot-putters, and the All-American fullbacks? Tell me, Boys, is there anybody here who weighs more than a hundred and thirty pounds?" It was a fantasy of course, and Houlihan made the speech shrewdly, because he knew it made the replacements laugh and like him, but there was a foolish element of fact in it, too.

As he was watching, Michael saw the Lieutenant take a bottle out of his pocket and drink from it. Pfeiffer watched the Lieutenant narrowly, rolling the dice slowly in his mud-caked hand. "Lieutenant," he said, "what do I see in your pocket?"

The Lieutenant laughed. "Cognac," he said. "That's brandy."

"I know it's brandy," Pfeiffer said. "How much do you want for it?"

The Lieutenant looked at the notes in Pfeiffer's hand. "How much you got there?"

Pfeiffer counted. "2000 francs," he said. "Forty bucks. I sure would like a nice bottle of cognac to warm up my old bones."

"4000 francs," the Lieutenant said calmly. "You can have the bottle for 4000."

Pfeiffer looked narrowly at the Services of Supply Lieutenant. He spat slowly. Then he talked to the dice. "Dice," he said, "Papa needs a drink. Papa needs a drink very bad."

He put his 2000 francs down. The two Sergeants with the bright stars in the circles on their shoulders faded him.

"Dice," Pfeiffer said, "it's a cold day and Papa's thirsty." He rolled the dice gently, relinquishing them like flower petals. "Read them," he said, without smiling. "Seven." He spat again. "Pick up the money, Lieutenant, I'll take the bottle." He put out his hand.

"Delighted," the Lieutenant said. He gave Pfeiffer the bottle and scooped up the money. "I'm glad we came."

Pfeiffer took a long drink out of the bottle. All the men watched him silently, half-pleased, half-annoyed at his extravagance. Pfeiffer corked the bottle carefully and put it in his overcoat pocket. "There's going to be an attack tonight," he said pugnaciously. "What the hell good would it do me to cross that goddamn river with 4000 francs in my pocket? If the Krauts knock me off tonight, they are going to knock off a GI with his belly full of good liquor." Self-righteously, slinging his rifle, he walked away.

"Service of Supply," said one of the infantrymen who had been watching the game. "Now I know why they call it that."

The Lieutenant laughed easily. He was a man beyond the reach of criticism. Michael had forgotten that people laughed like that any more, good-humoredly, without much cause, from a full reservoir of good spirits. He guessed that you could only find people who laughed like that fifty miles back of the lines. None of the men joined in the Lieutenant's laughter.

"I'll tell you why we're here, Boys," the Lieutenant said.

"Let me guess," said Crane, who was in Michael's platoon. "You're from Information and Education and you brought up a questionnaire. Are we happy in the Service? Do we like our work? Have we had clap more than three times in the last year?"

The Lieutenant laughed again. He is a great little laugher, that Lieutenant, Michael thought, staring at him somberly.

"No," said the Lieutenant, "we're here on business. We heard

569

we could pick up some pretty good souvenirs in this neck of the woods. I get into Paris twice a month, and there's a good market for Luegers and cameras and binoculars, stuff like that. We're prepared to pay a fair price. How about it? You fellows got anything you want to sell?"

The men around the Lieutenant looked at one another silently. "I got a nice Garand rifle," Crane said, "I'd be willing to part with for 5000 francs. Or, how about a nice combat jacket," Crane went on innocently, "a little worn, but with sentimental value?"

The Lieutenant chuckled. He was obviously having a good time on his day off up at the front. He would write about it to his girl back in Wisconsin, Michael was sure, the comedians of the infantry, rough boys, but comic. "O.K.," he said, "I'll look around for myself. I hear there was some action here last week, there should be plenty of stuff lying around."

The infantrymen stared coldly at one another. "Plenty," said Crane gently. "Jeep loads. You'll be the richest man in Paris."

"Which way is the front?" the Lieutenant asked briskly. "We'll take a peek."

There was the cold, slightly bubbling silence again. "The front," Crane said innocently, "you want to peek at the front?"

"Yes, Soldier." The Lieutenant was not very good-natured now.

"That way, Lieutenant," Crane pointed. "Isn't it that way, boys?"

"Yes, Lieutenant," the boys said.

"You can't miss it," said Crane.

The Lieutenant had caught on by now. He turned to Michael, who had not said anything, "You," the Lieutenant said, "can you tell us how to get there?"

"Well . . ." Michael began.

"You just go up this road, Lieutenant," Crane broke in. "A mile and a half or so. You will find yourself climbing a little, in some woods. You get to the top of the ridge, and you will look down and see a river. That's the front, Lieutenant."

"Is he telling the truth?" the Lieutenant asked, accusingly.

"Yes, Sir," Michael said.

"Good!" The Lieutenant turned to one of his Sergeants. "Louis," he said, "we'll leave the jeep here. We'll walk. Immobilize it."

"Yes, Sir," Louis said. He went over to the jeep, lifted the hood, took the rotor out of the distributor and tore out some wires. The Lieutenant walked over to the jeep and took out an empty musette bag from it and slung it over his shoulder.

"Mike." It was Noah's voice. He was waving to Michael. "Come on, we have to get back . . ."

Michael nodded. He nearly went over and told the Lieutenant to get away from there, to go back to his nice snug office and warm stove, but he decided against it. He walked slowly over and caught up with Noah, who was trudging in the mud on the side of the road toward the Company line a mile and a half away.

Michael's platoon was planted just under the saddle of the ridge which looked down on the river. The ridge was thick with underbrush, bushes, saplings, that even now, with all the leaves off, gave good cover, so that you could move around quite freely. From the top of the ridge you could look down the soggy, brush-dotted slope and across the narrow field at the bottom, to the river, and the matching ridge on the other side, behind which lay the Germans. There was a hush over the wintry landscape. The river ran thick and black between icy banks. Here and there a tree trunk lay rotting in the water, which curved around it in oil-like eddies. There was a hush over the drab patches of snow and the silent, facing slopes. At night there were sometimes little spurts of vicious firing, but during the day it was too exposed for patrols, and a kind of sullen truce prevailed. The lines, as far as anybody knew, lay about 1200 yards apart, and were so marked back on the map in that distant, fabulous, safe place, Division.

Michael's platoon had been there two weeks, and aside from the occasional fire at night (and the last burst had been three nights ago) there was no real evidence that the enemy was there at all. For all Michael knew, the Germans might have packed up and gone home.

But Houlihan didn't think so. Houlihan had a nose for Germans. Some men could sniff out authentic masterpieces of the Dutch school of painting, some men could taste a wine and tell you that it came from an obscure vineyard outside Dijon, vintage 1937, but Houlihan's specialty was Germans. Houlihan had a narrow, intelligent, high-browed Irish scholar's face, the kind you thought of when you imagined Joyce's roommates at Dublin University, and he kept looking out through the brush on top of the ridge, and saying, doubtfully and wearily, "There's a nest there, some place. They've got a machine gun set up there, and they're just laying on it, waiting for us."

Until now it hadn't made much difference. The platoon hadn't been going any place, the river presented too large an obstacle for patrols, and the machine gun, if it was there, couldn't reach them behind the safety of the ridge. If the Germans had mortars back in the woods, they were conserving them. But at dusk, the word was, a company of Engineers was to come up and try to throw a pontoon bridge across the fifty-yard river, and Michael's Company was to cross the bridge, and make contact with whatever Germans were holding the opposing ridge. After that, the next morning, a fresh company was to go through them and keep moving . . . It undoubtedly looked like a fine scheme back at Division. But it didn't look good to Houlihan, peering out through his glasses at the icy black river and the silent, brush-covered, snow-patched slope before him.

Houlihan was talking to Green over a field telephone strapped to a tree when Noah, Michael, Pfeiffer and Crane reached him. "Captain," he said, "I don't like it. They've been too quiet. There's a machine gun concealed somewhere along that ridge. I just know it. They'll send up flares tonight when they get good and ready. They'll have five hundred yards of cleared land and the bridge to lay it on to us. Over."

He listened. The Captain's voice scratched faintly in the receiver. "Yes, Sir," Houlihan said, "I'll call you when I find out." He sighed and hung up the receiver. He peered out across the river, sucking in his cheeks thoughtfully, looking pained and scholarly. "The Captain says for us to send out a patrol this afternoon," Houlihan said. "Keep going, in plain view, down to the river, if necessary, to draw fire. Then we can spot the place where the fire originates from, and he will get the mortars working on it and wipe it out." Houlihan brought his binoculars up and squinted through the gray afternoon at the innocent-looking ridge across the river. "Any volunteers?" he asked offhandedly.

Michael looked around. There were seven men who had heard Houlihan. They squatted in shallow rifle pits just under the line of the ridge and they took a great interest in their rifles, in the texture of the ground in front of them, in the pattern of the brush before their faces. Three months ago, Michael realized, he probably would have volunteered, proving something foolish, expiating something profound. By now, Noah had taught him better. He examined his nails minutely in the silence.

Houlihan sighed softly. A minute passed, with everybody thinking earnestly and almost solidly of the moment when the lead man on the patrol that would have to be made would draw the fire of the German machine gun.

"Sergeant," a polite voice said. "Do you mind if we join you?"

Michael looked up. The Services of Supply Lieutenant and his two traveling companions were making their way clumsily up the slippery hill. The Lieutenant's request hung in the air, over the men in the rifle pits, insanely debonair, like a line from a duchess in a Hungarian comedy.

Houlihan turned around in surprise, his eyes narrowing.

"Sergeant," Crane said, "the Lieutenant is here to hunt souvenirs to take back to Paris."

A fleeting and unfathomable expression crossed Houlihan's thin, long-jawed face, blue-black with beard. "By all means, Lieutenant," Houlihan said heartily, and at the same time with an unusual note of obsequiousness, "we're honored to have you, we are indeed."

The Lieutenant was panting heavily from the climb. He is not in as good condition as he looks, Michael thought. He is not getting his polo these days back in the Communications Zone.

"I heard this was the Front," the Lieutenant said, capitalizing it, taking Houlihan's helping hand. "Is it?"

"In a manner of speaking, Sir," said Houlihan. Nobody else said anything.

"It's awfully quiet," the Lieutenant said, looking around him puzzledly. "I haven't heard a shot in two hours. Are you sure?"

Houlihan laughed politely. "I'll tell you something, Sir," he said, in a confidential whisper. "I do believe the Germans pulled out a week ago. If you ask me, you could conduct a walking tour from here to the Rhine."

Michael stared at Houlihan. The Sergeant's face was open and childlike. Houlihan had been a conductor on a Fifth Avenue bus before the war, but, Michael thought, he could not have learned this on the run up from Washington Square.

"Good," the Lieutenant said, smiling. "I must say, it's a lot more peaceful here than it is back in our message center. Isn't it, Louis?"

"Yes, Sir," said Louis.

"No Colonels running in and out, bothering you," the Lieutenant said heartily, "and you don't have to shave every day."

"No, Sir," said Houlihan, "we don't have to shave every day."

"I hear," the Lieutenant said confidentially, looking down the slope toward the river, "that a man could pick up some German souvenirs down there."

"Oh, yes, Sir," said Houlihan, "a man certainly could. That field is covered with helmets and Luegers and rare cameras."

He's gone too far, Michael thought, now he's gone too far. He looked up to see how the Lieutenant was taking it, but there was only an expression of eager greed on the healthy, ruddy face. God, Michael thought disgustedly, who gave you *your* commission?

"Louis, Steve," the Lieutenant said, "let's go down and take a look."

"Wait a minute, Lieutenant," Louis said doubtfully. "Ask him if there are mines?"

"Oh, no," said Houlihan. "I guarantee there are no mines."

The seven men of the platoon squatted in their riflepits, looking at the ground, motionless.

"Do you mind, Sergeant," the Lieutenant said, "if we go down and browse around for awhile?"

"Make yourself absolutely at home, Sir," Houlihan boomed.

Now, Michael thought, now he is going to tell them it's a joke, show them what fools they are, and send them home. . . .

But Houlihan was standing motionless.

"You'll keep an eye on us, won't you, Sergeant?" the Lieutenant asked.

"I certainly will," said Houlihan.

"Good. Come on, Boys." The Lieutenant pushed clumsily through the brush and started down the other side of the ridge, with the two men following.

Michael turned and looked at Noah. Noah was watching him, his elderly, dark eyes steady and threatening. Michael knew that Noah was fiercely signaling him, in his silent gaze, to keep still. Well, Michael thought defensively, it's his platoon, he's known these men longer than I have . . .

He turned back and looked down the slope. The Lieutenant, in his bright brindle Abercrombie and Fitch trenchcoat, and the two Sergeants were sliding heavily down the cold, muddy incline, hanging on here and there to bushes and the trunks of trees. No, Michael thought, I don't care what they think about me, I can't let this happen . . .

"Houlihan!" He sprang up beside the Sergeant, who was peering, with a steady, fierce expression, across the river to the other ridge. "Houlihan, you can't do that. You can't let them go out there like that! Houlihan!"

"Shut up!" Houlihan whispered ferociously. "Don't tell me what to do. I'm running this platoon."

"They'll be killed," Michael said urgently, staring down at the three men sliding on the dirty snow.

"Well, now," Houlihan said, and Michael was frightened by the look of loathing and hatred on his fine, thin-mouthed, scholarly face, "which would you prefer, man? Why shouldn't some of those bastards get killed once in awhile? They're in the Army, aren't they? Souvenirs!"

"You've got to stop them!" Michael said hoarsely. "If you don't stop them, I'll put in a report, I swear to God I will . . ."

"Shut up, Whitacre," Noah said.

"Put in a report, eh?" Houlihan never took his eyes off the opposite ridge. "You want to go yourself, is that it? You want to get killed this afternoon yourself out there, you want Ackerman to get killed, Crane, Pfeiffer, you'd rather have your friends get it than three fat pigs from the Service of Supply. They're too good to be killed, is that it?" His voice which had

574

been trembling with malice suddenly became smooth and professional as he addressed the other men. "Don't watch them down on the field," he said. "Keep your eyes on the ridge. There'll only be two, three short bursts, you'll have to look sharp. And keep your eyes on the spot and call it out . . . Still want me to call them back, Whitacre?"

"I . . ." Michael began. Then he heard the firing and he knew it was too late.

Down on the field along the river, the brindle coat was slowly going down, deflating onto the ground. Louis and the other man started to run, but they did not get far.

"Sergeant," it was Noah's voice, very calm and level, "I see where it's coming from. To the right of that big tree, twenty yards, just in front of those two bushes that stick up just a little higher than the others . . . See it?"

"I see it," Houlihan said.

"Right there. Two or three yards from the first bush."

"You sure?" Houlihan said. "I missed it."

"I'm sure," Noah said.

God, Michael thought wearily, admiring and hating Noah, how much that boy has learned since Florida.

"Well," Houlihan finally turned to Michael, "do you want to send in your report now?"

"No," Michael said. "I'm not going to report anything."

"Of course not." Houlihan patted his elbow warmly. "I knew you wouldn't." He went over to the field telephone and called the Company CP. Michael listened to him, giving the exact location of the German gun for the mortars.

Now, again, the afternoon was totally silent. It was hard to remember that, just one minute ago, the machine gun had torn the quiet, and that three men had died.

Michael turned and looked at Noah. Noah was kneeling on one knee, holding his rifle with its butt in the mud, the barrel resting against his cheek, looking like old pictures of frontiersmen in the Indian wars far away in Kentucky and New Mexico. Noah was staring at Michael, his eyes wild and burning and without shame.

Michael slowly sat down, averting his eyes from Noah's, realizing finally the full implications of what Noah had tried to tell him in the replacement depot about going, in the Army, only to places where you had friends.

Just before the early winter dusk set in, the mortars started up. The first two were short, and Houlihan, at the phone, phoned back the corrections. The third one landed just where he asked for it, and the fourth. There was a curious little commotion on the other ridge, where the mortar had hit, a sudden, sharp shaking of the bare, tangled branches, as if a man had tried to stagger through them and had failed and fallen. Then it was quiet again and Houlihan said, over the phone, "That did it, Sir. Just one more in the same place for luck."

The mortar put one in the same place for luck, but there was no further movement on the other ridge.

As soon as it got dark, the Company of Engineers came through, struggling with pontoons and planks. Michael and the other men helped to get the cumbersome materials down to the water's edge. They passed a pale blur that Michael knew was the brindle coat, but he didn't look at it. The Engineers were almost halfway through with the bridge, working in the icy darkness, before the first flare went up. Then the artillery began on both sides. There was a little rifle fire, but it was scattered and wild, and the mortars worked on that. The German shells made an eccentric pattern, as though they didn't have many to spare and their forward observers were rattled by the heavy fire concentrated on the ridge. None of the shells hit the bridge. Three of the Engineers were wounded on the far side, and everyone was drenched by the splashes of the near-misses.

The flares, swinging over the river, lit the scene in a garish, unreal blue, making the struggling men in the river look paper-thin and insectlike. The first few men of the platoon which was leading the attack got across fine, but Lawson was hit, and fell into the river, and Mukowski.

Michael was crouched next to Noah, with Noah's hand on his arm, restraining him, as they watched first one man, then another, make his dash across the slippery, narrow planks to the other side. Somebody was hit and fell across the bridge and lay there, and the other men had to jump over him.

No, Michael thought, feeling his arm quiver under Noah's hand, impossible, they can't expect me to do this, they can't really expect it . . .

"Go," Noah whispered, "go, now!"

Michael didn't move. A shell landed in the river ten feet away from the bridge. The water spun up in a black thick curtain, hiding the man who was lying on the rocking and shaking planks.

Michael felt a hard fist hit him on the back of his neck. "Go!" Noah was screaming, "Go, *now,* you son of a bitch."

Michael got up and ran. A shell hit near the other side just as he crossed the first ten feet of the slippery boards, and Michael couldn't tell whether the bridge was still there or not. But he kept running.

A moment later he was over. A voice was calling, in the

darkness, "This way, this way . . ." and he obediently followed the voice. He stumbled into a hole and there was somebody else there.

"All right," the voice said harshly in his ear. "Hold on here until the rest of the Company is over."

Michael pushed his cheek sideways into the wet, cold earth. It felt refreshing and comfortable against his sweaty skin. He slowly stopped gasping for breath. He raised his head and looked back at the shadowy, paper-thin figures running across the bridge between the geysers of water. He took a deep breath. I did it, he thought. I advanced under fire. I can do it. I did what everybody else did. He was surprised that he was grinning. Finally, he thought, turning back toward the Germans, I am liable to be one hell of a soldier.

CHAPTER THIRTY-SEVEN

IT DIDN'T LOOK BAD, it looked almost like an ordinary Army camp, quite pleasant, in the middle of wide green fields, with the sloping, forested hills behind it. The barracks-like buildings were a little close together, and the doubled, barbed-wire fences, spaced with watch towers, tipped you off, of course—and the smell. Two hundred meters away, the smell suffused the air, like a gas that, by a trick of chemistry, is just about to be transformed into a solid.

Still, Christian didn't stop. He limped hurriedly along the road toward the main gate, through the shining spring morning. He had to get something to eat, and he needed information. Maybe somebody inside the camp was in telephone communication with a functioning headquarters, or had been listening to the radio . . . Maybe, he thought hopefully, remembering the retreat in France, maybe I can even pick up a bicycle . . .

He grinned sourly as he neared the camp. I have become a specialist, he thought, in the technique of personal retreat. It was a good skill to have in the spring of 1945. I am the leading Nordic expert, he thought, on disengaging tactics from dissolving military organizations. I can sniff surrender in a Colonel two days before the Colonel realizes himself what is passing through his mind.

Christian did not want to surrender, although it had suddenly become all the style, and millions of men seemed to be spending their entire time figuring out the most satisfactory means of accomplishing it. For the last month, most of the conversation in the Army had been an examination of that subject . . . In the ruined cities, in the sketchy and hopeless little islands of resistance set up across main roads and town-entrances, the discussion had always followed the same course. No hatred for the American Air Forces which had destroyed cities that had stood unmolested for a thousand years, no feeling of revenge for the thousands of women and children stinking and buried in the rubble, only, "The best ones to hand yourself over to are, of course, the Americans. After that, the British. Then, the French, although that is a last emergency. And if the Russians take you, we'll see you in Siberia . . ." Men with the Iron Cross, first class, men with the Hitler Medal, men who had fought in Africa and in front of Leningrad, and all the way back from Ste. Mère Eglise . . . It was disgusting.

Christian was not so certain as everyone else about the generosity of the Americans. It was a myth that a myth-ridden people had invented with which to comfort themselves. Christian remembered the dead paratrooper, swinging from the Norman tree, his face harsh and unrelenting, even then . . . He remembered the Red Cross convoy, with its pitiful horses, raked by the fighter pilots who must have seen the crosses, known what they stood for, and who had not held their hands . . . The generosity of Americans had not been spectacularly demonstrated over Berlin or Munich or Dresden, either. No, by now, Christian no longer was susceptible to myth. And it wasn't as though even the Americans had ever promised anything. Over the radio they had announced again and again that every guilty man or woman in Germany was going to pay for his crimes. At best, there would be years in prison camps and on work gangs, while they sifted the charges from one end of Europe to another. And what if some Frenchman had remembered Christian's name from Normandy, remembered the time he'd denounced the two men along the coast, after Behr was killed, and they had been tortured in the next room? You never knew what sort of record had been kept by the Underground, how much they knew. And God knows what that woman Françoise would have to say. She was probably in Paris now, living with an American General, filling his ear with venom. And even if they weren't particularly looking for you, once you were in their hands, any crazy Frenchman might happen to see you, and take it into his head to denounce you for some crime you never committed. And who would take your word, and who would there be to help you prove you were innocent?

And there'd be nothing to stop the Americans from handing over a million prisoners to the French, to take up mines and rebuild damaged cities, and anything would be better than being in the hands of the French for years . . . You'd never come out of that alive.

It did not fit in Christian's plans to die. He had learned too much in the last five years. He would be too useful after the war to throw it all away now. He would have to lie low, of course, for three or four years, and be agreeable and pleasant to the conquerors. Probably right back at home the tourists would come again for the skiing, probably the Americans would set up huge rest camps there, and he could get a job teaching American Lieutenants how to make snowplow turns . . . And after that . . . Well, after that he would see. A man who had learned how to kill so expertly, and handle violent men so well, was bound to be a useful commodity five years after the war, if he preserved himself carefully . . .

He didn't know what the situation was back in his home town, but if he could manage to get back there before troops got in, he could put on civilian clothes, and his father could invent a story for him . . . It wasn't so far away, here he was deep in Bavaria, and the mountains were just over the horizon. The war had finally turned convenient, he thought with grim humor. A man could fight his final action in his own front yard.

There was only one guard on the gate, a pudgy little man in his middle fifties, looking out of place and unhappy with his Volkssturm armband and his rifle. The Volkssturm, Christian thought contemptuously—that had been a marvelous idea. Hitler's home for the aged, the bitter joke had run. There had been a great deal of resounding talk in the newspapers and over the radio, to the effect that every man, of whatever age, fifteen or seventy, would, now that their very homes were threatened, fight like raging lions against the invader. The sedentary, hardened-arteried gentlemen of the Volkssturm had obviously not heard about their fighting like lions. One shot over their heads and you could pick up a whole battalion, with their eyes running, and their hands up in the air. Another myth—that you could take middle-aged Germans away from their desks and children out of school and make soldiers out of them in two weeks. Rhetoric, Christian thought, looking at the worried fat man in his ill-fitting uniform at the gate, rhetoric has deranged us all. Rhetoric and myth against whole divisions of tanks, armies of airplanes, all the gasoline, all the guns, all the ammunition in the world. Hardenburg had understood, long ago, but Hardenburg had killed himself. Yes, there would be a use, after the war, for men who had been cleansed of rhetoric and who had been once and for all inoculated against myth.

"Heil Hitler," said the Volkssturm guard, saluting uncomfortably.

Heil Hitler. Another joke. Christian didn't bother to answer the salute.

"What's going on here?" Christian asked.

"We wait." The guard shrugged.

"For what?"

The guard shrugged again. He grinned uneasily.

"What's the news?" the guard asked.

"The Americans have just surrendered," Christian said. "Tomorrow the Russians."

For a moment, the guard almost believed him. A credulous flicker of joy crossed his face. Then he knew better. "You are in good spirits," he said sadly.

"I am in great spirits," said Christian. "I have just come back from my spring holiday."

"Do you think the Americans will come here today?" the guard asked anxiously.

"They are liable to come in ten minutes, or ten days," said Christian, "or ten weeks. Who can tell what the Americans will do?"

"I hope they come soon," said the guard. "They are preferable to the . . ."

This one, too, Christian thought. "I know," he said shortly. "They are preferable to the Russians and preferable to the French."

"That's what everybody says," the guard said unhappily.

"God," Christian sniffed. "How can you stand the stink?"

The guard nodded. "It is bad, isn't it?" he said. "But I've been here a week and I don't notice it any more."

"A week?" Christian asked. "Is that all?"

"There was a whole SS battalion here, but a week ago they took them away and put us here. Just one Company," the guard said aggrievedly. "We are lucky to be alive."

"What have you got in there?" Christian nodded his head in the direction of the smell.

"The usual. Jews, Russians, some politicals, some people from Yugoslavia and Greece, places like that. We locked them all in two days ago. They know something is up and they are getting dangerous. And we only have one Company, they could wipe us out in fifteen minutes if they wanted, there are thousands of them. They were making a lot of noise an hour ago." He turned and peered uneasily at the locked barracks. "Now, not a sound. God knows what they are cooking up for us."

"Why do you stay here?" Christian asked curiously.

The guard shrugged, smiling that sick, foolish smile again.

"I don't know. We wait."

"Open the gate," Christian said. "I want to go in."

"You want to go in?" the guard said incredulously. "What for?"

"I am making a list of summer resorts for the Strength Through Joy Headquarters in Berlin," Christian said, "and this camp has been suggested to me. Open up. I need something to eat, and I want to see if I can borrow a bicycle."

The guard signaled to another guard in the tower, who had been watching Christian carefully. The gate slowly began to swing open.

"You won't find a bicycle," the Volkssturm man said. "The SS took everything with wheels away with them when they went last week."

"I'll see," Christian said. He went through the double gates, deep into the smell, toward the Administration Building, a pleasant-looking Tyrolean-style chalet, with a green lawn and whitewashed stones, and a tall flagpole with the banner fluttering from it in the brisk morning wind. There was a low, hushed, non-human sounding murmur, coming from the barracks. It seemed to come from some new kind of musical instrument, designed to project notes too formless and unpleasant for an organ to manage. All the windows were boarded up, and there were no human beings to be seen within the compound.

Christian mounted the scrubbed stone steps of the chalet and went inside.

He found the kitchen and got some sausage and ersatz coffee from a gloomy sixty-year-old uniformed cook, who said, encouragingly, "Eat hearty, Boy, who knows when we'll ever eat again."

There were quite a few of the misfits of the Volkssturm huddled uneasily in their second-hand uniforms along the halls of the Administration Building. They held weapons, but did so gingerly, and with clear expressions of distaste. They, too, like the guard at the gate, were waiting. They stared unhappily at Christian as he passed among them, and Christian could sense a whisper of disapproval, disapproval for his youth, for the losing war he had fought . . . The young men, Hitler had always boasted, were his great strength, and now these makeshift soldiers, torn at the heel end of a war from their homes, showed, by the slight grimaces on their worn faces, what they thought of the retreating generation which had brought them to this hour.

Christian walked very erect, holding his Schmeisser lightly, his face cold and set, among the aimless men in the halls. He

581

reached the Commandant's office, knocked, and went in. A prisoner in his striped suit was mopping the floor, and a Corporal was sitting at a desk in the outer office. The door to the private office was open, and the man sitting at the desk there motioned for Christian to come in when he heard Christian say, "I wish to speak to the Commandant."

The Commandant was the oldest Lieutenant Christian had ever seen. He looked well over sixty, with a face that seemed to have been put together out of flaky cheese.

"No, I have no bicycles," the Lieutenant said in his cracked voice, in answer to Christian's request. "I have nothing. Not even any food. They left us here with nothing, the SS. Just orders to remain in control. I got through to Berlin yesterday and some idiot on the phone told me to kill everybody here immediately." The Lieutenant laughed sourly. "Eleven thousand men. Very practical. I haven't been able to reach anybody since then." He stared at Christian. "You have come from the front?"

Christian smiled. "Front is not exactly the word I would use."

The Lieutenant sighed, his cheese-like face pale and creased. "In the last war," he said, "it was very different. We retreated in the most orderly manner. My entire Company marched into Munich, still in possession of their weapons. It was much more orderly," he said, the accusation against the new generation of Germans, who did not know how to lose a war in an orderly manner, like their fathers, quite clear in his tone.

"Well, Lieutenant," Christian said, "I see you can't help me. I shall be moving on."

"Tell me," the old Lieutenant said, appealing to Christian to stay just another moment, as though he were lonely here in the pretty, well-cleaned office, with colored drapes on the windows, and the rough cloth sofa, and the bright blue picture of the Alps in winter on the paneled wall, "tell me, do you think the Americans will get here today?"

"I couldn't say, Sir," Christian said. "Haven't you been listening on the radio?"

"The radio." The Lieutenant sighed. "It is very confusing. This morning, from Berlin, there was a rumor the Russians and the Americans were fighting each other along the Elbe. Do you think that is possible?" he asked eagerly. "After all, we all know, eventually, it is inevitable . . ."

The myth, Christian thought, the continuing, suicidal myth. "Of course, Sir," he said clearly, "I would not be at all surprised." He started toward the door, but he stopped when he heard the noise.

It was a flood-like murmur, growing swiftly in volume, swirling in through the open windows, past the pretty drapes.

Then the murmur was punctuated, sharply, by shots. Christian ran to the window and looked out. Two men in uniform were running heavily toward the Administration Building. As they ran, Christian saw them throw away their rifles. They were portly men, who looked like advertisements for Munich beer, and running came hard to them. From around the corner of one of the barracks, first one man in prisoner's clothes, then three more, then what looked like hundreds more, ran in a mob, after the two guards. That was where the murmur was coming from. The first prisoner stopped for a moment and picked up one of the discarded rifles. He did not fire it, but carried it, as he chased the guards. He was a tall man with long legs, and he gained with terrible rapidity on the guards. He swung the rifle like a club, and one of the beer advertisements went down. The second guard, seeing that he was too far from the safety of the Administration Building to make it before he was overtaken, merely lay down. He lay down slowly, like an elephant in the circus, first settling on his knees, then, with his hips still high in the air, putting his head down to the ground, trying to burrow it. The prisoner swung the rifle butt again and brained the guard.

"Oh, my God," the Lieutenant whispered at the window.

The crowd was around the two dead men now, enveloping them. The prisoners made very little noise as they trampled over the two dead forms, stamping hard again and again, each prisoner jostling the other, seeing some small spot on the dead bodies to kick.

The Lieutenant pulled away from the window and leaned tremblingly against the wall. "Eleven thousand of them . . ." he said. "In ten minutes they'll all be loose."

There were some shots from near the gate, and three or four of the prisoners went down. Nobody paid much attention to them, and part of the crowd surged, with that dull, flickering non-tonal murmur, in the direction of the gate.

From other barracks other crowds appeared, coming into view swiftly, like herds of bulls in the movies of Spain. Here and there they had caught a guard, and they made a community business of killing the man.

There were screams from the corridor outside. The Lieutenant, fumbling at his pistol, with his dear memories of the orderly defeat of the last war bitter in his brain, went out to rally his men.

Christian moved away from the window, trying to think quickly, cursing himself for being caught like this. After all he'd been through, after so many battles, after facing so many tanks, artillery pieces, so many trained men, to walk of his own free will into something like this . . .

Christian went out into the other office. The trusty was there alone, near the window. "Get in here," Christian said. The trusty looked at him coldly, then walked slowly into the private office. Christian closed the door, eyeing the prisoner. Luckily, he was a good size. "Take off your clothes," Christian said.

Methodically, without saying anything, the prisoner took off his loose striped-cotton jacket and began on his trousers. The noise was getting worse outside, and there was quite a bit of shooting now.

"Hurry!" Christian ordered.

The man had his trousers off by now. He was very thin and he had grayish, sackcloth underwear on. "Come over here," Christian said.

The man walked slowly over and stood in front of Christian. Christian swung his machine pistol. The barrel caught the man above the eyes. He took one step back, then dropped to the floor. There was almost no mark above his eyes. Christian took him by the throat with both hands and dragged him over to a closet door on the other side of the room. Christian opened the closet and pulled the unconscious man into it. There was an officer's overcoat hanging in the closet and two dress tunics and they gave off a slight smell of cologne.

Christian closed the closet and went over to where the prisoner's clothes lay on the floor. He started to unbutton his tunic. But the noise outside seemed to grow louder, and there was confused shouting in the corridor. He decided he didn't have time. Hurriedly, he put the pants on over his own trousers, and wrestled into the coat. He buttoned it up to the neck. He looked into the mirror on the closet door. His uniform didn't show. He looked hastily around for a place to hide the gun, then bent down and threw it under the couch. It would hold there for awhile. He still had his trenchknife in its holster under the striped coat. The coat smelled strongly of chlorine and sweat.

Christian went to the window. New batches of prisoners, the doors of their barracks battered down, were swirling around below. They were still finding guards and killing them, and Christian could hear firing from the other side of the Administration Building, although on this side, no one seemed to be trying to handle the prisoners at all. Some of the prisoners were knocking down a double door on a barnlike structure a hundred meters away. When the door went down, a large number of the prisoners surged through it and came back eating raw potatoes and uncooked flour, which smeared their hands and faces a powdery white. Christian saw one prisoner, a huge man, bent over a guard, whom he held between his knees, choking him. The huge man suddenly dropped the guard, who was still alive, and bulled his way into the warehouse. Christian saw him come out a minute later with his hands full of potatoes.

Christian kicked open the window and, without hesitating, swung out. He held by his fingers for a second, and dropped. He fell to his knees, but got right up. There were hundreds of men all around him, all dressed like him, and the smell and the noise were overpowering.

Christian started toward the gate, turning the corner of the Administration Building. A gaunt man with the socket of one eye showing in empty, scarred tissue was leaning against the wall. He stared very hard at Christian and began to follow him. Christian was certain the man suspected him, and tried to move quickly, without attracting attention. But the crowd of men in front of the Administration Building was very dense now, and the man with one eye hung on, right behind Christian.

The guards in the building had surrendered by now, and were coming out of the front door in pairs. For a moment, the newly released men were strangely quiet, staring at their erstwhile captors. Then a big man with a bald head took out a rusty pocket knife. He said something in Polish and grabbed the nearest guard and began to saw away at his throat. The knife was blunt and it took a long time. The guard who was being slaughtered did not struggle or cry out. It was as though torture and death in this place were so commonplace that even the victims fell into it naturally, no matter who they were. The futility of crying out for mercy had been so well demonstrated here, so long ago, that no man wasted his breath today. The trapped guard, a clerkish man of forty-five, merely slumped close against the man who was murdering him, staring at him, their eyes six inches apart, until the rusty knife finally broke through the vein and he slid down to the lawn.

This was a signal for the execution of the other guards. Due to the lack of weapons, many of them were trampled to death. Christian watched, not daring to show anything on his face, not daring to make a break, because the man with one eye was directly behind him, pressing against his shoulders.

"You . . ." The man with one eye said. Christian could feel his hand clutching at his coat, feeling the cloth of his uniform underneath. "I want to talk to . . ."

Suddenly Christian moved. The ancient Commandant was against the wall near the front door and the men had not reached him yet. The Commandant stood there, his hands making small, placating gestures in front of him. The men around him, starved and bony, were for the moment too exhausted to kill him. Christian lurched through the ring of men and grabbed the Commandant by the throat.

"Oh, God," the man shouted, very loud. It was a surprising

sound, because all the rest of the killing had taken place so quietly.

Christian took out his knife. Holding the Commandant pinned against the wall with one hand, he cut his throat. The man made a gurgling, wet sound, then screamed for a moment. Christian wiped his hands against the man's tunic and let him drop. Christian turned to see if the man with one eye was still watching him. But the man with one eye had moved off, satisfied.

Christian sighed and, still carrying his knife in his hand, went through the hall of the Administration Building and up the steps to the Commandant's office. There were bodies on the steps, and liberated prisoners were overturning desks and scattering paper everywhere.

There were three or four men in the Commandant's office. The door to the closet was open. The half-naked man Christian had hit was still lying there as he had fallen. The prisoners were taking turns drinking brandy out of a decanter on the Commandant's desk. When the decanter was empty, one of the men threw it at the bright-blue picture of the Alps in winter on the wall.

Nobody paid any attention to Christian. He bent down and took his machine pistol out from under the couch.

Christian went back into the hall and through the aimlessly milling prisoners to the front door. Many of them had weapons by now, and Christian felt safe in carrying his Schmeisser openly. He walked slowly, always in the middle of groups, because he did not want to be seen by himself, standing out in relief so that some sharp-eyed prisoner would notice that his hair was longer than anyone else's, and that he had considerably more weight on his bones than most of the others.

He reached the gates. The middle-aged guard who had greeted him and let him in was lying sprawled against the barbed wire, an expression that looked like a smile on his dead face. There were many prisoners at the gate, but very few were going out. It was as though they had accomplished as much as was humanly possible for one day. The liberation from the barracks had exhausted their concept of freedom. They merely stood at the open gate, staring out at the rolling green countryside, at the road down which the Americans would soon come and tell them what to do. Or perhaps so much of their most profound emotion was linked with this place that now, in the moment of deliverance, they could not bear to leave it, but must stay and slowly examine the place where they had suffered and where they had had their vengeance.

Christian pushed through the knot of men near the dead Volkssturm soldier. Carrying his weapon, he walked briskly down the road, back toward the advancing Americans. He did not dare go the other way, deeper into Germany, because one of the men at the gate might have noticed it and challenged him.

Christian walked swiftly, limping a little, breathing deeply of the fresh spring air to get the smell of the camp from his nostrils. He was very tired, but he did not slacken his pace. When he was a safe distance away, out of sight of the camp, he turned off the road. He made a wide swing across the fields and circled the camp safely. Coming through the budding woods, with the smell of pine in his nostrils and the small forest flowers pink and purple underfoot, he saw the road, empty and sunfreckled, ahead of him. But he was too tired to go any farther at the moment. He took off the chlorine- and sweat-smelling garments of the trusty, rolled them into a bundle and threw them under a bush. Then he lay down, using a root as a pillow. The new grass, spearing through the forest floor around him, smelled fresh and green. In the boughs above his head two birds sang to each other, making a small blue-and-gold flicker as they darted among the shaking branches in and out of the sunlight. Christian sighed, stretched, and fell asleep.

CHAPTER THIRTY-EIGHT

THE MEN in the trucks fell quiet as they drove up to the open gates. The smell, by itself, would have been enough to make them silent, but there was also the sight of the dead bodies sprawled at the gate and behind the wire, and the slowly moving mass of scarecrows in tattered striped suits who engulfed the trucks and Captain Green's jeep in a monstrous tide.

They did not make much noise. Many of them wept, many of them tried to smile, although the objective appearance of their skull-like faces and their staring, cavernous eyes did not alter very much, either in weeping or smiling. It was as though these creatures were too far sunk in a tragedy which had moved off the plane of human reaction onto an animal level of despair—and the comparatively sophisticated grimaces of welcome, sorrow and happiness were, for the time being, beyond their primitive reach. Michael could tell, staring at the rigid, dying masks, that a man here and there thought he was smiling, but it took an intuitive act of understanding.

They hardly tried to talk. They merely touched things—the metal of the truck bodies, the uniforms of the soldiers, the barrels of the rifles—as though only by the shy investigation of their fingertips could they begin to gain knowledge of this new and dazzling reality.

Green ordered the trucks left where they were, with guards on them, and led the Company slowly through the hive-like cluster of released prisoners, into the camp.

Michael and Noah were right behind Green when he went through the doorway of the first barracks. The door had been torn off and most of the windows had been broken open, but even so, the smell was beyond the tolerance of human nostrils. In the murky air, pierced ineffectually here and there by the dusty beams of spring sunshine, Michael could see the piled, bony forms. The worst thing was that from some of the piles there was movement, a languidly waving arm, the slow lift of a pair of burning eyes in the stinking gloom, the pale twisting of lips on skulls that seemed to have met death many days before. In the depths of the building, a form detached itself from a pile of rags and bones and started a slow advance on hands and knees toward the door. Nearer by, a man stood up and moved, like a mechanical figure, crudely arranged for the process of walking, toward Green. Michael could see that the man believed he was smiling, and he had his hand outstretched in an absurdly commonplace gesture of greeting. The man never reached Green. He sank to the slime-covered floor, his hand still outstretched. When Michael bent over him he saw that the man had died.

The center of the world, something repeated insanely and insistently in Michael's brain, as he kneeled above the man who had died with such ease and silence before their eyes. I am now at the center of the world, the center of the world.

The dead man, lying with outstretched hand, had been six feet tall. He was naked and every bone was clearly marked under the skin. He could not have weighed more than seventy-five pounds, and, because he was so lacking in the usual, broadening cover of flesh, he seemed enormously elongated, supernaturally tall and out of perspective.

There were some shots outside, and Michael and Noah followed Green out of the barracks. Thirty-two of the guards, who had barricaded themselves in a brick building which contained the ovens in which the Germans had burned prisoners, had given themselves up when they saw the Americans, and Crane had tried to shoot them. He had managed to wound two of the guards before Houlihan had torn his rifle away from him. One of the wounded guards was sitting on the ground, weeping, holding his stomach, and blood was coming in little spurts over his hands. He was enormously fat, with beer-rolls on the back of his neck, and he looked like a spoiled pink child sitting on the ground, complaining to his nurse.

Crane was standing with his arms clutched by two of his friends, breathing very hard, his eyes rolling crazily. When Green ordered the guards to be taken into the Administration Building for safekeeping, Crane lashed out with his feet and kicked the fat man he had shot. The fat man wept loudly. It took four men to carry the fat man into the Administration Building.

There was not much Green could do. But he set up his Headquarters in the Commandant's room of the Administration Building and issued a series of clear, simple orders, as though it was an everyday affair in the American Army for an Infantry Captain to arrive at the chaos of the center of the world and set about putting it to rights. He sent his jeep back to request a medical team and a truckload of ten-in-one rations. He had all the Company's food unloaded and stacked under guard in the Administration Building, with orders to dole it out only to the worst cases of starvation that were found and reported by the squads working through the barracks. He had the German guards segregated at the end of the hall outside his door, where they could not be harmed.

Michael, who, with Noah, was serving as a messenger for Green, heard one of the guards complaining, in good English, to Pfeiffer, who had them under his rifle, that it was terribly unjust, that they had just been on duty in this camp for a week, that they had never done any harm to the prisoners, that the men of the SS battalion who had been there for years and who had been responsible for all the torture and privation in the camp, were going off scot-free, were probably in an American prison stockade at that moment, drinking orange juice. There was considerable justice in the poor Volkssturm guard's complaint, but Pfeiffer merely said, "Shut your trap before I put my boot in it."

The liberated prisoners had a working committee, which they had secretly chosen a week before, to govern the camp. Green called in the leader of the committee, a small, dry man of fifty, with a curious accent and a quite formal way of handling the English language. The man's name was Zoloom, and he had been in the Albanian Foreign Service before the war. He told Green he had been a prisoner for three and a half years. He was completely bald and had pebbly little dark eyes, set in a face that somehow was still rather plump. He had an air of authority and was quite helpful to Green in securing work parties among the healthier prisoners, to carry the dead from the barracks, and collect and classify the sick into dying, critical and out-of-danger categories. Only those people in the critical category, Green ordered, were to be fed out of the small stocks of food that had been collected from the trucks and the almost empty storerooms of the camp. The dying were merely laid side by side along one of the streets, to extinguish themselves in peace, consoled finally by the sight of the sun and the fresh touch of the spring air on their wasted foreheads.

As the first afternoon wore on, and Michael saw the beginning of order that Green, in his ordinary, quiet, almost embarrassed way, had brought about, he felt an enormous respect for the dusty little Captain with the high, girlish voice. Everything in Green's world, Michael suddenly realized, was fixable. There was nothing, not even the endless depravity and bottomless despair which the Germans had left at the swampheart of their dying millennium, which could not be remedied by the honest, mechanic's common sense and energy of a decent workman. Looking at Green giving brisk, sensible orders to the Albanian, to Sergeant Houlihan, to Poles and Russians and Jews and German Communists, Michael knew that Green didn't believe he was doing anything extraordinary, anything that any graduate of the Fort Benning Infantry Officers' Candidate School wouldn't do in his place.

Watching Green at work, as calm and efficient as he would have been sitting in an orderly room in Georgia making out duty rosters, Michael was glad that he had never gone to Officers' School. I could never have done it, Michael thought, I would have put my head in my hands and wept until they took me away. Green did not weep. In fact, as the afternoon wore on, his voice, in which no sympathy had been expressed for anyone all day, became harder and harder, more and more crisp and military and impersonal.

Michael watched Noah carefully, too. But Noah did not change the expression on his face. The expression was one of thoughtful, cool reserve, and Noah clung to it as a man clings to a very expensive piece of clothing which he has bought with his last savings and is too dear to discard, even in the most extreme circumstances. Only once during the afternoon, when, on an errand for the Captain, Michael and Noah had to walk along the line of men who had been declared too far gone to help, and who lay in a long line on the dusty ground, did Noah stop for a moment. Now, Michael thought, watching obliquely, it is going to happen now. Noah stared at the emaciated, bony, ulcerous men, half-naked and dying, beyond the reach of any victory or liberation, and his face trembled, the expensive expression nearly was lost . . . But he gained control of himself. He closed his eyes for a moment, wiped his mouth with the back of his hand, and said, starting again, "Come on. What are we stopping for?"

When they got back to the Commandant's office, an old man was being led in before the Captain. At least he looked old. He was bent over, and his long yellow hands were translucently thin. You couldn't really tell, of course, because almost everyone in the camp looked old, or ageless.

"My name," the old man was saying in slow English, "is Joseph Silverson. I am a Rabbi. I am the only Rabbi in the camp . . ."

"Yes," Captain Green said briskly. He did not look up from a paper on which he was writing a request for medical materials.

"I do not wish to annoy the officer," the Rabbi said. "But I would like to make a request."

"Yes?" Still, Captain Green did not look up. He had taken off his helmet and his field jacket. His gunbelt was hanging over the back of his chair. He looked like a busy clerk in a warehouse, checking invoices.

"Many thousand Jews," the Rabbi said slowly and carefully, "have died in this camp, and several hundred more out there . . ." the Rabbi waved his translucent hand gently toward the window, "will die today, tonight, tomorrow . . ."

"I'm sorry, Rabbi," Captain Green said. "I am doing all I can."

"Of course." The Rabbi nodded hastily. "I know that. There is nothing to be done for them. Nothing for their bodies. I understand. We all understand. Nothing material. Even they understand. They are in the shadow and all efforts must be concentrated on the living. They are not even unhappy. They are dying free and there is a great pleasure in that. I am asking for a luxury." Michael understood that the Rabbi was attempting to smile. He had enormous, sunken, green eyes that flamed steadily in his narrow face, under his high, ridged forehead. "I am asking to be permitted to collect all of us, the living, the ones without hope, out there, in the square there . . ." again the translucent wave of the hand, "and conduct a religious service. A service for the dead who have come to their end in this place."

Michael stared at Noah. Noah was looking coolly and soberly at Captain Green, his face calm, remote.

Captain Green had not looked up. He had stopped writing, but he was sitting with his head bent over wearily, as though he had fallen asleep.

"There has never been a religious service for us in this place," the Rabbi said softly, "and so many thousands have gone . . ."

"Permit me." It was the Albanian diplomat who had been so helpful in carrying out Green's orders. He had moved to the side of the Rabbi, and was standing before the Captain's desk, bent over, speaking rapidly, diplomatically and clearly. "I do not like to intrude, Captain. I understand why the Rabbi has made this request. But this is not the time for it. I am a European, I have been in this place a long time, I understand things perhaps the Captain doesn't understand. I do not like to intrude, as I said, but I think it would be inadvisable to give permission to conduct publicly a Hebrew religious service in this place." The Albanian stopped, waiting for Green to say something. But Green didn't say anything. He sat at the desk, nodding a little, looking as though he were on the verge of waking up from sleep.

"The Captain perhaps does not understand the feeling," the Albanian went on rapidly. "The feeling in Europe. In a camp like this. Whatever the reasons," the Albanian said smoothly, "good or bad, the feeling exists. It is a fact. If you allow this gentleman to hold his services, I do not guarantee the consequences. I feel I must warn you. There will be riots, there will be violence, bloodshed. The other prisoners will not stand for it . . ."

"The other prisoners will not stand for it," Green repeated quietly, without any tone in his voice.

"No, Sir," said the Albanian briskly, "I guarantee the other prisoners will not stand for it."

Michael looked at Noah. The expensive expression was sliding off his face, melting, slowly and violently exposing a grimace of horror and despair.

Green stood up. "I am going to guarantee something myself," he said to the Rabbi. "I am going to guarantee that you will hold your services in one hour in the square down there. I am also going to guarantee that there will be machine guns set up on the roof of this building. And I will further guarantee that anybody who attempts to interfere with your services will be fired on by those machine guns." He turned to the Albanian. "And, finally, I guarantee," he said, "that if you ever try to come into this room again you will be locked up. That is all."

The Albanian backed swiftly out of the room. Michael heard his footsteps disappearing down the corridor.

The Rabbi bowed gravely. "Thank you very much, Sir," he said to Green.

Green put out his hand. The Rabbi shook it and turned and followed the Albanian. Green stood staring at the window.

Green looked at Noah. The old, controlled, rigidly calm expression was melting back into the boy's face.

"Ackerman," Green said crisply. "I don't think we'll need you around here for a couple of hours. Why don't you and Whitacre leave this place for awhile, go out and take a walk? Outside the camp. It'll do you good."

"Thank you, Sir," Noah said. He went out of the room.

"Whitacre," Green was still staring out of the window, and his voice was weary. "Whitacre, take care of him."

"Yes, Sir," said Michael. He went after Noah.

They walked in silence. The sun was low in the sky and there were long paths of purple shadow across the hills to the north. They passed a farmhouse, set back from the road, but there was no movement there. It slept, neat-white and lifeless, in the westering sun. It had been painted recently, and the stone wall in front of it had been whitewashed. The stone wall was turning pale blue in the leveling rays of the sun. Overhead a squadron of fighter planes, high in the clear sky, caught the sun on their aluminum wings as they headed back to their base.

On one side of the road was forest, healthy-looking pine and elm, dark trunks looking almost black against the pale, milky green of the new foliage. The sun flickered in small bright stains among the leaves, falling on the sprouting flowers in the cleared spaces between the trees. The camp was behind them and the air, warmed by the full day's sun, was piney and aromatic. The rubber composition soles of their combat boots made a hushed, unmilitary sound on the narrow asphalt road, between the rain ditches on each side. They walked silently, past another farmhouse. This place too was locked and shuttered, but Michael had the feeling eyes were peering out at him between cracks. He was not afraid. The only people left in Germany seemed to be children, by the million, and old women and maimed soldiers. It was a polite and unwarlike population, who waved impartially to the jeeps and tanks of the Americans and the truck bearing German prisoners back to prison stockades.

Three geese waddled across the dust of the farmyard. Chrismas dinner, Michael thought idly, with loganberry jam and oyster stuffing. He remembered the oak paneling and the scenes from Wagner painted on the walls of Luchow's restaurant, on 14th Street, in New York. They walked past the farmhouse. Now, on both sides of them stood the heavy forest, tall trees standing in the loam of old leaves, giving off a clear, thin smell of spring.

Noah hadn't said a word since they had left Green's office, and Michael was surprised when he heard his friend's voice over the shuffle of their boots on the asphalt.

"How do you feel?" Noah asked.

Michael thought for a moment. "Dead," he said. "Dead, wounded and missing."

They walked another twenty yards. "It was pretty bad, wasn't it?" Noah said.

"Pretty bad."

"You knew it was bad," said Noah. "But you never thought it would be like that."

"No," said Michael.

"Human beings . . ." They walked, listening to the sound of their composition soles on the road deep in Germany, in the afternoon in spring, between the aisles of pretty, budding trees. "My uncle," Noah said, "my father's brother, went into one of these places. Did you see the ovens?"

"Yes," said Michael.

"I never saw him, of course. My uncle, I mean," Noah said. His hand was hooked in his rifle strap and he looked like a little boy returning from hunting rabbits. "He had some trouble with my father. In 1905, in Odessa. My father was a fool. But he knew about things like this. He came from Europe. Did I ever tell you about my father?"

"No," said Michael.

"Dead, wounded and missing," Noah said softly. They walked steadily, but not quickly, the soldier's pace, thirty inches, deliberate, ground-covering. "Remember," Noah asked, "back in the replacement depot, what you said: 'Five years after the war is over we're all liable to look back with regret to every bullet that missed us.'"

"Yes," said Michael. "I remember."

"What do you feel now?"

Michael hesitated. "I don't know," he said honestly.

"This afternoon," Noah said, walking in his deliberate, correct pace, "I agreed with you. When that Albanian started talking I agreed with you. Not because I'm a Jew. At least, I don't think that was the reason. As a human being . . . When that Albanian started talking I was ready to go out into the hall and shoot myself through the head."

"I know," Michael said softly. "I felt the same way."

"Then Green said what he had to say." Noah stopped and looked up to the tops of the trees, golden-green in the golden sun. "'I guarantee . . . I guarantee . . .'" He sighed. "I don't know what you think," Noah said, "but I have a lot of hope for Captain Green."

"So do I," said Michael.

"When the war is over," Noah said and his voice was growing loud, "Green is going to run the world, not that damned Albanian . . ."

"Sure," said Michael.

"The human beings are going to be running the world!" Noah was shouting by now, standing in the middle of the shadowed road, shouting at the sun-tipped branches of the German forest. "The human beings! There's a lot of Captain Greens! He's not extraordinary! There're millions of them!" Noah stood, very erect, his head back, shouting crazily, as though all the things he had coldly pushed down deep within him and fanatically repressed for so many months were now finally bursting forth. "Human beings!" he shouted thickly, as though the two words were a magic incantation against death and sorrow, a subtle and impregnable shield for his son and his wife, a rich payment for the agony of the recent years, a promise and a guarantee for the future . . . "The world is full of them!"

It was then that the shots rang out.

Christian had been awake five or six minutes before he heard the voices. He had slept heavily, and when he awoke he had known immediately from the way the shadows lay in the forest that it was late in the afternoon. But he had been too weary to move immediately. He had lain on his back, staring up at the mild green canopy over his head, listening to the forest sounds, the awakening springtime hum of insects, the calls of birds in the upper branches, the slight rustling of the leaves in the wind. A flight of planes had crossed over, and he had heard them, although he couldn't see the planes through the trees. Once again, as it had for so long, the sound of planes made him reflect bitterly on the abundance with which the Americans had fought the war. No wonder they'd won. They didn't amount to much as soldiers, he thought for the hundredth time, but what difference did it make? Given all those planes, all those tanks, an army of old women and veterans of the Franco-Prussian War could have won. Given just one-third of that equipment, he thought, self-pityingly, and we'd have won three years ago. That miserable Lieutenant back at the camp, complaining because we didn't lose this war in an orderly manner, the way his class did! If he'd complained a little less and worked a little more, perhaps it might not have turned out this way. A few more hours in the factory and a few less at the mass meetings and party festivals, and maybe that sound above would be German planes, maybe the Lieutenant wouldn't be lying dead now in front of his office, maybe he, Christian, wouldn't be hiding out now, looking for a burrow, like a fox before the hounds.

Then he heard the footsteps, coming in his direction along the road. He was only ten meters off the road, well concealed, but with a good field of vision in the direction of the camp, and he could see the Americans coming when they were quiet a distance off. He watched them curiously, with no emotion for the moment. They were walking steadily, and they had rifles. One of them, the larger of the two, was carrying his in his hand, and the other had his slung over his shoulder. They were wearing those absurd helmets, although there would be no danger of shrapnel until the next war, and they weren't looking either to the left or the right. They were talking to each other, quite loudly, and it was obvious that they felt safe, at home, as though no notion that any German in this neighborhood would dare to do them any harm had ever crossed their minds.

If they kept coming this way they would pass within ten meters of Christian. He grinned without amusement, thinking of it. Silently he brought up his machine pistol. Then he thought better of it. There were probably hundreds of others all around by now, and the shots would bring them running, and then there wouldn't be a chance for him. The generous Americans would not stretch their generosity to include snipers.

Then the Americans stopped. They were perhaps sixty meters away, and, because of a little bend in the road, they were directly in front of the small hummock behind which he was lying. They were talking very loudly. One of the Americans, in fact, was shouting, and Christian could even hear what he was saying. "Human beings!" The American kept shouting, over and over again, inexplicably.

Christian watched them coldly. So much at home in Germany. Strolling unaccompanied through the woods. Making speeches in English in the middle of Bavaria. Looking forward to summering in the Alps, staying at the tourist hotels with the local girls, and there no doubt would be plenty of them. Well-fed Americans, young, too, no Volkssturm for them, all young, all in good condition, with well-repaired boots and clothing, with scientific diets, with an Air Force, and ambulances that ran on gasoline, with no problems about whom it would be better to surrender to . . . And after it was all over, going back to that fat country, loaded with souvenirs of the war, the helmets of dead Germans, the Iron Crosses plucked off dead breasts, the pictures off the walls of bombed houses, the photographs of the sweethearts of dead soldiers . . . Going back to that country which had never heard a shot fired, in which no single wall had trembled, no single pane of glass been shattered . . .

That fat country, untouched, untouchable . . .

Christian could feel his mouth twisting in a harsh grimace of distaste. He brought his gun up slowly. Two more, he thought, why not? The grimace turned into a smile. He began to hum to himself softly, as he brought the nearest one, the one who was yelling, into his sights. You will not yell so loud in a moment, Friend, he thought, putting his hand gently on the trigger, humming, remembering suddenly that Hardenburg had hummed at another time which had been very much like this one, on the ridge in Africa, over the British convoy at breakfast

. . . He was amused that he remembered it. Just before he pulled the trigger he thought once more of the possibility that there were other Americans around who might hear the shots and find him and kill him. He hesitated for a moment. Then he shook his head and blinked. The hell with it, he thought, it will be worth it . . .

He fired. He got off two shots. Then the gun jammed. He knew he'd hit one of the bastards. But by the time he looked up again after working fiercely to clear the jammed cartridge, the two men had vanished. He'd seen one start to go down, but now there was nothing on the road except a rifle which had been knocked out of the hands of one of the Americans. The rifle lay in the middle of the road, dark blue, with a pinpoint of sparkling sunlight reflecting off a spot near the muzzle.

Well, Christian thought disgustedly, that was a nicely botched job! He listened carefully, but there were no sounds along the road or in the forest. The two Americans had been alone, he decided . . . And now, he was sure, there was only one. Or if the other one, who had been hit, was alive, he was in no shape to move . . .

He himself had to move, though. It wouldn't take too long for the unwounded man to figure out the general direction from which the shot had come. He might come after him, and he might not . . . Christian felt that he probably wouldn't. Americans weren't particularly eager at moments like this. Their style was to wait for the Air Force, wait for the tanks, wait for the artillery. And, for once, in this silent forest, with only a half hour more light remaining, there would be no tanks, no artillery to call up. Just one man with a rifle . . . Christian was convinced that a man wouldn't try it, especially now, with the war so nearly over, when it was bound to seem to him like such a waste. If the man who had been hit was dead by now, Christian reasoned, the survivor was probably racing back right now to whatever unit he had come from, to get reinforcements. But, Christian figured, if the man who had been hit was only wounded, his comrade must be standing by him, and, anchored to him, not being able to move quickly or quietly, would make a beautiful target . . .

Christian grinned. Just one more, he thought, and I shall retire from the war. He peered cautiously down the road at the rifle lying there, scanned the slightly rising, bush-and-trunk obscured ground ahead of him, shimmering dully in the dying light. There was no sign there, no indication.

Crouching over, moving very carefully, Christian moved deeper into the forest, circling . . .

597

Michael's right hand was numb. He didn't realize it until he bent over to put Noah down. One of the bullets had struck the butt of the rifle Michael had been carrying, and, whirling it out of his hand, had sent a hammerblow of pain up to his shoulder. In the confusion of grabbing Noah and dragging him off into the woods, he hadn't noticed it, but now, bending over the wounded boy, the numbness became another ominous element of the situation.

Noah had been hit in the throat, low and to one side. He was bleeding badly, but he was still breathing, shallow, erratic gasps. He was not conscious. Michael crouched beside him, putting a bandage on, but it didn't seem to stop the blood much. Noah was lying on his back, his helmet in a small pale bed of pink flowers growing very close to the ground. His face had resumed its expensive, remote expression. His eyes were closed and the blond-tipped lashes, curled over his pale-fuzzed cheek, gave the upper part of his face the old, vulnerable expression of girlishness and youth.

Michael did not stare at him long. His brain seemed to be working with difficulty. I can't leave him here, he thought, and I can't carry him away, because we'd both buy it then, and fast, moving clumsily through the woods, perfect target for the sniper.

There was a flicker in the branches above his head. Michael snapped his head back, remembering sharply where he was and that the man who had shot Noah was probably stalking him at this moment. It was only a bird this time, swinging on a branch-tip, scolding down into the cooling air under the trees, but the next time it would be an armed man who was anxious to kill him.

Michael bent over. He lifted Noah gently and slid the rifle from Noah's shoulder. He looked down once more, then walked slowly into the forest. For a step or two, he could still hear the shallow, mechanical breathing of the wounded man. It was too bad, but Noah had to breathe or not breathe, unattended, for awhile.

This is where I probably catch it, Michael thought. But it was the only way out. Find the man who had fired the two shots before the man found him. The only way out. For Noah. For himself.

He could feel his heart going very fast, and he kept yawning, dryly and nervously. He had a bad feeling that he was going to be killed.

He walked thoughtfully and carefully, bent over, stopping often behind the thick trunks of trees to listen. He heard his own breathing, the occasional song of a bird, the drone of insects, a frog's boom from some nearby water, the minute clashing of the boughs in the light wind. But there was no sound of steps, no sound of equipment jangling, a riflebolt, being drawn.

He moved away from the road, deeper into the forest, away from where Noah was lying with the hole in his throat, his helmet tilted back away from his forehead on the bed of pink flowers. Michael hadn't figured his maneuver reasonably. He had just felt, almost instinctively, that sticking close to the road would have been bad, would have meant being pinned against an open space, would have made him more visible, since the forest was less dense there.

His heavy boots made a crunching noise on the thick, crisp, dead leaves underfoot and on the hidden, dead twigs. He was annoyed with himself for his clumsiness. But no matter how slowly he went, through the thickening brush, it seemed to be impossible to make no noise.

He stopped often, to listen, but there were only the normal late-afternoon woodland sounds.

He tried to concentrate on the Kraut. What would the Kraut be like?

Maybe after he'd fired, the Kraut had just packed up and headed straight back toward the Austrian border. Two shots, one American, good enough for a day's work at the tail end of a lost war. Hitler could ask no more. Or maybe it wasn't a soldier at all, maybe it was one of those insane ten-year-old kids, with a rifle from the last war dragged down out of the attic, and all hopped up with the Werewolf nonsense. Maybe Michael would come upon a mop of blonde hair, bare feet, a frightened nursery-expression, a rifle three sizes too large . . . What would he do then? Shoot him? Spank him?

Michael hoped that it was a soldier he was going to find. As he advanced slowly through the shimmering brown and green forest-light, pushing the thick foliage aside so that he could pass through, Michael found himself praying under his breath, praying that it was not a child he was hunting, praying that it was a grown man, a grown man in uniform, a grown man who was searching for him, armed and anxious to fight . . .

He switched the rifle to his left hand and flexed the fingers of his numbed right hand. The feeling was coming back slowly, in tingling, aching waves, and he was afraid that his fingers would respond too slowly when the time came . . . In all his training, he had never been instructed about how to handle something like this. It was always how to work in squads, in platoons, the staggered theory of attack, how to make use of natural cover, how not to expose yourself against the skyline, how to infiltrate through wire . . . Objectively, always moving ahead, his eyes raking the suspicious little movements of bushes and clustered saplings, he wondered if he was going to come through. The inadequate American, trained for everything but this, trained to salute, trained for close-order drill, advancing in columns, trained in the most modern methods of the prophylactic control of venereal disease. Now, at the height and climax of his military career, blunderingly improvising, facing a problem the Army had not foreseen . . . How to discover and kill one German who has just shot your best friend. Or maybe there were more than one. There had been two shots. Maybe there were two, six, a dozen, and they were waiting for him, smiling, in a nice orthodox line of rifle pits, listening to his heavy footsteps coming nearer and nearer . . .

He stopped. For a moment he thought of turning back. Then he shook his head. He did not reason anything out. Nothing coherent went through his mind. He merely transferred the rifle back into his tingling right hand, and kept on, in his thoughtful, rustling advance.

The log that had fallen across the narrow gully looked strong enough. It had rotted a little here and there, and the wood was soft, but it looked thick. And the gully was at least six feet across and quite deep, four or five feet deep, with mossy stones half buried in broken branches and dead leaves along the bottom. Before stepping out onto the log, Michael listened. The wind had died down and the forest was very still. He had a feeling that no human beings had been here for years. Human beings . . . No, that would be for later . . .

He stepped out onto the log. He was halfway across when it buckled, tearing, turning slipperily. Michael waved his hands violently, remembering to keep silent, then plunged down into the gully. He grunted as his hands slithered along the rocks and he felt his cheekbone begin to ache immediately where it had slammed against a sharp edge. The splintering log had made a sharp, cracking sound, and when he had hit the bottom it had been with a dull crash and a crackling of dried twigs, and his helmet had bounced off and rapped loudly against some stones. The rifle, he was thinking dully, what happened to the rifle . . . He was groping for the rifle on his hands and knees, when he heard the swift rushing sound of footsteps running, running loudly and directly toward him.

He jumped up. Fifty feet away from him a man was crashing through the bushes, staring straight at him, with a gun at his hip, pointing toward him. The man was a dark, speeding blur against the pale-green leaves. As Michael stared, motionless, the man fired from his hip. The burst was wild. Michael heard the slugs thumping in, right in front of his face, throwing sharp, stinging pellets of dirt against his skin. The man kept running.

Michael ducked. Automatically, he tore at the grenade hanging on his belt. He pulled the pin and stood up. The man was much closer, very close. Michael counted three, then threw the grenade and ducked, slamming himself wildly against the side of the gully and burying his head. God, he thought, his face pressed against the soft damp earth, I remembered to count!

The explosion seemed to take a long time in coming. Michael could hear the bits of steel whining over his head and thumping into the trees around him. There was a fluttering sound in the air as the torn leaves twisted down over him.

Michael wasn't sure, but he thought, with the noise of the explosion still in his ears, that he had heard a scream.

He waited five seconds, and then looked over the edge of the gully. There was nobody there. A little smoke rose slowly under the overhanging branches and there was a torn patch of earth showing brown and wet where the leaves and mold had been torn away, but that was all. Then Michael saw, across the clearing, the top of a bush waving in an eccentric rhythm, slowly dying down. Michael watched the bush, realizing that the man had gone back through there. He bent down and picked up the rifle, which was lying cradled against two round stones. He looked at the muzzle. It hadn't been filled with dirt. He was surprised to see that his hands were covered with blood, and when he put his hand to touch his aching cheekbone, it came away all smeared with dirt and blood.

He climbed slowly out of the gully. His right arm was giving him a considerable amount of pain, and the blood from his torn hand made the rifle slippery in his hand. He walked, without attempting to conceal himself, across the clearing, past the spot where the grenade had landed. Fifteen feet farther on, he saw what looked like an old rag, hanging onto a sapling. It was a piece of uniform, and it was bloody and wet.

Michael walked slowly to the bush which he had seen waving. There was blood all over the leaves, a great deal of blood. He is not going far, Michael thought, not any more. It was easy, even for a city man, to follow the trail of the fleeing German through the woods now. Michael even recognized, by the crushed leaves and familiar stains, where the man had fallen once and had risen, uprooting a tiny sapling with his hands, to continue his flight.

Slowly and steadily, Michael closed in on Christian Diestl.

Christian sat down deliberately, leaning against the trunk of the great tree, facing the direction from which he had come. It was shady under the tree, and cool, but shafts of sunlight struck down through the other foliage and lit, in oblique gold, the tops of the bushes through which Christian had pushed himself to reach this spot. The bark of the tree felt rough and solid behind his back. He tried to lift his hand, with the Schmeisser in it, but the hand wouldn't move the weight. He pushed annoyedly at the gun and it slithered away from him. He sat staring at the break in the bushes where, he knew, the American would appear.

A grenade, Christian thought, who would have thought of that? The clumsy American, crashing like a bull into the gully . . . And then, out of the gully, a grenade.

He breathed with difficulty. So far, he thought, so much running. Well, the running was now over. His mind seemed to slip in and out, like a faulty set of gears. The spring woods outside Paris and the dead boy from Silesia, lips stained with cherry juice . . . Hardenburg, on the motorcycle, Hardenburg with his face split away from its foundations, the stupid half-naked American firing from the mined bridge in Italy until the machine gun cut him down . . . Gretchen, Corinne, Françoise, the French will have us all yet . . . The vodka in Gretchen's bedroom, the sherry and brandy and wine in the closet, the black lace and the garnet brooch . . . The Frenchman pulling Behr's boots off on the beach after the planes, always the planes . . . "Listen, when a soldier joins an army, any army, there is a kind of basic contract the army makes with him . . ." Who said that, and was he dead, too? Fifty francs for a glass of brandy, served by an old man with rotting teeth. "The larger issue is Austria." And, "The end justifies the means" . . . This was the end, and what means did it justify? Other things . . . The American girl on the snowy hill. Just one more and I retire . . . The blundering, foolishly brave American, surviving by luck, accident, God's will . . . 1918 on the church wall, in chalk, the French knew, they knew all along.

The gears slipped in and out. It was getting very cold. The shafts of sunlight, which looked as though they were coming into the forest through narrow, slanted green windows, were getting thinner and thinner.

Two shots and the gun jammed. Finally, of course, it had to jam. My entire Company marched into Munich, still in possession of their weapons. It was much more orderly. The important thing was always to be able to lay your hands on a bicycle. How long, he thought, full of self-pity, can they expect a man to run?

Then he saw the American. The American wasn't cautious any more. He walked directly up to him, through the thin green sunlight. The American was no longer young, and he didn't look like a soldier. The American stood over him.

Christian grinned. "Welcome to Germany," he said, remembering his English.

He watched the American lift his gun and press the trigger.

Michael walked back to where he had left Noah. The breathing had stopped. The boy lay quiet among the flowers. Michael stared dryly down at him for a moment. Then he picked Noah up, and, carrying him over his shoulder, walked through the growing dusk, without stopping once, back to the camp. And he refused to allow any of the other men in the Company to help him carry the body, because he knew he had to deliver Noah Ackerman, personally, to Captain Green.

Dell Bestsellers

Nightwork

by Irwin Shaw

Superb entertainment from the author of
Rich Man, Poor Man

• An American who arrives in Europe with a hot $100,000 and a burning desire to enjoy the best of life and love while his money and luck hold out . . .

• An elegant fellow-American rogue who becomes his guide in a world of high-priced pleasures and high risk gambles . . .

• A Beautiful and sensual titled Englishwoman who chooses to be his companion on the razor's edge of the law and the most intimate side of love . . .

Put them all together with the storytelling genius of Irwin Shaw—and you have the most entrancing, romantic adventure he has written.

"Set against such backdrops as Washington, St. Moritz, Rome, Paris . . . with the most diverting pair of con men since *The Sting*, whose schemes are wild, wooly, and wonderfully profitable. Fun All The Way!"
—*Publishers Weekly*

A DELL BOOK (6460-00) $1.95

Frank Yerby's

magnificent historical novels have enthralled millions around the world . . .

REMEMBER IT DOESN'T GROW ON TREES

**ENERGY CONSERVATION -
IT'S YOUR CHANCE TO SAVE, AMERICA**

Department of Energy, Washington, D.C.

A PUBLIC SERVICE MESSAGE FROM DELL PUBLISHING CO., INC.